Tom Holt was born in London in 1961. At Oxford he studied bar billiards, ancient Greek agriculture and the care and feeding of small, temperamental Japanese motorcycle engines; interests which led him, perhaps inevitably, to qualify as a solicitor and emigrate to Somerset, where he specialised in death and taxes for seven years before going straight in 1995. Now a full-time writer, he lives in Chard, Somerset, with his wife, one daughter and the unmistakable scent of blood, wafting in on the breeze from the local meat-packing plant.

Find out more about Tom Holt and other Orbit authors by registering for the free monthly newsletter at www.orbitbooks.co.uk

TOM HOLT

Fishy Wishes

Contains
Wish You Were Here
and Djinn Rummy

www.orbitbooks.co.uk

An *Orbit* Book

First published in Great Britain by Orbit 2004
This omnibus edition © Tom Holt 2004

Wish You Were Here
First published in Great Britain by Orbit in 1998
Copyright © Tom Holt 1998

Djinn Rummy
First published in Great Britain by Orbit in 1995
Copyright © Tom Holt 1995

A CIP catalogue record for this book
is available from the British Library.

ISBN 1 84149 347 3

Typeset in Plantin by M Rules
Printed and bound in Great Britain by
Clays Ltd, St Ives plc

Orbit
An imprint of
Time Warner Book Group UK
Brettenham House
Lancaster Place
London WC2E 7EN

CONTENTS

WISH YOU WERE HERE

For John and Mary Creasey
And Joe Bethancourt:
Sweet Charioteers.

CHAPTER ONE

'Yes, sir,' said the tiresome old man, leaning back in his rocking chair, 'that there's Lake Chicopee right enough. Ain't no other lake like it in all of Iowa.'

Below them, the lake lounged motionless in the late morning sun like a well-fed cat in a window-seat. Because it's surrounded on all four sides by the crests of the Chicopee Hills, the wind seldom ruffles its surface, making it one giant mirror. Accordingly, unless you look closely, you don't actually see a lake; just a ring of ingrowing mountains and stalagmite pine trees surrounding an oval of blue. That, perhaps, was what the old man was referring to; or maybe he had something else in mind.

'Thanks,' muttered the motorist, glancing sideways at his watch. 'So to get to Oskaloosa we just follow this road until it brings us out on the . . .'

'They do say,' the tiresome old man continued, lighting his corn-cob pipe and blowing smoke in the motorist's face, 'that this here lake's haunted.'

The motorist coughed pointedly. In New York, blowing tobacco smoke in someone's face would get you arrested for assault with a deadly weapon. 'Is that so?' he said, trying his best to load each syllable with patent lack of interest. 'If I just follow this road as far as . . .'

'By an ole Injun spirit,' the tiresome old man said, 'name of Okeewana or some such. Now I lived in these parts all my life and I never seen her, but who's to say, huh? Who's to say?'

A scowl swept across the motorist's face like an empty polythene bag windblown across an empty car park. 'Who indeed? Look, I don't want to seem rude, but . . .'

'They do say –' The tiresome old man leaned forward, giving the motorist a unique opportunity to study at first hand the effects on tooth enamel of sixty years of chewing tobacco and industrial-grade bourbon whiskey – 'that if you're lucky and meet that ole spirit and jump in the lake after her, she'll grant you anything you truly wish fer.'

'Look –'

'And if you're *really* lucky,' he added, with an evil grin, 'you drown first.'

When the motorist's car had disappeared over the skyline – going the wrong way, but some folks just won't stop to listen – the tiresome old man smiled indulgently, shook himself like a wet cat and turned into a beautiful young girl. Then she stood up, disappeared the rocking chair, the quaintly tumbledown timberframe house and the white picket fence, and ran down to the shores of the lake. Duty done; time for a swim.

However long it was that she'd been here – it seemed like for ever, which is no time at all – in all that time she'd never grown tired of swimming in the lake. Sometimes she would be an otter, floating on her back or scudding like a sleek brown torpedo a few inches under the roof of the water, letting the bubbles stream after her like a dragon's tail. At other times she'd be a trout or a duck, occasionally a human; it all depended on the weather and the time of year, the mood she was in, whether she was working or off duty. There were all manner of delightful things to be in a lake; and that was only on this side of the surface. Underneath the reflection, on the mirror's flipside, the possibilities were, of course, infinite.

Today, it was her fancy to be a water-beetle. Having first scanned air and water for unfriendly birds and fish, she took a deep breath, drew down her mind into the tiny parameters of beetlehood and found herself balancing on legs thinner than her own eyelashes, standing on the surface of the water. It was a tricksy metamorphosis – the difficulty being how to get any purchase on the meniscus of the lake, rather like ice-skating with a single six-inch nail strapped point downwards on each foot instead of a nice wide blade – but the exhilarating effect of being able to scamper over the surface of an element that usually prided itself on always getting the last word generally made up for the time expended in mastering the art. As soon as that first, inevitable wave of shape-changer's panic had died away she began to feel the sheer bliss of unlimited choice, with nothing to interfere with her pleasure except a very slight breeze setting up a few trivial ripples, and the occasional wolf-whistle from the male water-beetles hanging round a belly-up dead fish a few yards further out. This, she reflected, is the life.

Her mind, or at least the tediously sentient part of it, was on the point of floating away when her insect vision caught sight of a human shape making its way down the southern slope of the encircling hills. A customer. Damn. With a faint buzz she opened her wing-case, spread her wings and sawed up off the surface of the water, making a noise like a tiny Japanese motorcycle engine.

She wasn't the only one to have noticed the newcomer. On the opposite side of the lake, high up in the branches of a tall pine tree, Talks to Squirrels shaded his eyes with his hand and did some complicated mental arithmetic.

Range: seven hundred and fifty yards. Windspeed: five, maybe seven miles per hour. Allowance for thermal currents rising off the warm surface of the lake: well, his best guess would have to do, so say five degrees. In which case, let x equal the coefficient of drag . . .

With an ease that mere quartz could never hope to achieve, his mind sifted the numbers, made the corrections, compensated for the effect of air-pressure on an irregularly knapped obsidian arrowhead spinning anti-clockwise against the wind on a sunny day and gave him the precise angle and the exactly quantified weight of draw on the bowstring that would have allowed him, if he was still alive, which he wasn't, goddamnit, to stick an arrow smack bang in the middle of the intruder's eyebrows. In his mind's eye he could see the spiralling flash of the arrow's fletchings against the blue sky, the pear-shaped curve of its descent, and (short pause, while his mind's eye changed lenses) the look of dumb incredulity on the sucker's face as he realised he'd suddenly and unexpectedly been taken dead. Hah! I'd have had you, you bastard, except for a technicality.

Remember the furious indignation you used to feel when you were young and the teacher kept you in after school for something you hadn't actually done? Quite. Think how much worse it must be to be kept in after life.

And it *hadn't* been his fault, damnit; because they'd

started it, with their treaties and railroads and forked-tongue promises. Fair enough, he hadn't exactly loathed every minute he'd spent in the armed struggle for his nation's liberty; but so what? How can it be wrong to enjoy doing well a job that has to be done? A skilled woodworker making a fine job of a difficult piece of carpentry is allowed to feel good about it; so why not a warrior? Hadn't been any of this fuss before *they* arrived. Great Spirits, but what wouldn't he give for just one more shot. Just one.

He sighed, and the world of the living would have heard the wind softly mussing the branches of the tree. While he'd been calculating and pondering on his wrongs, the scumbag had moved. Range now seven hundred and twenty yards, windspeed now dropping, let y be the effect of the archer's paradox. Ah, shit, it just isn't *fair* . . .

If only he hadn't fallen in the goddamn lake.

The beetle had landed.

It shook itself and studied the newcomer. Was he, it wondered, the observant type, the sort of man who'd notice a timberframe house with picket fence, stoop and rocking chair and realise that it hadn't been there a moment ago? Probably not; a dreamer, if ever it had seen one. Quite liable to fall in the lake of his own accord, simply by not looking where he's going.

Still, duty called. A heartbeat later, he tasted the bitterness of tobacco in the back of his throat, breathed out a thin plume of smoke through his nose and set the chair rocking.

'Howdy,' he said.

The young man looked up. For an instant the tiresome old man wondered if perhaps he'd underestimated the lad, because there was just a tiny flicker of puzzlement in his eyes as he looked up and saw the house for the first time. But if his subconscious mind had noticed anything, it kept it to itself. The young man blinked, said, 'Hello,' in an unfamiliar accent, and turned back to stare at the lake.

Unfamiliar? No, it was just that the tiresome old man hadn't heard it for a very long time. A Britisher, by the Spirits; a direct descendant, maybe, of the dim-witted clowns who'd passed this way three hundred years or so since.

Hum. Unlikely to be a direct descendant of that lot. Where they'd gone, people don't have descendants. A relative, maybe. Sixteenth cousin thirty-two times removed, something like that. A collector's piece, at any rate.

'Mighty fine view of the lake you get from here,' the tiresome old man observed. A blue cloud rose over his head and hung there for a moment.

'Yes.'

'They do say,' continued the tiresome old man, 'that this here lake's haunted.'

'I know.'

'Haunted by an ole – you do?'

The young man nodded. 'That's why I'm here,' he said.

'Gosh darn,' muttered the old man, taken aback. For technical reasons too complicated to explain, he knew he wasn't dreaming; but to get a mark who'd actually come here on purpose – hell, if he was inclined to be paranoid he'd be looking for a trap of some sort. 'Yup,' he continued lamely, 'the ole Injun spirit of Lake Chicopee . . .'

'Okeewana,' the young man recited, 'Daughter of the West Wind. If you throw yourself in the lake, she grants you your heart's desire.' He made a peculiar noise with surplus breath and his teeth, which the old man recognised as a sigh of rapture. God *damn*it! 'I saved up for two years to come here,' he added. 'In the Post Office. You know, I still can't believe I'm actually here.'

I know the feeling, the old man said to himself. I can't believe you're actually here either. Still; the thing to bear in mind when dealing with mortals is never to give them an even break. 'Where you from, son?' he asked, and blew a smoke-ring.

'Brierley Hill,' the lad replied. He couldn't be more than twenty-five; tall, unfinished-looking, the sort of man who doesn't look like he's dried properly until he's about forty. Looking at him, the old man felt an overwhelming urge to fold him up and put him neatly away. Somehow, he made the world look untidy. 'That's near Birmingham,' the lad went on. 'England.'

'Is that so?' Birmingham? After my time. Tentatively, he probed the youth's mind for an image of the place; the result was strange, to say the least. Hell, whatever will they think of next? 'Well, you sure's tarnation a long way from home here, bud. Is she like you figured she'd be?'

'No.' The lad shook his head. 'It's better. It's really – you know, amazing. All that water and stuff.'

So what did you expect to find in a lake? Porridge? 'And you reckon you know all 'bout ole Okeewana,' he continued, feeling ever so slightly as if he was advising his grand-mother to bore a small hole in the pointed end, taking care not to crack the shell. 'They do say . . .'

'It's been my ambition, like,' the boy went on. 'Ever since I was twelve. I got this book out of the library, *Myths And Legends Of Many Lands*. All in there, it was.' He paused, and seemed to be bracing himself as if to confess some dreadful sin. 'I like all that stuff, mythology and things.'

You do, huh?'

He nodded. 'I think it's great. I think I like the Aztecs best, but you can fly here direct from Birmingham and anyway, I can't speak Spanish. Plus the exchange rate's better. My mum works in a travel agent's.'

The old man frowned. Following the kid's train of thought was a bit like trying to find the end of a rainbow with your eyes shut. 'They do say,' he persevered, 'that if you was to jump in this here lake . . .'

He paused. He could feel vibes.

Talks To Squirrels! Put that thing down, for pity's sake, before you injure somebody.

Hell, 'Kee, I'm only practising. All I can do these days, practise. You should know that, better than me.

Cut it out, Squirrels, before I cut it out for you. And maybe later, if you're good –

Huh. You always say that. .

Actually, I've got a good feeling about this one. And if it does come off, you can have first crack at him. Promise. Honest Injun.

'Kee, that wasn't funny the first time you said it.

The youth was looking at him curiously, as if he could hear echoes of the unspoken words. The old man pulled himself together.

'Sorry, kid,' he said, rallying gamely. 'Reckon I was miles away. When you been living here long as me, you get so's you think you hear things that ain't there, if you know what I mean. And just now, darn it if I wasn't sure as I could hear that ole spirit calling to me . . .'

Thanks to his unique insight into what goes on under the surface of lakes, the old man actually did know the look on a fish's face just before it takes the baited hook; a sort of stupid, greedy, well-bugger-me-there's-lunch-just-hanging-there sort of a grin that generally tends to dissipate any sympathy you might have for the fish. Just such a look was spreading over the lad's face, swiftly and indelibly as blackcurrant squash on a white rug. *Yessir, got me a sucker*, rejoiced the old man's soul, as it slowly began to turn the reel.

And lay off the Tom Sawyer stuff, will you, 'Kee? You're about as convincing as a five-dollar Rolex Oyster, and you're giving me a pain.

'Really?' the kid was saying. 'You can actually, like, *hear* her? That's *unreal*.'

'Hey, son, you can hear her for yourself if you just mosey on down to the edge of the water.'

There are some fish so gullible you don't need to bait the hook. They're the ones who look up at the three-sixty-degree sky and say to themselves, *Hey, wonder what it must be like up there, and wouldn't it be just great to find out if only I could find some way out of all this boring old water.* They're the ones who say, a fraction of a second before the gaff cracks them on the head, that it's one small tail-flip for a fish but a giant splosh for fishkind.

'Wow!' said the kid. 'You know, I might just do that.'

With a big silly grin all over his face, he set off down the hill. The old man watched him go, sighed a little, and shook himself.

'Yes,' said the editor, leaning back in his chair and loosening his tie. 'That's one hell of a story.'

'I know.'

The editor swivelled his chair round and scrolled back through the text on the screen. Occasionally he paused to nod his head, grin and catch his breath.

'One hell of a story,' he repeated.

'Yes.'

'I particularly liked,' the editor said, 'the way you link it all up at the end. Must have taken some doing.'

'Not really.'

'Ah.' The editor rubbed his chin. Something; not a worry, not even a niggle, as such. On the other hand, the *Tribune*'s circulation was up four per cent and the *Globe* had run rings round him with the Hudson Bay radiation leak scare. Something like this could change all that. Overnight.

'I really liked the bit where you link that guy the President's hairdresser's uncle was at high school with to the car smash where that ecology activist's arm got broken, which has never been conclusively proved not to be a bungled CIA hit attempt.' He chewed his lower lip thoughtfully. 'That had, you know, overtones. Could mean absolutely *anything*.'

'Thank you.'

The editor grinned. 'And that bit about the leading US company supplying components to the Brazilian company that supplies components to the French company that made all the filing cabinet divider cards used by Sadam Hussein during the Gulf War. Masterly. No other word for it. Their stock's gonna go through the floor when this hits the stands.' He frowned, and made a mental note to call his broker.

'Yeah. It's a pretty damn good story.'

'Good?' The editor gestured vaguely. 'It makes Woodward and Bernstein look like a couple of old guys doing a gardening column.' He frowned. 'Just one thing,' he added. 'You couldn't work in anything about Kennedy, could you? Only we haven't had a good JFK conspiracy story for . . .'

'Three weeks.'

'OK, OK,' grumbled the editor. 'Three weeks is a long

time in journalism.' He flicked through the story again. 'Here,' he said, pointing. 'In this bit where you link Mark Twain with the rise of the Hitler Youth. Couldn't you kinda just squeeze it a bit and –?'

'No.'

'No?' The editor pulled a little face. 'Fair enough, I guess it's your baby. All right, how about here? The part where you claim the guy who's doing all the Senegal famine relief stuff is really Klaus van Mordwerk, the Butcher of Chartres. If you just . . .'

'No.'

'Huh? Pity. Because, you know that bit where you say his birth certificate says he was born in 1957 but it's all a fake because really he was kidnapped by aliens who whizzed him round the galaxy at seven times the speed of light, so he only looks forty years old even though really he's ninety-seven; if you were to imply that the same aliens were the ones who snatched Kennedy –'

'No.'

The editor shrugged. 'You know best,' he said. 'It's just I hate to see an opportunity going to –'

'That's the follow-up. For next week.'

'Ah.'

'I suggest you put Chlopeki on it. She needs the experience.'

The editor nodded, and reached for a cigar. He was just about to light it when it was taken from his hand, snapped neatly in two and dropped in the bin. 'Sorry,' the editor said sheepishly. 'I forgot.'

'Don't.'

'Which reminds me,' the editor added. 'That bit where you attributed Rasputin's madness to passive smoking while he was a novice in Kiev. Do you think we could work that up into a major feature? Only, we haven't had a passive smoking scare for, oh . . .'

'Two days.'

'Right. Yeah, well, we could call it a follow-up. You know; *write your congressman NOW!!!* kinda thing . . .'

A shrug. 'You can if you like. Look, I'm really glad you liked the story, but I haven't got time right now. I'll catch up with you when I get back, OK?'

'Back?' The editor looked up. 'You off somewhere?'

'Yes.' Linda Lachuk nodded. 'Iowa. Looks like something big.'

'Another one? Hey.'

'No.' Linda allowed herself a thin smile. 'That one you got there's just a bit of fun. The Iowa thing is *big*. See you.'

The editor opened his mouth and closed it again. 'Hey,' he said, 'bigger than this? What's the story?'

Linda shrugged. 'You'll see.'

'Just a little hint?'

'Let's see, then.' Linda sat down on the corner of the editor's desk. 'We've got a secret nuke installation that's causing ecological havoc, maybe even bending the fabric of the space/time continuum, and it's all tied in with the clandestine arms scandal, which means . . .'

'Huh? What clandestine arms scandal?'

'This one,' Linda replied. 'The big question will be, did the President know about the existence of the second-generation tapes? And then, when we bring in the women's health issues, not to mention the cute little furry animals angle . . .'

The editor's face slumped into a stunned grin, so that he looked like a lemming version of Cortes gazing with a wild surmise at the Grand Canyon. 'There's a cute little furry animals angle?' he breathed.

'There's always a cute little furry animals angle,' Linda replied casually. 'If not express, then implied. You just gotta look for it, is all.'

Which was true, the editor admitted, as he recalled Linda's own stunningly innovative slant on the farm subsidies story. Who else, he asked himself, would have dreamed of leading with a full-page close-up of the cutest little mouse you ever saw, under the screamer: CON-DEMNED TO DIE! ('*If secret plans now being rushed through Congress are allowed to go ahead, millions of cute furry mice like Wilbert will be ruthlessly exterminated as callous farmers sadistically prepare grain silos for expected megabuck bumper harvests . . .*') He closed his eyes, and grinned. 'Way to go, Linda,' he said. 'I can hardly wait.'

Linda nodded and stood up; and the editor reflected, not for the first time, that for one person to be so incredibly successful, so stunningly beautiful, so completely integrated and at one with her lifestyle, wasn't perhaps the way it was supposed to be with human beings. Maybe, he surmised, she's got this really awful-looking painting in her attic. Or maybe not. If she had, she'd have made a story out of it long since.

With an ethnic rights angle to it, probably. Not to mention the cute little furry animals.

Ninety feet above the surface of the lake, the duck air-braked, banked sharply and turned.

Because a part of its mind, unused even after all this time to lightning-fast changes of body, was still being a tiresome old man with a corn-cob pipe, the duck made its way slowly down the sky, taking care not to pull a wing muscle or dislocate an arthritic joint. The rest of its mind used the response-time lag to assess the situation and demand to know, one last time, where the catch was. Too easy, it screamed. Nobody, not even a goddamn Brit, is this daffy. It's got to be a set-up or something.

Got to be.

But, the duck reflected as it lowered its undercarriage and aquaplaned a silvery gash through a reflected mountain, if there's a catch, buggered if I can see it. Not that I'm in any position to pontificate right now, what with being a duck and all. Stupider creatures than ducks are hard to find, if you leave out the sort of life-form you can comfortably fit on a microscope slide.

Having gathered its wings in tidily to its sides and preened them with its bill, it turned to face the shore and settled itself down to watch. Any minute now, there was going to be a loud splash.

Four. Three. Two. One.

Splash!

When the kid stopped flying through the air and touched down on the water, he fell through the reflection of a rocky outcrop on the south-western crest of the hills, smashing it into thousands of tiny shards of image. As he struggled to keep his head above water, each shard was further fragmented, making the surface of the lake a mosaic of tiny bits of hillside, each one perfectly mirrored but no longer making up a whole recognisable anything. When the kid finally realised that the swimming techniques he'd learned in the municipal swimming baths of the West Midlands didn't seem to work in the admittedly unusual waters of Lake Chicopee, the reflection healed up over his head with surprising speed. Four and a half seconds after the first splash, the ripples had stopped and the mirror was unbroken once more.

You get seven years for breaking conventional mirrors.

That's a conditional discharge and an apology from the judge compared to the penalty for disturbing this one.

Glug. A last few air bubbles floated up and burst.

The duck put its head down, and dived.

Oh God, Wesley Higgins said to himself as the water filled his lungs, *I'm drowning*.

Entirely against his will, he breathed in water through his nose. It felt –

Good. Odd, that. Hell, it felt *healthy*. Fresh, clean water and plenty of exercise. Just what the doctor ordered.

Hang about. I'm not drowning. I'm bloody well floating. I'm floating on top of the water.

Surely not; but it felt like floating. Mind you, the water in his lungs felt like air, so who was he to judge? Every scrap of logic remaining in his oxygen-starved brain yelled at him that this was Death; if not the real thing, then an introductory free sample designed to encourage him to sign on for the full course of treatment. *No way he could still be alive*.

And yet here he was. Floating on his back, like a damn Poohstick. And alive too, by every indication he could monitor. For a start, don't drowned people float face down, just a few inches under the surface? He'd read some-where – at school, probably – that they do.

He opened his eyes and saw the sky, oval-encircled by a rampart of hills and a fuzzy ring of trees. All perfectly normal, except –

Except that they were all back to front, turned through a hundred and eighty degrees, mirror-fashion. For two pins, he could make himself believe that his body, the long, embarrassing thing he'd shuffled around in all these years, really was bobbing along upside down on the surface of the lake. And here he was, floating serenely on the underside and staring at the sky. And breathing the water.

Query: was the water safe to breathe in these parts, or should he have brought along an aqualung full of Perrier? Did they even have Perrier in Heaven?

Who said anything about Heaven?

The voice seemed to come from inside his head. Maybe, he reflected, this was how it started for Joan of Arc. One day she'd been relaxing in a nice pine-scented bath, just like I'm doing now, and suddenly there were voices in there between her ears; quiet, whispering little voices just like this one, saying wasn't it a scandal, all those English people coming over here buying weekend cottages and second homes, forcing property prices up, writing books about how comical the locals are, it's high time somebody did something about it. And the next thing she knew, of course, there she was tied to this big hunk of wood and some grinning bastard was waving a burning torch at her and saying, Now then, this may hurt a little. With hindsight, she'd have done better to buy a Sony Walkman and drown the buggers out till they went away.

Joan of Who?

Arc. It's a place. In France.

Excuse me, but I think you're wrong there. Because according to what you've got in your memory banks, it's either a segment of a circle or a big boat full of animals. No, hang on, I tell a lie. Here we are, Joan of Arc. Hey, going on what you've got in here about her, she doesn't seem like a terribly nice person.

'She was a *saint*, damnit,' Wesley said aloud. 'And who the hell are you, anyway?'

Would it help if I came out of your ear? No offence, but it's not exactly a welcoming environment, not unless you happen to be a bee.

Something went *pfzzzz*! in his ear, and a moment later he caught sight of a round, beady black eye, on a level with his own. It seemed to be inset in a pointed, furry head with a sort of Disney-cuddly face and whiskers. He looked at it. It looked at him.

'Hi,' it said. 'I'm an otter.'

First voices in his head, now talking animals; spiffing. Dying and going to Heaven would have been nice. Dying and going to hell – decidedly lower down on his list of preferences, but still well within the scope of his expectations. Dying and going to *The Wind In The Willows* struck him as insult added to injury, with ice, lemon and a sprig of mint.

'I expect you're wondering,' the otter said, 'what's going on.'

Wesley would have nodded; but as far as he could tell he was playing fast and loose with the laws of physics just by being there, lying on top of water he'd drowned in not two minutes earlier. The slightest movement on his part might draw attention to the fact that by rights he should be under the surface, not on top of it.

'Yes,' he said.

The otter dived, resurfaced, flipped over onto its back and drew alongside him, like a launch beside a tanker. 'I'm not surprised,' it said. 'This must all seem rather strange to you. In fact, you're probably thinking you must be dreaming or mad or something. All perfectly normal.'

If, half an hour earlier, someone had told Wesley that later on that day he'd find comfort and reassurance in something an otter had told him, he'd have been sceptical, hard to convince. Only goes to show what a difference thirty short minutes can make. 'Normal?' he whispered. 'What –?'

The otter waggled its wee forepaws. 'This,' it said, 'is Lake Chicopee. Remember? The place you've come all that way just to see?'

'How d'you know that?'

'You told me. And you recall what happens when you jump in Lake Chicopee when the water's still?'

'You drown.'

'Oh no you don't,' the otter contradicted cheerfully. 'If you were drowning you'd be saying things like *glblblblblbbbbb* right now, take it from me. When you jump in Lake Chicopee, your heart's deepest wish comes true.' The otter made a face which, on a human physiognomy, would be a smirk. 'And so it has.'

It crossed Wesley's mind that if his subconscious deepest wish was to be floating on a lake talking to an otter, maybe drowning was too good for him, but he decided not to say it out loud on diplomatic grounds. 'It has?' he said.

'You bet. Your deepest wish,' the otter continued, 'is to find release from this mundane, commonplace world by bursting into some wild, fantastic adventure in a magical realm where anything is possible. Am I right or am I right?'

Wesley considered for a moment. 'Well . . .'

'Oh come on,' the otter said briskly. 'I was in your mind, remember. I can see the interior of your home. A bedsit over a chemist's shop, right?'

'Well,' Wesley replied dubiously, 'yes, I suppose—'

'We open the door,' the otter went on. 'Directly in front of us on the wall is a map of Middle-Earth, framed. You know your way round it better than you know the centre of Birmingham.'

'Actually, that's not diffficult. They haven't got a one-way system in Middle-Earth.'

'To our left,' the otter continued, 'is the bookshelf,

covering the whole wall. And what do we find? Tolkien. C.S. Lewis. The complete works of Anne McCaffrey. Yards of the stuff, enough dreams to float the Graf Zeppelin. To our right, ignoring the unmade bed and the rather disgusting mound of used laundry, we have the mantelpiece, which is covered in skilfully painted lead figurines representing elves, dwarves, orcs, wizards, heroes, disturbed-looking young women with big swords and hormone imbalances, trolls, giants, self-propelled trees, dragons – they come in three sections, and the wings can be displayed in the open or folded position and God only knows what else. Melt that lot down and you could re-roof the Vatican.'

'No! I mean, you lay off my collection. Taken me years . . .'

'Ever since you were twelve,' the otter agreed. 'Have I proved my point, or shall we take a peek inside your wardrobe?'

'All right,'Wesley snapped. 'You can make fun all you like. I still don't see what that's got to do with lying on my back in a bloody lake talking to an otter.'

'You don't?' Amusement permeated the otter's voice like the writing in a stick of rock. 'Then you're being deliberately dim, friend. Oh, I didn't mention the life-size handcrafted Franklin Mint replica of Excalibur, on which you still owe nine instalments. Late at night you draw the curtains, take it down off the wall and do feints and little slashes with it. There's a great big hole in the wardrobe door you're hoping the landlord won't notice, though from what I saw of him while I was inside your head, he's not the sort of guy who's going to be fooled by chewing gum and shoe polish.'

Wesley thought hard. Excalibur. 'You're the Lady of the Lake?' he hazarded. 'But I thought –'

'This is a lake,' the otter replied. 'The rest's just a matter of morphology and capital letters. Principle's the same, I guess. What it all boils down to is, you're a very sad kid who's never grown out of fairy stories. Yes?'

Despite the various disadvantages he was obviously under, Wesley couldn't let that pass without rebuttal. 'No I'm not,' he replied. 'There's nothing wrong with me. I've got a car. I've got a responsible job in a building society.' He remembered something which struck him as being of great evidential value. 'I've got a personal pension plan,' he added triumphantly. 'With the Norwich Union.'

The otter looked at him. 'Bully for you,' it said. 'Do you want your heart's desire or not? Because if you'd rather go back to your bedsit and your spavined Metro and your screen in Mortgage Processing, you've only to say the word. And you'll prove my point, while you're at it.'

'Yes, please,' said Wesley. 'It may not be much, but it's what I am. And I'm not a loony, like you're trying to make out I am. And,' he added savagely, 'I don't talk to otters. Let me out of here.'

The otter looked at him gravely with deep black eyes.

'No,' it said.

Before he could argue further, the otter grabbed him by the scruff of the neck and started to tow him towards the shore. He struggled and tried to kick, but the water around him was thick and unbelievably heavy, like mercury, and he found that he wasn't strong enough to move it out of the way. Another thing; there were no ripples on this water as he moved through it, unwillingly and backwards. He simply slid through reflected mountains and trees, as if he was the image and they were real. He felt as if the lake was the screen and he was a movie being projected onto it. It wasn't the happiest of sensations.

'All right,' he said. 'Will you slow down, please?'

The otter, which had been cracking on at a fair rate, decelerated. 'Is that better?' it asked. 'If you're going to be sick, please don't throw up on the mountains, they stain as soon as look at them. We're nearly there, anyway.'

'Are we?'

'Nearly.'

Calvin Dieb parked his car at the side of the road under a tall fir tree, pulled his binoculars out of the glove box, and turned to look at the lake.

Lake Chicopee, Iowa; several thousand acres of the most enchanting, mouth-wateringly promising real estate he'd seen in the course of a long and vigorous legal career. It seemed to call to him; in the sighing of the trees, the soft splashing of the waters, the sound-kaleidoscope of bird-song. 'Develop me!' it was saying. 'Make me pay!'

Right opposite where he was standing, they'd have the shopping mall; and next to that, the drive-ins. On this slope, where he was standing, the first phase of residential, with its unrivalled view of the health complex below, phase two on the left, phase three on the right, and a big fluorescent plastic M dead ahead. If they decided to keep the water, the M would reflect nicely, especially at night.

It had taken God, he reflected, seven days to make this. His clients would take seven years, but they'd do a *proper* job. Not that he was knocking God; the guy hadn't had the advantages. For a start, He hadn't had the benefit of top-flight legal advice from Hernan Piranha and Cal Dieb. All in all, it was a miracle the roof hadn't fallen in yet.

But that's what lawyers are for; to put the Real in realty. He scanned the lake and caught sight of something moving on the surface of the water. A fingertip adjustment to his executive Zeiss binoculars revealed it to be just an otter, furrowing the water and pulling runs in the reflections like unravelling knitting. Dieb frowned. He'd heard horror stories of dream deals crashing headlong to the ground, their wing-wax melted by the presence on-site of one miserable rare bird or endangered frog. Only last month, he'd been talking to a guy at a seminar who'd nearly lost a deal because of Lexington's Vole; except that the guy had had the foresight to fly in ten crates of heather-buzzards from Colombia and have them turned loose one dark night when the protesters were too cold to keep a proper watch. The buzzards had scarfed up the voles inside a month; and, since the birds were even more protected than the wee rodents, there was nothing anybody could do. Then, when the food supply was exhausted, the buzzards had moved on, leaving the site clear for the diggers to roll. Best of all, the feathered pests had taken residence on a neighbouring development site owned by clients of a rival law firm, and put them out of business. It put a whole new slant on the term legal eagles.

Wonder what eats otters? Something must. He murmured a few words into his pocket dictaphone. Wolves? Bears? Giant turtles? Were otters a big deal anyway? Probably worth checking while he was here. He took his phone from his belt.

'Cindi? Is Jack there? Thanks. Jack, otters. Yeah. Look, I'm at the Lustmord Corporation site and it's ankle deep in goddamn otters. Can we waste the buggers or –? We can? Good work, Jack. Ciao.' He snapped the phone shut and put it away; another crisis averted, another five hundred bucks on the bill. It was turning into a good day.

But, he reflected as he swung the binoculars round, just

because otters weren't going to be a problem, it didn't necessarily follow that there weren't a whole load of other furry saboteurs out there all poised and ready to pounce. Now sure, he could wait for the report; but then he'd be getting the data at the same time as the clients, which wasn't his style. Far better to be able to turn to Frank Lustmord at their next meeting and say, 'Oh, and by the way, Frank, you'll be pleased to hear we've got the Van Sittaert's Rat situation nicely in hand.' And Frank would look worried and say, 'I didn't know we had a Van Sittaert's Rat situation, Cal,' and then he could say, 'This time next week you won't, Frank'; and that'd be worth another ten grand, possibly even a step closer to getting Lustmord's corporate acquisition business. Worth a little mud on the trouser leg, particularly since he was doing it on Frank's time.

He returned to the car, pulled on a pair of thousand-dollar gumboots and started off down the slope towards the lake. It wasn't easy going underfoot; bits of the hill tended to break off under his heel, roll down and go splash in the lake. He tried not to watch them; heights made him nervous, and if he were to fall and injure himself horribly, he wasn't quite sure who would be the appropriate person to sue. A fine fool he'd look, a man in his position, ending up all hideously mangled and not a cent in damages to show for it. Above all, he didn't want to fall in the lake, because he couldn't swim. Well, why should he? Never, in twenty years in the legal profession, had he found occasion to include in any of his bills the entry: *To swimming, pursuant to your instructions* .... *$1,000.00* – so why bother with it? If any swimming ever needed doing, he could hire some guy. From an agency or something.

He felt a stone break loose under his left foot, listened as it bounced and clattered down the hill and heard the splash as it hit the water.

Trouble is, there isn't always an agency handy when you need one.

Perhaps, he decided, quickly, it would be a good idea to stay exactly where he was until he'd had a chance to collate relevant data, assess the position as regards short, medium and long term eventualities, formulate a plan of action and only then implement it. He did so. Then he started to yell for help.

'Howdy, mister,' said a voice behind him. 'Fine day again. What you hollerin' fer?'

'I need help,' he replied, not turning round. 'I'm stuck.'

'Don't look stuck to me,' said the voice. 'What's the matter? Put yer foot in a bear-trap or something?'

Being rooted to the spot, he couldn't turn and look at whoever it was, but the voice alone was enough to rough out a picture in his mind. It was one of those folkloric, old-fashioned All-American voices that go hand in glove with the expression 'old-timer'. It wasn't a section of American society he was familiar with. Presumably they did go to law sometimes – all Americans go to law sooner or later – but they never walked into his office, quite possibly because they couldn't afford to talk to his receptionist, let alone him. He assumed they consulted check-shirted, chaw-chewing, four-wheel-drive-driving, stoop-sitting, harmonica-playing, sandpaper-chinned lawyers with offices over lumber mills in towns with quaintly evocative names; the sort who still use embossed letterhead. On the other hand, their legendary woodcraft and oneness with the environment probably made them experts in the field of getting people off dangerous hillsides. In any event, it was a fair bet that the concept of money as a reward for services had permeated this far by now.

'Get me off this goddamn hillside,' he said, 'and I'll give you twenty bucks.'

Behind him he could hear a wheezy cackle, like a bad telephone connection in a high wind. 'Say, mister, why don't you just walk back up the hill and save the twenty bucks?'

'I can't. I'm stuck.'

More cackling. 'You mean you're too darn scared.'

'Yes. Look, get me out of this and I'll make it fifty bucks.'

'You got it.'

As fingers like steel rods gripped his arm and wrenched him up the slope, he was already wondering whether he might not have been too generous in his offer. Twenty bucks cash and a Piranha & Dieb gift voucher, fifty dollars off the divorce of your choice, might have done just as well.

'You OK now?'

He opened his eyes. Below him, the lake sparkled. The otter, still ploughing its way through the water, was nearly to the shore. A few mallard pitched out near the western edge, shattering a mirror mountain.

'I think so,' he said. 'Jesus, I was scared there for a minute. It's a long way down.'

'Sure is, mister. I recollect you saying something about fifty dollars.'

Why am I not surprised? 'That's right,' he said, turning round. 'Will you take a cheque? Only I haven't . . .'

He stopped. Facing him was no grizzled old wood-whittler, as traditionally portrayed in the movies by Slim Pickens; instead, he was staring at a beautiful young girl, with straight black hair, skin the colour of peanut butter and the lissome grace of a top-flight defence attorney squirming his way past the prosecution's key forensic evidence.

'No cheques,' said the vision of loveliness, her full lips slightly parted. 'Strictly cash.'

Whereupon she put her foot in the middle of his chest and pushed him back down the hill.

CHAPTER TWO

'Sorry?'

'I said,' Wesley repeated, 'are we nearly there yet?'

'What? Oh, yes, right.' The otter nodded a couple of times. 'I was miles away,' it added. 'Look, here we are. You can wade from here.'

Whereupon it let go of Wesley's collar. After a few panic-stricken kicks he managed to get his feet onto something solid, and stood up, to find himself still waist-deep in water. Straight ahead of him was the lake shore. He waded towards it, and the water seemed to drift away from him as if it was some heavy, swirling gas. He wasn't at all wet. His knees hurt, and he had pins and needles in his feet.

'Hurry up,' the otter called.

There was something odd about its voice. Up till now, it had been a sort of falsetto squeak, the way you'd expect an otter to sound if you'd been brought up on cartoons. Now there was a rather more human tone in it; feminine, even.

'I'm coming as fast as I can,' he shouted back. 'My feet have gone to sleep.'

'Probably got bored waiting for the rest of you. I haven't got all day, you know.'

As Wesley limped up out of the water, a human figure appeared from behind a rock. The sight of it stopped him in his tracks.

Facing him was no sleek-furred water-mammal; instead, he was staring at a beautiful young girl, with straight black hair, skin the colour of peanut butter and the lissome grace of an elf-maid at a Broadway audition. Wesley, who had always tended to regard young women with the mixture of admiration and apprehension that a dedicated trainspotter might feel at the sight of a perfectly restored vintage steam locomotive coming straight at him down a tunnel at seventy miles an hour, wasn't entirely happy at the substitution. Somehow, he knew he'd be better able to cope with talking otters than girls; especially pretty girls.

'Welcome to your heart's desire,' said the pretty girl.

In the circumstances, Wesley took it quite well. It wasn't the usual sort of thing that girls, pretty or otherwise, tended to say to him. Even short, circular girls with complexions like the skin on cold custard tended to talk to him as if he was something they'd just trodden in. To be welcomed to his heart's desire by something out of one of the better-class mail order catalogues was something entirely new. It was as if, a second or so before the train hit him, he'd realised that it was a 1930s' Castle class Swindon-built double-chamber locomotive in fully authentic GWR livery, still retaining its original glass oil-valves.

'Oh,' said Wesley, beetroot-coloured from collar to hairline. 'You mean . . .'

'Get real,' the girl replied (normality has been restored; we apologise for any inconvenience). 'I mean, we're now on the other side of Lake Chicopee. You understand what that means?'

'No.'

The girl sighed. 'Fine. Then I'll tell you.' She sat down on the rock, pushing her hair back over her shoulders in a way that made Wesley want to climb a tree and hide in a hornets' nest till she'd gone away. 'I'm not sure how observant you are, but did you notice something about the lake? How perfectly it reflects everything around it?'

'Sure,' Wesley replied, truthfully as a newspaper. 'What about it?'

The girl swung her head, so that her hair swayed. 'The surface of the lake's a sort of mirror-fronted door, like the ones you get in shops and bathrooms. That's rather a confusing way of putting it, but you'll get the general idea later on. There's the side you come from; let's call that topside. We've come through that and now we're on the flipside. It's an exact mirror image of topside, except that here the rules are different.'

'What rules?'

The girl shrugged, doing things to parts of her anatomy that Wesley really didn't want to know about just then. 'Any rules you like, that's the whole point. On Flipside, the world's the way you want it to be.'

'Oh.'

'Or rather,' the girl went on, 'it's the way you *think* you want it to be. You made a wish when you jumped in the lake. Right?'

Wesley nodded.

'What you wished for, you got.' She smiled, rather unpleasantly. 'Whether you like it or not. Go forth and enjoy.' She yawned, putting one hand over her mouth and the other behind her head. 'You get the bill later.'

'The *bill* –?'

'Of course the bill. You think I run this place as a public

service? Yes,' she added, looking at him, 'probably you do. I don't suppose such concepts as overheads and maintenance and repair mean an awful lot to you. Remind me later on and I'll let you see last year's accounts.'

Her tone of voice made Wesley feel he ought to apologise, though he wasn't sure what it was he'd done wrong. The least he could do, he reflected, was try and show a little enthusiasm. The fact that he didn't really believe that any of this was actually happening was neither here nor there; even if it was only a dream, he reckoned that he stood a far better chance of waking up if he didn't antagonise anybody until he was safely back under his own duvet, with Old Mister Sun beaming in at him through the mildewed curtains. 'I'm sure you're right,' he therefore said, 'and I didn't mean any offence, honestly. It's just I didn't realise . . . I mean, I spent all my savings on the air fare, so if there's going to be a bill to pay, maybe we'd better call it a day now.'

The girl grinned at him, making him wonder exactly what she was. A few moments before, she'd been an otter. Before that, if his intuition was correct, she'd been an old man with a pipe. Now, with that grin on her face, she looked just like a wolf.

'I wouldn't worry about that,' she said. 'I don't render the sort of bill that money can pay.' She paused for effect, and then continued, 'After all, if it was money I was after, I wouldn't need to bother. Money's easy.'

Wesley blinked. He didn't know precisely how many adjectives there are in the English language – a hundred thousand? Quarter of a million? Five million? – but there were a hell of a lot, and virtually any of them seemed more appropriate than easy when applied to money. 'Gosh,' he said. 'You reckon?'

'Yes,' the girl replied; and it started to snow banknotes. Before Wesley had time to move, he was up to his shins in crisp, new thousand-dollar bills. He didn't need to hold one up to the light to see that they were genuine; somehow it went without saying. He took about a second and a half to recover from the shock; then he started grabbing with both hands.

'If it was just a matter of money,' the girl went on, as a sudden gust of wind blew a heavy drift of thousand-dollar bills straight into Wesley's face, 'my job would be a doddle. If giving you your heart's desire was as simple as sending you home with enough of those things to fill a large container lorry, believe me, I'd be absolutely delighted. Trouble is,' she said, with a sigh that made all the money vanish as suddenly as it had come, 'it isn't. Money wouldn't solve a thing. You'd just be a rich fuck-up instead of a poor one.'

'You know what they say,' Wesley muttered, his hands still tightly clenched on what was now nothing but empty air. 'A change is as good as a rest. I'm prepared to give it a go if you are.'

'That's terribly sweet of you,' the girl replied, vaporising a thousand-dollar bill that had somehow managed to get lodged down the back of Wesley's neck, 'but it'd only make me lazy. No, I know what you really want, and I intend to see that you get it.'

Wesley made a little whimpering noise and sat down on the ground. He wasn't sure he understood this dream. If his heart's desire wasn't the gorgeous girl and it wasn't all that wonderful money, what in hell was it? Later, he resolved, he and his heart were going to have a serious talk about the meaning of the word *priorities*.

'All right,' he said. 'You've told me what it isn't. Now tell me what it is.' A disturbing thought crossed his mind. 'Hey,' he said, 'if this turns out to be one of those timeshare presentation things and the free gift's really only a radio alarm clock, I'm not going to be happy.'

'Be happy. It's not that.'

'Then what is –'

'*Look!*'

Linda sat back in her seat, waved away the offer of a drink, and gazed out of the window at the clouds below.

Iowa.

She frowned. Deplorable but true; she knew only two things about Iowa. One, that it was big, dull and agricultural. Two, it was reputedly the birthplace of James T. Kirk.

Briefly she considered these two nuggets of wisdom and came to the conclusion that there wasn't a story angle in either of them. A pity; because, like Pythagoras, Linda lived her life by and for angles, and accordingly straight lines bothered her, in the same way as a vacuum is reckoned to bother Nature. As far as she was concerned, if you can't crack it open and pick news out of it, there's not much point in it being there. By those criteria, they might as well dig up Iowa and use it to line window-boxes in New York.

Nevertheless; by some divine mistake the Story to end all Stories was happening in Iowa. To be precise, at a place called Lake Chicopee, a little-known beauty spot situated in the exact geometric epicentre of nowhere.

She wrinkled her exquisite nose. As far as she could make out, there were Strange Happenings at Lake Chicopee. Mostly, it was people disappearing; but there were also uncanny sights and noises, weird manifestations, things appearing, disappearing and changing shape, things going bump in the night. She switched on her laptop and waited for the lights to stop flickering.

Seven people, five males and two females, all of them from out of state, had last been seen or heard of setting out to walk to the lake. No bodies, possessions, footprints or bloodstains had come to light, though for some reason the police department adamantly refused to drag the lake. Among the manifestations there was a long, low ship that appeared and disappeared, strange whispering voices in the woods, unexplained lights and animals and birds that were supposed to have changed their shape in clear view of what passed in Iowa for reliable witnesses.

Yes. Well.

Those, then, were the raw materials:

- Lake
- Remote
- People disappearing
- Boat appears and disappears
- Funny lights
- Cute furry animals changing shape

As the great silver bird sliced its cloud-splitting way like a light-sabre through wedding cake, Linda typed the ingredients in and read the list back two or three times, occasionally changing the order and flipping across to the readership profile database. Then she took a deep breath, flexed her shapely fingers, and set to work.

When a cook cooks, he gathers the ingredients before him and makes them into something. He doesn't wait for them to march into the pot and semaphore a message to the cooker to switch itself on. He doesn't agonise over whether the carrots really belong in the sauce or whether the parsnips are true. He goes to it with a container, a source of heat and a big sharp knife.

She paused, scrolled back and noticed an omission, which she rectified by typing in:

• Native Americans

– which was likely enough; and in any case, the casserole needed them. She had to have Native Americans or there wouldn't be an R to go with the C, the A and the P:

• Conspiracy
• Racism
• Animals
• Politics

Put 'em together and what do they spell? News.

Weird things happening in a remote spot = secret Government scientific research. Funny lights and things mutating = nukes. People disappearing – see above. A *ship* that appeared and disappeared; on a *lake* –

She furrowed her brows, bit her lip and let her mind off the leash.

Sherlock Holmes' law, as amended to fit the requirements of journalism. Once you have eliminated the unnewsworthy, whatever remains, however improbable, *will* be the truth . . .

Yes!

Submarines. Secret Government nuclear submarines. Neo-fascist CIA warmongers were covertly stockpiling Armageddon submersibles in America's heartland, not giving a damn about the catastrophic effects on the cute furry environment and the cute furry Native Americans, cold-bloodedly jeopardising world peace with the intention of . . .

Of?

Yes, murmured her internal devil's advocate. Why would anybody go to all that trouble? Not, of course, that a motive is essential; people will believe that the Government will do anything, provided they can be made to appear to be covering it up. On the other hand, there's nothing quite like a good solid motive for building a story that'll keep going for a week. Leave it all shrouded in enigmatic overtones and by Day Three you'll find yourself sandwiched in between the film reviews and the crossword.

Motive?

Linda clicked her tongue, reproaching herself for her lack of vision.

Obviously, they were doing it secretly because they were planning to give the submarines as clandestine military aid to a sinister foreign power.

Right.

Database; SFP/LIST.

Crossreference; readership profile database.

Only a fool would choose an SFP that'd offend half the readership. Merge; and –

'Oh,' she said aloud.

She looked at the screen. She raised an eyebrow. On the other hand, it must be right, or it wouldn't be on the screen. After all if you can't trust the database, what can you trust?

• Vatican City

OK, clandestine military aid to the Vatican. Saint Petergate. Pausing for a moment to speculate as to why the paper had so few readers among the Irish, Italian and Hispanic communities (bad business; must do something about that), she filled in the bare facts with some mental colour.

Vatican? Well, it was beginning to make sense. Most people knew next to nothing – she knew next to nothing – about the recently elected Pope Shane III, formerly Cardinal Archbishop of Adelaide. On the other hand, very little real hard news ever seemed to come out of Australia; and it stands to reason that any country that goes out of its way to be obscure and secretive must be up to something. She tapped a few keys, and the screen read:

• Australia – State Department backing – ultimate aim world domination.

Which was much more like it. After all, nobody ever claimed that Australians were a minority of any sort, so she could say whatever the hell she liked about them and nobody'd be in the least offended.

She sighed contentedly and looked out over the clouds again, consolidating the progress so far in her mind. In unspoilt idyllic environmentally sensitive Lake Chicopee, renegade CIA elements are funding a massive program of clandestine nuclear submarine building, with the sinister intention of funnelling Armageddon technology through the Vatican to the warmongers of the shadowy, secretive Australian ruling junta. Psychotic antipodean death squads with corks round their hats are systematically wiping out anybody who happens to stumble across this terrible secret, including the once flourishing Native American population, who stand by helpless as their proud cultural heritage is ground into dust under the jackbooted paw of the kangaroo. Meanwhile, your tax dollars are going to help fund the greatest threat to world peace since Genghis Khan.

She smiled, saved the file and closed her eyes. As she drifted into sleep it crossed her mind that one day the world might of its own accord produce enough genuine organically grown news to satisfy the needs of the global media, in which case she wouldn't have to do this sort of thing any more. Which would be a pity; but that day, if it ever came, wouldn't be in her lifetime. They'd just have to start up more newspapers and more TV channels and more radio stations, just to redress the balance.

Having bounced off a couple of rocks and a tree-root or two, Calvin Dieb came to rest in a tangle of briars.

Once he'd realised he wasn't dead a number of thoughts crossed his mind, all of them to do with money.

First; he'd been crazy to offer fifty bucks to someone to get him off the hillside, because in the event he'd been able to roll down it with only superficial scratches and bruises to show for it.

Second; in the time he'd taken to roll down the slope, he could have earned, at his usual charging rate of two thousand dollars an hour, eighteen dollars and forty cents.

Third; he would willingly pay the cash equivalent of ten hours of his time to anybody who would show him where that goddamn lunatic female had gotten to, and provide him with a large, sharp knife.

He stood up. Because of his involvement with the briar patch, this entailed a certain amount of ripping of his five-thousand-dollar trousers, but he was (a) past caring and

(b) so heavily insured that he was in danger of becoming a gravitational anomaly and attracting his own meteorite belt. Someone else was going to pay – heavily – for this whole episode in any case, so the hell with details.

Thoughts of money always inspire strong emotions in lawyers, and this particular train of thought aroused in Calvin Dieb a flashback of anger of the intensity usually reserved for rival law firms who filched his richer, more gullible clients. As he gained his feet and sent out search parties for his breath, his anger started to cool; or rather to temper, becoming harder and more capable of keeping an edge. Forget the sharp knife, he muttered to himself, and bring me a writ. And, more to the point, bring me someone I can sue.

After all, he told himself, as he removed a length of bramble from around his ankle, kill a guy and there's an end to it. Sue him and you can do to him in this life what the devils in Hell will do to him in the next, only rather more thoroughly. They didn't phase out trial by combat because it was too cruel; quite the reverse.

But all that could wait. In the morning, he'd have a team of investigators down here to get him the name, address and financial details of the crazy broad who'd pushed him, and in the afternoon he'd send in the cops and the process servers. Right now, he wanted to get back to his office, where iodine would heal his wounds and foreclosing on some poor bastard would salve his mind. He looked up at the gradient he had to climb, took a deep breath and reached in his pocket for his car keys.

His car keys . . .

Psychiatrists say that the fundamental subconscious anxiety that all men suffer from, and which underlies all their actions, is a morbid fear of castration. Wrong. Unzip any man's mind and you'll find, right down there in the dark, terrifying place where the soul never goes, a primeval dread of losing his car keys. Just think how many times a day you instinctively reach in your pocket or pat your hip, just to know they're still there. Upon Calvin Dieb, already thorn-ripped, humiliated and physically and mentally out of pocket some tens of thousands of dollars, there descended the horrifying realisation that he had been gelded of his keys and that his car, the external expression of everything he was, now sat useless and undrivable in the lay-by above.

Shit!

He stood for some ninety seconds, tracing by eye the path of his fall from the crest of the slope, where he'd encountered that goddamn female, down here to the very shore of the lake. Anywhere along that line his keys could have fallen out. It could take him hours – tens of thousands of dollars – to find them in all this scrub and undergrowth. On the other hand, it would take him at least nine thousand dollars to walk to the nearest town, another thousand or so to wait for a car or a helicopter to come out from the city and pick him up, not to mention all the pain and suffering involved in walking too far in boots as expensive as those he was wearing. It's an odd fact, but an undeniable one, that once you start paying four-figure sums for footwear you tend to end up with magnificently hand-stitched instruments of torture that reduce the backs of your heels to raw flesh if you do more than hobble from your car to the elevator; part of the price you have to pay for being rich, he'd always rationalised. As it happened, he had in the trunk of the car a pair of worn-out old sneakers, $4.99 from K-Mart, that were the nearest thing a mortal could ever experience to floating on a cloud. If he only had his keys, he could go back up there and put them on. If only . . .

OK. Forget the writ. Forget even the three fingers of single malt and the hot tub that had started to figure prominently in his subconscious thoughts. *What I really want now, more than anything in the whole world, is to find my goddamn keys* –

Just as the thought crossed his mind, he tripped over a briar-root, fell heavily, tumbled down a steep incline, hit a boulder and rolled off a rocky ledge into the still, calm waters of the lake.

A second or two later, an otter slid into the water and began swimming out towards him.

'*Look!*'

So Wesley looked. But there wasn't anything to see –

Except, in the far distance, a ship. No, the *reflection* of a ship, an upside-down mirror image of a dragon-prowed, clinker-built, square-sailed fifty-oar longship, a black pinewood killer swan with brightly painted round shields all along its sides in the manner of a Hawaiian flower wreath.

'Bet you never knew,' the female was saying, 'that the Vikings got this far. Well, they did. Two generations after Eric the Red reached Newfoundland, this lot –' she waved vaguely at the mirror-ship. 'This lot, fifty fearless explorers led by Thorfinn Piglet and Einar Bluetooth, sailed down the coast until they blundered into the mouth of the St Lawrence river, which they rather liked the look of. So they pottered down that, past Quebec, into Lake Ontario, where they ran into a little problem known to you and me as the Niagara Falls. Now we both know that there's no way on earth to get a ship by there; but they didn't, so they took it to bits, plank by plank and nail by nail and little-widgetty-thing-that's-always-left-over-once-you've-put-everything-else-back by little-widgetty-thing-that's-always-left-over-once-you've-put-everything-else-back, and they carried it down into Lake Erie, where they put it together again and went on their way; past Cleveland and Toledo, except they weren't called that then, of course; past Detroit, across Lake St Clair and down the St Clair river into Lake Huron.' The girl paused. 'Are you taking any of this in, by the way? I mean, you do know where all these places are?'

'What? Oh, yes,' Wesley lied. 'Course I do.'

'That's all right, then. I'd hate the awesome scope of their achievement to be wasted on you just because you think Lake Erie's in Cumbria. Anyway, off they go across Lake Huron, all the way round the fair state of Michigan, passing through the Mackmac straits into another whopping great big lake which happens also to be called Michigan, either through coincidence or a stunning lack of imagination. So there they are, skirting Lake Michigan, and they see Green Bay. They're sick and tired of Lake Michigan by now, so they hang a right and toddle down the Bay, down the Fox river, sometimes carrying that damn boat more often than it carries them because of all the falls and rapids and so on; then they bear right again and get lost in lots of itty bitty rivers, the sort that make a country look like it's got varicose veins. Just as they're starting to feel depressed, they trip over the Wisconsin river and follow that; and when it merges with the Mississippi, they follow that; and when they're bored with the Mississippi, they branch off down our very own local-river-made-good, the North Squash; and one quick taking-to-bits-and-putting-back-together-again later – they're really good at that by now, by the way; they can take that boat to bits and put it back blindfold and wearing two pairs of gloves – here they are in Lake Chicopee, bright-eyed, bushy-tailed and eager for whatever new nugget of happenstance Fate chooses to bestow on them.' The girl paused and gazed at the two-dimensional longship under the shadow of her palm, so that Wesley couldn't see her expression. 'In about five minutes,' she continued, 'they're due to hit the one submerged rock in the whole lake, sink and drown. Pity, really.'

Wesley stared at her. 'Why?' he demanded.

The girl shrugged. 'They felt like it. Not the sinking part, of course, the rest of it; they felt like going for a run out, and one of them had this boat, so why not? I think the captain muttered something about wanting to travel courageously where nobody had been yet. Some people are like that.'

'Yes, all right,' Wesley interrupted. 'I can understand that. But what I mean is, after that really incredible journey, why've they got to go and get drowned *here*, of all places? I mean, it's so flat. I mean calm,' he added, before the girl had a chance to point out that lakes are usually flat, which is what stops them falling off the edges of hills and turning into rivers. 'I mean, how the hell could anybody drown in *that*?'

'You nearly managed it,' the girl pointed out.

'Yes, but I'm not – I mean, *I* couldn't have sailed all the way up those rivers and down those lakes.' He stared at the reflection as it slid, noiselessly majestic, over the upside-down mountains. 'Isn't there something we can do to warn them?' he asked. 'Or are they, like, sort of *ghosts* . . .' He shivered a little as a pair of landing ducks splashed straight through the ship, sending bits of it rippling in all directions.

'I mean, is that why we can only see the reflection and not the actual boat?'

The girl watched the reflection slowly take shape again and shook her head. 'Not quite,' she replied. 'In about four minutes they'll hit the rock and come on down this side. Then we'll be able to see them.'

'But they'll be *dead*.'

The girl shrugged. 'You some sort of bigot?' she asked. 'I'll have you know, some of my best friends are dead. Wouldn't want my daughter to marry one,' she admitted, 'but that's not prejudice. It's just, think of all the problems their kids'd face, at school and so on.'

A light-bulb, no more than forty watts but still bright enough to see by, lit up in Wesley's brain. 'Just a moment,' he said. 'When they fall in the lake, you grant them their heart's desire, yes?'

The girl beamed. 'So you *have* been listening!' she cried, clapping her hands together. 'Oh, that's so encouraging. Yes, I certainly do.'

'By drowning them in a lake?'

'Yes.' The girl shrugged again. 'It's like I told you. They get their heart's desire, but it's up to me exactly what form it takes. Now, what these clowns really wanted was to go on an awfully big adventure. Ah,' she added, as the sound of wood splintering on rock echoed around the amphitheatre of mountains and lake. 'Party time!'

The reflection dissipated into another clutch of ripples, out of the centre of which a longship rose, submarine-fashion. Apart from a few wisps of pondweed draped round the top of the mast and a very upset-looking trout thrashing about on the deck, it seemed none the worse for its recent misfortune. The girl stood up and waved.

'Over here!' she shouted.

The ship changed course, until the dragon's head was facing them square-on. The oars started to move, keeping metronome time and sending out great sunbursts of ripples each time the blades hit the water. Wesley could hear wood groaning and rope creaking; he could feel the enormous amount of physical effort it took to propel the great heavy thing just a few yards across the water. It must be, he felt, like pushing a lorry that's run out of petrol.

All the way from Newfoundland, up rivers and down lakes, oarstroke by oarstroke. He felt sick, and his back started to hurt.

'Excuse me.' The voice was coming from the ship. 'Excuse me, please, young lady, but on the right way for Duluth are we being?'

'Duluth?' The girl shook her head. 'No, sorry, you're well out of your way here. About seven hundred miles, give or take a bit.'

'Bother!'

'To get to Duluth,' the girl went on, 'you want to head back to the Mississippi, right back up the way you came as far as Lake Huron; then stick to the north coast round into Lake Superior, carry on hugging the north coast and head west till you come to the pointy bit, you can't miss it. You took the wrong turning.'

'Silly old us,' the Viking shouted back, shaking his helmeted head. 'Joshing us the fellows will be when we are to home returning. Nevertheless the funny side visible is. Thank.'

'You're welcome.'

The ship swung round – Wesley could hear the cracking of joints as arms wrenched in their sockets with the effort – and headed back up the lake, the way it had come. Then it hit the rock again and sank.

'Why Duluth?' Wesley asked, after a long silence.

'Hadn't ever been there, I guess,' the girl replied. 'That's explorers for you. Marvellous people, Heaven only knows where the world would be without them. Actually, it was a cousin of Thorfinn Piglet who was the first man ever to set foot on the North Pole.'

'Gosh!'

The girl nodded. 'Bjorn the Stupid, his name was,' she said. 'He had to walk the last three hundred miles, all on his own. Hell of a journey.'

'He died too, presumably.'

'Oh no.' The girl shook her head. 'Lost quite a few fingers and toes and things through frostbite, but he made it home alive to the Viking colony at Brattahlid. Not all in one piece, but the majority of him.'

For some reason, that made Wesley feel a whole lot better. 'Well, then,' he said. 'So why do the books say it was Scott, or Amundsen, or whoever? I'd have thought –'

'Oh, he never *told* anybody,' the girl replied. 'Too embarrassed. You see, he was supposed to be heading in the other direction. But he got lost, went north instead of east. He'd only set out to deliver a load of timber a few miles up the coast. When they asked him why it'd taken him so long and what'd happened to his appendages, he made up some story about being set upon by polar bears. Nobody believed him, of course. They all assumed he'd got plastered and fallen off his boat into the ice-cold water.'

Wesley didn't say anything for a very long time. He didn't like this dream very much, he decided; it was too depressing, and unlike all his other horrible dreams, which usually involved him standing up in front of a crowded Wembley Stadium with no trousers on, it was just close enough to reality to be thoroughly unpleasant. He sent a memo to his inner brain saying, *Wake up now, please*, but nothing happened.

'There's a point to all this, isn't there?' he said at last. 'I mean, there's a moral or motto or whatever you call it.'

'Correct.' Without taking her eyes off the lake, the girl nodded. 'I suppose you could call it the vanity of human wishes, except that's a bit trite. Anyway, that's a sort of introductory session. Passive learning. All the rest of it's a bit more hands-on, or do I mean interactive? What I'm trying to say is, instead of just sitting there on your bottom and listening, you actually get to do things and have adventures. Isn't that fun?'

Wesley thought about it for a moment. 'No,' he said.

'You don't mean No,' the girl replied cheerfully. 'What you really mean, though you probably don't realise it, is Yes. Trust me, I know about these things.'

Wesley allowed his slump to melt into a crouch. 'Does interactive mean you're going to drown me too?' he asked. 'Or will you let me off with just losing all my fingers and toes?'

The girl smiled. Whether it was a nice smile or not, Wesley couldn't tell. 'Whether you get to keep your fingers,' she said, 'depends rather a lot on whether you pull them out. Come on.'

On the far western shore of the lake, under the shade of a tall pine tree, sat a border guard, waiting for her eggs to hatch.

Throughout the history of conflict, ever since the first primitive humanoid picked up a ploughshare and realised that, with the help of a forge and a big hammer, he could turn it into a moderately efficient sword, every army ever raised has sooner or later taken on the basic diamond-shape form of organisation. At the apex, the uppermost point, you have the top one per cent who make up your elite forces; the guys who swing through windows on ropes and hold off vastly superior numbers while swigging vodka martinis. In the middle come the squaddies, foot-sloggers and cannon-fodder; people of all shapes, sizes and qualities who complain a lot, do as they're told, make of it the best they can and die from time to time, even when the cameras are looking the other way. And, at the reverse apex, the whole thing dwindles away to the bottom one per cent; the incurably hopeless, incompetent and disaffected, neither useful nor ornamental. It's this section of the military community that gets ordered to stand in front of things and guard them. Wherever there's a mountain or tall building that might get stolen, or a lake or river that might burn down, there you'll find a little wooden kennel with a pointy roof, and in it a nerk with a gun, called a sentry.

In this instance, Jemima. So highly was she thought of by the rest of the Lake Chicopee Defence Force that they hadn't actually told her she was in it. It took an atypically bright young lieutenant in the Household Frogs to notice that whenever anything moved within ten yards of Jemima's eggs, be it a moose, a squadron of armoured cars or a falling leaf, Jemima started making a horrible noise which lasted until the thing went away again. All that remained was to move Jemima's nest thirty yards or so to the right, until it was within spitting distance of the border gate, and that was one more loophole effectively plugged, relieving a proper soldier of a boring job and leaving him free to perform the vital function of bashing the butt of his rifle on the ground every time his sergeant yelled, 'Hut!'

There were five of these vulnerable points – known as 'gates' for convenience, though they were more complex than that; think of them as ill-fitting lavatory windows round the back of the cinema of Time and Space, through which the recklessly brave can sometimes climb in to watch the film for free – and each one had a sentry. Because of the peculiar physics of Lake Chicopee, there was no knowing what lay on the other side of each gate at any given moment, or (more to the point) who or what might be trying to get through it. Hence the need for sentries, who had to be fearless, vigilant, not easily bored and, above all, expendable.

Jemima had just completed twelve hours sitting on her eggs facing north-south, and was performing the delicate manoeuvre of turning east-west, when a tiny movement caught her eye. No human, no featherless biped of any description, would have noticed it; nor would the latest state-of-the-art monitoring device, for there was no displacement of air, no microsubtle temperature change, no physical transfer of mass to get in the way of an infrared beam. In fact, it wasn't so much a movement as a minutely small editing of reality, whereby a few motes of dust stopped being in one place and found themselves in another.

'Ark! ' said Jemima. 'Ark ark ark ark ARK ARK ARK!'

'Oh for crying out loud, it's that bloody duck again,' said Cap'n Hat, bravest and boldest of the transdimensional smugglers of Lake Chicopee. 'I thought I told someone to deal with it the last time.'

His henchmen exchanged guilty looks. 'Sorry, Chief,' muttered Squab, Hat's stubble-chinned, eyepatched bo'sun. 'Slipped me mind. Here, I'll shoot the bugger if you –'

'Please don't,' Hat said wearily. 'Quacking ducks are bad enough without gunshots as well. Besides, you'd only miss.'

'No I wouldn't, Chief. I been practising.'

'Squab, my dear old mate, you couldn't hit a large building if you were inside it. Now shut up and let me think.'

Given the amount of noise the duck was making it was inevitable that somebody would come soon, if only to wring its neck. Caught as he was, in the open, in broad daylight, with two handcarts laden down with Flipside plunder that he'd really rather not jettison if he could help it, he was left with a meagre choice of three options; hang concealment and make a run for it, stand and fight it out, or try and find something to hide under. Dismissing the first two options, for he was essentially a realist, he ducked under an ivy leaf and gestured to his men to follow suit.

'Wassat damn racket?' yelled the distant voice of an owl.

'Just that duck again,' replied an equally distant frog. 'Prob'ly seen its own shadow or somethin'.'

'Take a squad an' have a look anyhow,' ordered the owl. 'Just in case.'

Swearing fluently under his breath, Hat peered round the edge of the leaf until he located the frog-squad. Typically, they were directly between him and the gate, which put paid to making a run for it. As for fighting; instinctively he reached for his pistol and thumbed back the hammer, but he knew as he did so that he was hopelessly outnumbered. Indeed, bearing in mind the calibre of the forces at his disposal, he was theoretically outnumbered even when there was nobody there at all.

'Nobody move,' he hissed.

'But, Chief –'

'Shuttup, Twist.'

'Chief, I need a pee. Would it be all right if I just crept very quietly over to those bushes and –?'

Hat was tempted; after all, when Twist crept unobtrusively he was about as hard to spot as an earthquake in central San Francisco. That meant he'd be pounced on and instantly nabbed by the patrol, thereby causing a diversion under cover of which –

'I said be quiet. Should've gone before you came out. Cross your legs and try not to think about it.'

The smugglers of Lake Chicopee, who make their living by scarfing up props and scenery from the infinite variety of Flipside, sneaking them Topside and selling them, are probably the most extraordinary parasites in the Universe. They're also, of course, a dangerous pest, since many of the commodities they bring across aren't supposed to exist on the obverse side of the lake; dragons and thunderbirds, magic rings, cloaks of invisibility, bottomless purses, seven-league boots and radio alarm-clocks that actually go off when they're supposed to. The damage they do in Reality is mirrored (of course) Down Under. Many's the time a long-lost prince has turned up to draw a sword from a stone only to find that someone's beaten him to it; and by the time he discovers it's missing, the sword has already been sold off a barrow in some street market, making a bemused Japanese tourist the rightful king of all Albion. In other words, the equilibrium is upset. Ripples get into the reflections.

The smugglers are not, therefore, terribly popular; hence the Defence Force, the sentries and the armed duck.

'Chief.'

'Shut up, Twist.'

'Yes, but, Chief –'

'Tie a bloody knot in it and be *quiet*!'

'I was only going to ask,' said Twist, 'why we don't just slip away through that tunnel.'

'Because, you stupid oaf – what tunnel?'

'That tunnel, Chief.'

And Twist pointed. Sure enough, there was a tunnel. It looked like the entrance to a mine (except that there was no way it could be, because it led directly under the lake; start digging into the floor there, and you'd break through and fall down out of the sky).

Hat stared at it. 'Where the hell did that come from?' he demanded.

'Dunno, Chief. Funny I never noticed it before.'

'You and me both.' Hat rubbed his chin. He had no idea how long he'd been around this lake; vaguely he recollected a time when a little trickle of water had come down the side of the mountain with a sheaf of estate agents' particulars in its current, taken one look at the bone-dry valley below and said, 'Yes!' In all that time, he'd never seen any tunnels or mineshafts or underground railways of rustic construction. What the –?

On the other hand, the frogs were closing in fast.

'This way,' said Hat.

CHAPTER THREE

CALVIN DIEB: INTERNAL MEMORANDUM
From: *subconscious mind & memory archives*
To: *awareness control centre*
Message: *Please remember that you can't swim*

Thank you, Dieb muttered under what little remained of his breath, I hadn't forgotten. Instead of wasting my time telling me things I already know, tell me some way I can get out of . . .

The rest of Calvin Dieb's breath, by far the majority, was floating on the top of the lake in bubble form. Another stream of bubbles headed towards it on an intercept course.

Sorry, can't help you on that score. Query whether you could sue your school for negligence/breach of contract in that they failed to teach you to swim when you were ten. Query also joining the estates of your deceased parents as co-defendants.

He was just drafting a scathing reply when something nudged his ear. Without actually ceasing to drown, he put drowning on hold for a moment or so. It was, he saw, an otter.

'Hello,' said the otter. 'Bears.'

'What?'

'And wolves, if they can catch us. But bears, mostly.'

'Bears? What about goddamn bears? And how come you can –?'

The otter flipped over and floated on its back. 'You were speculating earlier,' it said, 'about what sort of animals eat otters.'

'I – How did you *know* ?'

'Mind you,' the otter went on, paddling languidly with its back paws, like a small furry paddlesteamer, 'that wouldn't be much use to you, would it? Bears'd be even harder to get rid of than otters. Can't think offhand of anything on this continent that eats bears.'

'Look, I'm really sorry, I didn't mean . . .'

'Except,' added the otter, looking him in the eye, 'humans. I believe barbecued bear steak with onions is considered a delicacy in these parts.'

'No. I mean yes. I mean, do you want it to be?'

The otter shrugged. 'Don't make no never-mind to me,' it said. 'I'm not a bear. Not at the moment, anyhow. Welcome to Lake Chicopee, by the way.'

INTERNAL MEMORANDUM. *Hey, we're floating. Didn't know we could do that. How **are** we doing that? Hell, I thought you knew.*

'Thank you,' Dieb replied.

'You're welcome,' said the otter. 'Have a nice day now, d'you hear?'

Whereupon it rolled over, ducked its head under the water and vanished. Immediately, Dieb started drowning again.

'Hey!' he yelled. 'You in the fur! Come back!'

No reply –

– Except, just as he'd assumed he'd gone under for the last time, there he was floating again. Or at least, he was lying on his back on top of the water, staring up at a blue sky –

– A blue sky with trees and mountains in it. Having given the situation some thought, Dieb came to the conclusion that lying very still was probably the most sensible course of action. Lying on water wasn't something he'd ever tried before, and he wasn't sure he knew the rules. Maybe it was the same basic technique as walking on water. Which can't be all that difficult, at that. If God and crane-flies can do it, so could he.

'Hello again.'

This time, the otter was on the other side of him. It too was lying on its back, nibbling at a fish clutched between its front paws. The fish, Dieb noticed, was still vaguely alive.

'I meant to ask earlier,' the otter said. 'When you were drowning just now, did your entire life flash past you, the way it's supposed to? Sorry if that's a rather personal question, but I'm interested. I meet a lot of drowning people, you see, and about half of them say, "Yes, it does," and the other half say, "No, it doesn't," and I'd really love to do some serious research here. I mean, do you only get a memory flashback if you've lived a really happy life, or the other way round, or doesn't that come into it at all? What about you, for instance?'

Status report: *you're lying on your back in the water, talking to an otter. Why are you doing this?*

'I don't know,' Dieb replied. 'I mean, no, my life didn't flash before my eyes. And it's been a very happy life, I guess.' His face clouded for a moment as he said the words; and his brain's credit control department raised a query along the lines of *Why are you lying when you're not getting paid for it?* 'I guess,' he repeated. 'Yes, I'm sure. I mean, look at me. I'm the senior partner of one of the best goddamn law firms in the state. Annually, after tax, I take home –'

Suddenly, the fish between the otter's paws lashed out frantically with its tail, shot up into the air and crashed into the lake with a *plop!* and a shower of fine spray. The otter lifted its head and watched the ripples with the air of a park keeper watching people walking on the grass.

'Damn,' it said. 'I was just getting to the tasty bit.'

'It was still alive, for Christ's sake!' As he spoke, Dieb wondered at his own passion. Hell, it was just a fish. Now it was a partially eaten fish, still gamely swimming. Under normal circumstances, his instincts would have been to try and interest it in substantial personal injury litigation, but for some reason all he could think was: *Why bother? Why make a run for it when effectively it's dead already?*

'I might ask you the same question,' the otter replied.

'*What?*'

'Look at you.' The otter obeyed its own suggestion. 'Forty-nine years old, grossly overweight. Severe – I mean *severe* – stress-related disorders, badly aggravated by chronic alcohol and tobacco habits, virtually a suicide diet, no exercise ever; you're about five years overdue for the Great Meathook as it is, and you're exhibiting all the self-preservation instincts of a dishonoured samurai. But when you feel yourself drowning, you thrash about. Why bother?'

Calvin Dieb scowled. 'Ah, cut it out,' he growled. 'I get that all the time from the quacks, and I'm still here, aren't I?' A horrible thought struck him, precisely at the same moment as an unexpected wave splashed water into his face. 'I *am* still here, aren't I? Shit, did I die? Is this some sort of goddamn afterlife or something?'

The otter twitched its nose at him. 'Welcome to Lake Chicopee,' it replied, as if answering the question.

'Huh?'

'It's a moot point,' the otter went on. 'I won't bore you with the equations, so let's just say it's – what's that phrase you lawyers use when somebody asks you a question and you don't know the answer? Let's just say it's a grey area. On the one paw, you're definitely taking time out from your usual continuum. Your watch, for instance, won't work. Time doesn't work, come to that; it just doesn't seem to pass here, is all. Hey, that must be hell for you; I could ask you for all sorts of complicated legal advice and you couldn't charge me a cent.'

'Hey . . .'

'On the other paw,' the otter continued, 'don't try collecting on your life policies, because you can't, 'cos you're still alive.' It made a tiny hacking noise, presumably analogous to laughter. 'You're stuffed, Dieb, you know that? You can't earn money, and you can't collect for being dead. Since your only purpose in existing is to accumulate dollars, what the hell is the point in you?'

'Shuttup!'

At once, the otter flipped and dived. A surge of panic swept through Dieb like on a bad day on Wall Street, and he began to feel desperately heavy, as if he'd just stepped out of a twentieth-storey window. The water was just starting to get into his mouth when the otter popped up again, just by his left ear.

'But we digress,' it said, and at once Dieb was floating again. 'This is Lake Chicopee. You know the old legend?'

'Get me *out* of here!'

'The old legend,' the otter said, ignoring him, 'has it that if you make a wish and jump in this here lake, you get your heart's desire. Good, huh?'

'Fine. My heart's desire is to get out of –'

'Wrong.'

'I beg your pardon?'

'Wrong,' the otter repeated. 'Your heart's desire, as at 11:04 and sixteen-point-two seconds, which is the precise moment you hit the water, was to find your car keys.' That tiny hacking noise again. 'Your wish is my command, buster. You ready?'

'*Hey!*'

'Then here,' said the otter, 'we go.'

'That's it?'

'Sure is, miss.' The cab driver pressed a button, and the window on Linda's side wound down with an electric purr. 'Kinda pretty, ain't it?'

'Hm?' Linda shrugged, as if he'd asked her to perform some abstruse mathematical calculation. 'Yeah, sure. What do I owe you?'

'Call it thirty bucks, miss.'

'I'll need a receipt.'

'Huh?'

Linda frowned. 'It's what we call a piece of paper with the cost of the ride written on it.' She sniffed. 'They do use writing around here, don't they? Or do you muddle through with body language and smoke signals?'

'Just a second,' the cab driver said. 'I'll write it on the back of one of my cards. There, that do you?'

She nodded, took the card and put it away. 'Say, mister,' she said, 'you wouldn't happen to have seen any submarines in these parts at all?'

'Submarines.' The driver looked thoughtful. 'Can't say as I have. What with the lake being so far from the sea, and all. Course, I could be mistaken,' he added fair-mindedly. 'Don't reckon I'd necessarily know one if I saw one.'

'Quite.' Linda sighed. 'All right, then, how about Australians?'

'Australians?'

'That's right. People from Australia. Seen any?'

'Can't say as I . . .'

'Forget it.' Linda opened the door, threw out her bag and slammed the door shut behind her. 'Don't wait,' she added. 'When I'm ready to leave I'll ring through on my mobile.' She hesitated, as a disturbing thought occurred to her. 'Mobiles do work in these mountains, don't they? I mean, you can get a signal?'

'Can't say as . . .'

'It's all right,' Linda growled. 'If necessary, I'll walk. Don't let me keep you.'

The driver looked at her, smiled a thin little smile and drove away, much to Linda's relief. He reminded her a bit too much of her father, who had driven the station cab at Parsimony, Utah until they closed the station (not, mercifully, before she'd had a chance to use it to get the hell out of Parsimony, Utah and that whole goddamn way of life) and the resonances unsettled her. One of her dad's favourite apothegms was that you can take a girl out of Utah but you can't take Utah out of the girl; and it was remarks of that sort that tended to undermine her belief in language as a viable means of communication.

God, she muttered to herself, I *hate* the countryside. It's so . . .

Well. Quite.

Still, if there's a story in it somewhere, then it had to be tolerated; humoured, even. Even if it meant having to walk on grass and cross rivers and shelter under trees and all that crap. Feeling more than a little resentful, she hefted her bag onto her shoulder and set off towards the lake.

Whereupon the tiresome old man, who had been watching her through the eyes of an eagle circling a long way up above her head, pottered out of a sudden and unexpected timber shack and said, 'Howdy.'

Linda turned and looked at him, assessing him in his capacities as (a) threat, (b) informant and (c) eyesore. No to (a), yes to (c); she resolved to investigate (b) further.

'Hello,' she said, switching on her smile at the mains. 'You live around here?'

The old man nodded. 'Sure do,' he said. 'Been livin' here all my life. You come to look at the lake?'

Linda nodded. 'It's very . . .' She remembered the technical term the cab driver had used. 'Kinda pretty,' she parrotted.

It seemed that she'd said the right thing, because the old man smiled, revealing a set of teeth that reminded her of baked beans swimming in mustard. 'You said it, miss,' he replied, and wheezed; a general purpose combination laugh/cough. 'Kinda pretty all right. Though,' he added, after a tiny pause, 'they do say this here lake is haunted.'

Linda stepped up the smile by an amp or so. 'Really,' she cooed. 'How fascinating. You don't say.'

'That's right,' the old man said, doing something disgusting with his tongue. 'By the ghost of an ole Injun sperrit, name of Okeewana or some such. By Jiminy, miss, the tales I could tell you 'bout that ole –'

'Submarines.'

The old man hesitated, like a jammed machine. 'Beg pardon, miss?'

'Have you seen any submarines, by any chance? You know, ships that suddenly appear from out of the water and then –'

'You mean like that one?' He pointed.

Linda swivelled round like a small boy on an office chair and saw a *thing*; something that looked for all the world like a wood-carving of a dragon's head, just breaking the surface of the water, surrounded by ripples swarming like disturbed bees.

'A periscope!' Linda breathed.

'Keep lookin'.'

The thing rose steadily up out of the water, followed a moment later by what was unmistakably a mast, and then by a whole ship; broad-beamed, clinker-built, bristling with oars like a squashed-flat centipede. Brightly painted round shields encircled its bows, and a few disgusted-looking fish flapped wearily on the planks of the deck.

'Right,' said Linda contentedly. 'Thought so.'

Cursing fluently, Talks To Squirrels loosed his last arrow, following it with his eye all the way from his bowstring to the newcomer's heart: Bang on the money, as always; enough to make a man weep. He'd just put six consecutive arrows into a space the size of a playing-card at a range of a hundred and seventy-five yards, and the bugger hadn't even noticed. The irony, the cruel, savage, merciless irony of it was that when he'd been alive he'd been hard put to it to hit a sleeping bison at five paces.

Where the hell were they all coming from? Three of the sons of bitches, all in one morning; and he'd come out with just two dozen arrows and a small flint knife. The question was, if he sprinted back Flipside for more arrows and his business tomahawk, would the scumbags still be here when he returned, or would he come running back, armed to the teeth, only to find they'd moved on? Whereas if he stayed here, at least he could pelt them with insubstantial rocks and batter them around the head with non-existent tree-branches. It was a difficult choice to make. Or rather, it wasn't, since he wouldn't be able to stir so much as a hair on their heads even if he had a battery of cannon and a Gatling gun at his disposal. Quit kidding yourself, Talks.

Gloomily he shoved his bow back into its buckskin case, sat down on top of a disused anthill, wrapped his hands round his chin and sulked. When he'd made his wish, all those years ago, to be able to carry on fighting the paleface until the sun went out and the moon fell from the sky and the mountains slid down into the lake and were swallowed up, he hadn't pictured it working out quite like this. Admittedly, if you worked on the basis of mortal wounds delivered and direct hits inflicted, at the last count he had eighty-six thousand, four hundred and ninety-seven notches on his bowhandle; not bad going for a brave who used to be known as Trips Over Own Feet While Running Away. The figures were, however, deceptive, not least because of the duplication factor. At least twenty-seven thousand of those notches were multiple hits on the driver of the mail truck. He'd also killed old Mr Tomacek, who drove the garbage truck along the valley road once a week, sixteen thousand and eight times, and Mrs Bernstein from Owl Farm nine thousand, six hundred and twenty-four times. The first time he'd shot Mrs Bernstein, she'd been six; she was now a sprightly eighty-seven, and showing no inclination whatsoever to fall over and die, leaving Talks With Squirrels to draw the demoralising conclusion that shooting the buggers was actually good for them.

'Still,' said a small bird above his head, 'it keeps you out of mischief.'

'Get lost, you,' Talks replied without looking up. 'Since

it's all your fault, I'd be obliged if you'd keep your witty remarks to yourself.'

'My fault?' The bird flapped its tiny wings, caught a gnat in mid-air and returned to its perch. 'Here we go again. I'm sorry, but I can't see the point in going through all that again. I only came by to say that if you want to nip home for more arrows, they'll still be here when you get back.'

'Can't be bothered.'

The bird twittered cheerfully. 'Oh no you don't, Talks. Till the sun goes out and the moon falls out of the sky, remember? I don't recall anything about only when you feel in the mood.'

'But it's so pointless,' Talks growled wretchedly. 'I mean, what exactly does it *achieve*? Ninety-four times I've crushed young Duane Flint's head with a rock, and he's never had so much as a bad cold in his life.'

'At least you've learned something,' the bird replied. 'Pointless. Doesn't achieve anything. Out of the mouths of babes and dead Indians, huh?'

Talks shook his insubstantial head. 'Don't give me that,' he snarled. 'It's only pointless and doesn't achieve anything when they don't fall over when you kill them. Let me have one real shot – just one – and then we'll see . . .'

'Oh, you,' said the bird indulgently. 'At least you're consistent, I'll give you that. Consistent as five hundred generations of lemmings, but consistent nonetheless. Good shooting.'

'Ah, piss off.'

Wearily the ghost dragged itself to its feet and trudged away, mingling with the dappled shadows on the forest floor until it wasn't there any more. The bird watched him go, then shook itself, swung her legs over the tree-branch and dropped lightly to the ground. Shading her eyes with the palm of her hand, she gazed across the valley to where she was talking to Linda Lachuk; another customer, three in one day. She wasn't sure she liked these sudden flurries of new business; she was spreading herself pretty thin as it was. How people who *couldn't* be in two places at once ever managed to cope, she had no idea.

Time she wasn't here. Time she was –

– An otter, floating on its back in the middle of Lake Chicopee alongside a resolutely not-drowning lawyer.

'Here we go,' she said.

'How?' the lawyer replied. 'I can't swim, remember.'

'Then,' said the otter, 'maybe we should hitch a ride. Tell you what, the next ship that passes this way, we'll flag it down.'

'Oh, very –' Calvin Dieb didn't finish his sentence, because just then a Viking warship rose up out of the water next to him. It was probably at this point that the skeleton crew who'd been doggedly manning the key positions in his sanity got up from their seats, switched off the lights, locked up and went home. At any rate, he found himself lifting his right arm out of the water and waggling his thumb furiously.

'Hello,' said a voice from the ship. 'How can I of assistance be?'

'You, um, going anywhere near dry land?' Dieb heard himself say. 'Only I could really use a lift right now if you are.'

'Dry land,' the voice repeated, as if confronted with a disturbing new concept. 'Near dry land we may be passing. To be aboard welcome.'

'Well,' muttered the otter in his ear, 'what're you waiting for?'

Dieb reviewed the options available to him, the way he'd been taught in law school. Something they don't teach you in law school, although maybe they should, is that climbing aboard mysterious Viking longships that suddenly materialise in the middle of mirror-calm mountain lakes is, at best, something of a gamble.

Quite where they'd fit it into the syllabus is anybody's guess. Probably they'd have to shoehorn it in between second-year conveyancing and industrial tribunals procedure. It ought to be in there somewhere, all the same.

'Can one of you guys throw me a rope?' Dieb yelled.

'Certainly we can. Here a rerp is to you coming.'

'Ouch. I mean, thanks.'

'Now then, Thorvald, Oddleif, if to pull upon the rerp so kind you would be.'

Not long afterwards, Dieb was lying on the deck, panting like one of the fish he'd seen there when the ship first emerged, and wondering what he'd gotten himself into. Round him stood a ring of the most ferocious-looking warriors you'd ever hope to see outside of the more flamboyant parts of Los Angeles. Some of them were lacking an eye, others a selection of teeth or fingers. All of them had patches of smooth, shiny pink skin on their arms, legs and faces that bore witness to a time when they'd nearly come second out of two in a hand-to-hand combat with sharp weapons. If someone had told Dieb at that moment that the ship's hold was stuffed full of customised Harley-Davidsons, he wouldn't have been in the least surprised.

'How are you feeling?' asked a particularly serrated giant with a horned helmet and only one eye. 'Perhaps of warm milk a cup good would do you.'

'The water at this year time,' added an even larger Viking, 'cold is being. A chill you might be getting.'

'Scerns there are,' pointed out a third. 'Freshly today baked by Little Olaf.'

'Scerns?'

'Scerns, with yam and clooted cream,' the first Viking explained. 'Little Olaf, it is his mother's recipe.'

For the first time, Dieb realised that the second Viking, the one with arms like legs and only three teeth, was wearing a blue-and-white-striped pinafore. 'Little Olaf,' said the first Viking, 'is the cerk.'

'Ah.'

'Also there are dernuts.'

'Right.'

'And pastries Danske.'

'Great.' Dieb swallowed hard. 'I'd just love some, er, dernuts and a pastry Danske with my, ah, warm milk.'

Little Olaf departed, grinning, while the other Vikings produced a barrel for him to sit on, a blanket for his knees and a huge plump cushion with a rabbit embroidered on it.

'Hey, guys,' he said, trying to manufacture a smile that didn't look like a Jack Nicholson crazed grin. 'This is really, um, really decent of you. Thanks.'

'You're welcome. Ah. Here Little Olaf with the milk is.'

Dieb took the cup, doing his best not to notice that it was formed from a human skull, the eyesockets and ear funnels of which were filled with gold and massive uncut gemstones that traced a runic inscription which undoubtedly translated as *World's Best Cook*.

'While it warm is, be drinking.'

'Yeah, right.' He took a deep breath and drank. Yuk! Warm milk!

'And here, behold the dernuts.'

Still recovering from the milk, he glanced down and beheld the dernuts, still faintly glistening with oil. It made him nostalgic for the lake.

Which reminded him. What had become of that goddamn chatty·otter? If he'd managed to show it a clean pair of handstitched heels, he was at least that much ahead of the game.

'It's not that easy,' said a seagull perched on the rigging just above his head. 'Oh, and before you think to ask, they can't hear me.'

Dieb groaned, prompting a worried enquiry from Little Olaf about the quality of the dernuts. He made a conscious effort not to look up.

'Now then,' said the first Viking, who appeared to be some sort of leader. 'You are to where going?'

'Um,' Dieb replied. 'Actually, if it's no trouble for you guys, maybe you could drop me off at the shore. Anywhere round here'll do.'

For some reason, this seemed to disturb the Viking; he looked away and fidgeted with his bears' teeth necklace for a moment before answering. 'Clerse to the shore go we cannot,' he said. 'For fear the ship aground to be running. This very sad is, that help you we cannot.'

'Oh. Well, never . . .'

'As hosts in our duty failed you we have,' the Viking went on. 'Never in Valhall honour shall we have, if before as hosts our duty we our lives put. Scorn us will Thor. Upon us spit will the Valkyries. But our ship aground to run . . .'

'Hey guys,' said Dieb, nervously, 'please. Doesn't have to be here. Anywhere that's convenient for you will me do just fine.'

The Viking narrowed his eyes ferociously, until he put Dieb firmly in mind of Clint Eastwood trying to stare down a tax inspector. 'Saying that you sure you aren't our feelings just not to be hurting?' he said.

'Huh? I mean, quite.Yes. I mean no.'

Suddenly the Viking smiled, flashing two rows of teeth like

badly weathered tombstones. 'Then fine that shall be,' he said, standing up. 'Maybe now below you to go would like, sleep to be getting. Arriving at Duluth, calling you we shall.'

'*Duluth?*'

Immediately the Viking's face subsided into a look of utter self-reproach, so rearranging the scars that you could have played noughts and crosses in them. 'Right I was, and out of your way too far Duluth,' he exclaimed, jumping to his feet. 'Ashore at once to be putting you, and the ship aground to be running matter not at all will. Thorvald!'

'No,' Dieb said imploringly, 'please! Duluth'll be just great, I can charter a plane or something – I mean, Duluth's actually where I was headed anyhow. So that's great. Really.'

'Sure?'

'Positive. Word of honour. My, these really are mighty good, um, dernuts. Haven't had dernuts this good since I was a kid.'

The Viking sat down again, beaming like a lighthouse. 'Then to take with you in a bag of paper more shall you have. Olaf I shall instruct freshly them to bake.'

'Great.' The bridge of Dieb's mind sent a frenzied message down to Engineering: *Quick, for Christ's sake, fabricate some enthusiasm. How? We ain't got the recipe. Then improvise, dammit.* 'Looking forward to it. Yum!'

'And now to be excusing me,' the Viking said, standing up again. 'The ship to be running I must.' He wandered away, turning occasionally to smile and wave. Eventually, Dieb was left alone with his blanket, his cushions, several remaining pastries and the seagull.

'Duluth,' muttered the seagull. 'Wonder what's at Duluth?'

'I'm gonna find out, aren't I?' Dieb replied irritably. 'You know, this is costing me *thousands* –'

'No you won't,' the seagull said, preening its wing feathers. 'Ship's gonna hit a rock any minute. If I were you, I'd go up the rounded end.'

'Hit a rock?'

The seagull nodded. 'And sink. With all hands. That's a nautical expression meaning all these folks are gonna die. Not you, though.'

Dieb's jaw dropped, and for a moment – the first since he embraced the art of advocacy – he was fresh out of words. 'Die?' he repeated.

'Drown. Glug glug. Davy Jones' locker. But like I said, you make it, so where's the problem?' The seagull opened its beak wide, as if yawning. 'Means you can't sue them for anything, true, but what the hell, they haven't got that sort of money anyhow.'

Dieb opened and closed his mouth several times, like a fish drowning in air. 'But can't we warn them, for God's sake? Tell 'em to steer the boat to one side?'

'Compassion, Mr Dieb?' The seagull regarded him for a while, standing on one leg. 'That's a word for feeling sorry for people, in case you've never come across it before. No, can't warn them. Against the rules.'

'But . . .' Dieb looked around; at the blanket, the cushions, the home-made doughnuts, the gold-and-gemstone-encrusted skull . . . 'But they *rescued* me,' he said feebly. 'I *owe* them.'

'Nah.' The seagull shook its head. 'Moral obligation only. Nothing on paper. And besides, if they're all dead, who's to know?'

'But . . .'

The seagull spread its wings. 'Anyhow,' it said, 'this isn't getting your car-keys found, is it? Now remember; get up as near to the stern as you can without attracting attention, or else one of 'em might follow you – to ask how you're doing, offer you another doughnut, that sort of thing – and that'd be no good. The sucker might survive along with you.'

'But that'd be great. I thought you said –'

'Maybe I didn't explain properly. If any of these guys makes it, you don't get to find your keys. You'll have to stay here and drown too. Think about it. Pity there's always got to be a loser, but hey, that's litigation.' The seagull spread its wings and flew away before Dieb could answer.

He stood up. He looked once again at the blanket, the cushion, the home-made doughnuts, the skull. If any of these guys made it, he wouldn't. Then he looked over the side at the still, wet water, and remembered what it had been like being in that stuff, that fluid, alien element that makes no allowances. And on the bridge of his mind, the captain turned in his swivel chair and muttered, *Hell, we didn't ask to get involved in this. And the suckers'd have drowned anyway. Not as if them drowning's our fault.*

Which was true.

Picking up the blanket, and stuffing doughnuts in his pockets for later, he set off for the rounded end.

Janice DeWeese climbed over the brow of the ridge, her feet hurting like something the Spanish Inquisition saved for people it really didn't like, and looked down at a big, mirror-still lake.

'Hey!' she muttered. Her map, once she'd wrestled it out of her pocket and turned it the right way up, told her that this Lake Chicopee –

– Which was supposed to be over *there*. This was supposed to be a valley, not a lake. There should be a stream running through it, and a disused powder mill, and a small wooden hut put there by the Forestry Department for muggers and rapists to rest up in between jobs.

She'd come the wrong way.

Wearily she dropped herself on a fallen tree, cleaned her glasses on her sleeve and smoothed the map out again. Right; over there, the Squash river, so that was north. Over there, the tall pointy mountain with trees up to its neck, so that was west. Accordingly . . .

Accordingly, she was going to have to turn round and go back the way she'd come, seven miles of overgrown paths and savage inclines, if she wanted to get to Broken Heart by nightfall. Or, if she had the sense she was born with, she could go down to the lake and up the other side to join the road, which would take her to Claremont, the Greyhound bus and civilisation; and the hell with Broken Heart, pop. 361. She was faced with a long, long walk whichever way she went, and this lousy backpack wasn't getting any lighter. Some vacation, huh?

But, she reflected, as she scrabbled in her pockets for life-giving chocolate, this is the sort of vacation you get to go on when you're, to take an example entirely at random, twenty-eight, short and dumpy with a face like a prune. Vacations involving swimming-pools, long cool drinks, hot sun and slinky black evening dresses tend to happen to other sorts of people.

At least it had been something to talk about at the office, for a day or two. Something she could have talked about, if somebody had actually asked her. If somebody had asked her where she was going for her vacation, she'd have answered in a light, devil-may-care tone of voice that oh, she was backpacking across Iowa again this year. *Backpacking* across *Iowa?* Sure; don't you just love the freedom, the big open spaces? You can really be *yourself*. Oh yes, on my own, naturally; wouldn't be any point otherwise. If anybody had asked her, she could have been great. And if she ever got home again (could a person die of sore feet?) then she'd have some really spellbinding stories to tell, if anybody ever asked her.

The hell with it. She could go crawling round the moon on her hands and knees and nobody'd ever know. Last year, for instance; last year, she'd spent her entire savings on an overland expedition down the Nile, by boat, Jeep and camel. She'd slept under desert stars, huddled in her government-surplus sleeping bag while sandstorms howled, basted in red-hot winds and walked silent-footed through the dead cities of Ancient Egypt; she might as well have stayed in Pittsburgh, because (owing to a freak succession of cancellations) the expedition consisted of her and two seventy-year-old Egyptian guides who spoke no English, and when she got back to the office, sun-bleached and crispy-thin, Mr Marcowitz had said it was just as well she was back, the R304Es were all down again, they were knee-deep in pink PZ23s and could she take a look at the Xerox machine? Come five o'clock that first day back, she was into the chocolate again and hard put to it to remember anything about Egypt at all.

She dragged herself back onto her feet, speculating as she did so what the world would have looked like if she, not Chris Columbus, had discovered America. Easy; flat, with a big drop at the edges. Back the way she'd come, or on past the lake up to the road? The lake; why not? At least it'd be a different set of ankle-breaking trails and tendon-sapping gradients.

As she trudged, the phrase 'holiday romance' bounced about in her mind like a small child in a collection of

Oriental porcelain. That, as far as she could tell, is what vacations meant to the rest of the girls in the office; see bedroom ceilings the length and breadth of the USA. Quite probably some of them could write a learned textbook on the different types of light-fittings used across America. Not Janice DeWeese, though; all she got to see was mountains and lakes and rivers and deserts and sunrises and sunsets and fallen-down old buildings. Oh, she had often sighed as she gazed out across some breathtaking panorama someplace, to be an egg; because at least an egg gets laid *once* . . .

Me, though, I just look like one. Maybe, if I'd saved all that money I've frittered away on seeing the goddamn world and spent it on some really drastic cosmetic surgery; well, then I'd look like an egg with Sharon Stone's nose. Fact is, either you got it or you ain't; and I . . .

I get to see lots of countryside. Lewis and Clarke, and Jan DeWeese; to boldly go where no one with any sense has gone before. If I had any sense, I'd jump in this goddamn lake right now and do myself a favour. Oh, if only I didn't have a face like a prune. If only I was –

So musing, she stuck her foot in a tree-root.

Splash.

'Hang on,' Wesley grumbled. 'There's something in my shoe.'

'That'd be your foot, surely.'

'As well as my foot.'

'Never mind. We're nearly there now.'

Wesley laughed, although the sound he produced had as much to do with amusement as an oven has to do with efficient ice-cream production. 'I think you said that before,' he sighed.

'I did. This time, it's true.'

This time, it was a squirrel saying it. On the previous occasions the words had been spoken by a beautiful girl, a whitetail deer, a wild turkey, a brown bear, a pheasant, an elm tree and a derelict 1974 Chevy. This perpetual flitting from shape to shape was beginning to get on Wesley's nerves, and he said as much.

'Bigot.'

'Oh come on,' Wesley replied, stopping where he was and sitting down on a rock. 'It's hardly fair, is it? I mean, how am I supposed to have a sensible conversation with you when I don't even know what you are?'

'Don't see the problem myself. And do you mind not sitting on me when I'm talking to you?'

Wesley looked down. 'Oh, you're that now, are you? What was wrong with the squirrel?'

'Heights. And besides, we're here now.'

'Are we?' Wesley lifted his head and looked around him. It wasn't an enlightening experience; this patch of forest looked just like the patch they'd traipsed through an hour ago. He could even still see the lake below them through the trees. In fact, the lake didn't seem to have moved at all. Wesley voiced this suspicion.

'Well, it wouldn't, would it? Be reasonable.'

'Does you being a rock now have anything to do with us having arrived?'

'Yes,' replied the rock. 'Hey, you're beginning to get the hang of this.'

'OK,' Wesley said. 'Why, now that we're here, are you a rock?'

'Because bears don't eat rocks.'

'Bears? What bears?'

'Hey. I'm in no position to point them out for you, being

a rock and all, but if you stay there you'll see them soon enough.'

'Oh, for God's –' Wesley jumped up, swivelled his head two or three times, then looked up at the tree above him.

'Bears can climb trees,' said the rock. 'Rather better than you can.'

'Thanks a lot. What can't they do?'

'Oh, all sorts of things. For a start, they can't play musical instruments.'

'Apart from not play musical instruments.'

'Well,' said the rock pleasantly. 'I never yet heard of a bear who could pull a magic tomahawk from a tree and use it to defend himself with.'

'Neither can I.'

'Huh!' replied the rock scornfully. 'That's what you think. Why don't you give it a try? After all, this is supposed to be a learning experience.'

'Because,' Wesley said, 'there isn't one. Not in this tree, anyway.'

'What?' That's what a puzzled rock sounds like, folks. Now you know. 'How do you mean, there isn't one?'

'I mean there isn't one. Come on, I thought rocks were what they make silicon chips out of.'

'But there ought to be . . .' The rock fell silent. 'Oh. Sorry about this.' The rock vanished, and was replaced by the beautiful girl. Wesley took one look at the expression on her face and decided there were probably more ferocious things in the forest than bears, after all.

'Talks!' the girl shouted. 'Yes, you, Talks To Squirrels! Put it back!'

There was a *tchock!* noise directly above Wesley's head. He glanced up, and suddenly there was this sort of axe thing sticking in the tree, or rather hanging loosely from the bark. It had a stone blade and the haft was perhaps eighteen inches long and decorated with two threadbare eagle's feathers. It'd terrify the life out of you if you happened to be a small twig.

Wesley looked at it glumly. 'Magic tomahawk?' he asked.

'Magic tomahawk,' the girl replied, vanishing.

He reached up and managed to catch it before it fell out of the tree. 'Magic,' he asked, 'in what sense?'

'Give it a top hat and you'll never want for rabbits.'

Wesley was just about to pass an observation on the appropriate timing of comic remarks when the bears arrived. There were seven of them, and the smallest would just about have squeezed into a Ford Fiesta if you took the seats out first.

'If I were you,' muttered the rock, 'I'd run away.'

CHAPTER FOUR

Someone with rather less self-confidence might have found it just a trifle disconcerting.

Not Linda Lachuk. She had postulated submarines, as being journalistically right, and here submarines were. Naturally, if she ordained submarines, submarines would be provided. To have expected anything else would have been like Christ taking a hip-flask to the wedding at Cana.

'Ahoy there!' she shouted.

The ship turned obediently, like a good dog, and sliced a deep cut through the lake top towards her. An otter popped its head up above the surface, took a good look and vanished again, leaving a circle of ripples like a cup-mark on a newly french-polished table.

'Good morning, miss,' someone shouted from behind the dragon prow. 'And how you can we be herlping?'

Linda caught her breath. That was no American voice, booming out to her across the meniscus of one of Uncle Sam's most secret military installations. That high, nasal, sing-song quality – instinctively she sent a search-and-correlate memo to the librarians of her memory, ordering them to pull the file on *Crocodile Dundee*.

An Australian . . .

Actually, he didn't sound all that much like Paul Hogan; but there were other similarities, too striking to ignore. The blond hair. The leather jerkin. The necklace of wild beast's fangs. The big knife strapped to his midriff.

Probably, she rationalised, it's some kind of regional accent. Adelaide, or one of those places.

'Hi,' she yelled back. 'Are you Australian?'

'Your pardon begging?'

'Are – you – *Australian?*'

She scowled. Perfectly simple question; but by the looks of it, either he didn't understand or he was playing dumb. He shrugged his huge shoulders and plastered some kind of dumb friendly smile across his face. She tried again.

'From Australia,' she shouted slowly. 'Down under. Um. Oz.'

'Oz?'

'Yeah.'

'Ah!' The man nodded, with such overpowering friendliness that she half expected him to vanish and reappear a moment later with a rubber ball in his mouth. 'From Oseberg. Yes, from there am I. Presently.'

'Right. Now then –'

'My name,' he went on, 'is Lief the Lemming. To be helping you, in what manner?'

Linda breathed in. 'Your subm –'

The rest of her sentence was drowned out by a horrible noise, as the ship seemed to trip over something. It shuddered, from carved wooden periscope to pointed duck's tail thing at the other end. From below the deck came muffled cries of 'Excuse me, please,' 'Drat,' and, 'To be sinking, the ship!' They sounded surprised; but Linda wasn't.

They were being silenced.

Typical CIA trick. She should perhaps have thought about that, before she blew their cover with the direct accusation of Australianness. Still, couldn't be helped now. At least she'd be able to get some good shots of the boat sinking. Quickly she felt in her bag for her camera –

– And remembered. Damnit, no batteries in the misbegotten thing. Of all the rotten luck.

'Hey!' she shouted. 'Excuse me!'

Lief the Lemming froze in the act of lowering the ship's only lifeboat, and turned to look at her. 'Excuse me, please?'

Linda smiled. 'You wouldn't happen to have any batteries, would you? For my camera. Just plain old LR13s, if you can spare me a couple.'

'Batteries?'

'Yeah. You know,' Linda replied crossly. 'Power cells. C'mon, you gotta have some on that tub of yours. Or does everything in Australia run on clockwork?'

'Excusing me please a moment.' Lief left the lifeboat dangling six feet or so above the water and ducked down under the deck. From where she stood, Linda could hear a muffled conference but no distinguishable words. This was so *frustrating* –

'Little Bjorn,' said Lief, popping his head up above the level of the deck, 'speculating is batteries to mean instances of battery or common asserlt. To which truthfully answering, on a voyage long, tempers to be occasionally fraying but rarely in fisticuffs resulting, rather to be out of our systems got by exercise healthy and good and much of deck footberl playing. And now to excuse me, the ship . . .'

Linda folded her arms grimly. 'Quit fooling around, will you?' she growled, and the severe expression on her face made her look like an angel who's just been given a dodgy cheque. 'Don't act dumb with me. I want those batteries now, mister. The people have a right to –'

But at that moment the ship suddenly capsized, hit the reflection of itself in the still water and vanished into a bubble and an empty-bath gurgle, leaving Linda standing on the shore breathing hard through her nose.

Yes. Well. She'd see about that. Sooner or later, people were going to learn that the more you tried to put Linda Lachuk off the story, the harder she came back. OK, so it would have been nice to have gotten real live-action pictures of the sub going down; staged re-creations for the camera are all very well, but they lack that intangible spontaneity that you only get when there are actual people genuinely dying for real. Still, it wasn't the end of the world. There'd be other chances; and at the very least, she'd seen a palpably real submarine and spoken to a palpably real Australian. If they thought she was just going to shrug her shoulders and meekly walk away, they had a surprise coming.

She picked up her bag, shrugged her shoulders and started to walk (unmeekly) away. She had gone maybe ten yards when something warm and wet pressed against her ankle. She stopped.

It wasn't a wholly unfamiliar experience; but where she came from, something warm and wet rubbing against one's ankle usually turned out to be one of the guys from the sports page crawling back to his desk after lunch. She looked down.

It was an otter. It was long and sleek and cute, like a performing bratwurst, and in its mouth it held a packet of four LR13 batteries.

'Why, you little –' Linda stooped and lunged for it with both hands, but it slipped through her fingers and waddled jauntily into the lake. A moment later, as soon as she'd dumped her bag and kicked off her shoes, Linda dived after it.

The last thought to cross her mind before the water closed over her head was, *God, I really want this story!*

'Chief.'

'What now?'

'Where are we, Chief?'

'If I knew that, Twist, we'd be somewhere else by now. Shut up, there's a good lad.'

After half an hour in the tunnel it had occurred to all the smugglers, even the ones with oatmeal for brains, that something was wrong. A tunnel where a tunnel had no business being. A tunnel that hadn't been there before. A tunnel leading where?

'Chief!'

'So help me, Twist, just as soon as there's enough room I'm going to wring your bloody –'

'Light, Chief. Straight ahead. Can you see it?'

'Damnit, yes!'

'It's the sort of white twinkly stuff, there, just a bit to the left of where I'm –'

'Thank you, Twist, I have seen daylight before. Like when you're standing sideways on and I look through your ear.'

'Chief?'

'Forget it. Get a move on, will you? Let's get out of here, for pity's sake.'

A few anxious moments later Captain Hat scrambled out of a hole in the ground, looked round to make sure the coast was clear and hauled himself to his feet. His knees hurt; or, to be more accurate, his knees hurt most.

'OK, lads,' he called back down the tunnel, 'it's all right. Come on out, we're –'

He froze, and in consequence was butted in the rear by a procession of crawling, mole-like smugglers. He didn't seem to notice them.

'– Right back where we started,' he concluded quietly. 'Goddamnit, we've come round in a bloody circle.' He rubbed his eyes, opened them and looked again. 'Hey,' he murmured, 'that's crazy. Could've sworn we went in a straight line. Anyway, no sign of the frogs. Hurry up, people, we don't want to be standing out in the open like a lot of garden gnomes. Is that the lot? OK, let's move.'

They moved. Around them, the undergrowth popped and crackled, for all the world as if it was sniggering at them. They began to feel uncomfortable.

'No,' said Hat at last, as they passed the same tree for the fifth time. 'I refuse to believe we're lost. There's got to be some simple reason.' He peered through the branches of the trees at the lake, no more than a couple of hundred yards away as the crow, having fallen off its perch, slithers. Put him two hundred yards from Lake Chicopee and Hat would know where he was with his eyes shut, his ears stopped up, his nose and mouth blocked with clay and his hands and feet encased in concrete. All right, he'd be dead within a minute, but at least he'd know exactly where he was. He could easily picture himself losing his way on the back of his hand, but not here.

But . . .

'North-west,' he muttered. 'We haven't tried northwest yet. Come on, you lot.'

'Chief.'

Hat closed his eyes again. Give me strength, he prayed; not very much of it, just as much as it takes to throttle Mr

Snedge will do just splendidly. 'Well, Snedge?' he said sweetly. 'And what can I do for you?'

'Isn't that them Vikings over there, Chief? You know, the ones whose boat keeps sinking?'

Hat followed the line indicated by Snedge's grubby finger, and saw eight or nine bedraggled figures squelching up out of the lake below them. He recognised them all, though he wasn't sure what they thought they were doing on land. It was a big day for surprises, evidently.

'What I thought was, Chief, maybe we could ask them.'

Hat shook his head. 'Don't think so,' he replied.

'Oh. Why not?'

'Don't think we're terribly popular with them, Snedge. Not since we nicked their lifeboat.'

'Oh.'

Hat narrowed his eyes. 'Mind you,' he said, 'usually they drown. This time, apparently, they haven't.'

'Well, then. Maybe they wouldn't mind us asking.'

'They're still sopping wet, Snedge,' Hat replied thoughtfully. 'I mean, they didn't row their way to shore all nice and dry. I expect that when the time came and they started abandoning ship and they went to find the lifeboat, they still went through that good old where-is-it-I-don't-know-who-saw-it-last? routine.' He looked up at an unfamiliar tree – he'd known all the trees round this lake since they were seeds, and this wasn't one of them and sniffed. 'Mind you,' he said, 'they do seem to know where they're going.'

'Yeah.'

'Which is more than we do.'

'Yup.'

'OK.' Hat stood up. 'Let's follow them,' he said.

★

'Somewhere around here, I guess,' said Calvin Dieb, pointing at the rocky slope that fell away into the water. 'I think. To be honest with you, this whole place looks the same to me.'

The Vikings nodded, and started to look. They turned over stones, they prised apart tangled knots of bramble, they combed grass. While they were at it, Dieb looked up into the branches of the tree above him, and saw a squirrel.

'Bad move,' it said.

Dieb scowled. 'Sez who, tree-rat?' he snarled. 'Look, I saved these guys from drowning. They were all scheduled to die, and I saved them. Told them to get down the rounded end of the boat, and they did. Isn't that something?'

'Bad move,' the squirrel repeated.

'And,' Dieb went on, 'to show their gratitude, they've agreed to help me find my keys. Mutually beneficial, I call it. So what's so bad about that?'

'On the other paw,' sighed the squirrel, 'it's exactly what you're supposed to have done. Don't worry about the arrows. Be seeing you.'

'What arrows?' Dieb demanded, as two feet of straight, obsidian-tipped pine flicked past him and buried its nose in a tree. 'Oh, those arrows. Hey,' he yelled up into the branches, 'you didn't explain why I shouldn't worry about them. I'm sure there's a perfectly good reason, but . . .'

He didn't continue the sentence, because he'd seen something. Fifty yards or so away, the Vikings who'd been looking for his car-keys had suddenly fallen over. There were arrows sticking out of them. In fact, there were arrows everywhere, and sticking out of everybody except him. He dropped to his knees and put his hands over his head, whimpering. Something like a moustache brushed the little finger of his left hand. It was a moment or so before he realised it must have been the fletchings on an arrow-shaft, missing him by –

And then the trees echoed to a series of shrieks and whoops, as strange, savage buckskinned men poured out of every patch of cover large enough to hide a pheasant. They were after the Vikings; Dieb didn't look, but what he heard convinced him that they made a thorough job of it. There were shouts and screams, and from time to time heavy, dull bashing noises, the sort of sound an overweight lawyer with a morbid imagination might connect in his mind with a not-too-sharp flint axe mashing a man's skull. Distantly, in a remote part of his mind where he simply didn't care, he wondered whether it would hurt terribly much, and came to the conclusion that by the time it started hurting he'd be past feeling it. *But don't quote me on that*, added that remote part of his brain, remembering that it was part of a lawyer. *Hey*, it added, just before Dieb located it and yanked it off line, *why don't you call the cops?*

And then there was silence, except for distant low-voiced conversation in a strange language. What, he wondered, were they saying to each other, as they collected up their arrows and wiped their axes on the grass? Although he couldn't make out the words, it sounded like any conversation between people who spend a lot of their time working together. Hey, looks like this weather's set in for the rest of the week. Saw your sister's boy the other day; he's grown, hasn't he? You think the Redskins gonna make it to the Superbowl this year?

And then he thought he could hear words he could understand –

That bloody squirrel again –

'Yo, Talks.'

'Much obliged.'

'You're welcome, Talks.'

'Where'd this lot come from, then? I thought you said . . .'

'It's this clown I'm taking round. Not the English kid or the journalist or the droopy girl, the lawyer. Didn't do what he was told.'

'Ah.'

'I said to him, Don't try and warn them. So of course he did. Guessed he would. That sort always have to know best.'

Dieb cringed. *All his fault!* He recognised the feeling that flooded his body as if it was a leaky submarine; it was that oh-shit sensation he used to get as a young lawyer when he realised he'd failed to meet a time limit, missed out some procedural step, lost the deeds, whatever. Partly it was straightforward pain, as if his mind had been burnt and was still raw and seeping; mostly, though, it was a great gush of rage building up pressure inside him, searching for an outlet. When he'd been a young lawyer he'd hated everybody he could think of; his boss, for giving him work he wasn't fit to do; his secretary, for not reminding him; his colleagues, for not warning him; the client, for getting him into this mess in the first place. And God, of course. When he'd been a young lawyer, Calvin Dieb had sworn a lot at God. Now that he was a middle-aged lawyer, used to having the buck screeching to a halt at his feet every day of the week, he didn't hate anybody in particular (even now, he didn't hate the Vikings, or the Indians, or even the squirrel). He just hated. And, of course, he got even. Usually he got even first; if he had a philosophy of life, it was huddled round the concept of pre-emptive revenge.

It was very quiet now; either they'd gone away, or they

were all standing round him in a circle, waiting for him to open his eyes. He opened them. As far as he could judge, he was on his own.

'Hello?' he heard himself call out – Jesus, how stupid! No harm seemed to come of it, however. No more arrows, no more howling warriors, not even a chatty squirrel. It occurred to him that maybe he should go and see if any of the Vikings were still alive. If so, he could use the phone in his car to call for help, if only he could get into his car, which he couldn't, not without the keys. Unforceable locks, unsmashable glass, an alarm that boiled your eyes in your head at forty paces; it was one of the reasons he'd gone for that particular model, the security. If only, if only he could get back inside it and raise the windows and dead-lock the doors and call the National Guard and the Air Force on the phone, then everything would be all right.

If only he could find . . .

Survivors. There had to be survivors. With every muscle, tendon and nerve in his body clenched – except for victim photographs usable in evidence, he couldn't stand the sight of blood – he tiptoed down towards the lakeside –

(Oh God, what if they've scalped them? He didn't actually know what scalping really involved, but he was prepared to wager relevant money that it was truly horrible.)

And found it empty. Not a corpse. Not an arrow, or a tomahawk, or a splatter of blood. The whole scene was cleaner and tidier than a Swiss operating theatre.

A wave of relief and a surge of panic raced simultaneously through his mind, turning it into a jacuzzi of conflicting emotions. Maybe it hadn't happened, and nobody had been killed; in which case, he'd hallucinated it all, and he was going mad, and they'd lock him up in the funny farm and debar him from practising as a lawyer, and then the bank would foreclose on the house and his wife would be put out on the street –

Hang on, he remembered, I haven't got a wife. And the house is paid for, at least the town house is, and the apartment in Des Moines. The farm and the ski lodge weren't, but as far as he was concerned they could have those and welcome, what with interest rates and negative equity and all. Shit, he muttered to himself, I'm having an anxiety attack here and it's not even my anxiety. Get a *grip*, for Chrissakes.

All I have to do is find my keys, and I'm out of here.

'Try looking under that rock,' suggested a beaver, poking its dear little head up out of the water. 'No, not that one, the flat one to your left. I expect you're quite comfortable with the undersides of flat stones, in your line of work.'

Dieb winced, as if someone had carelessly stubbed out a cigarette in his eye. 'It's you again, isn't it? Goddamnit, why can't you just leave me alone?'

'Be like that. Only trying to help.'

'I am not lifting up that rock.'

'Don't, then.'

'Ah, shit.' He bent over, got his fingers under the edge of the rock and heaved.

'Hi.'

He stared, for maybe a fifteenth of a second; then he let go of the rock, but too late.

Peering up at him, his hair tousled, his glasses misted, his beard full of earwigs, was his partner, Hernan Piranha.

The biggest bear, a mountain of fur and muscle with a claw salad and teeth garnish, turned its head and stared at him.

'Er,' said Wesley, and dropped the tomahawk on his foot.

''Scuse me,' said the bear.

A sharp blow on the toe can be excruciatingly painful, and the agony deprived Wesley of the power of speech; no great loss, in the circumstances, since there was absolutely nothing he could think of to say to a huge bear in any case. He refrained from screaming, and as far as he was concerned that was his lot.

''Scuse me,' repeated the bear, in a deep, reverberating growl, 'but could we possibly borrow your axe thing?'

'M?'

'You see,' the bear continued, 'we forgot the tin opener. At least,' it added, turning its head just far enough to be able to give the bear to its right a vicious look, 'one of us forgot the tin opener, the same way she'd forget her own head if it wasn't tied to her shoulders with her neck, though that's an arrangement that might well be subject to review.'

'M?'

'Ignore him,' said the female bear. 'Have you got it? I asked, just before we left. Yes of course, he said, d'you think I'm thick or something. And then when we get here it's I thought you had it. Well –'

'I bloody never!'

'That's right, shout. That's your answer to everything, shouting.'

'Tin opener?' Wesley enquired.

The male bear nodded. 'For the picnic things. The corned beef and the potted shrimps and the crab paste. And some pillock,' he added, looking left this time, 'managed to snap off the little rings on forty-seven cans of beer, though God only knows how he managed it. I mean, forty-seven!'

'Picnic things?'

'That's right. And if you could possibly hurry it up, that'd be really great, because the rest of them are due along any minute now.'

'Every bear that ever there was,' confirmed the female bear.

'And if there's nothing for them to eat except bread and butter and orange squash, life might get a bit hectic, if you see what I mean.'

''S all your fault,' the female bear sniffed. 'This'd never have happened if we'd gone to Weymouth like I said.'

'Nobody wanted to go to bloody Weymouth 'cept you,' the male bear snapped, 'so shut your noise. You can see what I've got to put up with,' he added, as Wesley backed away another step and got a low branch in the small of his back for his pains. 'So if you could just see your way . . .'

Pulling himself together like a zombie jigsaw, Wesley picked up the tomahawk and held it at arm's length. 'Please,' he said, 'help yourself. Keep it if you like.'

'Can I really? Thanks.' The bear lumbered forwards, took the axe gently, as if carrying a captured crane-fly to the window, and waddled back to where a massive wicker basket was lying on the ground, being unpacked by the other bears. One of them, who had been trying in vain to bite through a tin of salmon, grabbed the tomahawk and drew the sharp tip of the top horn of the blade round the lid of the tin. ''Scuse paws,' it said, and then levered the severed lid back delicately with one clawtip. 'Hey, salmon,' it said. 'Always it's bloody salmon. What's wrong with pilchards?'

'In the other basket, stupid.'

'Ruddy marvellous picnic this is turning out to be.'

'Oh, go climb a tree,' snarled the she-bear. 'Some

people,' she sniffed, turning to Wesley as if expecting agreement, 'are never satisfied.'

'Ah, but bear's claws must exceed his paws, or what's a Heaven for?'

'Your father's off again,' sighed the she-bear. 'Who rattled his cage, then?'

'Excuse me,' said Wesley.

'Yes?'

'Excuse me,' he repeated, 'but I thought the picnic was for teddy bears.'

The bears looked at each other. 'What was that he said?' one of them asked.

'Teddy bears,' the male bear replied. 'I think he means that lot that go around on scooters wearing long thin trousers and big jackets.'

'Not our lot, then.'

'Actually,' interrupted the bear who was someone's father, 'I think he means soft, cuddly toys made in the shape of bears.'

'Don't start, Dad, please. You know it upsets the kids.'

Wesley bit his lip, rather harder than he'd intended. 'In fact,' he said, 'that's what I did mean. There's a song, you see . . .'

This time, the bears looked at Wesley. 'Come off it,' said the salmon-hater, 'that's silly. How could a lot of cuddly toys have a picnic?'

Wesley decided not to reply to that; instead, he watched the bears ripping open tins with the tomahawk. Despite the fact that they didn't have thumbs, which is supposed to make handling things like axes extremely difficult, they were getting through them at an impressive rate. There were also two enormous brown bears, who were digging a hole.

'Excuse me,' Wesley heard himself say, 'but what's the hole for?'

'To bury the litter, of course,' replied the she-bear who'd wanted to go to Weymouth. 'We're green, we are.'

'Speak for yourself.'

'I heard that.'

Sure enough, the two bears stopped scrabbling with their tennis-racquet paws and started shovelling the empty cans into the hole they'd made, swearing occasionally as a ragged tin edge snagged a glove-leather-soft paw-pad. It was at that moment that Wesley forced himself to admit that this was really happening, and it wasn't some bizarre sport of his imagination; because however weird and disturbed he might be, there was no way that he was capable of imagining *this*. Even his odder acquaintances, the ones who regularly chatted to angels or acted as franchisees for Martian Equitable Life, might get embarrassed and remember distant appointments if he started telling them about this.

'Thanks.'

The first bear, the one he'd lent the tomahawk to, was talking to him. He turned his head and smeared a bewildered smile on the front of it.

'Sorry?' he said.

'Thanks,' the bear repeated. 'For the loan of your axe. Did the job a treat. Would you like a pickled walnut?'

'I, er – yes, that'd be great. Fine.'

The bear reached out a treelike arm and put something small, black and shrivelled delicately into his hand. It looked like something a nine-year-old head-hunter might have brought home from school. He shuddered and said thank you nicely.

'Saving it for later?'

'Yes,' Wesley replied. 'Much later. I'll, er, appreciate it more then.'

'Suit yourself,' said the bear equably. 'Well, we'd better be getting along. See you around.'

'Will you? I mean, yes, right. Cheers for now, then.'

The bears waved their paws, turned and wandered off into the forest, until their lumbering backs merged into the dappled shadows. When Wesley was sure they'd gone, he opened his hand, looked at the strange black fossilised thing clutched in it, and threw it away. A squirrel ran down the side of the tree over his head, pounced on the reject walnut and ate it quickly.

'Waste not, want not,' it said with its mouth full. 'Sure you don't want some?'

'Very sure indeed.'

'Your loss.' The squirrel twitched its nose and spat something out. 'Well, maybe not,' it added. 'Anyway, how are you liking it?'

Wesley made a peculiar noise. '*Liking* it,' he repeated. 'Oh for God's —'

'You mean you aren't? That's a pity. Particularly since you saved up and everything. Hell, for that money you could have gone to Disneyland. I would've,' the squirrel added wistfully. 'Of course, Ihaven't had a holiday in, oh, twenty thousand years.'

'This is a holiday?'

'Supposed to be, yes.'

'A holiday!' Wesley burst out. 'So far I've nearly drowned. I've witnessed a shipwreck and I've been set upon by seven enormous bears. If that's meant to be a holiday, what the hell do you think I do the rest of the year?'

'I wouldn't call it being set upon, exactly,' the squirrel pointed out. 'As I recall, they gave you a walnut.'

'Set upon,' Wesley affirmed. 'By seven enormous bears. Look, is there a point to all this, because if so I'd like it if we could get to it now, please, so I can go home.'

'We're getting there,' the squirrel replied. 'I mean, we're past stage one, the suspension of disbelief.'

'Oh, I've suspended my disbelief all right. Lynched it, in fact. Now can I please –?'

'Not yet,' said the squirrel firmly. 'Boy, you ain't seen nothing yet.'

Funny bugger, Old Mister Instinct. At school, Janice DeWeese had been a keen swimmer. (See that rubber-capped, goggle-faced egg shape chugging up and down the school swimming bath, lacking a salt-caked smokestack but otherwise a dead ringer for the ship in the poem? That's her.) The human otter, they'd called her, to her face. And yet, when she got her head up out of the water and realised what was going on, she found she was doing the doggy-paddle; not very well, either. The thing that had somehow got into her mouth was either a newt or a small fish. The backpack wasn't helping, either.

In her defence, she could have argued that this wasn't the sort of water she was used to. Swimming-pool water, like tap-water, sea-water and pretty well any kind of water apart from the stuff you find in Lake Chicopee, flows. Push it aside, and it goes away. In other words, it's liquid. This stuff was more like runny aspic. You'd be hard put to drown in it, in the same way that it's hard to drown on a stone floor; but it wasn't much good for swimming in. It wasn't particularly – what was the word she was groping for? – wet.

'Gnurrgh!' she said.

'It's an acquired taste,' said a voice by her ear.

'Gnargh?'

'Not,' the voice added, 'that I'd go out of my way to acquire it, if I were you. There's things living in it that aren't house-trained.' The otter shrugged. 'Texture's not all that hot, either. You wouldn't want to irrigate your tender young seedlings with it, for fear of squashing them flat.'

'You're an otter!'

'Yes.' The otter twitched its nose. 'So?'

'But . . .'

'Look, if you've got a problem with that, I'm terribly sorry. But it's turning out to be a long day and I've got a lot on my plate right now, so if you could just accept the fact that you're talking to an otter, it'll save a whole lot of time.'

'But . . .'

'Ah, don't be like that. The others were all right about it, so why should you be any different?'

'Others?'

'Whoops, me and my big mouth. You can see I'm tired, can't you? Look, any minute now you're going to see this Viking longship, okay?'

'What?'

'Longship. They're called that because . . .' The otter shrugged again. 'Because they aren't short, I guess. That's beside the point. There'll be this ship, OK? Oh *bugger*, here it comes now. The thing I want you to remember is, don't worry if they drown, all right? I dunno, goddamn lousy tight schedules . . .'

The otter dived, leaving a string of bubbles like three dots at the end of a sentence. Janice realised that she'd stopped swimming, panicked and thrashed out with all available limbs. This at least did have some effect on the water around her; it made her go downwards. She was just about to have a go at underwater screaming when she heard something so unusual that she forgot all about drowning and bobbed back up to the surface again.

It was a wolf-whistle.

'Grrnyahgh!' she said, finally getting rid of the fish, newt or water beetle. At the periphery of her vision she could see something that looked vaguely like a ship. She craned her neck and looked round; and as she did so, she heard voices.

'Thorgrim! I am telling you how many times that not to be doing! Disrespectful it and sexist is!'

'Splut?' Janice murmured, puzzled.

'Apology,' said another voice. 'Ernly, away carried I was. It a long time been has. And loveliness such!'

'Ah!' agreed the first voice. 'Agreement. But the whistling not, to be so kind '

Jan kicked feebly against the jellied water. She couldn't remember having banged her head, but maybe the bang on the head was affecting her memory. 'Hey!' she shouted.

'Hello, gorgeous one,' replied the second voice. 'Often here are you coming? In this damp water all alone a nice girl doing what is?'

'That, Thorgrim, not much better is. A line that is so old whiskers on it there are . . .'

'Help!' Janice yelled. 'Somebody get me outa here!'

'To be saving you a privilege, entrancing one. If a little patience –'

'You, Skaldulf, too presumptuous are,' interrupted a third voice. 'You saving her who was it said it should be? On this ship others beside yourself –'

'First I was seeing her, of a lady dog offensive offspring!'

'My bones breaking sticks and stones may be, of a crow the excrement! And out of the way to be getting –'

'My dead body over, of a dog the breath! And your feet putting –'

Janice trod water, wondering what in all hell was going on. She could see the ship clearly now; a big wooden rowboat, with painted lids on the sides. The decks were lined with men, who were *looking* at her.

'Straws we could I suppose be drawing,' someone was saying. 'Straws here I happen to have, by some chance . . .'

'With your straws perhaps aware you are what you might do, Bjarni Oddleifsen. Now, my way out of.'

'The contrary, serpent –'

'*The ship, where it is heading!*'

There was a crash, as of stone on timber. There was a gurgling, like the water draining out of God's bath. There were complicated refined curses, and glugging noises. And then there was silence, except for the slight lapping of the water as the ripples were ironed away.

'Ah, shit!' Janice said.

CHAPTER FIVE

'Hiya, Calvin,' said Hernan Piranha.

Usually, Calvin Dieb could recover his composure so quickly that you'd never notice that he'd lost it. If a Greek god were to descend from the heavens and prove to him that without knowing it he'd murdered his father and married his mother, by the time the god had finished speaking, Calvin would have adjusted to the fact and be ready to explain precisely why killing your dad and marrying your mom was probably the brightest thing you could do if you really wanted to cut your tax bills. On this occasion, however, he stood with his mouth open, looking very much like a two-legged, expensively suited goldfish.

'Hi, Hernan,' he eventually replied.

There was, of course, a lot of subtext going on here. Inevitably, their spectacularly successful partnership was built on a solid foundation of implicit mutual mistrust. If, at the start of the office day, Calvin said, 'Good morning,' Hernan would spend the next hour and a half trying to work out exactly what Cal had meant by good. If Hernan said to Calvin, 'No, you drive,' Calvin would make damn sure he wiped any fingerprints off the steering wheel before getting out of the car. They were both, after all, Americans and lawyers. On finding Hernan under a flat stone in the middle of all this utter weirdness, therefore, he didn't ask himself, *What's Hernan doing under that stone?* but *What's Hernan up to under that stone?* And although paranoia was thrusting daggers of panic into his heart, it sure was comforting to see him, in a life-threatening sort of a way.

'Bet you're surprised to see me here, kid,' said Hernan.

'No, not particularly. Why?'

– And that was another thing; seventeen years Hernan Piranha had been calling him 'kid', and only last week he'd found out that the sonofabitch was actually three weeks younger than he was. At the time, he'd merely requisitioned another propane torch and barrelful of six-inch nails for the customised Hell he'd been designing for Hernan since the first day they'd met. Here and now, he felt a more immediate response was called for. Like calling him 'gramps' or something equally mordant.

'Because I don't usually hide under rocks in picturesque valleys is why, Cal. Or hadn't you noticed?'

Calvin smiled warmly. 'Jesus, Hernan, you know I'd never question your judgement on anything. If hiding under rocks is the right thing for you just now, then go for it.' He turned up the smile a volt or so, in his mind imagining those extra volts added to an already plentiful supply going up into the seat of Hernan's trousers from the electrodes of Old Sparky. 'I know you never do anything without a darned good reason,' he added. 'Oh, did Niedermeyers call back about that railroad thing?'

Hernan shook his head, not even bothering with an old ploy like that. For the first six years of their association, Calvin had managed to keep Hernan permanently twitching by asking him throwaway questions about entirely non-existent cases. The way in which Hernan ignored the question convinced Calvin of one thing, at least; this was his partner, in person, and not just some jerk from an agency made up to look like him.

But Piranha, damn him, was grinning all over his overfed-Chinese-god face. 'Admit it, Cal,' he said, 'you're just burning up inside to know what I'm doing here. But you're such a stubborn old cuss, you'll never ask in a million years. Am I right?'

'You go ahead and tell me, if it'll make you feel better. You know, it often does help to talk about these things.'

'Yeah. Well –'

'And you know, Hernan,' Dieb pressed on ruthlessly, 'that whatever happens, I'll always be here for you. Whatever happens.'

'Sure, Cal,' Piranha replied, eyes twinkling. 'With a knife up one sleeve and a sharpened stick behind your back, you old coyote. But it so happens that today, *I'm* here for *you*.'

'That's good to know, Hernan.'

'Because,' Hernan continued, holding up something small and shiny, 'I know you want these.'

The car keys, goddamnit! For a split second Calvin Dieb lost his cool, and grabbed. By the time his hand had moved the eighteen inches separating his fingertips from the keys, they'd vanished. Not that Hernan had perceptibly moved; his hand just wasn't there any more.

'Perhaps it'd help,' he said, 'if you thought of me as Jacob Marley.'

Thirty-two feet per second per second; eventually the penny dropped. When it did, Calvin Dieb took a step back, crossed his arms and said, 'Actually, I preferred you when you were an otter.'

Piranha shook his head, and turned into a beautiful

young girl with hair the colour of freshly laid Tarmac. 'Took you long enough,' she said. 'I thought you lawyers were supposed to be smarter than that.'

'I was humouring you,' Dieb replied as best he could. 'Can I have my keys now, please?'

The girl shook her head, so that her hair swung. 'Nope,' she said, sitting down on a rock and crossing her knees. 'Here, come and sit beside me.' She patted the rock beside her and smiled a dazzling smile.

'You can forget that, by the way,' Dieb said, doing so. 'Now that I've seen you as Hernan, there's no way it's going to work. So, you're gonna Scrooge me, are you? Well, you're welcome to try, but as your legal adviser I have to tell you, you're wasting your time.'

'Not my time,' replied the girl sweetly. 'Yours. Your time, which costs two thousand dollars an hour. If I were you, Mr Dieb, I'd co-operate.'

Dieb shrugged. 'OK,' he said, 'I'll co-operate. What've I got to do?'

'Find your car keys,' the girl said. 'That's all. A smart guy like you ought to be able to manage something simple like that. Hey, do you know that talking to you in your office for *one second* costs fifty-five cents? I mean, what can you possibly tell me in one second that's worth as much as a pint of milk or a game of pinball?'

'Easy,' Dieb replied wearily. 'In one second I can tell you Yes, or No. My yes or no could make you a fortune or save you millions. More to the point, whoever you are, what can you do in a second that's worth – oh shit, no, I didn't mean that –'

'Oh yes you did.'

'No, please, forget I –'

You could have skewered chunks of barbecued lamb on

the look in the girl's eyes. 'One second, Mister Dieb? You wanna see what I can do in one second?'

'No,' Dieb replied with uncharacteristic honesty.

'Tough. You ready? *Now . . .*'

One second later, Calvin Dieb opened his eyes, to find himself surrounded by bears.

Funny what a few hours can do to a man. Earlier that morning, if you'd offered him a choice of being surrounded by bears or having lunch with his ex-wife, he'd have chosen the bears so fast you'd scarcely have seen his lips move. Now, however, he'd have welcomed Thelma with open arms. For one thing, she'd scare off the bears.

Jesus, he made a mental note, but they're big fuckers. And how come they've got such big, sharp teeth? All his life, Calvin Dieb had lumped bears together with cashmere scarves and English tea and detective stories where the little old lady solves the mystery before the cops have even taken their hats off, all falling into the category of soft, cuddly things that you can only afford if you're hard and mean, really. Hard, mean bears were something entirely outside his experience; and something told him that these were seven hard, mean bears.

Hungry, too, by the look of them.

'Help?' he suggested, looking round for the girl. But she wasn't there. For all he knew, she was one of these goddamn wild animals. Not that the thought was comforting; rather, the reverse.

'There now,' he muttered. 'Good bears.'

The second largest bear growled at him; a low, rumbling noise like some horrible machine. Its eyes were small, circular and hostile, and it was paying him full attention. Inside its head, he could almost hear the wheels turning as it asked itself the only question it knew: *Food/notfood?*

There were six more like that. Great.

'However,' said a squirrel on a branch above his head, 'they do eat otters, so that's all right. If you had an otter problem, you'd be real glad to see these guys.'

'HELP!'

'Don't shout,' cooed the squirrel, 'it excites them. Movement, too. Now, I bet you're wondering how seven hungry bears are going to help you find your car keys.'

Having been advised to stay still and quiet, Calvin Dieb neither nodded nor spoke. Instead he concentrated on emitting inedibility vibes.

'Well,' continued the squirrel, 'here's the deal. There's an old Iroquois legend that a warrior who kills a bear in single combat and eats its heart raw gains great wisdom. If you had great wisdom, you might be able to find your keys. Well, what're you waiting for?'

The third largest bear straightened its back and rose up on its hind paws, rumbling ominously. One swat of its front paw would turn Calvin's head into bonemeal and jam. It opened its mouth and licked its lips.

'I know,' said the squirrel. 'You're waiting for me to let you have the magic tomahawk. Coming through!'

Something fell at Calvin's feet; or, to be precise, something fell on Calvin's big toe, just exactly where he had the bunion. It speaks volumes for his self-control that, instead of screaming and leaping in the air, he merely said, 'Eek!' in a muted whisper and stayed put. Meanwhile, the largest bear of all put its ears back and growled.

Calvin had a very unpleasant feeling that it was saying grace.

'The tomahawk, dummy,' the squirrel was yelling at

him. 'C'mon, for Pete's sake, it's magic, you won't really have to do *anything* and there'll be bits of delicatessen-style thin-sliced bear all over the place. Ah, come *on*!'

The biggest bear's shoulder muscles tensed; and here it comes . . .

But it didn't. Instead, there was a shrill, ear-splitting yodel that turned Calvin's blood to yoghurt, and something crashed through the trees on the end of a long rope. The something turned out to be a tall, slim, striking-looking woman with fiery red hair, a severe black pinstripe suit with massively padded shoulders and a skirt that came up to her chin, and eyes of cold blue flame. As soon as her feet touched the ground she whirled round, kicked high in a manner that would have made Bruce Lee's eyes water, slammed the megabear in what Calvin assumed was its nuts, punched out the two bears to its left and right with knife-hand blows that sounded like pistol shots, swooped to gather up the tomahawk with her left hand, threw it spinning through the air and caught it backhanded with her right, jumped and landed in a perfect axefighter's stance, threatening not just the cowering bears but the whole world.

'Hi, Thelma,' Calvin squeaked.

'You're pathetic, Cal,' his ex-wife replied, not looking at him. She was staring down the bears so ferociously that at any moment you'd expect them to melt into little pools of tallow. 'God, you haven't changed one bit.'

'That's right, Thelma. You chase away those goddamn bears and I'll be as pathetic as you like.'

'Hah!' By the time the echo of her shout died away, even the biggest of the bears had lumbered away, moving at lightning speed despite its obvious agony. The squirrel, meanwhile, had retired to the very top of the tree and was hiding behind a thick branch.

'Way to go, Thelma,' Calvin sighed, pulling himself up from the heap into which he had subsided. 'How's life in Chicago, anyway?'

'Hell of a lot better since I dumped you,' Thelma replied, tossing the tomahawk up and catching it again. 'Shit, Calvin, I've been tracking that big fucker for *hours*. Trust you to mess it all up for me.'

'Sorry, Thelma. Don't let me keep you.'

'I don't suppose you happened to notice which way it went. Or were you too busy pissing your pants?'

'I made the time, Thel. It went that way, up the slope and left by that fallen tree.'

Thelma nodded, stooped to pull the strap of her shoe back over her heel, flicked a blood-red lipstick round her mouth and stalked off up the slope. 'You know what, Cal?' she threw back over her shoulder. 'You always did lack that killer instinct. That's why you'll always be nothing.'

'Very true. Be seeing you.'

'I hope not, Cal.'

A moment later, she was gone. Calvin gazed after her with a mixture of horror and respect in his eyes, as the squirrel tentatively made its way down the branch.

'There,' Calvin said reverently, 'goes the best damn divorce attorney in the state of Illinois.'

'Hey.'

'Which is a big state, but not nearly big enough. Sorry, you were saying?'

'The bear,' said the squirrel. 'Actually, it went down the slope and into those bushes.'

Calvin nodded. 'I know,' he replied. 'But hell, what harm did it ever do me?'

'Admit it, Chief,' said Mr Snedge. 'We're lost.'

Captain Hat didn't answer. Instead, he sat down on the ground, took off the flamboyant, ostrich-feather-trimmed hat that was his trademark, and spun it slowly round his finger, as his eyes strayed out over the silver waters of the lake. They were about two hundred yards away, and they'd been trying to reach them for four hours.

'This,' he said eventually, 'is silly.'

'You bet, Chief. The lads and me, we were just saying . . .'

'Maybe,' Hat mused, 'we're going about this the wrong way. Maybe we should stay here and let the damn lake come to us.'

They sat in silence for ninety seconds; after which time, Mr Squab cleared his throat and said, 'Hasn't moved yet, Chief.'

Hat shrugged. 'Maybe it's shy or something. Everybody close their eyes, quit staring at it.'

They shut their eyes. Seventy seconds later, they opened them again.

'OK,' said Hat, 'at least we tried it, so we can eliminate that as a possibility. Any other suggestions?'

Just then, something large and heavy crashed past them, bulldozing a straight path through a briar patch. A moment or so later, something else followed it, leaving behind the impression of ferocious energy, short skirts and flaming red hair.

'Hey, Chief,' said Mr Snedge. 'What was that?'

'I think,' Hat replied, his chin rested on his hands, 'it was a huge bear being chased by an attractive older woman with some kind of axe.'

'Not an axe, chief. A tomahawk.'

'Really?' Hat sighed, without looking round. 'How come you're so sure?'

'I nicked it from her, Chief.'

Captain Hat closed his eyes. 'Snedge,' he muttered, 'I wish you'd stop doing that. One of these days it's going to get someone really pissed off with us, you know?'

'Sorry, Chief.'

Hat shrugged. 'Yeah, well. Neat piece of work, though. You sure she didn't notice?'

'They never do.'

'Pass it over, then, and let's have a look at it.'

A simple tomahawk it proved to be; knapped flint and pine and elk sinew, nothing more. Hat looked at it for a while, then closed his eyes, tossed it up in the air and caught it.

'Yo, Chief, where'd you learn to do that?'

Hat shook his head. 'No need,' he replied. 'It's one of those magic things. Hell, a snake could juggle with these babies and still catch them.'

'Magic, huh?' Squab didn't sound impressed, exactly. 'What's those curious symbols incised on the handle mean?'

'Symbols? Hey, he's right, let's see. *Made in USA by union labor.* CAUTION *Read safety warnings in manual before use.* Well, I guess that's another little mystery cleared up. Shall we try going up the trail instead of down it this time, or did we try that already?'

'We tried it, Chief.'

'Nuts.' Hat lay back, tipped the brim of his hat down over his eyes and folded his hands behind his head. 'Let's stay here, then. Perhaps if we stay here long enough, the universe'll get bored and go pick on someone its own size.'

'Chief.'

'What?'

'It can't do that, Chief, on account of nobody's the same size as the universe. That's called Einstein.'

'I stand corrected, Mr Squab. Let's just stay here anyway.'

Far away, a bird sang. An otter slipped into the water, strewing bubbles. A bear roared, either in rage or in terror.

'Chief.'

'Yeah?'

'Wasn't it Einstein who directed *Battleship Potemkin*?'

'That was Eisenstein, Snedge.'

'I thought Eisenstein was US chief of staff in World War Two.'

'I don't think so, Snedge. He was a Russian.'

'Hey! You mean like a spy or something?'

'You're thinking of Eisenhower, Snedge.'

'Ah, right. You mean the relativity guy.'

'That's him, Snedge. The very same.'

A plane flew overhead, very high. Just before it was due to pass directly over the lake, it changed course slightly and flew round it. They always did. Nobody, not the pilots, not flight control, ever knew why. In the distance, a long-ship sank.

'Chief.'

'Oh, cut it out, will you? I was just getting comfort-able.'

'Chief,' insisted Mr Squab, 'there's someone coming.'

Immediately Hat was on his feet, hat on, right hand on the butt of his pistol. 'Damnit,' he hissed, 'we're right out in the open, too.'

'It's them Injuns again, Chief.'

'You mustn't call them that any more, Snedge, they don't . . . Where?'

'Coming over the ridge, look. Hey, you remember the time we stole their . . .'

'*Hide!*'

'No, Chief, we stole their canoe, remember? Don't think they had any hides.'

'I mean conceal yourself, you dummy.'

'Sorry Chief.'

Linda Lachuk stopped in her tracks, turned round and looked. Nobody there. Odd; she could have sworn she was being followed.

She shrugged and carried on walking, just as the ninth consecutive arrow from Talks With Squirrels' bow hit her smack between the shoulder blades. It was archery of a kind that would have left Robin Hood weeping with jealous rage; nine hits within a half-inch circle at seventy-five yards. For the record, she'd also trodden right on the dead centre of the fragile platform of branches covering the deep pit full of sharpened stakes, put her feet in the trip-wires of four noose-and-bent-sapling beartraps and strolled through a direct frontal assault by Talks' entire war party without even blinking an eye. If she'd only known what kind of footage she was missing, she'd have died of frustration.

Just as she was beginning to feel that a nice sit-down and a cup of coffee would be really helpful, she caught sight of a building, fifty yards or so away under the shadow of a stand of tall pines. She stopped, turned off the path and sauntered up to the front door. It wasn't locked.

'Hello?' she called out. 'Press. Anyone home?'

The place seemed deserted, but the occupants couldn't be too far away; there was a roaring fire in the grate, and the red check tablecloth was laid for a meal. There were cute little wooden bowls, with cute wooden cups and spoons. A cute cottage loaf and an old-fashioned wood-handled breadknife sat on a cute wooden platter in the middle of the table. A big copper kettle hung on a hook in front of the fire.

Ah, said Linda to herself, a Tea Shoppe. Probably out back they keep the postcards, souvenir mugs and expensive home-made fudge. She sat down on one of the cute wooden chairs – oddly enough, there was only one she could sit on; the other two were too big and too small respectively; rural inbreeding, probably – and looked round for a waitress.

A moment later, one appeared. She was tall, slim, dark and beautiful, with hair like a black waterfall. 'Hiya,' she said. 'What'll it be?'

'Coffee.'

'Sorry,' the girl said. 'No coffee. All we got is milk.'

'Milk, then,' Linda replied. 'Is there anything to eat? A triple pastrami on rye with alfalfa sprouts and blue cheese relish, and . . .'

The girl shook her head. 'There's porridge,' she said.

'Porridge?'

'It's mighty fine porridge,' the girl said with a smile. 'Best in all of Iowa. With cream and honey.'

'Porridge, then,' Linda sighed. 'Oh, and while you're here, I don't suppose you know anything about the submarine base, do you?'

The girl chewed the end of her pencil. 'You mean the secret nuclear submarine base in the lake? The one that's a joint venture between the CIA, the Pope and the Australians?'

Linda nodded, unable to speak. For a split second, she even forgot her resentment about there being no pastrami.

'Sure,' the girl replied. 'Just wait there till I fetch your order, and I'll tell you all about it.'

She swayed gracefuly away, leaving Linda looking as if

she'd just been trapped in amber. *Yes!* The CIA, the Vatican *and* the Ozzies, with alfalfa sprouts, blue cheese relish *and* a fennel salad. Good menu they got here, she muttered to herself, except for the food.

Her daydream froze-framed, and splintered into fragments as she looked at the open doorway and felt the muscles of her stomach tighten into a hard knot.

In the doorway stood three bears.

'All right,' said the squirrel, 'we're here now.'

Wesley, who had been trudging along looking where he was going, stopped and surveyed.

'We came *here*?' he demanded. 'On *purpose*?'

The squirrel's tail quivered; body language for, *Yes, I know*. And it wasn't a prepossessing spot; all that picturesque scenery, all that awesome majesty of nature, the trees, the scree-covered hillsides, the silvery cascade of the waterfall – and here they were, at a garbage dump.

'But not,' the squirrel pointed out, 'just any old trash-heap. Look carefully.'

Wesley sniffed, his manner reminiscent of the food-taster to a psychotic Roman emperor who's just slapped an extra denarius on beer and ciggies. 'Must I?' he queried. 'Squirrel, this place smells like where I live. I don't *want* to look carefully.'

'Look carefully.'

'Oh, all right.' With his toe, Wesley tentatively nudged a parting into the overgrowth of nettles and briars. 'Like I thought,' he called back over his shoulder, 'it's nothing but a load of old – *oh my God!*'

'Impressive, huh?'

'But –' Wesley turned his head slowly. 'This hillside,' he said, slowly and nervously. 'It's not all –?'

The squirrel nodded. 'The whole hillside, as far as the eye can see. Just one huge great pile of bones. I'm telling you, if you were a dog with a weak heart, you'd be dead meat by now.'

'Er . . .' Wesley knelt down, uncomfortably aware of creakings and snappings underfoot. 'Might I ask what sort of . . . ?'

'It's all right, they're not human bones,' the squirrel replied. 'Just look at the size of them, for a start.'

Wesley peered closer. They were, indeed, *huge*; enormous ribcages and tibiae and femurs. And skulls too, of course. As soon as he saw them, he knew what the bones were.

'Buffalo,' he said.

'Bison,' the squirrel corrected him. 'Look around you, and you're looking at all that remains of roughly a billion bison. Hey, you're into making model kits; if you like, I'll get you some glue and you can piece a few of 'em back together again.'

'Shuttup!' Wesley felt the shudders coming on, but there was nothing he could do about it. 'Did you say . . . ?'

'A billion's maybe overdoing it, I couldn't resist the assonance. Well over ten million, though. Must be pretty close to eleven million. Can your mind conceive of eleven million of *anything*?'

'No,' Wesley answered without hesitation. 'Anything over four hundred is basically just lots.' He took a deep breath and managed to slow his shivering down a little. 'What is this place, Buffalo Bill's skip?'

'Hell, no,' the squirrel replied. 'Bill Cody and his type only helped sweep up the very last knockings. There used to be *lots* of bison in these parts at one time.'

'OK.' Wesley folded his arms and looked resolutely away. 'So what happened?'

'Before Buffalo Bill –' Wesley glanced up into the tree; the squirrel had vanished, and the voice was coming from immediately behind him. 'Before the red man, even, there were an awful lot of buffs around here. They had it good, too; no natural predators, plenty of suitable food and clean water, amenable climate – the living was easy if you stood six feet at the withers and weighed a ton and a half. In fact, it got so easy that the buffs found they had time for other things besides mere survival and reproduction.'

'Huh?'

'Music,' said the buffalo behind him. 'Poetry. Philosophy. The arts. And, shortly after that, the sciences too. Ten thousand years ago, these babies were highly civilised. Sophisticated, enquiring minds. Sensitive souls capable of savouring the beautiful and strange. Impeccable table manners.'

'Table manners?'

'Never spoke with their mouths full. Digested everything in the proper order. Table manners can get really sophisticated when you've got two stomachs.'

Wesley frowned. 'All right,' he said, 'point taken. So what happened to them?'

'Bit slow on the uptake today, aren't you?' replied the buffalo, pawing absently at the crust of the bonehill. 'They wiped each other out, is what. Par for the course, when a species gets so far above itself that it's got time on its hands. Remind you of anyone?'

'Um.'

'Actually,' the buffalo went on, swishing its tail, 'our lot at least had the common sense to use an ultimate weapon that didn't blow up the planet. As I recall, it was a highly selective synthetic virus that only affected the American bison. Wiped out ninety-nine per cent of the population in just under forty-eight hours.'

Wesley swallowed the nasty-tasting stuff that was creeping up inside his throat. 'And the other one per cent?' he asked.

'Oh, they'd made plans. Before the war started, they got the other bison to dig them nice deep bunkers, usually underneath lakes where the virus couldn't get through. Water filtered it out, you see. Then, when all the others were dead and the virus had died out along with them, up they came and got on with the job of rebuilding the breeding stock.' The buffalo sighed. 'It was sort of arse-about-face Darwinism, if you like. Survival of the most devious. The idea was that the genetic matrix of a bunch of creatures who could cheerfully send the rest of their species to their deaths must be pretty hot stuff; so if they could wipe out the rest of the species until only they were left to breed from, pretty soon they'd have a race of genetically perfect Superbastards; you know, the sort who not only inherit the Earth but duck out of paying the inheritance tax. Can you follow that line of reasoning? It has a sort of ghastly logic, don't you think?'

Wesley nodded. 'Where I come from,' he said, 'we call it government policy. The needs of the many outweighing the needs of the few. Sorry, you were saying.'

'Quite,' the buffalo replied. 'The misrepresentation of the people, and all that. In our case, though, the whole scheme blew a fuse at the last minute.'

'Really?'

'Really,' the buffalo confirmed. 'What actually happened was that immediately after the war started, just before the bunker hatches were due to be sealed, the cleaners who'd been ordered to spruce the place up a bit before the superbison moved in – you know, give it a last going-over with the Hoover, air the beds and so on – changed the locks and refused to come out. The superbison all died of the plague, and as a result the dumb beasts Bill Cody's boys polished off were all descended from a bunch of cleaners and carpet-shampooers; marvellously gifted at keeping the prairies neat and tidy, not much cop when it came to out-witting the white man and his stick that spoke thunder. I suppose you could say it served them right. After all, sur-vival of the most houseproud; it's not exactly a manifesto for a brave new world, is it?'

Wesley shrugged. 'It was a pity, all the same,' he answered. 'I mean, they couldn't exactly help the mess their ancestors made.'

'Sure.' The buffalo sounded unsympathetic. 'And if the egg you had poached for breakfast this morning had been allowed to hatch, maybe it'd have gone on to write Beethoven's symphonies. I wouldn't lose much sleep over it, though, if I were you. In the final analysis, what tastes better on toast, a symphony or a poached egg?'

Wesley shifted his weight off his left leg, which had gone to sleep. 'Is there any point in you telling me this,' he asked, 'or is it just to make me feel rotten about being human?'

The buffalo snickered into its beard. 'This is just the set-ting,' it replied. 'The adventure'll be along in a minute.'

'The adventure? What adventure?'

'Ah.'

'So you're the little bastard who's been sitting in my chair,' snarled the Daddy bear. 'Muriel, hold her arms.'

Linda rose to her feet like a firework from a milk bottle. As she did so, she heard the chair go *snap!* under her. 'Now just a minute,' she said.

'My chair!' yelped the bear. 'Look what the bitch's done to my chair! Goddamn thing isn't even paid for yet, and she's gone and bust it.'

Linda looked down, gulped and turned back, trying to fumble her face muscles into a smile. 'It's OK,' she croaked, 'really. The paper'll pay for any damage. Look, I'll give you my card, and . . .'

'Like hell you will. Junior, run and get the big hammer.'

Many years ago, when she was nothing but a cub reporter with a spiral-back notebook and a dream as big as Mongolia, Linda had been sent on a course. The title was *Handling Awkward Confrontations*, and the idea was to train the young newshound how to blarney her way past the fact that she'd been caught taking pictures of the secret military installation, resting her elbows for a one-fifteenth second exposure on the big sign saying *Photography Punishable By Death* while wearing a T-shirt of the local military dictator dressed in horns, cloven hooves and a frock. At the time, Linda had been rather more interested in following up a potential story about corrupt coursework-grading practices at that particular summer school, and she'd missed quite a few useful hints. Short-sighted of her, in retrospect (although in the end it had made a fine story).

There were, however, three magic words that usually worked in these situations. She tried them.

'I'm a journalist,' she said, and held her breath.

Daddy bear's brow furrowed. 'A what?'

'Journalist,' Linda repeated, in that patient voice grown-ups use when teaching backward children to read. 'I write things for the newspapers.'

'Newspapers?'

Before Linda could say anything, Mummy bear leaned

forward and whispered something in her partner's ear.

'Oh, right,' he said. 'That stuff. And you write the words, do you?'

Linda allowed herself to relax ever so slightly. 'That's right,' she said.

'Ah. Actually, I've often wondered, maybe you can tell me this. Why do they bother printing words all over the stuff when all you ever use it for is wiping your –?'

'Hey!' Linda objected.

Hard-bitten, cynical newshound that she was, Linda Lachuk still had a small, battered compartment in her soul labelled *Dreams – Handle With Care*. About the only thing in that compartment that hadn't been reduced to glass dust years ago was the quaint notion that whenever a story of hers got printed in a newspaper, people would actually read it and take it seriously. Although, generally speaking, she wouldn't give you the pickings of a piranha's teeth (you collect) for any matter of principle that wasn't good for two thousand words and a photo spread, all it took was somebody speaking blasphemously about the media to make her as ideologically ferocious as, say –

A she-bear defending her cubs? Well, why not?

The bear stared at her down its long snout. 'You say something?' it demanded.

'I said, Hey,' Linda replied. 'Want to make something of it, fuzzball?'

'Don't you call my husband a fuzzball.'

'Go on, Dad, eat her.'

The bear growled. 'Yeah,' he said. 'I want to make something of it.'

'Right now?'

'Right now.'

'Then perhaps,' Linda said, slowly taking off her jacket and rolling up her sleeves, 'you'd care to step outside.'

The bear frowned. 'But you're a girl,' it objected.

Linda nodded. 'Yeah,' she said. 'I'm the girl whose gonna shove your dumb face down your dumb neck, you fleabag. Now, you wanna step outside or not?'

The bear opened its mouth. 'You bet.'

'Me, too. Oh please, Mum, can I step outside, too? Oh, go on.'

'Let's all step outside,' snarled the she-bear. 'Nobody calls my husband a fleabag and gets away with it.'

Linda nodded. In her eyes flickered the light of battle. The three bears looked at each other, and their eyes said, *Right*.

'Go on, then,' grunted the bear.

'No, after you,' Linda replied, dipping her head in a disdainful bow. She stood up, crossed to the door and held it open for them.

'Right,' said the bear.

'Right.'

'Right.'

'Right.'

The three bears stalked outside, breathing heavily through their snouts; whereupon Linda slammed the door behind them, shot the bolts, dragged up a chair and wedged it under the handle and sprinted for the stairs. By the time the Daddy bear had smashed down the door, Linda had one leg over the sill of the bathroom window, and was calculating approximately how hard she'd hit the tin roof of the scullery ten feet below.

The answer was: quite hard, but not nearly as hard as, for example, three angry bears. She rolled down the roof, landed awkwardly on her right hip, swore, picked herself up and ran. Mummy bear reached the open window just as Linda disappeared into the trees, and although she threw several articles of crockery and footwear after her, she missed.

Some considerable time later Linda caught her foot in a low trailing bramble, measured her length on the ground and lay still. When her head came back on line she got up on her hands and knees and listened for sounds of pursuit. Silence, except for soft forest murmurs and the welly-booted tap-dancing of her own heart. Shaken them off. Phew.

'Damn,' Linda said aloud. OK, it was good to have escaped from the bears, but that didn't alter the fact that she'd been *that* close to getting a full eyewitness statement from that waitress which sounded set fair to link the CIA, the Pope and the Australians to this submarine thing.

If she was half a journalist, she'd go back.

Yes, reasoned the better part of her valour, and if you do go back, fairly soon you *will* be half a journalist; the bottom half, probably, all chewed and covered in scratch marks. And to die without having filed the story – what a terrible, terrible waste that would be. Once she'd filed the story – well, once they'd printed the story and she'd won a hatful of awards and done her acceptance speeches then all the bears in the Universe could come and eat her with English mustard and hack sauce for all she cared. Until then, she was the guardian of a Sacred Trust.

To cover the story . . .

Bring 'em back alive . . .

And me too, please, added discretion's better part, which had been kibbutzing on this train of thought. *If that's all right with the rest of me, that is.*

.The hell with it. There would be other witnesses. All she had to do was find them.

Pulling her shirt collar up round her ears – it was turning cold, and she'd left her jacket behind – she set off to do just that.

CHAPTER SIX

'I should've taken that job,' muttered Four Calling Birds, the second in command of the war band. 'Maybe then I'd have had a cigar store of my own by now.' He flopped down on a tree-stump, hauled off his left moccasin and evicted a small stone.

Talks To Squirrels, who was just as weary and footsore as his first officer but felt the need to set an example, scowled at him. 'Selling tobacco,' he sneered. 'Fine trade for a brave.'

'Look,' Four Calling Birds replied, 'if I had, I'd have killed a hell of a lot more palefaces by now than you have, and that's no lie. Why do we bother, Talks? It's a waste of –'

'Shut up!' Talks To Squirrels dropped to his haunches and hauled his comrade down out of sight, signalling to the rest of the band with his other hand to do likewise. 'Something's coming.'

'So what? Worse case scenario is, we'll fail to kill it or it'll fail to kill us. We're ghosts, for crying out loud.'

It turned out to be a large shaggy bear, lumbering on all fours. 'Only me,' it said, in a feminine voice. 'It's been one of those days, so I thought I'd take a break and see how things were going.'

'Same as usual,' Talks replied, getting up and brushing leaf-mould from his knees. 'Scragging the Vikings was fun, but apart from that it's been dismal.'

The bear shrugged. 'You're welcome,' she said. 'And in any case, next time it's their turn to massacre you. Your unique cultural heritage snuffed out by brutish foreign adventurers, all that jazz. Oh come on, Talks, don't make faces. You know it's only fair.'

'Takes me all my time not to burst out giggling,' Four Calling Birds said. 'Those Vikings couldn't massacre their way out of a paper bag.'

'True,' admitted the bear. 'But the punters don't know that.'

Talks To Squirrels shook his head. 'It's dishonourable,' he muttered, 'having to hold still while a load of amateurs massacre you. My mother didn't raise me to be cut down by incompetents.'

'She didn't? What a very narrow-minded woman she must have been.' The bear sniffed, and licked its paws. 'You know the rules, Talks. If you don't want to play you shouldn't have joined.'

Talks With Squirrels made a get-lost gesture with his hand and changed the subject. 'Awful busy all of a sudden,' he observed. 'How many of them are there?'

'Four,' the bear sighed. 'Simultaneously. Takes it out of a person, I'm here to tell you. Still, they've all done the Vikings, and three of 'em have done the bears. I always reckon that once you've got the bears out of the way, the rest's pretty well plain sailing. Still, if it keeps up like this I'm going to have to think seriously about taking someone on.'

'Really?' Three French Hens, the band's master-at-arms, looked up sharply. 'You mean, like an apprentice or something?'

The bear nodded. 'Just someone to answer the phone, make the coffee, do the ottering, nothing too taxing. Why? Interested?'

'Sure,' said Three French Hens. 'Beats this dead-end job,' he replied, ignoring the look on his CO's face. 'My mother didn't raise me to hang around for centuries after my death haunting no duckpond. Come to think of it,' he added, 'my mother didn't raise me, period, I was found in a basket and brought up by wolves. But you know what I mean.'

'Fine.' Talks To Squirrels threw his hands up in the air melodramatically. 'Get lost, the whole lot of you, leave it all to me to do. Don't reckon anybody'd notice if you did, at that.'

The bear extended a footstool-sized paw and patted him gently on the shoulder. 'Don't be like that, Talks,' it said. 'You're doing a fine job, really. And who knows, this time round or maybe the next, you might just strike it lucky and get sent Home. Well,' it added, as Talks expressed his cynicism by way of a vulgar noise, 'you never know. One of these days we'll complete the Cycle and you'll get exorcised. See if you don't.'

Talks shook his head. 'Going round and round and round and getting nowhere,' he grunted. 'Sounds just right for an Exorcise Cycle to me.'

The bear removed its paw. 'Save it for the customers, Talks,' it sighed. 'And cling on like grim death to the day job. By seeing you, guys.'

The braves waved as the bear lumbered away. The band relaxed. Some of them lit a fire. Two Turtledoves and Five

Gold Rings started to fix dinner. In the distance, the mountains stirred in their sleep.

'It's all very well her saying that,' Talks growled. 'But we've been through this – hell, I don't know how many times, and we're still here, damnit. All I can figure is, we must be doing something wrong.'

'Just worked that out, have you?' Four Calling Birds replied. 'With a response time that quick, maybe you should go work for IBM. Hey, anybody seen my tomahawk? I thought I left it under this tree.'

'Can't leave anything for a second round here,' Talks sighed. 'I'm telling you, if ever I get my hands on those no-good smugglers –'

'They'd go right through them,' Two Turtledoves interrupted. 'Forget it. We aren't scheduled to do the bears for a while anyhow.'

'Yes, but it's my –'

'Get another one from the Stores,' snapped Talks To Squirrels. 'Great Spirit, have you got nothing better to worry about than a goddamn stone axe?'

'No.'

Talks To Squirrels pulled a sad face. 'To be honest with you, neither have I. Probably explains why I'm depressed. Come on, let's go shoot some motorists. Mr Paliachiewski's due along any minute now with the bread van. Two squirrels' tails for the man who can shoot out his tyres in five shots.'

He set off up the hill. Behind him, the war band exchanged glances.

'Might as well,' Four Calling Birds admitted. 'It's not as if we're snowed under with more exciting things to do.'

''S'pose not. Hey, Birds, you got any idea where he gets the squirrel tails from? Being a ghost and all?'

'Mail order,' Four Calling Birds replied. 'And they're synthetic fur fabric, made in Indonesia.'

'Hey, that's amazing,' said Two Turtledoves, impressed. 'Where's Indonesia?'

Four Calling Birds furrowed his brow, until his eyebrows collided like furry trucks. 'Somewhere south-west of Chicago, I think. Out that way somewhere.'

'Oh. I thought that was Indiana.'

'No, he's the guy who swings in and out of old ruins on a rope, wearing a hat. They call him that because he comes from Indonesia.'

'Ah!' said TwoTurtledoves. 'I see.'

'Knowledge is power, Doves.'

'You bet, Birds. Last one up the hill gets an Iroquois haircut.'

'Well?' Wesley demanded.

'Sorry about this,' replied the bison, tight-lipped. 'Slight technical hitch, by the looks of it. Honestly, you can't leave anything these days except it's nailed down.'

Wesley raised one eyebrow, Mister Spock fashion. 'Excuse me,' he said, enjoying himself, 'but are you trying to tell me someone's *stolen* the adventure?'

'Not the adventure itself,' the bison replied, turning over a rock with its snout. 'Just one of the props, is all. Unfortunately, it just so happens it's one of the important ones. Goddamnit,' it added.

A thin, soft wind flicked over them, mussing up Wesley's hair and rufffling the fur on the bison's shoulders backwards, against the pile. Tiny ripples moved on the surface of the lake, frosting the glass of the mirror. The bison snuffed at the ground with its broad nostrils, then pawed dolefully with its front left hoof.

'Bugger,' it said.

Wesley got up from the bison skull he'd been sitting on. 'Fair enough,' he said, 'I suppose that means we'll have to miss out this adventure. Never mind, eh?'

'Oh no you don't,' grunted the bison. 'You'll have this adventure, and like it. And if you don't have it now, it'll be put in front of you every day until you do, so be told.'

'You sound just like my . . .'

'Ah,' said the bison, 'here we are. Now, I want you to imagine that sticking in this rock here, there's a sword.'

'*Imagine. . . !*'

'Yes, damnit,' replied the bison, annoyed. 'Come on, for God's sake, you're the one who lives in a world of fantasy and imagination, peopled by strange gods and the weird offspring of the subconscious. Imagining a sword ought to be a piece of cake.'

'That's not the point. Sure, I *can* imagine swords. I just can't see why I should have to. Like, I can sleep on the beach under a black dustbin liner, but that doesn't mean I'm satisfied when I get off the plane and find they haven't built the hotel yet.'

'Imagine,' repeated the bison, 'there's a sword in this here stone. Big shiny job, OK?'

'With a bejewelled hilt?'

'Naturally.'

'Runes?'

The bison considered for a moment. 'Probably not,' it replied. 'Wrong tradition. Make it sigils instead.'

'OK, I've got the sigils. Are the quillons straight or curved?'

'The whats?'

'Quillons. The arms of the crossguard, which I think ought to curve inwards, like a coathanger.'

The bison shrugged; no small undertaking, for a creature whose shoulders are higher than its head. 'Whatever's right,' it said. 'Far be it from me –'

'And the pommel,' Wesley went on, looking into space. 'Is the pommel disc-shaped, in the French style, or more of a semicircle with the flat edge facing the quillons, owing more to the Scandinavian –?'

'I think you're getting the hang of this,' said the bison, breaking out the emergency supplies of self-restraint. 'Now then, this sword –'

'Hang on, we haven't discussed the ricasso profile yet.'

'Take hold of the hilt,' growled the bison ominously, 'in your left hand. Above it, place your right. You there yet?'

'I think so. It'd help if you'd specified it was a two-hander. I'm having to do some pretty substantial revisions as I go along here. For example, the fifteenth-century Swiss zweyhander . . .'

'Both hands on the hilt.' snarled the bison. 'Ready? Now pull.'

'I can't.'

The bison looked up. 'You what?'

'I can't,' Wesley repeated. 'It's stuck in this rock.'

'Oh for fuck's – Imagine it isn't.'

'But it is. Rusted in solid. These finely tempered Solingen steels, they rust as soon as look at them.You'd need a gallon of WD-40 and a jackhammer to get the ruddy thing out.'

A bemused expression flitted over the bison's face, as if it had been God saying *Let there be light* and having the Void reply *Only if you've got fifty pence for the meter*. 'All right,' it said, slowly and patiently, 'imagine a gallon of WD-40 and a jackhammer.'

'WD-40. Jackhammer. OK.'

There was silence for a moment, disturbed only by the bison breathing loudly through its nose and Wesley making bda-bda-bda noises under his breath. When the bison felt it couldn't really take much more of the sound effects, it lifted its head and said, 'How's it coming along?'

'Not good, I'm afraid,' Wesley replied. 'You see, the rust's really taken hold here. We've got to be a bit careful if we don't want the bloody point to snap off.'

'I see.'

'Of course,' Wesley continued, rubbing his chin, 'we could try heating the rock with a propane torch until it's really hot and then splashing water on it. That'd crack the rock, and then maybe we could sort of ease the sword free.'

'Good idea,' sighed the bison. 'Why don't you try that, then?'

'Ah,' Wesley replied, 'but then you'd run the risk of taking all the temper off the sword itself and ruining it. You've got to be a bit careful with heat around best-quality steel, you know.'

The bison shut its eyes tightly, until the muscles of its eyelids hurt. 'Look,' it said. 'If you can get this sword, this *entirely imaginary* sword, out of that rock, that'll make you rightful king of all Albion. Doesn't matter if you snap off the tip or spoil the frigging temper, when you're king you can have the royal swordsmiths make you a new one. All you have to do . . .'

'But that's silly,' Wesley retorted. 'If it's an imaginary sword, how will anybody know I've actually done it?'

The bison made a small noise, in which bewilderment and rage were mixed in the same proportions as gin and vermouth in a dry martini. 'Look,' it whimpered furiously, 'they'll trust you, OK? You'll be their goddamn king, it

wouldn't even occur to them you might be lying. I thought
you were dead keen on royalty where you come from.'

'We are,' Wesley replied. 'At least, some of us are. My
mum is. But where I come from, there's a bit more to
being royal than pulling imaginary swords out of chunks of
masonry. If it was as easy as all that, the whole system'd fall
to the ground.'

'All right,' said the bison wearily. 'You wait there. Don't
move. Don't even breathe. I'll be right back.'

'Where are you going?' Wesley cried.

'To get you a real sword, of course. Because you're so
damn literal-minded you won't do the adventure unless
there's an actual sword. Which means I've got to go traips-
ing all the way down to the Stores, fill in a pink requisition
slip, a blue confirmation slip, a green –'

'Hang on,' Wesley shouted. 'I've nearly got this one free
now. I felt it move just now.'

'– Authorisation docket, a mauve receipt, a blue confirmation slip for the mauve receipt, an orange cashier's
voucher, a –'

'That's got it, here we – Oh my God!' Wesley stood for
a moment, a huge double-handed sword with curved quillons and a disc pommel wobbling in his hand; then he
remembered that swords of this style weighed anything up
to twenty pounds, and dropped it with a clang.

'Told you it was a piece of cake,' said the bison smugly.
'Hey, you forgot the sigils.'

'Um.' Wesley stared at the sword as if it was a cat he'd
just run over. 'Hey, does this mean I'm rightful king of
Albion?'

'Yup.'

'Wow.'

'All hail,' said the bison, in a bored monotone. 'Long live

the king. May the king reign for ever. You realise you've spoilt this whole adventure for me now.'

'Hey, I'm sorry. I was just . . .'

'Gallon of WD-40 and a jackhammer,' the bison went on. 'Never heard the like in all my born days.'

Wesley cupped his hands to his cheeks. 'Hey,' he whispered, 'you realise what I just did? I *materialised* that sword, just by imagining it. One moment there was just this rock, the next . . .'

'Missed a trick though, didn't you? I mean, any sensible person would have imagined a sword he was actually capable of lifting; but not you, oh no. You had to go and dream up something that weighs half a ton. All I can say is, look out Albion.'

'Yes, but . . .'

'Well then,' the bison muttered, as it started to walk away. 'If I were you, I'd get straight on with imagining a block and tackle and a fork-lift truck. I'd get a wiggle on as well, before the goblins show up.'

'Goblins?'

'You bet. You don't suppose you were issued with that thing just so as you could open sixteen-gauge steel envelopes, do you?'

'You never said anything about goblins.'

'Didn't want to alarm you. Not then, at any rate. Right now, I'd just love to see a little pool of yellow liquid form at the bottom of your trouser leg. You see, I belong to the school of thought that holds that blind gibbering terror brings out the best in people.'

'You –!' Wesley wobbled, as fear melted the bones in his legs. 'Get me out of here, for Christ's sake.'

'But I thought you wanted excitement, adventure and a chance to do heroic deeds.'

'Eeekl!' There was a scuffling noise just inside the wood, like feet scrabbling on loose stones, or whatever. Wesley swung round, desperately looking for the best direction to run in. While doing so, he noticed the other goblins.

'They have you surrounded,' said the bison placidly. 'Just to make sure you don't pass up this once-in-a-lifetime opportunity of doing heroic deeds. Actually, the phrase *once in a lifetime* may be a trifle unfortunate in this context, so let's say *unique opportunity*. Don't want to strike the wrong note, after all.'

Goblins was what they unmistakably were; no risk of confusing them with fluffy kittens or social workers. Each of them was about four feet high and the same wide, with shoulders like American footballers and wicked pointy teeth sticking out of the corners of their green-lipped mouths. The knuckles of the hands they weren't holding their scimitars in trailed on the ground. They all had big noses and little round, red eyes.

'Wesley, goblins,' said the bison. 'Goblins, Wesley.'

The goblins advanced, moving as fast and as erratically as spiders. As Wesley stooped to where the sword was lying, a particularly chunky and red-eyed specimen darted towards him, brandishing a scimitar –

– Which he dropped, as he backed away screaming, his hands over his eyes. Wesley squirted another long jet of WD-40 at him, just to make sure, and spun round on his heel to confront the goblins who were sneaking up behind him. They shrieked out the first few notes of their blood-curdling war-cry, but got no further than 'Eeeeee!' before the sound was drowned out by a staccato pounding, thudding noise that made the ground shake. Four goblins went down like sacks of potatoes; the others ran away, very fast.

'My,' murmured the bison, as Wesley peered round over

the sights of the Uzi in his hands, 'you've really taken to this conjuring-stuff-up-out-of-thin-air business like the proverbial duck to water. Do you mind not pointing that thing at me, by the way?'

'Sorry,' Wesley mumbled, staring at the slaughtered goblins. 'Fuck it, bison, I *killed* them. Oh God . . .'

'Wouldn't worry about it if I were you,' the bison replied, nibbling at a thistle. 'They'll be right as rain in an hour or so. Hungry, of course, but that's their look-out. I guess having to miss the occasional meal is something you learn to live with if your staple diet is people.'

Wesley shuddered from his toenails to his scalp. At some stage, the Uzi had vanished again, although the shiny golden spent cases still glittered on the ground at his feet. The WD-40 and the jackhammer had gone, too, but the sword was still there. 'You bastard,' Wesley said, with feeling. 'You –'

'Whether or not that counts as a glorious deed,' the bison continued serenely, 'is rather a moot point. I think I'll have to look it up and get back to you on that one. I must say, though, it shows initiative, not to mention a pragmatic streak I must confess I hadn't expected of you. You've gone up in my estimation a bit, young Wesley. You'd best change your trousers, though.'

Wesley gave the bison a long, hard look but didn't say anything. What he was thinking ran too deep for words, except for a few short, vulgar ones mostly beginning with B.

The bison shook itself and became the lovely girl again. 'Come on,' she said. 'I'd pencilled in this time for a coffee break, but we're running a bit behind schedule. This way.'

Janice swore.

Around here somewhere, there must be a telephone.

You'd have thought that, wouldn't you? A civilised country like America. In your dreams.

Not, she told herself as she sat down and fished a small boulder out of her boot heel, that there was any great rush, being realistic about it. If the people from the ship had all drowned (as she feared was the case) then they'd still be just as drowned even if she didn't make it to a phone booth before nightfall. More drowned, even. So why should she break her neck scrambling down semi-vertical deer trails and break her back scrambling up the other side? Pointless . . .

Hang on, she muttered to herself as she struggled with a recalcitrant bootlace, just a cotton-picking minute. For a girl who's just witnessed a major tragedy – Ship Sinks In Lake, Fifty Feared Drowned – she ought to be going through all kinds of ghastly mental trauma, with a side order of guilt and choice of emotional damage from the trolley. And here she was, sitting grumpily on a rock cussing out a bootlace.

Delayed shock? The anaesthetic effect? Probably. Truth was, however, that all she really felt was rather silly. Did those strange men really steer their ship onto a rock because they were too busy gawping at *her* to mind where they were going?

Is this the face that sank a thousand ships? Under normal circumstances she could believe it; also the face that smashed a thousand mirrors, cracked a thousand lenses, soured a thousand gallons of milk – she'd heard 'em all, over the years. But beguiling sailors into running their ships aground; not me, pal, you're thinking of some-one else. Surely.

Maybe I'm imagining it. Probably. After all, picture the scene, where she's telling it how it was to the police. Well, officer, they were all standing on deck whistling at me and saying nice things, and then they hit this rock. Yes, at me. Yes, I was wearing clothes at the time. No, I don't think they were all stoned out of their brains . . .

The sun, she muttered to herself, must be hotter than I thought. It's curdling my brains. Me? Nah.

She stood up and tramped painfully over a low rise, from the top of which she could see a pleasant sight: a road of sorts, more of a dirt track really but flat, regular and, best of all, human-made. The logic being; people don't make roads that lead nowhere. Follow this track and you'll end up someplace people are. Goody.

She walked down to the track and was following it in what she hoped was an easterly direction when she heard an even more hopeful sound: the rumble of an engine. Better still; because right then she'd had enough of walking to last her a very long time. The noise was coming from in front of her, where the track disappeared into the trees.

Not one engine. Lots of engines. One hell of a lot of engines.

And then they appeared; twenty or so big, garish black-and-silver motorcycles, all daddy-long-legs forks and spider-bodies a few inches above the ground, straight out of *Easy Rider* genre ripoffs but without the class. On the motorcycles rode vaguely humanoid shapes – huge, burly, hairy men with enormous black beards and arms as thick as legs. She stopped where she could, trying to still the instinctive panic as the bikes surged forward and seemed to flow all round her, their engines deep and growling as the voices of great bears.

Oh *cringe*, she thought.

The ursine nature of their appearance was probably

intentional, for they were all wearing black leather cutoffs, on the backs of which were embroidered fancy stitching; somebody's girlfriend? Somebody's mother? Or did they sit round in the evenings beside the campfire threading needles and borrowing each others' silks?

IOWA GRIZZLIES M.C.
OSKALOOSA, IO.

– and a stylised picture of a bear's head, open-mouthed and roaring. One of them even had an *actual* bear's head, and the rest of its skin, wrapped round him like a towelling-robe, or Hercules as depicted in antiquity. Actually, it looked decidedly seedy and moulted, and Janice felt it had probably come from the back room of a pawn-shop, a long time ago.

The bikes stopped, corralling her in. The bikers cut their engines simultaneously, like a platoon of marines coming to attention. That alone was more unnerving than anything else about them.

'Hey, miss. 'Scuse me.'

Janice tensed. Lacking gun, knife, can of mace, electric cattle prod or any other form of weapon, she was going to have to rely on her wits and her heels to get her out of this one. She tried to take a breath, but her lungs were too stiff –

'Only,' the biker was saying, 'we're lost, and we were wondering, is this the right road for Tucseehanna?'

Huh? Janice felt physically unbalanced, the way you do when you step off the escalator without looking down. She wobbled, and pulled herself up straight again. She didn't know quite what she'd been expecting, but a squeaky little tenor voice –

'Only,' the biker went on, 'Maurice reckons we should have taken a left back there on the Fawcett pike, but the map clearly says . . .'

And then Janice noticed the thing that had been staring her in the face, except that she'd been too busy panicking to notice.

They were all wearing dog-collars.

Not leather straps with lots of shiny big studs; clerical collars, as worn by ministers of religion. That, together with the odd tank-sticker that read *Bikin' For Jesus* and *Freeway To Heaven* and *God Rides A Harley*, pointed her in a direction which logic wanted her to follow, although sanity wanted nothing to do with it.

'Excuse me,' she heard herself whisper, 'but are you guys *priests*?'

'Sure are,' replied the biker, beaming. 'I'm Father Armand, this is Father Patrick, Father Maurice, Father Bernard and Father Duane. Pleased to meet you.'

'Very pleased,' murmured Father Patrick.

'You bet,' added Father Duane.

'Excuse me,' Janice croaked. 'It's just a bit –'

Father Armand smiled. 'Yeah, I know,' he said. 'Priests on bikes. People do tend to have a problem with that, to begin with. But basically, you know, we're just guys who're into bikes and into Jesus, and we like to get out of the city once in a while, you know, build a camp fire someplace, open a bottle of wine, sing a few psalms. You know,' he concluded, blinking, 'we kinda figure, if Bishop Odo of Bayeux could ride into the battle of Hastings on a big white horse, then it's probably OK if we ride Harleys.'

'Right on,' agreed Father Bernard. 'It's very, you know, American.'

'Um,' Janice replied. 'Actually, I'm not from these parts myself, so I really don't think I can help . . .'

As she was speaking, she began to feel ever so slightly uncomfortable; not that she'd been wildly comfortable before, when she'd been under the impression that she was about to be raped, murdered and quite probably eaten by a pack of human wolves. But this was a different sort of uncomfortable. The bikers were all *looking* at her.

Looking. More to the point, they were glazing. Yearning, even.

'Priests,' she said aloud. 'Catholic priests, right?'

'You bet,' replied Father Maurice, with a kind of strangled twist in his voice, as if he'd just remembered something he'd forgotten a long time ago. 'That's us,' he added wistfully. 'We're priests, all right.'

'Every one of us,' added a biker behind him. 'You know, like unmarried . . .'

'Celibate . . .'

'Aw gee . . .'

'Hey!' That was Father Armand, calling his people to order. 'Guys! Let's all just bear in mind who we are, OK?'

'Kinda hard to forget sometimes, Armand,' replied Father Patrick, sullenly. If the others were yearning at her, he was double-yearning, in spades. 'Especially when we happen to meet, like, an exceptionally attractive and charming young lady.'

'Guys!' Presumably Armand meant it as a mild rebuke. But since he was yearning at her too, with great big round eyes that'd have looked just fine on a Jersey cow but which were entirely inappropriate for a sworn-celibate man of God, it was hard to see what he intended to achieve. 'OK, so we're only flesh and blood. Still, I feel sure that a couple hours of silent prayer . . .'

'I only became a priest to please my folks,' Patrick was muttering. 'Family tradition, they said. Goddamn stupid Irish pride.'

'Hey!' Father Bernard interrupted him. 'You think that's bad, you should try being Italian. My momma said . . .'

It was, Janice realised, exactly that same *ohshit* feeling she'd had when the ship hit the rock. Inside her mind, the penny gave in to gravity and began its long descent.

'Guys,' she said, 'maybe I should be getting along. Er, go with God.'

'I mean,' Father Bernard went on, fingering the collar at his throat as if it was made of steel and too tight, 'don't you ever ask yourself, *Why'm I doing this? What'm I missing out on?* And sometimes . . .'

'Me too,' whispered Father Armand, nodding. 'Hey, guys, I think we ought to talk about this. What do you think?'

For a time the hills seemed to shake with cries of 'Yo!', 'Right on!' and similar exclamations. One or two of the bikers actually tore off their dog-collars and flung them to the ground. 'Heck,' one of them was saying, 'so what if I have devoted my entire life since I was a little kid to becoming a priest? So what? It's never too late to change.'

Do the individuals who act as catalysts to sudden great events occasionally feel just a trifle apprehensive about what they've started? Did Joan of Arc, on seeing the reaction to her petulant complaint about rich English second-home buyers pricing the locals out of the property market, ever wish she'd kept her trap shut? Does the spirit of Columbus, gazing down from the bar of Heaven at modern San Francisco, ever feel he'd have done better to tell the Spanish king that the whole lot was as flat as a pancake, marvellous site for a hydro-electric plant but a complete non-starter as far as colonisation was concerned?

Maybe. Certainly, Janice had her doubts about what she'd started. Thirty outlaw bikers she might just have coped with, assuming that death was something she could take in her stride. Thirty love-struck lapsed priests, on the other hand, wasn't something she wanted on her conscience.

'Excuse me,' she said, and ran.

'And what in hell is *that*?' Calvin Dieb asked, pointing. 'Triangulation point? New age TV mast?'

'It's a sword,' replied the lovely girl. 'In a stone.'

Calvin shrugged. 'Ask a dumb question,' he replied. 'And don't tell me what it's doing there, because I don't want to know.'

The girl stopped, and sat down under the sword. 'Sorry,' she said. 'This is what we came here for. If I were you, I'd pay attention.'

'Sure.' Dieb sighed deeply, and sat down on a rock. 'So this is Disneyland.'

'No,' the girl replied. 'It isn't.'

'No? All right then. It's Arthurian Park, and any minute now some guy's gonna come running in saying, *Ah shit, the clones've bust loose again.* That's so passé, you know?'

'Wrong again,' the girl replied, scuffing her toe on the chalky ground. 'Do you always think in clichés, Mr Dieb?'

Calvin thought for a moment. 'Not clichés,' he replied. 'Call it shorthand. Comes of being a lawyer, I guess. We always think in precedents; you know, instinctively try and pigeonhole anything new in with something we've come across before. Saves time and thought, which in our business equals money. At two thousand bucks an hour, you haven't got time to think, you just *do*.'

The girl nodded. 'Valid enough point, I suppose,' she said. 'So presumably, if you were to see a guy in a robe with a tea-towel round his head raising the dead to life, you'd say, *huh, a Lazarus job*. Yes?'

'Yup.' Dieb grinned. 'Hey, wouldn't that be a great trick if you could do it? The tax-planning applications alone would be stupendous.'

'Mr Dieb –'

'Not to mention,' Calvin went on, rubbing his hands together, 'the use you could make of it in insolvency litigation. Your client dies, you call all the creditors together and say, "Sorry, fellas, the guy just died and the whole estate's gone in legal costs, so forget it," and then a week later you can fetch him back and slap in an interim bill. Hell, with that I could run the competition clean out of town.'

'Mr Dieb –'

'Or divorce. In divorce, it'd be huge. Your ex-wife screwing you for two hundred grand a year alimony? So what? You die, and the settlement dies with you. Then up you get and walk away, a free man.'

'Mr Dieb,' said the girl. 'Behind you.'

'What the –? Oh, fuck!'

'Quite.' The girl smiled, tight-lipped. 'A Little Big Horn scenario, don't you think?'

Calvin Dieb started to back away, step for step as the ring of squat, grim bodies advanced towards him. On each leathery, green-tinged face was a look of cold rage. When his back was up against the blade of the sword, Dieb stopped and slotted a feeble grin into the hole in his face.

'Hiya, guys,' he croaked. 'It's been a while. How's things with you?'

The tallest and squattest of the advancing forms snarled at him, revealing sharp, pointed teeth. 'Dieb,' he snarled, 'we want a word with you.'

'You do, huh? Well, that's great, guys, I value new clients

over everything else, believe me. It's just that I'm a bit tied up right now, so if you could maybe call in at the office first thing Tuesday, maybe we could . . .'

'Get him!'

Four of the short, squat creatures darted forwards, fast as big black rats running up the clock, and tied him to the sword. Four or five others came close behind and started stacking billets of firewood round his feet.

'We took a vote on it,' explained their leader. 'In the end it was forty-five per cent for lynching, fifty-five for burning at the stake. Calvin Dieb, prepare to fry!'

'New clients,' murmured the girl, standing back with her arms folded. 'Mr Dieb, I may have got this all wrong but I don't think they want to hire you. Fire, however, would definitely seem to be on the agenda. You upset these people or something?'

'Hey!' Dieb tried to struggle, but the ropes were too tight. 'The case was a big break for me. Here was this major pharmaceuticals company, with this multi-million product liability suit against them. Of course I gave it my best shot, that's what I do. If it had been these guys who'd hired me, I'd have done my best for them too. It's the rules of the game, right?'

'Shut up, you,' snapped the leader. 'You're gonna burn. Hey, guys, anybody got some matches? These goddamn Zippos are supposed to light in any weather, but this one keeps blowing out.'

'Go on,' said the girl. 'You'd got as far as product liability.'

'Don't listen to him, lady,' one of the shapes interrupted. 'Try hearing our side of the story for a change.'

'Very well.' The girl nodded her head politely. 'Fire away, oops, rephrase that. Go ahead. Shoot.'

'What you say?'

'Shoot.'

'Hey!' The creature waved its hands in the air. 'Don't you confuse the issue. We got it down to lynching or burning and now you're saying shoot the bum. We spent long enough deciding as it is.'

'Tell the story,' said the girl.

'Yeah, well,' the leader replied. 'You see, we're all what you might call on the short side –'

'Not short. Altitudinally challenged.'

'Unfairly discriminated against as far as the y axis is concerned.'

The leader frowned. 'Yeah,' he said, 'whatever. Anyhow, along comes this big chemicals company, advertising this miracle enhance-your-height hormone treatment. Of course we go for it. We buy the filthy muck and smear it all over ourselves.'

'Yeah,' shouted a creature at the back. 'Like herrings to the slaughter.'

The girl raised an eyebrow. 'Herrings?' she asked.

'And then,' the leader went on, 'a couple months later, we look in the mirror and hey, we ain't grown none, but we've all gone this funny green colour, and we're sprouting muscles like Arnie's big brother, and we're all starting to grow these teeth . . .'

'You try eating an apple without laying your own face open. It's awful.'

'I see,' the girl said. 'So you sue the pharmaceuticals company, and Mr Dieb here defends them. Am I to understand that you lost?'

'Too darned right we lost,' grunted the leader. 'We end up having to pay this creep's costs, plus damages to the chemicals guys for defamation and God knows what-all else. Man, it was a *disaster*.'

'All his fault,' agreed a spare creature. 'Shoulda been an open and shut case. Instead, this scumbag shuts our mouths and opens our wallets.'

'Cost us so much,' the leader went on, 'we couldn't afford to go into hospital and have the goddamn treatment. We had to live with it.'

'Ah.'

'Which is why,' the leader concluded, 'we're gonna torch you. Here, Jules, make with the kerosene. C'mon, guys, one of youse gotta have some matches. Hey, lady!'

'Sorry.' The girl held up her hands. 'You could always try rubbing sticks together.'

'I've got matches,' Dieb said.

The leader rounded on him. 'Oh yeah?' he said. 'Well, you wasted your bread, pal, 'cos where you're headed you ain't gonna need them. Vernon, find me a couple of dry sticks, will ya?'

'In my jacket pocket,' Dieb continued. 'You're welcome to them, really.'

'Sure.' The leader scowled until his fangs drew blood on his chin. 'But to get to them, we've gotta untie you. And then you make a run for it, and we lose you. No way, buster. If we can't find any matches, then it's back to Plan A and we lynch you.'

'Fair enough,' Dieb said. 'Lucky you've got the rope.'

The creatures started to murmur among themselves. 'He's right, Phil,' one of them said. 'Burning or lynching, we've gotta untie the creep either way.'

'Just a minute,' the leader growled. 'Just a friggin' minute. Didn't somebody say something about shooting him?'

'Nobody's got a gun, Phil.'

Dieb cleared his throat. 'Actually,' he said.

The leader lost his temper. 'Oh yeah,' he cried. 'And it's in a shoulder holster inside your coat, all we gotta do is untie the rope. Gag the son of a bitch, someone, while I find a big rock. Nobody touches the rope, understood? This is a *lawyer* we're dealing with here, remember?'

'Hey,' Dieb said, 'I just thought of something. Why not use the sword?'

'Sword? What sword?'

'This sword I'm tied to,' Calvin said. 'You could cut my head off, slice my guts out, all that kinda stuff.'

The creatures looked at each other. There were cries of 'Neat!' and 'Let's do it.' The leader, however, jumped up and down on the spot, screaming.

'You guys really kill me,' he yelled. 'To use the sword, we gotta untie the rope. When will you ever *learn*?'

It was at this moment that Dieb, who'd been rubbing the ropes up and down against the edges of the sword, finally felt the last strands give way. While the leader was hopping up and down and his companions were shouting at him to calm down, Dieb tugged the ropes free, fell to the ground, rolled to his feet and ran, leaping over the nearest creature like an Olympic hurdler running for a bus and making it to the edge of the clearing before any of them realised what was going on. The leader dropped to his knees, sobbing 'Nooo!' while the others rounded on him, howling curses and kicking him, as if to imply that, in their opinion, he might not have handled the situation as well as he could have, all things being equal.

CHAPTER SEVEN

'**H**ey, you.'

Captain Hat froze, as if suddenly immersed in liquid nitrogen. He pushed aside the leaf directly above his head, and stared.

'You,' the Big repeated. 'I wonder if you could help me.'

Mother of God, there's a Big talking to me. They're not supposed to be able to see us, for Chrissakes! 'Er,' said Captain Hat, surprising himself with the level of fluency he was able to muster. 'Um,' he added.

'I was wondering,' the Big went on, 'have you seen any submarines around here lately?'

'Submarines?' Hat repeated. 'I mean, no. No, certainly not,' he said defiantly. 'I don't know anything about any submarines. And besides, I was miles away at the time. I have witnesses.'

'Oh.' The Big seemed disappointed, but not for long. 'Australians?'

'Australians. People from Australia.'

Hat's brow creased. 'You mean, like guys in big hats with corks all round them?'

The Big nodded, her eyes aflame with excitement. 'That's it,' she said. 'Australians. You seen any?'

'No.'

'Oh. You're sure about that?'

Hat nodded. 'Positive,' he said.

The Big bit her lip. 'No disrespect,' she said, 'but how can you be sure they *weren't* Australians? After all, they don't always wear the silly hats or the fluorescent beach shorts, you know. As often as not, they can look just like ordinary people. Especially when they're under cover.'

That one, Hat felt, was so far above his head that you could bounce TV signals off it. 'You may be right,' he said carefully. 'I hadn't thought of it like that. But I can't remember seeing any people who definitely *were* Australians. As in funny hats, psychedelic leisurewear or talking in Australian accents.'

The Big smiled patronisingly. 'That doesn't mean anything,' she said. 'Australia's a culturally diverse country these days. Some of 'em don't sound like Australians at all.'

'Gosh. That must be awfully confusing for the rest of them.'

The Big nodded. 'You bet,' she said, and winked knowingly. 'All right, then, what about high officials of the Vatican? You can always tell them, by their broad-brimmed hats.'

'With corks round them?'

'Don't be stupid. They're red. They call 'em birettas.'

'I thought that was machine guns.'

The Big sighed. 'You're thinking of Lambrettas,' she said patiently. 'Have you seen any guys in red robes and big hats?'

'Sorry,' said Hat. 'Of course, they might have taken them off, if they were pretending to be Australians.'

'Ah.' The Big frowned. Clearly, she hadn't thought of that. 'All right then,' she said, 'what about Australians or high-ranking Papal officers masquerading as perfectly ordinary people? Seen any round here lately?'

Hat considered how he should frame his reply. 'Not to my knowledge,' he said, inadvertently echoing a thousand generations of lawyers. 'But maybe *they* were pretending to be the CIA?'

'Could be,' replied the Big, stroking her chin. 'But that's just conjecture, surely?'

'Maybe,' agreed Hat. 'Maybe not. Things are often not what they seem.'

'True. In fact,' the Big went on, 'in my experience, the more they seem to be something, the more likely they are to be something else.'

'You mean, like the Australians?'

'A case in point.'

'Or the CIA.'

'Perhaps,' the Big said. 'Though they tend to be the exception that proves the rule.'

'Do they? Oh, right. Anyway,' Hat went on, feeling that maybe he'd got the hang of talking to Bigs now, 'the way I see it, anybody I might have seen who was actually wearing a red hat with corks round it and carrying a Lambretta in a shoulder holster, *by that very token*, would probably turn out not to be Australian at all. You see what I mean?'

'I do,' said the Big, her eyes shiny again, 'I do indeed. Naturally, it'd be the CIA, deliberately trying *not* to look like *anybody*. Which'd make a whole lot of sense, of course.'

'It would?'

'Think about it,' said the Big. 'It's all just common sense, really. Hey, you've been very helpful. Can I quote you on that?'

'Well . . .'

The Big shrugged. 'Yeah, OK, I understand. You've got your own back to watch, I can see that. I'll just describe you as "an authoritative source in the upper echelons of the administration". That do you?'

'That'll be fine,' Hat replied. 'And meanwhile,' he added, 'if I do see any submarines . . .' And, having the feeling the Big would like it, he winked conspiratorially.

'You bet!' The Big winked back. Between them, they were beginning to look like a set of indicators. 'And as far as I'm concerned,' the Big went on, 'we never had this conversation, right?'

'What conversation?'

'You've got the idea. Well, stay loose. Be seeing you.'

'Not if I see you first,' Hat replied, with heartfelt sincerity. Then he ducked down under the leaf and crawled like Hell into the undergrowth.

For a minute or so after he'd gone, Linda stood where she was, looking inconspicuous – a skill in which she surpassed several large lighthouses. Then, nonchalantly whistling, she started to walk. And carried on walking, until she suddenly stopped, said, 'Ouch!' and fell over.

The reason being, she'd walked into a large sword in a stone and taken a nasty bump on the head.

She stood up. She waited till the world stopped spinning. She looked at the thing she'd just walked into, and recognised what it was.

And then, inspiration struck.

Linda got these sudden flashes, when things just seemed to appear out of nowhere and dance in front of her eyes, grinning and howling, 'Scoop! Scoop!' It was in just such a flash, for example, that she'd formulated the award-winning theory that it was actually Santa Claus who shot John

F. Kennedy – or otherwise, why was there this worldwide conspiracy to convince everybody that he didn't exist? And so, as she stood gawping at the sword in the stone, Linda *knew*.

Arms. Illegal arms shipments. Vaticangate. *They were shipping the stuff out in rocks*. That was why none of the consignments had ever been traced.

It was so beautifully simple. What the government were doing was encasing the arms in huge blocks of concrete, dressing them up to look like Sicilian marble, and then shipping them out on submarines via the Black Sea ports. God, it was so obvious a deranged child's imaginary friend could see it. And now she could, too. This was great!

(Behind her, a goblin crept stealthily forward, muttering something under its breath about third time lucky.)

Oh God, my kingdom for a fax machine! Not being able to get the story out right away was hurting her, physically, like a dagger in her heart or an ingrowing toenail. The biggest news story of the century, bigger even than her exposé of covert US involvement in the Trojan War, and here she was in the middle of the wilderness, unable to communicate with the office. Oh, life can be so *rotten*. Bewildered by the senseless cruelty of it all, she slumped down on a curiously shaped rock and buried her head in her hands.

'This one,' hissed Goblin Corporal Snargh to Goblin Sergeant Gnazhgz, 'is going to be a piece of duff. You watch. Dizzy bitch isn't even *looking*.'

'Bit of meat on 'er, too,' Gnazhgz grunted back. 'Leftovers'll do cold for Monday. I got the in-laws comin' over, it's her mum's malachite weddin'.'

Snargh's craggy, looming brow furrowed. 'How many's malachite?' he asked.

'Two hundred an' ninety-six. Y'know, whenever I think I got it rough, I look at her dad and I think, two hundred an' ninety-six years of *that*, I'd rather be boiled in lead. Still, wouldn't do if we were all the same.'

'Yeah.' Tiny tumblers clicked into place inside Snargh's fallout-shelter-thick skull. 'Jussa minute,' he whispered. 'Granted she's a bit on the buxom side, but there's never going to be enough for all of us *and* your missus's family on Monday. Not even if you was to do a sort of pasta thing and grate the meat up small, like a carbonara or somethin'.'

Gnazhgz grinned, revealing a collection of teeth that would inspire passionate interest in a research dentist and blind terror in anyone else. 'Sarge's perks,' he replied. 'You lot can have the next one.'

'Hey!'

'Shurrup,' the sergeant hissed, clamping a betaloned paw over Snargh's mouth. 'She'll hear you.'

Snargh pulled the paw aside. 'Now just a minute, Sarge, that's not bloody well fair.'

'Who said anything about fair? This is the army, son.'

'Yeah, but.' Snargh's face contorted into an even more horrific expression than usual. 'You said that the last time,' he growled. 'All we got was a load of giblets and bits of pipe and stuff. I'm not standing for it, you hear?'

'Keep your voice down, or the whole bloody world will.'

'Don't care. Fair shares for all this time, OK? Or . . .' The tip of Snargh's nose began to quiver, a sure sign of high passion. 'Or,' he said icily, 'we'll damn well help ourselves and you don't get any.'

'Huh! You and whose army?'

'Yours. Hey, lads! Sarge is gonna rip us off again!'

Goblin heads turned. Goblin eyes filled with rage. If

Linda hadn't been so completely submerged in self-pity that a bomb could have gone off in her shoe without her noticing it, let alone think of phoning through the exclusive story to the newsroom, she'd have had an unrivalled view of nine goblin warriors all whispering angrily at once.

'Shove it, you 'orrible little goblins,' Gnazhgz rasped, in a voice like a cheese-grater on living flesh. 'Any more of it an' I'll friggin' well eat you. Got that?'

Lance-corporal Zhlaghpf, five foot one at the shoulder and squat as a troll who's been caught in a junkyard car compressor, stood up, breathing hard through his snout. 'You want me to take you up on that, Sarge?' he rumbled.

'Any time, Zhlaghpf. Any time you like.'

'Right.'

'Right.'

'Right.'

A moment later, instead of two goblins standing up and hissing at each other, there was a sort of goblin-rich cyclone-come-snowball rolling and whirling about among the rocks, into which the rest of the goblins were drawn one by one. Of the ten members of the squad, seven of them (namely Corporal Snargh, Lance-corporal Zhlaghpf and General Infantrygoblins Groghdng, Fluraghzd, Twlurgh, Shdlnog and Urghmpf) were trying their best to dismember Sergeant Gnazhgz and the Loyalist tendency; comprising General Infantrygoblins Brzhgnazh and Glarpfgh. Because the enthusiasm and sheer bulk of the mutineers exactly cancelled out the skill, experience and unspeakably dirty fighting habits of the loyalists, it was a completely even contest; and, since goblins invariably fight to the death, there could only be one outcome.

A quarter of an hour later, Linda pulled herself out of

her self-induced slough of misery with the thought that if all else failed, she could scribble a note, shove it in a bottle and sling it in the Squash River, and rose to her feet for the long walk back up to the road. She'd taken about twelve steps when she realised she'd just trodden on something squishy. She looked down.

'Urgh!' said the body at her feet.

'Sorry,' Linda said. 'Hey, you all right?'

'I'm dying,' croaked the goblin painfully. 'I got a hole in my lung, my head's caved in an' I think the buggers got half me liver.'

'Good God,' Linda replied. 'Ought I to call a doctor?'

The goblin shook his head feebly. ''Sall right,' he sighed, air wheezing through his punctured lung. 'I'll be right as rain in the morning. They rebuild us, you know.'

'Do they?'

'Clever bleeders. Take it out of our pay, of course, but that's the army for you. Might even get promoted this rebuild, if I can make 'em think it was in the line of duty.'

'Oh,' said Linda, reassured. 'In that case, maybe you could help me. Submarines.'

'You what?'

'Submarines,' Linda repeated. 'Nuclear submarines laden with huge blocks of marble. Have you seen any lately?'

'No,' groaned the goblin. 'Sorry. Why?'

'All right, then,' Linda persevered. 'How about Australians? Probably wearing hats with corks,' she added. 'Maybe even open-toed plastic beach sandals.'

'What you on about?' the goblin whimpered. 'I'm a Sergeant of goblin fusiliers, not a friggin' mind-reader.'

'Hats,' Linda repeated impatiently. 'You know, like Australians wear. Only, the chances are that anybody wearing a hat with corks is likely to be the CIA in disguise. You see, I have conclusive proof that . . .'

'Oh, tell it to the submarines,' snarled the goblin, and died.

Linda shrugged, stood up and looked around. There were other goblins lying about the place, she noticed, but they were apparently dead too. Very dead. She had no way of knowing just how clever the clever little buggers were, but as far as she could judge, the job facing them would have all the king's horses and all the king's men throwing up their hands in horror and sending for a plumber. A pity, but there it was. Even the most dedicated and imaginative journalists run into setbacks occasionally. By all accounts, Woodward and Bernstein thrived on them. She'd just have to keep plugging away. And in the meantime, she could always use the message-in-a-bottle idea, assuming she could find a bottle, a piece of paper, a cork and a pen.

She carried on up the hill.

'This here,' said the tiresome old man, leaning back in his rocking chair and grinning a toothy grin, 'is Lake Chicopee. They do say . . .'

'Save it for the customers,' replied the stranger irritably. 'I'm on a tight schedule. Now, what I'm basically interested in is productivity levels, turnaround times, cost-effectiveness ratios and any areas where costs can be cut without significantly reducing overall efficiency. So, if we can start with last year's budget outline and work forwards from that.'

Slowly the tiresome old man prised his pipe-stem off his lower lip and widened his eyes. 'You're an inspector,' he said.

'Didn't I mention that? I'm sorry.' The stranger pulled a

sheet of paper from the file in his hand and fluttered it under the old man's nose. 'You'll need to see this, I suppose. General requisition from the Area Manager's office, notifying you of a routine spot efficiency check. You're just about to tell me you never got a copy, right?'

'We sure didn't, mister.'

The inspector sighed through his nose. 'Marvellous, isn't it? Five hundred and seventy-four permanent administrative staff, and between them they can't manage to send a simple letter. Makes me look a complete fool, of course, but there you are. Anyway,' he added, cheering up slightly, 'just because they're pathetic at head office doesn't mean you lot out here can afford to let things slip. Right then, those budget figures . . .'

With a shudder, the tiresome old man metamorphosed into a beautiful young girl. The inspector didn't even notice. 'Ah,' she said, 'the figures. Now if we'd only known you were coming . . .'

'Not you as well,' replied the inspector, frowning. 'Why is it that nobody seems capable of keeping a few bits of paper in order? You know, I think it's high time we had a bit of a blitz on filing systems generally. The regulations clearly state –'

'Just a minute,' the girl interrupted hastily. 'I'll just run indoors and fetch the shoebox.'

As she ran, she distinctly heard the inspector wailing, 'Shoebox!' in a distressed voice, but she pretended she hadn't. Of all the lousy timing! Four customers roaming round the place needing looking after, and she had to have a goddamn inspector descend on her.

It was looking as if it was going to be a very long day.

She opened the door of the log cabin, rummaged around under a table and pulled a tatty old shoebox out from under a pile of dirty laundry and vintage washing-up. She opened it. It was empty.

'Hat!' she shrieked. 'Hat, you thieving little bastard! What have you done with my paperwork?'

Inside the cabin, there was a deathly hush and complete stillness; so deathly, in fact, and so complete that any fool would have known there was someone in the room, hiding and holding his breath. The girl counted slowly to ten.

'Hat,' she said quietly. 'One last chance, and then I set the cat on you.'

Slowly, the lid of the cookie-jar lifted. Under it was the head of Captain Hat, wearing a rather sheepish grin.

'Look,' he said, 'I can explain.'

With a movement that was both lightning fast and lissomly graceful, the girl reached over and grabbed Hat round the throat before he could dodge back down out of sight. 'So can I,' she growled. 'You're a thief and a smuggler, and I ought to pull your lousy head off right now. Am I warm?'

Being unable to speak, Hat nodded. The girl slackened her grip a trifle.

'OK,' she said. 'Give me my files back and we'll say no more about it. Of course, I reserve the right to break both your arms about it, but I won't *say* anything. Otherwise . . .'

'Um,' Hat whispered, turning puce, 'there may be a slight problem. You see . . .'

'Hat, I'm warning you.'

'I really am terribly sorry,' the smuggler gurgled. 'Wouldn't inconvenience you for the world. It's just that on the Other Side, your accounts represent a form of higher pure mathematics beyond their wildest dreams, and some of the big West Coast universities have research budgets that'd fry your brain. So . . .'

'Hat . . .'

'So obviously,' Hat went on, choking a little, 'I kept copies. Now, if you'll just let me go for five minutes . . .'

'I'm gonna *kill* you, Hat. I'm gonna squeeze you like a tube of toothpaste till your guts come out your ears. And that's just my version of friendly persuasion. Now, where's this copy?'

'In the crystal cave under the southern waterfall in a black tin box marked SWAG, oh Jesus, you're strangling me,' Hat replied. 'The key to the box is in the right-hand drawer of the old roll-top desk in Grendel's mother's office, please let go, oh *shit*!'

'Crystal cave?'

'Aargh!'

'Southern waterfall?'

'Nggh.'

'Black tin box marked SWAG?'

'Ggggh . . .'

'Key in right-hand desk drawer?'

'G.'

'Thank you,' said the girl, letting go. Hat fell back into the cookie jar, and she replaced the lid. Then she slammed out of the cabin and began to run.

'I suppose,' said the lovely girl, 'you could say that we've now completed Phase One.'

The sun, peering round a cloud, winked in the lake. A few ducks hopscotched on the reflected mountains, meeting themselves coming up as they crashed ripples into the face of the mirror. *What the hell do they wish for?* Wesley asked himself.

'To carry on being ducks, of course,' the girl replied. 'You just wouldn't believe how easy ducks have it.'

Wesley looked up. 'Really?' he asked.

The girl nodded. 'Masses to eat. No need to take thought for the morrow, what they shall wear and all that palaver. If they get right out into the middle of the lake, they're safe from every kind of predator, with the improbable exceptions of very large pike and –' the girl sniggered, though Wesley couldn't see why '– submarines. And so, every time they land on the water, they wish to carry on being ducks. These days I just leave them alone and let them get on with it. They know far more about being ducks than I do, so there's not a great deal they need me for.'

'Well, bloody good luck to them,' Wesley sighed. 'I'm glad somebody gets something out of this ghastly business. What were you saying about Phase One?'

The girl lay back on a flat rock, her arms behind her head, her hair trailing down and just brushing the meniscus of the water without disturbing it. 'The first part of the procedure,' she replied, gazing at the sky. 'The easy bit.'

'The easy . . .'

'You bet. The first three experiences are really only to get you in the mood, accustom you to the environment, give you an idea of the sort of thing that goes on here. The actual character-forming, problem-solving part comes later; that's when we start addressing your deep-seated personal shortcomings and inadequacies. In your case . . .'

Wesley stood up. 'Hang on,' he said. 'I thought this was where all my dreams come true. All that stuff about deeply seated –'

'Dreams,' the girl reiterated firmly. 'Admittedly, some of the dreams that are about to come true tend to be the ones you get after a late-night cheese salad, but what the hell, a dream's a dream.'

Wesley frowned. 'Usually I dream of playing the violin naked in front of packed concert halls. Or running away down corridors chased by big dogs and women with knives. There's also this really weird one where –'

'All that sort of dream,' the girl said calmly, 'comes out of your deep-seated personal shortcomings and inadequacies.' She propped herself up on one elbow, swept a curtain of hair away from her dark, cool eyes and added, 'You're not going to tell me you haven't got any? Personal shortcomings and inadequacies, I mean. Because if you are . . .'

'Look.' Wesley turned round twice and kicked a pebble savagely. 'Of course I have. Heaps of them. But I don't see how being attacked by goblins and watching Vikings drown is going to help me grow as a person. I thought it was more about sitting round in a circle in a school hall every Tuesday night talking about it with a lot of other – I mean, in the company of other people in the same position.'

'That's encounter groups,' the girl replied. 'Quite different. Not that I'm saying they don't work, up to a point. As I understand it, everybody goes away from them with the firm belief that they may be sad and pathetic, but at least there's twenty-nine other people in the same town who're even sadder and more pathetic than they are. Very useful stepping-stone on the path to self-reconstruction.' She smiled and slid off the rock. 'But this way's more fun.'

'Is it? I was the one the goblins wanted to eat, remember.'

'I said more fun. I didn't say who for. You ready?'

Wesley took a couple of steps backwards. 'What for?' he demanded.

The girl grinned; you might say 'playfully', if you'd ever

seen a cat playing with a dying bird. 'Let's put it this way,' she said. 'Nobody's going to expect you to play the violin.'

Wesley was just about to demand an explanation, coupled with a few explicit assurances about not having to take his clothes off, when the air was suddenly full of wingbeats, and a savage gust of air pushed him off his feet into the mud, face down. When he'd prised himself out of the mud and cleared a couple of gaps in the face-pack to see through, he saw a huge black, white-headed eagle, easily fifteen feet from wingtip to wingtip, lifting itself up into the air. Clasped in its talons, and struggling wildly, was the girl.

'Help!' she screamed. 'Don't just stand there, *do* something! This is not a drill!'

'Huh?'

'*Heelp!*' The girl's voice seemed to be ripped away from her by the slipstream from the eagle's wings. As he stared, he saw that its round cruel eye was fixed on him. There's an eloquence in eagles' eyes that beats verbal communication into a cocked hat.

'Hey!' Wesley shouted. 'What's happening?'

But the eagle and the girl were already small, receding dots against the sky. Wesley ran down to the water's edge, and stopped. There was nothing he could do anyway, except watch and see where it went.

First it climbed, soaring on the thermals that rose from the lake until it was nothing but a speck, a memory of its own outline. Then, just as Wesley was convincing himself that he'd lost sight of it and it was long gone, it started to descend, sweeping long, slow circles over the middle of the lake. Now it was directly between Wesley and the sun, but he kept track of it (rather cleverly, he couldn't help feeling) by watching its reflection in the water. Finally it spread its enormous wings and sailed lazily across the lake and up into the high mountain that stood at the lake's southern-most end. It climbed, put its wings back and glided in, pitching somewhere high among the rocks.

'Christ!' Wesley said, and sat down again. Except at job interviews, in exams and on his first and only date with Stephanie Northrop from Vouchers, he'd never felt so help-less or so bewildered in all his life.

Just then, someone shot him in the back.

'Hey,' said a voice behind him. 'You felt that!'

Slowly, Wesley turned round. 'Who the hell are you?' he asked.

'My name's Talks With Squirrels,' the Indian warrior replied. 'If you don't mind my asking, what exactly did you feel?'

'Like somebody just poked me in the back with a stick,' Wesley answered. 'Why?'

'Not agonising pain or your whole life flashing in front of your eyes?'

'Not really, no. Look, who are you?'

'And you can see me all right? I mean, I'm not blurry at the edges or anything? You can't look straight through me at the trees behind?'

'No. What was it you did just then?'

'Shot you,' the Indian replied, indicating the bow in his left hand. 'Right between the shoulder blades. Only this time, you noticed.'

'*This time?*'

The Indian nodded. 'I've been shooting you ever since you got off the bus,' he said casually. 'Direct hit every time. By rights, if you were to drink a glass of water, you'd make somebody a first-class watering can.'

'Hey!' Wesley wasn't quite sure how to react. On the one hand, he had this overwhelming urge to be very frightened indeed. On the other hand, by his own admission this lunatic had been using him as a dartboard for some time now, and he was apparently none the worse for it, so what was there to be frightened of? '*Who are you*?' he repeated.

Talks To Squirrels propped his bow against a tree and advanced, hand outstretched. 'I'm a war leader of the now extinct Shashkehanna nation,' he said, not without a certain audible pride. 'Prior to my death in 1703, I was the most feared and respected warrior this side of the Mississippi. Actually, since I died my average with the bow's gone up from 96.28 to 98.3, while with the tomahawk, at fifty yards . . .'

Instinctively, Wesley grasped the proffered hand. His fingers closed upon themselves, enfolding nothing.

'You're dead,' he said.

'In a sense,' the Indian replied. 'Look, it's a bit hard to explain really. Try this. You've heard of negative equity?'

Wesley nodded. He had friends who talked about little else.

'It's when you want to sell the house but you can't, because it's worth less than what's still outstanding on the mortgage, right?' The Indian shrugged. 'Well, that's basically how it is with me and Life.'

'I don't understand,' Wesley said.

'You don't?' The Indian sighed. 'It's not that difficult, for pity's sake. Look. In life, I made certain undertakings, right? I swore this really heavy oath by sun, moon and stars that I'd never rest till I'd killed every paleface between here and the Cedar River.' The Indian shrugged. 'I underperformed, I admit it. Due, in no small part, to misleading information and a serious underestimate of the number of palefaces I was up against. You see, my sources led me to believe there were only thirty-four of them.'

'Ah.'

The Indian nodded. 'But I made the undertaking, nevertheless, and now I'm a bit like a kiddie who's getting his plate of cold shepherd's pie put in front of him every meal till he eats it all up. And since there's even more palefaces around now than there were back in the early seventeen-hundreds, I guess I'm fairly comprehensively stuck. Like I said; negative equity.'

'Gosh.'

Talks To Squirrels shrugged, sat down on the rock and lit a pipe. 'I'm allowed to smoke, it's one of the advantages of being dead,' he explained. 'I'm intrigued, though. You see, there's no way you should be able to see me, let alone feel my arrows. Seems to imply that – nah, can't be that. Forget I spoke.'

'Seems to imply what?'

The Indian waved his hand dismissively. 'Please,' he said, 'don't ask. Too silly for words. Don't want you thinking Death's addled my brains.'

'Seems to imply what?'

'Well,' the Indian said, 'if you insist, and you promise not to laugh, it might be that you're becoming more real on this side than you ever were back where you came from.' He frowned, and blew a smoke ring. 'But that's just plain dumb, because for that to work, you can hardly have existed at all back where you belong. Now, how could that be?'

Wesley rubbed his chin. To his surprise, he felt a slight texture of bristles; curious, since usually a shave lasted him three days. 'Actually,' he said, 'it's not quite as daft as it sounds. You might say I didn't really exist all that much, back home in Brierley Hill. Then again, in Brierley Hill, who does?'

The Indian looked at him. 'Now you're the one talking gibberish,' he said. 'I guess it means you're more than usually perceptive. Psychic or something. Tell me, when you hold them do teaspoons curl and try and climb up your wrist?'

'No.'

'No? Oh well. Anyway, it was good talking to you. Have a nice day, now.'

'Just a minute.' Wesley leaned forward. 'I don't know if you can help me, but . . .'

The Indian raised an eyebrow. 'Look,' he said, standing up, 'no offence, but if you want me to try and make contact for you with someone who's Passed Beyond, then forget it. I may be dead, but all that ouija-board stuff gives me the creeps.'

'Listen,' Wesley said sharply. The Indian sat down again. 'It's nothing like that. A moment ago, I was standing here talking to a girl . . .'

'Nor,' said the Indian quickly, 'am I in a position to help you review your personal relationships. Being dead, you lose touch.'

'And an eagle abducted her,' Wesley continued severely. 'Just picked her up and carried her off to that mountain over there. The pointy one. I think I'm supposed to rescue her or something.'

'You are? Good Lord, how old-fashioned. I thought men these days weren't supposed to do that sort of thing any more. I thought it was all doing your fair share of the housework and not being afraid to cry.'

'Look . . .'

'You're sure she was being abducted? Maybe she just wanted her own space for a while, you know, to find herself or something.'

'Shut up,' Wesley said. 'Come to think of it, I'd probably be better off trying to handle this myself. Sorry to have troubled you.'

'Don't be like that,' the Indian replied. 'Just trying to be on your wavelength, that's all. Rescuing abducted maidens is bread and butter to me. It's all part of what being a warrior's all about. That's why they call us Braves.'

'Yes?'

'To our faces, anyhow.' The Indian leaned forward. 'That mountain over there?'

'Yup. The tall one with five trees near the top.'

The Indian nodded. 'Lots of eyries up there,' he confirmed. 'I can show you the secret path known only to the now extinct Shashkehanna nation, though actually it's quicker to follow the forestry trail. They've put in little finger-posts so you don't get lost.'

'Whatever,' Wesley replied. 'Can we start now, please, because –?'

'And when it comes to sorting out large, aggressive birds of prey.' The Indian smirked. 'Well, I was about to say "I'm your man," but "I *was* your man, once" would be rather more accurate. Still, with my skill and experience and your strength and courage –'

'We're stuffed,' Wesley said, sinking his chin in his hands. 'Marvellous, isn't it? Unless I rescue that bloody woman, I'm liable to be stuck here indefinitely. And what have I got to work with? Me, and a dead Indian.'

'The best kind, according to General Custer,' replied Talks To Squirrels cheerfully. 'And he should know, damnit. Hey, kid, what are we waiting for? Let's go show those eagles what we're made of.'

Wesley frowned. 'Oh yes, that reminds me. What *are* you made of?'

'Ectoplasm,' the Indian replied promptly. 'Marvellous stuff, except it's dry clean only. Come *on*, will you? I thought you were the guy who daydreams of adventure and glorious deeds.'

'Yeah,' Wesley answered wretchedly, 'that's me, isn't it? Hey, you. If I get killed in this ghastly place, will I have to hang around here for ever being a ghost, like you?'

'I'm not sure, but it's a very real possibility.'

'In that case,' said Wesley firmly, 'you go first.'

'Go *away*,' said Janice, irritably. 'And you, the whole lot of you. Go on, shoo!'

The goblins didn't move. Instead, they just crouched where they were, simpering at her. Bashfully, one of them reached out and offered her a flower.

'Get outa here!' Janice yelled, stamping her foot. 'Jesus, don't you freaks understand English?'

'Wie bitte, wunderschön Fraülein?'

'Oh . . .!' With painful effort, Janice closed her eyes and counted to ten. They were still there when she opened them again; ten lovesick goblins, grinning at her like something out of a Mills & Boon version of *Nightmare On Elm Street*. She decided to give sweet reason one last go before resorting to screaming and kicking.

'Guys,' she said, trying to sound friendly, 'no offence, but it's a non-starter, really. I mean, look at me, will you? I said look, damnit,' she added, as ten pairs of round red eyes gazed yearningly into hers, 'not gawp. Come on, let's keep some hold on reality here. You – are . . .' She swallowed hard before saying the word. 'Goblins. Orcs. Little short guys who eat people. Really neat, hunky goblins, I feel sure, and if I was a lady goblin I'd be tattooing your phone numbers on the back of my hand right this minute, you bet. But I'm *not* a lady goblin, now am I? I mean, do I look like a lady goblin? No, forget I said that. Just, um, take it from me. Like, you know, no fangs. Not quite up to speed in the talons department. I . . .'

She tailed off. It was hopeless. Whatever she did just seemed to make it all infinitely worse.

She would, she acknowledged, pay good money to anybody who could prevent the big scaly one at the back from playing the mandolin.

'All right,' she growled, 'you asked for it.' She stalked forward and kicked the nearest goblin on the point of the shoulder, as hard as she could.

The goblin grinned soppily at her, and blushed khaki.

'Heeelp!' she screamed, pulling half-heartedly at the hem of her windcheater. 'Help, anybody! Rape! Rape!'

She stopped yelling, and looked round defiantly. None of the goblins seemed to have moved an inch. If anything, they'd moved a bit closer. To protect her, probably.

'Oh, for Christ's sake!' she panted. 'Don't you guys ever –?'

That was as far as she got before an eagle suddenly swooped down and carried her away.

Calvin Dieb stopped running, looked round, saw no goblins and sank, exhausted, onto a tree stump. A moment later, a butterfly fluttered up and perched on his shoulder.

'That's you, right?' Dieb gasped.

'You got it,' the butterfly replied. 'Quick, aren't you?'

'Goes with the territory,' Dieb said, his eyes shut. 'God, I haven't run like that since, gee, the early eighties, maybe even since Jimmy Carter was President.' He opened his eyes and grinned. 'I remember that also seemed like a bad dream, at the time. Did I lose them?'

'The goblins? Sure. Happen to you a lot, that sort of thing?'

Dieb shook his head. 'Scarcely ever,' he replied. 'Which is odd, come to think of it. I mean, I guess I piss off more people in an average week than most people do in a lifetime, but for some reason none of them ever seems to want to get even. I mean, not with me personally, using the medium of physical violence.' Dieb shrugged. 'I'm not complaining. Just odd, that's all. I mean, if I did to me some of the things I do to other people, I guess I'd want to rip my lungs out.'

The butterfly fluttered its wings. 'Perhaps other people aren't as vindictive as you, Mr Dieb. Perhaps they're . . .' The butterfly was silent for a moment, while it searched for the right word. 'Nicer,' it said. 'You ever considered that?'

'Listen,' Dieb replied. 'Nobody ever made money in the legal profession being nice. It's like you don't make good ice cream with a blowtorch. It's just not the right technique.'

The butterfly didn't reply; instead, it spread its wings and flitted away.

'Hey,' Dieb called after it, 'what did I say? Come back!'

But the butterfly kept on flying, until it was nothing but a speck against the sky, and then just a remembered place where a speck was last clearly discernible. Dieb stood up, and then sat down again. 'Hey!' he said quietly.

And then the speck was visible again. It grew. And it grew. When it was larger than a butterfly, Calvin Dieb looked at it and saw that it wasn't a butterfly. It was something bigger, a long way away, closing in fast.

'Hey!' he said.

As it approached, coming in low across the lake, the underside of its huge wings and body were reflected sharply in the water; black and white wing feathers, white belly feathers, red feet, black talons. Its eyes were round and yellow, and it shrieked.

'Look,' Dieb said, backing away, 'I didn't mean anything against nice guys in general. I got a lot of respect for nice guys. Some of my best friends –' He checked himself; his instincts suggested that this was no time for playing origami with the truth. 'Some of my best friends,' he therefore said, 'have a lot of respect for nice guys. Well, not friends as such, more like business acquaintances . . .'

The eagle towered, put its wings back and dropped out of the sky towards him, talons outstretched. There was no point in trying to run, Dieb knew; another thing that goes with the territory is the sure and certain knowledge that there's no defence against things that drop on you from a great height. In Calvin's experience, that usually meant writs, but he had a shrewd idea that it probably applied to huge birds as well.

'Now you understand,' said the bird, halting its onslaught six inches or so from Calvin's head and hovering, 'where the expression *legal eagle* comes from. What's it feel like, being underneath for a change?'

Calvin lowered his arms from above his head and looked up. He could see the points of the talons; amazing how anything not made in a precision engineering workshop could be so sharp. 'Subtlety,' he said, in a rather wobbly voice, 'doesn't come easily to you, I can tell.'

'Lay it on with a trowel, that's my motto,' the eagle replied. 'I mean to say, where's the point in being subtle when you're trying to get a point across to a pig-ignorant jury? Chances are half of them are blacks and Hispanics anyway. That sort wouldn't understand subtlety if you smashed their teeth in with it.'

'Hey!' Calvin said. 'I may be a lot of unpleasant things, but nobody can say I'm a racist. I'm Jewish, for God's sake. We know all about that stuff.'

The eagle continued to hover, although its wings didn't move; it was as if the frame had frozen. 'So,' it said, 'finally there's something nice we can say about you, congratulations. You think that's a good reason why I shouldn't scarf you up in my nice sharp talons and rip your chest open?'

Calvin blinked. 'Is there any reason why you should?' he said.

'Yeah, sure,' the eagle replied, still motionless. 'I'm bigger than you are. I'm stronger and faster and smarter and I can afford the very best legal advice money can buy. That's what gives me wings, man, that's how come I can fly.' The eagle flexed its claws, lazily, with confidence. 'The law is my shepherd, Mr Dieb, wherefore shall I lack nothing. It maketh me to lie fluently in green pastures.'

'Hey,' Calvin said, benighted under the vast shadow of the bird's wings, 'cut it out, will you? I guess you made your point some time ago.'

The eagle opened its hooked beak wide. 'Objection overruled,' it said. 'I'm bigger than you, and I've got wings. Unless you've got a gun, or a better lawyer, you're mine.'

But Calvin stepped back and folded his arms. 'But that's not the way it is,' he replied, 'and you know it. I fight for the little guy, too. I sue the big corporations for the little kid who's been scarred for life by some firebug toy they couldn't be bothered to test properly. I take on the big hospitals when they've crippled some guy when they've cut corners to save a buck. Where there's some poor dumb broad whose old man's beating the shit out of her, I get her the injunction and the divorce. You get the hell off my back, bird, or I'll have the law on you.'

But the eagle flapped its wings, and they cracked in the air like a whip. Dieb felt the talons hook in the collar of his five-thousand-dollar coat, and suddenly his feet lifted off the ground. All the air was bumped out of his lungs, and the coat was strangling him where it pressed up under his arms. He felt as if he was being crucified.

'Legal eagle, huh?' said the bird, as they hung in the air, so high up that their reflection in the lake below was nothing but a tiny speck. 'So make your own way home from here.'

'Hey!' Calvin shouted. The eagle let go, and flew away, back to its eyrie in the southern mountains.

Although he instinctively knew it was inadvisable, Calvin looked down. And what a lot of down there was to look at, all of a sudden. Vast, unfathomable expanses of down, to be followed in short order by all the splat! he could possibly wish for. *No thanks*, he muttered to himself, and he spread his wings.

Now where in hell did they come from?

Not that I'm complaining. No way. I like them so much I think I'll buy the company.

He concentrated until he could feel the air tingling in the feathers of his wingtips, as his mind hunted feverishly through the manual for something about how to manoeuvre. But all it could find was the long legal note disclaiming liability, and a load of guff about use of non-standard spares invalidating the warranty. Legal eagle, he said to himself. Well, yes. Seventy-five per cent of being a lawyer involves being stuck in precarious situations and not knowing what the hell you're supposed to do next. The trick is not to let anybody else see that you don't know.

In this case, gravity. One false move, one slight hint that he didn't actually know how to fly this thing, and gravity would be up at him like a ton of bricks.

And what did he always tell himself, in these situations? *Hey, relax. We'll just wing it from here and see what happens.*

He relaxed, and spread his wings. And the sky rushed down at him like a falling roof.

CHAPTER EIGHT

'This it?' Wesley spluttered, hauling himself over a ledge of rock.

'Yes.'

'Oh, *good*.' His hands hurt; there was rather less skin on his knuckles than there ought to be, according to the specification, and he had cramp in his tendons running right up into his elbow. For a man who, twenty-four hours previously, had he thought about it, wouldn't have been entirely sure he *had* tendons, it was a sudden and not entirely pleasant reversal of circumstances.

'Ouch,' he observed. 'Ow.' He huddled on the ledge and hugged his arm ostentatiously, waiting for the Indian to sympathise.

'The eyrie's up there,' whispered Talks To Squirrels, nodding his head towards an opening in the cliff wall facing them. 'Chances are, your eagle's one of the ones that live there.'

'*One* of the . . .'

'Of course,' the Indian went on, his voice so low as to be scarcely audible, 'scaling the cliff'll be relatively straightforward. Presumably you've got a plan for what we do after that.'

Wesley looked at the cliff – forty-odd feet of smooth, slightly concave rock – and thought, *relatively straightforward*. 'Tell you what,' he said. 'You tell me how you'd set about it, and then I'll sort of chip in with my comments and observations. I'd hate for you to get the idea I was muscling in.'

'If you're happy with that,' the Indian replied. 'Well, if it was me, as soon as I'd scaled the cliff –'

'Uh.'

'Sorry?'

'No,' Wesley said, 'go on, please. Don't let me interrupt you.'

The Indian nodded. 'All I was going to say was, once I'd scaled the cliff I'd be thinking in terms of a direct frontal assault – you know, take out as many of them as I could, wave a torch around, set light to a few eagles, let them spook the rest, and hope I'd be able to find the girl and get clear before they knew what was happening.'

'Ah,' said Wegley. 'I see. And you think that'd work?'

'No,' the Indian replied brightly. 'How d'you think I got to be a ghost in the first place?'

'Oh.'

'And that was just normal-sized eagles,' Talks To Squirrels went on. 'One minute I was standing on this ledge fitting an arrow to my bowstring and thinking, This is easier than I thought, and the next minute I was tumbling back down the cliff, banging my head on stuff and saying *Eeeeee*. Of course, when you do it, maybe it'll all work out OK. After all, I'd never done anything like this before.'

'You hadn't?'

'I led kind of a sheltered life,' Talks admitted. 'Was I dumb, or what? I mean, only a complete idiot would imagine you could work something like this out from first principles.'

'Well, quite,' Wesley said.

'So,' the Indian persisted, 'what's your plan? I'm telling you, I can't wait to hear. You know, ever since that day I've been turning it over in my mind, asking myself, what'd I do different if I had my time all over again, and all these hundreds of years I haven't been able to figure it out.'

'You haven't?'

The Indian grinned self-deprecatingly. 'Pretty dumb of me, I guess. So, you gonna tell me now or do you want it to be a surprise?'

'Oh, a surprise,' Wesley said. 'Definitely a surprise.'

Calvin Dieb landed.

For a moment or so he wobbled, rocking backwards and forwards on his talons like an expensive china ornament on a high mantelpiece; then it occurred to him that he'd probably do better just by holding still. It worked.

'Help!' said a female voice.

He peered into the darkness of the cave behind him. His eagle eyes cut the gloom in a way that astounded him, and he made out a human shape huddled in a fissure of the rock. It was a girl, damnit –

– Well, a girl in a sense. A youngish, thirty-something woman, with big thick-lensed glasses, rather on the stocky side; maybe damsel would be pushing it. But in distress, definitely.

'It's all right,' he said.

'Huh?'

'It's all right,' he repeated. 'Just keep calm and everything'll be just fine.'

'Help! Help!'

Dieb cringed. In the confined space of the cave, her yowling sounded horribly loud. Whoever or whatever it was that she was afraid of (with good reason, presumably) would have to be deaf as a post not to hear. He made a shushing noise and edged towards her.

'You OK?' he whispered.

'*Heeeelp!*'

'Look.' He came closer; she shrank back. 'What's going on?' he asked. 'Who's keeping you here?'

The girl stopped caterwauling and stared at him. 'You are,' she said.

Calvin must have swallowed his breath the wrong way or something. He choked. 'What?' he spluttered.

'You are, you disgusting bird,' the girl repeated. 'You brought me here, damnit.'

'Did I?'

'Oh for fuck's sake. Yes, of course you did.'

'But . . .'

'*Heeeeeelp!*'

Calvin took a step backwards, and felt himself wobble again. He looked down and saw something under his savagely hooked claw. It was a human skull.

'*Shit!*' He jumped about a foot in the air, nearly stunning himself on the roof of the cave. As he landed and regained his precarious balance, a thought struck him –

Eagle.

Cave.

Skull.

Oh Jesus, he cursed inside his mind. *Of all the eagles in all the mountains in all the world, why did I have to change into this one?*

'Hey,' he said aloud. 'Just a minute, pipe down. Did I really bring you here?'

'Yes,' replied the girl, offended. 'You tend to notice these things.'

'Are you sure?' Dieb queried. 'I mean, are you certain it wasn't some other eagle? Dunno about you, but I can't tell 'em apart.'

'It was you,' the girl said unpleasantly. 'White diamond on the breast, split claw on the left foot, slight upward twist to the hook of the upper jaw. It was definitely you.'

'But it can't have been. No, really. You see, I'm not an eagle, I'm a lawyer.'

'HEEEELP!'

Oh for Christ's sake, what's this thing people have about lawyers? 'I'm a human being,' he said. 'I don't know if you're caught up in this crazy weirdness too, but I'm a perfectly normal lawyer who's been turned into this god-damn eagle thing, and I'm not going to eat you. Or anybody. Trust me.'

The girl scowled at him. 'You're just saying that,' she growled. 'Trying to lull me into a false sense of security.'

Suddenly, Dieb felt annoyed. 'Yeah, sure,' he replied. 'Well-known hunting technique of the larger raptors. Soon as they see a jackrabbit or a woodchuck or whatever down there on the prairie floor, they swoop down, call out, *It's OK, really I'm just a lawyer?* and the moment the rabbit comes back out of his hole, they nail him. Look, what've I got to do to convince you, file a suit or something?'

'You don't sound like a lawyer,' the girl said, after a pause.

'Given your attitude, I'll take that as a compliment. Hey, you think I'm threatening, maybe you should see my part-ner. Man, if I was a rabbit I'd far rather take my chances with the eagle.'

At least the girl had stopped screaming and quivering.

'All right,' she said, 'so really you're a lawyer. Still doesn't explain why you grabbed me and brought me here.'

'I didn't. No, please, just listen up, will you? Maybe it was an eagle grabbed you, and maybe, God help me, I'm that eagle now; but I wasn't that eagle *then*.'

'No?'

'Nah. That was the eagle. The *real* eagle,' he added quickly, as the girl started yowling again. 'The eagle whose fucking horrible body I've somehow gotten myself into Look . . .'

'It's OK,' the girl said. 'I believe you. It's OK.'

'You do?'

'Yes. It's what you said. Anybody who can come out with all that bullshit and really expect anybody to believe it has got to be a –'

'Yeah,' Dieb snarled, shutting his eyes, 'right. The point is, I'm not gonna hurt you, I'm just as confused as you are, and the sooner it cuts it out and we can get back to real life, the happier I'll be. So if we can both stop acting crazy and just think for a minute . . .'

The girl nodded. 'I guess so,' she said. 'What happened to you, then?' She stopped, and stared at him, as coinage tinkled on impact in her mind. 'Just a second, though,' she went on. 'You haven't fallen in love with me, right?'

'Look,' Dieb said, recovering rather faster than he'd imagined he would, 'don't get me wrong, but . . .'

'Everybody I meet,' said the girl defiantly, 'falls in love with me. Vikings. Priests. Goblins . . .'

'Did you say Vikings? And goblins?'

The girl nodded. 'And just don't make any remarks, OK? Because really, this isn't the time.'

'I've had Vikings,' Dieb said excitedly. 'And goblins too, I guess. How about bears?'

The girl shook her head. 'No bears. How about you? Any priests?'

'No. But don't let's get sidetracked. We both had the Vikings and the goblins, right? So whatever this garbage is, it's happening to both of us.'

'Maybe. Did you fall in the lake? I did. That's when everything started to go weird.' She scowled. 'Like, men started falling in love with me.'

'Ah.'

'Except you.'

'Um.'

'Which is great,' the girl went on, 'really. And I've been thinking; you know, about the weirdness. You see, all my life I've had this stupid notion about how nice it'd be to be one of those girls who have it really easy because they're attractive, and men just fall over backwards and jump through hoops the moment they see them.'

'You mean, like a bimbo?'

'That's the word I was looking for, yes. All I wanted to be was a genuine, twenty-two-carat peroxide bimbo. Well, that's what's happening to me, almost like someone's teaching me a lesson.' She paused for breath. 'Is that what's happening to you? Not being a bimbo,' she added quickly. 'Punishment by wish-fulfilment, or whatever.'

Dieb shook his head. 'Can't say it is,' he replied. 'I keep meeting these chatty birds and animals who try and psychoanalyse me, but all I really want to do is find my car keys.'

'Car keys?'

'Yeah, my keys. I dropped them. If I could only get into my car . . .'

The girl rummaged in her windcheater pocket, and produced a small, glittering bundle of metal. 'These keys?' she asked. 'I picked them up beside the —'

'*My keys!*' Calvin stared for a fraction of a second, roughly the amount of time it takes for light to travel a quarter of an inch, and then extended a taloned foot and grabbed.

But before he could touch them –

'Sssh!'

'Oh, shut up,' Wesley hissed back over his shoulder. 'It's all right for you, you're a ghost. You don't weigh anything, and if you fall off it won't actually matter. In my case –'

'Look!'

Wesley craned his neck over the lip of the ledge, and peered as far as he could into the cave. 'Oh, *shit*,' he whispered.

'You found him!'

'Yes,' replied Wesley, thoughtfully. 'So I have.'

'And he's about to eat the girl.'

'Could be. Could be. However, let's not jump to –'

The ghost hopped up onto the ledge, drew his bow and shot three arrows in the time it takes to blow one's nose. 'Look at that grouping,' he sighed. 'You could cover all three with a quarter. Pity.'

'Yes,' Wesley agreed. 'Quite.'

The Indian flattened himself against the rock. 'OK,' he said, 'your turn. All you've gotta do is sneak up behind him with that chunk of rock and flatten him.'

'That's all, huh?'

'Sure. Ain't life just full of anticlimaxes?'

Wesley reached out and wrapped his hand around the chunk of rock indicated. 'I'm not sure about this,' he muttered, 'ecologically speaking, I mean. I'm sure I read somewhere that eagles are protected.'

'Not this kind. I refer you to the Protection of Birds Act 1977, section 42, subsection 4(b). Go get the fucker.'

'Right,' sighed Wesley. 'Here goes.'

Rock in hand, he crawled forward.

'My keys *aaaagh*!'

The eagle slumped forward, and its beak hit the ground with a chunky crack, like a coconut falling on a rock.

'Hey!'

Wesley, who had shut his eyes a moment before swinging the rock, opened them again, and saw what he had done. He stood rooted to the spot, while many different reactions and emotions coursed through his mind like cars in an overcrowded multi-storey car park.

'What the hell did you do that for?' demanded the girl.

Wesley looked up, and saw, and said nothing. Instead he goggled.

'And who the hell are you, anyway?' the girl continued.

Despite the sleeting blizzard of pink hearts and fat cabbage roses swirling in front of his eyes and obscuring his vision, he could see that this wasn't the gorgeous female he'd been trudging round after all this time. This was a different creature entirely; squatter, more compactly built, probably much better suited to life on a planet with much higher gravity, with a face that reminded him curiously of a warthog in spectacles. Somewhere in the back of his mind, a thousand violins began to play.

'Er,' he said.

'What?'

It was, insisted the skeleton staff still on duty inside his head, time to explain. 'I . . .' he said.

'You what?'

'Um.'

The girl looked at him, and her glance struck him like a napalm attack on a tribe of snowmen. He stepped back, walking clean through Talks With Squirrels as he did so. The Indian, who had been only one arrow away from ten consecutive hits in the girl's forehead before Wesley jogged his arm, instinctively tried to reach out and catch him; but his fingers passed through Wesley's wrist, a fraction of a second before he stepped backwards over the lip of the cave and into thin air.

'Aaaaaagh!' he observed.

As the cry dopplered away, the girl scurried forward, yelling, 'Hey, wait!' – the sort of damn silly thing girls do say, under such circumstances. Talks To Squirrels sighed, looked down at the drop separating the cave mouth from the ground, sank his tomahawk into the back of the girl's neck and sat down in a corner, sulking.

'Hell!' said Janice.

For want of anything better to do, she tried to find the car keys, which she distinctly remembered dropping just after the funny man had nutted the eagle. Needless to say, they were nowhere to be seen.

Captain Hat, scampering down the mountainside with his latest trophy, was surprised and a little bit put out when a falling human body hit him on the head, squashing him flat. Quite apart from the inconvenience of having every bone in his body broken by the force of the impact, he dropped the car keys he'd just made away with; and, being pinned down under a human body, could only watch help-lessly as they rolled down the hill, bounced off a projecting rock and went *plop!* into the lake.

'Urgh,' groaned the human body.

'Excuse me.'

Hat peered up from under the body's armpit. There was a Big peering down at him. 'You again,' he said.

'What? Oh, yes. Hi.' Linda Lachuk crouched down on her knees and moved aside the body's arm. 'We've met already, haven't we?'

Hat nodded. 'You're the submarine spotter,' he said. 'Find any yet?'

'One,' Linda replied. 'But it sank. Hey, I found out they're smuggling the stuff out in rocks.'

'Is that so?'

Linda nodded. 'I don't know why I didn't think of it earlier, it's so obvious,' she said.

Hat shrugged. 'Often it's the obvious things that never occur to you,' he said. 'Ain't that the way, huh?'

'You're right. Anyway, I thought it might be a good idea to get up high, so I can see everything that's going on. Is that a cave up there?'

'Could be,' Hat replied cautiously. 'There's an eagle in there, mind.'

'Really? Hey, that's great. All the story needs to make it truly cosmic is a threatened-habitat angle.'

Hat nodded. 'I see,' he said, wriggling out past Wesley's elbow and picking up his hat. 'In that case, I guess I'd better leave you to it.'

'OK,' Linda said. 'And remember, if you see any submarines . . .'

'Sure,' Hat replied. Then he clamped his hat onto his head as firmly as it would go, tucked his shattered arms and legs tight into his body, deliberately fell over and rolled all the way down the hill to get his bones set.

Linda watched him go, shrugged, and set off up the slope, cursing the thoughtlessness of whoever was responsible for the terrain. Some people. No respect. She was just beginning to feel nicely cross when –

Goddamnit!

Heedless of the uneven ground she ran, sliding and staggering, to the foot of the cliff, which she immediately began to swarm up, totally without science but with boundless enthusiasm. No way a piffling sheer rock face was going to get between her and her story!

Above her head was the mouth of the cave. She waited until gravity was looking the other way, and jumped.

The very tips of her fingers hooked over the rocky ledge. Engaging her adrenalin drive and whacking the throttle wide open, she swung herself up, dropping her knee over the cavemouth's lintel just as the strength in her fingertips gave way. A few chunks of rock, dislodged by her entrance, rattled and bounced away down the cliff, taking their own sweet time before hitting the ground. She didn't notice. What she was seeing and hearing in the studio of her mind was far too enthralling for her to bother about crumbling ledges, vertiginous drops or the risk of a horrible death. As far as she was concerned, if a horrible death wanted to meet her, she might just be able to spare it five minutes a fortnight Tuesday, but it would be well advised to phone nearer the time and confirm if it wanted to avoid a wasted journey.

She hauled herself into the cave and lay on her stomach, panting, only an inch or so away from the object of her fascination. It was a hat.

It was round. And broad-brimmed. It had lots of corks hanging from it, attached to the brim by little bits of string. In other words, it was an Australian hat.

'*Yes!*' Linda gasped, reaching out to touch it. Her fingertips were just about to make contact with the outermost fibres of its fabric when, agonisingly, it was snatched away.

'Hey!' said a female voice.

Linda looked up. There was some sort of female attached to the hat by means of a podgy-fingered hand

and sixteen inches of arm. Linda blinked. Dear God, she prayed, sweet Lord in Heaven, don't let her be CBS News or the *Boston Globe*.

'What d'you think you're doing with my hat?' she demanded.

Linda stared at her, feeling as if she'd just found the Holy Grail only to find the words *Batteries Not Included* engraved on the rim. 'Your h-h-?' she stuttered.

'Yeah,' replied the female. 'My hat. Lay off it, will you?'

Linda fought back the panic. 'But I *need* that hat,' she gasped. 'Really, I do.'

The girl shrugged. 'So go buy yourself one,' she replied. 'They're only $12.99 from the big Government surplus store in Oskaloosa.'

Linda stared. 'You *bought* that hat?' she whimpered.

'Yes. So what?'

'But – but you're not *Australian*.'

'True.' The girl nodded. 'I'm two-fifths Irish, one fifth Polish, one fifth Italian and one fifth Swede, not that it's any damn business of yours.'

Linda swallowed hard. 'You just *bought* it? In a *shop*? You're certain about that?'

'Yes.'

'In Oskaloosa?'

'Yes.'

'Ah, *damn*!' Linda flopped down on the ground and lay still, while the bailiffs came for her remaining adrenalin. Then a thought occurred to her, and she looked up. 'Did you say one-fifth Italian?' she asked.

'Yes. Do you happen to know how to revive a stunned eagle?'

'No. And Polish, was that?'

'That's right.'

Linda chewed her lower lip thoughtfully. You had to be careful nowadays, but with a little careful scripting and some subliminal camera angles, Polish and Italian could be made to translate as *Vatican Secret Agent.* 'You don't,' she enquired tentatively, 'work for the Pope at all, do you?'

'What?'

'The Pope. No? Oh, never mind. Can I just *borrow* your hat, for a second or two. I just want to look at it.'

The girl shrugged. 'Be my guest,' she said. 'Here.'

Linda took it gingerly and examined it for telltale clues; a smear of submarine oil here, a few flakes of chipped marble there. She didn't find any; instead she saw, inside the lining, a label which read:

COUNTRY CLUB™

SIZE 60 CM

100% NYLON

MADE IN TAIWAN

Slowly she passed the hat back. She couldn't have felt more let down if she'd managed to get to see God, and God had made a pass at her. 'Oh well,' she said. 'One fifth Italian?'

'I think the eagle's about to come round.'

'Eagle?'

The girl pointed. 'Over there. About eighteen inches to your left.'

Linda looked round. 'Oh,' she said, 'that eagle. My endangered habitat angle.'

'Huh?'

It suddenly occurred to Linda that a word of explanation might be in order. 'I'm a journalist,' she said, and smiled reassuringly.

'You are, huh?'

'That's right.'

'Figures. Did you get the Vikings and the goblins too?'

Linda furrowed her brow. 'No,' she replied. 'What Vikings?'

'Oh.'. The girl looked disappointed. 'Then bang goes that theory. Shucks.' The girl shrugged. 'Then it's back to the drawing board, I guess. What are you going to do now?'

'Go back outside and watch for submarines,' Linda replied, puzzled that anybody should need to ask. 'Oh, that reminds me. Have you seen any?'

'Any what?'

'Submarines.'

'No.'

'Oh.' Linda thought for a moment. 'How about tanks and missiles and rockets and things? Probably encased in concrete blocks,' she added.

'Nope. Sorry.'

'Hell. I think your eagle's just woken up, by the way. He just tried to bite my ankle.'

'Actually,' said the girl, 'he's a lawyer.'

'A lawyer?'

'That's what he told me.'

Linda mused for a moment, wondering whether lawyers disguised as enormous eagles could somehow be worked in as background. 'Nah,' she said aloud, 'that's no use, they'd only say I was faking the pictures. If you see any submarines, you will let me know?'

'If you like. You haven't seen a set of car keys lying about, have you?'

'Car keys? No, sorry. Can you remember where you had them last?'

'Yes.'

'Well, there you are, then. Try and remember about the submarines.' She sighed, lowered herself carefully over the ledge and started to climb down the cliff, preoccupied.

Strange woman, said Janice to herself, as she knelt down beside the eagle. Almost at once, it raised its head and stared at her.

'My keys,' it said. 'My keys!'

'Ah yes,' Janice mumbled. 'Your keys. I'm afraid there's been a bit of an accident. You see . . .'

'My *keys*!!'

'They were here a short time ago,' Janice said. 'But first there was the lunatic with the rock, and then that crazy journalist, and I've looked everywhere, and they've gone.'

The eagle lowered its head and made a high, thin keening noise. Exhausted, Janice leaned back against the cave wall and closed her eyes. 'Do you have to make that horrible noise?' she snapped.

'Yes.'

'I thought you said you were a lawyer. Lawyers don't make high-pitched screaming noises.'

'How would you know?'

'They don't on *LA Law*,' Janice replied firmly. 'And they don't in Cleveland, either. My cousin's sister-in-law –'

'Look.' Calvin Dieb sat up, or as near to sitting up as his shape would allow. 'Somebody's playing games with us, it's obvious. Whoever it is who changed me into an eagle and did whatever's been happening to you has also stolen my goddamn keys. Agreed?'

Janice nodded. 'I hear you,' she said. 'So what do you reckon?'

'Right.' Dieb pulled his mind together, and tried to concentrate. 'I think you and I are just regular people. What about the other two?'

'The rock fiend and the reporter? Hard to tell. On balance, I think the reporter was, 'cos she seemed to be acting the way they usually do.'

'Oh? Like what?'

'Like she was only interested in what she wanted for her story, not what was actually going on.'

Dieb shook his head. 'Unless we're certain, let's assume she wasn't; safer that way. OK, so we know we're both all right. Obviously,' he went on, 'the most important thing is for us to stick together, not let them split us up. Agreed?'

'Agreed.'

'Fine. Now, th –'

He vanished.

'Ugh,' said Wesley.

'Feeling better?'

Wesley looked up. 'Oh Christ, it's you again. Why can't you just –?'

The beautiful girl raised a perfect eyebrow. 'Don't tell me,' she said. 'At your school you could either do tact or woodwork, and you're reasonably good at woodwork. Am I right?'

'No, actually. I always hit my thumb with the hammer. What's woodwork got to do with anything?'

The girl reached out a hand and pulled him to his feet. 'That was Phase Two,' she said. 'You failed.'

'I did?'

The girl nodded. 'You were meant to,' she added. 'In fact, it'd spoil the whole thing if you didn't.'

Wesley scowled, and looked up at the cliff face. 'Who was – I mean, who were those people? The eagle, I mean, and the . . .'

'The short, fat, pig-faced girl?'

'She's not . . .'

The beautiful girl snickered and turned away to hide her grin. *Yes*, muttered Wesley under his breath. Bet you could make a pretty neat chest of drawers, at that. 'It's all right,' she said. 'Don't worry about it.'

'The hell with you.' Wesley tried to push past, but the beautiful girl tripped him up and he went sprawling.

'She's gone now,' she said. 'There's no point climbing all that way up there again.'

'Where's she gone to?' Wesley gasped, scrambling to his feet.

'Somewhere you can't follow,' she replied, with a soupçon of grated harshness. 'I said, forget it. You had your chance to rescue a damsel in distress and win your only true love, and you blew it. Now we go on to Phase Three. You do still want to get out of here, don't you?'

'Of course I do.' Wesley hesitated, looking up at the cave. 'Of course I do,' he repeated, but with rather less conviction.

'Well then.' The girl grabbed him by the collar and spun him round; she made it look easy. 'And don't worry, you'll forget about her eventually. Give it fifty years or so and you'll hardly give her a second thought.'

Wesley considered saying something, but decided against it. Fury, heartbreak, despair and the like tended to muck up his vocabulary, leaving him with as much chance of hitting on the right word as finding a pint of fresh milk in a supermarket at ten to eight on a Saturday night. Instead, he tightened his fists until they hurt and relaxed them again.

'I see,' he said. 'Fine. Can we get on with Phase Three now, please? I'm getting rather sick of this game, and I'd like to go home as soon as possible.'

The girl giggled. 'I'd lay off trying to be angry with dignity if I were you,' she said. 'It makes you go all pink, like tinned salmon. Actually, I think you might rather like Phase Three, in the mood you're in. It involves quite a bit of . . .' She paused, flicking through her mental card-index. 'Hooliganism,' she said. 'Don't suppose you ever went in for that when you were a kid. Too scared of getting caught.'

Despite the bad reviews of his angry dignity, Wesley persevered with it. 'If you mean throwing stones through windows and spraying things on walls, you're right, I never did. Not because I was frightened –'

'*Look out!*'

Without even thinking, Wesley hurled himself to the ground, grazing the palms of his hands and bumping his chin, so that his teeth jarred together. 'Agh!' he said.

'Sorry,' said the girl, looking down at him. 'Didn't want you to get hit by the low-flying pigs.'

'Oh, very funny.'

The girl shrugged. 'It wasn't bad,' she said, 'but I don't suppose they'll be leaving out whole chunks of Groucho Marx and Noël Coward just to make room for it in the new edition of the *Dictionary of Quotations*. Are you going to get up, or would you rather crawl all the way to the next location? You can if you like, but it's rather a long way.'

When Calvin Dieb came to, he found himself tied to a stake.

Another thing he noticed was that it had suddenly gone dark, leading him to the conclusion that wherever he'd been while he hadn't been inside the body of Calvin Dieb, he'd been there for quite some time. The only light, in fact, came from the huge bonfire, around which a large number of people were apparently dancing. Fortunately, the light reflected well off the surface of the lake, so he could clearly make out the curious Native American folk costumes the dancers were wearing, and the strange multi-coloured pigments they'd applied to their bodies and faces. They were also singing, but Calvin had an ear for music the way a snake has a leg to stand on; so they could have been singing Country standards or *La Traviata* for all he knew. He couldn't make out any of the words, but that didn't mean anything either. He had an idea it wasn't the 'Star-Spangled Banner', but that was as far as he got.

'Hello,' he called out. 'Excuse me.'

Nobody seemed to hear; not surprising, given the volume of the singing. He tried to wave to get someone's attention, but the ropes prevented him.

'You haven't got it yet, have you?' whispered a voice in his ear.

'What?'

'I said, you haven't got it yet. What's going on, I mean.'

'Sorry, you'll have to speak up. The music . . .'

'YOU HAVEN'T GOT IT YET, HAVE YOU?'

'That's better. Got what?'

'Oh, for crying out loud. Stay there.'

A second or so later, a bat flittered out of the darkness into his face, making him flinch. It dropped out of flight and hung from the lapel of his coat, like a huge black inverted carnation. 'Can you hear me better now?' it asked.

'You? Oh, you. Yes, that's much better. Hey, you got any idea what's going on?'

'You bet,' replied the bat.

'Well?'

'You're going to enjoy this,' the bat chuckled. 'Right up your street, this is.'

Calvin raised both eyebrows. 'You reckon so? Maybe you don't know me as well as you thought.'

'Get outa here, will you?'

'Love to.'

'I mean, on the contrary. I *know* you'll enjoy this, because it's what you do best.'

'Being tied to things? Sorry, lady, wrong guy. It's my associate Mr Piranha who's into chains and whips and things.'

'Litigation,' said the bat, patiently. 'That is what you do best, isn't it?'

Dieb nodded, insofar as he could with a thick coil of rawhide rope tightened under his chin. 'But this doesn't look much like a lawsuit to me,' he added. 'The big fire, for a start. And the dancing.'

'Ah.' The bat shook its wings, reminding Dieb of someone shaking out an umbrella after coming in off the street. 'But this is a different kind of litigation.'

'Well?'

'This is litigation,' the bat went on, 'Cherokee style. Though I think they used to have something similar in Europe a long time ago. Actually, it was only abolished in England in the early nineteenth century, by George the Third. The guy must have been nuts, if you ask me.'

'Excuse me?' Calvin enquired. 'Are we talking about canon law or the Star Chamber or something? We didn't do legal history where I went, or at least you could do it but it meant missing Advanced Fee Augmentation, so I didn't bother.'

'Something like that,' replied the bat. 'Like I said, it's an old-fashioned form of litigation, but generally speaking it's quicker, cheaper, fairer and a hell of a lot less traumatic than what you guys do nowadays. So I thought you might find it interesting.'

'Cheaper?'

'Oh, much.'

'Ah. Well, thanks all the same, but . . .'

The bat opened its claws, spread its wings and dropped-cum-flew away, leaving Calvin puzzled and not entirely happy. An obsolete form of legal procedure common to both Europe and Native America. Actions on the case? Ejectment? Oyer and terminer? Tricky.

Two authentic-looking Native Americans with feathers on their heads and rather forbidding expressions left the dance and stalked over to him. They were holding what he assumed were authentic tomahawks and had presumably authentic whacking great knives stuck through their belts. Without a word they cut the ropes, hauled him to his feet and dragged him towards the fire. Amazing, how some of these re-enactment society guys really live the role.

As they came inside the circle of firelight, Calvin was just about to start protesting when, to his great surprise, he saw someone he recognised.

'Leonard?' he said.

'Calvin,' replied the tall, ambassador-like man in the three-piece dark blue suit. 'It's been a long time.'

'Sure thing,' Calvin replied, as the two authentic people let him go. 'I thought you were . . . I mean yes, it really has been a long time. How're you doing? How's retirement suiting you? Hey, you look years younger than when you were at Schadling & Blutsauger.'

'Thanks.' Leonard nodded politely, and the firelight glinted on his almost Presidential grey hair. 'I've been a new man since I quit the profession, Cal. All sorts of new interests, things I'd never have gotten into if I'd stayed behind that desk. So,' he added with a smile, 'as it turns out, you did me a favour when you turned the rest of the partnership against me and squeezed me out.'

Calvin grinned uncomfortably. True, he'd spent five years of round-the-clock intriguing and politicking to dispose of dear old Len, the last remaining barrier between him and the purple; but it was a bit tactless to bring the subject up almost immediately, after so long. 'These new interests,' he said, trying to lighten things up. 'Historical re-enactments, huh? Never thought that was your scene, Leonard.'

The older man stopped smiling. 'It isn't,' he said. 'Though, as a matter of fact, I truly am half Cherokee. You didn't know that, did you?'

'No, Len, I didn't. Gee, it only goes to show, you think you know a guy, and . . .'

'Yes.' Leonard made a small, economical gesture to someone standing just outside the firelight. 'It only does. Well now, Cal, you ready?'

'Huh?'

'For the trial. Actually it's a purely Western tradition that the defendant gets first choice of weapons, but since you're a guest here among my people I guess it's only polite to extend you the courtesy.'

Before Calvin could put into words the question marks and exclamation marks that were clogging the passages of his brain, a totally authentic Native American with a bear's skull on his head stepped forward holding two identical spears. Ah, thought Calvin.

'Among my people,' Leonard went on, 'this is how we do litigation. Apart from it doesn't make any money for anybody, I reckon it's got the other way licked on all counts.'

'Trial by *combat*?'

Leonard nodded. 'Dontcha just love it? Now by rights, being over sixty years old I could name a champion to fight for me.' He peeled off his coat, tie and shirt, to reveal rippling pectorals and bulging biceps. 'But I thought, what the hell, this is something I want to see to *personally*. And if it means I give you the advantage, then so what?'

'Hey,' Calvin muttered. He tried to step backwards, but there was something large and authentic right behind him, prodding him in the back with a knife. 'Just a minute . . .'

Leonard held up his hand. 'You're right,' he said. 'I was forgetting. You have the option of wearing the spirit armour. You wanna go for that, or shall we forget about it? Up to you.'

Calvin heard the word 'armour' and nodded. Immediately a man like a substantial rock formation loomed forward, slapped a thick hairy paintbrush three times across his chest and once across his face, and stepped back. Slowly, feeling very much like Oliver Hardy, Calvin wiped paint out of his eyes.

'Suits you,' Leonard remarked. 'Me, I guess I'll make do without and risk the consequences. You try getting that stuff off again, you'll see why. Pumice-stone'll do it sometimes, but usually you gotta use caustic. Now then, you ready to choose?'

Calvin looked at the spears. They were very long and heavy, and the blades looked revoltingly sharp. 'Say, Leonard,' he whimpered, 'I never imagined you'd be sore about leaving the firm, honest. If only you'd said something . . .'

Leonard gave him a look that made the spearhead seem like a pat of butter. 'You got an injunction, remember? If I so much as showed my face at the office, you were going to get me carted off to jail. And that was three days before I even got the letter suggesting I should retire.'

'Really?' Calvin felt his heart shrivel. 'Guess it must have gotten held up in the Christmas mail, Len. I didn't mean it to be that way. I always had the utmost respect for you. Always.'

'And I always thought you were an evil little shit, Cal. Now, are you gonna choose, or shall I just stick you where you stand?'

There was a lump in Calvin's throat. He tried to swallow it. 'Hey, Len,' he said. 'Let's just toss a coin or something, huh?'

'No way. I want this done *legal*. I mean, if you haven't got law and order, what've you got?'

Calvin stared at the spears. They were both big and horrible and he wanted no part of either of them. The only difference between them was –

– The one on the left had a set of car keys dangling from its shaft, about an inch below the blade socket. The one on the right had a bat hanging from it. It lifted its head a little, and winked at him. He pointed to the one on the left, and said, 'That one, please.'

'Sucker,' said the bat.

CHAPTER NINE

'Hooliganism,' said Wesley, thoughtfully. 'I don't suppose you'd care to amplify, would you? Only it's not a very precise description.'

The girl sighed. 'You want it all handed to you on a plate, don't you?'

'Talking of things on plates . . .'

'Whereas,' the girl continued, binding up her hair in a pretty red silk scarf, 'really, you should be working it all out for yourself. If you want to pass Phase Three and get out of here, I mean. Think about it. *Proper* heroes don't have it handed to them on plates. You don't catch Indiana Jones swinging into action with his bullwhip in one hand and an envelope with detailed instructions jotted down on the back in the other. He's got to make it up as he goes along. And so must you.'

'Nuts,' Wesley replied. 'Indiana Jones's got the full support of the studio behind him. Hundreds of scriptwriters. Thousands of technicians. Mr Spielberg, with a microphone and an eyeshade. And what have I got? You.'

'If you'd rather I left you to it . . .'

'You think I think that's a really terrifying threat, don't you?'

'Yes.'

Wesley shrugged. 'I could seriously fancy a hamburger,' he said.

'What?'

'A hamburger,' Wesley replied. 'With large fries and a thick shake, vanilla, if you've got any.' He sat down on an ivy-covered tree stump and took his left shoe off.

'Tough,' the girl replied impatiently. 'And we haven't got time for you to adjust your footwear, either. I'm not waiting for you.'

''Bye, then.'

The girl turned, strode on four paces, turned back and scowled at him. 'I'm serious,' she said. 'Lag behind and I'll leave you for the wolves.'

'I expect I'll cope.'

'You reckon?'

Wesley shrugged. 'Why not? There won't be any wolves. At least, not unless there's supposed to be wolves. All these Phases and so forth, it stands to reason. You've got your program to run, or whatever you call it, you can't afford to have me randomly eaten by wolves. Bet my life on it.'

'Don't joke about it,' the girl hissed menacingly. But Wesley didn't look up. Instead, he fished a small lump of rock out of his sock and discarded it.

'You need me,' he went on. 'Probably rather more than I need you. I know a bit about large organisations, working for a building society. Things have to be accounted for. Targets have to be met. My guess is, unless you deliver me to a certain place at a certain time, all neatly processed and enlightened or whatever, that's your quarterly quota figures up the spout and you'll have some explaining to do to who-ever it is you're answerable to. Am I warm?'

'Drivel,' replied the girl.

(But, in another part of the forest, she could see herself trying to explain a shortfall to the Inspector, who was peering at her over the rims of his spectacles and pursing his lips. *Lost a customer? Mislaid him, you mean? This is very serious. I'm afraid I'm going to have to mention this in my report, and . . .*)

'Fair enough,' Wesley said. 'So I called your bluff and I was wrong. Well, on my own head be it. I'm still not moving from this spot till I get something to eat.'

'But . . .'

'All I've had since breakfast,' he went on, 'is two peppermints and a gnat I swallowed by mistake just before I fell in the lake. I'm hungry. And don't tell me I can't be hungry because this isn't real time, because I know when I'm hungry, and I'm hungry. OK?'

'You're making a big mistake.'

'Am I? Oh well.'

'You'll be sorry for this.'

'Not half as sorry as you'll be when they hand you your cards and tell you to clear your desk by lunchtime. I imagine career opportunities for sacked fairies are few and far between. Perching on top of a Christmas tree, perhaps, but that's purely seasonal work.'

'I am not,' the girl growled, 'a fairy.'

Wesley nodded. 'Whatever,' he said. 'Hamburger. Fries. Shake. I shall count up to ten, and then I'm going back the way I came.'

'You'll get lost in the forest and the coyotes will eat you.'

'One. Two. Three. Four.'

'This is *fatuous*. Here I am making your most deep-seated fantasies come true, fulfilling your secret desires, turning you from a snivelling feckless little runt into a fully rounded, self-confident, quasi-heroic man of action, master of your fate and captain of your soul, and you've got the nerve to go on strike.'

'Five. Six. Seven. Looks like you succeeded with the self-confidence bit, doesn't it? Eight. Nine.'

'Did you say large fries?'

'Mphm.'

'Corn relish and dill pickle on the burger?'

'Sounds all right to me.'

'Have a nice day,' snarled the girl, as a paper bag fell in Wesley's lap. 'Enjoy your meal.'

'You see,' said Wesley with his mouth full, some time later. 'That wasn't too difficult, was it?'

'Huh.' The girl glowered at him and stole a chip. 'The sooner you start taking this thing seriously . . .'

Wesley sucked up the last inch of his milk shake; the solid lump of gritty ice cream that always makes your teeth ache. 'That's better,' he said. 'Now then, what's next?'

'I told you, you've got to try and figure –'

'One. Two. Three. Four.'

'Aaagh!' The girl screamed furiously, grabbed the paper bag and screwed it up into a ball. 'All right,' she said, 'it's like this. You'd better listen good, because if you miss anything . . .'

'I'm listening. Try and stay calm.'

'Over there,' the girl said, pointing, 'is a Cherokee village, some time in the last third of the nineteenth century. Your job is to rescue the prisoner . . .'

'Oh come on,' Wesley groaned. 'Not again.'

'. . . before he's burned at the stake by Chief Talks To Squirrels' war party. They outnumber you thirty-five to one, but you do have your trusty Spencer rifle, capacity seven shots, maximum effective range two hundred yards, and your equally trusty forty-five six-shooter, and this stick of dynamite. All you have to do is crawl up to the fire, evading or silently killing the guards, throw the dynamite into the fire, untie the prisoner under cover of the explosion and ensuing confusion, steal a couple of horses and ride away. Now, do you think you can manage that?'

'No.'

'Rifle,' said the girl grimly. 'Revolver. Dynamite. Penknife for cutting ropes with. Lump of sugar for the horse. Once you've escaped, ride up the other side of the valley and follow the big Dayglo orange signs saying *This Way*. Don't fall off the horse and don't rescue any Indians by mistake. You get bonus points for élan and flair, and an automatic fail if you get killed. *Ciao*.'

She vanished.

For nearly three minutes Wesley sat where he was, not moving and counting up to ten, over and over again. Then, slowly and with infinite misgivings, he picked up the rifle, making sure the end with the hole in it was pointing away from him, and tried to figure out how it worked.

There was a very loud noise.

'That leaves you six shots,' said a disembodied voice. 'You reload by cocking the hammer and pulling down the lever under the trigger. Shoot up any more of my trees and you'll be getting a bill. Oh, and by the way, the prisoner's a lawyer, but try and bring him back alive nonetheless.'

Wesley nodded. He'd just remembered something. 'Excuse me,' he said. 'What did you say that Indian was called?'

'Talks To Squirrels,' the girl replied. 'Why?'

Wesley grinned. 'Oh, nothing,' he said. 'Well, be seeing you.'

'You sound cheerful. I don't like that. Why are you sounding cheerful?'

'No reason. Cheerio, then.'

He stood up and began to saunter over towards the brow of the hill.

'Ah *shit*,' Leonard groaned.

Calvin Dieb let go of the spear, and Leonard fell over with a crash. Everything had gone quiet, all of a sudden.

'Sorry,' Calvin said.

'Shit,' Leonard repeated. He tried to pull the spear out of his side, but it had gone in too far. He coughed up a little blood, and fell back. 'This is *crazy*,' he said bitterly. 'Ever since I left the firm, I been practising spear-fighting. Twelve, sometimes eighteen hours a day. I'm so good, there's nobody in the whole world as good as me.'

'Sucks, doesn't it?' said Calvin, sympathetically.

'You're goddamn right it does,' Leonard agreed. 'And what happens? First pass, you trip over a tree-root, fall over and your spear goes right through me. It ain't fair, and that's the truth.'

He shook his head, pulled a wry face, and died. With a sigh, Calvin turned away; at which point he became aware of thirty-odd authentic warriors, all looking at him.

They thought it sucked, too.

'Hey,' Calvin objected, as they grabbed him and dragged him back to the wooden stake, 'I won, didn't I? It was a trial, and I won. OK, by rights he *should* have won, but he didn't, and I did. So what's the . . . ?'

'We going to appeal,' grunted the Chief. 'We implement

ancient Cherokee appeal procedure. Four Calling Birds, where kerosene?'

'Hey!' Calvin said again. 'But that's not fair!'

'All fair,' replied the Chief smugly, 'in love and litigation. You lawyer, you figure it out for yourself. Five Gold Rings, you fetch matches.'

Calvin thought quickly, as the kerosene glugged over his head. 'Can't I counter-appeal?' he said. 'There must be some way . . .'

'Easy.' The Chief nodded, and the feathers of his head-dress bobbed in the orange light. 'You go before judge sitting in chambers, obtain writ of habeas corpus and injunction, we let you go. Simple as that.'

'OK,' Calvin said eagerly. 'Just untie me and I'll do just that.'

'We no untie.' The Chief grinned. 'Figure we got you on a technicality,' he said.

Before Calvin could object further, someone shoved a kerosene-soaked rag in his mouth and blindfolded him. He heard a match rasp on a matchbox.

'Excuse me.'

The Chief turned round.

'Remember me?' said Wesley. 'We met earlier. You know, when we were chasing after that eagle?'

Talks To Squirrels' face melted into a grin. 'Hello there,' he said. 'How did you get on? Last time I saw you, you were falling to your death.'

Wesley shrugged. 'Annoying, wasn't it? Anyway, I'm here now. Thought as I was passing I'd just call in, say thanks for all your help.'

'Don't mention it,' Talks replied. 'My pleasure. Anything to pass the time. Hey, take a seat, make yourself at home. I've just got a bit of legal business to see to, and –'

'Actually,' Wesley interrupted, 'something you said set me thinking. And I might be able to help.'

'Really?'

Wesley nodded. 'It was what you were saying about how you're forever shooting people with your bow and arrow and they never take a blind bit of notice. I was really, you know, moved. I felt for you.'

Talks shrugged. 'You get used to it,' he said. 'After a century or so, you learn to take it in your stride.'

'Sure. But I was thinking, maybe if you stopped using a bow and tried something else instead. Say, a Spencer rifle, for instance.'

'Maybe.' Talks To Squirrels shrugged. 'Worth a try, I suppose. But I haven't got –'

'I have. Look. Also this very fine forty-five six-shooter. Or, if all else fails, what about a stick of dynamite? Just light the fuse, stand well back, fizz, *boom*! It's got to be better than bows and arrows, surely.'

'You bet,' Talks replied. 'If only we'd had this kind of gear back in 1703, maybe I'd never have gotten into this mess in the first place.'

'Quite possibly,' Wesley replied. 'Anyway, I knew you'd be interested, so I thought I'd give you first refusal.'

'That's mighty kind of you.'

'You're welcome. Go on, then, make me an offer.'

The Indian's brow furrowed. 'I don't know,' he said. 'Trouble is, we don't use cash here. We got beaver skins. You want any beaver skins?'

Wesley shook his head. 'Fur trade's gone to hell since your time, I'm afraid,' he said. 'What about gold? You got any of that?'

'You mean the soft yellow metal that comes out of rivers?'

'That's the stuff.'

'No. Used to have a whole load of it, but we slung it out. Pity. What about authentic Amerindian artefacts? We got heaps of them.'

Wesley considered, frowning. 'Tempting,' he said, 'but I think I'll pass on that one, thanks. I mean, if it was up to me I'd say yes, like a shot, but my accountant . . .'

Talks groaned sympathetically. 'Say no more,' he replied. 'Sometimes I ask myself, whose side are those guys on? Trouble is, I dunno what else we got that you might want.'

'Tricky, isn't it?' Wesley rubbed his chin for a moment; and then, apparently, inspiration struck. 'I know,' he said. 'How about a lawyer? You got any of those?'

Talks To Squirrels grinned. 'Mister,' he said, 'this is your lucky day, because it just so happens that we do.'

'Great! Can I see him?'

'There.'

'Where?'

'There. Tied to the stake.'

'Oh, him. You sure that's a lawyer? Doesn't look much like a lawyer to me.'

'Just a second.' Talks To Squirrels turned, drew a knife and prodded Calvin in the ribs with it. 'You. Talk some legal stuff, quick.'

'Sure thing. Whereas by a conveyance dated the fifth February one thousand nine hundred and seventy-two and made between the Ideal Tool Corporation of Oskaloosa Iowa a corporation established under the laws of the state of Iowa and having its office at Oskaloosa in the said state of the first part and Henry Carter Zizbaum also of Oskaloosa aforesaid of the second part all that real estate comprising some forty-two acres known as . . .'

'That'll do. Shuttup. Well, what d'you think?'

'Sounds like a lawyer to me,' Wesley admitted. 'Ask him his charges.'

'You.' Prod. 'Tell the man.'

'You bet. Two thousand dollars an hour plus disbursements plus local and national taxes, plus twenty per cent care and control plus an additional seven hundred fifty dollars an hour for matters of unusual complexity by prior agreement with the client.'

'Yup, he's a lawyer all right.' Wesley extended a hand. 'Deal?'

'Deal. Excuse me asking, but what the hell do you want him *for*? I mean, not trying to be funny or anything, but his best friends wouldn't call him ornamental, and as for useful . . .'

Wesley contorted his face into his best approximation at a knowing smile. 'Well,' he said, 'you'd be amazed.'

'Yes. Quite frankly, I would. He's a *lawyer*, for God's sake. I suppose you could cut him up small and feed him to your pet rat, but rats can be fussy devils . . .'

'You want the rifle? Or not?'

Talks To Squirrels shrugged. 'Your business, I suppose. Here you go, and don't blame me. No refunds, no part exchanges, and absolutely no liability accepted for loss, damage or insolvency, whether directly or indirectly caused. Goddamnit, he's got me talking like one now. Get him out of my sight, before I go all frothy at the mouth.'

He gave Dieb a powerful shove. Quickly, Wesley collected him by the arm and started to walk away. They were almost at the edge of the firelight circle when Dieb stopped dead, like a mule.

'Just a moment,' he said. 'My car keys.'

'*What?*'

'My car keys,' Dieb repeated. 'They're still back there,

tied to one of those spears. I'm not leaving without them.'

'Something up?' Talks To Squirrels called out behind them. 'If he's stopped moving, I'm told a kick up the ass works wonders.'

'Sounds good to me,' Wesley called back. 'Look, you,' he whispered to the lawyer, who was still doing Gibraltar impressions, 'keeping moving or I'll leave you here. Understood?'

'I want my keys,' Dieb replied. 'Without them, I'm stuck here for ever. I *need* them, OK?'

'They were going to burn you alive, for God's sake,' Wesley hissed. As he spoke, he heard a noise in the background; not a grating noise exactly, because well-oiled metal components sliding smoothly together don't grate, unless you've been careless and got sand in the works. More a sort of metallic whisper. 'I know these people, they're utter loons. So get moving, or . . .'

'Not without my keys. I'd rather die now. Sorry.'

So Wesley just stood there, like a rabbit in oncoming headlights, thinking *Oh God!* Behind him, he could hear Talks To Squirrels saying, 'I pulled the little lever thing, why doesn't it go bang?' and one of his cohorts suggesting that it would help if he cocked the hammer first. In the split second between Talks To Squirrels saying, 'God, yes, I forgot,' and the very loud bang, he made a mental calculation of the distance separating them from the trees and the time it would take to cross it, even at a mad sprint, and came to the conclusion that it was too late to worry now. He spent the rest of the nanosecond relaxing his muscles and wondering what getting shot really feels like.

'Bugger,' said Talks To Squirrels, thirty yards behind. 'Why's he still standing up? I was sure I'd got him.'

'Can't have done. Here, try again.'

The second bang followed; and still Wesley couldn't feel anything. The lawyer, too, was still resolutely on his feet, though he'd started to go green in the face.

'This sonofabitch thing ain't working. Here, Two Turtledoves, can you see what I'm doing wrong?'

'Sorry, Chief. At this range, they should both be stone dead by now.'

Wesley nudged the lawyer in the ribs. 'Ready to try running away yet?'

'I'm coming round to the idea, certainly.'

'Fuck it,' the Indian was saying, 'it's because I'm a ghost, isn't it? It's just the same with guns as it is with bows and arrows. All right, pass me the dynamite, someone. We'll soon see about that.'

'My keys,' Dieb whimpered.

BOOM! The ground shook, and the soundwave hit them before the explosion came anywhere near. As it was; well, you know that gust of hot air you get when you open the door of a fan-assisted oven after it's been going for an hour or so? Well, it was like that. Only rather more so.

'Gosh.' Wesley, still face down on the ground, could hear the lawyer's voice somewhere over his head.

'Hey, he was right.'

'Was he?' Wesley asked, without moving.

'You bet,' Dieb replied. 'About the dynamite working even though the gun didn't. They've blown themselves up.'

'You don't say.'

'See for yourself. Little bits of them hanging off the trees, like slices of pastrami. Wonder why we weren't incinerated too?'

'Because,' Wesley was about to suggest; but then it started raining morsels of barbecued Indian, and he didn't feel like saying anything for a while. 'Can we go now?'

'I'd still like to have a look for my keys.'

'Be my guest. I think I'll just stay here for a while.'

A few long, rather horrible minutes passed; and then Dieb came back. 'No sign of any keys,' he said sadly. 'The only chance is that they were thrown clear by the blast. In which case, they could be anywhere.'

'How terribly sad,' Wesley muttered. 'Were there any survivors?'

'Huh? Oh, you mean the Indians? No, we're OK on that score. You might just find enough bits to make up a whole one, but only if you weren't too bothered about the colours matching.'

'I see.' Wesley got up slowly, being very careful where he put his hands and knees. 'I rather liked him,' he said.

'Who?'

'That Chief bloke. He helped me out earlier on, when I had to stalk an eagle.'

Dieb blinked. 'This eagle,' he said. 'Did you happen to crack it over the head with a big lump of rock?'

'I believe so. Why?'

'That was me.'

'Oh.'

'You nearly smashed my skull in,' said Dieb. 'And I was just about to get my keys back, too. A second later, and I'd have had them.'

'Is that so?'

Dieb nodded. 'That girl was handing them to me, and then you came out of nowhere and nearly brained me.'

'Well I never. Small world, isn't it?'

They stood looking at each other for a moment, neither of them liking terribly much what he saw. 'Calvin Dieb,' said the lawyer at last, extending a blackened, blood-streaked hand. 'Pleased to meet you.'

'Wesley Higgins. Are you having all kinds of weird experiences, too?'

Dieb nodded. 'I fell in the lake,' he said. 'I guess that seems to be what causes it.'

'It is.' They started to walk away. 'It's because the lake's enchanted.'

'You don't say.'

'By an Indian deity called Okeewana,' Wesley said. 'If you fall in the lake, she makes your dreams come true, or that's what she told me, anyway. Would you believe it, I came all the way from Brierley Hill just to meet her. Took all my money out of the Post Office, used up a whole year's holiday, just to be blown up by a ghost.'

'I just lost my keys. My car's parked up beside the road, see, and if only I could find them . . .'

Wesley stopped in his tracks. 'The girl,' he said. 'You saw her too?'

'The chubby broad? Yeah, I saw her. Like I said, she'd found my keys, and if you hadn't bashed me over the head . . .'

'She's not chubby.'

'The girl I was talking to was. She looked like the Before picture in a slimming advert.'

'You thought so, did you?'

'Nice enough kid,' the lawyer went on, apparently not noticing the thin film of ice forming over the other man's voice, 'but definitely well insulated. The kind that gets real value for money out of a train ticket.'

Wesley made an effort and put aside his annoyance. After all, he reasoned, jerk or no jerk, this extremely unpleasant person was a fellow victim. Working together, pooling their resources, maybe they'd both stand a better chance of –

'You're no beanpole yourself, Mr Dieb,' he heard himself reply. 'In. fact, if there's anybody round here with an excessive weight problem, it's you. So where do you get off, making cheap cracks about people being fat?'

'Hey!' Calvin Dieb restrained himself. True, he didn't like people making remarks about the large proportion of him that just hung about round his middle waiting for a hard winter; least of all toffee-nosed Brits who went around beating up on harmless birds with lumps of masonry. On the other hand, here was another guy in the same jam as he was. Maybe if they stuck together, worked as a team . . . 'Who are you calling fat, you goddamn Limey punk? First you club me half to death, then you get me shot at by a bunch of crazy Indians –'

'*Me* got *you* shot at? Who was it who wouldn't run away because of his stupid keys?'

'I wouldn't have needed to run away if you hadn't attacked me, just when I was about to . . .'

In the darkness ahead of them, two horses stood, tethered and patiently waiting. The two men ignored them.

'May I remind you,' Wesley was saying, 'that you'd just abducted an innocent girl . . .'

'I did not. That was that goddamn eagle.'

Wesley sneered. 'I see. A different eagle, was it? Another huge mutant bird that just happened to be passing? Oh yes, I'm convinced, I really am.'

'You calling me a liar?'

'I am now, yes.'

'Why, you –'

And then, just when Dieb's fist should have connected with Wesley's jaw and Wesley's fist should have landed squarely in Dieb's eye, they both vanished.

★

The moment Linda heard the explosion, she turned and ran.

The scene of the blast wasn't hard to find. There are certain tell-tale signs you look for when you're an experienced newshound, such as huge gaping craters, scraps of smouldering cloth, rashers of roasted flesh; that's the sort of clue your dedicated investigative journalist can read like a book. As soon as Linda scrambled over the rise, her heart stopped still.

One hell of a blast, it must have been; chance of finding anybody even remotely photogenic still alive correspondingly remote. Still, she had to look.

After a lot of grubbing about under fallen trees and scrabbling round in the dirt, she found one survivor, trapped under a large stone dislodged by the explosion. With a display of strength that surprised her, Linda managed to heave the rock out of the way.

'Hello,' she said. 'I'm a journalist. What happened?'

'Explosion,' the survivor croaked. 'All – killed – except – me.' His face contorted with pain, and he started to cough up blood.

'Yes, I can see there was an explosion,' Linda replied impatiently. 'I'm not blind, for God's sake. What was it that blew? One of the Rapier missiles? A reactor core off one of the subs?'

'Dynamite,' the Indian gasped. 'Chief threw dynamite into fire. Big explosion . . .'

'The chief engineer threw dynamite into the fire?' Linda's brow creased. 'Why the hell did he do that? Wait a bit – was it some kind of internal power struggle between the Cardinals? Tribal infighting between the Queenslanders and the New South Welsh? Or . . .?'

'He wanted to see,' groaned the survivor, 'if it would work.'

'I got you,' Linda said, her eyes shining. 'Unauthorised testing of a revolutionary new secret weapon. We could get a worldwide embargo on all US goods if we play our cards right. But then –'

'No – secret. We – all – knew . . .'

'And so they had to silence you!' Linda gasped, and sparks crackled up and down her spine like arc-welding ants. 'A cover-up! They had you terminated so you wouldn't blow the gaff on the illicit arms shipments!'

The Indian moaned softly, and tried to prop himself up on one elbow. 'No,' he whispered, 'not that way at all. You got – wrong end of stick. Just accident, that's all.'

Linda gazed down at him sternly. 'That's what they told you to say, obviously,' she replied, her voice heavy with contempt. 'Don't try and kid me, buster, I'm a reporter. Now, where were the shipments for? Did the President know? Where did the submarines come into it? And exactly what was the Mafia's role in the overall plan?'

'You – crazy,' murmured the Indian, falling back. 'Nothing like that – at all. Only . . .'

Frowning scornfully, Linda straightened up. 'Ah, the hell with you,' she said. 'I'll get to the bottom of this somehow, and if you think for one moment you can palm me off with a load of –'

'Aaagh.'

She looked closely. The Indian appeared to have died; a variant on the old *No comment at this time* routine that even Linda Lachuk found hard to crack. Never mind, she told herself, as she walked on past the crater and the mangled bodies. If they think they can throw me off the scent this easily, they've got a shock coming.

Oh yes.

★

'Complete dead loss,' sighed Captain Hat, as he slumped into the rabbit-hole where the rest of his company had been waiting for him. 'Waste of bloody time. Absolutely nothing here worth pinching at all.' He snarled and reached for the bottle, which proved to be empty.

'Oh,' said Mr Snedge. 'That's a pity, seeing as how we're stuck here.'

Although he was tempted to refute his first officer's downbeat analysis, on principle, as being bad for morale, Hat decided against it. They'd be bound to ask him why he thought they weren't stuck here; and listening to their commanding officer admitting that he hadn't a clue where they were or how to get home again was likely to be even worse for morale than Snedge's defeatist whimperings. So he ignored them.

'I blame this crop of punters,' he went on. 'Deadbeats, the lot of them. I mean to say, here they are acting out their wildest dreams, and not one decent bit of kit have they come up with, between the four of them. No caskets of uncut diamonds, no chests bursting at the hinges with Spanish gold, nothing. All I got was a set of car keys, and I dropped them.'

Nobody commented; an indication that, contrary to all evidence, they weren't quite as thick as they looked. After he'd sulked for five minutes or so, Hat stood up and began to pace the rabbit-hole, stroking his beard thoughtfully and avoiding the piles of rabbit ordure that would have swallowed up a less observant man of his stature without trace. Something was nagging at the back of his mind.

'I can't help feeling,' he said at last, 'that I'm somewhere else.'

His men looked at each other. Over the past few thousand years they'd developed a non-verbal shorthand, suitable for eye-contact communication. This particular look meant, *Oh God, he's off again*. Accordingly, they stayed quiet.

'And it's because of where I am that we're here,' Hat went on. 'Does that make any sense to anybody?'

'No, Chief.'

Hat shrugged. 'That makes two of us, Snedge, because I'm buggered if I know what's going on. Mind you, that's about par for the course in these parts.' He stopped pacing and peered out through the hole at the daylight beyond. 'On balance, though, I rather think that the me who's somewhere else is hiding from someone and is rather keen not to be found. And that,' he added, closing his eyes, 'is probably why we're lost.'

''Scuse me, Chief?'

'On the principle,' Hat continued, with the air of someone trying very hard not to listen to what he's saying, 'that if we can't find ourselves, then neither can anyone else. Does that sound to you like the sort of thing we'd do? Anybody?'

Mr Twist rubbed his chin; fortunately, the skin of his hands was of the texture of boot leather, otherwise he'd have rasped himself down to the bone. 'Well,' he ventured, 'I heard dafter things in my time, Chief. Anything's possible.'

'True.' Hat nodded in acknowledgement of a valid point. 'We might all get taken rich. You might even shave. Talking of which, Mr Twist, there's something that's been worrying me for five hundred years. How can it possibly be that in all the time I've known you, you've managed to keep the stubble on your chin just precisely the same length? How come I've never seen you clean-shaven, or with a beard?'

'Dunno, Chief,' Twist replied unhappily, for it was

something that had often puzzled him as well. 'Though they do say,' he went on, 'as fingernails and hair carry on growing even when you're dead.'

'But you're not dead, Twist. And your hair never grows.'

'Maybe it don't grow *because* I'm not dead, Chief.'

Hat winced. Too much of that sort of logic can rot a man's brain. 'Anyway,' Hat said, as soon as he'd managed to jemmy his brain back into gear, 'we're still stuck here, with nothing to steal and not much hope of getting out of here unless . . .'

'Unless what, Chief?'

'Well, not really unless anything,' Hat conceded despondently. 'If I'm right, the only people who can let us out is us, and we don't seem to know how to go about it.'

Mr Snedge considered this for a moment. 'D'you think we're giving it our best shot, Chief? I mean, we would give it our best shot, wouldn't we?'

'Shut up, Snedge.'

'Yes, Chief.'

Hat stood up again, and resumed his pacing. Being the only sentient life-form among so many pillocks had its positive side as well; in the country of the thick, the half-witted man is king. On the other hand, it made for a certain degree of isolation, not to mention stress. It'd be nice if, just once, they got themselves into some horrible jam and someone else figured out how to get them out again.

''Scuse me, Chief.'

Hat looked round and recognised Mr Flurt, the company's master-at-arms, who also doubled as their quarter-master and, when necessary, a battering-ram. Compared with the prospects of getting a sensible remark out of Mr Flurt, blood spouts out of stones like something out of Sam Peckinpah's nightmares.

'Hm?' Hat said, allowing his mind to idle again.

'Well,' said Flurt, 'if it's us hiding, then if we knew who we was hiding from, we could go hide somewhere else where they still wouldn't find us.'

Just as Hat's subconscious was pressing the *Delete File* key to get all that gibberish out of his short-term memory, a gleam of sense caught his mind's eye. 'Say that again,' he ordered.

'If it's us hiding,' said Flurt, reciting carefully, 'then if we knew who we was hiding from —'

Hat pounded his fist into his cupped palm excitedly. 'Then,' he shouted, 'we could go and hide somewhere else where they still wouldn't find us! Of course. That's brilliant.'

'What's brilliant, Chief?'

'What you just said, Flurt. Honestly, there are times . . .'

'No, Chief,' said Flurt patiently. 'What's it mean?'

Hat allowed his excitement to subside a little. Other things come out of the mouths of babes and sucklings beside wisdom, as anybody who has to clean up afterwards can testify. 'I'll explain later,' he muttered. 'Right now, I've got to think.'

Indians!

Janice froze. For all that it was the last decade of the twentieth century, and people don't think that way any more, she still had a residual level of sludge at the bottom of her mind in which lurked, secretly nourished by the cowboy movies of her youth, an irrational fear of being overtaken in the middle of nowhere by a Native American war-party on the rampage. What she was afraid of, she didn't know; that's often the way with irrational fears. Maybe they'd say unkind things about her, or accidentally drop tomahawks on her foot.

She looked again. Yes, there were Indians, right enough; but these particular Indians were unlikely to pose a threat to anyone, in the short term at least. If nothing was done about them for several days, it'd be a different matter.

'Hello?' she said.

No reply; under the circumstances all to the good, because the last thing you want if you're of a sensitive disposition is dead people answering you when you say, 'Hello.' It's bad enough when they knock once for yes, two times for no and start playing silly buggers with the table.

'Um,' she went on nonetheless, 'are you guys all right? Can I help anyone?'

But they continued to be dead, and took no notice. Or at least, the ones near to where Janice was standing continued to be dead. Further off, where the briars and undergrowth obscured her view, there was something moving about.

Janice ducked behind a moss-covered rock.

'Bloody hell,' said a voice. 'Just look at this lot, will you?'

'They just don't think,' someone else replied.

Shivering, Janice peered over the top of the rock, and saw two men. They were wearing brown overalls and baseball caps with some sort of logo or crest on them, and they carried big red plastic toolboxes. One of them knelt down and picked up a stray arm.

'Just look, will you?' he said. 'Brand new 36D. Remember the trouble we had getting hold of these?'

The other man nodded as he unfastened his toolbox. 'They're buggers, they are. Bloody old UNF threads, you need a special grommet or they just flop about. Well, he'll have to make do with a 41 metric, 'cos that's the nearest I got. Don't suppose he'll live long enough to notice, the way they're carrying on.'

'That's if we've got a 41 metric,' said his colleague. 'I got a feeling we bunged the last one on one of them Vikings. I ask you, how can you lose a bloody arm when you're drowning?'

'They do it on purpose, if you ask me.' The man was doing something Janice didn't want to think about with a mangled torso and a ratchet screwdriver. 'Just to be awkward. Fifteen holes I counted in one of them goblins. Well, that's this month's body putty gone, and the others'll just have to lump it.'

Whatever it was they were doing, they were certainly quick about it. They worked with the certain, economical movements of men who know what they're doing and have been doing it for a very long time. Janice could hear clicks and clunks and the occasional whirr of a cordless drill.

'I only fixed this bugger dinner time,' growled one of the men. 'Came in with his head on the wrong way round. Only been trying to mend it himself, the daft sod. Here, you got a 97B in heads, twelve mil. by thirty-six?'

'Only in pink.'

The man shrugged. 'Sling it over,' he said. 'Don't suppose anybody'll notice under all that warpaint they wear.' Something round and soccer-ball-sized looped through the air and was caught. The drill whirred. A socket wrench clacked. The man swore.

'Taken all the skin off me knuckles,' he explained. 'Got any?'

'Here.'

'Ta. When's this lot got to be done by, anyway? There's a couple here ought to go back to the works.'

The other one shrugged. 'They didn't say,' he replied. 'They ought to keep a few back as spares, then we would-n't have all these rush jobs. I've had it up to here with getting the blame when arms fall off, and it's only 'cos I haven't had time to do a proper job.'

'Yeah. They just don't think.'

My God, Janice muttered to herself, they're repairing all those dead guys, this is *amazing*. Or maybe they aren't guys, maybe they're just robots. That'd still be pretty amazing.

'Hey!'

This time, the voice was coming from a few yards away. Janice ducked down again and held her breath.

'Hold yer water, son,' replied one of the men wearily. 'We'll get to you soon as we can. Only got one pair of hands, you know.'

'Here, that's a good one, Phil. Only one pair of hands.'

'What? Oh, yes, right. Go and see what he wants, will you, Dave? I've got this one's liver all in pieces, and you know how those little return springs jump out soon as look at them.'

The man called Dave gathered up his tools and trudged over to where the voice had come from. 'Call out, will you?' he said. 'Can't see bugger all in this long grass.'

'Over here,' the voice replied. 'Look, sorry to hassle you, but I'm due on in a minute and all that's left of me is a couple of toes.'

Dave located the source of the voice and stood for a moment or so, clicking his tongue and making well-I-dunno noises. 'Tell you what,' he said after a while, 'the best I can do for you is bung you in one of them other bodies, just for now. Then, when you've done your bit, I'll have you in down the depot and sort you out properly.'

'Ah shit,' replied the toes, disgustedly. 'Can't you just patch me up with a bit of insulating tape or something? It's only a non-speaking part.'

'I'll pretend I didn't hear that,' Dave replied frostily. 'You know what my boss'd say if he saw one of you buggers walking about all bodged up with sticky tape. Either you can go in someone else, or you'll have to wait till we get back to the works. It's up to you.'

'Bloody prima donnas,' muttered the toes. 'All right, then. But find me a good one, will you? And not that one, he's got rheumatism.'

Dave worked in silence for a while, clicking and clunking his way through a growing pile of small, bloody, oily bits. 'What the hell happened to you lot anyway?' he asked eventually. 'Looks like you got blown up.'

'We did.'

'How'd that happen, then?'

'If you must know, I threw a stick of dynamite on the fire.'

'You did?'

'Yes. It was in the scenario. I don't enjoy getting blasted into catfood, you know.'

'You lot, you just don't know how to look after decent kit. I mean, just look at this leg.'

'All right, you've made your –'

'With a bit of luck I might be able to salvage the universal joint, and that's it. Hold still, will you? Don't want to waste another heart valve, thank you very much. Now then . . .'

'Hey!'

'Shuttup,' hissed Dave. 'And keep still. There's something behind that rock.'

'So?'

'Stay there. Don't move.'

'Haven't really got any choice in the matter, have I?'

Janice contemplated flight, but not for very long;

because before she could sweet-talk her limbs into unfreezing, Dave was standing over her, looking very apprehensive and gripping a big spanner tightly in both hands.

'Oh balls,' he said.

'Excuse me?'

Dave scowled at her as if she were a crossed thread. 'You're one of them, aren't you?' he growled. 'A customer.'

Janice nodded.

'You're not supposed to see any of this.'

'No?'

'No.' Dave was looking at her differently now; that slightly bewildered, slightly boiled, slightly stuffed expression she was coming to know so well. 'No,' he repeated, letting the spanner drop. 'Well, er, no. Actually.'

Janice hauled herself back onto her feet, with rather more enthusiasm than dignity. 'I'm terribly sorry,' she mumbled. 'I'd better be going, then.'

'No, don't go,' Dave said, looking even more boiled and stuffed. 'I mean, no harm done, and we, er, don't want to seem unfriendly or anything.'

'But I'm keeping you from your work,' Janice protested feebly. 'I'm sure you've got ever such a lot to get on with, and . . .'

Dave made a dismissive, hang-spring-cleaning gesture. It was about as convincing as a four-dollar note, but he didn't seem to care. 'Let it wait,' he said. 'All rest and no play, eh? Why don't you, er, come and have a look at the, um trees and things. Flowers,' he added hopefully. 'Sure we can find a flower or two around here if we look hard enough.'

'Flowers?'

He nodded like a well-socked punchball. 'Heaps of 'em, probably, unless the blast shrivelled 'em all up. Let's go and take a look, shall we?'

He made a wild grab for her hand, but she whisked it away. *Oh Christ, not again. Why can't everybody just ignore me, like they usually do?* Unfortunately, she knew the answer to that. 'Look,' she said, trying to sound brisk and no-non-senseish. 'I know what you're thinking, it's been happening a lot lately, and I'm afraid it simply isn't on. It's not real, you see, it's only this dumb wildest-dreams thing, so per-haps I'd better just leave before we both say things we'll regret . . .'

He wasn't listening, needless to say. The look in his eyes was so intense that Janice could almost smell the formalde-hyde. It'd be so nice if he'd just go away.

'Excuse me saying this,' he burbled, 'but you've put me in mind of something, let's see, it's on the tip of my tongue, memory like a tea-bag, my wife says. Oh, that's it, a summer's day. You and a summer's day could be sisters, really.'

The word *wife* fizzed in Janice's mind like an aspirin in water. 'Talking of your wife,' she said, 'd'you think she'd take kindly to you comparing strange girls to summer days? I really think you should –'

'Don't care what *she* thinks, rancid old cow,' Dave replied savagely. 'I can think of all sorts of things to compare her to, but they've mostly got four legs and horns. The only day she puts me in mind of was back along last February, that time all the pipes in the roof froze solid and we had water dripping in the soup. Got a temper on her, too.'

'I . . .' Janice shrugged. Why risk getting involved, after all? Although, on balance, her sympathies were probably with Mrs Dave – it couldn't be pleasant washing his work clothes, given his trade, and the dirty marks he must leave on the towels didn't really bear thinking about – the fact that Dave's marriage appeared to have been made in Hell wasn't her fault, and she'd have nothing to reproach herself for if this particular brief encounter gave the wretched thing its final shove. 'Whatever,' she said. 'In the meantime, unless you get back to work right now, I'll tell your supervisor. You got that, or shall I write it down?'

'Actually,' Dave said, 'I'm the supervisor. Well, there's only two of us in the department, what with the cuts and all, but nominally I'm the supervisor and Phil's the foreman. Daft, really, but you try telling them anything.' He smiled, and the effect was something like a Death's head in a Comic Relief nose. A small, rebellious part of Janice sympathised, for in her time she'd been the unwanted admirer more often than she cared to remember, and she clearly recalled that one of the symptoms was being as unwilling to take a hint, or even a direct command, as a market trader is to take a cheque. Love is deaf as well as blind, and can construe, 'Get stuffed, you prune-faced warthog's arse', as a thinly veiled come-on. Sympathy, however, is all very well.

'Piss off,' she said.

'Sorry?'

'Piss off,' Janice repeated, elocuting. 'Go away, with prejudice. Go play with a dead body. Understand?'

'Oh.'

'I mean it. Given a choice between you and one of your dismembered corpses, I'd choose the corpse every time.' She paused, and grinned unpleasantly. 'Go jump in the lake,' she added.

'Jump in the lake?'

Janice nodded. 'It's over there somewhere. Big wet thing, with upside-down trees all over it.'

'Done that.'

'Huh?'

Dave nodded. 'Done that, what, eighty years ago. Back in the First World War. That's why I'm here.'

Janice didn't like the sound of that. 'And you're still here?' she asked. 'After all this time?'

'Yeah. Bummer, isn't it? You see, I used to be a doctor. Really keen on doctoring, I used to be. What I really wanted more than anything else was to be able to take people who'd got all smashed up, like the poor bleeders we used to fish out of the trenches and pick off the barbed wire, and put 'em back together again, good as new. So, when I fell in the lake . . .'

A dull, sick feeling slapped itself across Janice's mind. 'But that's crazy,' she said. 'That was a good thing to want, surely.'

'I used to think so, too,' Dave sighed. 'Never could see the harm in it.'

'But they're *punishing* you for it,' Janice said, horrified. 'You wanted to save people's lives, and they kept you here. That's *bad*.'

Dave shrugged. 'Got what I asked for, though, didn't I?' He chuckled bitterly. 'Can't complain on that score. The only difference is, in the trenches we used to get a couple of days off every month. Used to enjoy me days off, I did. Used to go into Armentières and play dominoes with the Canadians.'

Janice took a step or so backwards, ignoring whatever it was that felt soft and squidgy under her foot. Up till now, she'd felt confused and put-upon. Now she was starting to get angry.

'I've had about enough of this,' she said. 'I guess it's OK what they're doing to me, because I asked for it, in a way. But picking on a doctor because he wanted to make people better just isn't right.'

Dave frowned, puzzled. 'So what're you going to do about it?' he said.

'Complain,' Janice answered immediately. 'Demand to see the manager. Write my Congressman. I don't know. I'm going to do something, though, just you wait.'

'How about . . .?'

'Oh, get lost, I'm busy. I want to talk to someone in authority.'

'But . . .'

Whatever Dave said next, he said it to empty air.

CHAPTER TEN

Wesley fell over.

There was a simple reason for this. At the moment he disappeared, he'd been aiming a punch at a fairly substantial lawyer. When he reappeared, the space the lawyer should have occupied turned out to contain nothing but oxygen, nitrogen and a few trace elements of no great importance. Since there was nothing to stop the momentum of his fist, he accordingly fell over and landed, face down, in what had once been a bison's dinner. Subsequently it had gone clean through the bison and come to rest, in a collapsed pyramid shape, on the ground.

'Ack!' Wesley observed, sitting up and wiping it out of his eyes.

'Serves you right for playing rough games,' said the bison reproachfully. 'Bet you didn't expect to see me again.'

'Where'd he go?'

'The lawyer?' The bison's jaws moved methodically. 'Sorry, but you don't need to know that. Classified.'

Wesley said something succinct under his breath that summed up what he felt about classified information.

'Look,' he went on, 'this game, or ordeal, or whatever it's supposed to be. When's it due to finish?'

'When it's over.'

'Fine. Thank you ever so much. And when will it be over?'

'When it's finished.'

Carefully, trying not to get the former bison food on more of him than he could help, Wesley got to his feet and looked round. There had been a time, he freely admitted, when he looked at the world through rose-tinted glasses. In retrospect, that had been better, surely.

'Do you realise,' he said wearily, 'that not so long ago, I used to feel sad at the thought that the American bison was hunted to the verge of extinction. Now I only wish they'd done a thorough job.'

'So?' The bison turned its head and looked at him through soft, brown, stupid eyes. 'There's no point blaming me,' he said. 'I didn't start this. You came all this way specially, remember, just to meet me. Hey. You're on holiday, lighten up. Isn't this still more fun than being in the office?'

Wesley thought about that for a moment. 'Well,' he said, 'yes. But then again, so would hanging by my feet over a vat of molten lead. That doesn't actually prove anything. More to the point, we don't seem to be *achieving* very much. OK, I've had exciting experiences I'd have missed out on if I'd stayed in Brierley Hill, but they've all been horrible; except for meeting, um, her, but now she's gone again and it doesn't look like I'll get to meet her again.' He sighed. Below where he stood, the lake lay like a newly ironed duvet, lovingly hand-embroidered with a curious motif of upside-down mountains. 'If we've got to do this, can't we at least make it useful?'

'You mean profitable?'

'Well – yes, in the wider sense, I suppose I do. Well, quite. What's in it for me?'

'I see. You'd rather it was like a game show or something?'

'No,' Wesley replied firmly, 'of course not. I only meant –

But the bison had vanished, and the girl had come back; except that now she'd exchanged her fringed buckskin tunic for something skimpy and sequin-covered. She was also taller, blonde and totally different, though naturally still gorgeous.

'Better?' she said through a rose-rimmed hole in her smile. 'More in keeping with the way you perceive this experience?'

'Oh, don't be like that.'

'What's in it for me, you said,' the girl continued, the savagery of her tone of voice contrasting markedly with the toothpaste-ad smile it came out through. 'I now see that you're one of those people who wouldn't accept a first-class suite in the Kingdom of Heaven unless there was a radio alarm-clock thrown in free as well. All right then, buster, have it your way. This is your chance to win Fabulous Prizes. But don't come whining to me if you don't like this format after all.'

'No, look, really,' Wesley said, but the girl had stomped off in a huff and vanished, leaving only a Cheshire-Cat echo of her smile behind, like the green blobs you see with your eyes shut after you've stared into the sun. Since he had no idea what he was supposed to do now, Wesley sat down on a rock and waited.

But not for long. In fact, he just had time to think, *Oh for pity's sake*, before the sky went red on him.

*

'Here we are,' said the girl, with synthetic cheerfulness. 'Sorry to have kept you waiting.'

The inspector took the ledgers from her with a grunt. 'Now then,' he said, 'we can get started. I've had instructions to pay particular attention to operating systems, with a view to identifying any possible misapplication of resources, inefficient use of materials or funding, unnecessary duplications . . .'

He broke off, and looked ostentatiously around. He didn't say anything for quite some time.

'Sorry about this,' said the girl, avoiding his eye. 'It happens sometimes. Doesn't mean anything, of course. We're all used to it by now.'

The inspector didn't appear to have heard her. 'Perhaps,' he said, in a voice marginally more aggravating than the one he'd been using before, 'you'd care to explain why we appear to be standing in a theatre.'

The girl grinned. Sheepishly would be an underestimate. Sheep have more sense than to get themselves into messes of this magnitude. 'It's not a theatre,' she whispered, 'not as such. More like a TV studio.'

'Those people . . .'

'The audience.'

'Ah.' The inspector made a note in his notebook. 'I take it they're not full-time employees. I'd hate to think you were incurring regular expenditure . . .'

'Oh no.' The girl shook her head, perhaps a little more vigorously than necessary. 'Well, they are, full-time employees, I mean; but they're not just employed to sit. If you look closely, you'll see they're all Vikings and Indians in disguise.'

'Ah.' The inspector stole a quick look over the rims of his spectacles. 'Apparently they are. You keep a full-time staff of Indians and Vikings, then? Perhaps you'd care to explain . . .'

The girl cringed. 'Sorry to butt in,' she muttered, 'but would you mind awfully, er, saying something to them? A few jokes, just to warm up, get the sound levels right, that sort of thing? You see, you're actually the –'

'The what?'

'The host.'

'I *see*.' An expression of bewildered disgust migrated across the inspector's face. 'Could you perhaps explain the reason for that?'

'Oh, saving costs, of course,' the girl replied, crossing the fingers of both hands behind her back. 'We found that if we were prepared to be, you know, adaptable, turn our hands to different skills, we could save substantially on manning levels without in any way impairing the smooth running of the, um, whatever. Just a few jokes? Why did the chicken, that sort of thing? It's for a good cause.'

But the inspector only turned his head to the left, gave the red velvet backdrop a severe look, and jotted down something in his notebook. While he was doing this, a door in the wings opened and an unseen hand shoved Wesley into the middle of the stage.

'Excuse me,' whispered the girl.

'Hmm?'

'Sorry to interrupt, but the, um, first contestant . . .'

The inspector looked at her, and then at Wesley, and then back at her. 'I'm sorry,' he said, 'but this is going to have to go in my report.'

'OK, fine. Look, could you just, um, read what's on the card, please? Just this once. For me.'

During this exchange, Wesley had looked round, seen the faces of the audience like a great expanse of water lapping at his feet, tried to make a run for it, been retrieved by two of the larger Vikings in evening dress and frog-marched back to where he'd just run from. He now had the aspect of a caged crocodile in a handbag factory, and both arms held firmly up his back. He was being ordered to smile.

'Please,' begged the girl. 'Oh, go on.'

A refusal was just about to jump out of the inspector's rnouth and pull the ripcord when a little voice in the back of his mind said, *Well, why not?* He didn't know how it came to be there, or why on earth he should be listening to it; on the other hand – why not indeed? He looked down at the card the girl had given him, cleared his throat and tried to do something he hadn't attempted since he was a mere stripling of four thousand and six. He tried to smile.

'Hello,' he read, 'and welcome to Death Or Glory, the game where you only get the prizes if you're really unlucky.' He stopped, frowned and turned back to the girl, who nodded reassuringly. He went on, 'Now a big hand please for our first contestant, Wesley Higgins.'

For some reason, the Indians and the Vikings and the bears and the goblins and the other parts played by members of the company found this statement tremendously exciting, because they started to cheer and whoop and whistle as if he'd just announced free beer all round. While all that was going on, the girl handed him another card.

'Thank you, thank you,' he recited. 'And Wesley's first task will be, pause for effect – not the bits in brackets? Got you, right – to take all his clothes off and play the violin. Contestant, you have three minutes starting *now*.'

'Hey!' Wesley shrieked, as the Vikings started to

confiscate his clothes. 'I thought you said I wasn't going to have to . . .'

A third Viking shoved a violin into his hands. The audience was making the sort of noises audiences everywhere make under these conditions. It's probably fortunate that Charles Darwin never saw a game show studio audience, or else he might have started to wonder whether he hadn't got his celebrated theory of evolution the wrong way round.

As Wesley stood, wearing nothing except what was left of the bison by-product he'd fallen in, and doing his inadequate best to hide his embarrassment from a hallful of Vikings with one small violin, the inspector read out another card.

'Having the courage to confront our inner anxieties,' he read, in a voice that would have made the average Dalek sound like Laurence Olivier hamming it up, 'is a fundamental stage on the road to personality growth. By making our nightmares come true, we can confront whatever it is they really stand for, and resolve the inner turmoils that cause them. You have ninety seconds. Man, play that thing!'

Very reluctantly, Wesley lifted the violin to his chin, drew back the bow and let it glide across the strings. The result was perhaps the ghastliest noise ever made by catgut in the absence of the rest of the cat.

'Sixty seconds. And he's going to have to do a bit better than this if he wants to stand a chance of winning tonight's grand star prize!'

'But I can't –' Wesley started to say; then it occurred to him that anything further might lay him open to a charge of stating the obvious. He gritted his teeth, clamped his eyes so tightly shut that muscles in his chceks started to ache, and tried again.

And succeeded.

Admittedly, it was only *Baa Baa Black Sheep*, and there was little in it to prompt his colleagues at the day job to buy a big card for everybody to write farewell messages on; but considering that the nearest he'd ever come before to playing the violin was when he used to stretch rubber bands along his six-inch ruler at school and scrape them with a pencil, it wasn't bad at all. For the first time in a long while, Wesley felt –

– Proud? Good about himself? Maybe.

'Time's up,' read the inspector. 'And it looks like Wesley's won tonight's grand star prize. Which is –' He turned the card and found his place again. 'Death by what's that word? Oh, sorry. Electrocution, so let's have a big hand for . . .' He stopped reading, lowered the card, paused as directed, and raised the card again. 'Old Sparky!'

Whereupon the door in the wings opened; and someone dressed in a comic electric-chair costume waddled on, big felt smile stuck to the front of his seat, big white padded hands waving adorably, big live blue sparks arcing across his terminals –

Wesley opened his eyes. Time to wake up.

But he didn't wake up, and his eyes were already open.

When Calvin rematerialised, he found himself standing beside his car, with the keys in his hand.

Before that, he'd been just about to start a fight with someone, and then he *felt* himself disappearing; a very brief but entirely unmistakable experience, equivalent to watching yourself vanish before your very eyes.

'Tonight's star prize . . .'

He spun round on his heel, to find he was being

watched by a theatre full of people. Which meant he was in a theatre. Which meant that he was indoors. Which meant, though he wasn't quite sure why, that this wasn't his car.

Except that it palpably was. In the same way that a woman can always recognise her own new-born baby's cry in the middle of a wardful of howling infants, a man can always recognise his own car. Probably it's the same basic instinct; the natural and subliminal bonding between two souls formed from the same piece of stock. And if all that mystic stuff wasn't sufficient evidence, there were palpable physical signs; the tiny scratch on the front fender that nobody but he would ever know to look for, the minuscule abrasion on the front offside hubcap, the all but invisible scar in the paintwork under the filler cap where he'd once slipped with the filler cap key. His car; flesh of his flesh, chrome of his chrome, vinyl of his vinyl.

So what the hell was it doing here?

'A big hand, please . . .'

Who cares? He fumbled on the keyring for the doorkey. If only he could get inside, he'd be safe; he could triple-lock the doors, turn on the alarm, use his phone to call a SWAT team. According to the brochure, the quickest time in which the world's most accomplished automotive thieves had been able to break into this model had been twenty minutes. Give the boys in the flak jackets and baseball hats twenty minutes, and they'd have this whole lot looking like Monte Cassino on a bad day. Except for this car, of course; according to the literature, a direct nuclear strike might bubble off a couple of layers of paint, but that was about it. A serious car for a serious world, the brochure said; the picture its well-chosen phrases conjured up was of an intact, barely scratched car free-floating in the vacuum of space, while the exploded fragments of Planet Earth sailed harmlessly by on the interstellar winds. Once inside this mother, he'd be *safe*.

He located the key in the lock, pushing away the spring-loaded lock cover. He pushed.

The key wouldn't go.

'. . . For our second contestant, Calvin Dieb!'

The theatre exploded into pandemonium; howling, whistling, rebel yells and so on. Two large men in tuxedos materialised behind Calvin's shoulders. And still the key wouldn't go.

'Excuse me, sir,' muttered one of the men. 'Auto club.'

Whereupon he took the keys from Calvin's hand and put them in his pocket. As Calvin straightened up to punch him (although, without a stepladder, he'd have been hard put to it to do any significant damage), two huge hands pushed down on his shoulders, sitting him efficiently and with minimum dignity on the floor.

'Hey,' he whined, 'gimme my keys, will you?'

A giant hand reached down, gathered a fistful of lapels and lifted Calvin up by them. He found himself looking into the unfriendliest pair of eyes he'd seen in a long time; ever since, in fact, he'd been cross-examining a rape victim in the witness box and caught sight of his own reflection in a window.

'No keys,' said the proprietor of the unfriendly eyes. 'First you gotta play the game.'

The hand let go of his lapels and he slid back downwards, until he came to rest against the passenger door of the car. It was then that he noticed another man, this time wearing a spangly white tuxedo and reading aloud from a card.

'Your chosen subject,' the man said, 'is Law. You have

two minutes in which to answer one question – just one – correctly. If you do, then tonight's wonderful grand star prize, a complete set of keys specially custom-crafted to fit *your* car, will be yours to take home. If you don't, then you get to sit in . . .' The man lowered the card and counted under his breath before speaking again; when he did, his words were drowned out by the unison chant from the audience.

'Old SPARKY!'

Old Sparky? The electric chair? Calvin looked round quickly, to see if he had a chance of rolling under the car before the two tuxedoed monsters could stop him. Then he thought, Just a minute, one correct answer in two minutes? On Law? And they give me my keys?

He didn't exactly relax, in the same way as the polar ice never actually melts; but a different kind of tension thrilled down to his nerve-endings. If there was one thing he knew, it was Law. This was a gamble he'd be prepared to take.

'Your two minutes,' the man said, 'starting . . .'

And then he recognised him.

Strange, how quickly the mind can work when there's absolutely nothing that can be done in time to avert disaster. IBM never built anything with a better response time than the mind of a man who notices through the windscreen of his speeding car that the tall object five yards dead ahead is a tree. All that long interim, between the moment of initial recognition and waking up to find your arm full of plastic tubes, is filled with an almost infinite number of thoughts, suggestions and referrals from the self-preservation sub-committee and strong recommendations from the theology department; all marvellously good stuff, but there's no time to act on the advice.

The man smiled, and said, 'Now.'

'Hi, Dad.'

'In *State of Colorado v Stein*,' the man read out, 'was the third party's collateral warranty held to bind the defendant regardless of the terms of the original agreement?'

Dieb swallowed hard. 'Look,' he said, 'I really did mean to come to the hospital, it was just a bad day for me –'

'Incorrect. In actions for defamation, is slander actionable per se or must the plaintiff prove special damage?'

'I was all set,' Dieb went on, 'and then just as I was about to leave the phone rang, and it was this really important client –'

'Incorrect. In *Sharps v Rowan*, was the defendant's inability to fulfil the contract owing to intervening factors beyond his control sufficient to relieve him of his obligations to the plaintiff?'

'And about the funeral, I really did mean to go, but my dumb secretary'd booked me lunch with the board of Freemans', and you just don't call up old man Freeman and say, Sorry, can you do Tuesday instead? So . . .'

'Incorrect. Thirty seconds remaining. Briefly explain the maxim *res ipsa loquitur*.'

'Anyhow,' said Calvin desperately, 'I hope you liked the flowers. Sorry about the mix-up, I told my secretary you always liked carnations, but she must have gotten carnations and chrysanthemums mixed up. Besides, you wouldn't actually have seen them, would you? Not from where you . . .'

'Incorrect.' Calvin Dieb senior gave his son a big, friendly smile. 'Time's up, and gee, son, you've blown it! Which means –'

'Old SPARKY!'

As the cuddly, padded, smiling electric chair waddled in from the wings, and the two gorillas dragged Calvin towards it, his father waved to him, not unaffectionately. 'Son,' he said, 'you should have listened to Mom and me. Didn't we say if you threw in your job with the circus and ran away to law school, one day you'd be sorry? So long, son.'

'So long, Dad.'

Calvin Dieb senior turned to the audience and smiled. 'A big hand for Calvin Dieb junior, folks. Serves the little bugger right.'

He turned. Flashing blue light was reflected in his silver hair as he left the stage, a handkerchief pressed to his nose because of the smell.

In the chair, Calvin was just getting to the interesting bit when he vanished.

The Proprietor was dreaming.

It was a curious dream. It seemed to involve four blind mice, scampering round the shores of His lake, pursued by the farmer's wife, Sabatier XL stainless carver in her hand and a great big silly grin on her face. There were other ingredients to the dream – Indians and Vikings and goblins and talking bears and a thing like a walking armchair that fizzed blue, and a few others He couldn't yet see clearly. Everyone except the mice seemed to be enjoying themselves enormously; but this was wrong, because the dream was supposed to be for the mice's benefit.

It then occurred to the Proprietor that things which are good for you – medicines and cabbage and cold baths and quitting smoking and good healthy exercise and going to bed early – do seem, as often as not, to be horrible at the time. It's only afterwards that you appreciate their virtue; usually when you've grown up and have children of your own on whom you can inflict the torments of your youth.

The Proprietor wondered about that. He wondered why bad things taste nice, and good things taste nasty. He wondered why it was good to waste the golden sunlit afternoons of childhood doing piano practice so that, when you turn forty, you'd be able to play the piano indifferent-badly if only you had the time. He wondered why Youth must learn how to do long division so that Middle Age can tap a few buttons on a calculator. He tried to remember the things He'd been at pains to learn when He was young, but couldn't.

And He resolved; learning is to punish the ignorant for offences they would have committed if they hadn't known better. Having sorted out the point, definitely for ever, He slid back into full sleep.

The mice were still running; they ran through the briars and they ran through the brambles and they ran through the thickets where the rabbits wouldn't go, and still the farmer's wife followed them, and the sun flashed off the broad blade of her knife, in which were reflected many tall trees and mountains. This implied that He had missed the point, something He never liked to do.

So He wondered about the blind mice. He had already Resolved that learning is punishment; and when He came to look at them He could see that all four mice did indeed deserve to be chased, and that their tails had been forfeit for most of their adult lives. They needed to be taught a lesson. Well.

But they hadn't come to learn; they'd come to dream. One of them had capital-D Dreams like the New York sewers have alligators; one dreamed greed and selfishness and a callous disregard for everything beautiful and good that stood between him and a dollar; one lived in a dream so complete and so unreal that it wouldn't have mattered, except that she wanted to make other people believe it too; and one dreamed of being an unmitigated pest, which was antisocial behaviour by anybody's standards. Very well, then; let them have their dreams, and learn that their dreams are nightmares.

He tried to Resolve accordingly, but found that He couldn't.

Janice felt herself reappearing.

It wasn't anything like she'd imagined. As far as she'd always been concerned, you reappeared in a shower of tin-selly glitter, to the accompaniment of a melodious electronic twang, and the first thing you saw was the face of Mr Scott, peering at you over the top of his instrument panel. Then, if you were lucky, deferential security guards escorted you to the recreation room, where you could have a refreshing pink milk shake and a recycled currant bun.

The reality was rather different; a bit like the feeling you get when your leg, having gone to sleep, wakes up again. One of the things you don't readily do is move.

So, rooted to the spot, she looked round to find out where she was. She didn't like what she saw.

She was in an auditorium. High up, on scaffolding towers, there were TV cameras. White lights as bright as the Second Coming blazed at her, and beyond them was a sea of pink and red faces, some of them worryingly famil-iar. They appeared to be an audience, looking at her. She was on the stage.

She was also, she discovered, wearing a costume, or part of one. It was hard looking down, but she seemed to be wearing a sparkly sort of swimsuit; either that, or the parts of her that had to be at least vestigially covered had been smeared in glue and dusted down with sequins. There was glittery stuff in her hair, and enough paint on her face to do the outside of a block of flats.

And the audience was staring at her.

Sharing the stage with her was a tall, silver-haired type in a glittery white tuxedo and a smile that made the studio lights seem unnecessary, and also a stunningly sttractive girl with golden hair and eyes as blue as the mould on decomposing bread. They looked as if they were supposed to be the centre of attention. They weren't. She was.

By now, she knew the signs as instinctively as seaweed knows the weather. The whole goddamn audience was in love with her.

Vaguely remembering something she'd once heard about someone being a lion in a den of Daniels, she looked round for an escape route: but there didn't seem to be one. The MC and the dreamboat stood directly between her and the doorway in the wings. The only other visible way out was down off the stage and through the audience; an option as attractive to her as a short cut through a mine-field would be to a thirty-foot-long centipede.

The beautiful girl; didn't she know her from some-where? The eagle's cave? Something about submarines? She concentrated, and tried to hear what the MC was saying to her.

'Now then, Lindsey,' she heard, 'perhaps you'd like to explain your theory about the Vaticangate affair to our studio audience.'

'Right,' said the lovely girl. 'First, it's not Lindsey, it's Linda; or, to you, Ms Lachuk. Second, well, it's basically fairly simple. The beef is, they're bringing the stuff in somehow; I'm not sure of the details yet, but it seems to involve midnight airlifts using Mafia-owned Sea King hel-icopters. Then they encase it in blocks of – Hey!'

'Hm?' The silver-haired man, who'd been ogling Janice's legs, made an effort and turned back to the lovely girl. 'Sorry?' he said.

'The cameras,' she complained, 'why are they all on her and not me? I'm the one doing the story.'

'What? Sorry about that. I was miles away.'

'The cameras,' the angelically gorgeous female repeated angrily. 'And the mikes, too. I know about these things; they aren't picking up a single word I'm saying.'

'Huh? What did you say about the cameras?'

'Oh for crying out – Look, do you want me to give you my world exclusive scoop, implicating the US government and the Pope in illicit undercover arms shipments? Or would you rather all just gawp at the goddamn chubby bitch over there?'

The MC glowered at her. 'Not chubby,' he said sharply. 'Voluptuous.'

'Hey!'

'Or even,' he continued dreamily, 'Rubensesque. By God, there's enough meat on that to feed a family of five for Thanksgiving and still have enough for sandwiches clean through to New Year.'

Whereupon the audience burst out into an explosion of cheering, yowling and wolf-whistling that must have been plainly audible in Pennsylvania, and left Janice feeling torn between a desperate longing never to have been born, and a ferocious desire to scalp each and every one of them with a blunt putty knife. In the event, however, she did neither of these: instead, she carried on standing there, sweating through the makeup and looking like a cross between the Statue of Liberty and one of the young ladies who spend their days sitting in shop windows in Amsterdam. Probably the only person in the whole world who was more furious than her was the lovely girl; and that was a laugh, because she had all her clothes on.

'Hey!' she was howling. 'If this is your idea of a serious in-depth current affairs programme, you can . . .'

'Sorry? Oh hell, yes. I'd clean forgotten about you. Right then, Laura, er –' The MC glanced down at the card in his hand. 'Lachik, right? Laura Lachik, ladies and gentlemen, special current affairs correspondent for the *New York Globe*, who's going to give us the low-down on the latest . . . what was it again?'

'Oh for God's sake!' The dreamboat was scrabbling at her cleavage for the little concealed microphone. 'I've had enough of this. Here I am with the most significant news story in history, and all you creeps are interested in is that cow's legs. And they aren't even nice legs, damnit, they look like pink elephants' trunks.'

'Not just her legs,' replied the MC equably.

'Oh . . .!' The lovely girl was having difficulty tracing the course of the microphone lead, which had apparently been threaded through her underwear and out through a hole in her left shoe. 'The hell with you! I'm not standing for this. I'm . . .'

The MC was staring at her with baffled concern. 'But Ms Lachuk,' he was saying, calmly and quietly, 'I thought this was what you wanted. Peak air time, ten minutes all to yourself, your own script –'

'Stuff it!' With a yelp of pain as the flex bit into her hand, she yanked the mike off the end of the wire, pulled it free and stomped off into the wings, while the cameras followed her every step and the studio audience threw empty styrofoam cups. She was just about to slam out of the door when the length of wire she was trailing behind her snaked into the coils of spaghetti hanging out of the sound desk.

There was a sudden cracking noise, a puff of smoke and a big fat blue spark, which travelled along the wire and, catastrophically, up her skirt.

'Hey,' said the MC, pulling out his handkerchief and holding it over his nose. 'A big hand, people, please for Old . . .'

CHAPTER ELEVEN

Not long after his death, Wesley woke up.

He was lying on the grass. A very faint breeze was blowing, just enough to be noticed. Above him, a pine tree rose straight towards the sky, its branches scattering the sunlight. He tried to turn his head, and found he couldn't.

Panic.

Finally, when he'd found that none of him would move, and despair had taken possession of his mind and was measuring the insides of his eyes for new curtains, he stared down his nose and saw why.

Mostly, it was the ivy. For example, it was so hopelessly intertwined with the enormously long, straggly white beard he appeared to have grown at some stage that it anchored his head as effectively as a nail driven through his forehead. Other parts of the same ivy had overgrown his arms and legs, so that he lay under a sort of woven harness of the stuff like Daddy on the beach, buried in sand by his offspring while he slept. Some enterprising bird or animal had used his hair as nest lining material without first severing it from his head, with the result that there was a substantial build-up of twigs and leaves round his ears.

Although he couldn't see them, he was prepared to bet he had fingernails and toenails like the quintessential wicked witch, all long and curled and brittle. There was a beetle strolling up and down his nose, and there was nothing he could do about it.

Hair, beard and nails grow after death, they say; a curious fact which explains why the hairdressers of the great kings and pharaohs of the heroic age were buried side by side with their masters. Wesley ran a quick mental status check: unable to move, plus substantial hair growth, ditto nails suspected. But he was too well preserved in other respects to be dead; and besides, he was still breathing. There was also something else –

Ah yes, the noise. By his ear, something was buzzing with quiet persistence. It was a nondescript sound, but vaguely familiar. He concentrated on it, and had just worked out a hypothesis when the noise changed, proving his theory correct.

It wasn't going bzzzzzzzz any more; it was going *gloop-gloop-gloop-aargh*. It was a Teasmaid.

'Hello,' said the beetle on his nose. 'Sleep well?'

Wesley managed to bump-start the muscles he needed to talk with. 'Huh?' he said.

'Sleep well? Actually, that's a pretty dumb question. Still, you'll feel a bit more lively after you've had a nice hot cup of tea. That's one of your nice English customs, a cup of tea first thing after you wake up.'

'Asleep?' Wesley grunted. 'How long?'

'A hundred and sixteen years,' the beetle replied. 'I'm afraid you missed the whole of the twenty-first century. Still, it was very popular, so I expect they'll repeat it again soon. I'm assuming you've got cable?'

'A hundred and sixteen . . .?'

The beetle waggled its mandibles, presumably by way of confirmation. 'Rather longer than originally scheduled,' it said. 'You see, the idea is that by the time you wake up, everybody you could possibly have known will be long dead. Thanks to the wonders of twenty-first-century medicine, though, everybody lived much longer than ever before, so you've had to have a bit of a lie-in.'

'Just a minute,' Wesley croaked. His vocal cords, unlubricated for over a century, were scarcely functional, so that he sounded like Lee Marvin singing 'Wandering Star' with a sore throat. 'Everybody dead?'

'As nail in door,' the beetle replied cheerfully. 'But that's not going to worry you, is it? I mean, you always reckoned you never liked any of them anyway.'

Wesley's mind was moving sluggishly, but even so the big triangular warning sign that read *Rip Van Winkle* was rushing up towards him at one hell of a rate. 'What's happening?' he rasped, 'Who –?'

'At any rate,' continued the beetle, 'you missed the war; and anyway, it wasn't too bad here. Far enough away from a major city for there not to be much fall-out. Actually, the war was something of an anticlimax. Twenty-five per cent survival rate, as it turned out. Well, not here in America, of course, more like fifteen. But in Australia they got away with twenty-nine per cent, and Iceland scarcely copped it at all. I expect you'd like to try moving about now.' The beetle peered about, lifting its two front legs into the air. 'What we really need is a goat, they'll eat *anything*. A nice patch of brambles like that'd be like smoked salmon and caviare to a goat these days.'

'The war? What war?'

'What *war*?' The beetle scrabbled furiously with its front legs, then dropped down again. 'Of course, you don't know, do you? *The* war. The *big* war. World War – now let me see,' it added, counting. 'You know, it's at times like these you realise how useful it is having six feet. World War Five.'

'Five?' Wesley's jaw dropped as far as its beard-and-ivy cradle would allow. 'What about Three and Four, then?'

'Huh? Oh, right. Three and Four. Well, Three was something and nothing, really, except of course that your place, funny L-shaped island with a frilly top, it's on the tip of my – Britain, that's it. Doubleyou-doubleyou-three was more or less the end of the road as far as Britain went. And that other place. Um . . .'

'Ireland?'

'Europe. Still, no great loss, it was all worn out anyway. Doubleyou-doubleyou-four was when Japan and China and all those places got broken; and really, that was what ushered in the Forty GoldenYears of Prosperity for the US of A, because with no Europe and no Far East to get under our feet and keep asking us for favours, we could really get on with our lives, you know? All told, it was a pity it had to end. I suppose –'

'Yes?'

'I suppose,' said the beetle, thoughtfully, 'if we can't find a goat, a sheep would do. One of the new sheep. That's if you're feeling brave.'

In spite of the heavy traffic through the still heavily coned highways of his mind, Wesley was still able to spare a few million brain cells to pick up on that one. 'Why would I have to be feeling brave about sheep?' he said. 'Goats, yes, up to a point. But sheep –?'

'Ah,' said the beetle smugly, 'these are different sheep. You see, they inherited the earth.'

'I beg your pardon?'

'Well, it was promised them. I'm not saying they wanted it; I expect they'd have been happier with some furniture or a few pictures or a clock or something. But it said in the book of words, the meek shall inherit the earth. And they did.'

'Ah '

'But I've got to admit, it didn't make them nicer people, I mean animals.' The beetle opened its wing-case and closed it again. 'Isn't that always the way, when people inherit things? Never makes them happy. No, they changed.'

'They did?'

'Oh yes.' The beetle see-sawed backwards and forwards on its middle legs, as if nodding. 'They grew, for a start. Ten feet high at the shoulder they are now, fifteen some of them. And of course there was precious little grass left for them to eat, so they had to turn carnivorous.'

'Car –? You mean, they eat *meat*?'

'Most definitely,' replied the beetle, repeating the middle-legs manoeuvre. 'That's why there's no humans at all left in New Zealand. Plus, all their hair fell out, so they took to wearing human skins to keep themselves warm.'

'Dear God!'

'Very good at it, mind,' added the beetle. 'They make lovely thick coats and warm fleecy gloves and manskin-lined boots and everything. In fact,' the beetle went on, waving its mandibles at Wesley's abundant hair, 'I don't really think you'd want to meet a sheep right now. You know what they say, temptation beyond endurance. First thing you know, they'd make a three-piece suit out of you. Jesus, they're almost as bad as the lemmings.' The beetle rubbed its back legs together in an agitated manner. 'Believe me,' it said. 'You *don't* want to meet the lemmings.'

A surge of horror coursed through Wesley's nerves, like a bolt of lightning shinning up a strip of copper. A nanosecond behind it, taking its time and refusing to get excited, came a small detachment of cynicism. *Just a minute,* it was saying, *it's sheep we're talking about, right? Piano-stool-sized woolly nitwits who make town hall clerks seem intelligent, and the electorate look like they have a mind of their own. Come on, now, think about it.*

Wesley thought about it.

'This is one of those alternative futures, right?' he suggested cautiously. 'It hasn't happened yet, but it might *if.* Any minute now, Dr Sam Beckett will appear in a cloud of blue sparks, looking confused.'

The beetle vanished, and was replaced by a girl. Wesley was starting to feel fed up at the sight of her.

'Well done,' she said. 'That's more or less it, though I don't quite get the Beckett reference. Didn't he write gloomy plays about men in dustbins?'

Wesley shrugged. 'I don't think they showed that one in the UK. Anyhow, the point is that I *haven't* been asleep for a hundred and something years, and the world *isn't* terrorised by giant mutant killer sheep. Or at least,' he added, before the girl could speak, 'not in my universe it isn't. Please tell me I've got it right.'

The girl nodded. 'But,' she said, 'this is what *will* happen, unless something's done about it. You might say this future hasn't actually gone into production yet, but they've commissioned the script and started auditioning for the leading roles.'

Wesley mused on this for a moment. 'When you say something's got to be done about it, I have this awful feeling that what you really mean is that *I've* got to do something.'

'Not just you,' replied the girl, cheerfully. 'There's the others too. Well, two of them.'

'Ah yes.' Wesley frowned thoughtfully. 'I've been meaning to ask about that. Who are these others I keep bumping into? There's that lawyer I nearly had the fight with –'

'Calvin Dieb.'

'Right, yes. And the, um, girl.'

'Janice DeWeese.'

'Thank you. And the mad woman with the submarines, and the Indian, Talks To Squirrels . . .'

'The submarines lady is Linda Lachuk, and she's the fourth. Talks is, like, staff. So are all the others. It's just the four of you that's customers.'

'I see.' Wesley chewed his lower lip. 'And we're all sharing this horrible game, are we?'

'Not quite,' the girl said. 'You each get a set of experiences custom-fitted to your own problems and inadequacies. But we use the same sets and the same cast, is all.'

'Bit cheapskate, that, isn't it? Touch of the B-movie syndrome there, I'd have said.'

'Not at all,' the girl replied severely. 'Let's just say we're economical with fiction. And all that's beside the point. The point is, Phase Four involves saving the world, otherwise you don't get your grades.'

'I love your sense of perspective,' Wesley muttered. 'You're saying that unless we save civilisation as we know it, you'll send us to bed without any pudding. Anyway, what've we got to do? And I might as well warn you, if it involves dogs or spiders, you can count me out. Let the lawyer do it.'

'No dogs,' sighed the girl, 'and no spiders. Look, do you want me to explain, or would you rather we spent the last few hours before the point of no return finding fault with each other? It's all the same to me, because I can be a sheep just as easily as a human.'

'Explain,' Wesley said. 'Please.'

The girl shrugged. 'I was trying to,' she said. 'But you kept talking. The point is, doubleyou-doubleyou Five was a direct result of doubleyou-doubleyou Four, and doubleyou-doubleyou Four was the inevitable consequence of doubleyou-doubleyou Three. And doubleyou-doubleyou Three is due to be caused in about nine hours. Here, in Iowa.' She smiled, and added, 'Oh, and in case you were wondering, this is for real. Not a drill. OK?'

Wesley closed his eyes, trying to get his mind round it all. It was a bit like trying to fit a grand piano in a sock, but he did his best. 'All right,' he said. 'And what's going to happen in nine hours?'

'Quite simple,' said the girl. 'A top-flight attack journalist, writing for a leading schlock-horror New York tabloid, will put out this beautifully crafted, absolutely convincing story about global conspiracies and illicit arms shipments and Papal Armageddon and organised crime infiltration of Government and Lord knows what else. And, because the sheep and the lemmings actually inherited the Earth a long time ago but keep getting mistaken for people, the story goes over big. Networks all over the world pick it up. It gets splashed all over everywhere; which is a pity, because there's a lot in it you could take offence to if you happen to be, say, a small but well-armed non-aligned nation. Next thing you know, governments in all continents are issuing categorical denials, which is like having an affidavit from God that it's all true, as far as the media's concerned. In a frighteningly short time there's the usual media-induced hysteria – did you know it was that bunch of criminal psychotics who actually decide what happens on this planet, by the way? Not so much a democracy as a mediocracy. Then there'll be diplomatic incidents, and trigger-happy border patrols coming to blows all round the edges of four continents. After that it's only a matter of time before buttons get pressed, and, hey presto, the thing that just whizzed by in a puff of black smoke was the Third World War. Very short war, that was. Forty minutes after it had started, there wasn't much left to blow up.'

Wesley sat still for a long twenty seconds. 'I see,' he said. 'And this pillock journalist, the one we've got to stop; that wouldn't be the submarine fancier – what was her name again?'

'Linda Lachuk.'

'Fine. And how are we supposed to stop her sending in her copy?'

The girl grinned. 'That's easy,' she said. 'You kill her.'

Calvin Dieb opened his eyes.

For a moment, he was confused; but, active as ever, his brain was ready with two alternative explanations, both of which fitted the available data like a Florentine glove, almost before his eyelids were fully up.

Explanation One was that he'd died and gone to Heaven.

Explanation Two was that – finally – he'd woken up, and normality had been restored, we apologise for any inconvenience.

He looked again. Both explanations were wrong. Damn.

It had seemed promising at first, because the first thing he'd seen had been a judge's table on a raised dais under the good ol' Stars and Stripes. He was, in other words, in a courtroom; and yes, there was the jury hutch, there was the witness box, there were the cops and there were the cameras.

And there, unfortunately, was where the comforting illusion of reality faded; because he was sitting at the defendant's table and the man he was sitting next to was also, apparently, Calvin Dieb. Likewise the prosecutor. As far as he could see, he was the one on trial here. The good news was, he had Calvin Dieb to defend him. And the bad news was, Calvin Dieb was the prosecutor.

He tugged the sleeve of the Calvin Dieb next to him; the one who was lolling back in his chair doing the crossword. 'Hey,' he whispered urgently, 'what's –?'

'Shh.' He looked back at himself. 'Like I told you, stay cool. I got everything under control.' That smile; the one he'd practised in the mirror, all those years ago. 'Trust me,' he heard himself say. 'I'm your attorney.'

'Yes, but –'

Before he could complete the sentence, the usher called out, 'All stand,' and an automatic reflex operated the muscles of his knees.

Enter the judge.

In a way, he was relieved to find that the judge, unlike virtually everyone else in this nightmare, wasn't Calvin Dieb. Nor was he particularly surprised to see that the judge was, in fact, an otter. He wasn't even mildly perturbed when the otter, having taken its seat and found it couldn't see over the desk, shook itself and became a beautiful brown-haired girl.

The usher cleared her throat. 'In the matter of the Universe versus Calvin Dieb, Ms Justice Okeewana presiding.' Cameras started to whir. The judge leaned forward, and smiled.

'Mr Dieb,' she said, 'maybe it strikes you as odd that you've been executed first and tried afterwards. Let's just say I'm on a schedule, and this is the only way I could fit you in.' She turned her head, and nodded to the prosecutor. 'OK, Mr Dieb, you may begin.'

'Thank you.' The version of him on the other end of the table rose; and yes, damnit, it was Calvin Dieb; same smoothly oiled manner, same tactically perfect mannerisms. A stray thought, parked illegally in the back lots of his mind, wanted to know whether, since he was prosecutor, defendant and defence attorney, he'd be getting three fees, and if so, was there more of this kind of work available? A moment later, the stray thought was grabbed by the rest of the contents of Calvin's brain, and lynched. The prosecutor cleared his throat, as if he'd been conscious of the stray thought and had been waiting for it to subside, and placed his hands on the table, palms downwards. Do I do that? Yes, come to think of it, I do.

'Your honour,' the prosecutor said, 'the People's case against this man is exceptionally strong. We've all seen the evidence; from his business partner Hernan Piranha, who described him as, I quote, "a coyote". From his former wife, who referred to him as "pathetic" and told this court that he'd "always be nothing". From the victims of his ruthless ambition; the pharmaceuticals victims he cheated out of the compensation they so desperately needed, and his early guide and mentor, Leonard Threetrees, whom he callously ousted and, indeed, cold-bloodedly killed in front of this very court. We even have the testimony of Calvin Dieb senior, who cheerfully sent his own son to the electric chair.'

At Calvin's side, the defence attorney sprang to his feet. 'Objection,' he called out. 'In sentencing my client, witness was merely abiding by the rules of the game. There is no evidence to suggest that he did so cheerfully.'

Way to go, Cal, Calvin thought; but he didn't like the look on the prosecutor's face. It was his own malicious grin. Ah shit!

'Indeed,' the prosecutor said. 'As I recall, Mr Dieb senior's last words were, "Serve the little bugger right."' Oh Christ, Calvin thought, there's my very own triumphant smirk at the jury when I've just scored a really telling below-belt hit. 'Coming from the man's own father, members of the jury, don't you find that just a bit significant? Just a tad?'

Calvin looked round. The jury-box was, in fact, empty; but he felt he knew why without having to ask. It was because, no matter how weird the laws of physics might be in this lousy place, there's still no way you'd fit the entire population of the Universe into that little thing.

'But,' the prosecutor went on, 'the testimony I intend to rely on is that of the defendant himself. We've all seen and heard it, members of the jury. It speaks for itself.' He paused, like a lazy but skilful lion about to spring. 'That's what really makes this guy so much worse than all the other creeps and low-lifes we get in this court, because basically, even after everything he's been through, everything he's put everybody else through – and let's not forget those Vikings, members of the jury, for whose deaths he's solely responsible – he hasn't changed a bit. He's been scared, but he ain't sorry. The only thing that's been on his mind all along is to get his keys back and get the hell out of here, fast, before he wastes any more valuable, chargeable time. Even now, right this minute, there's a part of his evil little brain that's working out how he's gonna stick the last seven hours on Mr Lustmord's bill.'

Hey, how did he know that? Calvin wondered, and in so doing, knew the answer. Oh, but it was *depressing*. He glanced sideways at his defence attorney, who grinned back.

'I know,' his image whispered. 'But it's worse for me, 'cos I'm on a contingency fee.'

He was about to reply when he realised the prosecutor was looking straight at him. 'You heard that, members of the jury?' he said, with savage delight. 'Doesn't that just say it all? He hires himself to defend him, but he'll only get paid if he wins. I know he's a lawyer, sure, but what kind of guy sinks so low that he goes around ripping *himself* off? I don't think I really need to answer that one, folks. Just take a look and see for yourselves. The Universe rests.'

There was a moment of embarrassed silence; then the defence attorney stood up and addressed the bench. 'Your honour,' he said, 'if I can just confer with my colleague for a moment? Thank you.'

The two Calvin Diebs stood up and went off into a huddle over by the witness box; then the prosecutor sat down again, while the defence approached the bench. Although he was whispering to the judge, Calvin could hear every word.

'It's like this, your honour,' he was saying. 'It seems my colleague's on a contingency basis too, so we've agreed to split the fee between us and I'll throw the trial. I trust that meets with your approval? In the interests of justice, I mean.'

The judge nodded. 'Sure thing,' she said. 'Last thing anybody wants is for the scumbag to walk.'

Calvin – the Calvin Calvin hoped was the real Calvin jumped to his feet and started to protest, whereupon the court cop leaned over and dealt him a horrendous blow on the head with his nightstick. The last thing he remembered seeing in this life was the jury-box, crammed to bursting with the entire population of the Universe (Hey! Get a load of those guys from Ursa Minor! Count those prehensile ears!) and they were all waving and cheering like mad.

The defence attorney gathered up his papers, nodded to his colleague and left the court.

The prosecutor stood for a moment, looking down at the file open before him, and then across at the body slumped over the table, dead as a manifesto promise in mid-term. Then he felt something in his left hand, and unclenched his fist.

It was a set of keys.

He looked up at the judge, who nodded. 'You'll have to split them with the rest of you,' she said. 'That's the part of you that was prepared to sell the rest of you down the river, remember, so I guess your problems aren't entirely over. Still, it's an improvement. How about if you keep the ignition key and give him the filler cap key and the mascot?'

'He can have the mascot,' Calvin Dieb replied solemnly. 'We'll negotiate for the rest.'

'So long, Calvin.'

Calvin inclined his head. 'So long,' he said. 'And thanks, I guess. If ever there's anything I can –'

'You'll be sorry you said that,' answered the judge.

'Hey, it was just a figure of –'

Calvin vanished.

When Janice rematerialised, she found herself back in the forest. Having looked round carefully to make sure there were no Vikings, motorcyclists, eagles, doctors, gameshow hosts or other pests anywhere to be seen, she sat down on the trunk of a fallen tree, crossed her arms and waited to see what would happen next.

She didn't have long to wait. About twenty seconds later, she heard a soft hissing noise down by her ankle, looked down and saw a hat.

'Pst!' it was saying.

She frowned. There was something in the hat's demeanour – the angle of its brim, perhaps, or the slight droop in its feather – that suggested that it was about to try and sell her life insurance.

'Well?' she said.

'Wanna buy a map?'

Janice started. 'What kind of map?' she asked cautiously. 'If it's one where X marks the spot, and there's dead men's chests and so on, I really don't want to know.'

The hat rotated half a turn clockwise, then swung back again. 'Nothing like that,' it said. 'Listen, it's a map of how to get out of here. Only five hundred bucks. Guaranteed. No quibble warranty. This does not affect your statutory . . .'

'*Really* out of here?' Janice demanded. 'You mean, back into real life, where I don't have to hide in the bushes every time a male squirrel runs along a tree, just in case it falls in love with me and follows me about?'

The hat tilted backwards and forwards. 'User-friendly,' it urged. 'Easy to read, guaranteed not to crease or tear if used in accordance with manufacturer's directions.'

The frown on Janice's face thickened into a scowl, as if cornflour had been added. 'I don't care if it glows in the dark and hums Scott Joplin so long as it shows me the way out,' she replied irritably. 'Here, let's have a look.'

'Oh no you don't,' said the hat, moving back a pace or two. 'If you look at the map, you see the way out and you don't buy.'

'Forget it, then,' Janice said, forcing herself to sound indifferent. 'You see, unless I actually look at the map, I won't know if it's what you say it is. It's not that I'm calling you a liar,' she added quickly, as the hat started to vibrate. 'But you're a hat, for Chrissakes. How'd you know it's really real? For all I know, hat, you could be talking through yourself.'

'No money,' said the hat sadly, 'no deal.'

'Tell you what. I'll give you fifty bucks. How does that sound?'

'Insulting,' replied the hat sulkily. 'Hey, lady, what d'you do in your spare time when you aren't pulling gift horses' lips apart and sticking little mirrors in their mouths?'

Janice yawned. 'All right,' she said, 'seventy-five. But that's my last offer, 'cos that's all I got.'

'Seventy-five lousy bucks for your dream come true?' The hat slowly rotated. 'Lady, I *know* you're gonna be sorry. This is a once-only offer, remember, so . . .'

'What did you say?'

'Once-only offer,' the hat repeated. 'You're gonna be sorry.'

'No, before that.'

'Seventy-five lousy bucks for your dream come true?'

'That's the bit,' Janice said. 'Look, I can do seventy-five bucks cash, and the rest by card . . .'

The hat sniggered. 'Sorry, lady,' it said. 'Strictly cash. So long.'

'No, wait –'

The hat wasn't there any more. Janice looked for it under the repulsive-looking yellow fungus it had been leaning against, but there was no sign. She swore quietly and stood up, reasoning that if nobody was going to come and collect her, she might as well go and find somebody. With luck, whoever she found might be neither malevolent nor crazy. You never knew.

'Excuse me.'

She whirled round, overbalanced, and slipped, ending up in an undignified stack directly on top of the repulsive fungus. She looked up, and saw a man –

The hell with it; a *dazzlingly handsome, incredibly gorgeous* man in – she hated to have to admit it, but they were princely robes. He had a small gold crown nestling in the equally golden curls of his hair, and he was flanked on both sides by footmen in fancy dress and powdered wigs. And one of them was carrying a cushion.

And on the cushion –

'Excuse me,' the prince repeated, adorably, 'but would you mind awfully just, um, putting your foot in this, how shall I put it, slipper? That's if you don't mind, of course. I'd hate to think I was imposing, or anything.'

Janice stared at what was on the cushion as if it had been her head rather than a glass slipper. Not that it was what she'd call a slipper; where she came from, slippers had no backs and soft pink fur, and you kicked them under your bed when friends dropped by because you'd die of shame if they saw them. This object had a three-inch heel.

'Is that what I think it is?' she asked quietly.

The prince looked at her curiously. 'I don't know,' he said. 'That depends on what you think it is, surely.'

'I think it's the glass slipper left behind by the beautiful but mysterious maiden you danced with last night,' Janice muttered. 'Am I warm?'

'I don't know. If I had a thermometer we could take your temperature, I suppose.'

Janice frowned ever so slightly. 'No,' she said, 'what I

meant was, am I sort of right about the shoe? And the beautiful but mysterious maiden and all that.'

The prince nodded. 'I expect you heard the pronouncement,' he said, and his voice was like that soft rustling as you pull out the thin bit of corrugated cardboard they put into boxes of chocolates to stop the coffee creams getting squished in transit. 'I had it pronounced all over the kingdom, you see. I imagine you heard it somewhere, sort of out of the corner of your ear. Subliminally, I think they call it.'

Janice nodded. The footman advanced, bearing the cushion. Janice unlaced her left sensible walking shoe. The footman lifted the slipper off the cushion.

'Actually,' Janice said, as the footman slid the slipper over her toes, 'there's something that puzzles me. Mind if I ask you to explain it to me?'

'By all means,' replied the prince, smiling stunningly.

'Well,' Janice said, as the back of the slipper nestled up against her heel like a cat after the tinned salmon you're just easing out of the can, 'it's like this. You danced with this girl all night, and you thought she was so gorgeous you couldn't live without her, so you're searching the kingdom till you find her, yes?'

'That's right.'

'Your Majesty,' hissed the footman with respectful urgency. 'The slipper, your Maj —'

'OK,' Janice said. 'If she made this amazingly deep impression on you, how come the only way you can recognise this person is by whether or not a shoe fits her foot? I mean, wouldn't you be better off looking at girls' faces and seeing if maybe something goes *ching!* in the old memory banks? Quite apart from the fact that this slipper's a standard 5C fitting, which means that in the USA alone there's upwards of a million and a half girls it'd fit like a glove. Had you considered either of those points, by any chance.?'

'Your Majesty,' the footman persevered, maybe just a little louder, 'the slipper. It fi –'

'Gosh,' said the prince, biting his lip. 'I hadn't thought of that. Had you, Murdoch?'

'No, Your Majesty,' replied the other footman.

'How about you, Skellidge?'

The footman with the slipper didn't sigh; footmen, like Mr Spock, don't show emotion. But there was just the faintest hint in the way he didn't say anything, move or make a sound that implied the words, *Oh shit, here we go.* 'No, Your Majesty,' he said. 'If Your Majesty would care to look, Your Majesty might observe that the slipper fits.'

The prince started. 'It does?'

'Perfectly, Your Majesty.'

'Then – oh.' The Prince hesitated, and his divinely beautiful forehead crinkled. 'But, as the young lady just explained, that's not really conclusive evidence, is it?'

'No, Your Majesty.'

'All it does is whittle it down to a million and a half possible candidates.'

'Quite so, Your Majesty.'

'Just a moment,' Janice objected.

'Whereas,' the Prince went on, 'I really ought to be able to recognise the girl of my dreams when I see her, oughtn't I?'

'Yes, Your Majesty.'

'And,' the Prince went on, peering carefully at Janice's face, 'I'm afraid I can't remember ever having seen this young lady in my life before.' He sighed, and straightened up. 'Well anyway,' he said, 'it's not her, so we can eliminate her from our enquiries. So that leaves just –'

'One million, four hundred and ninety-nine thousand, nine hundred and ninety-nine to go, Your Majesty. In North America, that is. Elsewhere in the world . . .'

'Quite.' The Prince nodded gravely. 'Miss,' he said, turning to Janice, 'I'm most dreadfully obliged to you. You see, I was all set to marry the first girl this thing fitted, and then love her devotedly for ever. Thanks to you, though . . .'

Janice thought about that, and was left with the feeling you sometimes get when you've just turned the ignition key, and the key snaps cleanly off in your hand. 'On reflection,' she said feebly, 'I can see a few obvious flaws in my logic, so perhaps you shouldn't pay any attention to a word I say. In fact, if I were you I'd wipe it from my mind completely.'

The Prince smiled again; so warm a smile, you could dry socks over it. 'You're far too modest, Miss,' he said. 'It's only your clear thinking and exceptional insight that's saved me from making a truly, truly horrible mistake. I really am most awfully grateful.'

'Yes; but . . .'

With a grunt so soft that only a bat with a hearing aid could have heard it, the footman removed the slipper, wiped it out with a lace kerchief, and laid it carefully back on the cushion. 'And as a small gesture of appreciation,' the Prince went on, 'on behalf of the Kingdom as well as myself?'

'Yes?' Janice demanded breathlessly.

'I'd like you to accept this ten-dollar book token, with my compliments.' He snapped his fingers, whereupon the second footman stepped forward, put a white envelope in Janice's hand, bowed at an angle of precisely twenty-one degrees, and stepped back again.

'Gee,' Janice said, in a low, thin monotone. 'I don't know what to say.'

The Prince beamed at her. 'Think nothing of it,' he said. 'All right, Murdoch, back the way we came. There's an old chateau about three miles along the top road we haven't tried yet.' He was about to walk off, but turned and gave Janice a long, thrilling look. 'And don't worry,' he added, with a flash of his sparkling eyes. 'I feel sure that one day your prince will come. Just you wait and see.'

'You reckon?'

The Prince shrugged. 'Who knows? Don't give up the day job, though. Skellidge, the route map.'

The little procession departed, leaving Janice standing there doing active volcano impressions. It wasn't so much that she'd just trodden on the happy ending, she decided, as the fact that she'd been right, and they'd punished her for it. That made her think about the doctor, the one who'd been here since World War One just because he wanted to make people better. Then she remembered that she'd also turned down the offer of a ridiculously cheap escape out of all of this, and began to whimper.

She was snuffling away like a chain-smoking baby seal when a soft cough behind her made her turn. There, damnit, were Murdoch, Skellidge and the Prince.

'Excuse me,' said the Prince.

She looked at him warily. She knew what was coming; he had that dreadful pink-hearts-and-plastic-flowers look in his eyes that she had come, in a relatively short space of time, to know rather well.

'Um,' she said.

'I hope you don't mind me asking,' he said, 'but, um, what are you doing for dinner this evening?'

Janice took a deep breath. Oh, she reflected, it would be

so easy. After all, he was unspeakably attractive and his voice was like a violet-scented breeze humming in the neck of an empty milk bottle and all the cloudless skies of summer were reflected in his deep blue eyes –

'Huh?' she asked.

'Only,' he went on, 'if you're not frightfully busy I happen to know this really rather nice Sumatran restaurant where they do this really authentic . . .'

And not only the Prince. Skellidge was gazing at her like a lovesick traffic bollard, and Murdoch was respectfully pining away before her very eyes. Aaagh! she thought.

'Sorry,' she replied quickly. 'I'm, um, busy. I'm meeting someone. My, er, boyfriend. Well, when I say boyfriend, really I mean to say husband. He's a prince too, you know; or rather, more like a king. An emperor, actually. Sorry about that. Another time, perhaps.'

The Prince gave her a smouldering look down the side of his perfect nose. 'An emperor, huh?'

'That's right.'

'Anybody I'd have heard of? I know most of the emperors in these parts.'

Janice swallowed. 'Oh, he's not from round here,' she said, as casually as she could. 'Actually, our empire's ever such a long way away, in, um, Australia, but we're on a state visit, and there's this dreary old diplomatic function we've got to go to, so . . .'

'I see,' replied the Prince. 'In that case, I shall make a point of seeking out this emperor, putting him to the edge of the sword and claiming you for my own. Murdoch, mobilise the army. Skellidge, declare war on Australia. In fact,' he added, brightly, 'we could all save a lot of time, if I abducted you now and we did the fighting later. Would that be all right with you? It's just as well,' he added, 'that we've just finished upgrading our first strike capability, because that means my FT62s will have taken out Melbourne and Brisbane before we've finished our prawn cocktails. You do like prawn cocktails, I hope, only I've taken the liberty of ordering . . .'

'Hold it,' Janice said. 'Are you seriously telling me you'd bomb Australia and kill thousands of people just to get me?'

The Prince nodded. 'It's traditional,' he added. 'That's how a Prince shows he really cares. A declaration of war says more than flowers ever can.'

'Ah.'

'That's what all girls really want, you see. Well-known fact. Is this the face that launched a thousand bombs and burned the topless towers of Adelaide? That's psychology, you see. You need to know that sort of stuff when you hold the lives of millions in the palm of your hand.'

'I see.' Janice nodded slowly. 'You don't feel that killing thousands of people, as against the more usual bunch of flowers and box of chocolates, isn't maybe a bit . . . ?'

The Prince shook his head slowly. 'For beauty such as yours,' he said softly, 'what other tribute could there possibly be? You were born to be fought for –'

'You mean, like the Gaza Strip, sort of thing?'

'No,' snapped the Prince. 'Like Helen of Troy, except that you outshine Helen as the sun outshines the furthest star. And we've got to make sure that the body-count reflects that.'

'Right,' Janice said, walking slowly backwards. 'I hear what you say, but –'

'In fact,' whispered the Prince dreamily, 'on reflection I can't see that anything short of an all-out nuclear holocaust wouldn't be a positive insult. Murdoch, the smart missiles, quickly!'

As Murdoch bowed and produced an attaché case that opened to reveal a miniature control console with a shiny red button in the middle of it, Janice couldn't help wondering why the sheep on the hillside opposite were looking at her and rubbing their front hooves together.

CHAPTER TWELVE

L inda Lachuk opened her eyes.

So much, she reflected bitterly, for the ultimate scoop. At the precise moment when she connected with the live wire and felt a billion or so volts start to pump through her body, the thought uppermost in her mind had been that she was on the verge of getting the inside story on the biggest feature of them all; namely Death. *Hell*, she'd said to herself as she felt her heart stop beating, *if only there was some way to get my copy in, I'd die happy* –

And here she was, alive and apparently none the worse for wear, and she couldn't remember a thing about it. What, she wondered, had happened to her during that unquantified lost time? Had she died and gone to Heaven? Had she been chucked out of Heaven back down to Earth for pushing her way through the crowd of angels gathered round the celestial throne and demanding that God admit to his complicity in the Vaticangate scandal?

Hmmm –

Nah. Not without something like corroborative evidence. She'd probably be able to sell it to the California papers, but it wouldn't cut any ice in NewYork.

She sat up and looked about her; nothing but trees, rocks and the lake, lying flat on its back like a giant mirror.

Query; if you fall into a giant mirror, does that mean seven years' bad luck? If so, it would explain the rotten day she was having. So close, so very close to a story that'd guarantee her the Pulitzer Prize, and yet there was something she couldn't quite . . .

She stood up. Overhead, a thick wedge of ducks circled, watching her. A stream of bubbles a few yards from the shore showed the passage of an otter like a vapour trail. For a fleeting, treacherous moment, Linda wondered whether she mightn't have been better off right from the start if she'd gone into nature features instead of current affairs. From where she stood she could see yards, literally yards of potentially award-winning copy: waterfowl clowning adorably, small mammals furrily fornicating, butterflies doing whatever the hell it is butterflies do. Goddamnit, Linda thought bitterly, people get up and make cups of tea while a man stands talking into a lonely lens in the middle of some East European battle; but let someone go creeping up on a bunch of gorillas and the nation holds its breath. So what? Where the hell's the *story* in wildlife?

And then she noticed something.

The ducks weren't circling because she was there; it was the small party of men in faded green cotton shorts, wearing wide-brimmed hats with corks dangling from them, that had flushed them off the lake. And the string of bubbles wasn't an otter. It was a periscope.

Instinctively, Linda dropped to her knees, grinding her shin against a pointy rock as she did so. She didn't feel the pain; all Pain got was her answering machine, because she was far too preoccupied to take any notice. As carefully as she could, she crawled downhill towards the water's edge.

'G'day.'

Linda froze. Even the blood in her veins stood still.

'I said, G'day, miss. Where d'you want it?'

Slowly as a lazy glacier on its way to the dentist's, Linda turned her head. She was looking at a pair of plastic open-toed beach sandals. Raising her head a trifle, she could see a pair of brown hairy knees.

'Sorry?' she said.

'This flamin' block of stone,' the man said patiently. 'Where d'you want us to put it?'

'I . . . I'm not sure,' Linda stuttered. 'H-haven't made up my mm –'

The man gave her a long look, such as you'd use on a particularly stupid log. 'Tell you what,' he said. 'You just sign for it, here.' A clipboard moved down until it was on a level with her nose. 'Then we can be on our way, and you can put the ruddy thing wherever you want, soon as you've made your mind up. Got a pen?'

'Pen,' Linda repeated, trying to remember what a pen was. 'Oh, right, yes. Thank you, I have got a pen, yes.'

The man sighed. 'Then why don't you get it out and sign me flamin' chit? That's it, you got it. OK darlin', it's all yours. Careful with it, mind, it's all bombs and rockets and things inside.'

'What?' Linda shrieked; but the man wasn't there any more. In his place stood a huge concrete block, out of which were sticking nosecaps and tailfins and small areas of side panel with DANGER stencilled on them. As Linda crawled over to it, she noticed an envelope Sellotaped to the side; she ripped it open, unfolded the paper inside and read –

Delivery Note
Express delivery FOB to St Peters, Rome
Tractor spares
For the personal attention of His Holiness Shane III
Do not bend, drop or expose to naked flame

– all underneath an official-looking crest with an eagle and E PLURIBUS UNUM involved in it. Linda folded the note carefully, as if it were God's signed confession, and tucked it away in her top pocket.

Tractor spares! Hah! That's what they always say!

Well now, she said to herself, running a hand down the side of the block just to make sure it was really real, you wanted hard evidence, here it is. Now there's just the problem of how the hell to get it back home and in front of a camera. Piece of cake? Well, not quite.

Indiana Jones, she mused, never seems to worry about this sort of thing; and neither does James Bond, or the guys in Westerns who discover wagonloads of Confederate gold buried in the heart of the desert. The camera fades out, and the next shot is either THE END or our hero snogging the girl in a gondola floating down the Canal Grande. There's a cinematic convention that allows you to assume that somehow or other the heavy lifting gets done, the treasure is all neatly packed up in tea-chests and shipped back home, without even a squeak out of the customs men. Getting back to civilisation from here *without* a twenty-ton concrete block was probably going to turn out to be a bigger adventure than anything Mister Bond ever did in his life; and even if she somehow succeeded in getting this infernal megalith out to the airport and onto the plane, the baggage handlers at New York would probably manage to send it to Fort Worth along with the rest of her luggage, the way they usually did.

Which was something of a nuisance, all told, bearing in mind that she was the only person standing between civilisation as we know it and global Armageddon.

A bit over the top? Not likely; because unless she could somehow get this evidence away, break the story and stop the shipments, there could only be one outcome. Because whatever His Holiness wanted with all this hardware, it wasn't to turbo-charge his Massey-Ferguson, and it wasn't to hang on the Vatican wall. So; newshound to the rescue. It crossed her mind that, for most of the time at least, Superman was also a journalist. Must sort of go with the territory.

She gazed up at the block. Portable it wasn't. Rather, it was the sort of thing the Pharaohs used to build pyramids with. Even in the centre of Queens you could leave it lying about in the street for ten minutes and be pretty sure it'd still be there when you got back.

This was going to call for some imaginative thinking.

She thought for a while. Her imagination, quicker than lightning and, as often as not, every bit as destructive, graunched into action. She had an idea.

She stood up and walked down the hill.

The men in hats were still hanging about, muttering among themselves. The periscope was now about eighteen inches above water level. The ducks had slung their collective hook, but a couple of whitetail deer were standing tentatively on the opposite side of the lake, watching and looking as if they were making up their minds to write to somebody about it. Enter Linda, walking briskly.

'Hey,' she called out, 'you.'

'*G'day.*'

'You guys,' Linda snapped, fiddling with the large bit of tree-bark she'd managed to make look something like a clipboard. 'Quit loafing about there, and help me get the stuff on to the sub.'

Two of the hatted men looked at each other. One of them shrugged, and spat into the water. It was at this point that Linda reached in her pocket and brought out money.

'Where's the stuff you want shifted?'

'Over there,' she replied. 'Careful with it, there's bombs and all sorts.' The money vanished from her hand as quickly and completely as the ham from your sandwich when the pub cat's taken a fancy to it, and a moment later the submarine had surfaced and the block was being winched aboard on a derrick. Although her face remained a mask of polite disinterest, deep in her heart Linda allowed herself a huge, smug grin. True, the money was everything she'd had; until she could get to a bank, she was as broke as a child's toy on Boxing Day. It was worth the risk, though; and besides, fairly soon, sums like that would be too small for her to comprehend.

'Is that the lot?' demanded one of the men in hats.

'That's it,' Linda replied. 'OK, then, I'll just –'

Before the words had cleared the gate of her teeth, the conning tower hatch slammed shut, and the submarine slid under the water with the speed and grace of a diving otter, until only a string of sparkling silver bubbles remained to suggest that it had ever been there.

'Hang on,' Linda shouted, bewildered. 'Wait for me!'

The cork-hats looked at each other. 'You wanted to go too, huh?' they said.

'Yes, of course I do,' Linda snarled, jumping up and down on the spot. 'That's my evidence they've got in there.'

'You should have mentioned it,' observed the first cork-hat, reaching into a plastic coolbox and pulling out a can of beer. 'What a pity, eh?'

Linda stopped jumping for a moment and turned to him. 'Well, don't just sit there, you moron,' she yelled. 'Get on the radio and call them back.'

'Can't do that. Sorry. Against regulations.'

'The hell with – look, nobody'll know, couldn't you just –?'

The beer-drinker scratched the tip of his nose thoughtfully. 'Tell you what,' he said, 'for another three thousand –'

'I haven't got any more money, damnit,' Linda growled. 'I gave you every last penny –'

'Bloody cheapskate,' observed the cork-hat to his colleague sadly.

The colleague nodded, and stroked his beard. 'You wouldn't read about it,' he replied solemnly, as he retrieved a small yellow knob of chewing gum from the lining of his hat and began to chomp.

'Hey!'

The cork-hats stared at her blankly, shrugged and turned away. When Linda made further attempts to communicate they shooed her off with hand gestures and threw beer cans at her, a hint that even Linda felt she couldn't really ignore. Accordingly, she left, trailing her dreams like a bird with a broken wing.

Once she was safely out of earshot, the first Australian nudged his mate in the ribs with his elbow. 'Hey,' he said, 'how are we off for time? Actually, I got my Indian outfit on under this coat, so that's an extra minute or two.'

'So've I. Quick game of Goblins' Teeth?'

'Why not? Right then, nearest the nose to start.'

Linda meanwhile had reached the tree-line and carried on walking into the wood. She wasn't looking where she was going; understandably, because not only had she lost her evidence, she'd also arranged for the loading and despatch of enough thermo-nudear weaponry to blow up the world three times over. It's times like these, she told herself, I almost wish I'd stayed on the fashion page.

And, because she wasn't looking where she was going, she didn't see the cunningly disguised tripwire that released the bent-over sapling to which was attached the length of wire, the looped end of which Linda had just put her foot in. There was a twang, and a moment later she was hanging three feet off the ground, upside down, with reporter's accessories falling out of her pockets like heavy snow.

Any suggestions?

No?

Very well, she told her brain, in the manner of a teacher announcing that unless someone owned up she'd keep the whole class in after school, I'll just have to hang here till someone lets me go. She dangled, therefore, with the blood pumping through her head, like a solitary spider caught in a web put up secretly by the local flies' co-operative. One good thing, though; it gave her time to think before scampering off after that goddamned submarine.

There was a war in there; all neatly done up and packaged like sandwiches in a Tupperware box, but a war nonetheless. And it was thanks to her it was on its way, rather than just sitting beside the lake minding its own business.

She had to stop it. It wasn't just that the human race was only a matter of hours away from Armageddon. More to the point, that was her *story* in there.

First things first, however; there was the small matter of getting down out of this rope.

She considered her options and the resources available to her; which were? Difficult one, that. But, above all, she was a communicator, communicating was what she was good at. If she wanted out of here, it'd have to be a communication.

'*Help!*' she communicated.

'Hi,' said a voice below her. 'What're you doing up there?'

Linda opened her eyes. She'd been calling for so long that her voice had been sandpapered away, and most of the rest of her was so full of pins and needles that if only she could get down she'd be able to put all the haberdashery stores in the US out of business in a week.

'*Help*,' she whispered.

'Hey,' chimed the voice. 'Pleased to meet you, my name's Calvin Dieb.' Linda looked down and saw that Mr Dieb had stuck out a hand for a handshake.

'Can't move,' she moaned. 'Numb. Get me down.'

'Sure,' replied Mr Dieb. 'I'll need a ladder and maybe a knife or a pair of scissors. Haven't we met already?'

'Get me *down*.'

Mr Dieb nodded. 'No problem,' he said. 'A chair'll do if there's no ladder. You see, I just turned over a new leaf. Yessir, a whole new chapter's about to open in my life. From now on, I'm gonna change my attitude towards other people, especially people less fortunate than myself.'

'No chair. Please hurry. Going to –'

'No chair, huh? Pardon me asking, but how in blazes did you get yourself up there, anyhow?' Mr Dieb jumped a couple of times, reminding Linda of a small, yapping dog. 'Hey,' he said enthusiastically, 'maybe if I pull on this rope I could bend the tree down so you could – no, that's no good. I'd need someone else to hold the rope while I untie you, otherwise you'd just go *boing!* up in the air again. Still,' Mr Dieb continued, smiling cheerfully, 'there's gotta be a way, so if you'll just bear with me –'

Linda tried to move the pincushion that had once been her right arm; it was now so empty of blood, it would have served a vampire well as part of a rigorous calorie-controlled diet. 'Pull – rope,' she groaned, 'tie – to – tree.'

'Hah!' Mr Dieb tried to smother a giggle. 'Sorry, miss, I'm not laughing at you, don't do that kind of stuff anymore. You just reminded me of some red – Native Americans I ran into, is all. You sounded just like them, the way you were talking. Now, what was that you said? Pull on the rope and tie it to this tree here – hey, that's neat! Did I happen to mention I can see right up your skirt from here?'

Eventually, Linda hit the ground with a thump you could have felt through thick boots. Calvin Dieb got a substantial smack between the eyes from a branch of the sapling as it sprang back upright, but it didn't have much effect on his rate of speech or his born-again benevolence. Far from being annoyed, he blamed himself for being clumsy, and then helped Linda to her feet, nearly dislocating her shoulder in the process.

'Thanks,' she said, thereby proving that force of habit is the most durable thing on earth. 'Who are you, anyway?'

'Me? My name's Cal Dieb, I'm a lawyer.' The phrase, so automatic as to be faster than any conscious thought, seemed to jar on Calvin. He frowned. 'Well,' he said, 'up till now I've been a lawyer, but right at this moment I'm considering a change of direction in my life. You see, just lately – well, I won't bore you with all the pesky details, but I died, and now I'm just beginning to see how little I've really achieved in my life, you know, vis-à-vis making the world a better place. Actually, as far as I can see, not actively making the world a lousier place would probably be a giant leap forward for me in terms of personality development and realising my true potential as a human being, which I guess is why as of now I'm giving serious thought to doing something else, you know, feeding the poor and the sick and all. What do you think?'

'What do you know about the submarines?' Linda asked. As the words left her mouth, she wished she'd been really subtle and said it in an Australian accent, or Latin, just in case the guy replied in kind before he realised the implications. 'Are you with the Vatican?'

'Sorry?'

'The submarines,' Linda repeated. 'The big blocks of cement full of rockets. The Vatican.'

'The Vatican?'

She scrutinised Dieb's face closely, as if looking for secret microphones hidden among the hairs in his nose. 'You haven't seen any submarines?' she hazarded.

'Sorry.'

'Illegal arms shipments? Men in funny hats? Cool-boxes full of cans of beer?'

Dieb sighed. Here he was trying to help people, and his first effort was turning out to be a complete failure. 'I really wish I could be more help,' he said, with heartbreaking sincerity, 'but I guess the last thing you need is guys pretending to have seen submarines when they haven't, just because they think that's what you want to hear. Lawyers do that a lot, of course; you know, like, "Oh yeah, I think you've got some helluva case there," or, "No, I don't think it'll be all that expensive." Well, I'm through with all that from now on. When there's an unpalatable truth to be told, I'm just going to darned well out with it and tell it how it is. Like, really, what else is there in this life if to your own self you can't be true, huh? Don't you think so? Which is why, if I *do* decide to stay in the legal profession, I reckon I'm gonna start doing all that civil rights stuff, you know, oppressed minority groups and all? Take Native Americans, for example. You tell me, how many Native American judges are there in the whole of the City of New York?'

'Seventy-two,' Linda replied, remembering the figure from a feature she'd been working on. 'Sorry, how come we're talking about judges all of a sudden?'

Dieb hung his head. 'My fault,' he said. 'Sorry. There's me getting sidetracked when you're trying to ask me important questions. So I'll just shut up for a moment,' he said, settling himself comfortably against the trunk of a small rowan tree. 'Do please carry on with what you were saying.'

'What? Oh, er, right.' Linda wrinkled her nose, trying to remember. 'Illegal arms shipments,' she said. 'There was one here just a minute ago, but it went away. On a submarine.'

'I see.'

'I sent it, as a matter of fact.'

Dieb raised his eyebrows. 'Oh, I *see*,' he said, enlightened. 'You work for the Government.'

'No!' Linda replied angrily, 'I do *not* work for the Government, I just sort of accidentally got the arms loaded aboard the submarine.'

'By accident?'

'That's right.'

'Sort of an involuntary reflex action? Like Pavlov's dogs or something?'

Linda shook her head impatiently. 'I wanted to get the arms out of here so I could use them.'

'Really.' Dieb pursed his lips. 'How interesting.'

'As *evidence*,' Linda replied in exasperation. 'For the report I'm doing for the paper back home. You see, I'm a journalist.'

'Right,' Dieb said. 'So shipping arms is just a weekend job, then.'

'No, of course not. Like I told you, that was an accident. A mistake.'

Dieb smiled. It was an I-don't-believe-you-but-I-like-you-anyway smile, the sort you see a lot around mental hospitals. Rather a lot of Calvin Dieb's clients were familiar with that smile; the category of his clients whom you wouldn't believe if they told you the time while standing under the town clock. 'Ah well,' he said, 'don't suppose there's any harm done, so I wouldn't worry yourself about it if I were you.'

'Not *worry* about it!' Linda started to wave her arms about, as if she'd secretly always wanted to be a windmill but had never actually seen one. 'Jesus Christ, you fool, they're going to start *World War Three* with those weapons, and you say there's no harm done! We've got to stop them.'

'We've?'

'Well, who the hell else is there?' Linda stopped waving and flumped down on an anthill, her chin moodily cupped in her hands. 'Only, I don't see how we can. That submarine's probably halfway up Lake Erie by now.'

'Not unless it's really a salmon in disguise,' Calvin replied. 'For a start, there's an awful lot of waterfalls between here and the Lakes. Can't say as I can see how it's gonna get round them.'

'Waterfalls?'

Calvin nodded. 'That's places where the river kinda falls off a cliff, you know? Don't reckon as how the crew's going to be able to get out and carry a submarine down one of them. Can't see how you'd manage it even if you had a fleet of helicopters.'

Linda's face collapsed. It was as if she'd looked up at the

sky and had it fall in her face. 'But that can't be right,' she said, 'or how did the damn thing get this far in the first place?'

'Don't know.' Dieb shrugged. 'Maybe they built the thing here on the lake. I seem to remember the Germans built ships on site to sail up and down big lakes in Africa.'

'But . . .' Linda watched as, in her mind's perfectly focused eye, little charred fragments of her theory rained down all around her, like the scene in a Western where the bank robbers have used too much dynamite to blow the safe, and suddenly it's snowing banknotes. 'But I *saw* the sonofabitch thing, here, not five minutes ago. With my own eyes. There's got to have been a submarine, really.'

'I believe you,' Calvin replied. 'All I'm saying is, it can't have got far.'

Linda nodded; as if, in the Western scenario cited above, she'd just managed to catch one ten-dollar bill. 'You mean,' she said, 'the submarine's just for getting the weapons as far as the first waterfall?'

'Could be. You never know, with the government and all.'

'And then,' Linda whispered hopefully, 'they transfer the actual arms to a helicopter or something for the rest of the journey.'

'It's possible,' Dieb replied. 'Hell, anything's *possible*.'

'There, you see?' Linda smote her fist into the palm of her hand. 'So all we've got to do is find the first waterfall and there we are. We can intercept the shipment, capture it, and –'

'Yes?'

'I'm not sure,' Linda confessed. 'Still, we'll think of something.'

'You bet.'

'I mean,' she continued, 'we can cross that bridge when we come to it.'

'Of course.'

'And we mustn't count our chickens before they're hatched.'

'Goes without saying.'

'There's many a slip between cup and lip.'

'You said it.'

'Right, then,' Linda said, and she set her jaw in a determined line. 'Let's go, then.'

'With you all the way, honey.'

'Great.' Linda paused, and frowned. 'Er, which way?'

Calvin closed his eyes and pointed at random. 'How about over there?' he suggested.

'You positive about that?'

'If you want me to be, I am.'

'OK, then. That way it is.'

Grimly determined, icily calm, every fibre of his being dedicated to the mission he had embarked upon, Wesley stood on the top of a low rise and looked round.

'Um,' he said.

It was all very well setting out to kill a journalist. Nobody could find fault with the general principle. The mathematics are simple in the extreme: to find the optimum number of journalists that there ought to be in a perfect world, divide the actual number of journalists there are at the present time by itself, and subtract one. But Wesley's task was slightly harder, because he had to single out one particular journalist, and that of necessity involved finding her.

Not as easy as it sounds. Not, at least, in the environs of Lake Chicopee, where topography isn't a precise science.

It's hard to do a systematic search of somewhere that keeps rearranging itself with every step you take. To put it another way: there's not enough timber in all the rain forests of South America to make enough paper for a 1:2500 scale map of the seven square miles immediately surrounding the lake.

When you're looking for someone in unfamiliar territory, the sensible course of action is, of course, to ask a local. That's what Wesley decided to do. And fortuitously, there was a party of locals just appearing over the skyline to his left.

'Excuse me,' Wesley said.

'Hello?'

'Sorry to bother you,' Wesley called out, 'but have you seen a journalist?'

The party came closer. It consisted of a man in exotic ermine-trimmed robes, two footmen in powdered wigs and –

Her!

'A journalist, did you say?' said the Prince. 'Might have done. Truth is, I wouldn't recognise one if I saw one. What's this feller look like?'

'Um,' Wesley replied. 'Actually, it's a she. Sort of –'

'Yes?'

'Um.' Wesley shrugged, made a vague gesture with his hands. 'Sort of, er, gorgeous. Well, gorgeousish,' he added, trying not to look at the girl. 'If you like 'em tall and blonde and . . .'

'Ah.' The Prince rubbed his chin thoughtfully. 'Murdoch,' he said to one of the footmen, 'have we seen anyone like that around here lately?'

'No, sir.'

'You sure about that, Murdoch?'

The footman inclined his head gravely. 'Entirely, sir. Your Majesty will recall that, since Your Majesty's subjects are all exceptionally comely and tall, such a person would scarcely be conspicuous. However, we have been checking all the female subjects we encounter with the slipper.'

'Yes, of course. Silly me. How about you, Skellidge?'

'I regret to have to inform His Majesty, no.'

The Prince clicked his tongue. 'Sorry,' he said. 'Was it important?'

Wesley shrugged. 'Not really. Well, quite important, actually. Rather a matter of life and death, in fact.'

'Oh.' The Prince half turned and addressed her. 'How about you, my dear?'

'Mm. Mmmmm. Mmmm mm mmm mmm.'

'I beg your –? Oh, quite. Skellidge, the gag.'

Wesley hadn't noticed the gag, or the ropes, or the handcuffs. Now he did; and it occurred to him that maybe she wasn't too happy about accompanying the party. He took an advance on next year's courage ration and cleared his throat. 'Excuse me,' he said.

'Yes?'

'Um, why's she all tied up?'

'To stop her escaping,' the Prince replied. 'When you say a matter of life and death . . .'

'Would you mind—?' Wesley took a deep breath, aware as he did so that he was doing something really rather brave and quite remarkably stupid. 'Would you mind letting her go, please? If it's no trouble, of course.'

'But my dear fellow.' The Prince gazed at him, utterly bemused. 'If I do that she might escape. I can't fight a war for her sake if she's not there, it'd rob the whole thing of any significance whatsoever.'

'A *war*?'

The Prince nodded. 'The finest gift a man can give,' he replied proudly. 'Like they always say, carnage is a girl's best friend. And think what an anticlimax it'd be without her.'

Wesley thought for a moment. Hitherto, his experience of dealing with dangerous lunatics had been extremely limited; one of those things he'd always suspected he'd been missing out on, no doubt. However, where there's a loon there's a way. 'But surely,' he said, 'you've missed the point. With all due respect,' he added quickly, as Skellidge took a step forward. 'I don't mean to be rude, but don't you think you've got it the wrong way round?'

The Prince began to look worried. 'Whatever can you mean?' he asked anxiously. 'This is very important. Murdoch, the tablets of stone, quickly.'

'Well,' Wesley said, as Murdoch produced a slab of granite and a cold chisel from the pockets of his tailcoat, 'take Helen of Troy, for instance.'

'Always a good place to start,' the Prince agreed. 'So?'

'Well then,' Wesley said. 'Just ask yourself; in the end, who won? Who got the girl? Was it the kidnappers, or the people she was kidnapped from?'

'I see what you mean,' the Prince said slowly. 'Do go on, this is probably very relevant.'

'Think about it,' Wesley urged. 'Which lot was it that launched the thousand ships? And which side would you rather be, more importantly? Remember, it's the side who wins that gets the glory.'

For a while there was silence, except for the sound of steel on stone and a polite enquiry as to how you spell *importantly*. 'What you're saying is,' the Prince replied eventually, 'is that I'd do far better to let someone carry her off, and then fight the war to get her back. Is that it?'

'In a nutcase, sorry, nutshell, yes.' Wesley could feel moisture ooozing out of his pores, but decided it would be a tactical error to do anything about it. 'That way, you'd be right as well as romantic. You do see that, don't you?'

The Prince nodded. 'That only leaves the problem,' he added, 'of who's going to be mug enough to carry her off. Bearing in mind that he'd have to fight this amazingly destructive thermo-nuclear war shortly afterwards, I mean.'

'Thermo –'

'Absolutely,' the Prince said, his head bobbing like something hanging from a car mirror. 'Murdoch here's got seventy-five Pershing missiles trained on the major population centres right now, haven't you, Murdoch?'

'Of course, Your Majesty.'

'Oh.' Wesley hesitated. 'I see. And as soon as someone abducts the girl, you'll, um, press the –?'

'That's it,' said the Prince, smiling benignly. 'Our response time's really rather impressive, though I say it myself. Seventeen minutes and thirty-two seconds, and we could have most of Europe and the United States glowing so bright you could see them from Alpha Centauri. And that's just Phase One.'

'Gosh,' Wesley said. He looked at the girl out of the corner of his eye. True, she was ravishingly gorgeous, in a substantial sort of way. True, all he really wanted to do for the rest of his life was stand on one leg at a distance of twenty yards or so gazing adoringly at her. On the other hand; most of Europe and the United States . . . 'Well,' he said, 'I'm glad we've got that sorted out. And if I happen to bump into anybody who might be interested in abducting girls, I'll be sure to let them know.'

'Oh.' The Prince's face fell a little. 'Oh, I see. I'm dreadfully sorry, I'd sort of got the impression that you –'

'Me?' Wesley's nose twitched. 'Gosh, no, not me. I mean, usually I'd be only too happy, but I've got this journalist to find, matter of life and death, so . . .'

'Of course,' the Prince sighed. 'I quite understand. I'd better not keep you any longer, in that case. Much obliged to you, by the way, for clarifying that point about the war. Skellidge, make this chap a viscount or something.'

'Very good, Your Majesty.' Skellidge straightened his back a little and cleared his throat. 'You're a viscount,' he said. 'All hail.'

'Thank you,' Wesley said, walking backwards. 'Thank you ever so much. Well, must fly, 'Bye for now.'

The girl, who'd been painstakingly chewing through the gag all this time, chomped out the last few strands, spat and yelled out, 'Hey, come back!' just as Wesley disappeared over the rise and into the trees. However, since he didn't return, he couldn't have heard her.

CHAPTER THIRTEEN

The Proprietor began to stir.

He was, of course, fast asleep; but the images reflected on the still mirror of His mind were unquiet, and tiny ripples from the top side clouded His enormous dreams. He grunted, muttered, and stirred ever so slightly.

Then an image moved in His mind that really had no place being there; something which could never have got in there and certainly couldn't get out again. It was long and black and vaguely cigar-shaped, and it left a stream of bubbles behind as it slipped upwards out of existence.

The Proprietor didn't like it; not one bit. Having checked His memory, just to make sure He hadn't eaten a huge chunk of cheese shortly before He fell asleep, He came to a decision.

Damn, He thought.

'You sure it was this way?' Calvin Dieb enquired cheerfully. 'Only, it's at least an hour since we set off, and I'll swear I've passed that rock four times already. I remembered it particularly because it reminds me so much of my ex-wife's brother.'

Linda didn't reply. She was not, in truth, in the best of moods, and Calvin's blithe, carefree chatter was beginning to annoy her. She stopped, shaded her eyes with the palm of her hand and looked out over the lake.

'Hey!' she yelled. 'Over there!'

'Yes?'

'Look!' She jumped up and down five times. 'It's the submarine. Look, you can see its periscope, just breaking the . . .'

'Where? I can't see . . .'

'Where I'm pointing. Oh, come on, you dimwit, it's as plain as the nose on your face. Just there, where those ducks are swimming round.'

'What?' Dieb squinted. 'Oh yes. Well, I can see *something*, anyway. You sure it's not the Loch Ness Monster? I mean, you're always hearing reports of people seeing what they think are remarkable things, such as submarines, and they turn out just to be something mundane and ordinary, like sea-monsters.'

In spite of her excitement, Linda frowned. 'Mundane and ordinary? The Loch Ness Monster?'

'I reckon so,' Calvin replied. 'At any rate, it's a sight more mundane and ordinary than submarines that can shin up waterfalls. Which is probably just as well, don't you think?'

Linda left that remark well alone, and resumed her excited staring. She was so preoccupied, in fact, that it was quite a while before she noticed that there was someone standing beside her.

Four people, in fact; a man in peculiar clothes, something like a fur-trimmed dressing gown, two other men with powdered wigs on their heads, and the ugly girl she'd bumped into earlier.

Something about legs like pink elephant's trunks . . . No, she couldn't quite remember. Nevertheless, she had the feeling she didn't like the ugly girl. Call it a hunch; and hunches don't just materialise, you pay for them with hard-earned experience. No such thing as a free hunch.

'Excuse me,' said the man in the dressing-gown, 'but are you by any chance a journeyman?'

'Journalist, Your Majesty.'

'Sorry, a journalist? Only I gather there's one running around loose in these parts, and . . .'

Linda looked at him. 'Yes,' she said, 'I'm Linda Lachuk, current affairs correspondent of the *New York Globe*. Tell me, does that thing over there look like a submarine to you?'

The Prince nodded. 'I should say,' he replied, with a hint of pride. 'As a matter of fact, I know darned well it's a submarine.'

'You do?'

The Prince inclined his head. 'I should do,' he said, 'it's one of mine. Murdoch, the Aldis lamp.'

Linda's jaw fell like a drawbridge. 'One of *yours*?' she gasped. 'But that's crazy. I mean, you're not the President of the United States.'

'Very true. Actually, that's probably the nicest thing anybody's ever said about me. Thank you.'

'And you're not the Pope, either.'

The Prince's brow clouded slightly. 'True,' he replied. 'And, no disrespect for my Brother in Christ intended, but I can't really see what His Holiness'd be wanting with a submarine, what with his dominions being some way inland and all. He's got the Tiber, I suppose, but that's so polluted these days, the average nuclear submarine'd probably dissolve in it like an aspirin.'

'Right,' Linda replied, taking another good look at the Prince out of the corner of her eye. 'In that case, who the hell are you?'

'Me?' the Prince grinned pleasantly. 'I'm Prince Charming, of course. Why, didn't you recognise me?'

'Prince . . .'

The Prince nodded. 'Actually,' he said, 'don't be misled by the Prince bit, I'm actually the head of state. And yes, that's one of my submarines. The *Bloodspite*, actually, ex-Soviet navy, picked it up for a song at the liquidators' auction. One of the reactors is a bit dicky, but it's fine for just pottering about in. By the way, would you mind awfully if I were to ask you your shoe size?'

While he was saying this, the footman called Murdoch was flashing merrily away with the signalling lamp, and a succession of rapid blips of light appeared on the surface of the distant waters, presumably by way of reply. The Prince, meanwhile, had strolled over to where Calvin Dieb was sitting on a rock.

'Hello,' he said.

For a moment the new Calvin Dieb, friend to all humankind, flickered like a flame in a breeze. Basic survival instincts whispered things in his mind's ear about strange men in peculiar fur-trimmed outfits who sidle up to you and say, 'Hello.' The moment of apprehension passed, however, as soon as the Prince spoke again.

''Scuse my asking,' he said, in a pleasant sort of chummy drawl, 'but you wouldn't by any chance be interested in abducting women, would you?'

Calvin looked at him. An entirely different set of survival instincts took their places on the bridge of his mind, kicked their shoes off and switched on their work-stations. 'Pardon me?' he said.

'You *are* an American, aren't you?' the Prince went on, as if checking on an important detail he'd forgotten to clarify at the start.

'Why, yes,' Calvin replied. 'Though I should point out that abducting women isn't really part of the American heritage. Perhaps you were thinking of the Romans, or Vikings, maybe. We generally find we have more than enough of our own without stealing other people's.'

The Prince nodded. 'Fair enough,' he said. 'Only, you see, I need a whatchamacallit, *casus belli*. That's what diplomats say when they mean something to declare war about.'

Calvin looked at the Prince long and hard; and the old Calvin Dieb peered longingly through the bars of his cage and thought what a wonderful client this guy would have made – obviously rich, obviously deranged, obviously not too bright into the bargain. Legal dynasties have been built on such clients.

'You see,' the Prince went on, 'I've got this girl, you see, and she's so utterly, utterly gorgeous I feel I've got to fight the biggest and best war ever for her sake, just to tell the world how absolutely smashing she is, you know, but I can't do that unless someone abducts her, now can I? And so I thought, you being an American and America being such a big, powerful country . . .'

Calvin swallowed something that had suddenly appeared in his throat. 'You want to declare war on the USA?' he said.

'Well, it's a start,' said the Prince. 'It's always been my dream, you see, ever since I was just a kid; you know, to meet this wonderful, wonderful girl and fight for her sake, like the knights of old. And now, suddenly, here she is, and nobody to fight with. So darned frustrating, don't you know?'

'Excuse me,' Calvin asked quietly. 'Did you happen to, um, fall in a lake recently?'

The Prince frowned. 'Why, yes, as it happens I did. How did you know that?'

'Oh, blind guess.' Calvin thought for a moment; and the refrain was, in spite of his very best endeavours, *Well, why not?* After all, what possible harm could there be in turning his special skill, hitherto only practised to the detriment of his fellow creatures, to the service of the human race? To save them, in fact, from the prospect of universal extinction? And maybe make a buck along the way, no harm in that, the labourer is worthy of his hire. 'Excuse me,' he said, 'but let me put a suggestion to you and see if this makes any kinda sense. When you say war –'

'Yes?'

'Well,' Calvin went on, taking a deep breath, 'I know you say you've got your heart set on an actual shooting war, but has it perhaps occurred to you that a really prolonged and destructive lawsuit might not have the same effect, in the long run? You know, in terms of grand-scale expenditure of resources, pain, suffering and trauma inflicted, lives torn apart, national economies bankrupted, all the things you tend to associate with wars, but in a rather more controlled and civilised framework? Think about it,' he urged, observing the Prince's brow furrow. 'Maybe you remember a few years back there was all that hype about a new bomb that wipes out human life but leaves the real estate unscathed? Well, it's here and it's now and we call it litigation; and as Head of State, don't you owe it to your realm to have the very best? Huh? Am I right or am I right?'

The Prince's lips moved silently for a moment. 'You're saying,' he said slowly, 'instead of having a war over the girl, why not go to law about her instead?' His face clouded. 'All due respect, old thing, I'm not so sure about that. I mean, going to court, it's all a bit middle-class, isn't it?'

'Middle-class?' Calvin's face reflected the magnitude of the blasphemy. 'Going to law *middle-class*? Excuse me, Your Majesty, but have you any idea how much going to law costs these days? I mean, forget your yachts and your palaces and your private jets and all. If you want to talk about the ultimate status symbol, the kinda thing only the huge corporations and the divinely wealthy individuals can even dream of affording, look no further, 'cos what you need is a lawsuit. Damnit,' he went on, warming to the theme, 'any miserable little country can have a *war*. Bosnia can have a *war*. Only the serious players can afford serious lawfare. In fact,' he added, seeing in his mind's eye the twitch on the float that suggests that the fish is nibbling, 'before I'd agree to act for you I'd need to see some serious credentials from your banks.'

The Prince looked at him. 'You would?'

Calvin nodded. 'Definitely. And the audited gross national product figures for the last ten years. Sorry, but these days you gotta be businesslike.'

'Oh, quite.' The Prince nodded. 'I take your point entirely. Murdoch, the bank statements.'

Which is how, alone and unaided, Calvin Dieb very nearly saved the world. Unfortunately, while he'd been chatting up the Prince, Linda had been asking Janice whether she'd happened to notice any men in funny hats; and she'd replied that although she hadn't seen any men in funny hats, this was probably because she'd been captured and tied up and blindfolded at the time when the men in funny hats may well have been in evidence; whereupon Linda had asked whether, when she said tied up and held captive, she'd meant held captive like, say, a hostage; and she'd said, Well, yes, she supposed so; and Linda had suddenly realised that single-handedly rescuing the hostages and getting them home for Christmas would not only prevent the War but make the best possible finale to her story; and so she'd said, 'Skellidge, the sharp knife,' and Skellidge had handed her a sharp knife, and she'd cut the ropes and grabbed Janice by the wrist and said 'This way!'; and the Prince, observing all this, had asked Calvin which country Linda came from; and Calvin had replied that he was fairly sure she was American; and the Prince had smiled and said, 'Splendid, splendid. Murdoch, the button –'

And Murdoch had said 'Yes, Your Maj –' and then fallen silent and gone red.

'Murdoch?'

'I regret to say,' Murdoch replied painfully, 'that someone would appear to have stolen the button.'

'What?'

'The fire control button, Your Majesty. Colloquially referred to as the Doomsday –'

'Yes, I know all that,' replied the Prince impatiently. 'How do you mean, *stolen* –?'

'What is it, Hat?' Talks to Squirrels demanded, as the small and secret entrepreneur scratched his head and stared at his latest prize. 'Looks like some sort of briefcase.'

Hat shrugged his shoulders. 'Haven't the faintest idea,' he replied. 'Don't know why I bothered pinching it, to be honest with you.'

Talks considered for a moment. 'Because it wasn't spot-welded to the ground, Hat?' he hazarded.

'Ah yes, that was the reason.' Hat prodded the catches tentatively, recalling the time he'd swiped a similar case from someone who daydreamed of being Agent 006. Occasionally, in the cold weather, he felt it still. 'One of these damned combination locks,' he observed mournfully. 'Last one of these I got took us twenty years of trying different combinations before we got it open. And you know what was inside? Sandwiches. Or rather,' he added, 'a place where sandwiches had once been, a long time previously. Still, we might get lucky this time.'

Talks shrugged. 'Why not just bust it open?' he suggested. 'All it'd take would be a tomahawk spike behind the hinges there, and . . .'

Hat scowled. 'True,' he said, 'but that might just shave a few cents off the resale value, don't you think? No,' he went on, 'I guess I'll just have to be patient and keep plugging and plugging away . . .'

He pressed both catches at once, and the lid flew open. 'Hell,' he said disgustedly, 'it's empty.'

'No it's not,' Talks pointed out. 'There's things built into it. What're they, Hat? That red thing, and all the flashing lights?'

'I'm not sure,' Hat replied, fiddling. 'Could be a portable fax, or a laptop PC, or a photocopier. I guess this red button's the on/off switch.'

'Only one way to find out, Hat.'

'True.' Hat peered more closely. 'Only it does say DANGER in big stencilled letters. Do you think –?'

'Nah, that's just public liability stuff, their lawyers make them put that in just in case it gets hit by lightning while you're using it. You don't want to worry about things that say DANGER.'

'You don't?'

'Well, I don't. Mind you, I'm dead already, so I worry about very little.'

Hat nodded. 'All right, then,' he said. 'You press it.'

With a sad smile Talks With Squirrels put his ghostly hand right through the keyboard. 'Love to,' he said wistfully. 'But I can't. Sorry.'

'Fair enough. You're sure it'll be all right?'

'Of course. Trust me.'

'Trust me, I'm a dead Indian?'

Talks wrinkled his nose. 'Be like that,' he said. 'Would you trust me any better if I was alive?'

'Well, no. Less, actually.'

'There you are, then. Press the button.'

'I'm not sure . . .'

'Could be a CD player,' Talks said, his nose an inch or so from the button. 'Worth a buck or two, they are.'

Hat inclined his head. It looked safe enough; no wires, no leads, it must just run on batteries. Even if he did get an electric shock, the chances were it'd be so slight he'd hardly even notice it. 'The hell with it,' he said. 'Why not?'

'Go on, then.'

'You're *sure* it's safe?'

'How the hell could just pressing a button be dangerous? Gee, but you have one hell of a vivid imagination.'

Captain Hat bowed his head. 'Sorry,' he said. 'I was being silly. All right, then, here goes.'

He pressed the button.

And –

Beside His bed, the Proprietor's alarm clock started to scream.

And Wesley, who'd been running as fast as he could down the slope in the vague hope of getting to Hat before he pressed the button, put his foot behind a tangle of bramble, landed on his nose, said 'Ung!', scrambled to his feet, launched himself again, slipped athletically in a patch of mud and did the rest of the distance, quickly but with a minimum of dignity, tobogganing on his backside. He arrived just in time to slither straight through Talks to Squirrels (who nearly jumped out of his skin, but still recovered his composure in time to put three consecutive arrows in the back of his head in the space of four seconds; not bad for offhand shooting at a moving target) and land on top of Captain Hat, sending the briefcase flying.

A second and a half earlier, and he'd have been in time.

He was just propping himself up on his elbows and wondering (a) where the little bloke with the button had got to and (b) what the small, squishy, squirming thing he was lying on might be, when a fast-moving procession appeared over the skyline. It was led by Linda and Janice, running with more enthusiasm than wisdom straight for the bramble-patch. Seventy yards or so behind them came Calvin Dieb and the Prince, anybody's race with a hundred yards still to go, and Murdoch and Skellidge making quite reasonable time at a sort of stately canter.

All a bit pointless now, Wesley reflected; unless, of course, the Prince had some way of stopping the bombs his button had presumably launched. But he wouldn't *want* to, would he, any more than a bullet would suddenly decide to change course and go round rather than through you. Pity, that.

Even though he wasn't feeling at his blithest and best, he couldn't help smiling just a bit when Linda and Janice caught their feet in exactly the same brambles, did exactly the same little dance and arrived beside him in exactly the same way. He'd remembered thinking while he'd been bum-sliding down that self-same slope, 'I bet this'd be very funny to watch,' and this time he had the satisfaction of being the audience.

He'd been right. It was hilarious; more so, he guessed, with two of them doing it. Ah, well; last orders for humour at the bar, please, ladies and gentlemen.

'Hello,' he said. 'It's too late.'

'Huh?' Janice, who'd come to an abrupt halt on and around his legs, raised her head and looked at him as if he'd just turned himself into a strawberry flapjack. 'Too late for what?'

'Everything,' Wesley replied sadly, as the rest of the cast (who'd managed to avoid the brambles and the mud; spoil-sports, the lot of 'em) came panting up. 'This little pillock I'm lying on pressed the button.'

'What button?'

'Never mind. Doesn't matter. Forget I spoke.' Wesley stood up, apologised politely to Captain Hat, smiled politely at everybody else present and wandered away to throw stones in the lake. Or at it, rather, since he had a shrewd notion that everything was somehow the lake's fault anyway.

'Who was that?' Linda demanded, and although she didn't actually add out loud that the public had a right to know, her tone of voice implied it. 'And what's this button?'

Calvin Dieb cleared his throat. 'Something you obvi-ously didn't know about,' he said. 'A shame, really. You see, His Royal Whatever here wants to blow up the world, all in the name of pure, true love of course, so it's OK really, or at any rate it makes a refreshing change from pol-itics; and the deal was, if he could find someone to kidnap the, um, I'm sorry, I didn't quite catch the name, Ms –?'

'DeWeese,' Janice said. 'Janice DeWeese.'

'Very pleased to know you, if only temporarily. Anyhow, you kidnapped Ms Deweese –'

'I did not,' Linda objected. 'I rescued her. Didn't I?'

'Arguably,' Janice said.

Calvin held up a hand for silence. 'The way His Majesty saw it, you kidnapped her. And so his buddy in the wig and the fancy dress produced the good old doomsday button – that's it there, on the ground. And it seems like this small person here –'

'Hat,' said Hat.

'Gesundheit. This small guy appears to have walked off with it and, um, pressed it. Which means, I guess, we're all going to –'

'*Hey!*' Janice objected. 'Don't talk crazy, Mister who-ever-you-are.' She stopped, and squinted. 'Just a minute, aren't you that goddamn bird?'

Calvin nodded. 'I was,' he admitted, 'but I guess I grew out of it.'

Janice decided not to pursue that. 'Whatever,' she said. 'Still doesn't mean that button's actually going to blow up the world. It's not like any of this is *real*, for Chrissakes.'

'Who is this broad?' Talks to Squirrels demanded loudly, shooting Janice in the ear. 'And where does she get off saying we're not real?'

'But you're not,' Janice replied. 'And please have the good manners not to shoot people when they're talking to you.'

Talks shrugged. 'Does it matter?' he replied. 'After all, any minute now you're all just gonna be black outlines and puffs of smoke, which'll make shooting you even more pointless than it already is. I figure I might as well enjoy myself while I can.'

'But it's all just an illusion,' Janice protested loudly.

'Nothing really *happens* here. Even the people who get blown up get put back together again. It's just symbolism and stuff. Nobody's actually gonna *die*, are they?'

Calvin raised both eyebrows. 'One thing's for sure,' he said pleasantly. 'In about ten minutes or so from now, we'll all know the definite answer. And in the meantime,' he added, 'I don't see as there's a hell of a lot we can do about it. I suggest we all stop fussing about it and relax. You know, go with it. Be as one with the holocaust.'

There was a brief silence, broken only by Skellidge discreetly tapping Talks To Squirrels on the shoulder, clearing his throat head-waiter style and murmuring, 'Excuse me, sir, but do you have a reservation?'

'Just a moment.' This time it was Linda; and shortly afterwards there was a fine old debate going on, with Janice proposing the motion that it was all some kind of dream, Calvin being aggravatingly well adjusted about everything, Linda writing things down on her shirt-cuff to be used in evidence, the Prince nodding agreement with everyone in the intervals of looking up at the sky and then down at his watch, Talks to Squirrels shooting people and Captain Hat quietly examining the contents of their pockets for items of value. For his part, Wesley carried on throwing stones until he hadn't got any more stones to throw; at which point, he turned to the nearer of the two footmen and coughed.

''Scuse me.'

'Sir?'

'Which one are you?'

The footman thought for a moment. 'I, sir, am Murdoch.'

'Fine.' Wesley smiled pleasantly. 'Murdoch, the stones.'

'Certainly, sir. The sandstone or the flint?'

'Oh, let's make it the flint, shall we? It isn't every day the world gets blown up.'

Murdoch raised an eyebrow. 'Blown up, sir?' he enquired.

Wesley nodded. 'That's what that button thing was for, wasn't it?'

'No, sir,' Murdoch replied, bending at the waist as he produced a large, satin-lined box full of the finest selected Brandon flints. 'Certainly not, sir. That would be most injudicious, if I might say so.'

'Ah.' Wesley reached out for a flint, and paused. 'Which one's the coffee cream, then?'

'Sir?'

'A joke. Forget it.' He frowned. 'So the world *isn't* going to get blown up, then?'

'No, sir. You should be so lucky, sir.'

'Ah.' There was one particularly-fine flat-bottomed flint near the left-hand edge, and Wesley picked it out. 'You mean, something worse?'

'Something bigger, sir. Will that be all?'

Wesley nodded; then he drew back his arm and let fly. The stone spun from his hand, hit the surface of the lake and bounced, the way flat stones do unless they happen to have politicians living under them. It seemed to bounce for ever such a long time, and Wesley (who'd never managed to get a stone to skip more than twice before) watched it until it was nearly out of sight; at which point, it changed into a mallard drake and made a perfect landing out near the middle of the lake. Then he saw something else.

'Murdoch.'

'Sir?'

'What's that funny-looking greyish brown splodge?'

'Sir?'

Wesley pointed. 'On the hillside there, between the trees. It looks like someone's just poured gravy over the top of the hill.'

'No, sir. That would be the lemmings.'

'Ah.' Wesley double-checked his mental file, just in case there was something obvious he hadn't taken on board. 'Lemmings,' he repeated.

'Indeed, sir. The Doomsday lemmings, to be precise.'

'Right,' said Wesley, 'got you. Thanks a lot.'

'Sir.'

'Murdoch.'

'Sir?'

Wesley rubbed his chin, and said, 'Excuse me if this sounds a bit feeble, but I'm from England, and we don't actually have Doomsday lemmings there. Could you just sort of explain? A bit?'

Murdoch's lips twitched into a thin smile. 'Certainly, sir,' he said. 'You are aware, I take it, of the tradition that holds that all lemmings have a death wish, in pursuance of which they leap off cliffs into the waters below?'

Wesley nodded. 'There's a computer game, in fact, where you have to . . . Sorry, please go on.'

'And,' Murdoch continued austerely, 'you will be aware by now that to jump into this lake is to have your wish come true?'

'Yup.'

Murdoch turned and pointed at the grey tide washing over the bluffs into the lake, like beans in sauce slopping out of the tin. 'Their wish is about to come universally true, sir. Hence the expression, Doomsday lemmings.'

'Ah. Right. Sorry I asked.'

'My pleasure, sir.'

Wesley propped his chin on his hands and decided to

sulk. After all; buttons to blow up the world; Doomsday lemmings; all these people who'd been cropping up all over the place, sometimes real and sometimes not.

It was time, he said to himself, that someone sorted it all out.

Yeah, well. When, looking back over the history of the planet, wasn't it? But nothing ever was, not in real life. Confusion and chaos crash down from the high points of the past, spitting foam and spray; but they hit the surface of the present, and everything evens out into one flat, calm mirror. Nothing is solved or explained, but after long enough none of it matters. The worst part was that he'd come here deliberately.

He studied the lake, and the ridge of the mountains encircling it like someone curled up on his side, asleep under an eiderdown of trees. He'd long since given up trying to find his bearings; it was never the same twice, although he hadn't actually seen the mountains move or the trees being herded like sheep to another position. By way of experiment, he closed his eyes and opened them again; sure enough, the whole landscape was different when you looked closely. Where there had been a cliff – the one the lemmings had been jumping over – there was now a sparsely wooded incline running right down to the lake's edge. Where a rocky outcrop had stood a moment ago, there was now a low knoll crowned by a clump of thin, straggly fir trees. This is all a picture, he realised, in the mind of someone with an unreliable memory or a slapdash attitude towards continuity. Someone who doesn't think backgrounds really matter very much. Like me, for example.

Figures.

'Pretty, isn't it?' He looked round to see Calvin Dieb sitting beside him. 'Hey, you can just see my car from here.'

Wesley looked hard. 'You can?'

Dieb nodded. 'Well, not the actual car. You can just see the sun glinting on the windshield.'

'A reflection, you mean?'

'Yeah, a reflection. And don't bother saying it,' Dieb added with a grin, ''cos I'm way ahead of you. I realised. There is no car, only a reflection.'

Wesley didn't reply. The duck that had been his stone was still there, but it wasn't doing anything of note, even though it was now an otter. 'What do you think is going to happen?' he asked.

'Happen?' Dieb shrugged. 'Search me, pal. Does it matter?'

'Well, yes.' Wesley found a stone that hadn't been there a moment ago, a round pebble shaped like a duck's egg, and lobbed it smoothly into the water. It hit the surface and skimmed away out of sight. 'Even if it is all imagination, like whatsername says. I mean, if I believe it's happening, then surely it is. To me, I mean.'

'Maybe.' Calvin's shoulders rose and fell. 'I used to believe my life was happening to me, so what do I know? I used to think I was the big lawyer all American mothers want their kids to be. I used to think I had money and power and a superior intellect, which made it all right for me to do the things I did. I used to think my ex-wife didn't understand me. I used to think my Dad understood why I never called home. I even used to think I had a set of keys for my car. Only goes to show, huh?'

'But you did.'

Calvin nodded. 'That's the worst kind of fantasy,' he said, 'the kind that's true. And before you ask, yes, I missed the Sixties too.'

'Um.' Wesley shifted an inch or so away, trying not to be

too obvious about it. 'So you're going to chuck in the lawyering, are you? When you get back, I mean?'

Dieb looked at him as if he'd just offered him a dollar fifty for his soul. 'Chuck in the law?' he repeated. 'Hell, no. Why the hell would I want to do that, for God's sake?'

'But I thought . . .' Wesley groped for words in the lining of his mind's pocket. 'All this revelation and seeing the light stuff. I thought you meant you'd, oh, I don't know, decided to turn over a new leaf, live a nobler and more fulfilling life, that sort of –'

'Kid.' Dieb looked at him as if from a long way away. 'Just because I've finally realised what a shitty person I've been all these years doesn't make me want to stop being me. It just means I can stop feeling guilty, is all. I mean, if I'd discovered that deep down I was a really nice guy, caring and considerate and concerned about people, then I'd be worried sick. No way would you get me back in that office, not even if you called out the National Guard with firehoses.' He smiled. 'But I ain't. I'm a jerk. But now I can feel *good* about being a jerk. That's why I feel – well, kind of at peace, I guess. And you know, I suppose that's all I ever wanted. Deep down, I mean. How about you?'

Wesley shrugged. 'Oh, that's easy,' he said. 'I always wanted it to be like this. You know, magic and adventure and nothing really being what it seems. Which proves that you can be a really substantial idiot for a quarter of a century and never even know it.'

'Ah,' Dieb nodded. 'But do you feel at peace now you know you're an idiot?'

'No.'

'Oh, well. Whatever's right, I guess.' Calvin glanced down at his watch. 'A quarter of an hour, the prince guy said. If it's gonna happen, it ought to be roughly now.'

'Ah. That's . . .'
'Yes, isn't it?'
And it was.

It began with a slight nodding of the heads of the tall trees that stood on the crest of the hills at the north end of the lake. They nodded reluctantly and with an ill grace, as if they'd just lost an argument and were being forced to agree with their opponents' views. As they swayed, birds left them in prodigious quantities, until the sky seemed full of them.

Next, the shape of the hills themselves began to change. Earlier, those same hills had reminded Wesley strongly of a sleeping man lying on his side; the long, low slope to the west being the line gradually ascending from the feet to the rounded prominence of the hip; a valley where the line falls from the hip-bone to the slimmest part of the waist; another long, steadily climbing gradient to the highest point at the shoulder; another valley falling away to the level of the neck; another, steeper increment to the summit of the head on the far eastern side of the lake, and finally a sharp drop almost to the level of the water. Now, as the two men stared at the skyline, the mountains seemed to –

– Swivel, as the peaks of hip and shoulder dropped down –

– And rise, as shoulder and head lifted up, propped on one arm –

– And the knees bend, bringing the feet round –

– And then He lifts His torso from the waist and sits up, stretches His arms up until they're lost to the elbow in the clouds too high to disturb the uniform blue of the sky. And He yawns –

– Filling the amphitheatre of the lake with sound, and

rubs His hands into the sockets of his eyes, grinding away undergrowth and scrub and topsoil. He blinks, and yawns again, and stretches out His hands towards the surface of the lake, groping, as if He can't see –

– Without His spectacles. He's bigger now, of course; every moment He seems to become larger and larger, although He doesn't actually grow. He stays the same size, but where you're standing looking at Him becomes steadily further and further away. So; now He's big enough for the perspective to make sense, He picks up the surface of the lake and screws it into His eye, like Bertie Wooster's monocle.

'Grrnghzhgr,' He says, and yawns again.

He peers round, looking for His slippers. He sees them, brushes snow and cloud off the high points of the uppers, and jams His feet into them, treading down the backs.

The mountain has woken up, and wants His coffee.

CHAPTER FOURTEEN

'Yup,' said the squirrel, her cheeks full of part-masticated nut, 'that's him. The boss. Be careful how you talk to him, he can be a bit grumpy when he's iust woken up.'

'The boss,' Wesley repeated, as his mind tried to make sense of the sheer size of what he was looking at. 'You mean like – well, God or somebody?'

'God?' The squirrel nearly choked on its chewed nut. 'Hell, no. He's just the boss, is all. The Proprietor. The guy who owns this valley.'

'Ah.'

The Proprietor was standing upright now, and where the lake had been was an irrelevant emptiness filled with His shadow. The mountains were gone too, presumably; except that you couldn't see the space where they'd been because the Proprietor was in the way. He filled all available space, in the way light and air and water tend to do.

'You sure he's not God?' Wesley hazarded. 'There's a sort of family likeness, maybe something in the line of the jaw . . .'

'Nah,' the squirrel replied cheerfully, dropping nutshell crumbs on Wesley's head. 'He's just – tall.'

'Bet he has trouble buying shoes,' Calvin muttered.

'He can afford to have them specially made,' the squirrel replied. 'Believe me.'

Wesley looked down; he was feeling dizzy. 'What's he doing now?' he asked.

'Not much,' the squirrel said. 'Trying to remember what century this is, probably. Like I said, he's not at his best first thing.'

'Just a moment,' said Janice, shading her eyes with the palm of her hand. 'If he's the guy who owns all this, who're you?'

'Me?' The squirrel lifted her head, ran round the bole of the tree three times and came to a halt, standing at ninety degrees to the ground with her nose pointed downwards. 'I just run this place for him.'

'You're the manager?'

'That's right,' the squirrel said. 'He finds it easier that way. You see, it can be awkward when you're a giant, relating to people and all. They tend to feel a tad overawed, you know? But I can be anybody or anything I choose to be, so it's not a problem for me. Nowadays, he stays out of things right up till the end.'

'The end?' Calvin looked at her. 'Excuse me for nit-picking, but that's an ambiguous phrase. Is that end as in goodbye, world or end as in school's out?'

The squirrel shrugged, sending a ripple running from her shoulders to the tip of her bushy tail. 'You disappoint me,' she said wearily. 'Sorry, but you do. I thought you'd understand about perspective and scale by now, specially since you've seen the giant. Most people get the hang of perspective after they've been looking at him for a minute or so.'

'Pardon me for breathing,' Calvin muttered. The squirrel ignored him.

'The point is,' she said, 'what it's the end of depends on where you're looking from. Don't you see? If you were standing on the edge of the lake looking into it, what'd you see?'

'Water,' Calvin said. 'Pondweed. Maybe ducks. Sorry, was that the wrong answer?'

'You'd see,' the squirrel said, her tail twitching, 'your reflection. OK so far? Very good. You'd see this guy standing beside the lake, and behind him lots of trees and mountains and stuff, but they'd all be very small and far away. They'd look like they were all much smaller than the guy – that's you, of course; or else they'd be the normal size for trees and mountains, but the guy would be huge. Like a giant. You follow?'

Wesley nodded but Calvin shook his head. 'Sorry,' he said, 'but I don't reckon it'd stand up in court. I'd know the scenery was really bigger than me, 'cos it'd just be an optical effect. A trick; you know, like a figure of speech or something, like you use to make things seem other than they are. I know about these things, I'm a lawyer.'

The squirrel rubbed her nose with her paws and spat out a piece of walnut shrapnel. 'Yes,' she said, 'you probably are, at that. Still, we don't claim to succeed in every case. Fortunately, it's not us that have to live with the consequences.' She twitched her whiskers, changed into a beautiful girl and landed beside Wesley. 'Ow,' she said, 'my ankle.'

'Hey.' It was Linda this time, emerging from some reverie of her own, admittance by ticket only. 'That's no damn use. How'm I supposed to get that into a camera lens?'

'You could try standing back,' the girl said. 'But I wouldn't bother if I were you. Nobody'd believe it wasn't faked.'

Linda scowled horribly. 'Then where's the fuckin' *point*? What earthly good to me is something like this if nobody's going to believe it? I'd be the laughing stock of the profession.'

'That's interesting,' the giant said; and the force of His voice hitting them was like the great wind that blew Dorothy clean out of Kansas. 'The journalist believes it herself, doesn't she?'

'Sure,' Linda replied, hands on hips. 'But nobody else will.'

The giant laughed, like His counterpart in the sweetcorn commercials, except that He wasn't green or noticeably jolly. 'I like it,' he said. 'The journalist thinks that it doesn't matter if she believes something; unless she can make someone else believe it, it can't be true.'

'I didn't say that,' Linda replied irritably. Remarkable, the others thought, she isn't a bit afraid or overawed. 'What I said was, it's no use. Doesn't matter a toss if it's true or not. What good is something only I believe in?'

'This is wonderful,' the giant said. 'And I suppose that if she can make other people believe in something, whether it's true or not, is equally unimportant. This one's been wasting my time. That's two of them.' He sighed, and His breath made ripples in the air that broke up vision. 'Is that damned inspector still hanging around? We're going to be in trouble at this rate.'

Okeewana shrugged. 'Can't be helped,' she said. 'And I think the other two are going to be all right.'

'I'll come to them in a moment,' the giant replied. 'Don't confuse me, for God's sake, or I'll miss something. Let's deal with the lawyer and the journalist first. Ready?'

Okeewana nodded and produced notepad and pencil. 'Shoot,' she said.

'Right.' The giant thought for a moment. 'The journalist is easy,' He said. 'Obviously she's a dangerous pest and can't be allowed out again, but she'll be happy enough here. Find her something she'll enjoy, clear up the loose ends Flipside, put her on the staff. You can let one of the others go in exchange.'

The girl nodded, and turned a page in the book. 'What about the lawyer?' she said.

'His wish is granted,' the giant replied, 'and let it be a lesson to him. All his life, ever since he was a kid, he wanted to be the big lawyer, the guy who could make the right seem wrong and the wrong seem right. But all the time, while he was hacking and slashing his way, like psychotic Jack scrambling up the beanstalk, there were always these niggling feelings of guilt holding him back, making him doubt whether it was all OK, whether he'd be able to get away with it. Very good; his wish was that those aggravating doubts should stop. Let it be.' The giant paused, while the girl tapped some keys on a pocket calculator. 'What's the result?'

Okeewana nodded. 'It's fine,' she said. 'Happy ending.'

(She didn't say out loud what she saw; which was that seventy-two days later Calvin Dieb squeezed his partner Hernan Piranha out of the firm and almost immediately afterwards landed three new corporate clients of such staggering magnitude that even he was happy, for a while; and that three years to the day after that, he died, at his desk, of a massive coronary, aged forty-nine.)

'That's all right, then,' said the giant. 'Let's do the boot-faced girl next, shall we? Nice, easy job. She wanted to have men fall in love with her. Does she still want that?'

The girl looked at Janice, who made a peculiar noise. 'I guess not,' she said. 'Can she go?'

The giant nodded. 'From now on, she'll wake up every morning, look in the mirror and thank heaven she was born lucky.' He grinned. 'That just leaves the wetslap, yes?'

The girl nodded. Wesley was just about to ask Hey, what about him, when he realised –

'Difficult,' the giant said. 'After all, his wish was so peculiar. Do you think it's done him any good?'

'Hard to tell,' the girl replied. 'We've squeezed some of the godawfulness out of him, so I don't think he'd be too much of a nuisance if we let him go back. On the other hand . . .'

'Hey,' Wesley objected, but his voice was completely inaudible against the giant's soft tongue-click.

'I know,' the giant said. 'Yes, got it, I know what we'll do to him. All right, that about covers it for now. Any more?'

The girl shook her head. 'And next time there's going to be four at once,' she added, 'I'd appreciate a bit more notice, if that's no problem.'

'That's fair enough. Actually, you didn't do too badly, all things considered. What about that sonofabitch inspector, by the way?'

'Leave him to me,' the girl replied with a smile. 'Oh, and one last thing. You said I could lose one of the permanents now we've taken on the journalist. Any preferences?'

The giant shook his head. 'I'll leave that one to you,' he said. 'You know about these things.'

'Fine. Actually,' she added with a wicked grin, 'that'll help me deal with the inspector. Ciao, then.'

'Whatever.' The giant waved vaguely, took out His monocle, breathed on it, polished it on His sleeve and walked through it, leaving only a few concentric circles of ripples behind, and a duck sitting on water.

The girl put away her notepad and stood up. Wesley,

Calvin, Janice and Linda weren't there any more; even their reflections were almost completely faded off the face of the lake. 'OK, guys,' she said, 'show's over.'

'Good,' Talks to Squirrels replied. 'That was a hard day's work. Can't remember the last time I got killed so many times in one day.'

'You did good, Talks,' the girl replied. 'You all did,' she added, with a big smile. 'You too, Prince. You really had 'em going with that bomb stuff.'

Prince Charming bowed. 'My pleasure,' he replied. 'They're all on their way now, then?'

'At last.' The girl stood up, shook herself like a wet dog and became an otter. 'And before you ask . . .'

'Yes?'

'I haven't decided yet who gets to go home,' the otter said. 'But don't give me a hard time, OK? I'm thinking about it.'

She yawned and stretched; and as her arms rose above her head they became wings, and the dove flew away towards the mountains, which were back where they belonged and trying to get some sleep.

Linda emerged from the water like a bobbing cork, and felt for the bottom with her feet. The mud was only just deep enough to pull off one of her shoes. She stuck her arm in the water, grubbed around in the ooze until she struck footwear, pulled it out with an effort and squelched to shore.

She was sitting beside the road, wringing out her socks and wondering how long it took to get pneumonia, when a car drew up beside her. The window whirred down and a head poked through. On top of it was a round, broad-brimmed hat. From the brim dangled little bits of cotton. From the little bits of cotton hung corks.

'G'day, love,' said a voice from under the hat, 'but am I right for the submarine base?'

Linda froze, one half-wrung sock in her hand. She decided to adopt an experimental attitude towards the truth.

'Yup,' she said.

'Thank Gawd for that,' replied the funny hat. 'I was sure this was the right road, but Rocco here keeps insisting we should have hung a left at the secret nuclear testing site.'

'All right, Bruce, you made-a your point,' said the man in the passenger seat, who was wearing a scarlet dressing-gown, a rosary, one of those Lambretta hats, red gloves and a ring the size of a walnut. 'Hey, you seen a couple of cement lorries pass this way?'

Linda held her breath. 'You mean,' she said, as casually as she could manage, 'the lorries fetching the cement they use to make the concrete blocks they conceal the unautho-rised arms shipments in?'

'That'll be right,' the funny hat confirmed.

'They went, um, that way,' Linda said, pointing at random. 'About a quarter of an hour ago.'

'Huh!' The passenger snorted derisively. 'Late as usual. I told the President, "Boss," I said, "you no use that firm, not reliable. My brother-in-law, he very reliable, do you special deal." The President, he no listen. Pfui!' the passenger added. 'Come on, Bruce, time we go. Ciao.'

As the car drove off, Linda counted up to ten and pinched herself. Shit, she thought, if only I'd got that on tape . . .

Then she noticed the faint whirring noise.

She ripped back the zipper on her haversack. There, nestling among the socks and the underwear, was her pocket dictating machine. It was running, and on Record. Something must have jarred it – maybe the bump when she fell in the lake – and it had been recording away all this time . . .

She wound the tape back, and forwarded, and rewound, and backwards and forwards until she heard it. 'G'day, miss, but am I right for the submarine base?'

Reverently, she closed her eyes. There was, after all, a providence that looks after newshounds; one that shapes our ends, rough-hew them how we will. She started to grin –

And looked down at the lake, and saw the submarine.

A few moments later, she was scrambling back down the hillside. By the time she reached the shores of the lake it was fully emerged; and there, standing on the conning tower, were four women. They were all indescribably beautiful, in an otherworldly sort of way, and they wore robes of white samite; which turned out not to be a sort of cheese-cloth, as Linda had always assumed.

'Hail,' they said in chorus.

'Sorry?'

'Hail,' they repeated. 'Are you Linda Lachuk?'

Linda nodded. 'Yes,' she said.

'Linda Lachuk the *journalist*?'

She nodded again. 'That's me,' she said, not without a certain pride.

'Then you must come with us.'

'I beg your –?'

'To Avalon,' the fair ladies said, 'which lies in the Blessed Realms beyond the sundering seas. To cover the story of a lifetime,' they added.

'Huh?'

'The truth,' said the four ladies, as the wind billowed

their sleeves like sails. 'The truth about the Kennedy assassination. Come with us, and we shall show you.'

Linda paused, still holding one wet sock. 'Just a minute,' she said. 'Is this some sort of a wind-up, because . . . ?'

The ladies frowned, all at the same time. 'Certainly not,' they said. 'We thought you wanted to know the truth about that fateful day in Dallas, Texas, is all. But if you're too busy . . .'

'No!' Linda moved to spring forward and stubbed her toe on a rock. She didn't feel anything. 'Wait, please. Tell me, what did . . .?'

'Ah!' The ladies smiled enigmatically. 'You always thought, didn't you, that Kennedy was *shot*, that fateful day outside the Texas Book Repository.'

Linda nodded; and as she did so, she thought, *But he wasn't, was he? How could I have been so blind?*

'Whereas in fact,' the ladies said, 'what actually happened was that, using the staged assassination attempt as a diversion, we caught up JFK in a cloud of fire and carried him, still living, into Avalon, where he lives yet, along with King Arthur and Sir Francis Drake and Elvis Presley and Princess Di and all the rest of 'em. But we expect you'd already half guessed. Now hadn't you?'

Linda couldn't help herself. She nodded. 'There were some strong indications,' she murmured, 'if you knew what to look for.'

'Of course,' said the ladies, nodding sagely. 'And we guess you know he'll stay in Avalon, timeless and unchanging, until such time as the peace of the Earth is once again balanced on the razor's edge; whereupon he will come again into the world of men, riding in his manifest glory on the wings of the storm, and . . .'

'Yes?' Linda whispered.

'Start World War Three,' said the ladies. 'Come, time is short and we have far to go. How are you off for videotape, by the way? We have plenty, should you require it.'

'Thanks,' Linda said.

'Batteries?'

'What? Hell, I knew I'd forgotten –'

'We have many batteries,' said the ladies. 'Come. Your destiny awaits you. Only you can cover the story.'

'Yes,' Linda breathed, as if in a dream. 'Only me . . .'

'The public has a right to know. Come! Away! Away!'

And so Linda Lachuk, flower of all earthly journalism, took submarine for the fair isle of Avalon, that lies beyond the threshold of the dawn; and there she dwells yet, ageless and untiring, along with all the other antisocial pests they keep locked up there.

And all the headlines sounded for her on the other side.

As Calvin Dieb squelched his way out of the lake, his feet making wet-kiss noises at every step as the mud tried to steal his thousand-dollar gumboots, he noticed something small and shiny hanging on a bramble-branch that trailed down into the water. His car keys.

Hell, he muttered to himself, just as well I didn't lose them or I'd have been in real trouble.

After a short but knackering climb back up the hill he unlocked his car, which shrieked its alarm at him in friendly welcome, sat down heavily in the driver's seat and pressed the message button of his telephone.

– Hello, Mr Dieb, this is Cindi from the office. Your ex-wife called, can you call her back? She sounded – um, well, strange. Kinda, I don't know how to put this, friendly. She didn't yell. Well, not much. To start with. 'Bye, now.

– Hi, kid, this is Hernan. When can I have that goddamn

Pedretti Brothers file back, and Dan Vleek says lunch Thursday is OK. Who the hell is Dan Vleek, and when he says lunch, does he mean lunch, or just lunch? Call back immediately. Ciao.

– *Helloewe, Mister Deeb, this here is from Norway Olaf Bjornssen calling, me you not are knowing, a line of shipping I ern, you I am anxious to instruct a maritime insurance claim for to be pursuing. My nermber is . . .*

– *Hello, Calvin, this is Leonard. Been a long time, hasn't it? Maybe we could have lunch some day when you're free, there's a few things I'd like to talk over. Be seeing you.*

– *Hi, son, this is your dad here. I love you, son. I guess that's all. See you sometime, maybe. 'Bye.*

The last message gave Calvin quite a start, since his father had been dead these five years. In the end he figured it must be an old tape, not thoroughly wiped. He wiped it. Then he called Frank Lustmord.

'Frank? Hi, pal. Look, this Lake Chicopee thing. I'm at the lake now, and . . . You bet, guy, no substitute for seeing with your own eyes. And it's just as well I did, Frank, 'cos believe me, you got a serious problem here. Serious problem. Huh? Well, Frank, it's otters. Yeah, otters are a serious problem. Yes, Frank, like in serious *environmental* problem. Well yes, I guess you could, if you wanted to get blasted into mush by every TV station and newspaper from here to Seattle. You wouldn't be able to *give* the goddamn plots away free with gasoline, Frank, those green freaks'd have you looking like Hitler's elder brother, the one the family was too ashamed to talk about . . . Well, think about it, Frank, it's better you know these things *before* you spend twenty-seven million dollars . . . Yeah, well, you know, it's what we're here for, buddy. That's why you pay me, to think of these things. No, that's fine. That's great, Frank. What, *all* your corporate business? Why yes, sure, I'd be only too happy – sure thing, pal. See you around. Yeah, bye.'

Calvin put down the phone with a dazed grin smeared all over his face like a comedian's custard pie. He had no idea what had possessed him to tell Frank Lustmord that the otters were going to be a problem; because they *weren't*, goddamnit, he'd checked on that very point. But whatever the reason, it had worked, and now he had the Lustmord Corporation's business tied up and in the bag. It was as if he'd taken a shotgun to shoot his own foot off, missed and blown a hole in the ground that exposed a seam of gold-bearing quartz.

Or was it . . . ? Nah. Been out in the sun too long without a hat. There is no patron god of lawyers, and if there was one He'd be so expensive that not even lawyers could afford to go to Him. There's Kali Ma, of course, and the Father of Lies and Mercury, god of thieves; but they're retained occasionally on a sort of consultancy basis, not to be construed as implying any ongoing contractual relationship. The lawyer stands alone in the cosmos, or at least he clings to its back, inserts his proboscis and sucks. If he, Calvin Dieb, had managed to ensnare the Lustmord corporation, it was through his own unaided efforts, or the random workings of Luck, or because Frank Lustmord had offended his own personal corps of gods badly enough to let himself in for a level of punishment on which locusts, boils and frogs are too cissy even to be considered.

He shrugged, switched on the engine and engaged drive. Just before he pulled away, however, he caught sight of someone on the road ahead of him, waving. Normally, he'd have driven straight on past; but hell, it was his day for acting out of character. He put the car in neutral and wound down the window.

'What's the matter?' he asked.

'Are you Calvin Dieb?' the stranger asked. A strange stranger, by all appearances; wearing a sort of black dufflecoat thing with the hood up, and carrying a long bundle wrapped up in black cloth that might have been fishing-rods but probably wasn't.

'That depends,' Calvin replied. 'Who wants to know?'

'My card.' The stranger thrust a rectangle of black and red pasteboard through the window.

'Pleased to meet you, M –' Calvin broke off as he read the one word on the card. He looked at it again, and then back at the stranger, or as much of the stranger as he could see past the dufflecoat hood. 'Hi,' he croaked.

'I've been looking for you all over,' the stranger said. 'Your office said you might be here, so I came over.'

'Ah,' said Calvin, making a mental note to sack everybody when – if – he got back. 'Great,' he added. 'You found me.'

'Yup.' The stranger nodded. 'And in case you don't believe what it says on that card,' he added, throwing back the hood, 'these might go some way to confirming it. Yes?'

Calvin nodded. 'Say,' he asked, curious in spite of everything, 'don't mind my asking, but don't those things rip up the pillows when you sleep?'

'They would, if I ever did,' the stranger replied, combing a stray lock of jet-black hair back into place behind the right-hand horn. 'But I don't. Kinda goes with the territory.'

'That figures,' Calvin muttered. 'And what about the, uh, feet? What do you do about them?'

'Nothing. That's the joy of hooves, they don't wear out. Look, why I wanted to see you was, for some time now I've been thinking it was time I got myself a really good lawyer.'

Calvin frowned. 'I thought you got 'em all,' he replied. 'Eventually, I mean.'

'A good *living* lawyer,' Satan replied. 'Someone with expertise in contract work particularly.'

'Contract?'

'Sales and purchases.' Satan grinned disconcertingly. 'I need someone who can make an agreement that's *completely* watertight. For which,' he added, 'I'm prepared to pay top dollar. Interested?'

Calvin couldn't speak, but he could nod. He nodded.

'The package I had in mind,' Satan continued, 'was basically a three-year fixed term. During that time, of course, you can have anything you want.'

'Anything?'

'Anything. Your dearest wish. Your heart's desire. You name it, you can have it.'

'For three years?'

'Three years.'

'And after three years?' Calvin said, feeling as he did so that this was rather like shoving a mirror on a stick into a gift horse's mouth and asking it to say 'Aaah'. 'And after that?'

Satan shrugged. 'Then,' he said, 'we might consider a more permanent arrangement. What do you say?'

Calvin opened his mouth.

There's a word in the English language that could have been specially custom-coined to encapsulate Calvin's response. It's short, only three letters; it begins with Y and ends with S, and there's an E in it somewhere.

'Yes,' Calvin said.

Janice DeWeese scrambled out of the shallow water at the lake's edge, cursed her own clumsiness, sat down and took off her boots. By the look of it, there was enough water in her left boot alone to irrigate the Nevada desert. Marvellous, she thought; just wonderful. I've got a nine-hour hike to look forward to, in wet boots. This is probably going to turn out to be my best holiday ever.

She was emptying an equivalent quantity of water out of her right boot, and wondering how come the lake seemed to be as full as ever when so much of its contents had found its way into her footwear, when she became aware that someone was watching her.

Maybe under other circumstances she'd have been intimidated; not, however, under these. The prospect of a twenty-two-mile squelch in sopping wet clothes had made her quite possibly the most dangerous life-form in Iowa.

'Creep,' she called out imperiously. 'Yoo-hoo, creep, come on out of there, where I can throttle you. I'm gonna count to three and –'

'All right, all right.' The undergrowth to her right rustled a little. 'There's no need to get all snotty about it.'

The vegetation parted, and a very small anthropoid shape under an enormous hat waddled towards her. It looked like a mushroom; at least, it looked like the sort of weird mushroom you might see after eating too many weird mushrooms. In any event, it looked about as threatening as a bottle of ketchup, and not much bigger.

'Fine,' Janice said, with a yawn. 'Now piss off, before I cut you up and fry you.'

The rim of the hat tilted upwards, giving Janice a dim, overshadowed glimpse of a pointed nose-tip and two shining pink eyes. 'Very droll,' it said. 'All I need after the day I've had is amateur humour. I don't think I'll even bother with you now.'

The hat rotated through a hundred and eighty degrees

and was about to disappear back into the bushes when Janice snapped, 'Hoy!' in a tone of voice that'd have got her slung out of any army training camp for being too brusque. The hat stopped and swivelled back, like the turret of a floppy felt tank.

'Well?' it said.

'Just a minute, you,' Janice growled, stooping down to try and see under the brim. 'Just why were you looking at me, anyway?'

'Market research,' the hat replied.

'Market what?'

'Research. I thought you might be interested in buying something, that's all. But I can see I'm wasting my time.'

'How can you see anything, underneath that thing?'

'Ah,' the hat sighed, 'humour again. What is it with you people, anyway? With you it's nothing but humour, humour, humour all the damn time.'

'Sell me what?'

'Oh, you wouldn't be –'

'Sell me what, goddamnit?'

The hat wobbled, as if shrugging its brim. 'Oh, just some old stuff. Gold, diamonds, that sort of thing. Nothing that's any use for –'

'What did you say?'

This time the brim lifted at the front, until the long, droopy feather stuck in its band dipped in the mud. 'Gold,' it said. 'A dollar fifty a kilo. Diamonds. Ten dollars a kilo. Platinum. Ninety-five cents a kilo, or buy ten kilos of diamonds, get a kilo of platinum absolutely free. Can I go now, please?'

For a split second, Janice gawped, her mouth opening and closing again like a goldfish who's just been told it's won the Lottery. Then a bored expression took possession of her face and changed all the locks. 'Get outa here,' she said. 'Listen, shortass, I may be stupid but I'm not that stupid. An all-powerful supreme being couldn't create anybody *that* stupid, even if you gave him a pattern to work from. Go on, get lost.'

The hat bristled; that is, the pile of its felt seemed to stand on end. 'Are you calling me a liar?' it demanded. 'Well? Are you?'

'Yup.'

'Well, you're wrong, see? Because this is the genuine stuff. You want to see it?'

'No.'

'Tough, 'cos you're going to.' A tiny hand appeared from under the hat, clutching a fair-sized sports bag in defiance of all the laws of physics. 'Go on, open it.'

Janice shrugged, and pulled back the zip –

'Oh,' she said.

How she knew it was all good stuff, the genuine article, ninety-nine-point nine per cent pure, she didn't actually know; but she did. The gold had that dull shine that no brass can ever quite match. The diamonds had that cold, blue sparkle that glass has never quite got the hang of. As for the white stuff, she didn't actually know what platinum looked like but she was prepared to bet this was platinum. There was enough wealth in the bag to elect four presidents, assuming you could find anybody idiotic enough to want to do such a thing.

'Satisfied?' asked the hat, coldly. 'Right, then. Do the zip up and give it back, and I can be on my way.'

Janice shook her head. 'No way,' she said. 'Sorry, pal, but this lot goes with me. How much did you say you wanted for it?'

'The whole lot?'

'Yeah,' Janice said, her voice slightly wobbly, 'why not? The whole lot.'

'Well.' The front of the brim oscillated as the life-form under it made some calculations. 'I couldn't take less than forty dollars,' it said. 'For that, I'd throw in the bag, as well.'

'Forty dollars.'

'OK, thirty-five. Damnit, the diamonds alone are worth that.'

'Deal.'

'All right, if you insist, thirty-two fifty. Jesus, but you know how to – what did you just say?'

'I said Deal,' said Janice.

'Cash?'

'Sure.'

'I'd need at least ten per cent up front, and the rest by –'

'Here,' Janice pulled out three tens and a five from her top pocket and stuffed them under the hatband. 'Paid in full.'

'Really?'

'Really.'

'Wow.' The hand reappeared, grabbed the notes and pulled them in under the brim. 'Thanks. Hey, that's really – thanks.'

'Don't mention it,' Janice replied, gripping the bag firmly in both hands. 'Can I ask you a question, mister?'

'Sure thing. Shoot.'

'You won't take this the wrong way?'

'Guaranteed.'

'Then how come,' Janice asked, as calmly and rationally as she could, 'you've just sold me millions of bucks' worth of diamonds and stuff for thirty-five dollars? Not,' she added quickly, 'that I'm complaining. And you can't have it back, either.'

The hat rotated backwards and forwards through a hundred and eighty degrees. 'Don't want it back, lady. Thirty-five dollars in hard currency may not be all that much to you, but where I come from . . . Hell, you could buy where I come from for thirty-five dollars in US Treasury bills. In fact,' it added, after a moment's reflection, 'I might just do that.'

'Where's that, then?'

'In there.' The hat nodded towards the lake. 'And before you ask how can I live in a lake, please don't. I have this feeling that a serious credibility shortfall at this juncture might endanger our future trading relationship.'

'How can you live in a lake?'

'How can you live outside of one?'

Janice wrinkled her nose. 'You're a fish? Actually, I've seen those jellyfish, the ones with the big –'

'I am not a fish,' replied the hat austerely. 'If you must know, my name is Captain Hat, of the Lake Chicopee Free Traders Association. And where I live,' he added, 'we use that sparkly stuff for pebble-dashing houses.'

'Diamonds?'

'Sure. Whereas thirty-five dollars American –'

'I see,' Janice said, inaccurately. 'You've got a lot of, ah, unexploited mineral resources, then?'

'You could say that. It's props.'

'Props?'

'From the scenarios.' The hat tilted a few degrees. 'You know, the scenarios. The little shows they put on for the customers.'

'Customers?' Janice raised an eyebrow. 'You mean, this lake's some kind of holiday resort? Like a summer camp or something?'

'You could say that,' the hat replied. 'Better still, call it a theme park. But of course you . . . No, wait, of course, you don't remember a thing, do you?'

'Remember what?'

'About what happened to you, when you were in the lake.'

Janice rubbed her chin. 'Let's see,' she said. 'I fell in, I got wet, I splashed about a bit and then I got out again. Can't say there's any significant gaps in that.'

Although Janice couldn't see it, because of the brim of the hat, she could sense that somewhere in the shadows there was a big grin, generated at her expense. 'Right. Now then. Did your entire life flash in front of your eyes, all in one split second? Probably happened in the moment between your head going under the water and coming back up again.'

'No, I don't –' Janice paused. 'Hey, now you mention it, maybe it did. Or at least there was *something*. More like a dream, I guess. I can't remember anything about it, but . . .'

The hat repeated its nodding manoeuvre. 'That's it, then. I don't suppose you're going to believe this, but I'll tell you anyway. During that very short time, you went through this series of really weird adventures, courtesy of the ole Indian spirit that haunts the lake. She's called Okinawa, something like that.'

'Okinawa's a city in Japan.'

'Okeewana, then. Whatever. The way it works is,' the hat continued, 'if you fall in the lake and make a wish, the wish comes true. Doesn't have to be a *conscious* wish, either. It works just as well if there's something you're secretly daydreaming about, like in your subconscious mind. That can be very hairy, believe me. You had a pretty strange time of it yourself, come to that. I'd tell you about it, but you don't want to know.'

'Yeah?' Janice yawned. 'You're right, I don't. But what's all this about props and scenarios? If this is some roundabout way of telling me this stuff's all stolen –'

The hat quivered a little. 'Of course it's *stolen*,' it said. 'Who the hell do you think I am, Montezuma's rich brother-in-law? The scenarios are what happen on the other side of the lake.'

Janice turned her head towards the tall, round hill with trees on it that stood on the other side of the water. 'What, you mean over by that clump of fir trees? I can't see –'

'On the flipside,' the hat said patiently. 'The obverse.' A finger emerged from under the brim and pointed at the middle of the water. 'Under that.'

'Under the lake?'

'Not under,' said the hat, exasperated. 'On the other side. Come on, it's not a difficult concept, surely. Anyhow, when they do these scenarios, sometimes they get careless with the props, leave them lying about and all, and my boys and me – well, we help keep the place tidy. We have very strong views about ecology and stuff.'

'Tidy as in free of waste gold?'

The hat nodded. 'You bet. Gold's a good example; I mean, it's one hundred per cent non biodegradable, gold. Leave damn great chunks of gold lying around the place, it's there for ever.'

'And diamonds?'

'Diamonds are forever, too. Well-known fact. So we, er, recycle them.'

'I see.' Janice looked at the hat, and then down at the sports bag. On the one hand, she knew all about stealing and how wrong it was; but on the other hand, stealing from a fiction of the hallucinating imagination probably wasn't nearly so bad. On a par, perhaps, with murdering the imaginary friend you had when you were six. 'Well,' she said, 'you may be telling the truth or you may just have escaped from the home for deranged millinery, but to be honest with you, I don't give a damn. I think I'll go home now.'

'Good idea,' said the hat. 'I think I'll do the same. Call me superstitious if you like, but this place gives me the creeps.'

'This hillside?'

'This side of the lake. So long, Janice DeWeese.'

'Hey, how do you know my –?'

The hat started to scuttle, like some experimental model of soft-shell crab that got shelved when the funding ran out. 'I know all about you,' it said. 'Sister, what I don't know about you ain't worth knowing. You and those priests! Wow!'

'Hey!' Janice looked again, and realised that she was shouting at an empty landscape. She noticed something else, too.

'Neat,' she said.

It was a rainbow; a huge, scintillating, warm, humming rainbow, and one end of it was coming out of the sports bag. The other end, needless to say, was in the middle of the lake, and its reflection looked just like a big, friendly grin. It vanished as abruptly as it had appeared, and then it began to rain.

Janice looked down at the sports bag as she pulled her collar round her ears. All that gold, all those diamonds; she checked, and they were still there. With that much money, you could buy one hell of a lot of cosmetic surgery. Alternatively, with that much money you wouldn't need to, because with that much money you'd automatically become irresistibly attractive no matter what the hell you looked like; and the beauty that comes with obscene wealth never fades or tarnishes, and you can eat whatever you like, and there's no need to sit around for hours with grey slime on your face and slices of cucumber over your eyes. From now on for the rest of her life, Janice realised, she need never be alone or unadored again.

Nice thought . . .

Fairly nice thought . . .

Something to think about . . .

CHAPTER FIFTEEN

'So,' demanded Talks To Squirrels, 'who's it going to be?'

Lake Chicopee; the round blue centre of the round blue Earth. From the hilltop with the trees it looked like a small Earth, blue and green, white and brown patches where the trees and clouds and mountains were reflected in it. From higher still, on the other side of the sky, the big Earth looks very much the same; another world, a place to go away from and come back to, but made separate by an elemental barrier that only the mind can cross.

'I've decided,' Okeewana said, looking closely at her shoes.

'Yeah, right,' said the Chief Goblin impatiently. 'So share. Who is it?'

An otter waddled down the slope and slid into the water, leaving behind it a trail of bubbles, like a submarine. Like submarines and (to a certain extent) ducks, otters can make themselves at home on either side of the water, at least for a while, just as squirrels divide their time between the ground and the treetops. Whether they're different submarines, otters, ducks and squirrels when they're on the other side, nobody really knows. Only Man, the measure of all things, knows when he's truly in his element.

'I just want you to know,' the girl continued, 'I've given this a lot of thought. And my decision's final, so there's no point making a fuss.'

'OK, OK,' sighed a Viking. 'Understanding you all we are. The person name, so kind if you will be.'

The girl stooped, picked up a stone and threw it as far as she could. It hit the water with a tremendous splash.

'Me,' she said.

Everybody spoke at once; it was, in fact, what the writers of communiqués call a free and frank exchange of views, to the point of almost total unintelligibility. The gist of it, however, wasn't hard to grasp.

'You want to know why?' the girl said quietly.

Immediately, the babbling stopped.

'No,' said Mummy Bear.

'Tough,' the girl replied, 'because I'm gonna tell you anyway. I'm sick to the teeth of this place, is why. And I'm sick to the teeth of this lousy job, and I've had it up to here with you. I want to travel. I want to see the world. I want to *live* a little.'

'I tried that once,' said the doctor. 'Overrated. A bit like Japanese food.'

The girl shrugged. 'Anyhow,' she said, 'that's it, and it's final. I've got a job to go to, all lined up, even a body to do it in, so . . .'

'A body?' demanded the Goblin, his tongue involuntarily flicking round his lips, like the mortuary cat when they're scrubbing up for an autopsy. 'Lucky you.'

'Where'd you get that from?' asked Talks to Squirrels. 'You mean that crazy journalist bitch?'

The girl smiled. 'Not her,' she said. 'The Inspector. Captain Hat stole him for me, and now I'm going to be him. My replacement starts tomorrow, so I suggest you do a stocktake and get the place tidied up.'

'Replacement,' the doctor echoed. 'Hey, just a . . .'

But before he could say anything else, the girl jumped up, shook herself and leaped into the air. Her wings opened, and with a joyful quack she shot up above the trees, circled the lake three times and planed down, at full speed, right into the middle of the water, like a torpedo. Ripples welled out of the gash she made in the reflected sky, and faded away.

'It's a ruddy fix,' growled Prince Charming, his aristo-cratic drawl slipping. 'They ain't 'eard the last of this, not by a long way. I got a good mind to tell the giant.'

'Cut it out, will you?' sighed Talks To Squirrels. 'I reckon it's only fair, at that. I mean, she's been here ever since the lake was a boggy patch on a flat plain. If she's had enough, she's had enough. Let's go eat.'

He stood up, bent his bow, shot one arrow into the water at the point where Okeewana had dived in, three more into Daddy Bear and another two into Prince Charming's ear, and trudged away down the hill.

The rest of the redcoats watched him go in silence. Something he'd said had woken an old, submerged memory in all of them. They looked at each other.

'Eat?' said the Prince.

'That's food,' explained Baby Bear. 'We have food in our act, only it's not real, only pretend. Wax fruit and plas-ter bread and stuff.'

'Real food,' murmured one of the Russians.

'Smorgasbord,' whispered a Viking.

'Honey sandwiches,' breathed Daddy Bear.

'Children,' sighed the Chief Goblin. 'With sage and parsley and just a soupçon of turmeric.'

'I'd be quite happy with ham and eggs,' said the doctor, staring wistfully at the lake. 'And a couple of waffles with maple syrup, naturally.'

'And coffee,' the Prince interrupted. 'Dear God, real coffee. Made with genuine atoms and molecules, not like that 'orrible imaginary stuff you get in the canteen.'

The goblin nodded. 'What I wouldn't give,' he said, 'for a cup of real Blue Mountain coffee, with cream and lots of brown sugar; you know, the crunchy stuff that looks like bits of ground-up whisky bottle.'

'Quite,' agreed the Prince, looking at him sideways. 'My dearest wish, you could say.'

The doctor lifted his head, like a warhorse at the sound of the trumpet. 'Your heart's desire, even?'

'You're way ahead of me, Doc, I can see that.' The Prince grinned. 'Well, why not? In fact, we should get a staff discount or something.'

'Let's do it.'

'Yeah.'

The rest of the company looked at them. 'What are you two gibbering about?' Mummy Bear demanded. 'How do you mean, staff rates?'

'He means,' Daddy Bear said, his face split by a grin like a scale model of the Grand Canyon, 'staff rates. Wait up, you guys, I'm coming too.'

As the three of them began to run down the hill, straight towards the lake, there was a general tumbling of pennies from a great height. 'Oh, I *see*,' muttered Murdoch the footman. 'Heart's desire, right.' He shrugged. 'It might work, at that.'

'What might —?' Mummy Bear began to ask; then she

understood too, and a moment later she was running after them, folding her pinny as she ran. By the time she reached the water's edge, the doctor and the Prince had already jumped in. She wasn't all that far behind; and, with a loud rebel yell and a cry of: 'Madeira cake!' she closed her eyes, crossed her claws and jumped.

Wesley climbed out of the water and looked around.

'Oh,' he said.

Life can be very cruel, but it's scarcely if ever unusual; which is why it's legal as a form of punishment in the USA. The term 'life sentence', seen in that light, becomes rather frightening.

'Oh well,' Wesley said, and he waded ashore. Might have known, he muttered to himself. Must have been soft in the head, coming all this way and jumping in a lake, and really and truly expecting that the wish would come true. If he'd whispered, 'Double pneumonia,' under his breath as he jumped, he might just conceivably not have been disappointed. But he hadn't; so he was.

He looked round again, and then up at the sun, though he didn't actually know how to use it as an aid to navigating his way back to Brierley Hill. All this way, and for nothing. At times, life can be very, very usual.

Just as he'd made up his mind to try north, he heard a splashing noise coming from behind him and looked round, in time to see –

– A man in bedraggled ermine robes, eating a hamburger –

– A man in a white hospital coat with a stethoscope round his neck, eating a club sandwich –

– Three bears, eating muffins –

– Sundry Cherokee braves, in warpaint and clutching

feathered spears, on which were impaled appetising-looking bits of chicken tikka –

– Sundry Vikings, in armour and winged helmets, gnawing on whole chickens –

– Sundry Goblins, gnawing on something that looked sort of vaguely familiar –

– and some others he couldn't even begin to identify, all walking up out of the lake, grinning, laughing and talking with their mouths full. As soon as they saw Wesley they stopped dead in their tracks and saluted. One of them, apparently a Viking warrior with a chicken leg poking out through his beard, giggled.

'Er, hello,' Wesley said, out of a combination of nerves, embarrassment and force of habit. 'Can you tell me the way to Oskaloosa, please?'

None of the strange-looking people spoke. A goblin shook his head. A man in what Wesley guessed was a butler's outfit started peeling a banana.

'Oskaloosa,' Wesley repeated, wishing very much that he'd kept his mouth shut and kept on going. 'Do I go back up to the main road and bear east, or . . .?'

'You can't,' mumbled a bear through a mouthful of honey. 'Not allowed. Thought you'd have known that, Chief.'

Wesley began to get *that* feeling: the unmistakable one that starts in your throat and dribbles down like splodged-on gloss paint until it fills you right up. Rabbits and hedgehogs get it when they look up from the patch of hard, black, grassless ground they've just shuffled on to and see two very bright white lights coming straight at them.

''Scuse me?' he croaked.

'Are you going to do roll-call, then?' asked the man in the white coat. 'Because I've got a workshop full of Vikings with their heads in pieces, and once you lose one of those little eyelid return springs, you've got to tear the place apart to find it.'

'Roll-call,' Wesley parrotted. 'Sorry, I don't quite –'

The man in the wet ermine tutted. 'Sorry, Chief, we forgot. The routine is, roll-call followed by kit inspection followed by the day's assignments and 'anding out the luncheon vouchers, followed by sick parade and ten minutes when we can see you if there's anything we want to talk about, but we never do. You 'ave got the register, 'aven't you?'

'Register.' Wesley's mind filled with images of school (he always stood at the back and could never see a thing over the heads of the boys in front; he only knew what the Headmaster looked like because he'd seen a picture of him in a giveaway newspaper, and even then it was only a hazy mental image, because the vinegar had made the paper all transparent). 'Look, I'm not a hundred per cent sure I know what you mean. Are you sure it's me you –?'

'Wesley Higgins,' said a goblin, chewing a fingernail, not his own. 'You're the new manager, right?'

'Uh?'

The goblin glanced back at the rest of the crowd. 'She didn't tell him,' it hissed. 'Goddamn sneaky daughtero-fabitch didn't tell him. That's *bad*.'

'Tell me *what*?'

'Typical,' sniffed Skellidge the footman. 'Suppose she didn't want to give him the chance to refuse.'

'You can see her point,' whispered a bear. 'I mean, I'd have refused. Wouldn't you?'

'Refused what?'

'That the point is not. The point is after being to have told him common courtesy. Administrative smoothly the likewise.'

''Scuse me,' Wesley said; and he said it in a voice that faintly surprised him. 'Please tell me if I've got this wrong, but am I meant to be, you know, in charge?'

The strange-looking people nodded in unison, like a Hollywood script conference. 'You're the new manager,' the ermined bloke said. 'Congratulations and all that. Now, while I'm talking to you, do you possibly think I could put in for a new robe? Only water does tend to play 'avoc with me trimmings, I'll never get it quite right ever again.'

The doctor frowned. 'If he's having a new robe, then I really ought to get that impact screwdriver I put in for last month. I mean, it is actually a tool of my trade, and the time I waste having to drill out neck axis pins that've rusted in solid. I mean, fair's fair –'

'Yeah, but what about my new wrist?' whined a goblin. 'I've been waiting weeks, and if he's getting a screwdriver –'

''Scuse me –'

'Or,' the goblin went on, suddenly smiling, 'if it's easier, I could go on the sick until the delivery arrives. I expect it'd make the paperwork easier, too.'

'A new battleaxe four months I waiting have been. Fair fair's, as he the man said.'

'Quiet!' Once again, Wesley's voice surprised him, and he found himself automatically standing up straight and trying to shove an imaginary conker through where he remembered the hole in the lining of his jacket used to be. 'Now then,' the voice that was coming out of Wesley went on, 'let's get this straight, shall we? I'm supposed to be your new boss, right?'

'You got it, Chief.'

'So it would seem,' Wesley said irritably. 'Apparently from a great height, too. Would this be anything to do with me falling in the lake?'

'You go – I mean, yes, Chief. Your heart's desire.'

'Was it?' Wesley demanded, shocked. 'Can't have been. And anyway, it didn't work.' He looked up at the row of attentive, profoundly weird faces and mentally revised the last statement. 'I assume it didn't work. Did it work?'

'You bet, Chief.'

'And I wished to be in charge of you lot, did I? Seriously.'

The bear shrugged. 'You must have done,' he said.

'He did,' Skellidge broke in. 'I seem to remember it was something vague about wishing he lived in a magical fairy-tale land and how he wished he could be a noble or a baron or some such. According to the old saying, there's one thousand, four hundred and forty just like him born every day, in which case God help us all.'

Wesley hesitated. Someone had dumped a whole load of gubbins in his windpipe, making it hard for him to breathe, and his vocal cords had been repossessed by the finance company. Apart from that, he felt just fine. And he understood. In a sense. Up to a point.

'So it did come true,' he said. 'Gosh.'

'Bit slow, isn't he?' whispered a goblin. 'Mind you, I'm not saying that's a bad thing in a boss. Probably the reverse.'

'Yes, but there's slow and there's half-witted,' replied the doctor. 'And when you think about it, who's going to get the blame when everything goes wrong? Give you three guesses.'

So it had come true, Wesley repeated to himself. Amazing; but there it was. And now, presumably, his whole life would change for ever and he'd be . . .

His whole life. For ever.

Um . . .

Maybe what he was thinking seeped through on to his face, because one of the bears stepped forward and gave him a friendly pat on the back. 'Look,' said the bear, 'I know what you're thinking. And you're right.'

'I am?' Wesley replied, once his head had stopped reverberating. 'But . . .'

'What you've got to do,' said the bear, 'is look on the bright side. Be positive. After all, it's not as if you're leaving anything particularly wonderful behind, is it?'

'True,' Wesley conceded, as his memory put together a quick montage of all the things that were nice about his daily routine back in Brierley Hill. It didn't take long.

'You see?' said the bear. 'Look at it this way. Whatever it turns out to be like running this place, it can't possibly be worse than what you're leaving behind, surely.'

Wesley frowned. 'Actually,' he said, 'it could. I might get killed, or horribly maimed, or I might get a hideous disease or even just toothache, which'd be bad enough without dentists or antibiotics. And what about food and somewhere to live and, er, toilet facilities, and a pension plan so I can make sensible provision for my old age? Or there could be wars and violence and stuff. Or mosquitoes, and I haven't got one of those net things you sleep under, so what'd happen if I got malaria? And I don't suppose there's central heating anywhere, and it's supposed to be very difficult to light a fire if you don't know how, and I haven't got any matches or anything, and what am I supposed to do about clothes, or are they provided? Or . . .'

'Boss,' sighed the bear, 'shut up. Just take it from me, will you? It's better here. For someone like you, with an untrammelled imagination that can never find rest in the mundane, everyday . . .' The bear stopped talking and sucked its lower lip. 'Mind you,' it said, 'you do have a point. Hadn't you considered that before you made the wish?'

'Well, no,' Wesley replied. 'I just sort of assumed, you know. That there'd be food and proper toilets and somewhere you could have a bath without fish nibbling at you.' He stared at the bear with frightened, unsettling eyes. 'I don't think I want my heart's desire, after all,' he whispered. 'Especially not if I've got to be in charge of anything. I've never been in charge of anything in my whole life before.'

'You'll manage,' the bear replied, with at least forty-five per cent sincerity. 'Just you wait and see. And besides,' it went on, looking away, 'you haven't got a choice. You've got to be in charge. Goes with the territory.'

'Ah,' Wesley said. 'I see.'

'Should've been more careful what you wished for, huh?'

'I suppose I should,' Wesley said. 'And I'm very grateful to you and everyone else, it's really nice of you to go to all this trouble. But –'

'No buts, Chief,' said the bear. 'And you can't just jump back in the lake and wish for it all to go back exactly the way it was. Which is odd, when you think about it,' it added. 'Inconsistent, really.'

'Yes.'

'Like Life, in fact; which, of course, this is. You going to do roll-call now, then?'

Wesley shrugged. Projected against the backs of his eyelids he could see exactly what it was going to be like from now on; his future life flashing before his eyes, in fact, which was a subtle variation on the old drowning routine. It was endless, and boring, and there wasn't even death to look forward to, let alone lunchtimes and weekends and evenings and two weeks holiday a year. And no money, either; not that there'd be anything to spend it on, except for the pitifully few black-market goodies Captain Hat might be able to come up with – a new pair of socks once every ten years, a half-empty tube of toothpaste, three peppermints at the end of a ragged paper roll.

'It's like this,' said the bear, compassionately. 'You only get out of the lake what you put into it to begin with. And what you put into it is always you. Which means you always get you out of it, ultimately.'

'Great,' Wesley said, bitterly but with resignation. 'You've no idea how cheered up that doesn't make me. All right, where's the register? S'pose I'd better get on with it.'

'That's the spirit,' said the bear. 'Wish fulfilment's a bitch and then you die. She always used to keep the register under that rock there.' The bear walked back to join the rest of the redcoats, who were dwelling lovingly on the last few crumbs of their food. 'Some of them find it helps to have a hobby,' it said. 'Talks To Squirrels shoots people, for instance. The Vikings play Monopoly every Tuesday fortnight. They made the set themselves out of stones and bits of tree bark. I expect if you ask them nicely they'll let you be the little racing car.'

To begin with, they tell you there's magic. Elves live in woods, there are witches under the stairs and trolls in the airing cupboard. Father Christmas brings you presents if you're good, and the horrible green slimy thing that lives in the toilet cistern will get you if you aren't. There's magic, and there's justice, and you know where you stand.

Later on, they tell you there's no magic; but there's electricity and physics and computers and all sorts of machines for flying and killing and making you better, which do the same things as magic used to do, only cheaper and better and without the need for skilled labour. But there's no justice, there's not even any logic, and you know that if you stand there, chances are something's going to fall on you and make you go *splat*!

In the end you come to realise that there are still witches under the stairs and trolls in the airing cupboard, and the green slimy thing can take many forms and live in many places besides the cistern; and yes, jolly fat men do come down the chimney from time to time, but in reality they turn the place over and take your video and your CD player with them when they go. You do have the option of resisting, of fighting back with everything you've got; but don't let them catch you doing it, or you'll go to prison. Most of all, you come to realise that you've got nothing except what you stand up in, and that's somehow never enough.

Lake Chicopee exists all right; and the magic does work. The fact remains that the most anybody's ever got out of jumping into it is a bad cold.

The lake is quiet now. A few ducks chug up and down, steering with their feet. An otter ploughs a V-shaped wake through the reflected mountains. They have the sense not to be under the surface of the water, and to have no wishes whatsoever.

You only get out of it what you put into it, and what you put into it is never enough.

DJINN
RUMMY

For James Spartacus Hale
and Colin Wilberforce Lincoln Murray,
who, on 1 October 1994,
abolished slavery in Somerset.

CHAPTER ONE

67,811 pints today please, milkman.

Rule one in the licensed victualling trade: Know Your Clientele. Ignore it, and you might as well keep the doors locked.

Mr D. Jones had been in the business for a very long time, and he had long since learned everything there is to know about running a hotel, bar and bistro catering exclusively for drowned sailors.

It is, in fact, fairly straightforward. Good plain food; never under any circumstances allow the bar to run dry; strong tea with lashings of milk and sugar. And, of course, ensure that all tables are secured to the floor with half-inch carriage bolts.

He glanced up through the glass roof. Light never quite made it down as far as The Locker, but the water overhead was turning the precise shade of muggy dark olive that implied daybreak. Time to roll up the shutters, take the towels off the pumps and start a new day.

D. Jones folded the scrap of paper, pushed it into the bottle and rammed home the cork. Then he opened Number Six airlock.

A message in a bottle.

Having decided to kill herself, Jane went into the nearest chemist's shop.

'I'd like a large bottle of aspirins, please,' she said to the man behind the counter. He looked at her. In fact, as far as Jane was concerned, he made an unnecessarily thorough job of it, as if he was planning on doing an autopsy without the tedious business of cutting her up first.

'Aspirins?' he asked, making it sound as if she'd asked for the elixir of eternal youth.

'Aspirins,' Jane replied. 'Please. And could you hurry it up? I'm on my lunch break.'

The man, who was white-haired and very tall, sniffed. 'Any particular sort?' he asked. 'Or just aspirins?'

'Just aspirins.'

The man smiled. 'Not sure we've got any of those in stock, just aspirins. I'll have to look out the back. Don't go away.'

Before Jane could say anything, the man had darted away into the stockroom. She felt a strong inclination to make her escape while he was gone, but the voice of logic inside her head dissuaded her. *Come off it, girl*, it said, *you've made up your mind to commit suicide and you're afraid something bad might happen to you? In a chemist's?*

The man reappeared.

'You're in luck,' he said, extending a hand containing a big brown bottle. 'Just the one left. Directions on the label, that'll be two pounds seventy.'

It was, Jane couldn't help observing, a very old bottle. It had cobwebs on it. She'd read somewhere that out-of-date medicines could be very bad for you.

'Thanks,' she said. 'Just what I wanted. Keep the change.'

Now then; where? Did it matter? Anywhere she could be sure of a little bit of peace and quiet. Her flat. No, not her flat; they wouldn't find her for days (who would they be, she wondered) and by then she probably wouldn't be very nice . . . A hotel? She looked in her purse, which contained three pounds and seventeen pence, and no cheque book or credit card. She'd left them at home, on the basis that you can't take it with you. This, she muttered to herself, is getting tiresome.

A railway station. Yes. She was, after all, about to embark on a very long journey.

There was a station; and the station had one of those waiting rooms that make you decide to wait on the platform instead. Guaranteed privacy. She sat down, opened her bag and took out the bottle.

Note. Should she write a note? It was traditional, yes, but when you looked at it objectively, what the hell was the point? She had no family or other human associates to whom she owed an explanation; what made her think that the coroner was going to be interested in her tawdry little problems? They have a hard life, coroners; long hours, calls out in the middle of the night, constant association with lawyers, policemen and dead bodies. Boredom would probably be the last straw; and besides, she didn't have a pen with her, and a suicide note written in eyebrow pencil smacked of undue frivolity.

Goodbye, cruel world. She unscrewed the bottle . . .

WHOOSH!

'Thank goodness for that,' said the genie. 'For a moment there I was beginning to get worried.'

He hung in the air like a cloud of gunsmoke on a still, bright day; and as each second passed he became more substantial and more brain-wrenchingly incredible. There was a tinkle as the bottle hit the concrete floor and disintegrated into small, sharp brown fragments.

'You'd think,' he went on, 'I'd have had more sense, particularly in my line of business. First thing they teach you in genie school, if a strange man comes up to you, offers you sweets and asks you to get into his bottle, walk away, or better still, rip his head off and swallow it.' He sighed, and the effort made his component molecules sway in the air. 'Fourteen years this Tuesday fortnight I've been in that sodding bottle, and the sanitary arrangements left something to be desired, I'm telling you.'

He was no longer transparent; scarcely translucent. A shaft of light nudging its way through the dusty window hit the back of his head and, knowing what was good for it, refracted violently.

Genies are designed to be useful rather than ornamental, and this one was a masterpiece of the genre. There was enough ivory in its tusks to make cue balls for all the snooker tables in Europe.

'Who are you?' Jane said.

The genie frowned. 'Are you serious?' it demanded. 'Or just extremely sceptical?'

'You're a *genie*?'

'Hole in one.'

'A real genie?'

The genie clicked its tongue. 'No,' it replied. 'I'm a fake, you can tell by the lack of hallmarks. Of course I'm a real genie. What do you want, a certificate of authenticity?'

'What . . . ?' Jane felt her vocabulary clot. On the one hand, she had made up her mind to put an end to her pointless life, the existence of genies wasn't really germane to the various issues that had influenced her in making that decision, and time was getting on. If she didn't get a move on, she'd arrive in Heaven too late for dinner. On the other hand . . .

'Admit it,' she said, 'you're my imagination, aren't you? I've taken the pills and I'm hallucinating.'

'Thank you very much,' replied the genie, offended. 'Do I look like a hallucination?'

Jane considered. 'Frankly,' she said, 'yes.'

The genie considered this. 'Fair enough,' it replied. 'Maybe that wasn't the most intelligent rhetorical question I've ever posed. Do I take it, by the way, that you were planning on eating the pills?'

Jane nodded.

'Headache? Sore throat?'

'Bad dose of life,' Jane replied. 'Fortunately, the remedy is available over the counter without a prescription.'

The genie shook its head. 'Bad attitude you've got there, if I may make so bold,' it said. 'There's lots of things worse than life, believe you me.'

'Oh yes? Such as?'

'Such as death, for one,' the genie replied, 'spending a lot of time in bottles coming in close behind to clinch silver. Mind if I sit down, by the way? Cramp.' Like a closely packed swarm of bees it drifted down and hovered an inch or so above the bench opposite Jane. 'Mug's game, death is. All that standing about in queues and filling in forms. Compared to death, life is just a bowl of cherries.'

'Ah,' Jane replied, with a strong trace of ice in her voice, 'I wasn't planning on dying, I was planning on being reincarnated. So put that in your pipe and smoke it, Mister Clever.'

The genie nodded. 'Don't get me wrong,' it said, 'there's nothing bad about reincarnation *per se*, it's basically a very good system, cost-effective and ecologically friendly. It's just that, until they iron out the technical glitches . . .'

Jane frowned. 'I don't think you're a genie at all,' she said. 'I think you're actually the imaginary friend I had when I was five, only grown-up. You're just as irritating as he was, and you've got the same knack of poking your finger in your ear and wiggling it about when you're talking.'

'Do I do that?' The genie looked at its hand. 'Really?'

'Really.'

'Have you seen the length of my claws? How come I don't lacerate my eardrums?'

Jane shrugged. 'That's your problem, surely. Look if you really are a genie and you've been sent to make me change my mind –'

'Sent? Who by?'

'Search me. Is there anybody who sends genies, or do they just turn up? No, forget it, no offence but I'm really not interested. It's been lovely meeting you, really it has, but it's time I wasn't here. '

'Sure?'

'Positive.' Jane looked at the floor. 'I take it,' she said, 'the bottle was empty. Apart from you, of course.'

The genie nodded; or at least, it shimmered up and then down again, like an indecisive smoke signal. 'You want some aspirins, I take it?'

'Please.'

'Your wish is my –'

'Hold it.'

'Shit.' An expression of disgust flitted across the genie's face. 'I thought you'd say that,' it muttered. 'Perceptive, aren't I?'

Jane leant forward, her chin cupped in her hand. 'My wish is your command?'

The genie winced. 'Bloody marvellous,' it said.

'Humans, all they're interested in is one thing. My mother was right, it's wishes, wishes, wishes all the time with you people. Makes me sick.'

'Three wishes?'

'Absolutely correct. Still, since you're absolutely dead set on killing yourself, there really isn't much point, is there? Unless you want a hand getting the job done, that is.' The genie grinned toothily. 'In which case,' it said, 'absolutely delighted to oblige. Fourteen years in an empty bottle, one thing you do get is decidedly peckish.'

Jane shook her head. 'That,' she said, 'was before I had three wishes from a genuine genie. You've got to admit, it alters things.'

'Up to a point,' the genie said. 'I mean, we're talking parameters of the possible here. There are very strict rules about what we are and are not allowed to do for clients.'

'I'll bet.'

'So strict,' the genie went on, shimmering persuasively, 'as to make the wishes virtually worthless, in my opinion. Not worth the hassle. Forget all about it if I were you.'

'I think I'll give them a try, thanks all the same.'

'Gosh, there's a train just coming in, if you're quick you could jump under it and –'

'Three wishes,' Jane said firmly. 'Agreed?'

The genie sighed. 'In which case,' it said, 'you'd better have one of these.'

There was a rustle of pages, and a book appeared in Jane's lap. She picked it up and squinted at the spine:

OWNER'S MANUAL

'Demeaning, I call it,' the genie muttered. 'I mean,

owner, for God's sake. Makes me sound like a blasted lawnmower.'

Congratulations! You are now the owner of a Model M27 'Gentle Giant' general service domestic and industrial genie. Provided it is properly maintained and only genuine replacement parts are used (N.B. use of non-standard parts may invalidate your warranty) your genie should provide you and your civilisation with a lifetime of cheerful and near omnipotent service —

'Gentle giant my arse,' the genie interrupted. 'Well, giant maybe, but gentle . . .'

Jane read on for a while, and then closed the book. 'Three wishes,' she said.

'That's right. You saw the bit about the "Wish By" date, by the way? Very important, that.'

'Very well,' Jane went on, 'I'll have the first one now, please.'

'Fire away.'

'I'd like,' Jane said, 'another twelve million wishes.'

The genie's head jerked upright. 'Now just a cotton-picking minute,' it complained, 'that's not fair. There's no way . . .'

'Why not?' Jane smirked. 'Completely legitimate request, according to this book.'

'Rubbish. Like I said, there are strict rules.'

Jane nodded. 'I agree,' she said. 'Here they are on page four, paragraph two, three lines up from the bottom. Want to have a look?'

'I know the rules, thank you,' said the genie icily.

'As follows,' Jane continued. 'One, no wishes that change the very fabric of reality. Well, that's OK, if I can have three wishes I can have three billion, it's all the same in principle.'

'Matter of opinion,' grunted the genie.

'Two,' Jane said firmly, 'no wishes beyond the genie's power to fulfil. Obviously no worries on that score.'

'I've got a bad back, mind,' the genie interjected. 'Gives me one hell of a lot of jip in the winter months, my back does.'

'And finally,' Jane said, 'rule three, all wishes to be used within three hundred years of first acquiring the genie.' Jane glanced at her watch. 'By my reckoning that gives me till half past twelve on the sixteenth of June 2295. Agreed?'

'Twenty past twelve, I make it.'

'Then twenty past twelve it shall be.' Jane closed the book. 'Nothing in there that says I can't wish for more wishes. And if with my next wish I wish for another nine trillion and four wishes, there's absolutely nothing you can do about it. Is there?'

The genie scowled. 'I think this is probably something of a grey area, interpretation-wise,' it said. 'However, as a gesture of goodwill, would you accept six wishes in full and final settlement?'

'No.'

'You're not a lawyer by any chance, are you?'

'That's a horrible thing to say about anybody.'

'True.' The genie scratched the back of its head, and for a few moments bright sunlight seeped through the gashes made by its claws in the glittering air. 'All right then, tell you what I'll do. All the wishes you want for three years, how about that?'

Jane shook her head. 'For life,' she replied. 'But I promise I won't wish for anything too yuk, provided there's not an emergency or something.'

'God, you drive a hard bargain.'

'I know.'

'Can I go now?' The genie lifted its arm and sniffed. 'I mean, I'll be there as soon as you call, word of honour, but I'd really appreciate it if you'd just spare me a few minutes. You know, to freshen up, brush my teeth, that sort of thing. I won't be long.'

'That's all right.' Jane considered. 'What's your name, by the way?'

The genie looked embarrassed; that is, the million billion minuscule points of light of which it was composed flickered red, one after the other, all in the space of a fraction of a second. 'Just call me Genie,' it said quickly. 'That's what everybody else does, and it's much –'

'Name.'

The genie dimmed. 'Kawaguchiya Integrated Circuits III,' it mumbled.

'Kawaguchiya Integrated Circuits?'

''Fraid so.' The genie nodded stroboscopically. 'Commercial sponsorship, you see. Pays for all the running repairs, plus a twice-yearly check-up and insurance. People call me Goochie for short. If they dare,' it added. 'And even then, never more than twice. Myself, I prefer the acronym. It's more me.'

'Kick?'

'Kiss,' Kiss replied. 'The C is soft as in coelacanth, certain and celery. Like I said, though, just plain Genie does me absolutely fine.'

'With the light brown hair, huh?'

Kiss sighed and gathered together his photons with all the dignity he could muster. 'All things considered, I was a fool to leave the bottle. Be seeing you.'

He said; and vanished.

★

Much to Jane's surprise, he came back twenty minutes later.

'Would you like a cup of tea?' she asked.

'Thank you,' Kiss replied. 'Nice place you've got here, by the way.'

Jane raised an eyebrow. 'You like it?' she said. 'Personally, I think it's a dump.'

'Objectively speaking, it probably is. Sure beats an aspirin bottle, though.'

'I'll take that as a compliment,' Jane replied. 'Milk and sugar?'

Kiss shook his head – he was, Jane noticed, considerably more together than he had been; the gaps between the little points of light and shadow that comprised him were much smaller, and unless he stood with his back to the window you'd almost imagine he was solid. 'A slice of lemon, if you've got it.'

'Sorry.' Jane frowned. 'Hey, who's doing the wishes around here, anyway?'

Let there be lemon; and there was lemon. She handed him his cup (it was disconcerting to say the least to push one of her grandmother's Crown Derby teacups into a glistening dustcloud, but there was no crash) and bade him sit down. He repeated the hovering manoeuvre she'd witnessed before.

'I wasn't expecting you,' she said.

Kiss's eyebrows flickered sceptically. 'You usually lay out the best china just for yourself, do you?' he enquired.

'I don't remember giving you my address,' Jane replied.

Kiss snorted. 'Give me some credit,' he said huffily. 'I am, or was, one of the marshals of the hosts of heaven, rider of the tempest, companion of the cherubim. Looking someone up in the phone book is scarcely taxing my powers to the limit.'

'So how did you find out my name?'

'You write your name inside your handbag; evidently a throw-back to your schooldays. Rather endearing, I thought. Mind if I smoke?'

Jane frowned. 'Actually,' she said, 'I'm allergic to tobacco.'

'Who said anything about tobacco?'

Jane shrugged. 'Please yourself.'

A second or so later she became aware of the most delicious perfume; attar of roses or something like that. Two hundred quid for a tiny bottle sort of thing. She nodded approval.

'Actually,' said the genie, 'it's woodbines. Well, this is all very pleasant. So far, anyway.'

'Let's hope it stays that way,' Jane replied. She pushed her hair back up out of her eyes, and put on a serious face. 'I think it's time we did a little basic ground-work, don't you?'

The genie looked at her. 'Ground-work? You mean ploughing or something?'

'I mean,' Jane replied, 'I want you to tell me something about yourself. You see, I haven't got the faintest idea what a genie is, or where they come from, anything like that. Except that they come in bottles and grant you three wishes,' she added lamely.

'I see.' Kiss scratched the bridge of his nose. 'That's a bit like saying all you know about America is Eggs Benedict and the date of Groundhog Day. Not enough, in other words.'

'That's what I'd assumed.'

'Right, then,' the genie said. 'Now, where shall I start?'

Genies (Kiss explained) are fallen angels. That is to say, in the beginning they were created out of the Mind of God, to do the things for which angels are necessary. All I can say about that is, He's got one hell of a warped imagination.

Most genies got to be genies by backing the wrong side in the civil war between the archangel Michael and Lucifer, Son of the Morning. Not me, though; I was on the right side in that lot, albeit in the Pay Corps. As I remember, I spent the duration of the war either playing cards or wandering around with a clipboard trying to keep out of the way of the officers. Which suited me fine, by the way. Never saw a thunderbolt thrown in anger, and I play a really mean game of djinn rummy.

No, my departure from Heaven was the result of an unfortunate misunderstanding about a lorryload of black market stardust somehow going missing en route to HQ from King Solomon's Mines. I was, of course, framed, but would they believe me? Would they hell.

Well, after that I bummed around for a bit, doing the things genies generally do – You don't? Well, all sorts of things, really: raising storms, necromancy, digging up pots of gold at the ends of rainbows, riding the moon, changing princes into frogs, a few real estate deals, anything to pass the time and put a few dinars in your pocket. It's a good life if you like that sort of thing, though you do tend to end up mixing with heroes and grand viziers and a lot of other lowlifes, and you're really only ever as good as your last job. Particularly these days, with all the science and stuff. In fact, quite a few of the lads I used to hang out with have packed in the road and settled down as lift operators. No, not lift attendants, lift operators. You don't seriously think lifts go up and down all day with just a bit of wire and a few pulleys, do you?

And the movies, of course; special effects. You've heard

of George Lucas, I take it? Now that's one genie who really did make the big time.

Anyway, there I was, just sort of pottering about, minding my own business; and then, wham! Lamp time. It happens to all of us sooner or later, of course, it's genetic programming or something, like lemmings. Doesn't stop you feeling a right idiot when the stopper goes down, though.

Well, I was out of circulation for, what, five hundred years, five and a bit, and then – Sorry? Look, do I have to, because it really is very embarrassing? All right, if you insist.

I was at this party (Kiss said, cringing slightly) and there was this djinn, right? Tall, slim, blonde, pair of fangs on her like a sabre-tooth tiger; I mean, we're talking serious chemistry here and, besides, I may have been drinking. Alcohol has a bad effect on my metabolism, it has to be admitted. All I have to do is sniff a bottle of cough medicine and somebody has to take me home in a wheelbarrow.

Anyway, there we were and one thing led to another, and she said, 'Your place or mine?' and the next thing I remember was waking up in this lamp thing with a splitting headache and the lid coming off and me being shot out like someone had just shot a hole through the cabin wall at fifty thousand feet; and there's this magician type in a big pointy hat staring at me and saying, 'Hold on a minute, you're not the usual fiend, what's become of Mabel?'

Mabel, needless to say, was the looker with the luxury dentures, and she'd lured me back to her lamp, done a runner and left me there. I tried explaining, but it didn't do any good. '*Never mind, you'll just have to do instead,*' was all the sympathy and understanding I got out of him, the bastard.

Now here's a word of advice, from someone who's been there; if ever you get yourself indentured to a black magician, try to make sure it's not a black magician who's into the financial services stuff. It's bad enough as it is with the hurtling backwards and forwards through time and space, I-hear-and-obey-oh-mastering twenty-four hours a day, doing evil and getting yourself thoroughly disliked all the time. When you've got all that, plus you have to play snakes and ladders with the international currency markets, it can get to be a serious drag. You can imagine the sort of thing I mean: go sink a few of So-and-so's ships so I can mount a hostile takeover of his company. Oh look, the Samarkandi dirham's risen in early trading, go and raze their walls to the ground and eat their finance minister. I mean, where's the self-respect in that?

(At which point Jane interrupted to say it sounded awful. Kiss nodded sadly.

'It was,' he said. 'And you know what the worst part of it was? All this inside information floating around and me without a dinar to my name. A few lousy coppers in the right place and I could have been taken seriously rich, you know? As it was . . .'

'I see,' Jane said coldly. 'Do please go on.')

Anyway (said Kiss) eventually the Securities Commission caught up and it was a case of into the sack and off to the Bosphorus for him, and bloody good riddance too. Not, however, much fun for me, because I was in the lamp at the time. And in the lamp I stayed. For five hundred years, with nothing to do except play I Spy. Something, I need hardly tell you, beginning with L.

Just when I was starting to go lamp-crazy, though, off

comes the lid and there's this bloke in a sort of fawn safari suit peering in at me and saying something about typical thirteenth-century Bokhara ware, probably indicative of developing commercial links with the Ummayads. That's right, a blasted archaeologist. There are times when you don't know when you're well off.

You'll never guess what his three wishes were. Well, if you know anything about archaeology, maybe you can. As I understand it, in order to become an archaeologist you have to spend your youth stuck in some dusty old library reading books about bits of broken pot. You don't have time for going to parties, or girls. By the time you do have time, it's generally too late – unless, that is, you suddenly find yourself with a virtually omnipotent spiritual assistant and three wishes.

Anyway, after that I needed a year at the bottom of a disused mine-shaft just to recover and get over the embarrassment; after which I got a job as a clerk in a shipping office. It was the least exciting thing I could think of. I was right.

And then, just when I was thinking about what I was going to do next and how much fun I could have with superhuman powers and absolutely no social conscience, I got stuck in the bottle you so kindly extracted me from. No, I'm not prepared to go into details; and if you want any co-operation at all from me in the course of what promises to be a long and interesting working relationship, you'll respect my privacy on that one. OK?

'Superhuman powers?' Jane queried.

Kiss nodded. 'Pretty superhuman,' he replied, 'and I don't have to dash into the nearest phone box and change first, either. Although,' he added, 'all that stuff was a front. He didn't need to change at all, it was just part of the act.'

Jane's eyes widened. 'You mean Superman –?'

'No names,' Kiss replied, 'no pack drill. But it's true, there's more of us about than people think. We've sort of rehabilitated ourselves in the community, if you like to look at it that way.'

'I see.' Jane was staring out of the window. 'You know,' she said, 'I'm so confused about all of this that I almost believe in you. Am I going mad, do you think?'

Kiss paused before answering. 'You're still alive, aren't you?' he said. 'Seems to me that you're that much ahead of the game, so don't knock it. That reminds me. The suicide thing. Why?'

Jane shook her head. 'We'd better respect each other's privacy,' she said. 'Fair enough?'

'Your wish, etcetera. Right,' said the genie, 'what's it to be? Shall we kick off with the wealth beyond the dreams of avarice, get that out of the way before the banks close?'

'That's possible, is it?'

'Piece of duff.' Kiss yawned and picked a stray morsel of fluff out of his hair. It turned into a two-headed snake, burst into flames and vanished. 'Swiss francs are what we usually recommend, although gold bullion has a lot going for it. Up to you, really.'

Jane shook her head. 'Later,' she said. 'Let's just have a look at this book and see what it has to say. '

She opened the manual.

1.1 Getting To Know Your Genie

'Gosh,' Jane said.

'You're probably way ahead of me,' Kiss was saying, 'but just in case you were tempted to, don't look down. Or at least, not straight down. Vertigo is one of the things I can't do anything about, oddly enough.'

Below them, on Nevsky Prospekt, the traffic roared; so far below them that all Jane could see was one continuous stream of white light and another of red. Further away, the absurd spire of the Cathedral of St Peter and St Paul loomed up into the night sky, like a spear aimed at the moon . . .

'For God's sake look where you're going. We nearly flew straight into that pointy thing.'

'Sorry,' Kiss replied. 'I'm a touch out of practice at flying two up. It's a bit like riding a motorbike with a sidecar, really, you have to remember to compensate –'

'Look,' Jane interrupted, as they flashed past the Admiralty Tower with at least six thousandths of an inch to spare, 'where the hell are we?'

'St Petersburg.'

'*St Petersburg?*'

Kiss shrugged – under the circumstances, an act of carelessness verging on criminal recklessness. 'You said take me somewhere foreign,' he said, as Jane hauled herself back up between the base of his wings. 'St Petersburg's foreign. Can't get much more foreign than St Petersburg, if you ask me. That down there, by the way, is the Prospekt Stachek, and that impressive-looking thing with the crinkly walls is in fact a processed meat plant, would you believe. Designed by Rubanchik and Barutchev in 1929 –'

'Put me *down*.'

'As you wish. Anywhere in particular?'

'Yes. The ground. Quickly!'

The ground selected by Kiss for a landing strip turned out to be a pelican crossing on the Ulitsa Zodchevo Rossi, much to the chagrin of the driver of a lorryload of Brussels sprouts who was just about to drive over it. For the record, the lightning-fast swerve by which he managed to avoid running Jane and her invisible companion over was witnessed by no less a person than the acting secretary of the local bus-driver's co-operative, who offered him a job as soon as he was released from hospital.

'No offence,' Kiss said, as they crossed the road, 'but you're a lousy passenger. You may think that screaming *Oh God, we're going to die!* and grabbing hold of my left wing just when I'm doing the tricky part of the landing process is being helpful, but in actual fact . . .'

Jane sat down on the steps of a building and closed her eyes. 'I think,' she said, 'I'll take the train back, if it's all the same to you.'

Kiss was offended. 'I'd just like to remind you,' he said, 'that if you'd had your way, you'd have killed yourself by now. When it comes to a total disregard for the value of human life, I think you're the one who's into melanistic kettle spotting.'

Jane looked up at him angrily. 'To recap,' she said. 'Any wish I like, so long as it's physically possible?'

'That's right. OUCH!'

'Thank you.'

'There was no call,' Kiss said, rubbing the place on the side of his head where he had just thumped himself very hard, 'for that. If you're not happy about something, all you have to do is say. Remember that, and we'll get on just fine.'

Jane got to her feet. 'Now then,' she said. 'Yes, I'm convinced. You are a genie, and you exist. I think I'd like to go home. Slowly.'

'Your wish is my –'

'And peacefully. Straight and level. You think you can manage that?'

'I'll give it,' Kiss replied, 'my best shot.'

'Is that it?'

Kiss made no reply; he just took off his pinny, folded it neatly and put it back behind the door. Then he started the washing-up.

'And these little bits of grey grisly stuff,' Jane went on. 'You're sure they're really necessary?'

'Quails' guts Marengo,' Kiss replied. 'Where I come from, that's about as haut as cuisine can get. Fried in butter, or served as a crudite with a simple green salad . . .'

Jane put down her fork and folded her arms. 'No thanks,' she said. 'Just take it away and bring me a boiled egg. A hen's egg,' she added quickly; but not quickly enough.

'To hear is to obey,' Kiss explained smugly. 'Come on, eat it up before it hatches.'

Jane shook her head; and a moment later there as a faint tapping sound, like Ginger Rogers trapped inside a fire-proof vault. A hairline crack appeared in the side of the egg.

'People think,' Kiss said, removing the plate, 'that these little chaps became extinct because of severe climactic changes at the dose of the Cretaceous period. Truth is, nothing stupid enough to taste that good in an omelette deserves to survive. Oh look, here he comes. Whoosa pretty boy, then?'

A small, scaly head with three tiny bumps on its skull poked out through the shell and blinked moistly. Kiss clicked his tongue at it fondly a few times, and then vanished. When he reappeared, he was carrying a plastic tray and a styrofoam cup with a straw.

'More your style,' he said contemptuously. 'Still, it's early days yet. Next week we'll start you on ammonite cocktails and honey-roast mammoth.'

'Want to bet?'

'Your wish is my –'

'Oh, shut up.'

1.2 Setting Up Basic Routines

'For pity's sake,' Jane croaked, rolling over and peering at her clock. 'It's half past three in the morning.'

Over the end of the bed, a cloud of photons glistened cheerfully. 'Up bright and early, you said,' Kiss replied. 'Here, catch hold.'

To her disgust, Jane received a tray with a plate on it. On the plate was a hedgehog, curled up in a nest of dry leaves. There were cubes of cheese and pineapple impaled on its spikes. It was, Jane noted with relief, asleep rather than dead.

'You did say you wanted your breakfast still in its bed,' Kiss explained, 'so I didn't wake it up. Besides, hedgehogs are usually flambéd at the table, so if you'll pass me that box of matches . . .'

'Are you being stupid on purpose, or are you just –?'

'There's no need to be rude.'

1.3 Margins

'Right,' Jane said. 'Today we're going to set the world to rights.'

Kiss looked up from the sink. 'Fine,' he said. 'Is that before or after I do the washing-up?'

Jane blinked. 'I was being facetious,' she replied. 'Were you?'

'No,' the genie answered, squeezing the entire contents of the washing-up liquid bottle into the sink and turning both taps to full power. 'I'm never facetious where wishes are concerned, it's part of being a pro. You want the world set to rights, I'm your sprite.'

'I see.' Jane sat down and drank some tea. It was quite unlike any other tea she had ever tasted, while at the same time being unmistakably tea. She found out later that this was because Kiss made tea by uprooting a tea plant and dumping it in the pressure cooker for half an hour. 'And how do you propose going about it?'

'Easy.' The words *easy*, *no worries*, *piece of cake* had come to ring loud warning bells in Jane's mind; it usually meant that the genie was contemplating doing something so extreme as to boil the brain. 'The way I see it, all the misery and unhappiness in the world today is caused by governments, people like that. Just give me five minutes to get this baked-on grease off this grill-pan and I'll nip out and deal with them.'

'Deal with?'

Kiss made an unambiguous gesture with his forefinger and his throat. 'They've got it coming,' he said cheerfully. 'It'll be a pleasure.'

Jane spilt her tea. 'One,' she said, 'you'll do no such thing.'

'Oh, come on . . .'

'Two,' she continued, 'I thought there were rules about that sort of thing. I mean, what you can and can't do.'

Kiss shook his head. 'There are,' he replied. 'But topping a few politicians is entirely legitimate. It's only impossible things that I'm not supposed to do; you know, things that'd bend the nature of physics. There's nothing in the book of rules about criminal irresponsibility.'

'Ah.'

'I take it you're not keen on the idea?'

'I have to admit,' Jane replied, 'I'd prefer a more organic approach.'

The genie's massive brow wrinkled over. 'What, you mean bury them alive? Can do, just say the –'

'No.'

'All right, then, how about bury them alive in compost? You can't get more organic than compost.'

'I meant,' Jane said firmly, 'something a bit more constructive. Something that doesn't involve lots of people getting killed.'

The genie stared for a moment, then started to laugh. 'Set the world to rights and nobody gets killed? Hey, lady, where have you been all your life?'

Few compilers of folk-tale anthologies have recorded the fact, but all genies, regardless of the terms of their indenture or the nature of their employment, have an indefeasible right to one night off a week. Kiss had explained this to Jane in great detail, and had even taken the trouble of marking the whole of the relevant page of the manual in extra-fluorescent yellow marker pen.

Where, then, do genies go on their night off? There is, of course, only one place: Saheed's, in downtown Samarkand (turn left opposite the dye works till you come to a corrugated iron door, knock four times and ask for Ali). There, the stressed-out supernatural entity can relax, unwind and talk over the past week with other genies over a nice glass of cool goat's milk. Or so the theory runs. In practice, Ali the proprietor has had to have an annexe built into another dimension, because the fights on Quiz Nights threaten to upset the Earth's placement on its axis.

'It's amazing, it really is,' Kiss maintained, swilling the contents of his glass round to revive the head. 'The woman is completely weird. What exactly she wants out of life is beyond me entirely.'

His companion nodded sympathetically. 'Europeans,' he grunted. 'No more idea than next door's cat, the lot of them. I remember once, I was in this oiling can over France way, and –'

'Three weeks I've been with her now,' Kiss continued, absent-mindedly finishing off his companion's peanuts, 'and what have we done? Go on, guess. You'll never guess what we've done.'

'Probably not.'

'Nothing.' Kiss scowled. 'Absolutely bugger-all. Not proper genie stuff, anyway. It's all been ironing and shampooing the carpets and would you mind just running a duster over the sitting-room table? The score so far: ruby eyes of gods stolen, nil. Spirits of the dead raised, nil. Tail-feathers of firebirds plucked, nil. Hairs from the beard of the Great Cham abstracted, nil. Ankle-socks paired, four-teen. Potatoes peeled, thirty-two. Any more of this and I'm going to appeal to the Tribunal, because it really isn't on. Have another?'

His companion glanced at his wrist (genies don't need watches but are nevertheless creatures of habit). 'Since you're offering,' he replied. 'Just the one, mind, because I've got wealth beyond the dreams of avarice to fetch tomorrow, and you've got to keep a clear head for these fiddly little jobs.'

Kiss nodded and went to the bar.

'Two large djinns and tonic,' he said, 'ice and lemon in one.'

The bottle on the counter rocked backwards and forwards as if nodding, unstoppered itself and poured liquor into two glasses. Please note: customers who find they've left their money at home when dining at Saheed's don't just get away with doing the washing-up.

'Sounds like you've got yourself a right little ray of sunshine,' his companion observed, as Kiss brought back the drinks. 'What was that bit you said about further wishes?'

Kiss explained, again. His companion shook his head.

'I'm not sure about that,' he said, 'not sure at all. You should get the union rep to have a look at that for you. I mean, there must be something wrong with it, or else we'd all be in the smelly.'

'Lousy precedent,' Kiss agreed.

'Diabolical. They could take it up as a test case.'

'You reckon?'

'Worth a try.' His companion emptied his glass, wiped his mouth on the sleeve of his sixth arm, and stood up. 'Well, be seeing you. Don't steal any glass eyes.'

'Mind how you go,' Kiss replied absently. His companion withdrew, and a few moments later there was a brief outburst of muffled swearing as he discovered that while he'd been inside, some practical jokers had nailed his carpet to the carpet-park floor. (For the record, he arrived back home six hours late, soaking wet and frozen stiff, having had to make the return flight on a borrowed bar towel.)

Kiss lingered on until closing time, playing the video games in a desultory manner and beating the Dragon King of the South three times running at pool. It wasn't just that he was in no hurry to go home; there was something else troubling him, and he needed the noise and smashed-crockery sounds of his own kind about him in order to concentrate his mind. There was, he felt, something very odd going on, and in some way he couldn't work out he was involved in it, indirectly and at several removes. Whatever it was, it remained shadowy and obscure, with the result that he was too preoccupied to notice that he had just beaten the Dragon King a fourth time; which is to pushing one's luck as closing one's eyes and taking both hands off the wheel is to motorway driving. Not very long afterwards, he was rescued in the nick of time by the bouncer and deposited outside among the dustbins, where he passed a quiet night dreaming of jacket potatoes.

'What's it like,' Jane demanded, 'being a genie?'

They were digesting a leisurely picnic, a hundred feet or so up in the air directly above a spectacularly active volcano in the back lots of Hawaii. The venue had been Kiss's suggestion; it would save them having to take the empty fruit-juice cartons and boiled-egg shells home with them, he'd argued, if they could simply drop them into the most spectacular waste-disposal system on the planet. They were sitting on Kiss's own personal flying carpet (a three-ply Wilton Sportster with Hydra-Shock jute backing and a go-faster Paisley recurring motif) and Jane had just finished off the cold chicken.

'Dodgy,' Kiss replied, after some thought. 'You never really know where you are. I mean,' he continued, jettisoning an empty Perrier bottle, which liquefied twelve feet above the meniscus of the lava, 'potentially it's a really great lifestyle, if you can hack it and stay out of trouble. You've got eternal life and eternal youth, there's practically nothing this side of Ursa Major that can attack you without coming a very poor second, you can fly, you can materialise pretty well anything you like so long as it actually exists somewhere in the cosmos, and best of all you have absolutely no moral constraints whatsoever. I guess the nearest you could come in human terms would be a seven-foot-tall, extremely muscular movie star with a good agent and an even better lawyer. That's when the times are good, of course,' he added.

'And when they're not?'

Kiss shook his head. 'Bottles,' he said. 'Also lamps. Very bad news, both of them. I knew a genie once, in fact, got mixed up with one of those raffia-covered Chianti bottles made into a lamp. Poor bugger didn't know whether he was coming or going.'

'Confusing?'

'Just plain nasty,' Kiss replied. 'Take another mate of mine, Big Nick. I told him at the time – this was some years ago, mind – Nick, I said, stripping the lead off the Vatican roof is going to land you in very real grief, you mark my words. He didn't, of course, and look at him now.'

Jane squinted. 'I've heard of him, have I?'

Kiss nodded gloomily. 'I expect so. Big chap, white beard, red dressing-gown, reindeer, sack – thought you'd probably come across him.'

Jane's eyes widened. 'He's a *genie*?'

'There's more of us about,' Kiss said, 'than people realise.'

'And it's a punishment? All the delivering presents and happy smiling faces . . .'

'You try it and see how you enjoy it. I'm telling you, twelve thousand years in an oil-lamp would be paradise in comparison.' Kiss shuddered reflexively. 'And if that wasn't bad enough, the other three hundred and sixty-four days each year it's not just a bottle the poor sod's banged up in, it's one of those paperweights; you know, the sort you shake and it snows? I think you'd have to have a pretty warped mind to come up with something like that.'

Jane agreed.

'And it's getting worse, you know,' Kiss went on. 'Generally, that is. In the business. Admittedly in my young days there were more of the bad guys about – sorcerers and mages and the like – but at least they hadn't invented the unbreakable plastic bottle or the child-proof bottle-top. Makes my blood run cold, that does.'

Jane tried to imagine what it was like, being a genie, and found that she couldn't. Hardly surprising, she decided, but a trifle disappointing nevertheless. She dropped a paper plate over the side and watched it drift down and blossom, first into fire, then fine white ash, then nothing at all.

'And what about you?' Kiss said. 'Since we're obviously into a heavyweight experience-swapping trip, how about you telling me why the suicide thing? I have this feeling that it's something I ought to know, purely on a business level.'

Jane sighed. 'Why not?' she said. 'I expect you could find out if you wanted to.'

'No problem,' Kiss agreed. 'I could read your thoughts, for a start.'

'Could you?'

The genie nodded. 'It's frowned upon, of course,' he added. 'Not quite the done thing and so forth, especially within the parameters of the model genie/mortal relationship. But entirely feasible.'

'Hang on,' Jane objected. 'What happened to no moral constraints whatsoever?'

'It's not moral constraints, just peer group machismo. And we're drifting away from the subject rather, aren't we?'

'I suppose we are. Go on, then. Guess.'

'Guess why you wanted to kill yourself?'

'Mphm.'

Kiss frowned, and changed himself into a tree. Trees, as is well known, spend their entire lives trying to decide what they're going to do next, and therefore possess tremendous powers of concentration. It's only the lack of an effective central nervous system that keeps them from sweeping the board at chess tournaments.

'Unrequited love,' he said. 'Close?'

Jane scowled. 'Spot on,' she replied. 'Is it that obvious?'

'No,' replied the genie, with a hint of smugness. 'In fact, you've concealed it terribly well. I have the advantage, however, of superhuman intelligence. Not,' he added, 'that I use it much. Gives me a headache.'

'Me too.'

Kiss changed back into his customary shape: a nine-foot-tall clown, complete with red nose and a woolly ginger wig. 'Tell me about it,' he said.

'Nothing to tell, really.' Jane leaned over and stared at the seething flames below until her eyes hurt. 'His name was Vince, and he had the desk opposite mine at the Bank. In his spare time he played a lot of volleyball, his favourite food was pizza and he was saving up for one of those overland adventure holidays where you cross some desert or other in an open-topped truck. What I ever saw in him I can't for the life of me imagine, but there it is.'

Kiss nodded. 'It's the same with us and bottles,' he said. 'Only, of course, we eventually get out of the bottles, even if it does mean waiting till they biodegrade. As I understand it, your lot don't have that guarantee.'

'I don't know.' Jane sniffed. 'If you ask me, it's all a case of misunderstood biology. In fact, as an example of a very big hammer to crack a very small nut, it's hard to beat.'

Kiss rolled over on to his back and materialised a bottle of cold milk. He took a long pull, wiped the top of the bottle on the palm of his hand and offered it to Jane, who declined it.

'If you like,' he said, 'we can see what we can do about this Vince character. If you really want me to, that is.'

Jane shook her head. 'I don't honestly think it's something you can interfere with,' she replied. 'I thought you were only allowed to do the possible.'

Kiss shrugged. 'There would have to be an element of compromise,' he replied, 'and certainly you can't compel one mortal to love another. On the other hand, you can suggest to a mortal that he act affectionately towards another mortal if he doesn't want his ears ripped off and shoved up his nose. That'd be no bother whatsoever.'

'No, thank you.'

'Sure? The more I think about it, the more I warm to the –'

'Really,' Jane said. 'No thanks. '

'Suit yourself.' The genie yawned. 'So, what exactly do you want? I don't want to seem pushy or anything, but it's time you made your mind up about that. Most people have a shopping-list ready formulated before the cork's out of the bottleneck.'

'Well, I don't,' Jane said. 'Apart from the immediate things, I mean, like not having to clean the kitchen floor or go to work. Grand ambitions really aren't my style.'

'They don't have to be all that grand,' Kiss suggested. 'In fact, something modest but time-consuming would suit me down to the ground. A complete collection of

Bing Crosby records, for example; or better still, a determination on your part to have lunch in all the wine-bars in the Southern Hemisphere. I could handle that, if you could.'

Jane removed the straw from a fruit-juice carton and chewed it thoughtfully. 'Really,' she said, 'I suppose I ought to make the world a better place. Eliminate nuclear weapons, irrigate the deserts of Northern Africa, that sort of –'

'Oh dear, not *again*,' Kiss sighed. 'Sorry, but if I see one more North African desert, I shall probably be sick.'

'Oh. ' Jane looked startled. 'You mean you already . . . ?'

'We all have,' Kiss sighed, 'at one time or another. One of humanity's more predictable requests, I'm afraid. Exactly as predictable, in fact, as causing famine, pestilence and floods, which is Mankind's other great preoccupation. That's why we have the Concurrency Agreement. It was worked out by the Union, what, three thousand years ago, and just as well, in my opinion.'

Jane demanded footnotes.

'Simple,' Kiss explained. 'Suppose you have, say, fifty genies. You can bet your life that at any one time twenty-five of them are going to be indentured to do-gooders, let-the-deserts-bloom types; and the other twenty-five will be working for psychotic maniacs. We just set off one against the other, and things remain exactly as they are. Saves a lot of aggravation in the long run, and of course it gives your lot something to do into the bargain. Flag days, jumble sales, fighting wars, that sort of thing.'

'I see. How very depressing.'

'It is, rather. So, if you want me to convert the Nullarbor plain into a swaying forest of Brussels sprouts, just say the word, but you mustn't count on them staying there for more than a fiftieth of a second, if that. The rules are very strict.'

'Fine. I think I'd like to go home now, please.'

'Your wish is my –'

'Do you have to keep saying that?'

'Unfortunately, yes.'

CHAPTER TWO

A hot-air balloon bobbing uncertainly over a desert landscape.

Inside the balloon, a man and a girl, surveying the view with binoculars. There's nothing to be seen except sand and, in the far distance, huge rocky outcrops. No signs of life whatsoever. That suits the man and the girl perfectly.

The girl stoops down and picks up a metal cylinder, like a steel thermos flask. She opens it and rolls into the palm of her hand a single seed, no bigger than a grape pip. It sits, heavy for its size, in the soft skin of her hand. It looks, if anything that small and inert can manage such a feat, smug.

'Well?' asks the man. He has to shout because of the roaring of the wind, but his shout is so full of awe that it sounds like an extremely loud whisper; as if he was talking to a very deaf person in a cathedral.

'Here's as good a place as any,' replies the girl. 'Let's go for it.'

She leans over the side and reels for a second at the sight of so much nothing between her and the ground; then she deliberately opens her palm and lets the seed fall.

The seed falls . . .

And hits the ground.

WHUMP!

Was it a seed, or was it a bomb? Difficult to tell; there's a mushroom-shaped cloud standing up from the desert floor . . .

But that's not smoke or dust, that's foliage; a huge, thick stem supporting a giant bud –

– which bursts into a hot-flame-yellow flower with a raging red centre. The flower lifts towards the sun – you expect it to roar and shake its head like a lion – and the plant raises its two broad, leathery leaves like wings; and even up in the balloon, a thousand feet overhead, that's a threatening sight.

'Christ,' shouts the man, 'look at that thing grow!'

Look indeed; the plant is twenty feet high and still growing. Fissures run along the desert floor, marking the swift passage of the roots underground like lightning forking across a black sky.

'That,' the girl agreed, 'is one hell of a primrose.'

'Sorry?'

'I said that's one hell of a –'

'Speak up, I can't quite hear what you're –'

'I SAID, THAT'S ONE HELL OF A PRIMROSE.'

'Yes.'

No longer growing; instead, consolidating. The stem swells, to support the weight of the flower. The petals fan out, snatching photons out of the air like a spider's web. Hot chlorophyll pumps through the swelling veins. The roots tear into the dead ground like miners' drills. And stop.

'Hey up,' says the man, 'I think it's on its way.'

The primrose is rocking and bouncing up and down, for

all the world as if it's on a trampoline. Now it's swaying backwards and forwards, using all the leverage of its already phenomenal bulk to rip its roots free. In this particular part of the desert, nothing has stirred the ground since the seas evaporated and the wind ground down the rock and stamped it flat as a car park and hard as tarmac; fifty million years or thereabouts of patient landscaping, contouring, making good. A few more millennia, God might be saying, and we'll have a decent tennis court. Unless, of course, some bugger of a psychotic giant primula comes along and starts carving it up . . .

With a crack like bones breaking and much spraying of sand into the air, the roots come free; and for a few seconds they grope frantically in empty air until they touch ground, and –

– like a monster spider with wings and a huge yellow wind-up gramophone on its back, the plant begins to shuffle, on tip-root, sideways across the sand towards the distant shade of the outcrops.

'Gaw,' mutters the man, as well he might. For the Thing scuttling across the sand below him was his idea, and it was his genius (or his fault) that turned a little yellow wildflower commonly found in the fields and hedgerows of Old England into this: *Primula dinodontica*, the Ninja Primrose; or, to put it another way, one of the three components of the ultimate Green Bomb.

'Well,' says the girl, 'looks like that one works OK. Let's try the others.'

'I'm not absolutely sure about this . . .'

'Don't be so bloody wet. Here goes.'

From a second flask she takes another seed: flat, bean-like, about the size and shape of a small sycamore pod. Before the man can do anything, she's let it go.

WHUMP!

'. . . serious misgivings,' the man is saying, 'about the whole project. I mean, I never actually imagined for one moment –'

The primrose stops in its tracks. The tips of its roots, as sensitive as the nose of a bat, have felt the thump of the second seed landing, the explosion as the incredible potential energy contained in its brittle husk is released, the shivering of the earth as another set of iron-hard roots is driven deep under the surface. Like you, Mother Earth has this thing about needles . . .

'That,' remarks the man, rolling back the frontiers of statement of the stunningly obvious, 'is disgusting.'

A savage flashback into the racial memory – the myth of the hydra, the hundred-headed serpentine guardian of Hell's gate – except that instead of heads, this thing has pale blue flowers. Pale blue flowers writhing and twisting on their stems, petals snapping frenziedly at the empty air. The first Devil's Forget-Me-Not has been spawned.

'Two down,' yells the girl cheerfully, 'one to go. I'm really pleased, aren't you?'

The man says nothing; instead, he grabs for the third flask and hugs it to him. As the girl reaches for it, he backs away; forgetting that backing space in the basket of a balloon is strictly limited. *Safe* backing space, anyway.

'AAAaaaaaaah!' he remarks.

As he hits the ground (at which point, his troubles are definitely over) the flask is jolted out of his hand and flies wide, landing on a rock and smashing to pieces. A tiny, tiny seed, no bigger than a grain of salt, falls on to the flat stone –

WHUMP!

– which explodes into gravel as the third and finest

achievement of Operation Urban Renewal springs into instantaneous life. Its roots plough through the compacted sand like a torpedo through water as the single grotesque pod, the like of which hasn't been seen on earth since Hieronymus Bosch's window-box was destroyed by the Inquisition, splits and falls away, revealing a flower –

– You have to call it a flower, because botany is a naïve, trusting science which never for one moment imagined that anything like this could happen. A terrible, hideous flower, with jowls and warts and fangs and a big, purple lolling tongue –

– which tilts backwards towards the sun, and spits.

This is *Viola Aeschrotata*, the Hammerhead Pansy; proof, if any were needed, that the business of Creation is best left to the professionals. With a ghastly sucking noise, it ups roots and lurches at a terrific pace towards the other two flowers –

– who stop dead in their tracks, waggle their stamens and stare. A few seconds before, they had been marching grimly towards each other, with the express intention of pulling each other's leaves off. Now they exchange frightened glances, corolla to corolla. Jesus Christ, they are saying, what the fuck is *that*?

Pull yourself together, for crying out loud, empathises the Primrose. So long as we stick together, the two of us can have it for breakfast. What are you, a flower or a mouse?

But the Forget-Me-Not is backing away, its blossoms peeping out from behind its leaves. The hell with that, it broadcasts, have you seen the hairs on that thing? You want to be a hero, chum, be my guest. I'm –

With a lightning flurry of roots, the Pansy springs; and the Forget-Me-Not discovers, rather too late, just how incredibly quickly it can cover the ground on its enormous scaffolding of roots. There is a sickening plopping noise as, by sheer bulk, it crushes the Forget-Me-Not into the ground. The flower cranes on its stem and darts forward; the petals close; the carcase of the Forget-Me-Not shudders convulsively, and slumps.

In the balloon, the girl nods her head in unbounded satisfaction; and then, just to be on the safe side, has a good long pull on the hot-air burner.

For the Primrose, the desert is suddenly a very big, very open, very lonely place. The Pansy rises to the tips of its roots, swaying slightly; there is sap all round the bell of its flower.

OK. There is an infinity of magnificently pointless bravado in the vibes thrown out by the Primrose, as it rocks back on its roots and crouches, in a floral version of the classic knife-fighter's stance. Come on, weed, make my day.

No responding vibes from the Pansy; nothing at all. It emanates a vast negative aura, like a lawn-mower or a watering-canful of DDT. Every hair on the Primrose's leaves is standing on end.

Look. We can talk about this. The world's big enough for the two of us.

We're on the same side, you and me. Wildflowers united can never be uprooted.

Il faut cultiver notre jardin.

But from the Pansy, nothing. And now it has begun to move; slowly, rootlet by rootlet, dragging up vast moraines of sand and dust as it comes . . .

Sod you, then, the Primrose snarls, as its leaves pucker in horror. Go climb a trellis.

Ten or twelve seconds later, when it's all over, the Pansy

swivels its flower and looks around, until it is satisfied that there's nothing else alive within the range of its senses. That, as far as it is concerned, is how things ought to be. It ups roots and begins to crawl.

Five hours later, the girl in the balloon watches its dehydrated form wilt into a heap, thrash a last moribund tendril, and die. This, after all, is the Mojave Desert; even the roots of the Hammerhead Pansy can't dig deep enough here to strike water. Deserts have this aggravating knack of always having the last word.

Sow a few of those little white seeds somewhere where there's water, however – in the middle of New York, say, or Moscow or Paris or London, where water either runs in rivers through the middle or swooshes about a few feet under the surface in easy-to-find ceramic arteries – and it would be a very different story. The term 'flower power' would take on a whole new nexus of unpleasant meanings.

The girl smiles. The ultimate Green Bomb was now a reality. (And with friends like her, does the earth really need any enemies?) As the balloon drifts on its lazy course back home, she reflects contentedly on the progress of Operation Urban Renewal . . .

(. . . *Our environment is in deadly peril. The relentless spread of urbanisation threatens to poison and smother every last wild flower and blade of grass on the surface of the planet. Every pollutant, every waste product, every man-made toxin in the world originates in the Cities. The Cities, therefore, have got to go.*

Blasting them off the face of the earth by conventional means, however, would create as many problems as it solves. It has been calculated that a bomb powerful enough to take out, say, Lisbon, would generate enough toxic matter to poison eighty-seven per cent of the lichens and ribbon-form seaweeds in the Iberian peninsula.

How can we solve this dilemma, brothers and sisters of the Green Dawn? How can we cauterise the cancer of urban civilisation without killing the patient in the process?

We believe that we have found a way . . .)

It was regrettable, the girl mused, that the prototypes of the other two flowers should have been destroyed; not just because it would have been useful to be able to observe their progress but because it's always a tragedy, on general principles, when a living plant perishes. Would it be excessively animist and sentimental, she wondered, if she returned to the spot a little later and held some sort of brief, modest funeral?

No humans, by request.

The back bar of Saheed's was heaving. It was Karaoke Night.

Genies are, when the chips are down, simple creatures, as refined as the effluent from the *Torrey Canyon*, but with a strong instinctive sense of rhythm. There is nothing they enjoy more, after six or eight gallons of chilled goat's milk with rennet chasers, than grabbing a microphone in a crowded room and miming to Elvis singing *Heartbreak Hotel*. Since turning himself into a carbon copy of Elvis, correct down to the last detail of the DNA pattern, is child's play to a genie, the effect can be confusing to an uninformed bystander.

If this be offence, Kiss was a hardened recidivist, and on ninety-nine Karaoke Nights out of a hundred you could earn good money betting that he'd be up there, informing the Universe at large that ever since his baby left him he'd found a new place to dwell, if he had to jump queues and break bones to do it. Not, however, tonight.

Instead, Kiss was huddled in a corner with a half-empty plastic jerrycan of Capricorn Old Pasteurised on the surface of which icicles were forming, and a guest.

Of all the bars, he was thinking, in all the world, why did she have to come into mine?

'That one over there,' Jane was saying, 'looks exactly like Elvis Presley. Or was he a . . .?'

Kiss shook his head. Although there was no house rule prohibiting mortals, no genie had ever, in the long and illustrious history of the establishment, brought his employer there. The only reason there wasn't a rule against it was that in Saheed's there are no rules whatsoever.

Jane, however, had wanted to come. More than that; she had Wished to come, and accordingly here they were.

The agony had started, as far as Kiss was concerned, when Jane walked up to the bar, grabbed the menu and without looking at it ordered a bacon sandwich.

The barman had stared at her. 'A what?' he demanded incredulously.

'A bacon sandwich,' Jane had replied. 'Don't you know about bacon sandwiches? Well, it's very easy, you take two rashers of bacon –'

'Bacon,' replied the barman icily, 'is mortals' food. We don't serve . . .'

Without saying a word, Jane had turned to Kiss and smiled; a smile which could only have one meaning. I see and obey, oh mistress, your whim is my command. Oh fuck.

He loomed over the bar. He was good at looming. At Genie School you could do violin lessons or you could do looming. If you did the violin, you had to practise three hours a day in your spare time. Kiss had done looming.

'The lady,' he snarled, 'wants a bacon sandwich. You got a problem with that?'

'Yes,' the barman said, looming back, so that the two of them together reminded Jane of Tower Bridge a few seconds after a tall ship has passed through. 'We don't do mortals' food here. *Capisce?*'

'You do now.'

And the barman, who was only a Force Three genie with a maximum internal service pressure of a mere nineteen tons to the square inch, suddenly found himself cutting off rind and shovelling sliced bread into the toaster. As he brought the finished sandwich over to the table, Kiss could sense a certain degree of hostility in his manner.

After that, things had not improved. Jane's request, expressed in a loud, clear voice, that he introduce her to some of his friends, instantaneously made him the most unpopular person in the house, and genies whom he had known since Belshazzar was in nappies suddenly found it difficult to remember who he was, or even see him. So unnerved was he by this that he allowed Jane to beat him in two consecutive games of pool; the third he only just managed to win, on the black, by conjuring up invisible spirits to stand in the pockets whenever it was Jane's go.

'It is usually as busy as this?' she was asking.

Kiss nodded. 'Why are you doing this to me, by the way?' he continued. 'Was it something I said, or what?'

Jane raised an eyebrow. 'I don't know what you mean,' she said. 'I just thought it would be nice to see where you went on your night off. Part of getting to know each other better, that sort of thing.'

'I see. Well, thanks to you I've been banned for life, so from that point of view you've been wasting your time.

This is what I used to do on my night off, and therefore of historical interest only.'

'Ah, well,' Jane replied, 'it all helps to build up a general picture.'

Muttering something under his breath, Kiss returned to his goat's milk, while Jane looked around her. Something about her general deportment suggested to Kiss that any minute now she'd be asking when the interesting people were going to arrive.

'Hi, doll,' said a voice seven feet or so above her head. 'Want to dance?'

There is, of course, one in every bar: a nerd vain enough to believe that, contrary to all the teachings of experience, there is a woman somewhere who will one day say 'Yes'; realistic enough to focus his search for such a paragon upon the crippled, half-witted and partially-sighted. Or, in this context, even mortals. Kiss knew him well; a harmless enough genie in other respects, a trifling Force Two, cursed for ever to dance attendance on a small jar used for taking samples from suspected drunk drivers. Wearily he rose to his feet and clenched his fists . . .

'How nice of you to ask,' Jane said. 'I'd be delighted. '

The genie, whose name was Acme Better Mousetraps IV, blinked twice. 'You would?'

Jane nodded and smiled.

'Straight up?'

'Absolutely.'

'I can only do the valeta and the military two-step.'

'That's all right, we can learn together.'

She stood up. Acme Better Mousetraps IV leaned forward, picked her up awkwardly by one arm, and placed her on the palm of his hand.

'Right,' he said, as the genie on the stage informed

nobody in particular that they weren't nothin' but a hound dog. 'And *one*-two-three-*one*-two-three . . .'

Kiss shrugged, lolled back in his chair and drained the last few drops of milk into his glass. There was an outside chance that the two of them would discover how much they had in common, form a mature and lasting relationship and leave him in peace, but he doubted it. In the meantime, he resolved, he would just sit here quietly and hope nobody noticed him.

'Kiss, my man, what's the big idea?'

Kiss turned his head. 'She insisted on coming,' he replied, as Amalgamated Caribbean Breweries IX sat down beside him and filled two glasses with milk. 'Then, when Ambi asked her to dance, she accepted. I accept no responsibility whatsoever for anything that has ever happened ever. Is that clear?'

'Sure.' Acba sipped his milk and wiped his moustache. 'You got yourself one crazy mistress there, man. Rather you than me.'

'Can't fathom her out at all,' Kiss replied. 'So far, all I've done is domestic chores and a little light transportation. She hasn't breathed a word about wealth beyond the dreams of avarice yet.'

'No?' Acba raised an eyebrow. 'Hey, that's weird. Kind of spooky, you know?'

'Don't I just. The only thing I can think of is, her mind's on something else.'

'What?'

Kiss shrugged. 'Who knows?' he said. 'Or cares, come to that? Let's change the subject, shall we.'

'Why not?' Acba grinned. 'Hey, it's too bad you being tied up right now. There's something really heavy going down, and you won't get to have a piece of it. '

'Is that so?'

Acba nodded. 'The word's out,' he whispered, 'for Force Nines and above, excellent package including benefits for hard-working, committed candidate with a total disregard for the value of human life. I'm gonna try and get me a slice of that, no question.'

Kiss sighed. 'Sounds like it could be fun,' he agreed. 'Any idea what it's about?'

Acba shook his head. 'Whatever it is, it's serious men running it,' he said. 'That's all I know. Oh, and it's something to do with the Environment.'

'Oh,' said Kiss. 'That. In that case, it's probably just cleaning something. You're welcome to that. Let me know how it pans out.'

Acba nodded and stood up. 'Stay loose,' he said.

'Chance'd be a fine thing.'

During this time Abmi and Jane had danced two waltzes, one quick-step and a tango, all to the accompaniment of *Blue Suede Shoes*. For his part, Abmi was beginning to have serious misgivings about infringing the rule against impossibles.

'Well, thanks,' he said, lowering Jane gingerly to floor level. 'That was an experience, you know?'

'Oh. Have we finished dancing, then?'

Abmi smiled wanly. The tendons of his left arm were throbbing like wrenched harpstrings, and there were callouses all over his palm where Jane's heels had galled him. 'Hey,' he said, 'have you any idea what the guys will do to me, monopolising the foxiest chick in the joint? No way,' he added, with perhaps a scruple more vehemence than the context could accommodate. '*Ciao*, baby, I gotta fly.' Which he did. In fact, for the record, he put a girdle round the earth in twenty-seven minutes thirteen seconds and hid inside a wardrobe until he was sure Jane hadn't followed him.

Jane returned to Kiss's table and sat down.

'I have enjoyed myself,' she said. 'We must come here again.'

CHAPTER THREE

There was a queue.

You can tell of rationing. You can pontificate about the first day of the January sales. You can boast of your experiences in the line for day-of-performance tickets for *Phantom of the Opera*. But this was a queue to end all queues; so long that it projected sideways into several quite recherché dimensions, so crammed with repressed potential energy that it hovered on the brink of forming a black hole. It was, of course, an auditions queue; and nearly every genie in the Universe was in it.

When you have a queue comprising something in excess of 10^{46} supernatural beings who can flit through time and space with the reckless abandon of a Porsche with diplomatic plates hurrying to a meeting through the Rome rush-hour, queue-jumping ceases to be bad manners and becomes a challenge to the fundamental laws of physics. The Past became a frenzied jumble of genies bashing each other over the head and locking each other in cupboards so as to preclude their presence on the day in question; while a gigantic troll stood with folded arms in the doorway of the Future to keep back the stream of genies who reckoned they'd avoid the crush by fast-forwarding through Time. The Present was under the control of an only slightly less formidable young woman with glasses and a clipboard.

'Next,' she said.

At the back of the queue there was a hard core of genies who hadn't the faintest idea what the audition was for, but who felt sure that they were right for the part. The general opinion was that God was staging Aladdin, with a strong minority faction holding to the view that Springsteen had been taken ill on the eve of the big open-air concert in Central Park, and a stand-in capable of imitating him down to the last chromosome was urgently required. Both versions, although speciously attractive, were wrong.

The door to the small office where the auditions were taking place opened, and a dejected genie slumped out. A voice from inside called out, 'Don't call us, we'll –' as the door closed again.

Next in line was the Dragon King of the South-East. As the girl with the clipboard took his name and nodded him towards the door, he straightened his hair, shot his cuffs, and took a deep breath.

The Big Time beckoned. He strode through the doorway.

'Now is the winter of our discontent/Made glorious summer by this . . .' he said. The three men behind the desk gave him a look.

'He's too tall,' said the bald man wearily. 'Next.'

Dragon Kings are nothing if not adaptable. In the time it took for his vast brain to formulate the wish, he had reduced himself by twenty per cent.

'Too short,' muttered the skinny man with the glasses. 'Goddamn time-wasters.'

The Dragon King cleared his throat. ''Scuse me,' he said, 'but stature's not a problem with me. You give me the measurements, I'll come across with the body.'

'Voice too squeaky,' sniffed the freckled man with the cigar. 'OK, Cynthia, let's see the –'

'The voice needn't be a problem either,' the Dragon King interrupted, in a pitch that made the foundations of the building quiver. 'Just give me a hint, and I can –'

The freckled man looked up for the first time. 'Can he dance?' he asked the universe in general.

'Doesn't look like he can,' replied the bald man, raising his voice over the machine-gun cracking of the King's heels on the parquet. 'Two left feet.'

The King, by now rather flustered, took this for a specification, made the necessary modifications, lost his footing and fell over.

'Next,' said the skinny man. The Dragon King got up and silently left the room.

'Hey, Cynthia,' the bald man called out, 'are there many more of these deadbeats out there?'

'Quite a few, Mr Fornaldarsen,' the girl with the clipboard replied.

'Any of them look any good to you?'

'No, Mr Fornaldarsen.'

'OK, send 'em home.' The bald man glanced down. 'Except,' he added quickly, 'for this one. Recommendation from Zip Kortright.' He checked the name. 'Guy by the name of – goddamn stupid names these jerks have – Philadelphia Machinery and Tool Corporation the Ninth. Is he out there?'

'I'll just check for you, Mr Fornaldarsen.'

The door closed. After a moment, the three men looked at each other.

'Waste of time,' said the freckled man. 'Told you it would be.'

'We'll see this Philadelphia guy,' replied the skinny man. 'You never know your luck. Never known Kortright send up a complete turkey.'

The door opened – to be precise, it was virtually blown open by the noise of 10^{46} genies all protesting at once – and a tall, slim figure walked in, sat in the chair and crossed her legs.

There was silence.

'Hey,' said the bald man, 'it's a girl.'

'Correct,' said Philadelphia Machine and Tool Corporation IX. 'You see? Putting your lenses in this morning has already paid dividends.'

'What's Korty thinking of, sending us a girl?' snarled the skinny man. 'We don't need a girl, we need a guy.'

The girl parted her lips and smiled.

'On the other hand,' mumbled the bald man, 'have we actually thought this through? I mean, now I think of it I can see where, if we were to make the hero a girl . . .'

'It'd beef up the middle,' agreed the freckled man. 'There's that goddamn flat spot between the fight with the chainsaws and the bit where he blows up the Golden Gate Bridge. If we made him a girl, we could put in a bit with her and her kids, you know, mom stuff . . .'

'Like Cagney and Lacey,' agreed the skinny man.

'Excuse me,' said the girl.

The three men looked at her.

'Could one of you gentlemen possibly tell me what the film's about?'

'Hey,' objected the bald man, 'what's that got to do with you?'

'Well, now,' the girl said, flicking a few microns of cigar

ash off her knee, 'if I don't know what the film's about, how do I know whether I want to be in it?'

There was stunned silence; and the genie, who could after all read minds, watched with amused pleasure as the idea began to take shape in all three brains simultaneously.

She wants to know if it's the sort of film *she'd* like to be in.

If we want her, she might not accept.

She *must* be good.

The bald man cleared his throat. 'OK,' he said, 'it's like this. There's this guy —'

'Or girl,' interrupted the skinny man.

'Or girl, yeah, and she's got this brother who was killed in Viet Nam —'

'Big flashback sequence,' explained the freckled man. 'All the footage they couldn't use in *Full Metal Jacket*.'

'Only,' the bald man went on, 'really he wasn't, OK, it was just a dream, and in fact he's hiding out from the Mob —'

'Columbian drug barons.'

'Whatever, and then it turns out that in fact his girl —'

'Her guy —'

'Is working for the CIA, and is actually responsible for a string of serial killings —'

'He turns out,' elucidated the skinny man, 'to be a robot, but that's much later.'

'And then there's this big fight with chainsaws with this psychotic rogue cop —'

'He's a robot, too.'

'And then we have the big chase sequence and that's basically it. That's it, isn't it, guys?'

The other two nodded. 'Except for the bit where she spends three years working with disadvantaged Puerto Rican kids in the barrios of LA, of course,' the skinny man added. 'But that's really still at the concept stage right now. We're working on that.'

The girl frowned slightly. 'That's it, is it?' she asked.

'Yeah,' replied the bald man. 'Plus, of course, she gets killed in the first ten minutes, so all this is her coming back as a ghost.'

'We've already got Connery for God,' added the freckled man. 'Him or Streisand. Or both.'

'Both,' interjected the skinny man, 'and why not Newman as well? Goddammit, the guy's meant to be a trinity, why not really go for it?'

The girl considered, and stood up. 'No, thank you,' she said. 'Good afternoon.'

'We were thinking of calling it *Space Trek 9: The Search For* –What did you say?'

'I said,' said the girl, 'no, thank you. Goodbye.'

The bald man stood up, and then collapsed back into his chair. 'Hey,' he said weakly. 'I don't remember even offering you the goddamn part.'

'That was just as well, then, wasn't it?' said the girl. 'Thank you for your time.'

'Hey, wait a minute . . .'

Half an hour later, the girl left the office. In her bag she had a signed contract, and a cheque, and the star role in what was now to be called *A Thousand And One Dalmatians II: The Search for Spot*.

Three hundred yards down the street, she stopped, looked carefully around and turned himself back into a man. Well, a genie. Genies, as noted above, have a certain leeway in matters of morphology.

Some of them also have a certain amount of low cunning.

*

Kiss stood back to admire his handiwork, and saw that it was good. Well, he thought it was good, anyhow. And, since he was a genie and gifted with supernatural good taste in aesthetic matters (not that he ever used it if he could possibly help it; his personal preference when it came to interior decor was plaster ducks and little straw donkeys with 'A Present From Marbella' written on them) he knew that he was right. These matters are, however, essentially subjective . . .

'No,' Jane sighed, 'it's still not right. God should be older.'

Kiss sighed, and squeezed a big dollop of white on to his palette. 'You're making,' he said, 'a big mistake, I hope you realise that. Generations yet unborn will curse you for this.'

'Older,' she said. 'And more cuddly. Do it.'

Kiss winced, and assumed painting position: flat on his back, hovering eighteen inches from the ceiling. Overhead, the greatest artistic masterpiece ever, the fresco *God Creating Adam And Eve* glowed in a scintillating melange of colour. He soaked a rag in white spirit, and dissolved God.

'Fine,' he snarled. 'Why don't I just wipe the whole damned lot and do the ceiling over in woodchip and white emulsion?'

'I'm the one who's got to live with it,' Jane replied evenly. 'All I said was, would you help me with decorating the new flat. You were the one who thought it'd look nice with paintings . . .'

'Or perhaps,' Kiss went on, 'you'd prefer cuddly rabbits and kittens and adorable little puppy-dogs with ribbons round their necks. If so, just say the word. I mean, your wish is my –'

'If you say that just once more,' Jane told him, 'I shall scream.'

Offended, Kiss painted in silence for a while. Under his brush, the splodgy void which had once shown a fierce, jealous, enigmatic God piercing the veil of shadows to lob in the lightning-bolt of Life took form again to reveal the loving, all-compassionate Father of Mankind. Not bad, Kiss had to concede, but the first one was better.

'That's more like it,' Jane called up. 'Much more friendly. The other effort gave me the creeps.'

Gave you the creeps? You silly mare, that was God, it was meant to give you the creeps. I should know, remember. 'Oh, good,' Kiss mumbled through the brush gripped between his teeth. 'Your last chance for a few pink rabbits,' he added. 'Then I'm going to slap on the varnish.'

'No, that'll do fine.' Jane yawned. 'And as soon as you've done that, we can choose the carpets.'

'Carpets.' Carpets weren't what he'd had in mind. What he'd had in mind was eight hundred tons of mirror-polished Carrara marble, whirlpools of dancing white figures that would make you think you were walking on clouds. 'Anything you say,' he grunted. Women, he thought.

'If I said,' he suggested, floating back to ground level and dunking his brushes in a jam-jar of turps, 'that what you're forcing me to do violates my artistic integrity so much that even looking at it makes me feel like I was walking barefooted over red-hot coals, would it make any difference?'

'No.'

'Fair enough. Now, when you say carpet, obviously what you have in mind is a collection of masterpieces from the golden age of Persian carpet-weaving, featuring works by such immortal masters as –'

'Beige,' Jane interrupted, 'so as not to show spilt tea.

And it's got to be hard-wearing, because I don't want little bits of fluff getting everywhere. Ready?'

Let there be carpet, said Kiss. And there was carpet.

'That's fine,' Jane said, as the rolls of beige Wilton unfurled of their own accord and slid smoothly into position. 'Just what I wanted.' Carpet tacks materialised in a bee-like swarm, buzzed angrily for a moment, and flew with devastating velocity to bury themselves in the floor. 'I know it's not what you'd have liked . . .' she added, with a hint of remorse.

Kiss looked up from air-traffic-controlling the tacks. 'Actually,' he said, 'if it was my place we were doing up, it'd be lino. But you said you wanted it to look nice, and I do try to be conscientious. I have trouble, though, with conflicting signals.'

'Nice,' Jane replied, 'as in what I think is nice. Sorry if I didn't make myself clear.'

'Got you,' Kiss muttered. 'You may not know much about art but you know what you like. That sort of thing?'

'That's the general idea.'

Kiss nodded despondently and, out of residual malice, materialised pink curtains, a pile of lacy cushions and a four-foot teddy bear.

'Yes,' Jane said, nodding. 'Yes, I like that. '

'Fine. I think I was better off inside the bottle.'

'Maybe you were. Let's have some lunch, shall we?'

Kiss nodded, and instantaneously there was a table. It was covered with cloth of gold and laden with dishes of honeydew and jugs of milk of paradise. 'Or would you,' he asked, 'prefer scrambled eggs?'

'No, this looks fine. '

'You're sure?'

'I'm sure. I like yogurt.'

Conversation was slow over lunch; there was still a thin, oil-like smear of resentment over the surface of Kiss's mind, and Jane had her head buried in a furniture catalogue. This didn't do much to improve Kiss's temper (*Formica anything you like, dear God, but not formica*) and, being dutiful, he resolved to snap himself out of it by being affable.

'Funny bit of gossip going the rounds at the moment,' he said. 'Apparently, there's been some bloke going round trying to recruit genies for some job or other.'

'Oh yes?'

Kiss nodded. 'Offering good money, apparently. Which shows how much whoever it is knows about genies, if you stop to think.'

'Really.'

'If you think about it, I mean,' Kiss went on, trying hard to maintain the affability level. 'I mean, trying to bribe a genie with promises of wealth beyond dreams of avarice is like offering a fish a drink. Still, there's been a lot of interest.'

'Is that so?' Jane said, her face still obscured by the catalogue. 'Well I never.'

Kiss ground his teeth silently. *Small-talk*, said the training manual, *is the mortar that cements together the foundations of the ideal genie/mortal relationship. Talk to your mortal and you will find that empathy inevitably follows.* Something told Kiss that whoever wrote that hadn't been on active service for several thousand years.

'Oh yes,' he ploughed on, 'ever such a lot of interest. I'd probably have put in for it myself if I'd been at a loose end. Whatever it is,' he added lamely.

Jane closed the catalogue. 'Now then,' she said briskly. 'Kitchen worktops.'

★

The door opened.

Nobody walked through it, and nobody stood in the door-frame. After a moment, it closed itself again. The three people sitting at the table looked at each other.

'Good afternoon.' There was a brief flash of blue light and the genie Philadelphia Machine and Tool Corporation IX materialised in the air, hovering precisely one metre over the table-top. 'Sorry if I'm late, but I had a press conference.'

Better known to millions of cinema-goers as the star of *A Thousand And One Dalmatians II* under the name of Spot (and the corporeal trappings of the cuddliest, most adorable puppy ever) Philly Nine floated gently down and folded his arms. Each of the three members of the interview panel got the impression that he was face to face with the apparition; which wasn't the most comfortable illusion in the universe, not by some way.

'Um,' said the Chair at last. 'Thank you for, er, making the time.'

'No worries,' the genie replied. 'The job sounds interesting.'

'Yes.' The Chair tried to keep the hesitation out of her voice. 'The pay,' she went on, 'is excellent. I expect you want to hear about the money first.'

'Not really,' the genie replied, making his body translucent just to be aggravating. 'Let's see, now, I had one per cent of the gross for making this film I've just done, which at last count came to seventy million dollars, but so what? All I have to do to make seventy million dollars – silver dollars, if I want – is whistle. Like me to show you?'

'Yes,' said the Chair, quickly. 'I mean,' she added, 'if that's all right with you, of course . . .'

Suddenly it was snowing banknotes. Thousand-dollar

bills. Great big coarse sheets of money, drifting and floating in the air, settling in drifts, skittering in the draught from under the door. You didn't need to look to know they were genuine. For a while, the three committee members were a blur of fast-moving arms.

The money vanished.

'Easy come,' sneered the genie, 'easy go. And you reckoned you were going to pay me.'

'All right,' panted the Chair, catching her breath. 'Point taken. You are interested in the job, aren't you?'

The genie nodded, like a will-o'-the-wisp dangling from the rear-view mirror of Satan's Cortina. 'It sounds like it might be fun,' he said. 'From what I've heard, that is. Why don't you tell me all about it?'

The second member of the committee took a deep breath. His right hand was tightly closed around a thousand-dollar bill that had somehow failed to dematerialise, and he wanted to divert the genie's attention. 'Our organisation,' he said, 'is a radical group devoted to the cause of ecology. The way we see it, saving the planet is up to us, because nobody else is fit to be trusted with it. OK so far?'

The genie dipped his head.

'As part of our programme,' Number Two went on, 'we intend to destroy all cities with a population in excess of one hundred thousand. The reasons . . .'

With a slight crease of the lips, the genie waved the reasons aside. Number Two swallowed hard, and went on.

'In order to do this in an ecologically friendly way,' he said, finding the words strangely hard to expel from his throat, 'we have developed several new strains of . . . of –'

'Wildflowers,' interrupted the Chair. 'Pansies, forget-me-nots, that sort of thing.'

The genie grinned. 'I know,' he said. 'I'll admit, I was

impressed. For puny, stunted, pig-ignorant mortals, not bad.'

'Well.' The Chair, too, found that her throat was suddenly dry. 'We need someone to sow the seeds . From the air.'

'Over all the cities simultaneously,' added Number Three, 'so as to create the maximum effect. If all targets are engaged at the same time, they can't come to each other's assistance.'

The genie nodded; a token of respect, the gesture implied, from one thoroughly nasty piece of work to another.

All three committee members suddenly began to wish they were somewhere else.

'And you want me,' drawled the genie, 'to do this little job for you, is that it?'

The Chair nodded. She had a splitting headache, and she felt sick. 'If you'd like to, of course.'

'I'd love to.'

'Ah.'

'It would mean,' the genie went on, 'the deaths of countless millions of innocent people. Deaths by the most bizarrely hideous means imaginable. Wanton, barbaric genocide.' The genie smiled pleasantly. 'Sounds like a bit of all right to me.'

Number Two cleared his throat. 'A certain inevitable level of casualties . . .' he began, and found that he couldn't continue. The genie's eyes seemed to push him back into his chair.

'Smashed into pulp by the petals of a giant primrose,' he said, slowly, with relish. 'Horrific, bizarre, and with that ultimately humiliating soupçon of frivolity that marks the true evil genius. I like it. '

Sweat was pouring down the Chair's cheeks like condensation down an office window. 'It's them or us,' she gasped. 'People or plants. We're talking about the future of the planet. You do see that, don't you?'

The genie frowned thoughtfully. 'I see that you're a bunch of raving lunatics,' he said calmly, 'but so what?' He beamed. 'That makes you my kind of people. Glad to be on the team.'

Number Two tried to stand up, ineffectually. 'Of course,' he said, 'the whole project is still subject to review. We aren't actually committed to anything yet . . .'

'You are now.'

For a fraction of a second, a very small fraction indeed, Number Two had a vision of what it would be like. For some reason, the city he visualised was Oslo. He vomited.

'These,' the genie went on, holding up a cloth bag the size of a large onion, 'are the seeds of the flowers you so thoughtfully made possible. Anything possible, I'm allowed to do.' The image shimmered and glowed, like the heart of the fire. 'Thanks,' he said, and turned his eyes on the Chair. 'I'm sorry,' he said, 'I didn't quite catch your name.'

'Fuselli,' croaked the Chair. 'Mary Fuselli.'

The genie grew, filling the room. 'Apt,' he said, as the glass in the windows began to creak with the pressure. 'Mary, Mary, quite contrary, how does your garden grow?' The windows exploded and the Chair, Number Two and Number Three blacked out. Two seconds later, the pressure inside the room squashed them as flat as paper.

Philly Nine smiled, wiped human off his sleeve, and soared away into the upper air.

★

Faster than a thought he flew, breaching the Earth's atmosphere in a shower of sparks and soaring in a wide, lazy orbit around the Equator. As he went he amused himself by catching satellites and crumpling them in his fist like foil jam-tart cups. The further away from the planet's gravitational field he flew, the larger he became. A tail of fire flickered behind him, and dry ice knotted his hair.

From this altitude, the planet was mostly white and blue. The genie considered it impassively. It had, he felt, a sort of glazed, ceramic look, like a spun-glass Christmas tree ornament.

Or a very old bottle.

And, like all his kind, he had this problem with bottles. Bottles, in his opinion, were there to be broken.

And if one blue bottle should accidentally fall . . .

Kiss, genie-handling a huge roll of beige Wilton across the enormous expanse of the living-room floor, hesitated and glanced up through the window.

He swore.

Jane looked up. 'Problem?' she asked.

'Yes.' Kiss nodded. 'At least, there might be. Look,' he said, 'sorry to run out on you in the middle of the job, but could you see your way to managing without me for half an hour? There's something I've got to see to.'

'Can't it wait?'

Kiss shook his head. With a crack the roll of carpet snapped open, flattened itself, hung for a moment six inches above floor level, and started to rise.

'I promise I'll be back as soon as I possibly can,' Kiss shouted. 'Sorry about this,' he added and vaulted into the middle of the carpet which bucked like an unbroken horse, pawed at the windows with its front corners, smashed the glass and shot out into the air with Kiss sitting cross-legged on its back.

Philly Nine tutted. He was having trouble with the fiddly little knot the seed-sack was tied up with.

'Hey,' said a voice directly below him. He glanced down, and saw a flat brown rectangle. The slight quivering of its outer seams reminded him of a stingray floating in clear water. He frowned.

'Is that you, Kiss?' he queried.

'Philly!' replied the voice. 'Long time no see! And how's the world been treating you?'

The carpet closed in, drawing level with the hovering figure of Philly Nine, standing in the empty blackness trying to bite through a single strand of cord with teeth the size of office blocks.

'Not so bad,' Philly replied. 'What brings you here, my old mate?'

Kiss shrugged. 'Thought I'd catch a few spacewinds on my new rug. Like her?'

'Not bad,' Philly replied. 'Not bad at all. Like the stabilisers. You any good at knots?'

'I have my moments. Bung it over, whatever it is, and let me have a go.'

Philly Nine hefted the bag, and then checked himself. Coincidence, he thought; there are only seven Force Twelve genies in the whole Universe, and at this crucial moment here's two of them sharing one small, remote postage-stamp of empty space. 'It's OK,' he replied. 'I think I can probably manage. So,' he added nonchalantly, 'where've you been hiding yourself lately?'

Kiss twitched his features into a rueful grin. 'In an aspirin bottle,' he replied, 'of all places. And me, of all people. Well, you know how brown glass gives me a headache.'

'Been out long?'

'Not very. And you?'

Philly Nine shrugged. 'I've been hanging out.' he replied. 'You know, ducking and diving, pulling a few scams. Made a film, would you believe. Boy, that was some experience.'

'Yeah?'

'Yeah. Spooky stuff to be around, film. You hold it up to the light and you're ready to swear blind there's guys trapped inside the stuff.'

Kiss shook his head. 'I think it's just science, Philly,' he said. 'You know, mortal stuff.'

'I suppose so. ' Philly Nine folded his hands over the cloth bag. 'Well,' he said, 'nice to see you again, don't let me keep you.'

The carpet continued to hover. 'What've you got in the bag there, Philly?'

'Wildflower seeds,' Philly Nine replied. 'I'm doing my bit for the Green movement. Nothing to interest you.'

'Wildflowers?'

'That's right.'

Kiss raised an eyebrow. 'That's not like you, Philly,' he observed quietly. 'You were always, how can I put this, an evil genie.'

'It's very kind of you to say so, Kiss, my old chum.'

'My pleasure.' There was a moment of silence, disturbed only by the faint sighing of the interstellar winds. 'So why the change of direction?'

'Nah,' Philly answered. 'Me, I'm consistent, always have been. And if I were you, I'd go and fly your doormat some-place else.'

'Think I'll just hang around here for a minute, if it's all the same to you.'

'Suit yourself.' Philly Nine stuffed the cloth bag ostentatiously up one sleeve, and folded his arms across his chest. 'I'm in no hurry. All as broad as it's long, as far as I'm concerned.'

'Good waves, up here,' Kiss said; and, by way of illustration, he let the carpet slip on the spacewinds. A long, slow ripple snaked its way down the length of the carpet. Kiss began to hum:

'If everybody had a carpet
Across the galaxy
Then everybody would be floatin'
Like Ursa Minor B . . .'

'Cut it out,' Philly urged. 'You know as well as I do you never did like carpeting. Made you space-sick just going out on the ionosphere. What exactly are you doing here, Kiss?'

Kiss smiled. 'Stopping you,' he replied. 'Gosh, from here you can see the big pimple on Orion's nose. Fancy a peppermint?'

'I see.' Inside his sleeves, Philly's fists clenched. 'And why would you want to stop me, Kiss? I never did you any harm.'

'Never said you did, Philly. Always the best of pals, you and me. '

'Quite.'

'What have you got in the bag, Philly?'

Philly Nine smiled; and white lightning snapped out of his eyes, slamming into Kiss with traumatic force and sending him and his carpet spiralling away into emptiness.

Philly grinned and took out the bag. A tiny pinch of his fingernails and the knot loosened easily.

He turned the bag over, let go of the neck and shook it . . .

. . . and found himself inside a bubble, bobbing jauntily with the starbreeze. Above him, Kiss looped his Wilton, waved, and ducked behind the Moon.

'Bastard!' Philly yelled. On the floor of the bubble, seeds had landed. He rolled his left fist into a ball and smashed it into the wall of the bubble . . .

. . . which stretched.

Philly Nine noticed with some misgivings the rapidly thickening carpet of flowers round his ankles. They had already stripped the shoes off his feet (and Philly's shoes were rather special, even by genie standards; hand-stitched gryphonhide uppers, phoenixdown insocks and monomolecular polysteel soles; the gussets arc-welded in the hottest part of a supernova; the heel reinforced with the enamel from the teeth of a fully-grown snowdragon, the third hardest material in Creation. Imelda Marcos in her wildest dreams never imagined shoes like these . . .)

'Hey,' he yelled, 'let me out of here!'

'You'll have to grant me three wishes first.'

Philly began to get impatient. 'Kiss,' he shouted. 'If you don't quit horsing around and let met out of this contraption, I'll kick your arse from here to Jupiter. '

'Three wishes, Philly. You know the score.'

Petals like steel traps were slowly ripping his socks to shreds. Hand-woven from the fibres of firebird feathers (the second hardest material in the Universe) they had been custom-built to withstand the phenomenally corrosive properties of genies' sweaty feet. 'No dice, scumbag,' Philly roared. 'Get me out of here and I might just let you live. Otherwise . . .'

The last scrap of sock was digested, and Philly Nine suddenly became acutely aware that the hardest material in the Universe is the petal of a psychotic flower. 'All right,' he screamed. 'One wish. But I'm warning you, you're going to regret –'

The bubble popped; and Philly Nine was falling, helplessly entwined in roots and leaves, towards the Earth's atmosphere.

'The wish is,' came Kiss's voice from far away, 'that in future . . .'

Philly hit the atmosphere like a fly hitting a windscreen. For a fraction of a second the pain of impact paralysed him; and then he was through. Scrabbling frantically he managed to pull himself up on a handy thermal, and floated agonisingly in the upper air.

He glanced down and breathed a long, slow sigh. All the wildflowers had burnt up on re-entry – as had his shorts, his underpants and his impossibly expensive designer Hawaii shirt.

'. . . In future,' sighed the winds around his head, 'if you're going to be evil, make a mess of it. Have a nice day.'

Thirty-six hours later, the hole Philly had made in the ionosphere was still there. It was closing, but there was still a gap large enough for, say, a few wildflower seeds to drift through.

These days, nobody can seriously doubt that plants have the power to communicate; and the more self-aware the plant, the greater the power.

Ready? asked the Primrose.

Ready, replied the Forget-Me-Not. *Let's go.*

What about him?

Who?

Him.

Oh, you mean the . . .

Yes.

You ask him.

GRAAAOOAARR!!!

I think it's safe to assume he's ready too. OK, chaps, here goes.

They dropped in.

CHAPTER FOUR

Jane looked up.

'Where,' she asked, 'have you been?'

'Saving the world,' Kiss replied, materialising just in time to take the weight of the picture Jane was trying to hang straight. 'Bit more left, I think.'

Jane stood back, nodded and made the adjustment. 'What from?'

'Annihilation by overgrown carnivorous plants, if you must know. Has it occurred to you that this one would look much better over there by the alcove?'

'I beg your pardon?'

'Over there,' Kiss repeated, pointing. 'And then you could have the one of the three fluffy kittens playing with the ball of wool over there, where nobody would be able to see it, and that'd be verging on the ideal –'

'No,' Jane replied, frowning, 'before that.'

'Overgrown carnivorous plants?'

'Mphm. You are just kidding, aren't you? Only I never seem to know . . .'

Kiss looked offended. 'I am not kidding,' he replied grumpily. 'I was just looking out of the window when I saw a disturbing fluctuation in the infra-red, which turned out on closer examination to be an old mate of mine heading into orbit with a small cloth bag stuffed up his shirt . . .'

'You must have remarkably good eyesight. '

'I have, yes. Anyway, when I caught up with him it turned out the bag was full of nightmare carnivorous plant seeds, and he was just working out where to sow them. Fortunately, the silly sod hadn't realised that if you try and drop something through the Earth's atmosphere, it burns up, so as it turns out I needn't have bothered. All right?'

Jane stared. 'Are you serious?' she demanded.

'No,' Kiss said, pointedly not looking at the picture of the three kittens. 'Most of the time I'm aggravatingly frivolous. If you mean am I telling the truth, the answer is yes.'

'A *friend* of yours was trying to destroy the *planet*?'

'Well, sort of.' Kiss yawned, and stretched. 'Actually, he's just this bloke I've known for, oh, donkey's years; and he wasn't planning on destroying the Earth, just all non-vegetable life forms. Or at least I assume that was what he had in mind. My split-second spectroscopic analysis of the plant seeds leads me to believe that that would have been the inevitable result. Bloody great primroses,' he added with a grin. 'With teeth.'

'Hadn't you better tell me what's going on?'

Kiss shook his head. 'Tricky,' he said. 'You remember what I told you about being limited to the possible? However; to start with the primary question, Is there a God? we really have to address the . . .'

Jane asked him to be more specific.

'Guesswork, largely,' Kiss replied, materialising an apple and peeling it with his claws. 'My guess is that somebody hired my old chum to destroy the human race. Somebody a bit funny in the head, I shouldn't be surprised.'

'This chum of yours –'

'A genie,' Kiss explained. 'A Force Twelve, like me. That's pretty hot stuff, actually, though normally I wouldn't dream of saying so. We rank equal and above the Nine Dragon Kings, just below the Great Sage, Equal of Heaven. We get fuel allowance but no pension.'

'And this particular . . .'

'He goes by the name,' Kiss said, straight-faced by sheer effort of will, 'of Philadelphia Machine and Tool Corporation the Ninth, or Philly Nine for short. Remarkable chiefly for how little time he's had to spend in bottles. He's a shrewd cookie, Philly Nine, always was. Mad as a hatter, too, of course.'

'I see.' Jane sat down on a desperately fragile Tang-dynasty vase, the molecular structure of which Kiss was able to beef up just in the nick of time. 'So he's dangerous.'

'You might say that,' Kiss responded, spitting out apple pips, 'if you were prone to ludicrous understatements. If midwinter at the South Pole is a bit nippy and the Third Reich was, on balance, not a terribly good idea, then yes, Philly Nine is dangerous. Apart from that, a more charming fellow you couldn't hope to meet. Plays the harpsichord.'

Jane blinked twice in rapid succession. 'Oh God,' she said.

'Ah yes,' Kiss replied, 'I was just coming on to that. If we posit the existence of an omnipotent supreme being –'

'Will you shut up!' Jane looked around for something solid and reassuring in which she could put her trust. Unfortunately, everything she could see had the disadvantage, as far as she was concerned, of having been materialised or otherwise supplied by a genie. Eventually she found her left shoe, which she had brought with her from the life she'd been leading before all this started to happen. She hugged it to her.

'Sorry, I'm sure. Do you want me to make a start on the conservatory?'

'All this,' Jane mumbled. 'It is real, isn't it? I mean . . .'

Kiss clicked his tongue. 'Try banging your head on it if you're in any doubt. I have to say, I find all this ever so slightly wounding. I mean, I do my level best to make things nice for you, and the first thing I know you're questioning its very existence. Gift horses' teeth, in other words.'

'I thought I told you to be quiet.'

'You asked me a question.'

'Did I? Sorry.' Jane closed her eyes and tried to clarify her mind. 'Will you help me with this?' she asked.

'Depends,' Kiss replied huffily, 'on whether I'm allowed to talk.'

'Oh, stop being aggravating.' Jane took a deep breath. 'There I was,' she said, 'an ordinary person –'

Kiss cleared his throat. 'Jane Wellesley,' he recited. 'Age, twenty-eight. Height, five feet one inch. Weight –'

'Thank you, yes. Following a distressing scene with someone I had thought really cared about me –'

'Vince. Vincent Martin Pockle. Age, thirty-one. Height, six feet two inches. Eyes a sort of –'

'Either help,' Jane snapped, 'or go and empty the dustbins. Following a distressing scene, I resolved – stupidly, I admit – to kill myself. When I opened the aspirin bottle, out jumped a genie.'

'At your service.'

'Or so it seemed. At any rate, at the time I accepted you at face value, and I've been doing so ever since.'

'So I should damned well –'

'Ever since,' Jane went on, 'I've been ordering you to do seemingly impossible things, and you've apparently been doing them. The things you bring appear to be real.'

'You and I are going to fall out in a minute if you carry on with all this seems-to-be stuff,' Kiss growled. 'The last person to call me a liar to my face, namely the erstwhile Grand Vizier of Trebizond, spends most of his time these days sitting on a lily-pad going rivet-rivet-rivet and wondering why people don't bring him things to sign any more. I invite you to think on.'

'And now you tell me,' Jane continued, 'that another genie – was he one of the ones we met at that peculiar night club?'

'No.'

'Another genie is planning to destroy the human race, using overgrown carnivorous plants. And it's not,' Jane added, after glancing at her watch, 'April the first. Now then, what the hell am I meant to make of all that?'

Kiss shrugged. 'The best you can,' he replied. 'It's called coping. Like I said, some people find it helps to posit the existence of an omnipotent supreme being. I know for a fact He does. Other people,' Kiss added, materialising a decanter and a soda syphon, 'get drunk a lot. It all comes down to individual preferences in the long run.'

'Look –'

'As a matter of fact, He's all right, and so's the second one, Junior. It's the Holy Ghost you've got to watch out for. Forever walking through walls with its head under its arm, which for someone in its position is taking light-hearted frivolity a bit too far, in my opinion. Still, there it is . . .'

'Kiss . . .'

'Not to mention,' the genie continued, 'jumping out during seances and banging things on tables. And, of course, trying to exorcise it is an absolute hiding to nothing. Sorry, you were saying?'

'What *is* going on?'

The genie shrugged. 'Can't rightly say,' he replied. 'By the looks of it, some raving nutcase or other's decided to annihilate his own species. When you've been around as long as I have, you get used to it. You get used to pretty well everything eventually.'

'I see.' Jane started to pick at the stitching on her shoe. 'Happen a lot, does it?'

'Once every forty years, on average. Usually, though, it's just a war. When We get involved, it tends to get a bit heavy. Still, like I told you the other day, for every genie commissioned to destroy the world there's another told off to save it, so things even out in the long run. Last time I looked, the planet was still here.'

Jane opened her eyes. 'I think I'm beginning to see,' she said. 'Sort of. Just when this other genie – Pennsylvania something?'

'Philadelphia Machine and Tool. Actually there is a genie called Pennsylvania Farmers' Bank III – Penny Three – but he's no bother to anyone.'

'This Philadelphia person,' Jane continued coldly, 'is going to wipe out the human race, you suddenly pop up and stop him doing it. That's why all this is happening. And I'm . . .'

She stopped. She felt cold. In her anxiety, she broke the heel off her shoe.

'Look.' Kiss frowned, summoning up soft, heavenly music in the far distance. 'Nice try, but it doesn't quite work like that. Things aren't all neatly ordained and settled the way you seem to think – unless, of course, you posit the existence of a . . .'

'But it makes sense,' Jane protested. 'Someone wants the world destroyed. I want it saved.'

Kiss clapped his hands. 'Ah,' he said, 'now we seem to be getting somewhere. That sounded remarkably like a Wish to me.'

'Did it?'

Kiss nodded. 'I reckon so. You Wish the world to be saved. I take it,' he added, 'that you do?'

'I suppose so.'

'Give me strength!' Kiss took a deep breath. 'Either you do or you don't, it's not exactly a grey area. Toss a coin if you think it'll help you decide.'

Jane shook her head. 'Of course I want the world saved,' she said. 'Or at least, I suppose I do. The last thing I can remember before all this was wishing it would all go away.'

'That's just typical sloppy mortal thinking,' Kiss replied crossly. 'This is what comes of giving your lot free will without making you send in the ten coupons from the special offer box lids first. You mortals,' Kiss went on, with a slight nuance of self-righteousness in his voice, 'think that just because you come to an end, the world comes to an end too. Well, I'm an immortal and I'm here to tell you it doesn't. If you ask me, they should print *Please Leave The World As You Would Wish To Find It* in big letters on the inside of wombs and coffins, and then there'd be no excuse for all this messing about. I'm sorry,' he said, calming down, 'but there are some things I feel strongly about. Well, stronglyish, anyway.'

'Sorry,' Jane said meekly. 'I'm not really used to all this yet.'

'That's all right,' the genie replied, turning the music up a very little. 'Look, take it from me, you want the world saved.'

'Right.'

'Save the world,' Kiss continued, 'and you get merit in Heaven.'

'If we posit its existence, of course.'

Kiss sighed. 'Everyone's a comedian,' he grumbled. 'Look –'

'Save ten worlds and you get a free alarm clock radio –'

'That,' snapped the genie, 'will do. It's quite simple, as far as I'm concerned. The human race is the measure of everything that's prosaic and mundane. If there weren't any humans, there'd be no point being a genie, because there wouldn't be anyone to be bigger and stronger and cleverer than. So, as a favour to me, I suggest you Wish the human race saved. OK?'

Jane squinted into the middle distance, trying to see what the world would look like if she wasn't there. She couldn't.

'Put like that,' she said, 'how can I refuse? But hang on,' she added. 'I thought you said all the nasty plant seeds had got burned up. Doesn't that mean . . .?'

Kiss grinned unpleasantly. 'It means,' he said, 'that my old mate Philly Nine has failed. If he'd succeeded, the human race would have been annihilated. Since he's failed, with all the loss of face that entails . . .' The genie laughed without humour. 'That means,' he went on, 'he's honour bound to get even. Which means,' he concluded, materialising a paint roller and a five-gallon tin of pink emulsion, 'you lot really are in trouble. Are you absolutely dead set on having pink, by the way? It'll make the whole room look as if it's been whitewashed with taramasalata.'

Jane considered for a moment and then nodded. 'Yes,' she said firmly. 'Definitely pink.'

*

According to the ancient proverb, the worst words a general can ever utter are, 'I never expected *that*.'

In consequence, the military pride themselves on having anticipated every possible contingency. There are huge underground bunkers beneath the floor of the Arizona Desert staffed by teams of dedicated men and women whose sole purpose in life is to dream up the Weirdest Possible scenario, and make plans to meet it.

Some of these scenarii are very weird indeed.

Witness, to name but a few, the elite Special Boot Squadron (the task-force poised to counter an attempt by a hostile power to subvert democracy by glueing the soles of everybody's shoes to the floor while they sleep); the Royal Cleanjackets (the crack special force permanently on yellow alert for the day when alien commandos infiltrate all the major dry-cleaning chains across the Free World); not to mention Operation Dessert Storm (the fast response unit designed to deal out instantaneous retribution in the event of low-level bombing of non-military targets with custard).

The heavy burden of co-ordinating these various forces lay, at the time in question, on the broad shoulders of Major-General Vivian Kowalski: officer commanding, Camp Nemo. When the day arrived that was to be remembered ever after as the Pearl Harbor of weirdness, Kowalski had just returned from a tour of inspection of the Heliotrope Berets (the hair-trigger-trained haute couture force whose centre of operations is a tastefully decorated concrete bunker directly under the Givenchy salon, Paris). As a result he was feeling rather jaded.

It was good, he decided, to be back.

Returning to his spartan quarters, he removed the HB uniform he had worn for the tour (sage cotton jacquard battledress by Saint Laurent, worn over Dior raspberry silk chemise with matching culottes), lay down on his bunk and covered his face with his hands. It had been a long, hard day.

The telephone rang. The red telephone.

In an instant Kowalski was on his feet, dragging on his discarded uniform and gunbelt. Twenty minutes later, his helicopter landed on the White House lawn.

'Hi there, Kowalski,' the President greeted him, yelling to make himself heard over the roar of the chopper engines. 'Excuse my asking, but why are you wearing a dress?'

In clipped, concise military language Kowalski explained, and they went inside. In the relative peace of the Oval Office, the President explained. He didn't mince his words.

When he'd finished, Kowalski read back his notes and chewed his lip.

'Gee, Mr President,' he said. 'We never expected anything like *that*. Who do you think's responsible?'

The President shrugged. 'No idea,' he replied. 'Does it matter? The important thing is, what do we do? I assume you guys have something up your sleeves out there in the desert that'll zap these mothers into the middle of . . .'

He tailed off. Kowalski was shaking his head.

'Sorry,' he said. 'I guess we overlooked that possibility. You gotta admit,' he went on, countering the implied criticism in the Chief's eyes, 'giant self-propelled carnivorous wildflowers terrorising Florida has got to be one of the longest shots of all. Besides,' he went on, 'since you saw fit to trim the budget . . .'

'OK.' The President made a small gesture with his hands, guillotining the recriminations stage of the conference. 'So tell me, Viv. What have we got?'

Kowalski scowled and scratched his head. 'Assuming,' he said, 'that saturation bombing with all known weed-killers – you've tried that, yes, of course.' He grinned. 'I'm afraid you're going to have to let us work on that one for a while,' he said.

'But you do have a solution?'

'No,' Kowalski admitted, 'but I know somebody who might.'

The main reason why the world is still here is that genies have little or no initiative.

Command them to do something and they obey. It's not unknown for them sometimes to interpret their instructions with a degree of latitude – for example, if their instructions can be interpreted, however loosely, as a mandate to destroy the human race, and they happen to be psychotic Force Twelves with a personal grudge against mankind in general. Under such circumstances, they spring into action with all the vigour and energy of a super-charged volcano.

But without some tiny speck of mortal authority around which to build their pearls of malevolence, even the nastiest genies can do nothing. And, fortunately enough, mortals unhinged enough to give them that authority are few and far between.

In the most secret bunker of all, half a mile under the bleakest spot in all New Mexico, there is a door.

A big, thick steel door with a combination lock. For the unimaginative there is also a notice, in huge red letters, saying 'DO NOT ENTER'.

Open the door and you find a flight of steps, going down. Just when exhaustion and the disorienting effect of the darkness and the smell of must and stagnant water is about to get too much for you, the steps end and there is another door. It, too, is big, thick and made of steel. There is a notice, in big red letters, saying 'AUTHORISED PERSONNEL ONLY'.

Open that door and you find yourself in a small room, the size of the average hotel fitted wardrobe. The room is empty, apart from a chunky steel safe.

Inside the safe is a bottle.

WHOOSH!

Kowalski reared back, banged his head on the door and sat down hard. Suddenly the room was full of genie.

'Hello,' said Philadelphia Machine and Tool Corporation IX, grinning unpleasantly. 'Your wish is my command. What's it to be?'

Slowly, his eyes not leaving the apparition that surrounded him, Kowalski levered himself up off the floor with all the agility of a dropped fried egg climbing back into a frying pan. 'Hi,' he replied. 'Are you the genie?'

Philly Nine gave him a look.

'Yeah,' Kowalski said, 'I guess you must be. I'm –'

'I know who you are,' Philly Nine replied. 'What can I do for you? To hear,' he added, with a chuckle that belonged to some private joke Kowalski didn't even want to understand, 'is to obey. Shoot.'

The soldier explained; and as he did so the genie nodded sympathetically. The expression in his fiery red eyes didn't for one instant betray the savage triumph pumping through his heart.

Had it ever occurred to Kowalski to wonder, he asked himself, why a genie should have *volunteered* to be indentured to a bottle? Why, when all other genies in the history of Creation would do anything – anything at all – to avoid it, Philly Nine (a Force Twelve, no less) had deliberately and at his own request allowed himself to be bound to serve whoever removed the lid of this nasty, smelly glass container? Did the words *ulterior motive* have no place at all in this man's vocabulary?

'I see,' he said, when Kowalski had finished speaking. 'Nasty business. I take it,' he went on, choosing his words with the skill of a lawyer on a fraud charge, 'you want me to do something about it?'

Kowalski nodded. 'Positive,' he said.

'And may I take it,' the genie purred, 'that I have a certain degree of discretion in how I go about this? So long as I get the job done, of course?'

'Naturally,' the soldier said. 'This thing has sure got us licked. Anything you can do –'

'Oh, I can think of a few ideas,' the genie said. Being a Force Twelve, one of the seven most powerful non-divine beings ever to pass through the Earth's atmosphere, he was just about able to keep a straight face. 'A few tricks up my sleeve, that sort of thing. When would you like me to start?'

'Immediately,' Kowalski replied. 'If that's OK with you.'

A wide, slow smile crept like the first spill of lava from the cracks of Vesuvius across Philly Nine's large, handsome face. 'No problem,' he said. 'You just leave everything to me, and we'll see what can be done.'

Kowalski permitted himself a sigh of relief. Just for a moment back there, he'd been worried. 'That's fine,' he said, 'If there's anything you need . . .'

Philly hesitated. A few atomic bombs might, he felt, come in handy, particularly when it came to apportioning the blame afterwards. On the other hand, he had just been given carte blanche by a mortal – not just any mortal, he added with infinite smugness, but a duly accredited representative of the government of the United States of America – and asking for a fistful of nukes might just lead to awkward questions being asked and tiresome restrictions placed on his mandate. After his carelessness in wiping out the mortals who had given him his original opportunity, which he had then squandered (to his infinite shame), he had managed against all probability to get a chance at getting his own back. Best not to risk blowing it just for a handful of fireworks.

'Thanks for the offer,' he said therefore, 'but I should be able to manage. Have a nice day, now.'

He vanished.

Tinkerbell, Grand Khan of the Hammerhead Pansies, lifted its flower and roared.

The echoes died away. Then, from every corner of the Everglades, came answering roars, howls, shrieks and trumpetings. To the east it could make out the long, shrill howl of the primroses, under the command of Feldkommandant Trixie. From the north came the dull thunder of the forget-me-nots, and the laboured snorting of their High Admiral, Zog.

Where the bloody hell, Zog was asking, *are we?*

Tinkerbell twiddled its stamens in contempt. The forget-me-nots were, after all, an inferior species; and as soon as the job in hand was over, there was a place reserved for them somewhere near the bottom of the compost-heap of Creation. In the meantime, they might still conceivably be useful, if only as green mulch.

High overhead the F-111s continued their futile buzzing like so many demented mayflies; and, for those of them ill-advised enough to fly too low, with approximately the same life expectancy.

With a high wave of its right leaf, Tinkerbell motioned its column to proceed, and the mud churned around their thrashing roots. In the far distance, a reverberating *splat!* indicated that Zog had just tripped over its own tendrils.

Of all the seeds in Philly Nine's bag, only thirty-one primroses, twenty-six forget-me-nots and nineteen pansies had made it through the hole in the atmosphere safely to the ground; and at first Tinkerbell had wondered whether the forces at its disposal were going to be sufficient. As time passed, however, and each individual flower had started to grow and put forth flowers, it realised that its fears were unfounded. The three varieties had been designed to take root in the dry, barren dust of the cities. The rich, wet mud of the swamps was a thousand times more nutritious, and the plants had grown accordingly. Mud, however, is all very well, but for high-intensity carnivores it lacks a certain something. They were feeling, to put it mildly, decidedly peckish.

It was, therefore, fortuitous that the United States Third Armored Division should have chosen that moment to attack.

Ah! Seventy-six telepathic vegetable intelligences simultaneously registered a giant surge of relief. *Lunch!*

The army's battle plan was simple. Lay down an artillery barrage guaranteed to extinguish every trace of life in a thirty-square-mile area. Then another one. Then one more for luck. Then send in the tanks.

For the next ten hours it was noisy in that part of Florida, and visibility was poor because of the smoke. When the noise had subsided into a deadly silence, and the breeze had cleared away most of the smoke and fumes, there was nothing to be seen except desolation –

– and seventy-six enormous flowers towering over a nightmare scrapyard of twisted metal.

Better? asked the primroses.

A bit, replied the forget-me-nots, spreading well-fed roots among the debris that had once been a complete armoured division and burping. *But you know how it is. You quickly get tired of all this tinned food.*

With a sonic boom that shattered windows and played merry hell with television reception all over the state, Philly Nine flew over Miami, heading for the pall of smoke.

Swooping low, he turned a jaunty victory roll over the straggling column of refugees that clogged the interstate highway in both directions for as far as the eye could see. A ragged cheer broke out at ground level. The poor fools! If only they knew.

The wildflowers weren't hard to find; they were, by now, the tallest things in Florida. Spread out in a loose column, they were lurching at an alarming speed along the deserted tarmac of a ten-lane expressway. Huge lumps of asphalt came away each time their roots moved. Behind them the earth was a glistening muddy brown.

Philly Nine skirted round them in a wide circle, easily evading the outstretched tendrils of the forget-me-nots. As he flew, he hugged himself with joy. This was going to be fun!

He was, however, still in two minds. His original plan had been an unquenchable wave of fire that would shrivel up the flowers and then sweep irresistibly onwards, north-east, until the entire continent was reduced to ash. On mature reflection, however, he couldn't help feeling that that was a waste of the opportunity of an eternal lifetime. America is, after all, only one continent, surrounded on all sides by oceans. As he studied the column of marauding flora weaving its grim course, he couldn't help reflecting that this lot would probably be more than capable of having the same net effect if left to their own devices. What he wanted was something a bit more universal in its application; something that wouldn't grind to a jarring halt as soon as it hit the beaches . . .

Philly Nine stopped dead in mid-air and slapped his forehead melodramatically with the heel of his hand. Of course! He'd been looking at this entirely the wrong way round.

He accelerated, heading due north. In a quarter of an hour he was over Alaska; at which point he slowed down, rubbed his hands together to get the circulation going and looked around for something to work with.

At the North Pole he alighted, materialised a roll of extra-strong mints, popped the whole tube into his mouth and chewed hard. Then he took a deep breath, and exhaled.

The ice began to melt.

A word, at this stage, about Insurance.

There are your big insurance companies: the ones who own pretty well everything, who take your money and then make you run round in small, frantic circles whenever you want to claim for burst pipes or a small dent in your offside front wing. Small fry.

There is Lloyds of London: the truly professional outfit who will insure pretty well any risk you choose to name so long as you're prepared to spend three times the value of whatever it is you're insuring on premiums. As is well known, Lloyd's is merely a syndicate of rich individuals who underwrite the risks with their own massive private fortunes. Slightly larger fry, but still pretty microscopic.

What about the real risks; the ones that have to be insured (because the consequences of something going wrong would be so drastic), but which are so colossal that no individual or corporation could possibly provide anything like the resources needed to underwrite them?

(Such risks as the sun failing to rise, summer being cancelled at short notice, gravity going on the blink again, the earth falling off its axis; or, indeed, severe melting of the ice-caps, leading to global flooding?)

To cover these risks there exists a syndicate of individuals who possess not mere wealth, but wealth beyond the dreams of avarice.

Wealth beyond the dreams of avarice? Sounds familiar? Suffice it to say that the registered office of this syndicate is a small, verdigrised copper lamp, presently located at the bottom of a locked trunk in an attic somewhere in the suburbs of Aleppo.

For the record, nobody has yet been able to work out exactly what Avarice dreams about, on the rare occasions when it sleeps. It all depends, the experts say, on how late it stayed up the night before, how comfortable the mattress is, and whether it ate a substantial amount of cheese immediately before going to bed.

One of the many advantages that genies have over mere mortals is that they need no sleep. This is one of the few things that makes it possible for a genie to wait on a human being hand, foot and finger without something inside its head snapping. Eventually the mortal will go to sleep, giving the genie eight or so clear hours in which to recuperate and catch up on its social life.

Kiss had got into the habit of spending these few precious hours each day down at the gym, working out. When genies work out, by the way, they don't bother with weights, rowing machines and permanently stationary bicycles. What they exercise is their true potential.

When his bleeper went, therefore, Kiss was in the middle of a simulated battle with thirty thousand blood-crazed snow-dragons. To make it interesting, and spin the exercise out for more than six minutes, he had both arms and one leg tied behind his back, and he was blindfolded and chained to the wall. This made it difficult for him to reach the telephone.

'Yes,' he snapped into the receiver, deflecting a ravening hologram with his toes as he did so. 'What is it now?'

'I think you should get back here as quick as you can,' said Jane's voice at the end of the line. 'Something rather serious has cropped up.'

'Really?' Kiss tried to keep the weary scorn out of his voice, but not very hard. 'Let me guess. Your eyebrow pencil's broken and you want me to sharpen it. There's a very small spider in the bath. You can't find the top of the ketchup bottle . . .'

'The ice-caps have melted and nine-tenths of the Earth's surface is under water. Can you spare a few minutes, or shall I try to find an emergency plumber?'

'I'm on – get off me, you stupid bird – no, not you. I'm on my way.'

Grunting something under his breath about one damn thing after another, he shook himself free of his adamantine chains, swatted the remaining six thousand dragons with the back of his hand and pulled on his trousers over his leotards.

'Don't switch anything off,' he called out to the attendant. 'This won't take a minute.'

★

I don't know, he muttered as he raced across the night sky.

Never a moment's peace, he complained, as he grabbed a mop and a bucket out of the empty air.

It's not much to ask, an hour or so at the end of the day just to unwind a bit and relax, he said to himself, as he stopped off at the South Pole to fill the bucket with ice. *But no, apparently not. A genie's work is never done.*

He sighed, shrugged his shoulders and pulled out a handful of small hairs from the back of his neck.

Kiss, save the world. Kiss, thwart the diabolical plans of that crazed megalomaniac wizard over there. Kiss, empty the ashtrays and do the washing-up. I dunno. Women!

He rolled the hairs between his palms, spat on them and threw them up into the air. For a moment they hung between the earth and the stars; then they fell and, as they did so, changed into so many full-sized replicas of himself, each with a mop and a bucket of ice. Each replica pulled out a handful of its own hair and repeated the process.

'Ready?' asked the original Kiss. The replicas nodded.

'What did your last servant die of?' they chorused.

'That's enough out of you lot. Get to it!'

In the Oval Office, Kowalski and the President faced each other over the big desk.

'To begin with, Viv,' said the President, 'I was worried. For a moment there, I was beginning to think you'd maybe overreacted.'

Kowalski squirmed slightly, but not enough for the President to notice. 'You did say –' he began.

'Sure.' The President smiled. 'I should have had more faith in you and your guys. But next time –'

'I surely hope there won't be a next time,' Kowalski said, with conviction.

'Me too,' agreed the President. 'Still, it won't have done the polls any harm. Nothing the voters like more, when the chips are down, than a little display of All-American true grit. And the way your guys handled the evacuations was first class.'

Kowalski nodded. What the President didn't know, and with luck would never find out, was that the really big emergencies were the easy ones. For a really big emergency, like evacuating America, all he had to do was phone the insurance people and let them handle it. Which they had done.

'And the, uh, mopping-up operations afterwards,' the President continued. 'I guess I take my hat off to you there, Viv.'

Kowalski's eyes narrowed. 'You aren't wearing a hat, Mr President.'

'I was speaking figuratively, Viv.'

'Ah.' Kowalski left the semi-smug expression on his face, but inside he was still confused. The insurance people hadn't said anything about mopping up the floods. Leave it, they'd said, it'll go down of its own accord in a year or two. If it's still bad in eighteen months, send out a dove.

So who had done the business with the mops and the dry ice? He wished he knew.

Of course! How could he have been so stupid? The genie, of course, Philly whatever-his-name-was. Who else could it have been?

'No problem,' he said. 'We've got guys on the payroll for every contingency, Mr President, like I keep saying. '

'That's good to know, Viv.' The President smiled. 'Just like magic, huh?'

'There you go again,' replied Kowalski uncomfortably. 'You and your figurative speaking.'

*

Philly Nine sat on the peak of Everest and counted up to ten.

Don't get mad, he told himself, get even.

You bastards are going to pay for this.

As for the details – well, they'd look after themselves. They always did. Sooner or later some other idiot of a human being would give him an opening, and he'd be back. What was forty years or so to an immortal?

Provided, of course, that no interfering little toerag of a Force Twelve saw fit to stick his oar in, saving the planet with a twitch of his little finger before zooming away into the sunset. Some people, he reflected bitterly, don't know the meaning of the word solidarity.

Yes, indeed. He broke off the summit of the mountain, brushed it clear of flags and ate it. Kiss would have to go, or he might as well stay in bed.

But how? Force Twelves can't just be brushed lightly aside. Or even heavily aside, or aside with overwhelming force. It would be like trying to knock down a pterodactyl with a fly-swatter.

There are, however, ways and means. And of all the ways of killing a cat, Philly Nine reflected, drowning it in cream sure takes some beating.

There is a child.

His father was a brutal, sadistic bully; his mother a nymphomaniac married to a man (not the child's father) many years older than herself, and crippled into the bargain.

Left to his own devices for most of his formative years, the child developed serious personality disorders at a very early age. By the time he turned thirteen, he was effectively past hope of cure.

Partly it was heredity, partly it was environment; partly, it was the child's own basically vicious and perverted nature, which nobody ever took the slightest trouble to correct.

By the time he turned thirteen, the boy had developed a morbid fixation with shooting people. Because of his unusually privileged position, he's able to indulge this ghastly obsession with total impunity.

Look at him. Fourteen years old, dressed from head to toe in camouflage gear, with a Stallonesque headband and pimples. He's lying on his bed reading *Soldier of Fortune* magazine, and beside him on the duvet lies a state-of-the-art Macmillan sniper's rifle, with a Bausch & Lomb 21X scope and integral flash suppressor. When he gets bored with doing nothing, he'll go out into the street and start using it.

There's nothing anyone can do about it. Nothing at all. Despite the fact that this murderous infant ruins the lives of countless innocent people every day of the week, the authorities are powerless to act. They simply accept the situation and look the other way.

Because the child is a Force Thirteen genie – the only one – and his name is Cupid.

CHAPTER FIVE

High up in the Himalaya mountains, the very roof of the world, Kiss crouched low on a ledge a mere inch or so wide, held his breath, and waited.

'It's vitally important to us genies,' he could hear himself saying to Jane in an unguarded moment, 'that we retain our unique cultural heritage and ancient folkloric traditions and way of life.'

Jane had nodded sympathetically, gone away and read up the subject of what genies traditionally did. Accordingly, he had nobody to blame but himself.

'Come on, you goddamn treacherous sonofabitch,' he muttered under his breath. The mutterings froze in the sub-zero air and fell away, tinkling, down the sheer side of the rock-face. Fortunately, the wind drowned the noise.

On the blind side of the jagged outcrop of rock to which Kiss was clinging perched a bird. Not just any bird; the rarest, most fabulous, most acutely perceptive, biggest and worst-tempered bird in existence. Its plumage was a scintillating shower of jewelled colour, sparkling and shimmering in the clear, sharp light. It had a wing-span of fifty feet and claws that could disembowel an elephant as easily as undoing a zip.

'Cone on, my son,' Kiss whispered. Although he couldn't see the bird, he could hear the soft click as its heavily bejewelled, scalpel-sharp beak pecked at the trail of peanuts he had carefully laid the previous afternoon. Fortunately the phoenix, although rare, magical and incredibly dangerous, is not particularly intelligent. When it suddenly finds a trail of dry roasted peanuts extending along a ledge towards the mouth of a cave thirty thousand feet above sea level, it doesn't stop to ask how on earth they got there. Yum, it thinks, lunch.

This, together with the incalculable value of their tail-feathers, is probably the real reason why phoenices are so rare.

There are easier ways of obtaining phoenix feathers, however, than snaring them with peanuts and pitfall traps. The inhabitants of the Himalayas hit on a much more efficient method not long after the discovery of gunpowder. Genies, however, have obtained phoenix plumage the hard way since time immemorial, and so, regretfully, Kiss had left behind the Mannlicher-Schoenauer .600 Nitro Express rifle that common sense suggested was the best way of going about the job, and had instead packed peanuts, string and a folding shovel.

Peck, peck, peck. Aaaaargh! Crunch. About time too, Kiss sighed, and shuffled quickly along the ledge and round the corner, to peer down into the pit he had spent six hours digging the previous evening.

A baleful red eye glared up at him out of the darkness.

'All right,' croaked a hoarse voice. 'It's a fair cop, guv, I'll come quietly. I don't think,' it added.

Kiss frowned. 'Be reasonable,' he said. 'A couple of

feathers and you can be on your way. There's no way you can get out of there otherwise.'

From the pit, the sound of unfriendly cackling. 'You want feathers, chum, you come down here and get them. It's quite cosy in here out of the wind, I'm in no hurry.'

The genie rubbed his chin, nonplussed, and drew his collar tighter around his numb ears. His plan, although admirably simple and flawlessly executed, had only extended as far as getting the phoenix into the trap. Once he'd reached that stage, he had assumed, the rest of it would somehow take care of itself.

'Don't be stupid,' he growled. 'You're just being a bad loser. You make with the feathers, I'll make with the plank of wood. Agreed?'

'Up yours.'

'I can starve you out.'

'I carry six months supply of nutritional material around with me in the form of subcutaneous fat,' replied the bird smugly. 'If that's your game, you'd better have brought plenty of sandwiches.'

Kiss pursed his lips. The full extent of his preparations consisted of a thermos flask of, by now, lukewarm tea and the remainder of the peanuts. True, he could fly back to Katmandu, stock up on chocolate and be back in thirty seconds, but he had an idea that by the time he returned the phoenix would be out of there and circling overhead with its bowels puckered ready for pinpoint-accuracy bombing. Phoenix guano is the third most corrosive substance in the entire cosmos.

'I'll roll a rock on top of you,' he ventured. 'See how you like that.'

'You'd crush the feathers,' the bird replied. 'A right prat you'd look going back to the princess or whoever it is you're doing this for holding something looking like a second-hand pipe cleaner.'

'All right,' Kiss conceded. 'So it's a stalemate. Let's negotiate.'

'Bugger off.'

Tiny silver bells started ringing in Kiss's brain. 'Fair enough,' he said, 'if that's the way you want to play it, don't say I didn't give you every chance.'

The red eye blinked. 'Bluff,' it snarled. 'Look, you sling your hook and we'll say no more about it. Can't say fairer than –'

Kiss began to sing.

When they choose to do so, genies can sing well; heart-breakingly, soul-meltingly well. A genie can, if he sets his mind to it, sing solo duets; even barbershop.

Alternatively, they can sing badly. Very badly indeed.

By dint of stuffing its pinion feathers into its ears and banging its head sharply against the side of the pit, the phoenix managed to hold out for an amazing seventeen minutes, during the course of which Kiss sang *Sweet Adeline*, *Way Down Upon The Swanee River*, *Mammy*, *Alexander's Ragtime Band* and three complete renditions of *Seventy-Six Trombones Followed The Big Parade*. Indeed, it was only when he took a deep breath and announced that there were fifty-seven thousand green bottles hanging on a wall that the phoenix screeched like a Mack truck braking on black ice and started throwing feathers.

'Thank you very much,' Kiss called out, stuffing feathers into a sack. 'Do you want a receipt?'

'Shut up and go away, please.'

'And no sneakily crawling out and coming after me, you hear?'

'I wouldn't dream of it. Not unless I saw an affidavit

certifying you'd had your larynx removed first.'

Kiss slid the plank down into the pit, waved cheerfully, said goodbye and stepped off the ledge.

As he floated to the ground he entirely failed to notice the small figure huddled in the lee of the rocks, snapping furiously at him through a telephoto lens.

'That's him,' said Philly Nine. 'You think you can do it?'

'I dunno.' Cupid frowned. 'Let's see her again.'

Philly Nine shrugged and produced the other photograph. In it Jane was clearly visible, third from the left, second row down, holding a hockey stick.

'Couldn't you get something a bit more up to date?' Cupid demanded;

Philly shrugged again. 'If necessary,' he replied. 'I didn't think it mattered. Anyway, I thought you were supposed to be blind.'

Cupid smiled wearily. 'Man, there's all sorts of dumb things I'm supposed to be,' he replied. 'And this photo is fifteen years out of date. Get me something better and then we can talk business.'

'Wait there,' the genie said. Forty-five seconds later he was back.

'That's more like it,' said Cupid, appraising the picture with a professional eye. 'It's not going to be easy,' he added, after a few moments of close scrutiny.

'Come off it,' Philly said. 'To you, a piece of cake. Five minutes of your time, that's all I'm asking for.'

'Rather longer than that,' Cupid replied. He tried holding the picture sideways, but it didn't seem to help.

'Look.' Philly frowned. 'You owe me, remember?'

About a thousandth of a second later, he wished he'd kept his mouth shut. The child was looking at him in a way that made his blood run cold.

'Mister,' Cupid said, 'I'm a Force Thirteen, I don't owe nobody *nothing*. You'd do well to remember that, unless you want to spend the rest of your life sending boxes of chocolates to a red-arsed monkey. Understood?'

'Sorry.'

Cupid made a small gesture with his hands, signifying that the apology was accepted. 'All I'm saying is,' he went on, 'it's a tough assignment. The ballistics alone are gonna need a lot of careful planning. This ain't gonna be cheap, I can tell you that for nothing.'

Philly Nine smiled. 'That,' he said confidently, 'isn't a problem. Just so long as you can do it.'

'Yeah.' Cupid nodded. 'I can do it.' He laughed without humour. 'It'll be one for the trade press, I'm telling you. For a start,' he went on, 'there's the problem of the actual projectile. For her, it's got to be a frangible spire-point, or the chances are I'll just blow her away. For him, though, we're talking tungsten-core, full satin jacket stuff, the full treatment. Means there's no chance of a second shot if I miss the first time.'

'You won't miss, Coops. You never do.'

The boy shrugged. 'Always a first time. And supposing I do manage to do the job on them; I still gotta get myself outa there. Once your buddy here realises what I've done to him, he ain't gonna be pleased. '

Philly Nine stood up. 'You'll find a way,' he said confidently. 'That's why you're the best. It'll be worth your while.'

Cupid glanced back at the photographs and grinned wryly. 'It'd better be,' he said, did a thumbnail impersonation of a lovestruck marmoset, and vanished.

Jane hesitated, feather duster in hand, and looked around her.

'What the hell,' she said aloud, 'has come over me?'

It was, looked at objectively, an awe-inspiring sight. Suffice it to say, her mother would have approved. She had ambivalent feelings about that.

Yes, it was tidy. Yes, it was clean. Spotlessly so, in fact. Any passing visitor could have eaten his dinner off the floor without any health risk at all, although he might have found it more convenient to use a plate. Furthermore, the curtains matched the carpets, the carpets matched the loose covers and the loose covers matched the lampshades. It was exactly the sort of interior that furniture polish advertisements are filmed in, and a Swiss mother-in-law couldn't have found a microbe or a granule of dust anywhere.

'Yetch,' thought Jane.

Eight years' living on her own had accustomed Jane to a rather more bohemian environment: second-hand furniture, the floor hidden under discarded clothes and newspapers, a sink full of crockery and a kitchen floor that went crunch! when you stepped on it. She liked it that way. It was a statement, she'd always told herself, about her spiritual enfranchisement as a woman of the last decade of the twentieth century, the logical extension of the glorious principle to which Emmeline Pankhurst devoted her life.

And now look at it. 'Why?' she demanded. No reply.

Perhaps, she mused, catching herself in the act of plumping up a cushion, it's simply a case of reverting to type. That in itself was a disquieting thought, for the women in her family were the sort that ironed socks and regarded any meal that didn't contain at least two boiled vegetables as a badge of heresy. No, it couldn't be that. It had to be something else.

It had to be something to do with the genie. Looking at

the scene before her, she realised that what it lacked was a man, entering stage left and being told to take off his muddy shoes and not to sit on the chairs in those trousers. The genie, however, didn't by the wildest stretch of the imagination fall into that category. The only thing he – it – would be likely to tread into the carpets would be stardust or blood, and quite often it didn't even wear legs, let alone trousers. Nor could it possibly be a case of the genie's taste subconsciously subverting her own. Left to himself, Kiss would have done the place out like a cross between the palace of Versailles and Sinbad's cabin. Perhaps . . .

Perhaps, Jane reasoned as she automatically straightened a picture, it's an instinctive reaction; an urge to counter the intrusion of bizarre supernatural forces into her life by making her environment as brain-numbingly mundane as possible. Well, she was made of sterner stuff than that. She fished a magazine out of the paper rack, opened it and laid it face down in the centre of the floor. Then she straightened it, folded it neatly and put it away again. It was all she could do to stop herself ironing it first.

'This must stop,' she said firmly. The words seemed to soak away into the soft furnishings like water in a desert. Bad vibes.

That nest of tables hadn't been there this morning, had it? If anyone had told Jane a month ago that she'd ever deliberately own a nest of tables, she'd have laughed in his face. Yet there they were; with little coasters on them, to stop cups leaving rings on their sparkling glass tops. In her natural environment, cups grew on every available flat surface like mushrooms, and you had to give them a little tweak to break the gasket of solidified coffee that glued them down before you could remove them. And that, Jane knew in her heart, was the way it was meant to be. Not like this. She felt like a daughter in her own home. It was intolerable.

As soon as Kiss got back from whatever errand she'd sent him on, she resolved, she'd tell him to clear it all away and put it back exactly how it had been, down to the last smeared glass and overstuffed dustbin bag. Until then, she would go out.

Where, though? She didn't know. The last four weeks, she realised, had been spent in an orgy of home-making, with occasional breaks for picnics in exotic places. She hadn't yet come to terms with the fact that she no longer had to work for a living, or go out shopping, or do anything at all. Which left her with nothing whatever to do.

There had been, she recalled, some talk of saving the world, and as hobbies go, she supposed it would do to be going on with; more socially useful than needlework, and cheaper than collecting Georgian silver snuffboxes. It wasn't, however, the sort of thing you could do every day of the week. She needed something else, and she was damned if she was going to spend the rest of her life buying clothes or going to cocktail parties. She wanted . . .

Adventure? God forbid! Travel, to see strange sights and brave new worlds? She could go anywhere with a wish; but without the hanging about in departure lounges and lugging suitcases off carousels that gave travel its true meaning. All genuine wanderers know that it is better to travel uncomfortably than to arrive. Simply closing your eyes and finding yourself in Madagascar was as pointless as staying at home and arranging plastic flowers. What the hell did she want out of life?

But the idea of telling the genie, thank you very much, the rest of eternity's your own, was somehow repellant; it would be such a waste, like telling God you'd had a better offer. All the wish-fulfilment dreams you've ever had, there for the asking; no, there was no way she could say goodbye to all that. It would be cowardice, she'd never forgive herself, and she'd have to go back to doing her own washing-up.

There must, she reassured herself, be some purpose to all this. Although she'd never taken much interest in fairy stories when she was a girl, she could at least remember that genies didn't just happen to people out of a clear blue sky; there was always a plot of some sort, a sequence of events leading up to the genie, and a series of adventures following its arrival, concluding in the overthrow of evil, the righting of wrongs and the happiness ever after. To jump straight from the middle of the story to the end would violate the first law of narrative, and the laws of narrative make the laws of thermodynamics look weedy in comparison. Break the laws of narrative and you don't get let off with thirty hours' community service; they lock you up in a story and throw away the bookmark. No, something was going to happen, whether she liked it or not, and it was probably going to involve a life-and-death struggle with the forces of darkness. Gosh, Jane said to herself, what a cheerful prospect to look forward to. And aren't I the lucky one?

Why me, though? Well, why not? Presumably everybody else was busy. That was the sort of question she would have to leave to whoever was telling the story.

She glanced at the clock. Even if she was going to have to save the world, she reckoned, she'd probably still have enough time to wash her hair first.

In an upstairs window of the house opposite, Cupid adjusted his headband, chambered a round in his rifle and drew a skin-tight leather glove on to his right hand with his teeth. Through his telescopic sight (with the special rose-tinted filter) he could see Kiss trudging wearily back across the sky, his arms full of feathers. The girl was still under the hair-dryer, reading a book. The timing was going to have to be absolutely right.

No worries. Back in the old bow-and-arrow days, it was true, he had occasionally made a mistake. Now, however, he had technology as well as destiny on his side, not to mention the steadiest trigger finger in the Universe. At anything less than six hundred yards, provided the visibility was even half-way adequate, the course of true love was guaranteed to run smooth. He breathed in and felt his heartbeat slow down.

Now the genie was floating in through the window. The girl was looking up from her book. Here, the genie was saying, where do you want me to put all these feathers? Cupid half-closed his left eye and took up the slack on the trigger.

The first shot brayed out in the still air – only Cupid could hear it, of course – followed by the rattle of the bolt as he worked the second round into the chamber. No need to ask whether the first bullet had found its mark; the genie's mouth had already flopped open in that uniquely gormless way that can only mean one thing. With a half-smile, Cupid brought the crosswires to bear on Jane's heart and let his finger tighten round the trigger . . .

A spider, which had been spinning its web directly overhead, fell on the back of his neck. At the last moment, just as the sear slipped its bent, he twitched sharply, jerking the rifle sideways –

– and a potted fern, which had accompanied Jane from one flat to another for the last six years without really being aware of her existence, suddenly noticed with heartstopping intensity how entrancingly her hair curled round the nape of her neck –

– swore, worked the action and steadied the butt in the pocket of his shoulder. Ignoring the spider, which was trying to tunnel down under the collar of his combat jacket, Cupid half-emptied his lungs and eased off the trigger. For a split second the image before his eyes blurred, as the rifle jumped in a fierce spasm of unleashed energy. Then the picture cleared . . .

Gotcha! The room opposite was suddenly full of pink hearts, floating in the air like big, fat balloons. The whole street was heavy with the stench of roses.

Quickly and carefully, making no more noise than a stalking leopard, Cupid gathered up his equipment and got the hell out.

Fire crackled in the withered stems of the mistletoe, casting an eerie red glow on the lichen-covered stones of the circle. It illuminated seven faces.

'Ready?'

'Yup.'

The Chief Druid winced slightly. Although he was aware of how vitally important it was to attract keen new blood to the Circle, so that the ancient secrets could be passed down to generations yet unborn, he still hadn't come to terms with young Kevin's attitude. The sceptical part of him still harboured a suspicion that Kevin, who was an insurance broker, had only joined in the hope of picking up new clients.

However.

'We shall now,' he said gravely, 'link hands and invoke the Goddess.'

'Ready when you are, Humph.'

Ready when you are, Humph. It was at time like this that he wondered whether there was any point in passing down the ancient secrets. There was a sporting chance, he reflected gloomily, that if the Goddess did materialise Kevin would immediately leap forward and try to sell her a unit-linked endowment policy.

'Everybody join hands,' he went on, 'and keep holy silence in the presence of . . . Are you all right back there, Mr Prenderby?'

'Yes, thank you, Chief Druid.'

'It isn't time for your pills yet, is it?'

'Not for another half-hour, thank you, Chief Druid.'

'That's all right, then.' The Chief Druid glanced round. His flock were waiting, with all the silent embarrassment of grown men asked to hold hands with other grown men who they'd probably see again the next day, but wearing suits and ties rather than long grey woollen gowns. He cast another sprig of mistletoe on to the fire and took a deep breath.

WHOOSH!

'Stone the flaming crows!' The Chief Druid recognised the voice of Shane, who was on an exchange visit arranged with the Order's New South Wales congregation. He cringed. Just his rotten luck, he said to himself. The one time the Goddess actually manifests herself in my Circle, and the first person to greet her is this antipodean lout.

'Hello, boys,' said the Goddess.

She stood in the centre of the fire, which had leapt up to meet her like a large, friendly dog. Red tongues of flame licked round her, and her head was surrounded by a chaplet of pale blue light.

'G'day, Miss.' The Australian shook his hand free from

the clammy paw of Mr Prenderby (who looked like he was going to need his pills sooner than usual) and extended it gingerly. A long, yellow, spotted snake materialised out of the fire and curled round his forearm as far as the elbow:

'And what,' drawled the Goddess, 'can I do for *you*?'

'Excuse me.' Kevin's voice. The Chief Druid couldn't bear to watch. It shouldn't be like this, he told himself; it wasn't like this in the books.

The Goddess turned her head and smiled politely, like the Queen being introduced to the teams at half-time during the Cup Final. Kevin smiled back, instinctively using the wide grin he used for Putting Clients At Their Ease.

'Excuse me,' he said, 'but I take it you are the, um, Goddess? No offence, but I think we ought to just . . . rivet-rivet-rivet.'

The Circle froze, and the only sound was the sobbing of the wind and the frantic croaking of the small yellow frog that had once been Kevin.

'Satisfied?' asked the Goddess. 'Or would you like me to do something really convincing?'

The six druids fell simultaneously to their knees.

'Now then,' said the Goddess briskly, 'to business. Any requests, anybody?'

No reply. The Goddess clicked her tongue.

'Oh come *on*, people,' she said, 'I'm sure you didn't drag me all the way down here just to chat about the weather. Anybody for a bumper harvest? Rain for the crops? The winner of the 3.15 at Chepstow?'

The Chief Druid ran a desperate scan through the jumbled mess between his ears, but nothing occurred to him. He briefly considered saying, 'All hail!', but decided that She'd take that as a reference to the weather, a subject she apparently wasn't inclined to discuss.

·

'Well,' said the Goddess, 'if nobody wants anything at all, we'd better just fast forward to the wicker-cage bit, and then call it a day.'

For crying out loud, somebody say something. The Chief Priest swung a hasty glance round the Circle, but nobody was moving. They were all frozen like snakes watching a mongoose; except for Mr Prenderby, who had nodded off again.

'I see.' The Goddess sighed. 'Well then, the wicker-cage it is, then. And whose turn is it to be burnt alive this evening? I do hope somebody's remembered to bring some matches.'

'I have a request, Majesty.'

The Chief Druid's relief was short-lived, because the words were still hanging in the crisp night air when he realised that the voice that had spoken them was his own.

'Splendid,' the Goddess said. 'Right, what'll it be?'

'Um.' The Chief Druid felt his tongue dragging like sandpaper across the roof of his mouth. 'Do you know,' he went on, 'it's just slipped my mind for a moment.'

'Has it really?'

'Yes, Majesty.'

'Would it help,' the Goddess went on, 'if I just quickly read your mind? It won't take me two seconds.'

'Please don't trouble yourself, Majesty.'

'It's no trouble.' Suddenly the Chief Druid was horribly aware of the Goddess's eyes; he could feel them poking into his brain like knitting needles. No question at all that she could see exactly what he was thinking.

'I see,' said the Goddess. 'Yes, I can see your request in there, plain as day.'

'You can?'

'Of course I can, silly.' The Goddess smiled at him. 'You want me to afflict the world with seven plagues, don't you?'

'I do? I mean, yes, of course. How clever of you to –'

'You want me to trample the Unbeliever like a worm under the claw of the gryphon. You want me to unleash the fury of the Nine Terrible Winds, and visit the wrath of Belenos upon the heads of the ungodly.'

The Chief Druid nodded. As he did so, he was aware that he was on the receiving end of some pretty old-fashioned looks from the rest of the Circle (particularly Mr Cruickshank, who taught Drama at the local junior school and had a Greenpeace sticker in the back window of his Citroen) but he ignored them. 'Quite right,' he stuttered. 'My sentiments exactly, er, Majesty.'

The Goddess nodded. 'Fine,' she said. 'Ordinarily, that'd be a pretty tall order, but since it's you –'

'Excuse me.'

The Chief Druid's head whirled round like a weathervane in a hurricane. Mr Cruickshank had raised his hand.

'Yes?'

'Excuse me, Goddess,' said Mr Cruickshank, his eyes nearly popping out of his head, 'but, if you don't mind me asking –'

'Yes?'

'These seven plagues . . .'

'Ah yes.' The Goddess dipped her head placidly. 'Mr Owen will correct me if I'm wrong,' she said, dropping a smile in the Chief Druid's direction, 'but what I think he had in mind was plagues of hail, brimstone, frogs, sulphur, locusts, giant ants and burning pitch. That's right, isn't it?'

The Chief Druid felt his head nod.

'In any particular order, or just as it comes?'

'Oh, as it comes. Whatever's the most convenient for you.'

'Thank you.' The Goddess considered for a moment. 'In that case,' she said, 'I think we'll set the ball rolling with locusts. Is that all right with everyone?'

A flash of blue lightning rent the night sky, and six heads rapidly nodded their agreement.

'You're sure? It's your request, after all.'

'No, really,' gabbled the Chief Druid. 'Locusts, by all means.'

'Locusts it shall be, then,' the Goddess replied. 'Will Tuesday be soon enough, do you think?'

The Chief Druid shuddered. He had spent that afternoon planting out his spring cabbages. He assured the Goddess that there was no hurry.

'Oh, I think I should be able to manage Tuesday. Now then, any more for any more?'

Apparently not. A few seconds later, the Goddess was gone. As she sped through the fog and filthy air, she gave herself a little shake and turned back into the genie Philadelphia Machine and Tool Corporation IX.

A genie with a mandate.

The small yellow frog that had once been Kevin hopped slowly across the blasted heath.

Right now, he might be a small yellow frog; but not so long ago he had been an insurance broker, and we have already seen how insurance is like a pyramid –

(Huge, incomprehensible, hideously expensive, completely unnecessary and specifically designed only to be of any benefit to you once you're dead? Well, quite; but also . . .)

– a pyramid, with tens of thousands of little people like Kevin at the bottom, and a small number of very big people indeed at the top.

If one of the little people at the bottom shouts loud enough, one of the big people at the top will hear him.

Exhausted, the little yellow frog crawled the last few agonising inches and flopped into a stagnant pond. For two minutes he lay bobbing in the brackish water, gathering his strength.

They will hear him, because there is money at stake; and money is the ultimate hearing aid.

The little yellow frog stretched his legs and kicked feebly. A small string of bubbles broke the surface of the water. Deep down, among the pondweed and the mosquito larvae, Kevin rested, took stock of his position, and reflected on what he had to do next.

First, he had to file a claim. Without the policy document to hand, he couldn't be sure that there wasn't something in the fine print that excluded being turned into a frog from the All Risks cover; Act of Goddess, probably. But there was no harm in trying.

Second, he had to report to his superiors.

The loss adjusters at the top of the pyramid have a refreshingly dynamic approach to their art. Instead of simply coming on the scene when the dust has settled and trying to make the best of a bad job, they prefer to think positive. The best way to adjust a loss, they feel, is *retrospectively*.

Not long afterwards, a small yellow head appeared above the surface of the pond, blinked, and turned its snout towards the waning moon.

'Rivet,' it said. 'Rivet-rivet-rivet.'

CHAPTER SIX

'Would you like, Jane asked, 'a cup of tea?'

Kiss nodded, unable to speak. Genies, of course, can't stomach tea. The tannin does something drastic to the inexplicable tangle of chemical reactions that makes up their digestion. He grinned awkwardly.

'I brought you some feathers,' he mumbled, and thrust the bundle at her. She simpered.

'Gosh,' she said. 'Aren't they pretty? Let me put them in some water.'

She grabbed the feathers and fled into the kitchen, leaving Kiss to speculate as to what in hell's name was going on.

Heatstroke? He hadn't been anywhere hot. Malaria? Genies don't get malaria. A recent sharp bang on the head? No. Then what . . .?

Eliminate the impossible –

'Impossible!' he said aloud.

– and whatever remains, however improbable –

'No way,' he muttered. 'Biological impossibility.'

– must be the truth . . .

'*Shit!*' he said.

And yet. Weirder things have been known. It's a fact

that human beings (and genies count as human for this purpose) can get attached to almost anything, with the possible exception of Death and lawyers. And there was something indescribably charming about the way the corners of her mouth puckered up when she smiled . . .

'Oh, for crying out loud!' the genie exclaimed. And then the truth hit him. He peered down at his chest and saw, on the left side, a small round hole in his shirt. A few minutes later and it wouldn't have been there; the holes Cupid makes in cloth heal themselves in about a quarter of an hour, on average.

The bastard, Kiss said to himself. The absolute bastard.

But what could he do about it? Well, he could try changing himself into a woman – a piece of cake for a Force Twelve – but he had the feeling that that wouldn't make things better in the slightest degree; in fact, it would complicate matters horrendously. The same was true of turning into a cat, an ant or a three-legged stool.

He could get hold of that bloody aggravating child and twist his head off. That would make him feel better, for a while; but he knew perfectly well that even Cupid was incapable of undoing the damage. All he could realistically hope for was that with the passage of time the wound would heal of its own accord. But how long? With mortals, he knew, the process usually took somewhere between three and sixty years, and he didn't have that much time. Marriage, of course, was a recognised form of accelerating the process, but even so . . .

And why? The question flared in his mind like an explosion in a fuel dump. What possible reason could Cupid have for a stunt like this?

He could think of a reason. Cold sweat began to seep through his pores.

The door opened and Jane sidled through, holding a teacup and a large cut-glass vase full of soggy-looking phoenix feathers.

'There,' she said, 'don't they look nice?'

Kiss nodded dumbly. He had been an observer of human behaviour long enough to know perfectly well what came next; that excruciatingly embarrassing hour or so that you always get when two people realise that they're in love, but both of them would rather be buried alive in a pit full of quicklime than raise the topic in conversation. There would also be much staring at shoelaces, averting of eyes, feelings of nausea and meaningless small talk marinaded in sublimated soppiness.

'It was really kind of you to get them for me,' Jane was saying. 'It's something I've always wanted, a vase full of feathers. I think I'll put it here, where I can look at it when I'm sitting on the sofa.'

Jesus wept, Kiss thought, if only you could hear yourself! 'I'm glad you like them,' he heard himself reply. 'It was no bother, really.'

'I'm sure it was.'

'No, it wasn't.'

First, Kiss's subconscious was saying, we'll take the little bastard's rifle and wrap it round his neck and then shove it right up his . . .

'You sure?'

'Sure.'

There are rules, very strict rules, about when a genie may or may not read the mind of a mortal to whom he is indentured. Kiss broke them all. It was some small comfort to him to find that Jane's innermost thoughts were along more or less the same lines as his. *What on earth is going on?* he noticed with approval. *It can't really be, surely,* he was pleased to see. *What, him?* he read, with somewhat mixed feelings. *Pull the other one, it's got bells on it* was, he couldn't help feeling, just a trifle too emphatic. Without realising he was doing it, he made a few subliminal alterations to his bone structure and general physique.

Look, screamed his soul, this is ludicrous. Why don't you just tell her what's really happened, and find some way of sorting it out?

His consciousness turned to his soul and told it to get lost.

Yes, but . . .

Don't you understand plain Arabic? Bugger off. Can't you see the lady and I don't want to be interrupted?

'More tea?'

'Yes, please.' *You idiot, can't you see what's happening? Are you just going to stand there and let them . . .? Hey, there's no need to get violent, I was just going anyway . . .*

'Would you like a biscuit?'

'No, no, I'm fine, thanks.'

'You're sure?'

'Sure, thanks all the same.'

'It'd be no trouble at all.'

'No, really, I'm fine.'

As he spoke, Kiss marvelled at the moral fibre of the human race. A lesser species, faced with all this mucking about as an integral part of the procreative process, would have died out thousands of years ago. Salmon battling their way up waterfalls were quitters in comparison.

'Was it cold out?'

'Sorry?'

'I said, was it cold out? The weather.'

'No, it was fine. A bit nippy actually up the Himalayas themselves, but otherwise very, um, clement. For the time of year.'

'They must be very interesting,' Jane croaked. 'The Himalayas, I mean.'

'Yes, very.'

'And you had no trouble finding the phoenix?' Jane went on. It was painfully obvious that she was suffering too, but there was nothing at all he could do about it. He was having to call upon hidden resources of superhuman power just to stop himself from standing there with his mouth open like the rear doors of a cross-Channel ferry.

'No, it was easy enough. I just looked for some rocks with lots of white splashes and bits eaten out of them.'

'Ah. Right.'

Inside his heart, the bullet began to decompose. Cupid's bullets do that; the outer jacket, which is pressure-formed out of 99 per cent pure embarrassment, is soluble in sentiment and dissolves, leaving the bullet's core: 185 grains of cold-swaged slush. Any minute now, Kiss knew, he'd be staring at the carpet and muttering that there was something he'd been meaning to say to her for some time.

'Jane.'

'Yes?'

'There's something I've been meaning to say to you for some time.'

'Me too.'

'Sorry. Fire away.'

'No, no, you first.'

Thanks a heap. 'It's like, well –'

'Yes?'

He took a deep breath and said it. While he was saying it, the small part of him that was still functioning normally, albeit on emergency back-up systems and with a chair wedged behind the door in case the build-up of pink slop outside tried to force its way in, was working feverishly on the original very-good-question, Why?

Why should Philly Nine go to all the trouble and expense of hiring the ultimate hit-man, breaking all the rules in the Genies' Code of Conduct (it was cold comfort, but as soon as the Committee got to hear of this, Philly Nine was going to be spending a very long time in a confined space looking at green, curved, opaque walls) just to get his own back? Genies don't . . .

('. . . *Feelings that are, well, stronger than just ordinary friendship and, well, I guess that what I'm trying to say is . . .*')

Genies don't conduct their feuds like that; they hit each other with solid objects, sometimes even mountains and small asteroids, and pelt each other with lightning and divert major rivers down the backs of each others' necks, but at least they're open about it. And, once the air had been cleared and the damage to the Earth's surface has been made good and the mountains put back in their proper place, they forget all about it and carry on, as if nothing had happened. This sort of thing . . .

('. . . *and I was sort of hoping that if you somehow might find you feel sort of the same way about me then we might sort of . . .*')

And then the penny dropped. The shock was so great that for a few moments Kiss was suddenly taken stone-cold sober, and he stopped in mid-sentence and stared.

'The bastard!' he said. 'The complete and utter bastard!'

Jane looked up sharply. 'I beg your pardon?'

'Sorry.' The tide of slush, temporarily checked, started to flow again. 'I was miles away. As I was saying . . .'

Let's do everyone a favour and fade out on Kiss for the moment . . .

('. . . *Make me the happiest man, well, genie, in the whole wide world* . . .')

. . . And just consider the situation, calmly and without getting carried away. Ready? Good.

What do you get if you cross a genie with a human being? Answer, you don't, because you can't. It's a simple matter of chemistry; or physics; or, when you come right down to it, mythology.

Genies do not, of course, exist. This doesn't mean that there aren't any. There are, as should be now be only too obvious, rather more of them than the universe can comfortably accommodate. Any cosmos that contains fragile, breakable things, such as planets, is better off with a ratio of as near to zero genies per cubic kilometre as possible.

Genies exist at a tangent to reality. They intrude into the continuum we inhabit, in much the same way as an iceberg intrudes into a major shipping lane. Only a tiny proportion of the huge complex of forces that go to make up a genie is ever present on this side of the thin blue line at any given time. Of the genie known as Kiss, for example, 87 per cent is sprawled across the Past and the Future like a cat sitting on the Sunday paper.

Let your imagination do its worst, and then you will agree that any sort of lasting relationship between a genie and a human being is out of the question. And if that wasn't bad enough, please also bear in mind that regardless of the physical shape it chooses to adopt, a genie always weighs a minimum of 72 tons and has a normal skin temperature of 700 degrees Celsius. It takes as much effort for a genie just to shake hands with a human without crushing him to pulp or shrivelling him up into ash as it would have to expend on juggling with the Pyrenees while standing on one leg on the head of a pin. And relationships are hard enough as it is without any added complications.

There is, however, an escape clause. It's totally irreversible and unbearably romantic, and its consequences to the genie are so horrendous that it has never been used; but it does exist.

A genie can become a human.

Think about it. Never to be able to fly again; never to uproot mountains or conjure up storms, change shape, travel through time, work magic. To forswear eternal life, and accept the inevitably of old age and death. To throw away divinity and embrace mortality, and all for love.

A hiding to nothing, in fact.

But the option exists; and it's a basic rule of life in an infinite universe that if something is possible, no matter how dangerous, unpleasant or downright idiotic it might be, sooner or later some fool will do it. Because it's there.

Or because they have no choice.

While we're on the subject of genies, consider this. Given that genies are by temperament cruel, arbitrary, uncaring, destructive and deeply interested in wealth beyond the dreams of avarice, isn't it inevitable that at least some of them should end up in the legal profession?

The offices of Messrs Fretten and Swindall are on the fifth floor of a large Chianti bottle with a hole drilled in the side and a bulb stuck in the neck, somewhere in the fashionable suburbs of Baghdad. This is no dog-and-stick operation over a chemist's shop in the High Street; even the receptionist is a Force Nine genie, with the power to harness the winds, raise the dead from their graves and convince callers that Mr Fretten really is on the other line and will call them back as soon as he's free.

(A staggering achievement, considering that Mr Fretten has been imprisoned in an empty gin bottle on a back shelf of the golf-club bar ever since Jesus Christ was a teenager; but there it is. There are at least two callers who have been holding for six hundred years.)

Hoping very much that wealthy beyond the dreams of avarice meant just that, Kiss made an appointment and took a strong easterly trade wind to Baghdad. Having given his coat to the receptionist, handed over a bottomless purse by way of a payment on account and read the March 1453 edition of the *National Geographic* from cover to cover, he was ushered into Mr Swindall's office and permitted to sit down.

'It's like this,' he said. He explained.

'You're stuffed,' said Mr Swindall, a big, fat bald Force Twelve with six chins. 'Completely shafted. He's got you on the sharp end of a very long pointy stick and there's bog all you can do about it. Forty thousand years in a Tizer bottle will seem like paradise compared to what you're about to go through.'

'Oh.'

Mr Swindall grinned. 'As neat a piece of buggeration as I've ever been privileged to hear about,' he went on. 'You've got to hand it to this friend of yours, he really knows how to insert the red-hot poker. If he came in here tomorrow I'd offer him a job like a shot.'

'I see.' Kiss frowned. 'I thought you're supposed to be on my side,' he said.

Mr Swindall nodded. 'Oh, I am,' he said. 'One hundred and twelve per cent. But face facts, you're dead in the water this time. Won't do yourself any favours by burying your head in the sand.' Mr Swindall rubbed his hands together. 'Now then, first things first. You'd better make a will.'

'Had I?'

'Absolutely.' The lawyer nodded, setting his chins swinging. 'After all, now that you're going to snuff it – pretty damn soon by our standards – it's imperative that you set your affairs in order. In fact, you're going to need some pretty high-level tax planning advice while you're at it, because there'll be none of this beyond-the-dreams-of-avarice stuff once you're one of Them.' A slight cloud of worry crossed Mr Swindall's shiny face. 'You did pay in advance, didn't you?'

'Yes.'

'That's all right, then. Next you'll be needing somewhere to live, so I'll just give you a copy of our housebuyer's special offer package; and it'll be some time before you get used to not being invulnerable any more, so we'll put your name down for a couple of personal injury actions in advance. It's a good scheme, this one; it means you can start paying for the lawyers' fees before you have the accident. Ah, yes,' said Mr Swindall, rubbing his hands together and grinning like a hyena, 'we'll be able to provide you with a full range of legal services before you're very much older, you mark my words.'

'I see. Thank you very much.'

'Don't mention it. Oh yes, and of course there'll be the divorce as well . . .'

'The div . . .'

Mr Swindall smiled sadly. 'You don't think it'll last, do you? Be realistic, please. Ninety-nine-point-seven per cent of marriages between supernaturals and mortals don't last out the year, so if I were you I'd put a deposit down now while you've still got a few bob in your pocket. Much easier that way.'

Kiss raised his hand. 'Just a minute,' he said. 'Before we get completely carried away . . .'

'We are also,' Mr Swindall interrupted quickly, 'authorised by the Divine Law Society to conduct investment business, so if you'll just fill in this simple questionnaire . . .'

'Before,' Kiss insisted, 'we get completely carried away, what's the procedure for doing this . . . ?'

'The renunciation of eternal life?' Mr Swindall opened a drawer and pulled out a thick sheaf of forms. 'Piece of cake. You just fill these out, in quadruplicate, and take them with the prescribed fee to the offices of the Supreme Court between 9.15 and 9.25 on the first Wednesday in any month, and six months later you'll have to attend a short hearing in front of the District Seraph . . .'

It took Mr Swindall twenty-seven minutes to describe the procedure.

'It's as simple as that,' he concluded. 'And if you run into any problems along the way, just give me a shout and I'll put you back on the right lines. Now, where were we? Oh, yes. For a mere thirty per cent commission, I can put you on to some very nice unit trusts which ought . . .'

'The forms, please.'

'You don't want to hear about the breathtaking new equities portfolio we're putting together for a select few specially favoured clients?'

'No.'

'Oh.' Mr Swindall frowned. 'Oh well, sod you, then. The receptionist will give you the final bill on your way out.'

Organising a plague of locusts, even if you're a Force Twelve genie, is several light years away from a doddle, as anyone who's ever organised anything will readily appreciate.

First, catch your locusts. Actually producing nine hundred million locusts wasn't a problem. Let there be locusts! And there were locusts.

A plague of locusts. The phrase trips easily off the tongue. But consider this. The average locust needs a certain amount of food each day, or it dies. Nine hundred million locusts, gathered together in one spot awaiting distribution in plague form, need nine hundred million times that amount. Neglect to provide nine hundred million packed lunches, and before very long you'll have a plague of nine hundred million dead locusts; untidy, but no real long-term threat to humanity.

Another point to bear in mind is that locusts are in practice nothing more than the sports model of the basic production grasshopper; and grasshoppers hop. Up to six feet, when the mood takes them. Trying to keep nine hundred million of the little tinkers together long enough to organise properly structured devastation parties is, in consequence, not a job for the faint-hearted.

Furthermore, they chirp. They stridulate. The sound they produce is extremely similar in pitch, frequency and tone to the sound of fingernails on a blackboard. Nine hundred million locusts stridulating simultaneously takes noise pollution into a whole new dimension.

Half an hour into the plague, Philly Nine was beginning to wish he'd gone with the flow and specified a plague of frogs instead.

The final straw was the huge flock of ibises which suddenly appeared, hovering in the air just out of genie stone-throwing range and darting in whenever Philly's back was turned to gorge themselves on the biggest free lunch in ibis history. The few who overdid it to such an extent that they were unable to get off the ground again met with appropriate retribution; but there were plenty more where they came from.

Three hours into the plague, with nothing achieved except a massive feed bill, a net loss from starvation, desertion and enemy action of about seventeen million locusts and a lot of very happy ibises, Philly Nine sat down, put his head in his hands and began to whimper.

The locusts, who had finished off the latest consignment of rice (sacks included) and were beginning to feel peckish again, ate his shoes.

'Excuse me.'

Philly Nine looked up. Hovering above his head was a helicopter, out of whose window hung a man with a clipboard and a megaphone.

'Excuse me,' the man yelled above the roar of the engine and the chirping of the locusts, 'but are these insects yours?'

Philly nodded. By now they'd finished off his socks and were working their way up his trousers.

'Then I'm very sorry,' the man went on, 'but I'm going to have to ask you to move them. They're causing an environmental hazard, you see, and we can't have that. There's regulations about this sort of thing.'

Philly Nine laughed bitterly. 'Move them,' he said. 'Right. Where would you suggest I move them to?'

'Not my problem,' the man replied. 'But while we're on the subject, I take it you do have a permit for livestock transportation?'

'What?'

'A permit,' the man said. 'Transportation of livestock without a permit is a very serious offence.'

'No, I haven't,' Philly growled. 'What precisely are you going to do about it?'

The man shook his head. 'I'm sorry,' he said, 'but if you haven't got a permit, then I can't allow you to move these insects. They aren't going anywhere until I see a Form 95, properly endorsed by the Department of Transport . . .'

'But you told me yourself to get them shifted.'

'Agreed,' the man said, nodding. 'But not without a permit.'

'All right,' Philly snarled, just managing to stay calm. 'So what do you suggest I do?'

'Not my problem. You could try getting a permit.'

'How do I do that?'

The man sighed. 'You can't,' he said. 'Sorry. In order to apply for a permit, you have to give twenty-eight days' notice in writing to the Inspector of Livestock Transportation, and like I just said, you haven't got twenty-eight days because you've got to remove them immediately on environmental grounds. Bit of a grey area in the regulations, I'm afraid. Oh, and by the way . . .'

'Yes?'

The man pointed with his clipboard towards the ibises, which had settled down en bloc in the middle of the swarm and were munching a broad swathe through it with impressive speed. 'You're not allowed to do that, I'm afraid.'

'Do what?'

'Do or permit to be done anything which tends to prejudice the well-being of an endangered or protected species. If any of those ibises dies from over-feeding, I'm afraid it'll be your head on the block.'

'I see.'

'So I suggest you move them on. Although,' the man continued, 'disturbing the habitat of an endangered or protected species is also forbidden, and the expression habitat does include any well-established feeding-ground –'

Philly slowly got to his feet. 'All right,' he said, 'it's a fair cop. Looks like you're going to have to impound my locusts.' He grinned. 'No hard feelings,' he added. 'I know you guys have a job to do. OK, they're all yours.'

The man in the helicopter shook his head. 'Sorry,' he said, 'but we can't do that. Regulations state that we can't accept surrender of property from members of the public without an authorisation from the Secretary of State, and to get an authorisation we'd need to give twenty-eight days' notice . . .'

'Fine.' Philly's mental computer fixed on the helicopter, estimating its airspeed and mass, and calculating the necessary trajectory a good gob and spit would need to follow in order to hit the man square in the eye. 'So what are you going to do?'

The man frowned. 'I hate to have to do this,' he said, 'but if you won't co-operate you leave us no choice. All right, Wayne, over to you.'

Wayne? Who's Wayne? Philly Nine looked sharply round, just in time to see a tall figure in overalls standing over him with an empty milk-bottle in his hand. He tried to dodge, but he slipped on a wedge of squashed locusts, lost his footing and staggered backwards into the bottle. A cork appeared, blotting out the light from what had suddenly become a very small, cramped universe.

'Twenty-eight days,' said a small voice, very far away. 'For contempt. When you get out, we'll also be filing a civil suit for public nuisance and forty-six breaches of the planning regulations. Sorry.'

Nine hours later, the locusts ceased to be a problem. Starvation, ibises and a freak virus which spread like wildfire had accounted for them all; all except the one which had hopped into the milk bottle just before the cork was inserted.

Twenty-eight days turned out to be a very long time.

Genies can do, and have done, pretty well everything; but one field of endeavour in which they have little experience, for obvious reasons, is organising stag nights.

Call to mind the old adage about not being able to organise a highly convivial party in a brewery. Focus on that thought.

'We ought,' insisted Acme Waste Disposal Services III, a small Force Two, 'to have a stripagram.' He scratched his head. 'It's traditional,' he added, 'I think.'

The other members of the Committee shrugged and waved to the bartender for more goat's milk. These were uncharted waters.

'What's that?' asked Nordic Oil IX.

Awds Three frowned. 'What I've heard is,' he said, 'you hire this female mortal to come along and take her clothes off.'

'Why?'

'And then she sings a song or recites a poem or something.'

'No wealth-beyond-the-dreams or anything?'

Awds Three shook his head. 'Nope,' he replied. 'Off with the undies, do the song, say the poem, and that's it.'

'How very peculiar.'

'And sometimes,' Awds added, wishing he hadn't raised the subject, 'they jump out of cakes.'

'Get away!'

'So I've heard,' the genie mumbled. 'Never seen it myself, but . . .'

There was a puzzled silence.

'Let's just go over this one more time,' said a thoughtful genie by the name of Standard Conglomerates the First.

'There's this female mortal imprisoned in a cake, and . . .'

'Not imprisoned, exactly . . .'

'. . . and she jumps out and *doesn't* grant three wishes . . .'

'As I understand it. Like I said, this is all strictly hearsay . . .'

'. . . festoons the floor with her dirty laundry . . .'

'Hey, we don't have to do her laundry for her, do we, because I've got sensitive skin . . .'

'. . . sings a song and goes away again. For which,' he added, 'she expects to be paid money. And this,' he concluded, 'is fun.'

'Male bonding,' suggested Nordic Oil.

'I think that's extra.'

Stan One drew a deep breath. 'I think we'll pigeonhole that one for the time being, people. Which leaves us with excessive drinking . . .'

'Well, that oughtn't to be a problem, provided they skim the cream off first . . .'

'Excessive drinking,' Stan One continued, 'singing raucous songs and being sick in people's window-boxes in the early hours of the morning.' He paused. 'It's all a bit jejune, isn't it?'

'What sort of cake, exactly?'

'That's what mortals do,' Awds replied defensively. 'Don't blame me, I'm only repeating what I've heard.'

Stan One shrugged. 'If he's dead set on becoming a mortal, I suppose that's what he's got to learn to expect. ' He took a long pull at his goat's milk and spat out a tiny knob of rennet. 'The sooner he starts, I guess, the sooner he'll get used to it.' He grimaced; not entirely because of the rennet.

'Because if it's one of those creamy ones with jam in the

middle, she won't half be sticky and yeeuk by the time she's jumped up through the middle of it. Bits of glacé cherry in the hair, all that sort of –'

'I think,' said Imperial Unit Fund Managers IV, a big, slow genie, 'that at some stage we have to tie shoes to a car.' Awds shook his head. 'You're wrong there,' he said. 'It's horses you tie shoes to. Cars have tyres.'

'Oh. Sorry.'

'Damned odd, the whole thing,' mused Stan One. 'Anyone know why he's doing it?'

There was a general shaking of heads. 'For charity?' suggested the Dragon King of the South-East. 'One of these sponsored things?'

Impy Four shook his head. 'Can't see how it'd work,' he replied.

'Well,' replied the Dragon King, 'he's becoming a mortal, right? So he gets people to sponsor him, so much a year, to see how long he'll live. So suppose we sponsor him, oh, five gold dirhams a year, and he lives say twenty years . . .'

'That's a bit extreme, isn't it?'

The Dragon King shrugged. 'People do weird things for charity,' he said. 'I heard once where this bloke allowed himself to be chained in the stocks and have wet sponges thrown at him.'

Awds shook his head. 'I don't think it's that,' he said. 'I think it's more *cherchez la femme*.'

'Find the lady? You mean like a card game?'

'And anyway,' interrupted a slender Force Six, 'from what you say, all you have to do to find mortal females is look in the nearest Victoria sponge. There's got to be more to it than that.'

'I think,' said Awds, 'he's in love.'

A long, difficult silence.

'Just say that again, will you?' asked Stan One, slowly.

'I think he's in love,' Awds repeated, red to the tips of his ears. 'Just a rumour, of course. No idea where I heard it.'

'With a mortal?'

Awds nodded.

'A *female* mortal?'

'It's only what I've heard.'

Another long silence.

'Well,' said the Dragon King briskly, 'if he's doing it for charity, then I reckon I'm good for ten dirhams a year. Any takers?'

Jane frowned.

'The first one again,' she commanded, 'but without the sequins.'

There was a voiceless sigh, and out of nothingness appeared a dress. It was long, white and shimmering. Twenty thousand tiny white flowers sparkled on the sleeves. So light and insubstantial was the material that a gnat sneezing in the jungles of Ecuador set the hems dancing. It hung in the air, full of some sort of nothing that accentuated its breathtakingly graceful lines. Jane thought.

'All right,' she said. 'Let me see number three just one more time.'

'Sign here.'

Philly Nine took the clipboard, squiggled with the pen, and handed them back.

Sulphur, he thought. Nice, inanimate, noiseless sulphur. Ninety-nine-point-eight-nine per cent pure. Easiest thing in the world, a plague of sulphur.

'Just stack it neatly over there,' he said. 'Thanks a lot.'

The delivery man nodded, and started shouting directions to his colleagues. The long queue of lorries started to move.

''Scuse my asking,' went on the delivery man, 'but that's a lot of sulphur you got there.'

Philly Nine looked up from the bill of lading. 'Sorry?' he said.

'That's an awful lot of sulphur you got there, mate,' the delivery man went on. 'You want to watch yourself.'

Philly Nine favoured him with an icy grin. 'I know what I'm doing,' he said. 'Believe me.'

'OK,' replied the delivery man, as the genie stalked away and broke open a crate. 'So long as you realise that this stuff's highly . . .'

Philly Nine wasn't listening. To distribute sulphur in plague form: first, grind it up into a fine powder. Use this to salt rain-clouds all over the Earth's atmosphere. The sulphur will dissolve in the rain-water, forming (with the help of a little elementary chemistry) H_2SO_4, otherwise known as sulphuric acid. He chuckled, took a long drag on the butt of his cigar and threw it aside.

There was a flash –

'. . . inflammable.'

CHAPTER SEVEN

Kiss lay on his back, stared at the ceiling, and screamed. And woke up.

Genies rarely have nightmares, for the same reason that elephants don't usually worry about being trampled underfoot. With the possible exception of bottles, there's nothing in the cosmos large enough or malicious enough to frighten them, or stupid enough to try.

There are, however, exceptions. Kiss reached out for something to wipe his forehead with, and breathed in deeply.

He'd dreamed that he could no longer fly; that all his strength and power had deserted him and that one day, not too far in the future, he was going to die. As if that wasn't bad enough, he was going to have to spend what little time he had doing something futile, degrading and incredibly boring – the term his dream had used was a *full-time job* – just to earn a little money, money well within the dreams of avarice, simply to keep himself alive. And on top of that, what little time he had left over wasn't going to be spent in the back bar of Saheed's, playing pool, because his wife got upset if he kept going out in the evenings.

Weird dream. Talk about morbid . . .

His eyes shot wide open, and then closed again.

There must be some way out of this.

There were times, even now, when Vince felt just a little bit wistful about splitting up with Jane. Sure, she was difficult, querulous and, not to put too fine a point on it, on the chubby side of plump. And she had moods. And she didn't like Indian food or the right music. And her voice, when you got to know it well, had that tiny edge to it that eventually had roughly the same effect as a dentist's drill on an unanaesthetised tooth; on the other hand . . .

Lucky escape, Vince congratulated himself. Lucky escape.

Not, he realised as he switched out his bedside light and set his mind adrift for the night, like Sharon. True, Sharon had just enough brain to make up a smear on a microscope slide, but there were compensations. Sharon was what one might have expected to result if Pygmalion had been a photographer working on Pirelli calendars rather than a sculptor. He grinned at the darkness, and slipped away into sleep.

And dreamed a very peculiar dream.

He dreamed that he was asleep; and over his bed stood a huge, monstrous shape, towering above him like Nelson's Column, all gleaming muscles, fiery red eyes and big canine teeth. And it seemed as if the vision spoke to him, saying . . .

Listen, sunshine. Jane loves you and you love her. If you know what's good for you, that is. Get my drift?

And in his dream he had cried out and tried to wriggle away; but the monstrous vision had grabbed him round the throat with a huge, clawed hand, and had said –

Now you may be thinking, all that's over, I don't want to risk another broken heart. Well, there's other bits that can get broken too, take my word for it, not to mention tied in knots and yanked out by the roots. So you can either listen to the promptings of your secret heart, or you can spend the rest of your life drinking all your meals through a straw. Think on.

And then he'd woken up.

'AAAAAA!' he'd started to say; but before he could develop this line of argument the dream had stuffed a pair of socks into his mouth, lifted him up by the lapels of his pyjama jacket and held him about an inch from the tip of its huge, flaring nose.

'Not,' the dream went on, 'that I'm trying to influence you in any way. Heaven forbid. Just ask yourself one question. Is this Sharon the sort of girl who'd stick by you, come what may? Would she always be there to plump up the pillows, change the bedpans, maybe wheel you down the street as far as the library once a week? You reckon she is? Well, very soon you may well be ideally placed to find out. Sleep tight, punk.'

Then he fell, landing in an awkward heap on the mattress, and the dream turned out just to have been a dream after all. After three-quarters of an hour, he'd stopped shaking enough to switch out the light and . . .

In case I forgot to mention it before, looks aren't everything. And even if they were, it'd be a bit academic anyway if you couldn't see, on account of both your eyes having been pulled out and rammed up your ears. Hypothetically speaking, of course.

With a fantastic effort, Vince managed to ungum his mouth. 'Hey,' he said.

In case you've lost it, I'll just write Jane's phone number on your chest with this red-hot – oh, you can remember it? That's fine, then. Just remember, all the world loves a lover.

Vince gurgled and closed his eyes; then opened them again. Made no difference.

Last point, before I go. If I were you, I'd lay off the cheese last thing at night. Gives you bad dreams. Cheerio.

There was an old fisherman and he had three sons. They were called Malik, Ibrahim and Asaf.

Malik was very brave. Often when the wind was blowing in from the Gulf and the waves were so high that they seemed to splash against the clouds, Malik would take the boat and come back with his nets bursting with big, fat fish. Eventually Malik passed all his exams and became a chartered surveyor.

Ibrahim was very wise. Many a time, when the fish refused to leave the bottom and everybody else's nets were empty, Ibrahim would bring his boat to shore and his nets would be so heavy with fish that it took five men to lift them out. In due course, Ibrahim won a scholarship and qualified as an accountant.

But Asaf was always lazy and good-for-nothing, and while his father and brothers were out with the nets he would stay at home lying on his bed and dreaming of far-off lands and beautiful princesses. As a result, when his two brothers had both left home and his father came up lucky in a spot-the-infidel competition in the *New Islamic Herald* and retired, Asaf was left with nothing but a leaky old boat, a lot of split old nets and the prospect of a lifetime in the wholesale fish trade. Which served him, of course, bloody well right.

On one particular day, Asaf had been out since first light, and when evening came he still hadn't caught a single fish. Sadly he looked out over the Gulf, towards the burnt-out oil rigs that stood out from the leeward shore, and sighed. As he did so, a little voice inside him seemed to say, 'Throw out your net just once more, Asaf, and see what Providence may bring you!'

And why not? Asaf asked himself, and he flung the net out as far as he could throw it, and started to draw it in. As it came, he could feel how light it was; no fish again this time, he reflected sadly, isn't that just my bloody luck?

He was just about to stow the net away and head for home when he saw, hidden in the corner of the net, a tiny jewelled fish no bigger than a roulette chip. He picked it up in his cupped hands and was on the point of throwing it back when something caught this attention. He checked himself, and looked down at the little tiny body squirming in his hands.

'Just a cotton-picking minute,' he said.

The fish kicked frantically, opening and shutting its round little mouth. Asaf peered down at it and frowned. Then, quick as a flash, he grabbed his thermos flask with his other hand, shook out the dregs of tea, filled it with sea-water and dropped the fish into it.

'Hello,' he said.

The fish released a stream of bubbles, flicked its tail and darted down into the bottom of the flask. Asaf considered for a moment, then covered the neck of the flask with the flat of his hand and shook it up and down for a few seconds.

'You're not a fish, are you?' he said.

The fish flopped round through 180 degrees and burped drunkenly. 'Fair crack of the whip, sport,' it gurgled. 'What d'you take me for, a flamin' King Charles spaniel?' It froze, mouth open in a perfect O. 'Ah, shit,' it added.

'Quite.'

'Let the cat out of the old tucker-bag there, I reckon,' the fish went on, hiding its face behind a fin. 'All right, fair dos, I'm not a fish.'

'Sure?'

'Fair dinkum,' the fish replied. 'Since you ask, I'm the Dragon King of the South-East, and if you've quite finished . . .'

Asaf stroked his chin. 'A Dragon King,' he mused. 'I read about your lot once. You grant wishes.'

The fish thrashed its fins irritably. 'Look, mate,' it spluttered 'get real, will you? If I could grant flamin' wishes, my first wish'd be *I wish I wasn't stuck in this bastard jar.* My second wish –'

'Other people's wishes, I mean,' Asaf corrected. 'The poor fisherman catches you, he takes pity on the poor little fish trapped in his net and throws it back, and next thing he knows he's knee-deep in junk mail from the financial services boys. It's a standard wish-fulfilment motif in Near Eastern oral tradition,' he added. 'Usually three.'

'Three what?'

'Wishes,' Asaf replied, 'for fulfilment. Now we'll start off with a nicely balanced eight-figure portfolio made up of say fifty per cent gilt-edged government stocks, twenty-five per cent offshore convertible . . .'

The fish squirmed. 'Sorry,' it said.

'I beg your pardon?'

'No can do.' Fish can't sweat, but the Dragon King was, by definition, not a fish. 'Look, mate, if it was up to me it'd be no worries, straight up, Bob's your uncle. But . . .'

'*But?*'

'Yeah,' replied the fish. 'Dragon King of the South-East, remember? With responsibility for the Indian Ocean, southern sector.'

'You mean,' said the fisherman, 'Australia?'

The fish nodded. That is to say, it moved up and down in the water, using its small rear fins as stabilisers. 'And New Zealand,' it added, 'not forgetting Tasmania. But excluding the Philippines. And where I come from, blokes don't wish for the sort of thing you do.'

'They don't?'

The fish shook its head; the same manoeuvre, but in reverse. 'One, all the beer you can drink. Two, sitting in front of the TV watching the footie with a big bag of salt and vinegar crisps. Three, more beer. Interested?'

'Not particularly.' Asaf frowned. 'In case you didn't know, this is a Moslem country.'

'Is it? Jeez, mate, get me outa here quick. Talk about a fish out of water . . .'

'Quite.' Asaf lifted the flask and began to tilt it sideways towards the deck of the boat. 'Are you sure that's all you can do?' he said encouragingly. 'I'll bet you anything you like that if you really set your mind to it –'

'Watch what you're flamin' well doing with that . . .'

Asaf nodded, and restored the flask to the vertical. 'What you need,' he said, 'is more self-confidence. And I intend to give it to you. Inexhaustible wealth, now.' He started to count to ten.

'Just a minute.' The fish was cowering in the bottom of the flask, frantically feathering its tail-fin for maximum reverse thrust. 'Um, will you take a cheque?'

'No.'

'Plastic?'

'No.'

'Then,' said the fish, 'it looks like we got a problem here.'

'We have?' The flask inclined.

'Yes.'

Asaf shrugged. 'Fair enough, then. What can you offer?'

The fish oscillated for a moment. 'How about,' it suggested, 'a really deep bronze tan? You know, the outdoors look?'

'Don't be stupid, I'm a fisherman.'

'Right, good point. I guess that also rules out a magic, self-righting surfboard.'

'Correct.'

'All right, all right.' The fish twisted itself at right angles and gnawed its fins. 'What about stone-cold guaranteed success with the sheilas? Now I can't say fairer than that.'

'Yes, you can. To take just one example, inexhaustible wealth.'

The fish wriggled. 'Stone-cold guaranteed success with *rich* sheilas?'

Asaf nodded. 'I think we're getting warmer,' he said.

'Rich, good-looking sheilas?'

'Marginally warmer. Still some way to go, though.'

'Rich, good-looking sheilas who don't talk all the flamin' time?'

'Better,' Asaf conceded, 'but I still think you're missing the point somewhat. I think if you zeroed in on the rich part, rather than the sheilas aspect . . .'

'I got you, yes.' The fish turned over and floated on its back for a second or two. 'What about,' it suggested, 'rich old boilers who'll pop off and leave you all their money?'

Asaf shook his head. 'Too much like hard work,' he said. 'And besides, you're displaying a very cynical attitude towards human relationships, which I find rather distasteful. Let's stick to rich, shall we, and leave the sheilas element to look after itself.'

'Could be a problem with that,' the fish mumbled. 'The sheilas are, like, compulsory. Chicks with everything.'

'How depressingly chauvinistic.'

'Yeah, well.' The fish waggled its tail-fin. 'Sort of goes with the territory, mate. You don't have to treat 'em like dirt if you don't want to,' it added hopefully. 'I mean, if you want to, you can buy 'em flowers.'

Asaf sighed. 'Gosh,' he said, 'how heavy this flask is. If I have to stand here negotiating for very much longer, my arm might get all weak and . . .'

'All *right*, you flamin' mortal bastard!' the fish screeched. 'Just watch what you're doing with that thing.'

'Well?'

'I'm thinking.' The fish swam in slow circles, occasionally nibbling at the sides of the flask. 'OK,' it said. 'But this is the best I can do.'

'I'm listening.'

'Just the one sheila,' said the fish persuasively. 'And she's stinking rich –'

'Beyond the dreams of avarice?'

'Too right, mate, too right. Richest chick this side of the black stump. And all you've got to do is rescue her, right?'

Asaf scowled. 'You haven't been listening,' he said. 'All I'm interested in is the money. Climbing up rope ladders and sword-fights with guards simply aren't my style. I get vertigo.'

'No worries,' the fish reassured him. 'I'll handle all that side of things, just you see.'

'Sure,' Asaf growled. 'In case you hadn't noticed, you're a two-inch-long fish. Don't you think that'd prove rather a handicap when it comes to rescuing wealthy females?'

'Huh!' The fish sneered. 'Now who's the bigot?'

'But . . .'

'Just 'cos I'm small and I've got fins . . .'

'Be reasonable,' Asaf said. 'You can't escape your way

out of a thermos flask. How are you going to cope with heavily guarded castles?'

'I'll have no worries swimming the moat,' the fish replied. 'Anyway, I'm only a fish right *now*. As soon as I can get home and out of this flamin' fish outfit, I can go back to being a dragon. Dragons can rescue anybody, right?'

'I suppose so.' Asaf rubbed his chin. On the one hand, the Dragon King hardly inspired confidence. On the other hand . . . He looked down at the boat, the empty nets, the threadbare sail. 'Very well, then. So long as it's guaranteed success.'

'Trust me.'

'I was afraid you'd say that.'

'Look . . .'

'All right,' Asaf said. 'So what do I do now?'

The fish darted up the meniscus of the flask. 'Just chuck me back in,' he said, 'and then row to the shore. I'll be there waiting.'

'Straight up?'

'On me honour as an Australian,' the fish replied solemnly. 'No bludging, honest.'

'Oh, all right then.' Asaf jerked the flask sharply sideways, emptying its contents into the sea. There was a soft splash.

'Waste of bloody time,' he muttered to himself. Then he rowed to the shore.

He was just pulling his boat up on to the beach when there was a sharp WHOOSH! immediately behind his back, and sand everywhere. He turned slowly around and saw a very old, very battered Volkswagen dormobile, with lots of stickers inside the windscreen. He frowned; and suddenly realised that instead of his comfortable old fishing

smock, he was wearing strange new clothes: a denim jacket
with the sleeves cut off, shorts, trainers and no socks.
There was also some sort of sticky white stuff all over his
nose and lips.

Hey!' he said angrily.

WHAM!

Hovering over his head was a huge, green scaly lizard.

'G'day,' it said. 'Jeez, mate, you don't know how good it
feels to get me proper duds back on again after being
squashed inside that poxy little fish skin. Ready to go?'

Asaf stepped back. He had to retreat quite some way
before he could see the whole of the dragon. He began to
wish he hadn't started this.

'Hey,' he said, 'what's going on? Who are you, anyway,
the local area franchisee for the Klingon Empire?'

The dragon chuckled. 'I'm a dragon, mate,' he replied.
'What did you expect, a little skinny bloke with glasses?
Now, are you ready for off?'

'Off where?'

'Off to see this incredibly rich sheila,' the dragon replied.
'Now I'd better warn you, she's not exactly a real hot
looker, but so what? Like we say in Oz, you don't care
what's on the mantelpiece when you're poking the fire.'

'All right,' Asaf muttered. 'But what's with the broken-
down old van? Why the stupid clothes?'

The dragon looked offended. 'We're going on our trav-
els, right?'

'I suppose so, yes.'

The dragon's lips parted in a huge smile. 'Well,' he said,
'if we're going walkabout, we might as well do it properly.'

Asaf was on the point of objecting vehemently when it
occurred to him that the Dragon King was perfectly right.
Wherever you go, he remembered his brothers telling him,

whichever inhospitable corner of the globe you wind up in, you can always be sure of finding three tall, bronzed Aussies in beach clothes and a beat-up old camper. And you can bet your life that when the chips are down, they're not the ones whose fan-belt breaks three hundred miles from the nearest garage.

The Dragon King waved a giant forepaw and vanished. A moment or so later, when he'd recovered, Asaf noticed that the dormobile now had a chrome dragon mascot on the bonnet where the VW insignia ought to have been.

'This is silly,' he told himself. Then he climbed into the van and turned the key.

Love, according to all the best poets, works wonders. Under the influence of love, men and women scale impossible mountains, brave tempestuous seas, face down dangers that any rational human being would run a mile from; love does for the heart and the soul what a five-year course of anabolic steroids does for the muscles. Mankind will do virtually anything for love.

Blind terror, however, knocks love into a cocked hat.

It wasn't love, for example, that brought Vince, white as a sheet and jumping like a kitten at loud noises, round to Jane's front door at nine o'clock sharp, clutching a huge bunch of flowers and wearing the tie she'd given him at the office Christmas party (hastily unwound from a dripping tap and ironed).

The door opened.

'Hello, Vince,' Jane said. 'What lovely flowers! Goodbye, Vince.'

The door started to close. Love at this point would have given it up as a bad job and gone home.

'Jane,' Vince said. 'Hi there. It's been a long time.'

'Not nearly long enough. Get lost.'

Through the quarter-open door, Vince could see strange things: miles of plush carpet, acres of richly patterned wallpaper, stacks and rows of colour-supplement furniture. Somewhere in his subconscious, the change in Jane's environment registered. He smiled, trying as he did so to keep his teeth from chattering.

'I think we ought to talk,' he said.

'Do you? Why?'

'Um.' Vince dredged his mind for something to say and, in the silt at the bottom of his memory, came across a phrase. It had lodged there, muddy and forgotten, ever since he'd idled away a day's flu watching one of the afternoon soaps.

'We've got to sit down and talk this thing through,' he said solemnly. 'Otherwise we might regret it for the rest of our lives.'

Jane considered. 'You might,' she said. 'Depends on how thick-skinned you are. If being called a heartless, two-timing little scumbag is likely to scar you for life, I'd suggest you leave now. Mind you,' she added, 'I expect you're well used to it by now. Must happen to you all the time.'

'Does that mean I can come in?'

Jane sighed. 'I suppose so. It'd make shouting at you easier.'

Weak-kneed, Vince crept into the living-room . . .

AAAAGH!

There, sitting on the sofa, apparently putting a plug on an electric hair-dryer, was the Monster. For a fraction of a second it raised its eyes and looked straight at him; during which time he did his level best to swallow his own Adam's apple.

'Vince,' Jane said in a bored voice, 'this is Kiss. Kiss, this is Vince. I didn't ask him to come here,' she added.

The Monster was on his feet. 'That's all right,' he said, 'I was just going. I expect,' he added, 'you two have a lot to talk about.'

'No, we don't,' Jane said. 'It doesn't take long to call somebody a bastard.'

'See you later,' said Kiss, and walked out through the wall.

Vince sat down heavily in an armchair. 'Your friend –' he said.

'Fiancé,' Jane interrupted.

'Ah.'

'Bastard.'

'Yes.'

'What do you mean, yes?'

Vince tried to think what he did mean, but his brain wasn't working too well. 'Um,' he said.

What you mean is, yes, I admit I behaved like a bastard, but I promise I'll make it up to you. Got that?

It isn't actually possible to jump out of one's skin, but Vince did his best. The voice seemed to be coming from two inches inside his left ear.

'Do you mind not squirming about?' Jane asked wearily. 'You'll damage the furniture.'

'Sorry.'

I'll say it one more time. I admit I behaved like a bastard. Go on, say it.

'I admit,' Vince said, staring straight ahead, 'I behaved like a bastard . . .'

'Good.'

But I promise that I'll make it up to you. Come on, say it. And try and put some feeling into it, for God's sake.

'But I promise,' Vince gasped, 'that I'll make it up to you. Somehow,' he added.

Don't ad lib.

'Sorry.'

'What?'

Sorry for all the pain my heartless and misguided behaviour must have caused you. Now, however . . .

'Hang on,' Vince said. 'Sorry for all the pain my heartless and misguided behaviour . . .'

'Oh, for crying out loud!' Jane exploded. 'Look, buster, whoever writes your scripts for you, tell him not to pack in the day job.'

The part of Vince's subconscious currently under enemy occupation smirked.

Stupid cow. No! Don't say that. Listen, Jane, I can explain everything. Go on, you fool, cat got your tongue?

'Listen, Jane, I can explain everything.'

'So can I. You're a bastard. Explanation complete.'

Any suggestions?

Shut up. Jane, when two people feel the way about each other that we do, it's never too late to start again.

'Jane,' Vince enunciated, 'when two people feel the way about each other that we do, it's never too late to start again.'

'Would you like,' Jane asked, 'a cup of tea?'

A whoop of triumph rocked Vince's inner brain, playing havoc with his centre of balance. Yo, buddy, we're in! Go for it!

'Yes, please,' Vince said.

'Won't be a tick.'

Jane retreated into the kitchen. As soon as the door had closed, Vince felt a tremendous rushing in his ears, and –
WHOOSH!

'Hi,' he mumbled. 'How'm I doing?'

The genie gave him a cold, hard look. 'If I couldn't read your mind,' he growled, 'I'd swear you were deliberately trying to bugger this up. Fortunately for you, I can see you're shit-scared and you wouldn't dare. So just do exactly what I say and everything'll be just fine.'

'Sure,' Vince muttered. 'Er, excuse me saying this, but what exactly do you want me to *do* to her?'

The genie raised an eyebrow. 'Marry her, of course. What do you think?'

'Ah.' Vince cowered slightly. 'In that case,' he said, 'I'd rather have the violent and painful death, if it's all the same to you.'

For a moment, there was sympathy in the genie's eyes. 'Look, chum,' he said, 'it's you or me, right? And I'm bigger than you, which means it's you. Sorry, but that's the way it goes. At the moment,' he went on, deleting the sympathy and replacing it with a glare of heart-stopping ferocity, 'we're doing this the easy way.'

'But she's so damn *sloppy*.'

Kiss winced. 'Do you mean sloppy as in over-sentimental, or sloppy as in extremely untidy?'

'Both.'

'Agreed. Believe me,' he added, 'I'm really grateful to you for doing this. It's not just the fact that I can't stand the woman, I assure you. It's just that unless I can get her to let me off the hook, I'm going to have to become a mortal in fourteen days' time. Hence,' he added meaningfully, 'the sense of urgency. I'll make it up to you one day, genie's honour. Unlimited wealth, all that sort of thing. In the meantime, however . . .'

The door started to open. With a stifled *Oh shit!* the genie vanished, and Vince once again became aware of a dull presence against his inner ear, as if he'd just been under water.

'Tea,' said Jane.

'Thanks.'

'Drink it while it's hot.'

You heard the lady.

Vince smiled broadly and drank. A fraction of a second later most of the tea had turned into a fine mist, sprayed all over the room.

'Oh dear,' said Jane. 'Something go down the wrong way?'

By way of response Vince choked, gasped and made a peculiar gurgling noise in the back of his throat. He was still smiling, but only because some paranormal force had grabbed control of his jaw muscles and frozen them.

'Perhaps,' Jane continued sweetly, 'it's because I put five teaspoonfuls of salt in it instead of sugar. When you've finished retching, you can leave.'

Strewth, whispered the voice in the back of Vince's brain with horrified admiration, *she really is a tough cookie, your girlfriend.*

Vince stood up slowly, wiped tea off his face, closed his mouth tightly and pinched his nose hard between thumb and forefinger. Then he blew.

PLOP!

Kiss hit the floor like a sack of potatoes, rolled and came to rest against the opposite wall. He was dripping wet and shaking.

'Well,' Vince said, scrambling for the door, 'been nice seeing you again, Jane. All the best to you and your . . . All the best. Bye.'

The door closed behind him.

CHAPTER EIGHT

Philly Nine sighed. He was having a hard time.

The brimstone had been a complete washout. Literally – it had started raining just as he was lugging the crates of the stuff off the lorry, and industrial spec brimstone is water-soluble.

The frogs had been an absolute nightmare. They'd just sat there. No sooner had he shooed one consignment of, say, five thousand out of the delivery pond than the previous batch had hopped back in and sat down, resolutely croaking and wobbling their chins at him. Magically generated flash floods dispersed them for a while, but their homing instinct was such that at least ninety-five per cent of them were back home within the hour. They way they got through pondweed was nobody's business.

'Sign here,' the Frenchman said. 'And here. And here. Thanks, monsieur. It's a pleasure doing business with you.'

Philly nodded sombrely, and waved as the convoy of trucks rattled away into the distance. If you stretched the definition to breaking point, a worldwide chain of

Provençal Fried Frogs' Legs bars might be taken to con-
stitute a plague, but it probably wasn't going to bring the
world to its knees; not, at least, in the short term.

What, he asked himself wretchedly, next? His own fault,
he reflected, for letting himself be carried away by the
gothic splendour of the language. If he'd been content to
settle for a nice straightforward plague of, say, plague, the
entire human race would by now be coming out in suppu-
rating boils, and he'd be home and dry. As it was . . . He
took out the crumpled envelope on which he'd jotted down
his notes.

X   Locusts
X   Sulphur
X   Brimstone
X   Frogs
     Hail
     Giant ants
     Burning pitch

Never usually a quitter, Philly sighed, folded the envelope
and put it away. Was there, he asked himself, really any
point in going on?

And then he remembered.

The brochure. The smiling face. The slogan, 'We're here
to help you.'

'Of course!' he said aloud, and his face broke into a
silly grin. Virtually the only useful thing they teach you at
Genie School: don't bother learning the Knowledge
itself, so long as you know where to go to look it up. He
took out his diary and thumbed through the business
cards wedged in the inside flap until he found the right
one.

THE GENIE ADVISORY SERVICE
Central office: the Djinn Palace, Street of the Lamp-Makers,
Samarkand 9
Have you got a problem? Bring it to us!
Your wish is our command!

GAS headquarters had only recently relocated to an
imposing suite of purpose-blown bottles in a crate round
the back of Number 56, Street of the Lamp-Makers, and
there were the inevitable settling-in problems associated
with the migration of any large enterprise. For example,
the phones weren't working yet, only twenty per cent of the
staff knew where the toilets were, and all the files had been
sent to a hurricane lamp in the Orkneys by mistake, along
with most of the typewriters and the coffee machine. Apart
from that, it was business as usual.

After five minutes in the waiting room reading a back
number of the *National Demonological*, Philly was greeted
by a small, round genie who extended a tiny, moist paw
and introduced himself as 'GAS 364, your Personal
Business Adviser'. GAS 364 chivvied him into a small cell
with two deep armchairs, a vase of flowers and a large
framed print of Picasso's *Guernica*, offered him coffee, and
asked what the problem was.

Philly explained.

'Right,' said GAS 364, 'got you. The old, old story.'

'It is?'

GAS 364 nodded. 'Bitten off more than we can chew,'
he said, smiling. 'Trying to swoop before we can glide. It's
basically a time management/resources allocation problem.'

'Ah. Is that serious?'

'Depends.' GAS 364 waggled his hands. 'There's a lot of

variables. How your operation is structured, for example, lateral as against vertical command groups, properly demarcated zones of responsibility, incentive-related leadership packages, that sort of thing.'

'Gosh,' Philly said. 'Actually, there's only me.'

GAS 364 rubbed his various chins. 'Sole practitioner, huh?' he said. 'Now that means a whole different subgroup of potential dysfunction hotspots. The left hand not knowing whether the right hand's been left holding the baby. And, of course, carrying the can.' He shook his head. 'You know,' he said, 'if only you'd come to see us earlier, a lot of this could well have been avoided. But there we are.'

'Are we?'

GAS 364 spread his hands in an eloquent gesture. 'Are we indeed?' he said. 'Like we always say, you can't destroy the world without breaking eggs.'

Philly's brow clouded for a moment. 'Eggs,' he said. 'You're thinking of the giant ants?'

'Let's stay off the specifics for the time being,' GAS 364 replied, glancing at his watch, 'and zoom in on the generals. Which means, first things first, software.'

'Software?'

'Mortals,' GAS 364 translated. 'As opposed to hardware, meaning us. It's basically a question of approach, you see. You sole practitioners, you simply have no idea of how to delegate.'

'Delegate? Delegate the annihilation of the human race?'

GAS 364 nodded. 'The only way,' he said. 'Think about it. Sure, you're a Force Twelve, rippling muscles, big turban, the works. But at the end of the day, when pitch comes to shove, there's just you. Just you,' the genie repeated, 'to open the mail, answer the telephones *and* wipe out all sentient lifeforms on the Planet Earth. Result: you're overstretched.

Which means,' he went on, leaning back and folding his hands behind his head, 'when the van arrives with the crates of frogs, you can't cope. As we've seen.'

Philly nodded. 'So?'

'So,' GAS 364 replied, 'let somebody else do the donkey work for you. Get the software to do the actual extermination stuff, while you maintain a general supervisory and administrative role, which is what you're supremely qualified for. It's as simple as that.'

Philly, who had just begun to feel he was dimly glimpsing what the small genie was driving at, scowled. 'Please explain,' he said.

GAS 364 beamed at him. 'Easy,' he said. 'Start a war.'

'Hello,' Jane said.

Kiss got up slowly and started wringing out his wet clothes. 'Hello,' he replied.

'He's gone.'

'Has he?'

'Yes. You're all wet.'

'Yes.'

'Just as well,' Jane said, 'that you can't catch colds.'

'Isn't it.'

They stood for a while, looking at each other. Between them, so nearly solid that it was almost visible, the question *What were you doing in Vince's ear?* hovered in the air.

Somebody once defined Love as never having to explain what you were doing in somebody's ear. It's not a particularly accurate definition.

'Fancy a picnic?' asked Jane.

'Don't mind.'

'Or we could stay in and I'll cook something.'

Kiss smiled feebly. 'Let's have a picnic,' he said.

For want of anywhere better to go, they went to Martinique. It wasn't the most joyous picnic in history –

(For the record, the most joyous picnic in history was the time seven Force Fives decided to have a barbecue in the back garden of a house in Pudding Lane, London, in the year 1666. The genies had a great time and London got St Pauls, various Wren churches and a nursery rhyme or two by way of belated compensation.)

– and after they'd eaten the sandwiches and drunk the champagne they sat in silence for a full seven minutes, looking at the dark blue sea.

'Jane,' Kiss said eventually.

'Yes?'

How to put it, exactly? How to explain that the ferociously passionate feelings they both harboured were nothing but a device contrived by a supernatural fiend as part of his plan to annihilate humanity? How to explain all that, *tactfully*?

'Nothing.'

Jane poured the last dribble of the champagne into her glass. It was lukewarm and as flat as a bowling green. 'I thought that was very romantic,' she said.

Kiss suppressed a shudder. 'What was?'

'You hanging around like that when Vince was there. I think you were jealous.'

Well of course, you would. 'Ah.'

'Were you?'

'Sorry? Oh, yes. Yes, I was.'

'You needn't be.'

'That's good to know.'

Jane picked at the strap of her sandal. 'The moment I saw him,' she went on, 'I knew it was all over between us. In fact, I can't imagine what I ever saw in him, really.'

'Can't you?'

'No.'

Kiss breathed in. For some reason, he found it harder than usual. 'I quite took to him, actually,' he said. 'Not a bad bloke, when you get to know him. I expect.'

'Oh Kiss, you *are* sweet.'

That particular phrase, *Oh Kiss, you are sweet*, stayed with him the rest of the day and deep into the night, with the result that he couldn't sleep. By two-thirty in the morning, it had got to him so much that he put on his coat and went to Saheed's.

In the back bar he met two old friends, Nordic Industrial Components IV and Consolidated Tin IX. They were sitting in a corner sharing a big jug of pasteurised and playing djinn rummy.

'Hi,' he said, joining them. 'Would you guys say I was sweet?'

Nick and Con stared at him. 'Sweet?'

'You heard me.'

Nick shook his head. 'To be frank with you, Kiss, no.'

'I'm very relieved to hear it. Same again?'

Three or four jugs and a game of racing genie later, Nick asked why he had wanted to know.

'Oh, no reason. Somebody accused me of sweetness earlier on today, and it's been preying on my mind.'

'Ah.' Nick dealt the cards. 'Well, my old mate, you need have no worries on that score. Who's to open?'

'Me,' said Con. 'Three earthquakes.'

'See your three earthquakes,' Nick replied, 'and raise you one famine.'

'Twist,' said Kiss. 'I think it's a horrible thing to say about anybody.'

'Agreed,' said Con. 'Who said it, and what had you in mind by way of reprisals?'

'My fiancée,' Kiss said. 'Your go, Nick.'

'Your *fiancée?*'

'That's right.'

'See your famine and raise you a pestilence. Since when?'

'Recently,' Kiss answered. 'Can we change the subject, guys? I'm trying to enjoy myself.'

'Your pestilence,' said Con, 'and raise you one. This is pretty heavy stuff, Kiss. She must be some doll if you're thinking of packing in the genieing on her account.'

'Repique,' Kiss said (he was banker), 'and doubled in Clubs. My clutch, I think.'

'Buggery.'

'That's forty-six above the line to me,' Kiss went on, jotting down figures on a milk-mat, 'and one for his spikes, makes seventy-seven to me and three to play. My deal.'

'I've had enough of this game,' said Con. 'Let's play Miserable Families instead.'

So they played Miserable Families; and two hands and a jug of pasteurised later, Kiss was ninety-six ahead and held mortgages on seventy-five per cent of Antarctica, which was where Con lived.

'No thanks,' Con said, when Kiss suggested another hand. 'I get the impression your luck's in tonight.'

'Tell me about it,' replied Kiss gloomily.

'This girlfriend of yours.'

'Fiancée.'

'Quite.' Con paused. Generally speaking, genies don't kick a fellow when he's down, just in case he grabs hold of their foot. There are, however, exceptions. 'Lucky in cards, unlucky in love, they say.'

'They're absolutely right.'

Nick grinned. 'I take it,' he said, 'you're not overjoyed?'

'It's that bastard,' Kiss blurted out. No need to say who the bastard was. 'He hired Cupid to shoot me. It's not,' he added dangerously, 'funny.'

There was a difference of opinion on that score. When he had regained control of himself, Nick asked why.

'He's going to destroy the world . . .'

'Not *again*.'

'. . . and he wants me out of the way first. I call it diabolical,' Kiss concluded, draining his glass. 'He shouldn't be allowed to get away with it.'

'Oh, I dunno,' Con replied mildly. 'All's fair in –'

'Don't say it. Not the L word.'

'War,' Con continued. 'You've got to hand it to Philly, he has brains. And vision. And that indispensable streak of sheer bloody-minded viciousness that you need to get on in this business.'

Kiss frowned. 'Well, so have I,' he said. 'Trouble is, *she* won't let me use it.'

'Bossy cow!'

'Or at least,' Kiss amended lamely, 'she wouldn't like it. And as things are at the moment . . .'

Nick winked. 'Say no more,' he said. 'What you need, I think, is a little help from your friends.'

Kiss looked up. 'Really?'

'We might consider it,' Con replied. 'Get a mate out of a hole. Can't watch a good genie go down, and all that.'

Kiss's frown deepened. 'But what can you do?' he asked. 'Philly's a Twelve and you're both Fives. He'd have you for breakfast.'

Con cleared his throat. 'We weren't thinking of that,' he said. 'No, what we had in mind . . .' He looked at Nick, who nodded. 'What we were thinking of was more by way of getting your beloved off your back. Weren't we?'

'Could be fun,' Nick agreed. 'How long have you got?'

Kiss shuddered. 'Thirteen days,' he said, 'before the papers go through. Any ideas?'

Nick poured the last of the pasteurised into his glass and chuckled. 'I expect we'll think of something,' he said.

Battered Volkswagen camper van speeding across the desert.

The Dragon King was beginning to get on Asaf's nerves. After a long struggle, he had managed to jury-rig the primitive radio so that it could receive Radio Bazra's easy listening music channel; but he needn't have bothered, because he couldn't hear a thing over the Dragon King's Mobius-loop renditions of *The Wild Colonial Boy*. It would have been slightly more bearable if the King had known more than 40 per cent of the words. As if that wasn't enough, the King had taken his shoes and socks off, and his feet smelt.

''Twas in eighteen hundred and sixty-two,' the King informed him for the seventeenth time that day, 'that he started his wild career/Tum tumpty tumpty tumpty tum tee tumpty tumpty fear/He robbed the wealthy squatters and . . .'

'Do you mind?'

The King looked up. 'Yer what, mate?' he enquired.

'Do you mind,' Asaf said, 'not singing?'

The King looked hurt. 'Sorry, chum,' he said. 'Thought a good old sing-song'd help pass the time.'

'You did, did you?'

'No offence, mate.'

'Quite.'

The King turned his head and looked out of the window. 'I spy,' he said, 'with my little eye, something beginning with . . . S.'

'Sand.'

'Too right, sport, good on yer. Your go.'

'No, thank you.'

'Fair enough.' The King sighed and opened a can of beer, which hissed like a bad-tempered snake and sprayed suds all over the place. Asaf wiped his eye.

'That's another thing,' he growled. 'This car smells like a brewery.'

'Glad you like it.'

'As a matter of fact, I don't. Can't you wait till we stop?'

'Anything you say, boss.' He drained the can and chucked it out of the window. No point, Asaf reflected, in raising the subject of pollution of the environment and the recycling of scrap aluminium. Deaf ears.

'Not much further now, anyway,' the King said, 'till we reach the first Adventure.'

Asaf applied the brakes, bringing the van to a sudden halt. 'What do you mean,' he asked dangerously, 'adventure?'

The King looked at him. 'Gee, mate, this is a quest, right? You gotta have a few adventures in a quest. Don't you worry, though, she'll be right.'

'Who will?'

'It'll all go beaut,' the King translated. 'No worries on that score. Trust me.'

'I was afraid you'd say that.'

The next half-hour was relatively painless. True, the King hummed *Do You Ever Dream, My Sweetheart* in a Dalek-like drone under his breath, but with the radio and the groaning of the suspension over the rocky, potholed road, he was scarcely audible. It could have been worse, Asaf rationalised. It could have been *My Way*.

'Here we are,' the King said, pointing with his right forefinger into the middle of the trackless waste of their left. 'Anywhere here'll do.'

Asaf sighed and pulled over, leaving the engine running. 'Now what?' he said.

The King chuckled. 'You'll like this,' he said. 'Right up your alley, this is. Watch.'

A flicker of movement in the far distance caught Asaf's eye. The King handed him a pair of binoculars, through which he could see a girl on a donkey being hotly pursued by three men on camels. The girl had a good lead on her pursuers, but they were gaining fast.

'The low-down is,' said the King, 'the chick is the daughter of some Sultan or other, and the three blokes on the camels are wicked magicians. All clear so far?'

Asaf nodded.

'Well,' the King continued, 'she's running away from them because she's just stolen the Pearl of Solomon, which gives them sort of magic powers. You go to meet her, she gives you a magic bow and three arrows. You fire the first arrow at the first magician –'

'Excuse me . . .'

'And,' the King continued, 'he turns back into a beetle– that's what he really is, you see, a beetle – and you tread on him and that's that. You fire the second arrow –'

'Excuse me . . .'

'The second arrow at the second magician, and *he* turns back into a scorpion, which is his true shape, and you drop a rock on him. You shoot the third . . .'

'Excuse me,' Asaf shouted. The King looked up.

'Sorry, mate, am I going too fast? The first . . .'

'I won't do it.'

The King stared at him with a wild surmise. The

surmise couldn't have been wilder if he'd just said that Dennis Lillee was a slow bowler.

'I don't want anything to do with it,' the fisherman reiterated. 'You're asking me to aid and abet a theft, commit murder . . .'

Jeez, mate, they're *insects*.'

'Insectide, robbery with violence, obstruction of the highway and heaven knows what else, for no readily apparent reason –'

The King was almost in tears. 'For crying out loud,' he said, 'it's a flamin' *adventure*. What sort of a bloke are you?'

'Basically law-abiding,' Asaf replied coldly. 'Has it also occurred to you that I might miss? With only a very scanty knowledge of archery and just three arrows –'

'It's a magic bow, you dozy bastard!' the King yelled. 'You can't miss. Believe me.'

'It's still wrong,' Asaf replied. 'If there's a dispute between these people, they ought to take it to the proper authorities.'

The donkey was quite close now, and slowing to a gentle trot. The camels, however, were accelerating.

'*Look*,' shouted the King. 'Unless you rescue the chick, she won't be able to give you the three white stones, which –'

'What three white stones?'

'The three *magic* white stones which have strange and supernatural powers, you stupid drongo!' the King snapped. 'Of all the . . .'

Asaf sighed, and opened the door. 'Oh, all right,' he said. 'But I'm not shooting anybody, and that's final. You wait here and don't interfere.'

He climbed out of the camper. His legs were stiff with cramp after the long drive, and his left foot had gone to sleep. He hobbled over to where the donkey had come to an expectant halt.

'Allah be praised!' the girl exclaimed. She was radiantly beautiful, and around her neck hung a single white pearl which shone with a strange inner light. 'Quick, my prince, take this bow and –'

'Be quiet!' Asaf snapped. 'I'll deal with you in a minute.'

He trudged past her and stood between her and the camels, which slewed to a halt. The lead camel-rider drew a curved blue sword and brandished it ferociously.

'Out of the way, infidel,' he snarled, 'or I shall cut off your head!'

Asaf shook his head. 'Don't be silly,' he said briskly. 'And for your information, I'm not an infidel.'

The camel-rider reined in his steed and frowned. 'Yes, you are,' he said. 'By definition,' he added.

'Rubbish.'

The other two camel-riders drew their scimitars and waved them, but with rather less enthusiasm.

Asaf didn't move. 'Well?' he said.

'Well what?'

'Ask me a question about Islamic belief and culture. That'll show whether I'm an infidel or not.'

'It's just an expression,' the second camel-rider started to say, but his superior shushed him.

'All right, Mister Clever,' said the first camel-rider. 'What's the first verse of the fortieth chapter of the Koran? You don't know, do you? I thought you . . .'

Asaf cleared his throat. 'This book is revealed by Allah,' Asaf recited in a loud, clear voice, 'the mighty one, the all-knowing, who forgives sin and accepts repentance, the bountiful one, whose punishment is stern. Want me to go on?'

The camel-riders looked at each other.

'OK,' said the first camel-rider. 'So you're not an infidel. Now will you please shove off and let us get on with our work?'

Asaf stayed where he was. 'Bet you don't know the next bit,' he said.

The camel-rider glowered at him. ''Course I do,' he said.

'Go on, then. Prove it.'

'Huh.' The first camel-rider sniffed. 'There is no god but Him, all shall return to him, none but the unbelievers dispute the teachings of Allah –'

'Excuse me,' the second camel-rider interrupted.

The first camel-rider whirled round in his saddle. 'What?' he said.

'It's not teachings, it's revelations. The revelations of Allah.'

The first camel-rider scowled. 'It says teachings, son of a dog!' he growled. 'Do you dare –?'

'Actually,' muttered the third camel-rider, 'he's quite right, it is revelations. Here, have a look. At the bottom of the second page, three lines up.'

'What!' roared the first rider. 'You dare to contradict me, spawn of filth! I shall cut off –'

'Here, look for yourself, it's there in black and . . .'

'He's right, you know, Trev. It does say . . .'

There was the sharp, brittle sound of steel clashing on steel. Asaf sighed, shook his head sadly, and sauntered back to where the girl was waiting.

'Idiots,' he muttered softly. 'All right, give me the stones and sling your hook.'

'Allah be praised, oh my prince,' said the girl nervously, rather as if she'd been expecting a rather different cue. 'Thanks to you –'

'Yes,' Asaf said. 'We'll take all that as read, shall we? The stones, please.'

Behind him there was a roar of triumph. The third rider lay slumped on the sand, and the first rider was brandishing his sword again.

'If I were you,' Asaf said, 'I'd hand them over and get the hell out of here before those two sort out their differences. Keep straight on down this road about ten miles and you'll find a telephone box. Phone the police. OK?'

The girl nodded, confused, and handed him a white cloth bag which held something heavy. Before she could say anything else, Asaf turned on his heel, hobbled back to the van and slammed the door.

'I trust,' he said, putting the van into gear and driving off, 'that there's not going to be much more of this sort of thing, because a man can only take so much pratting around before his patience starts to wear thin. I'm telling you this,' he added, 'just so's you'll know. OK?'

'OK, mate. Actually . . .'

Asaf turned his head and gave the King a long, cold look. 'Don't tell me,' he said. 'There's more.'

'Fair crack of the whip, chum, it *is* a quest.'

Asaf glanced quickly in the mirror, slowed down and started to turn the van around.

'Hey,' the King protested, 'what are you . . .?'

'Going home,' Asaf replied. 'Look, I may just be a simple fisherman, but I have my self-respect. So let's just call it quits. You get out of my life and stay out, and everything will be fine.'

'But the sheila,' the King said. 'It's all fixed up!'

'Then unfix it.'

'I can't!'

Asaf stopped the van. 'What,' he asked quietly, 'does that mean?'

The King bit his lips. 'Like I said,' he replied mournfully. 'Everything's set up. You *wished*, remember?'

'Wealth without limit was what I wished for,' Asaf replied. 'There wasn't anything in the original specifications about running amok killing and stealing half-way across the blasted continent.'

'For pity's sake, mate, this is my job on the line here. I've made arrangements . . .'

Asaf leaned back in his seat and closed his eyes. 'All right,' he sighed. 'On three conditions.'

'Anything.'

'One, you don't sing.'

'No worries, mate, not another note.'

'Two,' said Asaf, 'we keep these stupid adventures to the basic minimum. No magic spells, no more beautiful maidens than absolutely necessary, and positively no gratuitous folklore. Agreed?'

'You got it.'

'Three.' He leaned forward and turned the key in the ignition. 'Keep your bloody shoes on.'

Two genies, rather the worse for six pints apiece of semi-skimmed with double-cream chasers, lurched out of Saheed's and hailed a taxi.

'Where to?'

'Isson this bitta paper,' mumbled Nick. 'Fastasyoulike.'

'You're the boss,' replied the taxi. It hovered for a moment, straightening out its corners, and lowered itself to ground level. The genies climbed aboard.

'Home, James,' Con declaimed, 'an' don't spare the Axminster.'

The carpet rose like a very flat Harrier, made itself stiff in every fibre of its being, and shimmered away into the night sky.

The cold air, rushing past their ears, served to cut the milk fug, and by the time they arrived at the destination scribbled on the milk-mat both genies were – not sober, exactly, but at least 90 per cent in charge of their principal motor functions. The ideal state, in other words, for attempting something very silly indeed.

'Right,' said Nick. 'You ready?'

'As I'll ever be,' Con replied. 'Here, I'm not so sure this is a very brilliant idea . . .'

'Shuttup.' Nick rubbed his eyes and said the shape-changing spell aloud. It worked. 'Your turn,' he said.

'I still think –'

'Get on with it.'

'All right.' Con mumbled the magic words; and he too changed shape. The carpet braked smoothly and began its descent.

'Here, Con,' Nick whispered. 'Remind me. Which one am I supposed to be?'

Con shrugged. 'I've forgotten,' he admitted. 'Let's have a look at you.'

'Well?'

Con rubbed his chin. 'I think,' he said after a while, 'you're the tall one. Wossisname.'

'I see. So you're . . .?'

'The other one.'

'Fine. I'm glad we've got that sorted out.'

The carpet came to rest. The two genies climbed off and paid the fare, and then looked round. Nobody about. Probably just as well. What they were doing was, of course, unethical and probably highly illegal by genie standards.

On the other hand, virtually everything genies do is.

'Here goes.'

'Break a leg.' Con extended a slightly unsteady arm and rang Jane's doorbell.

'What do you mean,' Nick asked, 'break a leg?'

'It's something mortals say,' Con replied as the porch light came on. 'Something to do with good luck.'

'It's not good luck breaking a leg,' Nick said doubtfully. 'Not if you're a mortal, that is. Takes weeks to mend, a mortal leg does.'

'It's just an expression.'

'Bloody silly one, if you ask me.'

The door opened and Jane stood in the doorway. She was wearing a pink winceyette dressing-gown and fluffy slippers.

'Ah,' said Nick, as smoothly as he could (but another half of pasteurised would, he realised, have been a wise precaution), 'good evening, um, miss. My name's Robert Redford and this is my friend Tom Cruise. Our car's broken down and we were wondering if we could borrow your phone.'

Jane frowned. 'It's two o'clock in the morning,' she said.

If Nick was fazed for a moment, he didn't show it. 'Exactly what I was saying to Mr Cruise,' he replied. 'Face it, Tom, I told him, chances of there being a garage open at this time of night are practically nil, so we'd better phone the breakdown service. And then, would you believe it, neither of us had any change. So we thought . . .'

In the background, the carpet lifted smoothly into the air, waggled its seams and glided away. 'You'd better come in,' Jane said.

'Thanks.'

Jane shut the door. 'You're genies, aren't you?' she said.

'Ah.'

'It's the carpet,' Jane said over her shoulder, leading the way through into the living-room. 'It's a dead giveaway, that. Also,' she added wearily, 'you obviously haven't seen Mr Redford for quite some time. Not that he hasn't worn quite well, but . . .'

Con took a deep breath. 'Hey,' he said, 'is this guy really a genie? Gosh, isn't that . . .?'

'And so are you,' Jane sighed. 'You're still wearing your slippers.'

The soi-disant Tom Cruise glanced down at his feet, which were encased in curly-toed gold slippers with jewels stuck to the uppers. 'Damn,' he said.

'Sit down,' said Jane.

Nick smiled feebly. 'Listen, Miss,' he said, 'this has all been a big mistake, and . . .'

'Sit *down*.'

They sat down.

'And take those silly faces off, for heaven's sake.'

They changed back into their proper shapes.

'Sorry,' Nick said.

'And so you should be.' Jane folded her arms and gave them each a look that would have made a woolly mammoth feel at home. 'Men!' she added.

'I'm sorry?'

'Typical male idea of a joke,' Jane went on. 'Oh gosh, Kiss is getting married, let's go and play a joke on him. Puerile.'

'Ah.'

'Posing as extremely handsome film actors, you said to yourselves, let's make some excuse to get in to her flat, so that when he comes round the next morning he'll jump to the wrong conclusion, get madly jealous and they'll have a row. How utterly childish!'

Nick swallowed hard. 'Yes,' he said, 'I see that now. How silly of me.'

'Me too,' Con mumbled. 'Won't be doing anything like this again in a hurry, you can bet your life.'

Jane glowered at them. 'Actually,' she said, 'you're closer to the truth there than you think. Stay there.'

She swept out, and came back a few seconds later with two tomato ketchup bottles and a saucepan. 'It's just as well,' she said, 'that I was planning on making a bolognese anyway.'

She emptied the bottles into the saucepan, put them down on a coffee table, and snapped her fingers. 'Right,' she commanded. 'In you get.'

The two genies stared at each other.

'You can't be . . .'

'You heard me. Come on, jump to it.'

Quickly, the two genies assessed their position. On the one hand, Jane had invoked no magic spell or charm sufficient to force them into the bottles. They didn't have to go. They would be perfectly within their rights to stay exactly where they were and simply explain, calmly and rationally, exactly what they thought they were playing at.

WHOOSH!

Jane nodded and screwed down the lids. Then she put the bottles away in the kitchen cupboard and went back to bed.

CHAPTER NINE

S tart a war.
    Using hail, giant ants and burning pitch.
Piece of cake.

The atmosphere was electric.

Around the packed arena, a hundred thousand spectators watched dry-mouthed as the synthesized fanfare
sounded, the gates opened and –

– the teams appeared!

They had said it couldn't happen, not in our lifetimes.
The political, cultural and ideological gulf was too great,
they said. They'd been wrong.

As the teams ran on to the field, one man sat back in his
seat in the President's box and swelled with pride like an
overfed bullfrog. Rightly so; he had devoted the last three
years of his life to making this moment possible. He had
dreamed the impossible dream, and it had become a reality.

The first ever international sporting event between the
pathologically hostile Latin American states of San Miguel

and Las Monedas. The symbolic resolution of a feud that threatened the peace of the whole world. Here, in the Stadio Ricardo Nixon, San Miguel City, the differences of these two bitter rivals would be fought out, not with tanks and bombs but the click of heels, the swirl of petticoats, the snap of castanets. The great Tango Showdown between the San Miguel Tigers and the Las Monedas Centurions was about to begin.

Secretary General Kropatchek sighed with pure pleasure. One small two-step for a man, he reflected, a giant entrechat for Mankind.

The contestants lined up, magnificent in their gaudy splendour. Nervously, the orchestra tuned their instruments for the last time. One false note, they knew, could even now lead directly to Armageddon. The Master of Ceremonies took the field – just for today, he had dispensed with the curule chair and his customary robes, and was dressed in a simple purple tuxedo – and read a brief prayer before shouting, '*Ariba!*' and standing well back. The contest began.

In the clear blue sky, a small black speck appeared, too small to notice . . .

Accounts of what happened next vary, naturally. If you believe the San Miguel version, a Starfighter of the Las Monedas air force swooped down low over the arena, discharged a drop-tank of napalm on to the dead centre of the specially installed dance-floor, and roared away. The Las Monedians, of course, say that it was a San Miguel MiG that dropped the incendiary device. The truth will probably never be known. The truth, in circumstances like these, is generally irrelevant anyway.

What did matter was the sudden explosion of activity in the President's box. As the flames roared up to the sky from the middle of the stadium, the delegates from the two countries flew at each others' throats and started throwing punches, plates of vol-au-vents and souvenir programmes. Their aides, meanwhile, were yelling into their radio handsets, demanding punitive air strikes and massive retribution. Secretary General Kropatchek managed to escape to safety, but only by stunning a passing waiter, snatching his tray and edging out backwards handing out canapés.

Three hours later, just before hostilities could begin in earnest, a hasty cease-fire was lashed together: involving a three-mile neutral zone along the common frontier, a UN peacekeeping force and a unilateral ban on all forms of ballroom and flamenco dancing throughout the front line states. It held. Just.

Which pleased the human race no end but irritated Philly Nine, who had put a lot of thought and effort into the attack, and had quite reasonably expected a result. Back to the drawing board.

High in his solitary eyrie, he watched the tanks withdraw, clicked his tongue, and took out his crumpled envelope.

He ran his pen down the margin and drew a cross.

X Burning pitch

Ah well, he muttered to himself. Better luck next time.

One small random particle, working its way steadily towards the centre . . .

'That signpost,' said Asaf, with deadly patience, 'says *Ankara, 15km.*'

The Dragon King lifted his sunglasses and squinted.

'Too right, mate,' he said. 'Well, stuff me for a kookaburra's uncle.'

Asaf breathed out slowly through his nose. 'I may yet,' he replied. 'Admit it,' he went on. 'We're on the wrong road.'

The King looked out of the window. 'Hell,' he said, 'it all looks different from down here. I'm used to the aerial view.'

Asaf snarled, put the camper into reverse and started to back up. The King put a hand on his arm.

'Just a second there, mate,' he said. 'While we're here, we might just as well . . .'

He tailed off. Asaf scowled.

'We aren't lost, are we?' he said accusingly. 'You've lured me out here for another of your goddamn poxy adventures. Admit it.'

'Fair dinkum, mate, you'll like this one. Stand on me.'

Asaf stamped on the accelerator, sending the camper hurtling backwards. 'Oh no, you bloody well don't,' he snapped. 'Not after the last time.'

'Yes, but –'

'And the time before that.'

'Hang on just a –'

'*And* the time before that, with the talking shrub. I nearly died of embarrassment.'

The King shut his eyes, took a deep breath and stalled the engine. Or rather, he caused the engine to stall. Then he tried his best at an ingratiating smile.

'Adventure,' he said weakly, 'is the spice of life.'

'Get out.'

'Pardon me?'

'Get out of my van,' Asaf growled. 'And you can bloody well walk home.'

'You haven't seen the adventure yet.'

Just then, at precisely the moment when Asaf was leaning across to work the passenger-door handle, a beautiful white gazelle sprang out in front of the camper, stopped dead in its tracks, raised its head for an instant and then ran on. Asaf stared.

'Is that the adventure?' he said.

The King drew breath to explain, thought better of it and nodded. 'You see?' he said. 'Told you you'd like it.'

Asaf frowned. 'I must be mad,' he muttered. 'Stark staring –'

'She'll be right, mate. Trust me.'

Still muttering, Asaf climbed slowly out of the camper, shut the door and walked slowly towards the gazelle, which had stopped about seventy-five yards away and was feeding peacefully on a discarded cheese roll. He had covered half the distance when –

WHOOSH!

It seemed as if the ground split open at his feet, as a huge apparition reared up and loomed over him. Generally humanoid in form, it had three heads, five arms and the legs of a wild goat. Out of the corners of its mouths projected weird curling tusks, and in its hands it held a variety of archaic but imagination-curdling weapons. It crouched in a fighting pose and said, 'Ha!'

'Oh, for pity's sake,' said Asaf, disgustedly. 'Not you again.'

And justifiably; because all three of the monster's heads were the same, and the face on each of them was identical to the one Asaf had so far encountered on one camel-riding magician, one magic-carpet-riding Grand Vizier, one man-eating Centaur, one seven-headed magic bird and, improbable as it may seem, one evil but enchanting houri. It was a face that was starting to get on Asaf's nerves.

'Tremble!' the monster commanded, a mite self-consciously. It was the tone of voice a policeman might use when arresting someone who, on closer inspection, turned out to be his elder brother.

'Bog off,' Asaf replied. He turned on his heel and started to walk back to the van.

'Wretched mortal, I shall devour . . .' the monster started to say; then it realised that its audience was fifteen yards away and walking briskly. It scampered after him; a manoeuvre that wasn't helped by the goat's feet.

'Wretched . . . mortal . . . I . . .' it puffed. 'Here, wait for me!'

Asaf turned and scowled, hands on hips. 'Look,' he said, 'I told you the last time. I'm not interested. Go away.' He turned and quickened his pace, and the monster had to sprint to keep up with him.

'But I shall devour . . . oof!"

Before the monster could halt its teetering run (imagine Godzilla in a pair of two-inch-heel court shoes, each shoe on the wrong foot) Asaf had whirled round and prodded it hard just below the navel. It wobbled for a fraction of a second and then sat down hard on a sharp boulder.

'Ouch!' it said. 'That hurt.'

'Good.' Asaf grabbed a pointed ear and twisted it. 'Look, chum, so far I've killed you twice, imprisoned your soul in a bottle, thrown you off a cliff and nailed your ears to a tree. What exactly do I have to do to you before you get the message?'

'I'm only doing my job,' the monster replied.

'Find another job, then,' Asaf snapped. 'Carpentry, for instance. Plumbing. Chartered surveying. Anything which doesn't involve meeting me ever again. Otherwise,' he added, 'I shall get seriously annoyed. Got it?'

'Finished?'

'Yes.'

'Thank you.' The monster clicked its tongues. 'Now then, where was I? Oh magnanimous one, spare my life and I shall . . .'

'Hold on,' Asaf interrupted, turning the ear in his hand a few degrees clockwise. 'This doesn't involve three wishes, does it, because I've had all that and as far as I'm concerned you can take your three wishes and you can –'

'No, it doesn't,' replied the monster irritably. 'And my ear is not a starting handle. Thank you very much.'

'Get on with it, then.'

'Spare my life,' growled the monster, 'and I shall show thee the most wondrous treasure.' It glanced up with its unencumbered heads. 'Interested?'

'Not very,' Asaf replied. 'But it's an improvement. Go on.'

'Not three leagues from here,' said the monster, 'there lies an enchanted castle, under whose walls –'

'Hold it.'

'Well?'

'Three leagues,' said Asaf. 'What's that in kilometres?'

'Fourteen and a half,' snapped the monster. 'Not fourteen and a half kilometres from here there lies an enchanted castle, under whose –'

Asaf shook his head. 'No way,' he said. 'A fifteen-kilometre detour on these roads, there and back, that's best part of an hour. We wouldn't reach Istanbul till gone nine.'

'Hoy!' the monster broke in angrily. 'We're talking about a wondrous treasure here.'

'Sorry,' Asaf replied. 'Not even with free wine-glasses.'

He gave the ear a final twist, for luck, and let go. 'So long,' he said. 'I have this strange feeling we'll meet again soon. Till then, mind how you go.'

'Gold!' the monster yelled after him. 'Silver! Precious stones!'

'Balls,' Asaf replied.

'You can't do this,' screamed the monster. 'I've signed for it now, they'll have my guts for –'

'I expect you're used to that by now,' Asaf said. 'Ciao.'

'Bastard!' The monster shook its many fists, spat into the dust and started to sink into the ground. Asaf walked a few more yards, and then stopped.

'Hey!' he said.

The monster paused, waist-deep in the earth. 'Well?'

'Did you say gold?'

'Yes.'

'And silver? And precious stones?'

'Yes.'

'Stay there, I'll be right with you.'

Asaf turned and hurried back. The monster was leaning on its elbows, drumming its fingers on a rock.

'You really like causing problems, don't you?' it said. 'You do realise I'm stuck here till they can get a maintenance crew out?'

'Gosh,' said Asaf. 'Sorry about that.'

'Either you can materialise,' grumbled the monster, 'or you can vanish. One or the other. You try mixing the two, you get stuck.'

'That was thoughtless of me,' Asaf admitted. 'By the way, I don't think I caught your name – your actual name, that is. Like, when you're off-duty.'

'Neville.'

'I'm Asaf.'

'Hello.'

'Hello. Now, about this gold.'

'And silver.'

'Quite. How exactly do I set about –?'

'*And* precious stones.'

'Great.' Asaf broadened his smile a little. 'Can you give me specific directions, because then I won't have to trouble you to come with me, I can just : . .'

The monster shook his heads. 'Oh, no, you don't,' it said. 'This time we do it by the book.'

Asaf sagged a little. 'Do we really have to?' he asked.

'Yes.'

'Sure? I mean, wouldn't it be far simpler if you just drew me a map or something?'

'Out of the question,' Neville replied. 'First, you've got to fight the hundred-headed guardian of the pit, and then –'

'Hang on,' said Asaf. 'This hundred-headed guardian. That'll be you, right?'

Neville bit his lips, then nodded. 'That's right,' he mumbled.

'And I win, right?'

'Yes.'

'And you get killed.'

'Yup.'

'Again.'

Neville furrowed all his brows simultaneously. 'Yeah,' he said. 'A bit pointless, really, isn't it?'

'Futile, if you ask me.'

'Anyway,' Neville went on, 'after you've killed the hundred-headed guardian, then you've got to guess the secret riddle of the Mad Witch of the North –'

'You again, right?'

Neville nodded. 'In a frock,' he added. 'Three sizes too small, too. Stops your circulation.'

'Must be awful.'

'It is. After that,' he went on, counting off on his fingers, 'there's the monstrous cloud-stepping ogre –'

'Guess who.'

'Followed by the wicked Grand Vizier who tries to have you thrown in the snake-pit . . .'

'You again?'

'No,' Neville replied, 'that's my cousin Wilf.'

'Ah. Let me guess, you're the snakes.'

'You got it.'

'I escape, naturally?'

'Naturally.'

'The snakes, I anticipate, aren't quite so fortunate?'

Neville shuddered. 'I do so hate death by drowning,' he added. 'Makes your ears go pop. I always get this headache, stays with me the whole of the rest of the day.'

'In fact,' Asaf said, 'the way I see it, I'm going to have to spend the rest of today, and probably most of tomorrow as well, kicking shit out of you, and it's all a foregone conclusion anyway.'

'Wretched, isn't it?'

'Childish,' Asaf agreed. 'Look, couldn't I just beat you to a jelly now and get it all over with in one go?'

There was a long pause. 'Put like that,' said Neville slowly, 'it does sort of make sense.'

'In fact,' Asaf went on, 'a token clip round the ear would probably do just as well.'

Neville frowned. 'I'm not sure about that,' he said. 'Standing orders specifically require –'

'Yes,' Asaf interrupted, 'but who'll ever know? I won't tell anybody.'

'You won't?'

'Scout's honour.'

The monster thought about it for a while. 'Can I get you to sign a receipt?' he asked. 'Just for the books, you understand.'

'Sure,' said Asaf.

'Deal!' The monster cried, and it reached down into the bowels of the earth. A moment later its hand reappeared holding a parchment, a quill pen and a bottle of ink. 'So much more sensible this way,' it said.

'Quite.'

'So if you'll just sign here . . .'

'Where your finger is?' asked Asaf, unscrewing the ink bottle.

'That's it. Goodbye, idiot!' he added. 'See you in Hell!'

And, so saying, it grabbed Asaf by the scruff of the neck, squashed him head-first into the ink bottle and screwed down the cap.

And vanished.

Meanwhile, the small frog that was Kevin, the insurance broker, had filed his report. It made interesting reading.

Only a genie of Force Seven or above could have deciphered the pattern of nibble-marks on the lily-pad, and known that they read:

rivet-rivet-rivet-rivet-
RIVET-RIVET-RIVET-RIVET!!!!!-RIVET!!!!!!

Only a genie of Force Eight or above, fluent in frog, could have translated the message and grasped its terrible significance.

Only a genie of Force Nine or above would have the authority to take the necessary remedial action.

Only a genie of Force Eleven or above (or God, at a pinch) would have the necessary technical knowledge and basic common sense required to put that remedial action into effect.

Fortunately, the report found its way on to the right desks, was understood and taken seriously. The necessary action was proposed, approved and set in hand.

As for the frog that was Kevin, it found itself coming to terms with its new lifestyle rather more quickly than it had originally anticipated. Not only were the hours better and the pressures less; the inhabitants of the pond were remarkably receptive to the idea of insurance and he was doing excellent business when a heron, new to the area, swooped down and ate him.

Regrettable; but that's nature for you, and it's a comfort to reflect that his last conscious thought must have been relief that his loved ones would be adequately provided for by a comprehensive insurance package specially tailored to his needs and circumstances.

Or would have done, if he'd had any loved ones, and if the policy hadn't contained a special no-herons clause. But it's the thought that counts.

A scrumpled ball of paper looped through the air and added itself to the small pyramid on top of the waste-paper basket.

Philly Nine yawned. It was late, he was tired, and he wanted to go to bed. Giant ants . . .

He got up and prowled round the room. Nobody to blame but himself, of course; he'd chosen giant ants of his own free will. He could have had anything he liked, but no, he had to be clever.

Ants, for pity's sake.

He sat down on the arm of a chair, closed his eyes and rallied his thoughts. What, he demanded of himself, do ants *do*?

Well. They build nests. They run around aimlessly. They get into picnic baskets and scamper about over the boiled eggs. This, Philly had to admit, wasn't exactly the stuff of Armageddon.

They chew things up. With their snippy little mandibles, they make mincemeat out of old dry timber. They dig. When you pour boiling water on them, they die.

He looked up at the clock on the wall, and shuddered. Would it be possible, he wondered, to claim a typographical error and instead have a plague of giant aunts? More scope there, he felt sure; something you could get your teeth into . . .

Nah. It'd be just his luck to get found out; to annihilate humanity and then have the whole thing set aside on a technicality. Long gone were the old, free-and-easy days of his imphood when near enough made no mind. These days, you had to be precise. No good putting a princess to sleep for ninety-nine years, three hundred and sixty-four days, twenty-three hours and fifty-nine minutes. You could bet your life there'd be some weasel-faced little sod with a clipboard and a stopwatch somewhere, just willing you to foul up.

Ants. Harmless, industrious, ecologically-friendly ants. Bastards.

He snatched another piece of paper out of the packet and started to scribble.

An anthill, he wrote, *so big that it cuts off the light from a major European city. Giant ants undermining Beijing, so that it falls down to the centre of the earth. The New York subway system infested with giant ants . . .*

Scrumple. Whizz. Flop.

He stood up again, and then sat down. *Giant* ants. Yes. Perhaps.

Giant ants, he wrote. *What causes giant ants? And whose fault would it be?*

Pay dirt. Ideas started to flood into his mind like water through a breached sea-wall, and he scribbled furiously. So furiously in fact, that it was half an hour before he realised he was writing on his best white linen tablecloth.

Giant ants. Yes. Yes indeed.

What do you call it when a genie has a really good idea? Genius.

It was late. Even Saheed's, which is never empty, was down to its last hard core of residual customers; a few sad types sitting at tables, two more playing the fruit machine, and one very sad customer with his foot on the brass rail.

'Don't you think you've had enough?' murmured the barman.

Kiss scowled at him. 'Not yet,' he grunted, and pushed his empty glass back across the counter. 'Yogurt. Neat. No fruit.'

The barman shrugged. He was, of course, only doing his job, and it was none of his business; but the idea of a Force Twelve wandering about with an attitude problem and five quarts of natural yogurt under his belt wasn't an attractive one. He filled the glass and shoved it back.

Time, he said to himself, to start a conversation. More goddamn unpaid social work.

'What's up, mac?' he enquired softly. He assessed the symptoms; it wasn't difficult. 'Trouble with your girl?'

Kiss nodded.

'You could say that,' he replied.

The barman nodded sympathetically. 'Found herself another guy, huh?'

'No.'

'I see. Just plain not interested, you mean?'

'Far from it,' Kiss sighed. 'That's the problem.'

Well, thought the barman, it takes all sorts. 'You mean,' he said, 'you can see it's all over between you, but you can't figure out how to tell her? That's tough.'

'No,' Kiss yawned, 'it's not that. We're in love. Head over heels in bloody love.' He snarled. 'Made in heaven, you could say.'

'Ah.' The barman shrugged. 'But there's some reason why you can't get together, is that it?'

Kiss lifted his head and looked at him. 'What is this,' he asked, 'some sort of blasted sociological survey?'

'Just passing the time, mac. Talking of which . . .?'

'Put another one in there,' Kiss said. 'With a cream chaser.'

'You're the boss, mac.'

'And stop calling me mac.'

'You got it, chief.'

There was a frantic chiming from the direction of the fruit machine and suddenly the floor was covered in oranges and lemons, tumbling out of the pay-out slot and rolling around on the floor. One came to rest beside Kiss's heel. He stood on it.

'I mean,' he said suddenly, in the general direction of the barman, 'it's not my fault, is it? I never asked to be the one to save the world.'

'Yeah,' said the barman. 'Have you seen what time it is, by the way?'

'I don't give . . .' Kiss leaned over, picked up an orange

and squashed it into pulp between his thumb and middle finger. 'I don't give *that* for the world. None of my damn business.'

'You said it, chief.'

'But it's my damn responsibility!' Kiss scowled horribly, and then looked down at his hand. 'Hey, have you got a towel or something?'

'Just a second.'

'So why,' Kiss continued, wiping his hands, 'does it have to be me? Go on, you tell me, it's your stinking planet. Why me?'

The barman shrugged. 'Somebody's got to do it?' he suggested.

Kiss shook his head. 'Not good enough,' he said. 'I'm a genie, right? We're . . .' He closed his eyes, fumbling through a fog of draught yogurt for the right words. 'Free spirits,' he said. 'No. Loose cannons. We do our own thing. That's unless somebody gets us by the balls and makes us do theirs. But that,' he concluded defiantly, 'goes with the territory. We can handle that.'

'Glad to hear it, buddy.'

In the background there was a dull squelch, as the fruit machine tried unsuccessfully to pay out a grapefruit through a four-inch slot. Kiss sighed.

'You don't want to hear all this, do you?' he asked.

The barman looked at him with old, warm eyes. 'I can take it,' he said, 'I've heard worse.'

Kiss nodded. 'You must have heard it all,' he said.

'Maybe.' The barman picked up a glass and polished it. 'But maybe I wasn't listening.'

Somewhere in Kiss's brain, the dinar dropped. 'You're a genie?' he asked softly.

'You bet, squire.'

'What Force?'

The barman shrugged, breathed on the rim of the glass in his hands and eased away a mark. 'Twelve,' he replied.

'Twelve?' Kiss looked at him. 'Then what the blazes are you doing in a dump like this?'

The barman looked back, and his eyes were like the view through the wrong end of the binoculars. 'Hey,' he said. 'You know how it is when you're bound by some curse to a bottle?'

Kiss nodded.

'Well, then.' The barman half-turned and with an eloquent but economical gesture he indicated the shelves behind him. 'Me,' he said, 'I got *lots* of bottles.'

'Gawd!'

'It's not the way I'd have liked things to pan out,' the barman agreed. 'But you find yourself in a situation, what can you do? Me, I serve drinks to people. That's from six pee-em to maybe four-thirty ay-em. The rest of the time . . .'

Kiss leaned forward. 'Yes?'

'The rest of the time's my own,' the barman replied. 'Same again, is it?'

On his way home, Kiss turned out the cupboard under the stairs of his mind and found it to be mainly full of junk. There he found the ironing-board of duty, the broken torch of hope, the unwanted Christmas presents of obscure function that represent the random operations of fate, the dustpan of experience, the stepladder of aspiration, the hoover of despair; there also he found the raffia-covered Chianti-bottle table-lamp of love, which had seemed such a good idea at the time, which promised to cast light where before there was darkness and which now got under his feet whenever he wanted to get out the ironing-board. Its shade was as pink as ever, but its bulb had gone.

Not, Kiss hastened to add, my fault. I'm the goddamn victim; and she is as well, of course, but *she's* not expected to give up being a Force Twelve genie. His thoughts returned to the genie behind the bar at Saheed's; another Force Twelve fallen on hard times. They could form a support group; well, not a group. The best they could do with the manpower available would be a very short, truncated heap.

I've got to get myself out of this. But how?

The inside of an ink-bottle turned out to be remarkably spacious, all things considered.

Admittedly, you have to sit with your knees round your ears and your arms behind your back; and it doesn't do to sneeze violently for fear of knocking yourself silly on the walls. The fact remains; getting six foot of retired fisherman inside three inches of bottle without pruning off several indispensable components is some achievement. Try it and see.

'Let me OUT!'

Some people, it seems, are never satisfied. There are successful young executives in the centre of Tokyo who pay good money for not much more *lebensraum*, and are glad to get it.

'Are you deaf or something? Let me OUT!'

Asaf paused to catch his breath. Yelling at the top of one's voice in a confined space is physically demanding and, besides, it didn't seem to be working.

If I were a baby bird, he said to himself, and if this was an eggshell, I could peck my way out.

Ah, but it isn't. And you're not.

It would be overstating the case to say that Asaf stiffened, because after nine hours in the bottle he was pretty conclusively stiff already; but he went through the motions.

There is someone, he said to himself, in here with me. Hope he's as uncomfortable as I am.

Not really. You get used to it after a while.

This time, Asaf felt a definite twitch in his sphincter.

Don't be like that.

'What?' Asaf said aloud. His voice, he couldn't help noticing, seemed to be coming out through his socks; something to do with the rather unusual acoustics inside an ink-bottle.

Hostile. I can definitely sense hostility. I'm only here because I thought you might be feeling lonely.

'How the hell am I supposed to feel lonely in something this size?'

Fair point. I'll be going, then.

'Wait!'

Silence. But then again, he reflected, there would be, wouldn't there? Since, apparently, whoever it was in here with him was either a disembodied spirit or . . .

A telepath. Bit of both, actually. Go with the flow, that's always been my motto.

'Who are you?'

Name? Or job description?

'Both.'

All-righty. My name's Pivot, and I'm the duty GA.

'GA?'

Guardian angel. Since whatever it was was simply a suggestion of words in his mind, there was no way it could actually sound embarrassed. But it somehow gave the impression.

'Bit late, aren't you?' Asaf grumbled. 'Nine hours ago I could have used you.'

I know, Pivot replied. *But like I said, I'm duty GA for this whole sector. I got held up on a call the other side of Bazrah. I came as quick as I could.*

'I see.' Asaf took a deep breath; or at least, the top slice of one. 'Well, now you're here . . .'

I can keep your morale up and comfort you with homely snippets of folk wisdom and popular philosophy.

'That's it?'

Sorry.

'Like, It's a funny old world, that sort of thing?'

You've got the idea.

'Fine. Well, I expect you've got lots of other calls to attend to, so don't let me . . .'

I know, replied Pivot sadly, *it's not exactly a great help. But that's all I'm able to do for you under the scheme. Lots of people actually do find it remarkably helpful.*

'I see.'

If you were being tortured, of course, or even briskly interrogated, that'd be another matter entirely. I could remind you of your rights and exhort you to display fortitude and moral courage in the face of adversity.

'Gosh. Well, it's just as well I'm not, then, isn't it?'

There was silence in Asaf's mind for a while, and he spent the time thinking all the most uncharitable thoughts he could muster, in the hope of persuading Pivot to leave quickly.

It'd be different if you were a fee-paying client, of course.

'Sorry?'

Morale-raising and verbal comfort are all I'm allowed to offer under the scheme. If you want to go private, of course, I'm sure I could be even more helpful still.

'Such as?'

Such as getting you out of here, for a start.

'Done.'

Plus, there's our fully comprehensive after-care package, of course. We don't just ditch our clients the moment they get out of the bottle; oh dear, no. We can offer advice on a wide spectrum of issues, including financial advice, investment strategy, pensions . . .

'Whatever you like. Just get me out of –'

If you'd just care to sign this client services agreement. There, there and there . . .

Asaf growled ominously. 'I'd just like to point out,' he said, 'that my hands are wedged against the side of this bottle so hard my circulation stopped about seven hours ago. I think signing anything's going to be a bit tricky.'

Oh. Oh, that is a nuisance. Because, you see, the rules say I can't really do anything for you unless you sign the forms. I have my compliance certificate to think of, you know.

Asaf gritted his teeth. 'I promise I'll sign them the moment I'm free,' he said. 'Word of honour.'

Ah yes, Pivot replied, *but how do I know you're not a FIMBRA agent in disguise? You could be trying to entrap me.*

'Why not take the risk? I'll have you know I'm shortly going to come into wealth beyond the dreams of avarice.' He paused significantly. 'I shall need,' he said, biting his tongue, 'all sorts of financial advice, I feel sure.'

Is that so?

'Definitely.'

Life insurance?

'As much as I can lay my hands on. '

Pensions?

'By the bucketful. I shall want as many pensions as I can possibly get.'

Stone me. It's been months since I sold a pension. Are you sure you're not a FIMBRA agent?

'Absolutely bloody positive. Now, could you please get me out of this fucking bottle?'

At the back of his mind, Asaf could feel Pivot wriggling uncomfortably. *I still have bad feelings about all this. The rules really are terribly strict.*

'Couldn't you . . .' Asaf squirmed with agony as a spasm of cramp shot down his spinal column. 'Couldn't you sign them for me? As my agent or whatever?'

Hum. Not really. Not unless you sign a power of attorney. I happen to have one with me, by the way.

'Oh, for crying out loud . . .'

I'm sorry, sighed Pivot. *I'd really love to help, but you know how it is. Now, are you ready for some homely snippets yet? We could start with, 'It's always darkest before the dawn', or we could . . .*

'No!' Asaf jerked violently in protest, and in doing so fetched the back of his head a terrific crack on the wall of the bottle. 'Just you dare, and the moment I'm out of this sodding contraption –'

He stopped in mid-snarl. The walls were creaking. Obviously, the blow from his head had damaged the glass. Now if he could only . . .

I've also got one about not beating your head against a brick wall, continued Pivot helpfully. *And I can customise it to refer to the sides of glass bottles for a very modest . . .*

Crash. The glass gave way and suddenly Asaf was out, sprawled full-length – six feet of cramp and muscle spasms – on a flat field of grass. There were shards of broken bottle sticking into him in all sorts of places.

There, I told you we'd have you out of there in no time, said Pivot, recovering well. *That'll be, let's see, seven minutes at a hundred dirhams an hour, so by my reckoning that's . . .*

Asaf lifted his head, and thought long and hard about what he would like to do to the next supernatural being who crossed his path. By the time he'd finished, something told him he was very much alone.

CHAPTER TEN

Jane looked around her, and clicked her tongue.

She was bored.

Not just bored in the nothing-to-do sense; she was bored to the marrow, half-past-four-on-a-Sunday-afternoon-in-Wales bored. And nothing much, as far as she could see, to be done about it.

Bloody genie! What the hell was the point of being able to have anything you want if all you have to do in order to get it is want it?

Still, she consoled herself while moving a small china ornament two inches to the right, once we're married there won't be any more of *that*. No more of this supernatural nonsense. We can just be ordinary people . . .

Ordinary people . . .

Yes, well. At least ordinary people can go shopping. When you're the proprietress of a Force Twelve genie, one thing you can't do is shop. No sooner have you written down something on your list than it's there, delivered in a fraction of a second, very best quality, from Harrods. But what's the point of having things if you can't shop for them first?

Jane steeled herself. She was a free woman, with an inalienable right to shop. And shop she would.

She glanced down at her feet and noticed that on the patch of floor directly below her, approximately five feet by seven, there was no rug. Everywhere else there were rugs; the very finest rugs ever, whisked here by arcane forces and precisely, down to the last fibre, what she'd wanted. Well, it would have to stop somewhere, and here was as good a place as any. She would go *out*, and *buy* a rug.

The resolution once made, she softened slightly. All the other rugs in the place – all the furniture and fittings, come to that – were her choice, and she knew for a fact that Kiss didn't really like them much. A bit thin on the barbaric splendour, he considered, while maybe slightly overstressing the cosy and colour-coordinated.

There, now. Two birds with one stone. She would buy a rug, in (she almost hugged herself with pleasure at the thought) a *shop*, and it would be the sort of rug Kiss would like. Persian or something. She could stand a coffee-table on it so that she wouldn't have to see it, but he would still know it was there.

Problem; although all Oriental carpets looked exactly the same to her, she was sure she remembered something about each one being unique, and some sorts being wonderfully marvellous works of art, and others being the sort of thing that's left unsold after a church bazaar. Obviously, it was incumbent upon her to buy one of the approved models.

Why is life so *complicated*?

The thought had scarcely crossed her mind when she caught sight of a book on the arm of the sofa. It was big and fat, and on the cover it had a photograph of a Persian rug. She picked it up.

It was written in Arabic.

That aside, it was promising; it was full of pictures of rugs, all of which looked pretty well identical to her, but it stood to reason that nobody, not even an Arab in the grips of vanity-publishing mania, would go to the trouble of producing a chunky great tome full of pictures of just one rug. Even if he was desperately attached to it, he'd probably just have its portrait painted and let it go at that.

Therefore, she argued, this must be a book, belonging to Kiss, on the subject of rugs; approved rugs, presumably. All she had to do was go to an emporium, find a rug which looked tolerably similar to the pictures in the book, and buy it. Problem solved. She dumped the book in her bag and went out.

Arguably, a more perceptive person might have noticed the wires coming out of the spine, and wondered what business a book had with sockets and electrodes.

The young man (his name was Justin) was tall and thin. L.S. Lowry would have hired him as a model widhout a moment's hesitation. He was wearing a hairy tweed jacket whose sleeves appeared to have eaten his hands right down to the middle joints of the fingers. He seemed nervous.

But not as nervous as the other man (his name was Max). If Justin resembled a golf club, Max was a dead ringer for the ball.

'Now you've got the number?' Max said.

'Yes, Uncle.'

'And you'll phone me if there's any problems? Any problems at all?'

'Yes, Uncle.'

'And you know where everything is?'

'Yes, Uncle.'

Max chewed his lip. 'The key to the safe is in the coffee tin on the top shelf of the stockroom, just under the –'

'Yes, Uncle.'

'And you're sure you'll be all right?'

'Yes, Uncle.'

There's only so much you can do, thought Max; and I'll only be gone two hours, and there's never any customers on a Thursday afternoon, and all the prices are clearly marked, and I've told him nineteen times not to let anybody haggle . . .

'Justin.'

'Yes, Uncle?'

'Remember, don't let anybody haggle. The prices as marked are non-negotiable. You've got that?'

'Yes, Uncle.'

. . . Twenty times, so what could possibly go wrong? no, don't even think, that. Just keep everything crossed, and hurry back as soon as possible.

'Oh, and Justin.'

'Yes, Uncle?'

'Don't buy anything.'

'No, Uncle.'

It's impossible, Max reassured himself, completely out of the question, that the boy could be as dozy as his mother. For a start, he seems able to remember to breathe regularly without anybody having to remind him. The shop will be in safe hands. Everything's going to be all right.

'Is there anything,' he said, taking a deep breath, 'you want to ask before I go?'

'No, Uncle.'

Max shut his eyes, broadcast a prayer to any passing gods and smiled wretchedly.

'Right,' he said, winding his scarf round his neck, 'it's all yours.'

He took three steps towards the door, stopped and looked round. Of course he would see it all again, and when he came back everything would be all right. But there was no harm in taking one last, long look, just to be on the safe side.

''Bye, Uncle.'

'See you, Justin.'

The bell on the door clanged and Justin was alone with the shop, the till, the books and seventy square miles of the choicest, rarest, most valuable Oriental carpets in the whole of the United Kingdom.

He sneezed.

Carpets attract dust, and dust played hell with Justin's sinuses. The next two hours, he just knew, were going to be very, very long.

He sat down behind the desk and found his place in his book, trying his best to breathe in through his mouth only. He hadn't read more than five or six pages when the bell tinkled. He looked up.

'Can I help?' he asked, and froze.

During the previous night, when he'd been lying awake fretting about having to mind the shop on his own the next day, he had finally managed to reconcile himself to the thought that there might be customers. He had squared up to that one, looked the imposter Fear straight in the eye and stared him down. It hadn't occurred to him, however, that there might be female customers. Young female customers. If the thought had crossed his mind, come to that, he wouldn't be here now.

'I expect so,' Jane replied, looking round. 'I want to buy a rug.'

'Gosh.'

'Looks like I've come to the right place.'

'Crumbs.'

'I mean,' Jane went on, with that awful feeling you get when you know you've got to keep talking because the silence that'll follow when you stop will be too embarrassing to contemplate, 'you look like you've got a very wide selection.'

'Have we? Yes.'

Jane subsided. What she really wanted to do now was leave the shop and never come back; but it looked like there was a sporting chance that the implied rejection would drive the young man behind the desk to slash his wrists, if he didn't break his thumbnail getting the big blade out first. She was stuck.

'Gosh,' she said, selecting a carpet at random, 'what have we here?'

The young man said nothing. His expression seemed to suggest that as far as he was concerned, all carpets were too ghastly for words and he wanted nothing to do with them, ever, not in this world or the next.

'No,' Jane muttered, 'maybe not. Or rather,' she added quickly, in case the negative vibes might just be the final shove that would send him over the edge, 'it's a really nice carpet, but not quite in keeping with . . . Yes, this one's even nicer. Don't you think?'

The young man lifted his head and gazed at the example she'd put her hand on. 'Do you want to, er, *buy* . . .?'

His tone of voice suggested that Jane was trying to seduce him into committing some luridly unnatural act. 'Well,' she mumbled, 'I do quite like . . .'

'I'll look,' said the young man, 'in the book.'

He ducked under the counter, and for an awful moment

Jane wondered if he was ever going to reappear. Just when she was steeling herself to go and see what he'd done to himself under there, he bobbed back up again with a shoebox full of tatty notebooks.

'It'll be in here somewhere, ' the young man said hopelessly.

Oh Christ, Jane thought, I'm going to be here for the rest of my life. Kiss, where the devil are you when I need you? Beam me up quick.

'Look, if it's any trouble . . .'

The young man favoured her with a look that wouldn't have been out of place on the face of a sheep in an abattoir. 'I'm quite capable of looking it up, thank you very much,' he said, with a sort of hideous mangled dignity that made Jane wish very much that her father had never met her mother. 'I'll try not to keep you.'

'I'll buy it anyway,' Jane whimpered, 'if that's all right with you, I mean.'

The young man didn't reply. He was nose-deep in the box. It looked very much as if he was going to be there for some considerable time.

Eventually, just as Jane was wondering whether she could surreptitiously roll herself up in the carpet like Cleopatra, wait till he'd gone and then make good her escape, the young man lifted his head and coughed nervously.

'Excuse me.'

'Yes?'

'Can you see a ticket on it anywhere? It should say 2354/A67/74Y.'

'Ah.' Jane examined the carpet. 'Doesn't seem to be.'

'No?'

'No.'

'Oh.' The young man winced, as if the book in his hand

was red-hot. 'I'd better just look, I suppose,' he muttered, and crossed the floor towards her. 'Maybe it's on the back of something. There *should* be one somewhere,' he added poignantly.

They were both standing on the carpet. 'Can I help?' Jane asked.

'It's all right, really, I can manage.'

'What does it say in the book?'

'It's a . . .' The young man squinted. 'Sorry, I can't quite pronounce it. Bokhara something or other.'

'And that's what you think this is?'

'I think so. Mind you, I'm really not an expert. If you wouldn't mind waiting till Uncle gets back, I'm sure he'd be able to . . .'

Oh no, thought Jane, I wasn't born yesterday. This is one of those traps, like the Flying Dutchman or the Lorelei. You promise to wait ten minutes, and five hundred years later you're still there, and everybody you ever knew on the outside has died. 'Here,' Jane said, press-ganging the first words ill-advised enough to come near her, 'I've got a book here, let's see if there's a picture we can identify it from.'

She opened Kiss's book, and as she was rather preoccupied she failed to notice the slight hum, or the pale blue glow from the endpapers.

God, she thought. I wish I was out of here.

COMPUTING

The voice was inside her, tiny, clear and sharp. She was sure she'd heard it. Oh wonderful, now I'm going potty. If ever I get out of this alive, it's going to be wall-to-wall lino for ever and ever.

I wish, she added in mental parenthesis, Kiss was here.

DOES NOT CORRELATE

'Did you say . . .'

'Sorry?'

'Nothing.'

Definitely, Jane said to herself, I want to be out of here. Immediately.

WHOOSH!

'Good on yer, mate,' said the Dragon King of the South-East, emerging from behind a pile of coiled-up rope.

'Look . . .'

'Like a rat,' the Dragon King continued, 'up a drain. No worries. Like they say out Paramatta way: you can take the bloke out of the bottle, but you can't take the bottle out of the bloke.'

This remark was so puzzling that Asaf dismissed his daydream of making the King swallow his own tail, and he sat down on a barrel. 'Where the hell am I?' he asked.

'On the high seas, me old mate,' the King replied. 'On your way to seek fame, fortune, and the sheila with the big –'

'Please be more specific.'

The King smiled; that is to say, the corners of his jaws lifted, and his bright, small blue eyes sparkled even more than usual. 'We're on a ship,' he said.

'I had in fact come to that conclusion already. What bloody ship, and why?'

The King chuckled. 'Because,' he replied, 'you'd get pretty flamin' wet trying to cross the old surf without one. Eh?'

Asaf sighed. It wasn't, he said to himself, fair; not on him, and not on everybody else. Why should the rest of the world be deprived of their ration of idiots just so that he could have an embarrassing profusion?

'Where,' he asked, 'are we going?'

'Pommieland,' the King said. 'The old country. Gee, you'll love it there, mate. It's really beaut, trust me.'

'England?'

'That's the ticket.'

Asaf frowned. 'But that's crazy.'

'That's where she lives, chum. The jam tart with the . . .'

'Fine.' Asaf drew in a deep breath and counted up to ten. 'And this ship . . .'

'Hitched a lift with an old cobber of mine, actually,' said the King. 'A really bonzer old bastard, do anything for you. Knows these seas like the back of his hand.'

Something horrible seemed to slide down the back of Asaf's neck, only on the inside. 'Please,' he said, raising a hand feebly, 'reassure me. Tell me we haven't hitched a lift with Sinbad the Sailor.'

'You know Simbo?'

'Heard of him,' Asaf muttered. 'But –'

'Simbo and me,' the King went on, 'we go way back. Me and old Simbo . . .'

Asaf lay back on the deck and covered his face with the edge of a redundant sail. 'I think I'd like to go to sleep now,' he said. 'And if I don't wake up, never mind.'

'But –'

'Look!' Asaf sat bolt upright, and stabbed the King in the left pectoral with his forefinger. The scales, he noticed in passing, were harder than his fingernail. 'This time last week,' he said, 'I was content. Not happy, but content. I had a sleazy little hovel with a hole in the roof, my own poxy little business that wasn't going anywhere, fish three times a day, some grubby old clothes, several people I hadn't borrowed money off yet. I was content. And then you turn up, with your bloody three wishes –'

'Steady on, mate . . .'

'I will not steady on!' Asaf shouted. 'Take me home again, now. And that's a wish.'

The King sighed, filling the hold with damp green steam. 'I know what it is,' he said, 'you're hungry. A bit of good honest tucker inside you and you'll be as right as —'

'NOW!'

'Sorry.'

'What?'

'No can do,' replied the King awkwardly. 'It's a bit late for all that now, mate. You should have thought about it before you came.'

'What the hell do you mean?' Asaf growled. 'You got me here, you get me out. And while we're on the subject, what the fuck was all that stuff with that damn bottle?'

'How about,' said the King – he was disappearing, fading into the pale sunlight that streaked down into the hold through an unfastened hatch – 'a nice egg and tomato sarny? Or I can do you pilchards.'

'But . . .'

The King had gone, leaving behind him a few airborne sparkles and a memory of the word 'sarny'. Overhead, the unsecured hatch slammed shut, and Asaf heard the sound of bolts shooting home. He sat for a moment, speechless with rage and confusion. Then he shrugged, folded the corner of sail into a pillow and lay down.

'I hate pilchards!' he shouted, and closed his eyes.

And here's the latest, warbled the television, *on the nuclear tests story. And we're taking you live to our man on Pineapple Atoll. Danny, can you hear me?*

Philly Nine grinned, propped his feet on the footstool and used the handset to turn up the volume.

Loud and clear, Bob, chirruped the reporter, who had replaced the studio set on the screen. Behind him there was a view of blue skies and coconut palms. *And the latest seems to be that we now have confirmation of the existence of the giant ants. The giant ants have, in fact, been sighted. By me. I saw them.*

The reporter seized up and stood, gazing into the camera lens. After a gentle prompt from the studio, he continued.

So far, he said, *we've sighted sixteen of the giant ants. They're big, like twenty feet tall at the shoulder, and they're making a real mess of the landscape, I can tell you. Also, attempts to deal with them by way of aerial dusting with ant powder and dive-bomb attacks with kettles of boiling water have proved basically futile. A spokesman for the World Wildlife Fund who chained himself to the leg of one ant in protest against these culling attempts has been eaten, but otherwise there are no reports of casualties.*

It was the studio's turn to say something, but nothing was said. The reporter, by now smiling disconcertingly, continued.

More importantly, the diplomatic exchanges over how these ants came to mutate so drastically is really beginning to hot up. I think all the superpowers are now in agreement that the mutation was caused by clandestine nuclear weapons tests, although I should add that there haven't been any seismic readings to confirm this theory. Where everyone seems to disagree is over who actually did the test. In fact, everybody is accusing everybody else, and the situation really is beginning to get a bit fraught. In fact, we could be looking at the end of the multilateral disarmament initiative here, so for anybody out there with a redundant coal-cellar, the message is, start taking bookings now, because . . .

As the screen hurriedly reverted to the studio set, Philly Nine lay back in his chair, closed his eyes and smiled.

I did that, he told himself smugly, with my little hatchet.

WHOOOOOOSH!

The carpet streaked across the sky like a flat, embroidered meteor, skimming off satellite dishes and the older pattern of weather-vane as it went by sheer force of air displacement. The wonderful aerial view available over its side was wasted on Jane, who was lying flat on her face clinging on to two clenched handfuls of carpet. Justin had blacked out.

'Where to, lady?'

Jane looked up, received an eyeful of fast-moving air and ducked down again. However, she saw enough in the fraction of a second's viewing time she had before the air-blast sandpapered her eyeballs to confirm to herself that there was nobody else on the damn rug but herself and the wimp. The voice was, therefore, entirely her imagination.

'No, I'm not. I'm your automatic pilot for what I hope will prove to be a relaxing and pleasurable flight to the destination of your choice.'

'Bugger off.'

'Pardon me?'

'I said bugger off,' Jane barked over the howling of the turbulence. 'I know you're just a hallucination inside my head, and I'm not standing for it. Go on, hop it, before I set my subconscious on to you.'

There was a pause. If it's possible for a pause to sound hurt, it did.

'You're the boss,' said the voice (and for some reason, it didn't have to shout; it was as clear as a bell over the background noise). 'However, I feel I should point out that I'm not in any way a figment of your imagination. If it helps you to relate better, you can call me George.'

Jane set her jaw firmly. She refused absolutely to be drawn into conversation with her own unbalanced mind sitting on a flying rug doing close on Mach One at just above rooftop level over Croydon. Especially a part of her own unbalanced mind called George. Never lower your standards for anyone, as her mother used to say.

'To explain,' George continued. 'The rectangular object you took to be a book is in fact a state-of-the-art carpet navigation system, compatible with all leading designs of magic floor coverings. Once installed on the carpet of your choice, the system automatically activates the carpet's propulsion and guidance systems, and receives directional input direct from your brainwave patterns by telepathic interfacing, made possible by our revolutionary fifth-generation textile chip technology. You said get me out of here fast, so . . .'

'I did?'

'You thought it,' George corrected itself. 'And that's good enough for me. Your wish is my –'

'NO!' Jane howled. 'Not another one!'

'Pardon me?'

'Look.' In her wrath, Jane knelt upright, oblivious to the enormous volume of nothing directly below. 'I have had it up to here with bloody genies, all right? My wish is not your bloody command. To hear is not to obey, O mistress. Got that?'

'We copy.'

'Good. Now get me down off this bloody contraption, fast as you like.'

George said nothing. The carpet continued flying straight and level, only appreciably faster. Had Jane been in the mood, she could have glanced down and seen an Alp, real close.

'Are you deaf or something?'

'On the contrary,' replied George affably. 'All our products have new enhanced sensor capability uprated to provide for instantaneous spoken inputting. This feature alone –'

'Then do as you're told and put me *down!*'

'Sorry.'

For a count of maybe three Jane was, literally, speechless; partly because she was so angry she couldn't speak, partly because something small and airborne flew into her open mouth, and the momentum of the collision nearly knocked her over the side. She struggled to her knees again and thumped the carpet with her fist.

'What d'you mean, sorry? I told you –'

'You told me,' George interrupted, 'that your wish was not my command, and that when I heard I shouldn't obey. You got it?'

'But look, I didn't mean . . .'

'Sorry. But you're the sentient being, I'm only a computerised guidance system. Policy formulation's down to you.' George paused, as if for effect. 'You guys are supposed to be good at that.'

'But . . .'

'Further clarification,' George continued, as they missed one snow-capped peak by a few thousandths of an inch, 'would, however, be appreciated. For example, when you say something, do you want me to ignore it completely or do the exact opposite?'

Jane blinked twice. 'Do the opposite,' she said quickly. '*Don't* put me down. Fly *faster.*'

'Thanks.'

The carpet flew on: same course, same momentum,

Jane screamed and clouted it with the heel of her shoe.

'Just checking,' said George. 'You told me to do the exact opposite. I'm programmed to disobey all orders, therefore I ignore you. That right?'

'No. Yes. Both.'

'Thank you.'

The carpet flew on.

Kiss sat bolt upright. He felt as if a truck had just ploughed into the back of his neck.

Someone was calling him – someone frightened, in danger, in need of protection. No prizes for guessing who.

Bloody woman!

Moon of his delight, entrancing vision of sublime loveliness who gave a purpose to his existence, yes; but bloody woman nevertheless. What, he asked himself bitterly as he searched for his left shoe, has she gone and done now? Locked herself out of her car? Forgotten which level of the multi-storey she'd parked on? Something, he felt sure, like that.

Without dawdling, but without unduly frantic haste either, he dressed and put on his curly-toed shoes. As if, he muttered, he didn't have enough to do. Clean handkerchief. Where in buggery are the clean handkerchieves?

Let there be clean handkerchieves. Problem solved.

Not, he added, that we'll be able to do *that* for much longer. Oh no. And who'll come whizzing along across the tops of the clouds then whenever she's at the station and wondering whether she's left the gas on?

Pausing only to collect the milk off the doorstep, he somersaulted up into the sky, looped the loop and traipsed away through the empyrean.

*

Jane looked up.

On a scale of one to ten of Sensible Things To Do, that was maybe a Two; above putting your hand in a moving circular saw or enrolling in law school, but definitely below, say, investing in gilt-edged stock or leaving a burning oil refinery. She regretted it almost immediately.

Before the regret set in, however, making her stomach turn over like a well-tossed pancake and tightening her intestines into a small knot, she saw a broad, gently undulating expanse of sand. It might have been a beach somewhere, except that beaches tend to have blue edges, and this lot didn't. In fact, it didn't seem to have any edges whatsoever.

The desert.

Which desert, Jane neither knew nor cared. All that registered with her as relevant information was that she was probably a very long way from Haywards Heath.

'Help,' she said.

Said rather than screamed; she was, at heart, a reasonably practical person, and there was nobody who could help her as far as the eye could see. That was assuming that Justin, who was beginning to come round, wasn't likely to be much use. On the basis of her experience of him so far, that seemed a pretty safe assumption.

Now then, she reassured herself, don't let's go all to pieces. Kiss'll be along in a moment, he'll switch this blasted thing off and we can all go home. My wish is his command, after all. And, she remembered, it was his bloody gadget that got her into this mess in the first place.

Having nothing better to do, she reflected for a while on that. Of all the stupid, careless things to do, she mused, leaving something like that lying about. She looked at the device, which was sitting smugly on the top edge of the carpet. Perfectly reasonable to assume that it was a book. It looked exactly like a book: pages, spine, covers, the works. What sort of an idiot leaves something like that lying around, just begging innocent passers-by to pick it up and leave it on carpets?

Not, she added quickly, that she didn't worship the ground he stood on (or, to be accurate, more usually hovered about six inches over); but that was either here nor there. Being absolutely adorable and gorgeous is no excuse for rank carelessness. She'd have a word or two to say to him when he finally condescended to show up.

Yes, and where in blazes was he, anyway? Genies, she felt sure, were capable of moving from A to B at the speed of light; and here she had been, for what seemed like hours and hours, stuck on top of a fast-moving flying tapestry over a desert. She'd have expected prompter service from the electricity board.

'Grrng,' said Justin.

It was, as far as she could remember, the most sensible thing he'd said since she'd met him. She turned round, smiled, and said, 'It's all right.'

Justin blinked and lifted his head. 'The shop,' he said. 'Uncle.'

'Everything's under control,' Jane said, as reassuringly as she could. 'One of your carpets took off, with us on it, and I think we're over a desert somewhere, but my genie'll be along in a minute and he'll take us home. So long as you don't look down . . .'

Justin, of course, looked down.

'AAAAAAAAGH!' he observed.

'Well, quite,' Jane said, 'my sentiments exactly, but there's no need to worry, honestly. You see, it's a magic carpet.'

'A ma –'

'Or at least,' Jane amended, 'it is now. I put a book on it, you see.' She turned up the smile a notch or so. 'I expect we'll all have a jolly good laugh about this as soon as we get back home again.'

'Your *genie?*'

'That's right,' Jane replied. 'No, don't back away, you'll fall off the edge.' The carpet wobbled vertiginously as Justin converted his shuffle backwards into a lunge forward. 'There now, you just lie still and everything will be –'

'Put me down,' Justin said, with a degree of urgency in his voice. 'Put me down put me down put me *down!*'

The carpet juddered slightly.

'Your wish is my command, O Master.'

Suddenly the world was at thirty degrees to itself, and Jane felt herself slide forward. The book, also; it flopped over and was just about to plummet over the side when Jane, stretching full length, managed to catch it. She wasn't sure she understood any of this at all, but it seemed reasonable to assume that if the book fell off the carpet would lose its supernatural capacity and turn back into an ordinary domestic floor covering. And ordinary domestic floor coverings as a rule don't fly.

'Ah,' said Jane. 'You again.'

'Mistress.'

'Look, I know we got off on rather the wrong foot back there in the shop,' said Jane, 'but I think it might be a good idea if we made friends and started again, don't you? Before we fly into a cliff or something.'

'There are no cliffs on our projected route, Mistress.'

'Look . . . Look, forget about cliffs. Just don't take any orders from him, all right? He's not quite . . .'

'Mistress?'

Justin was staring at her, wondering perhaps why she
was talking to the carpet. Could he even hear the bloody
thing, she wondered. 'All right,' she whispered, 'you do it
your way. Only for pity's sake, do look where you're
going.'

'Our fully automated guidance systems,' replied the
carpet huffily, 'are computer-aligned to ensure a comfortable, incident-free itinerary. State-of-the-art LCD displays
let you know at a glance –'

'LOOK OUT!'

The carpet swerved viciously, just in time to avoid the
ground. Jane opened her eyes again, to see the carpet
apparently on top of her. And then, after a heart-stopping
roll, underneath her again.

'Sorry. I mean, systems error.'

'Shut up and fly.'

'To hear is to –'

There was an uncomfortable twentieth of a second.

'Don't,' Jane hissed, 'even consider it.'

'But you said –'

'I'm warning you.'

'Your express wish,' said the carpet, flustered, 'was that
I ignore anything you tell me to do. Your wish is my command. Oh, *sugar*!'

The carpet hurtled groundwards. Jane shrieked.

'Mistress?'

'Don't worry about it,' Jane said quickly. 'When I said
look out, you ignored me. Very sensibly, however, and
quite independently of anything I may have coincidentally
said, you decided not to crash and took appropriate action.
Got that?'

'Yes, Mistress,' said the carpet gratefully. 'Although
strictly speaking I should ignore that too.'

'You just try it.'

'Sorry?' said the carpet. 'Did you just say something?'

The carpet levelled, and Jane patted a hem. 'That's the spirit,' she said.

'Excuse me.'

Jane looked round and saw Justin, clinging with both hands, his face buried in the pile. 'Yes?'

'I don't want to be a nuisance,' Justin mumbled through the fabric, 'but do you think we can go home soon? Uncle will be . . .'

Jane wasn't listening. She was looking, unbelievably, down.

'Gosh,' she said.

Underneath the carpet was the sea – a huge, flat blue spread, extending from horizon to horizon. Jane considered for a moment.

'If we jump,' she said aloud, 'we'll land in the sea.'.

'I can't swim.'

'I can. And you've got to learn sometime.'

'Why?'

'Because . . .' Jane searched her mind for a reason. 'Because it'd be very handy if, for instance, you were sitting on a carpet miles above the surface of the sea and somebody were to push you off.'

'Who'd do a thing like ?'

'That depends,' Jane said firmly, 'on how co-operative you were being at the time.'

You would think, reflected Asaf bitterly, that after escaping from a small glass bottle, escaping from a ship ought to be a piece of cake. Not a bit of it.

Wearily, he lifted the cask of nails above his head and tried once again to use it to smash through the battened hatch. By dint of ferocious effort he managed to deal a featherweight biff to the objective before his arms crumpled and the cask fell heavily onto the deck at his feet, narrowly missing his toes.

For one thing, his thoughts continued, although I didn't know it at the time, I probably had help getting out of the bottle – well, I definitely got help – whereas they want to keep me on the ship. Also, he couldn't help reflecting, the bottle hadn't been surrounded by deep, cold water; and the ship was.

That is, he parenthesised, always supposing I actually *am* on a ship and this isn't all some sort of tiresome metaphysical illusion, the sort of thing Captain Kirk and the crew of the *Enterprise* seem to spend most of their working hours in. The bottle now, that probably was an illusion. Bloody small illusion; and they might have had the decency to illude the ink out first. Then again, he was beginning to feel that whoever was doing all this to him had a fairly limited imagination.

Sinbad the Sailor, for crying out loud. Whatever next. Puss in Boots?

Now then. Be practical. This is a ship. I am a fisherman, I'm at home on ships. Ships hold no terrors for me . . .

Not strictly accurate. During his fishing career the only ship he'd ever been on was his father's vessel, and that wasn't a ship, it was a boat. Definitely a boat. And as between that boat and this ship, there were many significant differences. There wasn't any water coming up through the floor, for example; likewise, you could scratch your ear on board this thing without the risk of hitting someone in the eye with your elbow.

However, he rationalised, all sea-going craft have certain things in common. Not that he could think of anything offhand that might be of use to him; but he felt sure he was somewhere on the right lines, pursuing this . . .

The ship moved.

More than that; it seemed to jump up in the air. Leaping about is, of course, something that ships as a rule simply don't do (ask any fisherman); but since this was probably an illusion anyway, Asaf wasn't prepared to be dogmatic about anything. Right now, he'd have settled for an illusion that wasn't showering articles of displaced cargo on his head.

He was just struggling out from under a crate of some description which had fallen on him, soliloquising eloquently as he did so, when he noticed the light. A lovely great shaft of sunlight, slanting in through a now open hatch.

Told you, he muttered to himself. Told you it'd be a piece of cake.

'Now then,' Jane said, treading water, 'the first thing I'd like you to do is kick with your feet.'

'Aaaaaaagh!'

'It's all right, I've got hold of your neck, you can't – oh, bother.' She kicked hard and managed to get Justin's chin clear of the water. 'Now if you'd have done what I told you –'

'Help!' Justin screamed. 'Help help help heblublublublub . . .'

'You're not trying, are you?' Jane said wearily. 'Look, it's really very simple, any child can do it. You just paddle with your feet, and let your body sort of float . . .'

Jane suddenly realised that she was in shadow, and glanced upwards. There, directly over her head, was the carpet.

'Your wish,' it said politely, 'is my command.'

Jane scowled. 'I thought I'd told you to clear off,' she said.

'I wasn't,' the carpet replied, 'talking to you.'

'What? Oh. Oh you mean him.'

'*Help!*'

'Yes,' said the carpet. 'His wish, my command. So if you'd just shift over a bit, I can –'

'What about me?'

'What about you?'

Jane spluttered as a wave flipped a cupful of salt water into her open mouth. 'You've changed your tune a bit, haven't you?' she observed. 'Not long ago it was all "Our state-of-the-art microcircuitry, designed to make life easy for you".'

'That was different,' the carpet replied severely. 'I was in user-friendly mode then. Now I can please myself.'

'Charming.'

'You're welcome. Now, are you going to shift so that I can rescue my client, or are we going to hang about here all day chatting?'

'You're just going to ignore me, then?'

The carpet shrugged; that is to say, it undulated from its front hem backwards. 'That's what you told me to do, remember? Do you people understand the concept of consistency?'

'Help help *he*glugluglug . . .'

Jane bit her tongue. 'Tell you what I'll do,' she said. 'I'll let you rescue him if you agree to rescue me too. Now you can't say fairer than that, can you?'

The carpet hovered for a moment, thinking.

'I also,' Jane added, as casually as she could, 'happen to know a Force Twelve genie, and I was thinking, if he got hold of one of those carpet-beater things, you know, the ones shaped like a tennis racket . . .'

'All right then, all aboard that's coming aboard. I can take you as far as the ship.'

'Ship? What ship?' Then Jane remembered. 'Oh,' she said. 'That ship.'

That ship. The quaint old-fashioned one with the big square sails which they ought by rights to have crashed straight down on top of, if it hadn't somehow moved a hundred yards sideways at the very last moment. She'd forgotten all about it.

'Well?'

'That,' Jane said, 'will be just fine.'

CHAPTER ELEVEN

The reason why Kiss hadn't shown up yet was that he'd bumped into an old friend.

'Why the hell,' said Philly Nine, picking himself up off a bank of low cloud, 'don't you look where you're damn well . . . oh, it's you.'

'Hello there,' Kiss replied. 'How's you?'

'Oh, mustn't grumble. And you?'

'Persevering. Keeping busy?'

'Mooching about, you know. Nothing terribly exciting, but enough to keep me off the streets.'

'Ah, well. Is that a war I can see starting away down there?'

Philly turned and peered over his shoulder through the thin layer of cumulo-nimbus. 'Where?' he asked.

'Sort of south-east. Look, you see that mountain range to your immediate right? Well, follow that down till you meet the river, and . . .'

'Got it,' Philly said. 'Gosh, yes, it does look a bit like a war, doesn't it? Tanks and planes and things.'

Kiss gave him a long, hard look. 'One of yours, Philly?' he asked quietly.

'Gosh, what is it today, Thursday . . . Oh, *that* war. Yes. well, I may have had something to do with it.'

'You and your obsessive modesty.'

Philly shrugged. Far below, in the vast deserts of Mesopotamia, fleets of armoured personnel carriers speeding across the dunes threw up clouds of dust that blotted out the sun. 'It's only a little war,' Philly said.

'Small but perfectly formed?'

'One likes to keep one's hand in.'

Kiss frowned. 'Like I said, Philly, you're too modest. Why do you do it exactly?'

'Why do I do what?'

'Start wars. I mean, is there some sort of annual award for the best war, like the Oscars or whatever? First of all I'd like to thank my megalomaniac fascist dictator, that sort of thing?'

Philly smiled, a little sadly. 'It's what I do,' he replied.

'You're very good at it. Have they started shooting yet?'

Philly glanced at his watch and shook his head. 'Two abortive peace initiatives to go yet,' he answered. 'Give it another couple of hours, we might be in business. Things are so damn slow these days.'

Kiss fingered his chin thoughtfully. 'This war,' he said. 'Going to lead to anything, is it?'

'I do my best,' Philly replied. 'If you don't do your best, why bother to do anything at all?'

'I see. So it might be the start of something, well, big?'

'Fingers crossed.'

'Civilisation as we know it? Goodbye, Planet Earth?'

Philly smiled. 'Great oaks and little acorns, old son,' he said cheerfully. 'You never know.'

'Fine.' Kiss took a step forward. 'I hate to have to say this, but –'

'But you can't allow it?' Philly grinned at him. 'If I were you, I'd consider all aspects of the matter rather than relying on a snap judgement.'

'All aspects of global thermonuclear war are easily considered, Philly, and I don't hold with them. Cut it out, now.'

'Think,' Philly replied. 'Supposing the world is destroyed, right?'

'With you so far.'

'Well.' Philly Nine folded his arms. 'In that case, there's no way you'd have to marry that girl. Off the hook, you'd be, and absolutely nothing anybody could do about it. Just consider that for a moment, will you?'

There was a long moment of silence.

'Now you'll tell me,' Philly went on, 'that I'm contemplating something of a hammer-and-nut situation here. On the other hand, I can think of one hell of a lot of married men who'd say this was a classic case of omelettes and eggs. No disrespect intended, Kiss, old son, and I'm sure she's a charming girl, but when you actually stop and think it through . . .'

Kiss froze, his lips parted to speak in contradiction. Deep inside him, in the cubbyhole in his soul where his true identity lived (knee-deep in washing up and dirty laundry, overflowing ashtrays and discarded styrofoam pizza trays) a little voice piped up and said, *You know, he's got a point there, over.*

Balls, replied the rest of him. This is the temptation of the foul fiend. Rule One, don't listen to foul fiends. Any pillock knows that, over.

Yes, but think about it, will you? Not having to stop being a genie. To thine own self be true. Love means not being allowed to take your socks off in the living room. You would do well to consider all the pertinent aspects of the matter before committing yourself to any course of action, over.

Bugger off, over.

Yes, well, don't say I didn't warn you. Over and out.

'I hear what you say,' Kiss said, 'But no thanks, all the same. I reckon that if I can't sort out my domestic problems without conniving at Armageddon it'd be a pretty poor show – and besides, I live here. And you know what a drag it is finding somewhere decent to live these days. Carbon-based life forms don't grow on trees, you know.'

'Suit yourself, then,' Philly replied, and hit him with a thunderbolt.

'G'day.'

Asaf spun on his heel, missed his footing on the wet deck and sprawled against the mast, barking his shin.

'You again,' he snapped. 'I thought I'd seen the last of you.'

The Dragon King, hovering in a cloud of purple smoke, looked offended. 'Lighten up, cobber,' he replied. 'I'm a dragon, remember? And dragons don't bludge on their mates. She'll be right, you'll see.'

'What the hell are you talking about, you insufferable reptile?'

'Look, mate.' The Dragon King contracted his formidable eyebrows, until he looked for all the world like a bejewelled privet hedge. 'No offence, but I reckon I've had about enough of your whingeing for one adventure, thank you very much.' He nodded towards the sky. 'That sheila,' he continued. 'She's on her way.'

Asaf blinked. 'The rich one?' he asked.

The King nodded. 'Too right,' he replied. 'In fact, she

should be along any minute now. So let's have a bit less of the complaints, right?'

'Right.' Asaf frowned. 'You're sure about that?' he queried. 'I mean, we are in the middle of the sea. I don't really see where she's going to . . .'

WHOOSH.

The carpet zagged down like a turbocharged pigeon, braked in mid-air and hovered. God knows how it managed it, but it somehow gave the impression that it had an invisible meter, and that it was running.

Jane opened her eyes. If the truth be told, she wasn't one hundred per cent taken with what she saw.

She appeared to have come to rest half-way through a dragon; in fact she was wearing the bloody thing round her neck, like a horse collar.

Now that, she said to herself, really is uncalled for. God knows, I've tried to be reasonable throughout this whole nightmarish business, nobody can say I haven't given it my best shot, but this really is . . .

The dragon was floating about ten feet above the deck of the ship; as was the carpet, which appeared to have come to rest half in and half out of the dragon's right shoulder. Seen close to, the dragon looked as solid as a Welsh fullback, but Jane couldn't feel anything there. Probably, she decided, just as well.

The dragon's head pivoted slowly on its long, elegant neck and turned towards her.

'G'day,' it said. 'Asaf, this is Jane. Jane, Asaf.'

Jane glanced down and saw that there was indeed a human being on the deck of the ship – a youngish man with a mop of black hair and a prominent nose, wearing a

green anorak. He seemed to be staring at her in, well, disbelief.

'You're joking,' he said.

The dragon appeared disconcerted at this. 'No, mate,
straight up. Get stuck in.' It winked a round blue eye.

'No way,' the man said angrily. 'If you think I've come all
this way . . .'

'Don't you come the raw prawn with me, mate,' the
dragon replied irritably. 'Jeez, what's a bloke got to do
before you're satisfied?' He scowled, and mouthed the
words Loads of money . . . The man shook his head.

'Money,' he said firmly, 'isn't everything. Look, is there
some sort of ombudsman I can take this up with, because –'

'Excuse me,' said Jane.

'Ombudsman!' growled the dragon. 'You take the
flamin' biscuit, you do. When I think of some of the stringy
old dogs –'

Yes, but just look, will you? There's absolutely no way –'
'Excuse me.'

'Scheherezade,' continued the dragon, 'had a face on
her that'd curdle milk. You don't know when you're well-
off, mate.'

'I am definitely going to complain to *someone* and when
I've finished with you, you'll be lucky to get a job swimming round and round in a small glass bowl –'

'Excuse me,' said Jane, 'but I think your ship is sinking.'

'You keep out of this,' snapped Asaf. 'Now then, I don't
propose wasting any more breath on you. I shall be seeking
legal advice on this, and –'

'Stone the crows, mate, she's right. Hey, there's water
coming up through the –'

'Don't change the subject. My brother happens to be an
accountant and I reckon we're looking at breach of

contract, breach of statutory duty, trespass to the person and a bloody great claim in respect of pain, suffering, inconvenience, loss of earnings . . .'

'Bugger me, she's about to split. You want to get out of there quick, I'm telling you . . .'

'. . . false imprisonment, failure to report an accident, fraud, dangerous flying . . .'

'Look . . .'

The ship sank.

Funny, the way some ships just go under all of a sudden. Others hang around for days, leaning over on one side and allowing the survivors plenty of time to choose their eight gramophone records from the ship's library. This one, however, just went glop! and fell through the surface of the water like a lead weight.

Sinbad the Sailor watched her go down from the comfort of the one lifeboat, and shrugged. On the one hand she had been his ship, in which he had crossed all the oceans of the world, and inevitably a part of his soul went down with her. On the other hand, he had just renewed his insurance.

The cramped living quarters, he thought. The smell of stale bilgewater. The rats. The ship's biscuits, some of which were hard enough to polish diamonds with. The crew.

As he watched the last few bubbles rise and fade, therefore, his feelings were mixed. About 40 per cent happiness, and the remaining 60 per cent pure unalloyed pleasure.

Kiss picked himself up off the clouds and snarled.

To every cloud, the wiseacres say, a silver lining. Be that as it may; this one, as far as Kiss could judge, was lined with big lumpy chunks of rock, half-bricks and the like. In his list of My All-Time Favourite Things To Land On, it didn't score highly compared with, say, feather mattresses or trampoline cushions. It was also soggy and full of water vapour.

All in all he was working up a pretty good head of aggression. And the healthiest way to vent off the perfectly natural and wholesome aggression which lies buried in all of us is, of course, to thump somebody. Ask any psychiatrist.

Fortunately, he didn't have far to look for someone to thump. Not far, and upwards.

Philly Nine looked down nervously. There was something about Kiss's demeanour, and the way the cloud he was lying on was turning into fizzing steam, that made him feel uncomfortable and uncertain about his immediate future. He decided to try diplomacy.

'Now then,' he said pleasantly, 'you don't want to be late for your date, do you?'

'Yes.'

'But think,' Philly reasoned, 'of that sweet little girl of yours, counting every second before you come swooping down to rescue her. Think of the grateful smile on her face, the words of praise, the –'

'Are we thinking of the same person?'

'What about your honour as a genie? Her wish is your command, remember.'

'When I catch you,' Kiss replied calmly, 'I'm going to rip your lungs out.'

'If you catch me,' Philly replied, and fled.

'Excuse me,' said Jane.

Asaf glanced up from the piece of driftwood he was clinging to and frowned. 'What?' he said.

'I said excuse me.'

The sea, fishermen say, is a cruel playfellow. Actually they tend to express themselves in earthier, more basic terms, but that's the gist of it. For his part, Asaf had never really come to terms with the being-surrounded-on-all-sides-by-water aspect of fishing, despite his best endeavours, and consequently wasn't really in the mood to make new friends. His tone, therefore, was abrupt.

'Piss off,' he said.

'Be like that,' Jane replied equably. 'All I was going to say was, if you wanted a lift to dry land, I can take you as far as the coast. Probably,' she added, for she was a realist.

Asaf glowered up at the carpet, hovering about three feet over the waves. 'I don't believe in you,' he growled. 'Go away.'

'Don't believe in me?'

'You heard me. You're some sort of fatuous mythical practical joke, like everything else that's been happening to me lately. On the other hand, I do believe in this piece of driftwood. It's not much, but right now it's all I've got. Sling your hook.'

'HELP!' observed Justin.

Asaf lifted his head; suddenly, he was interested. By force of circumstance he was rapidly becoming attuned to the finer nuances of adventures, and it occurred to him that not many false visions of magic carpets have shit-scared young men clinging to them yelling 'HELP!' A nice touch, he had to admit. Either that, or it wasn't a mirage after all.

'Your friend,' he said.

Jane looked round. 'Oh, him,' she said. 'Yes?'

'Is he real?'

'I think so.'

'Ask him.'

Jane shrugged. 'Excuse me,' she said.

'HELP!'

'Yes, but are you real? I mean, do you exist? Only the gentleman down there in the water . . .'

'HELP HELP HELP!'

Jane nodded and turned back again. 'I would take that as a Yes,' she said.

'I see.' A small wave partially dislodged Asaf's grip on the driftwood and he floundered for a moment. 'That puts rather a different complexion on it, don't you think?'

'Sorry?'

'I wasn't,' Asaf replied, 'talking to you.'

'Oh.'

The Dragon King, who had drifted back into existence a few inches above the wave-tops, wiped his mouth on the back of his paw and nodded. 'Too right, mate,' he said. 'Sorry, forgetting me manners. You fancy a cold one?'

'Not now.' Asaf gave him a cold stare. 'Look, for once be straight with me. Are those two for real?'

'You bet your life.'

'That,' Asaf replied, 'is what I'm rather hoping I won't have to do. '

'Yes,' said the King, 'they're real. And by the way,' he added in a whisper, 'that's her.'

'We'll discuss that later. Now, how do I get on that thing without it tipping over?'

'She'll be right mate, no worries. Just take a jump at it, and . . .'

Splash.

'Thanks,' said Asaf.

'That's all right,' Jane replied, preoccupied. She was wondering how the hell she'd managed to get the carpet to swoop low over where Asaf had landed in the water and scoop him up with its front hem. Pretty snazzy rug-handling, by any standards. And she couldn't remember what it was that she'd done.

Asaf cleared his throat diffidently. 'You said something,' he mumbled, 'about dry land.'

'Yes.'

'Well, if it wouldn't be too much trouble . . .'

'It'd be a pleasure,' Jane replied. 'Any dry land in particular?'

Like a blue crack in the firmament, a long streak of lightning snaked its way across the sky and earthed itself savagely in Kiss's neck, hurling him seven miles through the air. There was a loathsome smell of singed flesh.

Thirty-fifteen.

Roaring with pain and fury, Kiss reached up into the air and grabbed a handful of cloud. As soon as it touched his hand the water vapour froze, until the genie was clutching the hardest, most fearsome snowball in history. He whirled round three times and let fly. On the other side of the horizon, hidden from sight by the curvature of the earth, someone howled.

Thirty-all.

'You as well?' Jane said.

Asaf was about to express surprise, but thought better of it. Think about it logically, he told himself. Perfectly normal seeming young woman and wimp, floating about on carpet above the Indian Ocean. Reasonable to assume that they were in the same sort of fix as he was.

'Me as well,' he replied. 'I've got this confounded bloody nuisance of a Dragon King who's giving me three wishes.'

'I've got a genie,' Jane said, making it sound like some sort of horrible illness. 'Wretched, isn't it?'

'Absolutely. My name's Asaf, by the way?'

'Jane. Pleased to meet you.'

Asaf settled himself rather more comfortably on the carpet. 'There I was,' he said, 'minding my own business . . .'

'I was about to kill myself, when this Thing jumped out of a bottle . . .'

'. . . Dragged me half-way across the bloody continent . . .'

'. . . His wish was my command, he said.'

'Really? Mine keeps saying that.'

Jane nodded. 'I think they all do. Not that it means anything.'

'Quite the opposite, in my experience,' Asaf agreed. 'So how long have you had yours?'

Jane frowned. 'I'm not quite sure,' she said, 'but it feels like absolutely for ever.'

Asaf shuddered. 'I know the feeling. And they're so damned smug about it, too.'

'Mine was supposed to rescue me,' Jane said, with a glint of anger in her voice. 'The one time I actually asked him to do something useful, and where is he?'

'To hear is to obey, I don't think,' Asaf agreed. 'Just who the hell do they think they are, anyway?'

Jane glanced at him sideways. A fellow sufferer, she thought. Nice to know I'm not the only one.

'So yours has been mucking you about, has he?' she asked.

'Don't ask.'

'We could start a victims' support group.'

Asaf thought for a moment. 'Pretty limited membership,' he said.

'Well, there's you, me and him for a start.'

'Him? Oh yes, him.'

Jane looked round at Justin, who had folded a corner of the carpet over his head and was lying very still. 'Are you all right in there?' she asked.

'Help,' Justin replied. 'I want to go home.'

'I think he's eligible for membership,' Asaf said. 'How did he get involved?'

'From what I can gather, it's his uncle's carpet.'

'Ah.' Asaf wrinkled his brow. 'Sorcerer's apprentice, you mean?'

Jane shrugged. 'I think he was just minding the store.'

'Typical.'

The mountain hung in the air for a moment, 800 feet above the ground. Then it fell.

For a fraction of a second before it hit the ground, there was a shrill scream of agony and rage. Then silence, except for the sound of Philly Nine brushing granite dust off his sleeves.

Deuce.

The dust settled. Birds began to sing again. The inhabitants of the nearby village poked their heads out of their windows, wondering why there was now a mountain in the middle of what had previously been a flat alluvial plain.

And then there was a faint humming sound a long way under the surface of the earth. It could conceivably have been a high-speed drill, or someone digging extremely fast with his bare hands.

Kiss broke through the surface like a missile launched from a submarine and soared into the air, spitting out boulders as he went. As he passed the mountain's peak, he stuck out a hand and grabbed. The mountain lifted.

'Look, grandad,' said a child in the village. 'You can see it from the window. A great big mountain, just like I said.'

Grandad, woken from his afternoon nap and not best pleased, rubbed his eyes and looked blearily through the window. 'Where?' he asked.

'Oh,' said the child. 'It was there a minute ago.'

'Hello, Bruce,' said one of Saheed's regulars. 'I thought you'd be out looking after your customer.'

The Dragon King of the South-East sneered into his glass. 'Got fed up with the whingeing little blighter and left him to get on with it,' he replied. 'I've done my bit. If the stupid bloody wowser can't find his own way to the happy ending from there, he doesn't deserve it. Fancy another?'

'Why not?'

'Mind you,' continued the King, clamping his offside rear talon firmly around the brass rail, 'I won't say it was easy. Took some doing, though I say so meself.'

'I bet.'

'There comes a time, mind,' the King went on, 'when a bloke's just got to turn round and walk away. You carry on spoon-feeding these bludgers and the next thing you know, you can't call your life your own.'

'Wretched, isn't it?'

The King nodded. 'Anyway,' he said, 'there we go. And it wasn't all crook, 'cos I was able to do a mate a favour along the way.'

'You don't say.'

The King grinned and nodded. 'Yeah. That sheila that Kiss was having so much strife with. Reckon I've offloaded her on me mark. Two birds with one stone, eh?'

'Clever.'

The King looked contentedly at the side elevation of his

glass. 'Reckon so,' he said. 'Reckon he owes me a couple of cool ones next time he's in.'

'You reckon?'

'Yup.'

Advantage –

The voice hesitated. Being an ethereal spirit, with no real existence within any conventionally recognised dimension, it had no hands with which to turn the pages of the book of rules, and it couldn't quite remember the precise wording of Rule 74. A tricky one, in any event. A grey area.

In the red corner: let your mind's eye drift to a barren plateau in the very centre of the desperately bleak Nullarbor Plain, to where a huge basalt outcrop has suddenly appeared from nowhere. While the seismologists stare at each other in blank amazement, and the cartographers draw lots to see whose turn it is to go flogging out there to draw pictures of the bloody thing, a relatively tiny form whimpers and struggles directly underneath it, pinned to the deck like a butterfly to a board. That's Kiss.

In the blue corner: the equally godforsaken north-east corner of Iceland has suddenly sprouted a new and exceptionally virulent volcano, which is pumping out red-hot lava with the frantic enthusiasm of a Japanese factory on the Emperor's birthday. Up to his neck in the lava outflow is Philly Nine.

Advantage –

Excuse me . . .

YES?

Is it possible to have a draw?

SORRY?

A draw. Like, when both sides are hopelessly stalemated and it's obvious nobody's going to win. Is that allowed?

I DON'T KNOW, replied God. I'D HAVE TO LOOK THAT ONE UP.

Could you? Only I think the sooner I give a decision, the happier they'll be. It can't be much fun for either of them.

HAVE YOU TRIED TOSSING A COIN?

The voice hesitated. On the one hand, what the big guy says, goes. On the other hand, there's such a thing as professional integrity: being able to face your reflection in the shaving mirror each morning, although of course in the voice's case that was pretty much a non-starter anyway.

Actually, if you don't mind, I'd rather we went for an outright decision on this one. Or at least a draw. If that's all right by . . .

YOU'RE THE EXPERT. DO WHATEVER YOU THINK IS RIGHT.

OK, fine. In that case . . .

JUST GIVE ME FIVE MINUTES, IF IT'S ALL THE SAME TO YOU.

Sure. Um – why?

BECAUSE IF I'M QUICK I SHOULD BE ABLE TO GET PRETTY GOOD ODDS ON A DRAW. THANKS FOR THE TIP.

Question, thought the voice. What sort of an idiot would take a bet from God? Answer: an idiot who didn't want to spend the next five million years at the bottom of the burning fiery pit, I suppose.

Um . . . You're welcome.

Like a bat out of hell following a spurious short-cut, the carpet raced through the sky over Stoke-on-Trent.

'Where can I drop you?' Jane asked.

Asaf looked down. The hell with it, he said to himself; I've come this far.

'Wherever suits you,' he replied. 'I'm pretty much at a loose end at the moment, as it happens.'

'Ah,' said Jane. She bit her lip. 'Fancy a quick coffee?' she added.

Asaf considered the position and decided that, all things considered, what he hated doing most of all in all the world was deep-sea fishing.

'Sure,' he said. 'Why not?'

'What do you mean,' Kiss demanded angrily, 'she's gone?'

Sinbad the Sailor shrugged. 'I suppose she got tired of hanging about waiting for you to rescue her,' he replied. 'I mean, no disrespect, but you did take your time.'

'I got held up,' replied the genie stiffly, 'saving the world.'

'It can be a right bummer, saving the world,' Sinbad said, 'especially when nobody thanks you for it.'

'You're telling me.' The genie sighed, letting his eyes drift out across the broad ocean. 'There are times, you know, when I really wish I was still in the bottle.'

'Well, quite. You know where you are in a bottle.'

'Peaceful.'

'Nobody to tell you what to do.'

'No telephone.'

Sinbad hesitated for a moment. 'Not your old-fashioned style bottles, anyway. No Jehovah's Witnesses.'

'And no bloody women,' Kiss added. 'Here, you haven't got such a things as a bottle handy, have you?'

'Afraid not.' He blinked and looked away. 'Sorry to change the subject,' he went on, 'but about this saving the world thing you were doing.'

'Yes?'

Sinbad paused again, wondering how to put it tactfully. 'If you've saved the world,' he said cautiously, 'presumably it doesn't matter that the whole of this sea is swarming with bloody great big nuclear submarines.'

Kiss wrinkled his brow. 'Oh, shit,' he said, 'the war. I knew I'd forgotten something.'

At the bottom of the sea, far below the parts where the divers go, even further down than the gloomy bits where the light never reaches and you get the fish that look like three-dimensional coathangers, there is a doorway. And a car park. And a garden, with benches and lanterns. And a big sign, with fairy lights:

THE LOCKER

it says; and in smaller letters:

David Rutherford Jones,
Licensed to sell wines, beers, spirits and tobacco for consumption on or off the premises

and then, going back to the bigger type:

LINERS WELCOME

The eponymous Mr Jones was quietly changing the barrels in the cellar, reflecting on the recession and how improved computerised weather forecasting was eating the heart out of the deep-sea licensed victualling business, when he became aware of an unfamiliar noise far away overhead. He stopped what he was doing and listened.

A humming noise. Like possibly engines.

A grin fastened itself to his peculiar, barnacle-encrusted face, and he ran up the cellar steps to the bar.

'Sharon,' he yelled, 'Yvonne! Defrost the pizzas! We've got customers.'

Women, Kiss reflected as he soared Exocet-like through the darkening sky. I have had it up to here with bloody women.

And not just women, he conceded, as he swerved to avoid an airliner. Human beings generally. In fact, I'm sick to the back teeth of all the damned creepy-crawlies that hang around this poxy little dimension. Come to think of it, for two pins I'd wash my hands of the whole lot of them.

The thought had scarcely crossed his mind when he became aware of something tiny and sharp, folded into the palm of his left hand. Inspection confirmed his instinctive guess. Two pins . . .

'Shove it, Philly,' he snarled at the clouds above him. 'I'll deal with you later.'

Ah yes, the war.

No names, no pack drill. We will call the opposing parties A and B.

Army A had occupied all Europe as far east as the Bosphorus, only to find themselves stuck in a traffic jam that reached from Tashkent to Samarkand. Army B had swept up through Central Asia in the time-honoured manner and had broken through as far as Baghdad before realising they'd forgotten to switch off the gas and having to go back.

Fleet A and Fleet B were both pottering about in the Mediterranean, trying to keep out of each other's way until somebody had the courtesy to tell them what the hell was going on, exactly.

Air Force A was scrambled, on red alert, absolutely set

and ready to go as soon as the rain subsided a bit. Air Force B was engaged in frantic high-level negotiations with the finance company which had repossessed its entire complement of fighter-bombers.

In other words, stalemate; at least as far as the conventional forces were concerned. Not, of course, that conventional forces count for very much these days –

In the bunker, with half a mile of rock and concrete between themselves and the surface, the Strategic First Strike Command Units of both sides were locked in a desperate struggle with forces which, they now realised, were rather beyond their abilities to manipulate

'Look,' said the controller at SFSCU/A, 'it's perfectly simple. A child could understand it. If you press this one here, while at the same time pressing this one and this one . . .'

The senior technical officer shook his head. 'That's the automatic failsafe, you idiot,' he said. 'I reckon it's got to be the little red button here. If you look at the manual . . .'

'All right, let's look at the goddamn manual. *Congratulations! You have just purchased –*'

'I think you can skip that bit. '

'Right, here we are. *To commence War press START followed by C and E. The word READY? should then appear on the monitor –*'

'There isn't a button marked START, for God's sake.'

'It must be the little red one here –'

'No, look at the diagram, that's just for when you want to set the timer . . .'

'Actually, I think that's only for the Model 2693. What *we've* got is the Model 8537 . . .'

'You could try giving it a bloody good thump. You'd be amazed how often that works.'

'How about ringing the other side? They'd probably know how to make the bloody thing work.'

'Well, actually, I think they've got the Model 9317, which has a double-disk RAM drive, so . . .'

'I wonder what this button here does?'

WHOOSH!

Lightning, they say, never strikes twice. This was true before the introduction of free collective bargaining. Nowadays, lightning tends to work to rule.

Cupid, however, is resigned to the fact that he often has to do the job on the same target several times. This doesn't bother him particularly, since he charges the same fee for a repeat and there's usually less preparatory work the second time around. In the final analysis, so long as he shoots somebody and gets paid for it, he isn't too bothered.

A long, silver-tipped round slid frictionlessly into the chamber of the Steyr-Mannlicher, and he folded down the bolt with the heel of his right hand. He centred the crosshairs of the sight, breathed fully in and half out, and . . .

Her again. God knows, he thought dispassionately as he squeezed the trigger, what they all see in her. Probably, he reflected as he ejected the spent case and chambered the next round, why they need me.

He raised the rifle and took aim. Deep breath in –

'G'day, mate. How's she coming?'

Startled, Cupid jerked involuntarily and the shot went high. A portrait of Abraham Lincoln, which for some unaccountable reason hung over the sofa in Jane's living-room, glanced down and thought, 'Gosh . . .'

'You idiot,' Cupid hissed. 'Now look what you've made me go and do.'

'Jeez, sorry, mate,' whispered the Dragon King. 'I only stopped by to see how you were making out. Didn't mean to make you jump.'

'Shut up and stay still,' Cupid snarled. He chambered the third round and tried to recover his composure.

'Always wanted to watch a top-flight pro like yourself at work,' the King continued. 'I think it's marvellous, the way you fellers –'

Cupid forced himself to relax. 'Look,' he said, 'if you don't shut up and keep still, the next one's for you. You got that?'

Since the only female in sight was Jane, the King froze as effectively as if he'd been carved from stone. Cupid closed his eyes, counted to five, and raised the rifle to his cheek.

Deep breath in. Centre the crosshairs. Half breath out, and – steady . . .

Bang.

'SWITCH THAT BLOODY THING OFF!'

The King looked suitably mortified. 'Sorry, chum, I really am, only they make me carry this damn bleeper thing, it's in case anybody needs to call me in a –'

Cupid breathed out through his nose. 'Thanks to you,' he said, 'and a freak ricochet, the microwave is now hopelessly in love with the sink unit, which in turn is besotted with the electric kettle. I hope you're satisfied.'

'I've switched it off now. Sorry.'

'You haven't got a digital watch that bleeps, have you?'

'No.'

'Ticklish throat? Feel a sneeze coming on?'

'Nope.'

'Splendid. Now, since I happen to have one shot left. perhaps we can get on with it.'

Chamber the round. Lift the rifle. Centre the crosshairs. Deep breath in. Half breath out. Cuddle the trigger, and –

'Nice one!' exclaimed the King. 'Right up the –'

'I was aiming,' Cupid sighed, 'for the heart. But it doesn't actually matter all that much, not in the long run.'

'That's all right then,' said the King happily. 'Now, will you take a cheque?'

What Cupid didn't realise was that one of his shots – the one that nailed Abe Lincoln, for what it's worth – rebounded off the edge of the frame and ended its journey in the carpet. *The* carpet.

Carpets, especially the sentient, magical variety, are no fools. The specimen in question had been dozing quietly in front of the fire, resting after an unusually taxing day, when it became aware that someone was shooting at it. It did what any sensible item of soft furnishing would have done in the circumstances, and got the hell out of there.

For the record, it still had Justin on it. The negative Gs generated in the descent from 40,000 feet had knocked him out cold, and Jane and Asaf had been too wrapped up in each other to pay him any mind.

The carpet, then, zoomed off into the empyrean and kept going. As it flew, however, it found itself reflecting on its life so far, with particular reference to its solitary nature and the lack, to date, of sympathetic female companionship.

(We use the term female in this context for convenience only. Technically, what the carpet was longing for was companionship of the inverse-weft variety; but for all practical purposes, it amounts to the same thing.)

It was just beginning to feel sad and moody when something whizzed past its hem, leaving behind a blurred memory of a sleek cylindrical body and a tantalising whiff of perfume.

'Cor!' thought the carpet. 'That was a bit of all right.'

It did a double flip and followed the object's vapour trail.

What it was in fact following was an M43 ballistic missile with a 700-megaton warhead, launched after half an hour of frantic debate in the B-team bunker when the assistant scientific officer rested his coffee cup on the instrument panel.

The carpet sped on through the sky, established visual contact and fell hopelessly in love.

'Hi,' it said, swooping down parallel with the missile and shooting its hems. 'My name's Vince. What's a gorgeous metallic tube like you doing in a place like this?'

The missile made no reply, but there was a twinkling of LED readouts on its console that might be equated with a fluttering of eyelashes.

'Like the tail-fins,' the carpet persevered. 'They suit you.'

The rocket slowed down, ever so slightly. A product of ninth-generation missile technology, the M43 is officially classed as semi-intelligent, presumably so that it feels at home in the company of military personnel. It's intelligent enough, at least, to recognise a basic chat-up line when it hears one. When you're an instrument of mass destruction, however, you don't tend to get many offers. Public executioners, lawyers and people who work for the Revenue tend to have the same problem.

The rocket bleeped.

'Say,' said the carpet, as suavely as a piece of knotted

wool can manage. 'How about you and me grabbing a bite to eat somewhere? I happen to know this little place . . .'

The other nuclear missile, fired by Side A, shot over Kiss's head, neatly parting his hair with its slipstream.

Pausing only to use profane language, the genie hurried after it, caught it with his left hand and disarmed it with his right. He did so deftly, confidently and with the minimum of fuss, because the very worst epitaph the Planet Earth could wish for would be 'Butterfingers!'

Having programmed it to carry on into a harmless orbit, he sat down on a sunbeam and recovered from the retrospective shakes. A sense of humour was one thing but this time, in his opinion, Philly Nine had gone too far.

'Want to make something of it?' Philly demanded, materialising directly over his left shoulder.

'Oh, come on,' Kiss replied wearily. 'We've been here already, remember? Beating the shit out of each other with mountains, chasing about across the sky, all that crap. I'm really not in the mood.'

'Tough,' replied Philly Nine. 'Because I am.'

Kiss frowned. 'You are, are you?'

Philly nodded. 'Because,' he amplified, 'you're starting to get on my nerves. Nothing personal, you understand.'

With exaggerated effort, Kiss stood up. 'Has it occurred to you,' he said, 'that since we're both Force Twelve genies, there's absolutely no way either of us can beat the other?'

'Yes. I don't care.'

'You don't?'

'No.'

Kiss scratched his head. 'You wouldn't prefer to settle this by reference to some sort of game of chance, thereby introducing a potentially decisive random element?'

'Not really. Two reasons. One, you'd cheat. Two, I want to bash your head in, and drawing lots would deprive me of the opportunity.'

'I wouldn't cheat. '

'Says you.'

'When have I ever cheated at anything?'

'Hah! Can you spare half an hour?'

'I resent that.'

'You were supposed to.'

The light bulb beloved of cartoonists lit up in Kiss's head. 'It's no good trying to provoke me,' he said. 'Sticks and stones may break my bones . . .'

'Good, I'd like to try that.'

'You know what your trouble is, Philly? You're unregenerate.'

'That's probably the nicest thing anybody's ever said about me.'

'It needn't be drawing lots, you know. We could try cutting a pack of cards, or throwing dice. Or snakes and ladders. Best of five games. Wouldn't that be more fun than scurrying round trying to nut each other with granite outcrops?'

'No.'

'Sure?'

'Positive.'

Kiss grinned. Blessed, he'd read on the back of a cornflake packet once, are the peacemakers, and he'd done his best. That, he felt, qualified him for the moral high ground; and the nice thing about the moral high ground was being able to chuck rocks off it on to the heads of the unregenerate bastards down below.

'In that case . . .' he said.

★

'You're not going to believe it,' muttered a technician in Bunker A, 'but one of our missiles has gone off.'

'What?' The Controller swivelled round in his chair. 'And I missed it?'

'Presumably. You can't remember pressing anything marked FIRE, can you?'

'Just my bloody luck,' grumbled the Controller. 'We start World War Three, and I miss it. That's a real bummer, that is. It would have been something to tell my grandchildr . . .'

He tailed off as the inherent contradiction hit him. The other inhabitants of the bunker shrugged.

'Never mind,' said the wireless operator. 'We've got plenty more where that one came from. Now, try and remember what it was that you did, exactly.'

'More wine,' breathed the carpet heavily. 'Go on, let's finish off the bottle.'

The atomic bomb shook its warhead. Nuclear weapons aren't accustomed to intoxicating liquor, and it was starting to see double. All it wanted right now was to go home and sleep it off.

'A brandy, then? Coffee? We could go back to my place and have a coffee.'

It occurred to the bomb that if it showed up back at the silo with its exhaust residues smelling of drink, it would have some explaining to do. It nodded, and lurched against the table for support. Suddenly it didn't feel too well.

'Waiter,' said the carpet, 'the bill, please.'

The waiter was there instantly, assuring the carpet that this one was on the house, and could it please take its friend somewhere else quickly, because . . .

The bomb hiccuped. Geiger counters on three continents danced a tarantella. The waiter threw himself under the table and started to pray.

Cautiously, the bomb got up and promptly fell over. Fortunately for generations of cartographers yet unborn, it fell into the carpet, which lifted gracefully into the air and flew away.

Justin chose that particular moment to wake up.

He opened his eyes. Next to him, he noticed, there was a big black cylindrical thing, like a cross between a sea-lion and a fire extinguisher. There was stencilled writing on its side: THIS WAY UP and HANDLE LIKE EGGS and DANGER! The casing was warm.

The shop! He remembered about the shop. He glanced at his watch; Uncle would be home by now, and he'd be absolutely livid. He had to get back to the shop as quickly as possible.

'Excuse me,' he said.

The carpet frowned at him; that is to say, some of the more intricate woven motifs seemed to crowd more closely together.

'Not now,' it hissed. 'Can't you see I've got company?'

'We've got to get back to the shop,' Julian said. 'Now.'

'That's all right,' the carpet replied in a loud whisper. 'That's exactly where we're going right now. Be there in about five minutes.'

Julian breathed a sigh of relief and snuggled up closer to the warm flank of the ICBM, which had started to tick.

'That's all right, then,' he said.

CHAPTER TWELVE

Never in the history of superhuman conflict have two Force Twelves ever tried to fight it out to the bitter end.

Generally speaking, they've got more sense. They know that it's next best thing to impossible – nothing is definitively impossible in an infinite Universe, but there's such a thing as so nearly completely impossible that even an insurance company would bet on it never happening – for either participant to kill the other, or even put him out of action for more than a minute or so. It's a simple fact that, in this dimension at least, genies can't be killed or injured, although they can of course do a hell of a lot of damage to anything else in the vicinity. Think of a bar-room brawl in a John Wayne Western, and you get the general idea.

They can; however, feel pain; and so they do their level best to avoid fighting each other in any meaningful sense. A direct hit from a mountain hurts, and is best avoided for that very reason.

The battle between Kiss and Philly Nine was, therefore, something rather special; and when word reached the back bar of Saheed's, there was a sudden and undignified scramble for the exit. This was going to be something to see.

'GO ON, YOU BLOODY FAIRY, RIP HIS EARS OFF!' shouted a small Force Two, who had climbed a lamppost to get a better view.

'Which one are you cheering for?' asked a colleague. The Force Two shrugged.

'Both of them,' he replied. 'I mean, it's bound to be a draw, so . . . COME ON, PUT THE BOOT IN! STOP FARTING AROUND AND BREAK SOMETHING!'

'But if neither of them's going to win, what's the point in cheering at all?'

The Force Two shrugged. 'It's a poor heart that never rejoices,' he replied. 'CALL THAT A RABBIT PUNCH? MY GRANNY HITS HARDER THAN THAT.'

'As I recall,' commented the other genie, 'your granny was Cyclone Mavis. Wasn't she the one that pulled that coral island off Sumatra right up by the roots and plonked it down again fifty miles to the east?'

'So I'm being factually correct. Where's the harm in that?'

Half an hour later, the two combatants paused for a breather.

'It's only a small point,' panted Kiss, picking shards of splintered basalt out of his knees, 'but what are we going to do about paying for the breakages?'

'Split 'em between us, I suppose,' Philly replied, lifting a small Alp off his ankle and discarding it. 'That's probably simpler than trying to keep tabs as we go along.'

'Fair enough,' Kiss replied. 'Otherwise it'd be like trying to work out the bill in a restaurant. You know, who had what, I thought it was you that ordered the extra nan bread, that sort of thing.'

'Ready for some more?'

'Yeah, go on.'

'Or do you want to phone whatsername? She's probably wondering where you've got to.'

Kiss shook his head. 'More important things to do,' he replied wearily. 'I mean, she can't expect me to phone her if I'm fighting for my life against overwhelmingly superior demonic forces, can she?'

Philly rubbed his nose. 'I dunno,' he said. 'You know her better than I do.'

Kiss thought about it. 'Maybe I'd better just give her a quick call,' he said. 'I mean, she may have started dinner or something.'

Philly put his head on one side and gave Kiss a thoughtful look. 'That'd take priority over mortal combat with the prince of darkness, would it?'

'You haven't had much to do with women, I can tell.'

'I suffer from that disadvantage, yes.'

'Don't go away, I'll be right back.'

Easier said, Kiss discovered, than done. When eventually he found a public telephone (he was in the middle of the Mojave Desert at the time) he discovered that all his loose change had shaken out of his pockets during the fight, and his phonecard was bent and wouldn't go in the slot.

Easier, he realised, given that I'm capable of travelling at the speed of light, to nip round there in person. He gathered up his component molecules and jumped –

There is a perfectly reasonable scientific explanation of how genies manage to transport themselves from one side of the earth to the other apparently instantaneously; it's something to do with trans-dimensional shift error, and it is in fact wrong. The truth is that genies have this facility simply because Mother Nature knows better than to try and argue with beings who only partially exist and who have all the malevolent persistence and susceptibility to logical argument of the average two-year-old. Let them get on with it, she says; and if they suddenly find themselves stuck in a rift between opposing realities, then ha bloody ha.

– and, before the electrical impulses that made up the thought had finished trudging along his central nervous system, he had arrived. He felt in his pocket for his key.

And stopped. And sniffed. Fee-fi-fo-fum, he muttered under his breath, I smell the blood of a Near Easterner somehow connected with fish. Or rather the socks. And the armpits. Not to mention the residual whiff of haddock which is so hard to lose, all the deodorants of Arabia notwithstanding.

Funny, he thought.

He opened the door and strolled in; to find Jane, his betrothed, apparently joined at the lips with a skinny dark-haired bloke in a salt-stained reefer jacket and grubby trainers.

It's at times like this that instinct takes over. An instinct is, by its very nature, impulsive. Instinct doesn't stand on one foot in the doorway thinking, 'Hey, this really lets me off the hook, you know?' before discreetly tiptoeing away to see if it's too late to get the deposit back on the wedding cake. Instinct jumps in, boot raised.

Three seconds or so later, therefore, Asaf was lying in a confused huddle in the corner of the room wondering how he had got there and why his ribs hurt so much. Jane was standing up, gesticulating eloquently with her right hand while trying to do her blouse up with her left; and Kiss was leaning on the arm of the sofa, listening to what Jane had to say and thinking, Shit, I think I've broken a bone in my toe.

And just what precisely, Jane was asking, did he think he was playing at? And what made him think he had the right –?

'Hold on,' Kiss interrupted. 'That bloke there. Are you trying to tell me he was *supposed* to be doing that?'

It wasn't a way of putting it that Jane had foreseen, and for a moment it checked the eloquence of her reproaches. 'Yes,' she said. 'And –'

'This, not to put too fine a point on it, *mortal* –'

'Here,' broke in Asaf, 'who are you calling a mortal?'

'You.'

Asaf fingered his ribs tentatively. 'Fair enough,' he said. 'Hey, are you another one?'

'Another what?'

'Another bloody genie. Because if you are . . .'

WHOOSH!

'G'day,' said the Dragon King, materialising next to the standard lamp and knocking over a coffee table. 'Perhaps it'd be a good idea if I explained . . .'

Somebody threw a glass decanter at him. Who it actually was we shall probably never know, but there were three obvious suspects. He ducked, looked round to see where the decanter had met the wall, and winced at the sight of good whisky gone to waste.

'Not you *again*,' Asaf said. 'Not on top of everything else. Haven't you people got anything better to do?'

Kiss froze. 'That reminds me,' he mumbled.

'Shut up!'

Asaf, Kiss and the Dragon King all stopped talking at the same moment. 'Thank you,' said Jane. 'Now listen.'

They listened.

'First,' she went on, 'you with the scales and the beer-belly. I don't know who you are or what you're doing in my front room, but if you leave now and never come back I might just be generous and pretend you were never here in the first place.'

'Well, cheerio then,' said the King; and vanished.

'Next,' Jane continued, turning to Kiss, 'you. I have had enough of you. First you clutter up my flat with lethal gadgets that fly people half-way across the world; then, when I send for you to come and rescue me, you're nowhere to be seen; and finally you come bursting in here like the bloody Customs and Excise and beat up my friends. This is your idea of hearing and obeying, is it?'

'But he was –'

'In fact,' Jane ground on, 'I'm beginning to get just a little bit sick of the sight of you. In fact, I wish you were back in your damned bottle, where you bel –'

WHOOSH.

'Excuse me,' said Asaf nervously, extracting himself painfully from the corner of the room, 'but what the hell happened to him?'

'Who cares?' Jane replied. 'Left in a huff, I expect. Now, where were we?'

HELP!

HELP!

HELP! LET ME OUT, YOU IDIOTS, I'VE GOT TO SAVE THE SODDING PLANET!

In an aspirin bottle, no one can hear you scream.

This business with bottles. It has perplexed some of the finest minds in the Universe, almost as much as the peren-nial enigma of why the cue ball sometimes screws back off the pack for no good reason and goes straight down the centre left-hand pocket.

Some say that bottles are the gateways to other universes (generally small, cramped universes with convex sides, smelling of stale retsina), and that a genie imprisoned in a bottle has stepped sideways into an alternative reality. It's all, they say, part and parcel of the wish syndrome, whereby each wish calls into being an alternative reality where the wish comes true, however improbable this may be.

Another school of thought holds that a genie embottled is only a tiny part of the totality of that genie. Genies exist simultaneously in innumerable different dimensions, and by bottling one all you do is shove most of him out of this dimension and into the others, leaving only a token presence behind.

The French say that bottling genies is something that should be done at the *château* of origin, or not at all.

The major petro-chemicals manufacturers say that putting genies in bottles is fine by them, but wouldn't it make more sense to use plastic non-returnable bottles with screw tops, which means you can keep them longer before they go flat?

Genies take the view that getting put in bottles is just one of those things that happens to a guy at some stage in his life, and if it wasn't that it'd be something else, and there are probably worse small, confined spaces to pass the odd millennium in, for instance coffins, so why worry? This goes some way to explain why genies have never ruled the Universe.

Force Twelve genies, however, are a cut above the general production-line standard, and therefore can't afford to be quite so laid back all the time. Some of them have responsibilities – planets to save, and so forth. This means that from time to time they find it hard to be philosophical about the cork going back in. Some Force Twelves, indeed the elite few who have more moral fibre than a square yard of coconut matting, even resent it.

'Women!' said Kiss aloud. The word echoed round inside the bottle and died away.

Never mind. If it's any consolation, when the planet gets blown up in a few minutes I expect the force of the blast will shatter the bottle and you'll be away clear. It's an odd thing, but in any significant explosion, glass is usually one of the first things to go.

Kiss looked up, and then down, and then from side to side. 'Do I know you?' he asked.

I'm the duty GA. I'm having a busy shift, actually, because I was talking to another guy in more or less the same fix as you not that long ago.

'Go away.'

Beg pardon?

'I said go away. I've got enough to put up with as it is.'

There was a pause.

Why is everybody so blasted hostile? I'm only doing my job.

'Take the day off. Go and spend some quality time with the family.'

It's a pity you feel you have to adopt that attitude, you know, because the GA service really does have a great deal to offer to people in your position. If you weren't so cramped in there, I could give you some leaflets which –

'No leaflets. Piss off.'

It's this crisis of confidence which is bringing the profession to its knees. Me, I blame franchising. Under the old system –

'I said –'

Under the old system, you see, I could have brought gentle subliminal influences to bear on that mouse . . .

'Piss . . . What mouse?'

The mouse presently scampering along the mantelpiece on which your fragile glass bottle is resting, three feet above a tiled fireplace. Like I was saying, I could have subtly suggested to that mouse that it might find it a good idea to run along this mantelpiece terribly fast, regardless of the risk of accidentally brushing up against your bottle and dislodging it.

'Ah.'

Whereupon the bottle would have fallen to the floor and smashed, and . . .

'Yes, thanks,' Kiss said. 'I think I was there way before you. Now, about this mouse . . .'

Small for its species, sort of greyish-brown, whiskers, answers to the name of Keek. Unusually gullible, too, even for a mouse. The faintest suggestion that there's a small crumb of mozzarella just to the side of your bottle, and all your problems would have been over. Pity, really.

'Gosh.'

Yes. As it is, the voice continued sadly, *all I can do is offer moral support and axioms of an uplifting nature designed to help you to come to terms with the harsh reality of your situation without too much culture shock. For instance, 'It's a long road that has no turning.' 'It's always darkest before the dawn.' Actually, that's not quite true, because generally speaking just before dawn you get that rather attractive pastel-pink light just above the horizon, which always puts me in mind . . .*

'Excuse me . . .'

. . . of a strawberry milk-shake. Sorry, did you say something?

'The mouse. Now where is it?'

About eight inches to your immediate left. It seems to be eating a microscopic crumb of some sort, probably toasted crumpet.

'I wonder if you might possibly . . .'

No, it's gone again. Something must have disturbed it. That's a real shame, in my opinion. A good mouse is hard to find, I always think.

'Gone?'

'Fraid so, yes. Now then, where were we? Had I got on to 'if at first you don't succeed' yet?

Kiss slumped against the side of the bottle. True, in even the most spacious bottle slumping room is generally at a premium, but he managed quite nicely under the circumstances.

'Listen to me,' he said. 'Any minute now, the air is going to be blue with fucking great big nuclear bombs. Unless I do something about it, these bombs are going to blow up the planet. Now, can you do anything to help?'

That does put rather a different complexion on it, the voice admitted.

'I rather thought it might.'

Quite so. In that case, I think either, 'You can't make omelettes', or 'It's no use crying over spilt milk', would be rather more appropriate. Or possibly even, 'It is better to have loved and lost than . . .'

This, Kiss reflected, is what comes of getting involved. If I was back in the bar right now, along with the rest of the lads, none of this would matter. True the planet would go pop, but so what, there's plenty of planets. Let's have another cup of coffee and another piece of pie. But as it is . . .

'I think I'll pass on all of those, thank you. So unless you've got anything actually positive to suggest . . .'

Try singing.

'Right, that does it,' Kiss snarled. 'Unless you're out of my head in a five seconds flat, I'm going to bash my brains out against the side of the bottle. One-Mississippi. Two-Mississippi. Three-Mississippi.'

He paused and listened. Nothing. Good.

Won't be long now. Time, ladies and gentlemen, please. Haven't you got afterlives to go to?

He waited.

Try singing. Try *singing*, for God's sake. Yes, of course! Now why the hell hadn't he thought of that for himself?

The bomb had fallen asleep.

Just, grumbled the carpet to itself, my bloody rotten luck. First time I've been on a promise in God knows how long, and she goes and falls asleep on me. Marvellous.

The carpet flew on regardless. It was, after all, a gentle carpet. Take her back to the shop, let her sleep it off there.

As if things weren't bad enough, it noticed as it flew, she snores. Or rather, she ticks loudly in her sleep. Amounts to the same thing, in the long run.

Question. Since it's such a painfully obvious solution, why hasn't anybody thought of doing it before?

Answer. Because genies are generally too bone-idle and pig-ignorant to try anything. Put a genie in a bottle and he'll stay there till somebody lets him out. After all, they have all the time in the world.

Kiss cleared his throat, swallowed, and sang.

'Do-rey-mi-fah-so-la-tee-*do*!'

Nothing. He tried again, an octave higher. Then an octave higher still. That was enough to make his eyes water and his teeth ache.

Excelsior.

'*Do-rey-mi-fah-so-la-tee-DO!*'

He paused to massage his throat and jaw. Come on,

Kiss, if some fat lady in a blond wig and a hat with horns on can do it, so can you. Higher still.

'DO-REY-MI-FAH-SO-LA-TEE-DO!'

He broke off, coughing like a terminal tuberculosis case and wiped his eyes on his sleeve. Reckon I'm just not cut out for this sort of work, he told himself.

Indeed. Very apt.

'*DO-REY-MI-FAH . . .*'

Success; and just in time, too. Another note higher and he'd have been in no fit state to save green shield stamps, let alone the world.

Subjected to a harmonic stress equivalent to seven fat elephants jumping up and down on it, the bottle flew into pieces. Kiss tumbled out, cutting himself to the bone on broken glass as he did so, hit the tiled floor of the fireplace, swore horribly and scrambled to his feet; all in one nice, fluid movement. All around him windows were falling out, decanters were splitting, light bulbs were popping. The mouse was curled up in a ball in the coal-scuttle, its paws jammed in its ears. Only the picture of Abraham Lincoln seemed not to mind, probably because its mind was on other things.

'Now then,' Kiss said aloud, as he aimed himself at the window. 'That was the easy bit.'

He jumped.

The sky, when he got there, was a bit like the Rome rush-hour. Nose to tail intercontinental ballistic missiles, all hopelessly snarled up, their proximity-actuated guidance systems completely up the pictures, all at a complete stand-still; honking, swearing, waggling their fins in unconcealed fury, trying to nudge past on the inside, ignoring the traf-fic-light beacons helpfully shot up into orbit by Side A's mission control centre, and generally not improving the situation. Kiss crossed from Europe to Asia by walking across the backs of bottleneck bombs.

There is no need, Kiss realised, to save the world. Just sit back and let old Captain Balls-Up do it for you.

Nevertheless he was here now, he might as well make himself useful.

He rolled up his sleeves, materialised a whistle and a pair of white gloves, took his stand on a small wisp of cloud a few feet over the seething mass of bombs, and started to direct the traffic out of orbit in the general direction of Ursa Major. It took him about half an hour, during the course of which his ankles were lightly singed by overheating rocket motors and a Class 93 ran over his foot. Apart from that, it was a doddle.

That left just the one bomb, presently sleeping it off on a mattress improvised out of priceless Turkestan rugs in Justin's uncle's shop. Kiss didn't know about that one, of course. Nobody can know everything.

Right, he said to himself, done that. That was more of the easy bit. It was time he got on with the job in hand.

'So there you are,' said Philly Nine, whooshing into existence a foot or so above his head. 'Pretty long phone call, if you ask me.'

'I got held up,' Kiss admitted, 'but I'm back now.'

'Good. Shall we get on with it, then?'

'Only too pleased. Oh, by the way, I got rid of all those missiles.'

Philly looked at him. 'Oh,' he said. 'You did, did you?'

Kiss nodded. 'They were cluttering the place up a bit,' he said, 'so I shooed them away. Hope you don't mind.'

'Plenty more where those came from, I expect,' Philly replied. 'Production lines probably working double time right this very minute. Honestly, Kiss old thing, you are naïve.'

In his time, which was roughly coeval with the Universe, Kiss had been called a wide selection of things, but this was a new one. 'You think so?' he said.

Philly nodded. 'You honestly think you can save the world by getting rid of a few bombs? Dream on, chum, dream on. All they'll do is build some more. Idiots they may be, but what they lack in basic survival instinct they make up for in dogged persistence. And of course,' he added, 'I shall be there to offer whatever assistance they require.'

'Will you now?'

'I confidently predict that I will be.'

'We'll see about that.'

Leonardo da Vinci, had he been there, would have wept.

So would Shakespeare, and Goethe, and Tolstoy. And Beethoven and Mozart and Jelly Roll Morton, and Sophocles and Flaubert and Rubens and Molière and Wordsworth and Brahms and Petrarch and Diaghilev and Jane Austen and Tintoretto and probably Virgil, Buddy Holly and Sir Arthur Conan Doyle.

All these people laboured, in their separate ways, to entertain and amuse the human race. But what the human race really wants to watch, in the final analysis, is a good, dirty fight.

Ernest Hemingway, on the other hand, would have loved it. Sir Thomas Malory would have been taking notes. Homer would have been sitting somewhere on a balcony wearing a straw hat and saying, 'Ah yes, but you should have seen Hercules back in '86, he had a copybook cover drive off the back foot that would have put these young whippersnappers to shame.' Chaucer would have missed the fight itself, since he'd have been tearing round the deserted streets trying to find an open betting shop.

It was a good fight, by any standards. Most fighters are inhibited by the fear that, unless they exercise at least some degree of circumspection, they may end up getting permanently damaged. Since Kiss and Philly Nine had no such worries, they were able to give their full attention to trying to beat the crap out of the opposing party.

Genies, for whom poetry inevitably begins with the words 'There was a young lady of . . .', and in whose world-view painting is something involving scaffolding, long brushes, ladders and being indentured to someone whose windowsills need doing, are connoisseurs of the fight beautiful, and as far as they're concerned the Marquess of Queensberry is a pub in Camden Passage. For the first time ever, Saheed's was deserted, except for a small knot of spectators peering out through the skylight.

'Strewth,' observed the Dragon King of the South-East. 'I never thought that was even possible.'

'Well, now you know,' replied a Force Six who had money invested. 'Wouldn't like to try it myself, mind.'

'You could do yourself an injury,' agreed a Force Three, who had the binoculars.

'Anybody know,' asked a small Force Two, whose view was obstructed by about ten larger genies and a few cardboard boxes, 'what the fight is about, exactly?'

There was a thoughtful silence.

'Good and evil?' suggested the Six.

'All violence is a symptom of the underlying malaise in carbon-based society,' said the Three.

'They do that,' agreed the Two. 'They lurk in among the rubber trees and jump out on people with big curly knives.'

'You what?'

'And in Sumatra and parts of Burma, too. I think it's something to do with the heat.'

A large chunk of rock, part of a mountain that had been pressed into service as a knuckleduster, hurtled down from the sky. The genies ducked.

'It's all right,' said the Three, looking up. 'Landed on Daras. Are they allowed to use weapons? I thought this was strictly a bare-knuckle job.'

'You want to go up there and remind them, be my guest.'

'Fight fair, yer rotten bludger!' shouted the Dragon King. The others looked at him.

'Yes, well,' he said, shamefaced. 'I mean, fair crack of the whip, lads. One of them is trying to save the world.'

'So?'

'Would you mind moving your bloody great elbow? You're blocking my view.'

'I think,' said a tall, thin Force Eight, 'it's something to do with a girl.'

'What is?'

'The fight. I think it's about some girl or other.'

'Surely not?'

'It's as good a reason as any. I mean, the fight's got to be about *something*. All fights are about something.'

'Oh.'

CHAPTER THIRTEEN

The fight was getting bogged down. It had, in fact, reached something of a stalemate.

'All right,' suggested Philly Nine, 'try this. You let go of my throat, and then if I simultaneously take my teeth out of your left ankle . . .'

'I don't think that'll work,' Kiss mumbled after a moment's thought. 'All that'll happen is we'll fall over.'

Philly, who was turning purple, clicked his tongue. 'Well,' he said, 'we'd better think of something, unless we want to stay locked together like this for ever and ever.'

'Agreed. The sooner the better, as far as I'm concerned.'

'How about if –?'

Whatever Philly's suggestion was, it never got a hearing; because before he could make it both genies were knocked spinning by a long-range intercontinental ballistic missile.

'Shit,' gasped Philly, who'd been winded, 'what the hell was that?'

Kiss floundered his way out of the soft cloud-bank into which he had fortuitously tumbled. 'Don't ask me,' he replied. 'It was long and metallic and –'

He broke off and ducked as a large and colourful carpet,

flapping its edges frantically like a manta ray in a hurry, shot past, calling out, 'Stop! I didn't mean it!' at the top of a voice which Kiss only heard in the back of his brain. The two genies dusted themselves off and floated level with each other.

'One of yours?' Kiss asked.

'Never seen it before in my life.'

'Well, it's solved one problem for us.'

'True. Shall we carry on, then?'

'Might as well.'

'Where were we, exactly?'

'Hmm.' Kiss stroked his chin. 'Well, as I recall, you had me in a scissor lock and were trying to bite my leg off, and I –'

'Not a scissor lock,' Philly interrupted. 'More of a Polynesian death-grip, surely?'

'No, you're wrong there. Isn't that the one where the left knee comes up under the opponent's armpit?'

'You're thinking of the Mandalay wrench.'

'No, that's the one where –'

This time the bomb hit Kiss in the small of the back, catapulting him neatly into orbit. Philly had the presence of mind to duck, only to be swatted flying by the bunch of roses the carpet was frenziedly waving. He had just recovered his balance from that when a tall, thin apprentice carpet salesman landed around his neck, jarring his spinal column and sending him spiralling towards the ground. He couldn't have been more than ten feet off the ground, and travelling at a fair pace, when he managed to break the spin and pull out of it.

He landed and shrugged off the apprentice carpet salesman, who landed in a gooseberry bush and lay still, making faint whimpering noises. Philly looked down at him.

'Are you all right?' he asked.

'Heeeeeeeeeeeeeelp!'

Philly considered for a moment. 'Yes,' he said, 'you're all right. Don't go away, now.'

'Have they gone?' Kiss asked, when they were once more face to face.

'I think so,' Philly replied cautiously. 'Can't see them, at any rate.'

'You got any idea what they're playing at?'

'Not really, no. Looks like the rug's got the hots for the bomb, if I'm any judge.'

'How can a rug be in love with a bomb?'

'Dunno. Still, one of them's colourful and flat and the other one's dull grey and round, and they do say opposites attract.'

Kiss bit his lip. 'I ought,' he said, 'to go and defuse that bomb before it does any damage.'

'It'll keep. Looks like the rug's doing a pretty good job, anyhow.'

The genies shook their heads, as if to say that they wouldn't mind fighting to the death over the destiny of the world if only the world would show a little respect.

'Right,' Philly said at last, 'back to the job in hand. What say we start again from scratch?'

Kiss raised an eyebrow. 'You sure?' he asked. 'I had you ahead on points.'

'Did you?'

'Sure.' Kiss nodded. 'I was giving you six for the head-butt, nine for the savage blow to the left temple with the giant redwood and seven for the combined half-nelson and stranglehold on the windpipe.'

'OK,' Philly replied dubiously, 'but I wasn't counting that because of the nutcracker hold you had on my right elbow at the same time.'

'I don't remember that.'

'Maybe you had other things on your mind. Anyhow, I put us more or less dead level, so . . .'

'That's very sporting of you, Philly.'

'Don't mention it.'

They drifted a little way apart, each looking for an opening. Somehow the aggro seemed to have gone out of the whole thing, and both genies started to feel just a trifle sheepish.

'This is the point,' suggested Kiss, putting the mutual feeling into words, 'where one of us should say, "This is silly, there must be a better way of settling things".'

'Doesn't that come later?'

'Could do. Or we could do it now.'

'Get it over with, you mean?'

'We could skip it if you like,' Kiss replied accommodatingly. 'After all, you're trying to destroy the planet, I'm trying to save it, so there's not all that much scope for creative bargaining. On the other hand . . .'

Something, Philly noticed, had gone in his back. He winced. 'Quite,' he said.

'I mean, it's a bit daft when you think about it.'

'Two intelligent beings . . .'

'Two supernatural beings . . .'

'And not just your average thing that goes bump in the night,' Philly added. 'I mean, Force Twelves, not many of them to the pound avoirdupois, if you get my meaning.'

'Better things to do with our time, wouldn't you say?'

'Exactly.'

Philly looked down at the world beneath him. From the vertiginous height they were presently occupying, he could see all the kingdoms of the Earth spread out before him like a giant map. Hmmm, he thought. Bloody untidy, with all those green and brown splodges and the blue stuff just slopping about anyhow. Not a straight line to be seen anywhere. On the other hand . . .

Kiss looked down at the world beneath him and thought of bottles, and all the time he'd had to spend in them over the years. No more earth, he thought, no more bottles. No more women. No more having to fetch and carry after snot-nosed mortals who happen to unscrew a cap.

'How about,' suggested Philly, picking his words carefully, 'I just destroy a bit of it?'

'Which bit had you in mind?'

'Well . . .' Philly peered down through the swirling clouds. 'How about Australia?' he said. 'I mean, nobody's going to miss Australia, are they?'

'Not immediately, certainly,' Kiss conceded. 'But it's a big place, Australia. And somebody's got to be fond of it,' he added doubtfully.

'All right, then,' said Philly. 'What would you say if I left you Queensland?'

Kiss pursed his lips. 'Don't know if that'd work, actually,' he said. 'I mean, geography's not my strong point. Could be that the other bits are holding it up or something.'

'All right then,' Philly replied. 'How about Tasmania? That's just an island, for pity's sake.'

Kiss remembered something he'd heard once. 'No man is an island,' he said sagely.

'Well, of course not,' Philly responded. 'I don't know about you, but I can count on the fingers of one hand the number of flat people with frilly edges entirely surrounded by water that I know to speak to.'

'I didn't mean it literally,' Kiss replied. 'What I was getting at is, you can't really go knocking off hundreds of thousands of people, even if they are Australians. I think it's something to do with divine justice.'

'Divine justice!' Philly sneered. 'Don't you give me divine justice. Fifty talents they fined me, and I was only doing ninety-five, top whack. And they made me blow into a little bag.'

Kiss frowned. 'I'm not saying I hold with it,' he said. 'All I'm saying is, it's there. And –'

'And what?'

Kiss shrugged. 'I'm not sure, really. Only it's probably a good idea. On balance. In the long run. I mean, I think things tend to come out in the wash, in the fullness of time.'

'I see. And because of that, you'd begrudge me Tasmania?'

'Look, Philly, if it was up to me you could have Tasmania in a paper bag with salt, vinegar and a lemon-scented napkin. But you've got to face facts. Destroying Tasmania would be . . .'

'Would be what?'

'. . . antisocial.' Kiss scooped up a handful of cloud and began picking at it. 'Not a very nice thing to do. A bit unnecessary.'

Philly sighed. 'All right,' he said. 'Tell you what I'll do. Scrub round Tasmania, how'd it be if I just destroyed a bit nobody wanted at all? Some desert or something? Now nobody could object to that, could they?'

Kiss scented a chink in the argument. 'In that case,' he said quickly, 'why bother at all? I mean, if nobody's going to mind? Like, if it's a desert anyway, surely you'd be wasting your time. And how could anyone tell the difference once you'd finished?'

Philly frowned. 'I would,' he replied. 'It's a matter of

principle, really. Something I promised myself a long time ago.'

Kiss stared. 'A matter of *principle*?' he repeated incredulously.

'Yeah. What's so funny about that?'

'Genies can't have principles. If they could, what'd be the point of having humans?'

'To be honest with you, Kiss, old mate,' Philly said, with a slow smile, 'I never could see the point in having humans. That's why I decided, a long time ago, to do something about it.'

There was a long silence.

'Well,' said Kiss at last, 'I suppose we'd better carry on with the fight, then.'

'Reckon so.'

'Pity, though.'

'It always is,' said Philly, and hit him with a railway station.

'Sorry to interrupt,' said Asaf, 'but there's something going on.'

'Hmm?'

The interruption, Asaf admitted to himself, was not entirely unwelcome, because he was starting to lose the sensation in his lower lip. He untangled himself from Jane, got up and walked over to the window.

'Not to worry,' he said, having looked. 'It's only two genies fighting.'

Jane scowled and started to button up her blouse. 'They're starting,' she said, 'to get on my nerves.'

'Who?'

'The genies,' Jane replied. 'I think it's time I did something about it.'

The word 'You?' froze on Asaf's lips. True, his experience of female facial expressions was limited, since where he came from they tended to go around with curtains over their faces (and no bad thing too, he remembered, calling to mind some of the blind dates his brothers had fixed him up with in times gone by. Actually, the blind ones hadn't been so bad; it was some of the deaf-mutes who made him cringe with embarrassment, even now); there is, however, a basic defence mechanism built into the male psyche that reacts quickly to flashing eyes and deep frowns, and sends men of all races and creeds dashing out of the house in search of an all-night florist.

'Absolutely,' he said, therefore. 'If you don't mind, though, I'll just –'

'Get your coat, it's turned cold.'

It occurred to Asaf, as he scuttled after Jane down the stairs, that he still had an indentured genie of his own on the payroll, with at least one ungranted wish still in reserve. 'I wish,' he muttered to himself, 'she wouldn't go dashing off getting us both involved in things.'

Sorry, mate. This time you're on your own. G'day.

'In that case,' he said aloud, 'you'd better give us a lift.'

Jane stopped at the foot of the staircase, looking impatient. 'Come on,' she said. 'We haven't got all day, you know.'

'Sorry. I was just arranging us some transport.'

'Transport?'

'G'day.'

The Dragon King materialised, filling the stairwell and substantial parts of the up and down stairs as well. Huge, Asaf noted, magnificent, brutal and stuck. Probably better off with a taxi.

'Good idea,' said Jane briskly. 'You.'

The Dragon King winced. 'G'day, miss. What can I do you for?'

'That fight. I need to stop it now. Take us there.'

'Um.' The dragon looked at her, mentally comparing the respective risks of going within a hundred miles of a fight between two crazed Force Twelves and refusing a direct order from Jane. 'Straight away, miss,' he said. 'No worries.'

They scrambled on to his back. A moment later, the stairway was empty.

A long time ago, when God created the world –

A feature common to all building sites is the presence of many, many long pieces of timber with nails stuck in them. Nobody knows where they come from, or what they're designed to achieve. What they actually do is wait until the grass has grown up round them and then spring out on passing builders, preferably when they're carrying precarious loads of fragile objects. When the building is completed they are sometimes ritually burned, but as often as not they stay, forgotten and untouched.

It was just such a piece of timber, undisturbed since the Fourth Day (on which He dug out the footings and poured the concrete) that Philly Nine was using to batter Kiss about the head. Given the origin of the thing, it was not surprising that the bent, rusty nails were in fact made from extruded amethyst. This didn't stop them hurting.

Kiss wasn't taking this lying down. More sort of crouched on one knee, cleverly managing to ward off most of the blows from his body with his head, and groping with his left hand for a large chunk of rock (Malta) he'd noticed out of the corner of his eye a while back.

'Hey, you!'

Philly paused, club upraised, and looked round.

'You talking to me, chum?' he said to the Dragon King of the South-East, who was hovering sheepishly over his left shoulder.

The King shook his head vigorously. In Wisconsin, they thought the result was snow.

'Didn't say a word, mate, straight up,' he said, smiling meekly.

'I thought you just spoke to me.'

'Nah. Try the sheila between me shoulder-blades.'

'What she . . . oh, her. What does she want?'

'*Hey!*'

Philly glanced down, lowering the club a degree or so. 'Do I know you?' he asked. 'Not that it matters much, but if we are acquainted, I shall send a wreath to your funeral. That's,' he added, 'always assuming they find enough of you to fill a coffin. Being realistic, though, a doggy bag might be more suitable.'

'Oh, shut up,' Jane replied. 'And put down that silly stick before you put someone's eye out.'

Philly frowned and lashed out with the club. What with residual particles of self-doubt and guilt, combined with extreme irritation at not being able to make much impression on Kiss's head with one of the nastiest blunt instruments in the cosmos, he had just about reached the stopper of his bottle (genies don't have tethers), with the result that his sense of chivalry was down there with the Polly Peck shares. Fortunately, the King's nose came between Jane and the plank.

'Missed,' Jane called out. 'You want to saw that thing in half.'

'Do I? Why's that?'

'Then you'd have two short planks. Company for you.'

'Very droll.' He tried the reverse sweep, but this time the

King ducked and suffered no more than a slight scratch to his right ear from one of the nails. With a sigh, Philly swept round on his heel and belted Kiss again, knocking him back off his feet.

'Missed again,' said Jane smugly.

'Third time lucky.' Philly swung the plank, feinting high and then changing tack in mid-blow. The resulting impact missed Asaf's head by a few thousandths of an inch and found its mark on the King's back.

'Fair go, mate,' the King squealed. 'What harm have I ever done you?'

'Call it pre-emptive revenge,' Philly replied. 'In the meantime, could you try and hold still? It's harder than it looks, swatting something that small.'

Jane bristled and turned to Asaf, giving him what used to be known as an old-fashioned look.

'Well?' she said. 'Don't just sit there. Do something.'

The bomb was confused.

It was dizzy, sick, miles and miles off-course and beginning to see spots in front if its eyes. Furthermore, it had the feeling that running away from an amorous carpet wasn't really the sort of thing self-respecting atomic bombs are supposed to do.

It slowed down and activated its rear-view sensors. The carpet was nowhere to be seen.

Bombs are nothing if not logical. This goes with the territory. A fat lot of good an emotional, sensitive, caring bomb would be to anybody. Probably cry all over its own fuse.

The logical argument was this:

* I do not want to be chased about any more by this frigging carpet.

* If I go off, everything within five hundred miles will
be turned into little grey wisps of curly ash.

* Including the carpet.

It sniggered, and armed itself.

'What,' Asaf asked, 'did you have in mind?'

By way of reply, Jane just looked at him.

'Right,' he said, 'fine. Just leave it to me.'

Kiss, meanwhile, had dragged himself back up to cloud
level, having collected on the way a massive charge of static
electricity which someone had left lying about in the bottom
of a cloud he'd passed through. Observing that Philly was
preoccupied with trying to brain the Dragon King with his
oversize telegraph pole, he took the opportunity to connect
his new plaything up to the inside of Philly's knee.

The results were quite entertaining.

Doctors, he recalled, as he watched Philly soar steadily
upwards, use a similar technique to test their patients'
reflexes. Nothing wrong with Philly's reflexes, as far as he
could make out.

He waited where he was for a moment or so, on the
offchance that gravity might have something to say about
Philly's movements. He counted to twelve. Probably safe to
assume that gravity knew when to leave well alone.

'Hello,' he said.

'Where the hell were you?' Jane replied.

'I –' He checked himself. Oh woman, he murmured to
himself, in our hours of ease uncertain, coy and hard to
please; when pain and anguish rack the brow, an even
greater nuisance thou. 'Sorry,' he said.

'And you just sat there,' Jane continued, 'while that great
oaf tried to hit me.'

'Yes.'

'And you call yourself a genie!'

'I tend to exaggerate.'

'Aren't you going after him?'

'No.'

'You mean you're afraid.'

'Naturally. I do also have a nuclear missile to see to, but that's only a flimsy excuse. Really it's because I'm a coward.'

'You haven't heard the last of this.'

'I should think not. Excuse me. 'Bye.'

'I haven't finished with you yet!' Jane called after him, as he dwindled away into a tiny dot on the horizon. 'Honestly!' she summarised.

Beside her, Asaf made a vague oh-well-never-mind noise. 'Any how,' he said, 'that's sorted that out. Can we go home now, please?'

Jane looked around and noticed, as if for the first time, that she was sitting between the wings of a dragon thousands of feet above the surface of the earth. 'Gosh, yes,' she said. 'Let's do that right away.'

'I was hoping you'd say that.'

'Well, go on, then. It's your stupid dragon.'

'Sorry, yes. Now then, I wish –'

As he said the words, he chanced to look up; and the terms of his wish changed slightly. In its amended form, which he didn't actually vocalise, it consisted of, *I wish the other genie, the one who got hit by the electric shock and jumped up miles into the air, wasn't coming back.*

Unfortunately, as the Dragon King hastened to point out to him, that one was asking a bit too much.

'Here, bomb,' Kiss called. 'Here, nice bomb. Bommy bommybommybommy.'

No reply. And no sign of the poxy thing, as far as the eye (even his) could see. How do you attract bombs, exactly? Bomb-nip? Rattle an empty uranium canister?

'Oo vewwy naughty bomb,' He experimented. 'Oo come here *this minute*, or else no . . .'

He paused. What do bombs like best?

He squirmed. No prizes for guessing what bombs like best.

'If you don't come here *this very minute*,' he essayed, 'the nasty Peace Movement will get you.'

Of course, he rationalised as he swung low over San Francisco, it might just be that he was looking in the wrong place. But he didn't think so, somehow; he could smell bomb – a strong, not very pleasant smell drifting back from the possible future – and it was definitely coming from this direction.

'Come out with your fins up,' he shouted (but it turned into a whimper somewhere between his larynx and the atmosphere). 'I have this planet surrounded.'

He heard a click. It was a tiny sound, no louder than, say, a safety-catch being thumbed forward or a life-support machine being switched off. But he heard it, because it was the sound he'd been listening for.

'Now then,' he wailed, 'there's no need to take that attitude.'

Think, you fool, think. Somewhere out there is a bomb, armed and dangerous – a small, functional intelligence, probably scared and confused, trying to know what's the right thing to do.

Get real, Kiss told himself, this is a fucking *bomb* we're talking about here. Bombs aren't like that. When was the last time you heard of a three-hundred-megaton warhead being talked down off a twelfth-storey parapet by highly trained social workers?

There it was, a little high-pitched whining of artificial brainwaves, like a gnat in a sandstorm. And what was it saying?

It was saying, *Nothing personal*.

Swearing under his breath, Kiss did a back somersault that would have ripped the wings off even the latest generation of jet fighter and doubled back, head, down, in the direction of Oakland.

Thirty seconds, and counting.

'You're too late,' Jane said, arms folded, face a study in defiant satisfaciton. 'He's gone to catch the bomb, and he'll defuse it. You've –

'Did you just hear something?' Philly interrupted.

'No. What?'

'Sounded to me like a faint click.'

'That'll be Kiss,' said Jane, smugly, 'defusing the bomb.'

Nine seconds, and counting.

Mortals, who tend to think of their lives as the shortest distance between the two points Birth and Death, have a bad attitude towards Time. They accuse it of being inflexible, doctrinaire, officious. In the collective imagination of the human race, Time wears a peaked cap and carries a thick wad of parking tickets.

This is unfair. Time does, in fact, have a considerable degree of discretion. True, it rarely exercises it in favour of mortals (because of their bad attitude), but even so, most of us will have experienced moments when Time has seemed to slow down or stop altogether. The tragedy is that in those moments we're usually sailing through the air, staring at an oncoming car on our side of the road, or realising with a feeling of sick horror that the sound of key in lock means that our spouse has come home earlier than anticipated. We therefore lack the leisure and the objectivity to give Time its due.

Nine seconds and counting. Kiss, being a genie (and having done Time an enormous favour years ago in a rather shabby incident involving yogurt, rubber tubing and a goat) kept his head and called in, so to speak, his marker.

Sniff, sniff, sniff. The smell of bomb was overpowering, but still he couldn't see the bloody . . .

Gotcha! Big steel tube, leaning nonchalantly against a row of other steel tubes, which Kiss identified as liquid nitrogen canisters propped up against the wall of some factory or other. He braked sharply, leaving pale grey skidmarks on the sky, and swooped down.

The bomb saw him and flinched.

'There, there,' he said, 'it's all right, I'm not going to hurt you.'

That, replied the bomb, *must be the stupidest remark I've ever heard.*

Kiss blinked, and then realised that what he was hearing was his own brain's instantaneous translation of the subtext of the bomb's computer intelligence's extraneous drive-chatter; the equivalent of the dead-cat-dragged-over-velvet noise you get when you switch on the tape deck to full volume with a blank tape in it. Gosh, he said to himself, I'm so much cleverer than I ever realised.

'OK,' he replied, 'point taken, let's approach this from a different angle. What harm have we ever done you?'

I'm sorry?

'Us. Sentient life forms. What harm have we ever . . .?'

Let me see. You made me, for a start; that involved being hacked out of the living rock and run through heavy rollers and then heated in a blast furnace until I melted and then poured into a mould like I was jelly or something and then shoved through more rollers and then punched full of sodding great rivets and drilled full of holes with a drill that makes your dentists' drills seem like feather dusters and then packed full of horrible ticklish uranium and shoved down a long, dark tube in a submarine hundreds of feet under the sea and then shot out again, which feels like being farted out of God's arse, let me add, and a fat lot you care about my vertigo and then . . .

This, Kiss realised, is starting to get a bit counter-productive. 'Fine,' he said, 'you've got real grievances, I admit, but is this really the best way to settle them? I mean, really?'

The bomb's sensors treated him to a withering stare. *I'm a bomb, for fuck's sake, this is what I'm supposed to do. Why don't you creeps make up your damn minds?*

'Ah,' Kiss replied quickly. 'The I-was-only-obeying-orders defence. That won't wash, you know.'

So what? I'm about to be blown into my constituent atoms, right? And you're suggesting that something bad might happen to me afterwards? Grow up.

Eight seconds and counting. More like seven and four-fifths. Fortunately, Kiss's pores didn't have enough time to start sweating, or he'd have been drenched.

'How would you feel,' he asked, 'about bribery?'

There was a tiny flicker of interest in the readout patterns. *How do you mean, bribery?*

'We pay you, anything you like, if you don't blow up. How does that grab you?'

Like I said, I'm a bomb. What the hell is there that I could possibly want?

Kiss turned up the gain in his brain. 'I'm sure we could think of something,' he said. 'Anything you like, anything at all. A velvet-lined silo. Raspberry-flavoured rocket fuel. A nice little land-mine to cuddle up to in the evenings?'

What's raspberry?

'You see?' Kiss shouted, waving his arms. 'A whole Universe packed with scintillatingly thrilling sensations, and you haven't experienced any of them. You haven't *lived*. But think how different it could all be, if you'd only –'

Of course I haven't lived, I'm a bomb. And how the blazes am I supposed to experience all these wonderful sensations of yours? All I'm built to do is fly and go bang.

'We can fit you with new sensors, of course,' Kiss replied. 'Audio, visual, sensory, you name it. Just think of it. Ice cream, music, the scent of primroses after a heavy shower, the sunset over the Loire valley . . .'

I could experience all that?

'No problem. And that's just the start of it. If you'd just use your imagination, there's no end to what we could show you.'

Fuck.

Kiss blinked. 'What?' he said.

I said fuck. It'd have been really nice, I bet. Too late now, of course.

'Too late?'

Use your common sense. I'm armed and about to blow. You don't think there's anything I can do to stop it, do you?

'But –'

You honestly believe I can switch myself off? Get real. As far as bombs are concerned, free will is a lawyer's marketing gimmick. God, I wish you hadn't said all that stuff about what I could have had. You've really upset me now.

Five seconds and counting. Time was doing its best, but there are limits. At the back of his cosmic awareness,

Kiss could feel the world tapping its foot and saying, Come on, *do* something.

Do what?

Anything. Anything is better than nothing.

Nothing. Generally defined as an absence of anything, nothing is usually produced by some catastrophically traumatic event; an atomic bomb, say, going off in a confined space. Such as a galaxy.

Kiss thought, and something came. If he'd been a cartoon, a bubble with a light bulb in it would have appeared above his head.

Sugar and spice and all things nice, that's what supernatural beings are made of. Among other things; including a pretty substantial amount of pure, crude energy. Kiss had never bothered to learn the physics (he'd spent physics lessons practising simple levitation on the underwear of the girl sitting next to him) but he had an idea that what he was mostly made of was raw power. Which accounted for his being able to fly and materialise physical objects, not to mention the chronic indigestion.

And to every action, there is an equal and opposite reaction; which he had only been able to understand in terms of a very fast car hitting a very solid lamp-post.

Indeed.

The trouble was, if he used himself as the lamp-post, he was likely to get seriously bent.

Omelettes and eggs. Three seconds and counting. Yes, he screamed in his mind, the complaint of every poor fool since time began who'd suddenly found out he's been cast to play the hero, but why me? And the inevitable answer: because you're here, and there's nobody else. Because we didn't think you'd mind. You don't mind, do you?

Kiss moved.

Here, protested the bomb, *what the devil do you think you're playing at? It was bad enough with that goddamn nymphomaniac carpet . . .*

'Shut up,' Kiss replied. He wrapped his arms tight around the bomb, and closed his eyes.

No seconds, and counting.

CHAPTER FOURTEEN

I expect you're right,' said Philly Nine wearily. 'No doubt he's disarmed the bomb in the very nick of time, and all my hours of hard work gone straight down the pan. Which only leaves me,' he added, taking one step forward, 'the consoling thought of what I'm now going to do to you.'

Jane's eyebrows shot up like Wall Street after a Republican landslide. 'Me?' she snapped. 'What on earth have I got to do with it?'

'A whole lot,' Philly replied, flexing his fingers purposefully. 'If it hadn't been for you, he'd never have thought to interfere. All this is your fault.'

'Rubbish.'

'Your fault,' Philly repeated, pale with anger. 'Your god-damned meddling can't-mind-your-own-business fault. Well, you can take it from me, it's the last time you'll –'

'Excuse me,' said Asaf.

The shock stopped Philly Nine dead in his tracks. The feeling was hard to describe, but it was something along the lines of the way you'd feel if you were sitting in, say, the roughest dockside bar in San Francisco and a four-foot-six eighty-year-old missionary tottered in on a zimmer frame and offered to fight any man in the place.

'What?'

'Please,' said Asaf, standing up, 'don't talk to the lady like that. You'll upset her.'

'You *what*?'

'And if you upset her,' Asaf continued, 'you'll upset me. So please, cut it out. OK?'

The Dragon King, who had been trying to look unobtrusive to the point of virtual translucence, suddenly snapped out of existence. He rematerialised as a vague presence at the back of Asaf's mind, hammering on the door of the Instincts Section, Self-Preservation department, which appeared to be locked.

Cripes, mate, are you out of your tiny mind? This bastard'll have you for flamin' breakfast.

'I know what I'm doing,' Asaf replied. 'You go away and leave this to me.'

Don't say I didn't warn you.

Philly Nine narrowed his eyes. 'Are you serious?' he said.

'Yes.'

'*You* are threatening *me*?'

'If you choose to look at it that way, I suppose I am.'

It had been a long day, and Philly had had enough. 'You're dead,' he said softly. 'Dead and buried. Now then . . .'

And then he stopped. In fairness, he tried to back away and run for it, but somehow he couldn't. Rabbits who go foraging for food in the middle lane of a motorway often experience the same effect.

'Please . . .' he said, and then his tongue packed up, immobilised like the rest of him.

'I really don't want to do this,' Asaf said, 'but you leave me no choice.'

He was holding a bottle. To be precise, it was one of those small screw-top plastic botdes they sell fizzy drinks in nowadays. Slowly, his body language broadcasting determination and regret in equal proportions, he advanced.

Philly's tongue came back on line just before the neck of the bottle touched him. 'You can't make me get in there,' he hissed. 'Absolutely no way. There is literally no power on . . .'

'In you get.'

'I steadfastly and categorically refuse to –'

'In.'

Wildly, Philly stepped backwards and groped behind him for something to cling on to. Try as he might, he couldn't take his eyes off the neck of the bottle; it seemed to summon him.

'As you can see,' Asaf said gently, 'this is no ordinary bottle.'

'You're lying. It's just a bog standard pop bottle, and I'll be damned if I –'

Asaf's face creased in a smile that had nothing whatsoever to do with humour. He levelled the bottle as if it were a gun, and beckoned.

COME

'*Shan't!*'

COME.

'Good Lord,' Philly gibbered, both arms linked round a granite outcrop, 'you didn't honestly think I was serious about destroying the world, did you? It was just a joke, honest. I mean, why on earth would I possibly want –'

WHOOSH.

Asaf shook his head sadly, screwed on the cap and held the bottle up to the light. It was transparent plastic; but there was nothing to be seen inside the bottle except the usual few beads of condensation clinging to the sides. And they had been there before.

'Gosh,' said Jane.

With a sigh, Asaf swung his arm back and threw the bottle up into the air. There was a sudden terrifying clap of thunder, a streak of lightning that made Jane think the sky had finally come unzipped, and then nothing.

'A pity,' Asaf said. 'But there it is.'

There was a flutter of air and the Dragon King hove back into existence, hovering a few feet above the ground. He was shaking slightly, and his wings were creased.

'Stone the flaming crows,' he said. 'I never seen the like in all my . . .'

Asaf nodded to him. 'Thanks,' he said.

'You're welcome, mate, no worries. Any time.'

Jane looked from one to the other, and made a sort of feeble questioning gesture with her left hand. She couldn't think of anything to say.

'It was his bottle, you see,' Asaf said, in a matter-of-fact tone of voice. 'I guess he must have been carrying it around for years. Boy, how he must have hated himself.'

'*His* bottle . . .'

Asaf nodded. 'Fell out of his pocket or his scrip or whatever genies have, when that other genie hit him with the thunderbolt. I guessed it might come in handy, so I picked it up. It was the dragon who drew my attention to it.'

'Pleased to be of service,' mumbled the King.

'It was the way the dragon jumped up in the air and made a little screaming noise when he saw it that put me on the right lines,' Asaf continued. 'And while you two were having your slanging match, it suddenly occurred to me. Why would a genie, of all things, carry a *bottle* around with him? Particularly the sort of bottle he could never ever escape from. Shatterproof, you see. And non-biodegradable.'

Jane waited for a moment, and then said, 'Well?'

'Simple.' Asaf sat down and opened a roll of peppermints. 'Because he wanted to be put in it. Subconsciously, I guess. I mean, that ties in with all the rest of it. The wanting to destroy the world, and that stuff. What he really wanted to destroy was himself.'

Jane's mental eyebrow rose sharply. This all sounded a bit too glib, too Lesson Three, Psychology For Beginners for her liking. Any minute now and he'd start talking about sublimated urges, cries for help and traumatic potty-training in early childhood. However, she held her peace.

'Added to which,' Asaf went on, 'there's the simple logic of the thing. All those chances he had to destroy the world, and he couldn't actually do it. Bearing in mind what he was, that could only mean he didn't want to do it. You do see that, don't you?'

Jane frowned. 'I don't quite . . .'

'Well,' Asaf replied through a mouth full of peppermint debris, 'it really does stand to reason. If you're a genie and you want to destroy the world, you don't muck about, you just get on with it.'

'Unless,' Jane interrupted, 'somebody stops you.'

Asaf shook his head. 'A genie who wanted to destroy the world wouldn't have gone about it in a way that would have given anybody any opportunity to stop him. Isn't that right?' he asked the King, who nodded.

'Fair dinkum,' he said. 'Five-minute job. Melt an ice-cap, release a plague virus, anything like that. All this pissing about with flowers and ants . . .' He shook his head in sage contempt.

'All self-delusion on his part,' Asaf went on. 'Really, it was basically just a cry for help –'

Ah, thought Jane. Thank you.

'– because, deep down, he couldn't stand being him. Thinking about it, you can see his point.'

'And when it came right down to it,' the King joined in, 'when the chips were down and push came to shove and he actually could have destroyed the world if he wanted to, he just –'

'Lost his bottle?'

'You could,' Asaf said, frowning, 'put it that way. If you had less taste than the average works canteen Yorkshire pudding, that is.'

Jane drew in a deep breath and looked at the sky. It was still, she noticed with relief and approval, there. As were all the other necessary odds and ends: the ground, for example, and the hills and the sea. Whatever the hell had been going on, it had stopped. Which was probably just as well.

'That's that, then, is it?' she said.

'That's that.'

'Good.' She turned round and beckoned to the carpet. 'Let's go home.'

The shop door opened.

'Justin,' called the proprietor, 'I'm back. Anything happen while I was away?'

'Not really, Uncle.'

'Anybody buy anything?'

'No, Uncle.'

The proprietor glanced round. 'Just a second,' he said. 'Where's the big Isfahan that was in the corner there? You know, the one with the goats.'

Justin swallowed. 'A customer,' he said, 'sort of borrowed it.'

'Borrowed it?'

'On approval,' Justin said.

'I see. Leave a deposit?'

Justin reached under the counter and produced the big, fat, heavy sack he'd discovered in his hand when he'd woken up and found himself back in the shop. As it touched down on the desk, it chinked; and there is only one substance in the whole of the periodic table that chinks. Two clues: it's yellow, and before the development of specialist dental plastics they used to make false teeth out of it.

'I guess so,' he said.

Think what the sea can do to a coastline in thirty million years. The shock wave from the blast had the same effect on Kiss's body in about a fifth of a second.

Souvenir hunters would have been disappointed. Not even the characteristic black silhouette etched on the glazed earth; just nothing at all to show that Kiss had ever existed.

He was disappointed. Optimist that he was, right up till the very last moment he'd somehow believed that when the smoke cleared he'd still be there; a bit singed, perhaps, and threadbare, like a character in a Loony-Tunes cartoon, but nevertheless basically in one piece. The stern reality that faced him when he came round, however, was that he was now in more pieces than the mind could possibly conceive.

Gosh, he said to himself (or rather, selves), so these are smithereens.

On the other hand, he reflected, it's not use moping. It's

times like these when you just have to pull yourself together and . . .

Pull yourself together. Easier said then done.

He considered himself, hung in suspension above the surface of the planet like one aspirin dissolved in twenty million gallons of water. Spreading yourself a bit thin these days, Kiss, old son, he reflected. On the other hand . . .

Yes, he noticed, that's interesting. He realised that every single atom of his former body still had the consciousness of the whole, so that instead of there being just one Kiss, there were now several billion. A shrewd operator, he reflected, could turn this situation to his own advantage.

A gust of high-level wind reminded him of the downside. True, there were billions of him, but each one on its own was about as ineffective as the average civil rights charter. It's molecules united who can never be defeated. A solitary atom on its own, with nothing except the moral support of its fellows, is effectively dead in the water.

And likely to stay that way. Think of all the aggravation it takes to get together a mere twenty or so people for a school reunion, and then multiply that by ten billion.

Another aspect of the matter that he had to admit he didn't like much was the fact that each individual consciousness seemed to be fading rapidly. How long since the blast – one second, maybe two – and already he was starting to sound in his mind's ear like a cassette recorder with flat batteries.

There was, he recalled, a technical term for all this. What was it again? Ah, yes. Death.

Now there's a thought. If I die, I'll get to collect on my insurance policy.

(For he had indeed, many years ago and when under the influence of curdled whey, taken out a life policy with the

most senior underwriter of them all. He had regretted it
ever since, because (a) in the normal course of things he
was immortal, and (b) he had nobody to leave the proceeds
to even if he collected.)

Proviso B was still as valid as ever, but that was pretty
well beside the point. So anxious was he to find a silver
lining for the mushroom cloud that he was prepared to
overlook the pointlessness of the exercise. Accordingly, he
summoned up what energy he still had, and put a call
through.

This wasn't, in fact, difficult; since bits of him had been
dispersed to every nook and cranny of the planet, it wasn't
surprising that one stray atom had lodged in the Chief
Underwriter's ear. This made notifying the claim fairly
simple.

'Hi,' he said, 'my name is Kiss, policy number
6590865098765. I'm dead, and I want to make –'

YOU CAN'T.

The particle buzzed softly, confused. 'How do you
mean, I can't?' he demanded. 'If you want the policy document, it's in a tin box under a flat stone in a crater in the
Sea of Tranquillity. I can draw you a map if you like.'

YOU CAN'T CLAIM. SORRY.

'Well, of all the . . .' He would have expanded on this
theme, but one of the seraphim who sit on the right hand
of the Chief Underwriter pointed to the burning sword
lying across its knees and made a pretty unambiguous gesture with it, implying that taking that tone with the Boss
would result in extreme loss of privileges. The Kiss-parti-
cle subsided a little.

'Something in the small print?' he enquired. 'Some sort
of all-purpose cow-catching exclusion clause?'

NOT AS SUCH, NO. THE CLAIM WOULD BE

PERFECTLY VALID. IT'S MORE A MATTER OF FEASIBILITY, REALLY.

'Ah.' The batteries were very nearly flat now, and it was taking him all his strength just to stay awake. Nevertheless, he was intrigued. 'In what way?' he asked, as politely as he could.

SIMPLE. THE TERMS OF THE POLICY. I'M SURE YOU SEE WHAT I MEAN.

'I'm sorry, I don't think I quite . . . Oh. Oh yes, I see. Yes. Quite.'

A particle can't grin, but the bit of Kiss in question came very close to succeeding. The Chief Underwriter's ear began to itch.

'It's just as well you reminded me of that,' he chirruped. 'Left to myself, I'd never have seen it that way.'

SHIT.

An insurer's nightmare.

There's a strong argument for saying that paying out any money to anybody under any circumstances whatso-ever produces the same effect on your average insurer that two pounds of mature Cheddar eaten as a bedtime snack has on other people. But by any standards, the problem facing the Chief Underwriter as the bits of Kiss embarked on their final decay into oblivion was a honey.

The policy promised to pay Kiss, on his demise, the sum of ten thousand celestial dollars.

(There was a lot of other guff about with profit and pro-visions in the event of surrender prior to the contractual maturity date, but we can skip all that. Not germane to the issue in hand.)

Let's just pass that concept round the room and see what we come up with.

When Kiss dies, he gets ten grand. It can also be construed as saying that each time Kiss dies, he gets ten grand. Nothing at all in the small print about this being a one-off payment.

As noted above, there are currently tens of thousands of millions of Kisses (each one with the same consciousness, the same self-awareness, the memory, the persona, however you like to put it; at this point the vocabulary tends to get a bit fancy, but the idea is clear enough), all of them scheduled to die at precisely the same moment. Each one entitled to claim under the terms of the policy.

Now that's an awful lot of lettuce.

Which is not to say that the Chief Underwriter can't afford it. Somewhere buried in a cave in Galilee, or deep in some unexcavated catacomb in Rome, or maybe stashed away in a secret chamber under a Crusader castle somewhere, there's a tablet of stone in a cedarwood box that says, This guy's cheque will not bounce.

There is, however, more to it than that. In a word, inflation. More precisely, a desperately overheated money supply, leading to an inevitable devaluation, with knock-on effects on the divine economy which would throw countless angels on the dole and spell ruin for all those saints that from their labours rest who have to make ends meet on a celestial pension. Put it another way, things could hardly be worse if God suddenly fell off his yacht and drowned.

As the Chief Underwriter realised, a fraction of a second before his unwonted lapse into vulgarity, there's only one thing that can save Heaven at this point.

A miracle.

HAVE A SEAT, said the Chief Underwriter. *AND A*

CIGAR. I THINK WE CAN COME TO SOME SORT OF AN AGREEMENT.

Wherever it was that Philly Nine actually went to, when he got there he found a table and a plastic bucket.

Inside the bucket were hundreds and hundreds of brightly coloured little plastic bricks.

Philly stood for a long time, staring at the bricks and thinking 'What the . . .?' Probably his mind wandered during this time, because the next thing he knew was that he had taken two bricks out and slotted them together. Each brick had little knobs on the top and little holes on the bottom that the knobs fitted into; and some of them were square and some of them were rectangular, and there were a lot of other excitingly different shapes and sizes.

Without really thinking what he was doing, he pulled the bucket towards him, sat down on the floor and began to build.

And in the evening, he looked upon everything that he had built, and saw that it was good.

And the evening and the morning were the first day.

'Thanks,' Kiss called out as he ran down the steps.
DON'T MENTION IT. ANY TIME.

A satisfactory outcome, all told. The simple task which all the king's horses and all the king's men had so conspicuously failed to do for Humpty-Dumpty had taken the Chief Underwriter's staff about seven minutes. And there had been time to suggest a few subtle design improvements along the way.

True, Kiss reflected as he strolled back down the sky, he'd had to agree to forgo a quite bewilderingly large sum of money to which he was, strictly speaking, contractually entitled; but he wasn't too bothered about that. It wasn't, he decided, that you couldn't take it with you, because you could. It was just that there wasn't exactly a superfluity of things you could spend it on once you'd got there.

Right. What shall I do now?

Well, I could pop into Saheed's for a milk sour and a game of pool. Or I could put a girdle around the earth in twenty minutes. Or I could check out the thermals. Heaps of things I could do. The rest of Time's my own.

Or I could go and see if Jane . . .

He stopped dead in his tracks, and swore. It's a basic ground rule of genie life that you don't allow yourself to get involved with mortals, and he should by now know that better than anyone. And if there was one mortal in particular who merited complete avoidance . . .

Because of her, he reflected, I've been humiliated, threatened with imminent loss of divine status, involved in a series of horrible fights with a fellow Force Twelve and finally blown to bits. By any standards, that's taking the old wish/command nexus to its absolute limits.

The sequence of thoughts reminded him of something, and he closed his eyes and listened. Nothing. He knew without having to enquire further that as far as this dimension was concerned, Philly Nine no longer existed. The threat to the world was over. Another tick on the list of Things To Do.

Well, that milk sour surely does sound inviting. I think I might just as well . . .

He looked down. He had arrived, doubtless through sheer force of habit, a few feet above the block of flats where Jane lived. That bloody woman. Hah!

There could be no doubt whatsoever, he reflected as he walked in through the front door of the building and summoned the lift, that as far as his indentures were concerned, he was free and clear. She'd had far and away more than her bottle-top's worth out of him. Under no obligation whatsoever.

Nevertheless, he rationalised as he rang the doorbell, it'd be a shame to part on bad terms, and their previous parting hadn't exactly been cordial. Besides, he never had given her the obligatory bottomless purse, and he felt conscientious about that. Like the little silver inkstand-cum-paperweight you get given when you're knocked out of a TV game show after the very first round, the bottomless purse wasn't optional. It came with the territory.

Rather to his surprise, the door was opened by the Dragon King of the South-East.

'G'day, mate,' said the King. 'I was just leaving. Done me stint on this job.'

'Me too.'

The King shook his head. 'Right bunch of wowsers if you ask me,' he muttered, 'the lot of 'em. Glad to be through with 'em at last.'

'Quite.'

'That bloody sheila . . .'

'Indeed.'

'Well.' The King hesitated for a moment, as if considering whether some gesture of solidarity – a slapped back, perhaps, or a matey hand on the shoulder – would be more likely to result in the offer of a cool one down at Saheed's or an instinctive left hook to the jaw. He must have been a pessimist at heart because he smiled, shook his head and trotted off down the stairs. In human form this time, naturally. Eventually, even Dragon Kings learn by their mistakes.

Kiss stood for a few minutes, a hand on the half-open door. I don't really need to say goodbye, he told himself.

The more usual form of ending a mortal/genie relationship was a string of vulgar abuse and a puff of evil-smelling green smoke. Nevertheless. Trends are there to be bucked, and fashions led. He pushed the door open and walked in.

About fifteen seconds later he came out again, moving fast and a sort of deep scarlet colour from the hairline to the collar-bone.

It only goes to show, he muttered to his immortal soul as he bolted down the stairs, humans and genies are on different wavelengths altogether, and probably for the best. As a genie, he hadn't thought twice about strolling in unannounced on two mortals of different sexes who were just embarking on the traditional living happily together ever after. Exactly what went on under such circumstances was, he realised, not something he'd ever given much thought to, in the same way that the bricklayers don't generally hang around to see what colour carpets eventually go into the house they've just built. By the time the happy ending was properly under way, he was usually long gone and starting on another job.

Well, now he knew; and, from what he'd seen, he was well out of it. For one thing, it looked so damn undignified. Not to mention uncomfortable. Cramp would be the least of your problems.

Each to their own idea of a good time. Compared to, say, a good game of pool, however, he was amazed that it had lasted as long as it had.

A good game of pool. And a quart or two of natural yoghurt with the lads, a really hot curry and so to bed. What could, in all honesty, be better?

Jane stirred, brushed aside the heavy residue of sleep and reached out towards the pillow beside her.

Nothing.

Or rather, a note. With a frown like gathering thunder-clouds, she picked it up.

BACK ABOUT SIX-THIRTY

she read; and underneath, obviously added as an after-thought,

GONE FISHIN'

'An' another thing.'

The other regulars propping up Saheed's back bar bestowed on him the look of good-natured contempt that relatively sober people reserve especially for those of their fellows who've had more natural yoghurt than is good for them. One of them said, 'Yes?'

'Humans,' said Kiss, 'have no sense of proportion.'

'Really?'

'Really.'

'You mean, their heads are too big for their bodies, that sort of thing?'

Kiss shook his head, a courageous act under the circumstances. 'You're thinking,' he said, 'of perspective. They're quite good at perspective, actually, give the buggers their due. Used not to be, of course. Anyway, where was I?'

'Proportion. Lack of sense of, prevalence of among the more ephemeral species. You were pontificating.'

'Yeah. 'Specially women. Women have no sense of pro-portion,' Kiss said, swilling the dregs of cream round in his virtually empty mug, 'whatsoever. All they care about is –'

'Yes?'

'Carpets. And curtains. And loose covers. And what colour the bloody things should be. I mean, I ask you.'

'What?'

'Sorry?'

'What do you ask us?'

Kiss blinked. 'I ask you,' he continued, after a moment's regrouping, 'what the hell difference the colour makes to a cushion. I mean, are red cushions softer than blue ones, or what?'

'I think they like things to look nice. After all, they're the ones who spend all their time at home, so I suppose it's –'

'Balls,' said Kiss, with grandeur. 'I mean, can you tell me without looking what colour your trousers are?'

'As a matter of fact, I can. They're a sort of pale beige, with a faint –'

'All right, then, all right. Can you tell me what colour your bathroom curtains are? Go on, you can't.'

'True, but since I'm a river-spirit I don't actually have a bathroom. The rest of my place is done out in blues, greens and browns, and that's in the lease.'

Kiss scowled. 'You know what I mean,' he said. 'All women care about is fripperies. Stupid, pointless things which –'

'And I suppose,' interrupted the river spirit, 'that we devote all our time to higher issues. Like darts.'

'Applied ballistic research,' someone broke in. 'Very important study.'

'Betting on horse-races.'

'Advanced probability mathematics.'

'Combined with equestrian genetics.'

'And meteorology, don't forget. Depending whether the going is hard or soft.'

'I thought that was flying rocks and stuff.'

'Look,' Kiss broke in, 'all right, we may not exactly cram each something minute with sixty seconds of whatsit, but in our case it doesn't matter. Only matters if you're gonna die some day. Ruddy women, now, they're all going to go to their graves and nothing to show for it except a load of soft furnishings. Absolutely futile, if you ask me.'

The river spirit shrugged. 'So?' he said. 'What of it? Mortals are mortals and we're us.' He grinned. 'Vive la difference,' he added.

'Yeah, well . . .'

'Fancy a game of dominoes?'

'Now you're talking.'

After leaving Saheed's, Kiss wandered slowly up through the clouds and perched for a moment between the upper and the lower air. It was just after sunrise, and the big red splodge was beginning to give way to the first blue notes of a new day. From where he sat, Kiss could see the whole of the daylight side of the planet. He shaded his eyes with his hand and had a good look; something, he realised, that he hadn't done for a long time.

There was a lot to look at. All over the surface, and par-ticularly in the yellow sandy bits, the armies who had failed to get to the war on time were slouching listlessly at home, trying to remember as they did so what the hell all the fuss had been about. There now, Kiss told himself, if it hadn't been for me . . .

So? What of it? Mortals are mortals and we're us. If ever they do blow up this planet, we can just move to another one. Who gives at toss, anyway?

As he watched, the Earth turned. Night retreated to the right and advanced to the left. One step forwards, bal-anced for ever by one step back. How it ought to be, of course. Except that if you got together say a hundred genies, and by dint of some miracle you persuaded them all to work together, you could get them to haul another star in from another solar system and so position it that it could be day on both sides of the planet simultaneously. Sure, you'd have to make some adjustments to the mechanism, so that the seas didn't dry up and that sort of thing; but it could be done. All manner of things could be done.

Probably just as well, Kiss told himself, that they aren't.

On an impulse, he spread his arms wide and drifted down to the surface. He wasn't aiming for anywhere in particular, and he ended up hovering a few feet above the water, somewhere in the middle of the sea.

There was nothing except water for miles in every direction; nothing to be seen except the regiments of waves, marching in perfect formation in accordance with the orders of the moon. Nothing, except a tiny speck, so small that he couldn't even tell how far away it was.

For genies, though, thinking is doing, and without a conscious decision he found himself hovering directly over the speck, which turned out to be the neck of a floating bottle.

That rings a bell.

Mortals, Kiss recalled, when cast away on desert islands, sometimes write messages and put them in bottles, in the hope that somehow, at some time, somebody will find them and do something: notify the next of kin, or the coastguard, or more likely the insurance company. And although it might be considered a futile gesture to launch so tiny and frail a communication into so much savagely indifferent water, you had to admit it showed a bit of class. A random particle of optimism fired blindly into infinity in the hope of hitting the bull, of achieving something worthwhile. The fact of death and the promise of hope; between the two of them mortals had a rough time of it, and they coped remarkably well.

Through the opaque green glass, Kiss could see a scrap of paper neatly folded and tucked in underneath the cork. His heart unaccountably high, he dived and picked the bottle out of the water as neatly as a Japanese fisherman's cormorant. Pop went the cork (not whoosh, this time) and he unfolded the message, which said:

NO MILK TODAY
signed
D. JONES

'Marvellous,' said Kiss disgustedly; and he was reflecting bitterly on the nature of anticlimax when an idea struck him.

A message in a bottle. Yes, why not?

Without giving himself time to think, he jumped down through the neck of the bottle and dragged the cork in tight after him. Then he leaned back, smiling contentedly, waiting to see what would happen next.